ONCE UPON AN ISLAND

Once Upon An Island

JOSEPH CANNING

To Carol,
for her patience.

The right of Joseph Canning to be identified as the author of this work is hereby asserted in accordance with the Copyright, Designs and Patents Act 1988.

All characters and events in this publication are entirely fictitious. Any resemblance to any person or persons, living or dead, or to actual events, is purely coincidental.

ISBN-13:978-1514330746

ISBN-10:1514330741

*First published 2006 This edition 2015
Copyright © Joseph Canning 2015.
All rights reserved.*

ONE

THE LONG, bleak estuary of the Langwater eats into the curve of the sinking eastern coastline for almost eleven miles, at its mouth and for much of its length three or so miles across, but in places broadened even further where wide, tentacled fleets and ragged inlets gouge deep into the flatness of the land. It lies at the base of the East Anglian bulge, a windswept waste of mudflats and marsh, created and preserved by the motions of the sea, at low water bisected along its entire length by a broad main channel from which shallow, silted creeks wind landwards across the sucking ooze of the riverbed, at high tide filled to its uppermost reaches by a creeping, grey-green flood that drowns even the great trenched banks of saltings which fringe its shores and choke its inlets.

This is the world of the lonely hunter drifting in his punt upon freezing, mist-shrouded waters through the deep November dark, the domain of the harsh-shrieking white gull wheeling and diving over dulled-silver channels far out from the land, the haunt, too, of heron and piping curlew, of wild duck, widgeon and wader, shellduck, teal and pintail, of mallard and Brent geese winging their way silently homeward in the purple winter twilight to the false sanctuary of their nesting places amid the desolate salt marsh where the wildfowlers wait with their guns.

Truly, a man had to be born to that silent vastness to be inured to the bleak loneliness of the place, to dwell content within so dreary a region of the sea throughout the slow procession of his years and to labour in the flat, marsh-drained fields along its shores heedless of the rigours of his life. I was born to the estuary, but I was never inured to it, even though for sixteen of the first seventeen years of my life I lived on Norsea, the mile-long, half-mile-wide, eye-shaped island which lies in the middle of the estuary, a mile out from the mainland northern shore opposite the small village of Gledlang. I had arrived on

Norsea as a baby a year after my own father had died, pushed there across the narrow sand and shale causeway which links it to the mainland by my mother in a pram festooned with white ribbons, so I was told, when she had married Ben Wigboe, the island's bailiff. From that day on, Norsea had become my home and my world: in time, too, from my fourteenth birthday onwards, its fields became my workplace, the white gulls over the river my constant companions, the saltings, the creeks and the interminably-winding seawall which encloses and defines the estuary my whole environment: and the wind, the ever-blowing wind which comes off the open sea, my daily discomfort. All I ever thought was of leaving it, of someday going out into the world and seeing all the things I knew were there to be seen and perhaps never returning: so you will understand my surprise when Richard Wigboe came back that chill, mid-April morning of Forty-Seven, two years after the war had ended: Ben's son, my step-brother.

Richard Wigboe returned to Gledlang just as he had left it, stealing back into the village in the secrecy of the dark, unseen and unheralded, the prodigal half-remembered in tales of youth told by men grown into middle age reappearing among them as suddenly as he had vanished from the monotony of their lives nineteen years before. Posey Gate was the first to see him when he cycled up Shoe Street just after six on his way to milk the cows on the Stanson sisters' farm: not recognising one whom he had known years before, the old farmworker saw only the huddled figure of a stranger slumped upon the broken circle of the ciderstone embedded in the earth beside the iron-wheeled pump in the Square, his head bowed upon his arms as if asleep, a flat cap pulled down over his forehead and the collar of his dark overcoat turned up as if to hide his face.

Why Richard waited on the ciderstone instead of coming on to his old home on Norsea, my home, the draughty, timbered period-farmhouse in the centre of the island, I do not know: perhaps it was because, even at that moment, he was unsure of the wisdom of his return: perhaps he just did not know the time of the morning tide and did not think he could yet cross the causeway, which snakes out from the island's westernmost tip: or perhaps he was just too tired after his long walk and needed to rest.

Not till the rising sun had tinged the eastern sky with pink and the bright winking diamond of the morning star had faded in the chill light of a new dawn did he rise wearily from his place and trudge down the long slope of Shoe Street, past the curving line of plaster-fronted cottages where the old bakehouse stood, past the redbrick cottages halfway down with their crooked windows and sagging roofs, past the low, thatched, black-timbered cottage at the bottom, half hidden behind a high hedge, then on through the white gates of Boundary farm and along the rough, potholed chase which runs between the vast sprawling acres of apple and plum orchards there to the estuary shore itself.

Only when he stood again atop the broad, grass-covered seawall, which stands as high as a house and winds away on either side for mile after endless mile, past creek and salting, inlet and hard, from the Gap up in the next county round to the wharves and dockyards of London itself – only then would he have seen the tree-shrouded outline of Norsea emerging from the morning gloom, remote, distant and brooding across the brown, salt-sheened expanse of the Stumble mudflats.

TWO

I WAS still abed in the old farmhouse, cocooned in blankets and burrowed deep in the hollow of the mattress, thankful that I had had the foresight to lay my army surplus greatcoat and my tattered working jacket upon the bed and sleep in all my clothes: for, to the rough-hewn country youth I then was, pyjamas were an eccentricity about which I did not care and a luxury which I could not afford. On cold nights I slept in all my things, shirt, vest, trousers, pullover and socks, reasoning quite sensibly that, that way, I was better able to withstand the douche of cold air washing over me when first I tugged back the covers and crawled from my bed in the pale light of yet another freezing dawn.

Twice already my mother had sought to scold me from that warm haven, but the thought of spending another day working alone in the freezing emptiness of the fields served only to send me wriggling deeper into the hollow so that only the bleached straw thatch of my hair was visible above the coats and covers.

At last the expanding parallelogram of sunlight on the far wall touched the corner of the marble-topped washstand and glinted on the handle of the china jug and the rim of the white basin: I knew then that the long drawn-out agony of my waking must end and my moody, shuffling descent be made to the kitchen below. In the next room, Ben, my step-father, was still asleep, sending up such a bronchitic wheezing and snorting through constricted tubes and tired lungs that it sounded as if one moment someone were operating a set of punctured bellows, the next labouring at an unoiled pump handle.

As if to remind me that I could no longer delay, from the kitchen below came the furious rattling of a poker against the bars of the grate as my mother, always the first to rise, raked out the ashes of the previous night's fire from the range. Then footsteps padding across the bare linoleum and the clank of a metal handle told me that water was being poured from the pail which stood just inside the back door and which I filled assiduously each evening from a squeaking-handled pump a quarter-mile from the farmhouse.

I had paused at the top of the stairs where the two landing boards creaked to pull on my boots when I saw Richard for the first time through the narrow gap between the banisters and the low ceiling of the passageway: he was standing before the kitchen door, a soiled brown canvas kitbag at his feet, cap in one hand and the shoulders of his dark overcoat glistening with patches of dew. At that moment, of course, he was simply a stranger: and so dulled by sleep was I that the oddity of someone standing in our passageway at that unearthly hour did not immediately strike me as anything unusual.

He had left Norsea before ever I was born, three years before, to be exact, the day after his mother's funeral, so I had once been told: he was just seventeen when he rose in the winter dark of a freezing January dawn while Ben was still asleep and trudged across to the mainland through driving lines of sleet and snow. I know the blizzards which can blow in that region so I know that, before he was even halfway across, Norsea's tall elms would have disappeared in a curtain of white behind him, while the trail of his footprints through the slush of the causeway would have vanished almost as soon as they were made: as if Nature were colluding with him to hide all evidence of his flight.

If Ben and my mother ever spoke of him in my presence, which was seldom, they did so by referring only to 'him' or 'he,' as though they thought the gangling, dull-eyed youth, with a red-tanned face and haystack hair, who sat yawning and sniffing opposite them at the kitchen table would not know about whom it was they spoke: but I knew, I knew: I had made it my business to know. Now Richard Wigboe, my step-brother, was back!

In the few seconds in which I saw him before he lifted the latch and stepped out of my sight into the presence of my mother, I sensed a nervousness about him, as though he were listening to the sounds from within and trying to determine who was making them, unsure whether to enter or indeed whether he should have ventured that far through our unbolted front door.

I heard Richard's voice first. 'I'm sorry – I – I thought Ben Wigboe still lived here,' he stuttered, obviously not expecting the apparition which greeted him, especially one so fearsome looking as my mother as she angrily raked at the cold grey ash: cheeks finger-streaked, hair hanging down in a wild disorder from the fury of her exertions, stockings rolled down over her ankles and wearing her oldest and most frayed flowered pinafore.

There was a pause as the two eyed each other, then Richard, still apologetic, added: 'I'm – I'm Richard Wigboe – Ben Wigboe's son. I – I used to live here.'

THREE

SOMETIMES, without even seeing the look on a person's face or hearing their words, you sense their shock: no words come when words should come: there is a vacuum, a pause, and when the words are spoken they are blurted out hurriedly, as if to mask something: surprise, embarrassment, shock. Such a thing happened to my mother that morning: for a full six or so seconds there was silence as she stared back at the figure in the doorway of her kitchen: then the storm burst.

'I know who you are! You don't have to tell me that!' she snorted, scornfully. 'I may only be a woman, but I'm not stupid! I knew who you were the moment you opened that door. You don't have to tell me that!' The emphasis was on the 'me,' naturally: nothing infuriated my mother so much as the person who underestimated her intelligence: it fairly rankled with her.

She must have stood up at this point, for I heard the poker drop into the hearth: that did not stop her from talking, of course. 'Lord, I ought to know who you are, didn't I?' she went on in the same angry tone. 'I'm your step-mother, aren't I? I married your father, didn't I, fifteen years ago? Clara Coe that was – Clara Coe-Wigboe that is now, so help me. Same name as you and lived here ever since I married your father. I'd be a fine one if I didn't know my own husband's son, wouldn't I? I know you even if you don't know me.'

'Step-mother? Oh!' Richard sounded aghast. 'I'm sorry, I didn't know. I had no idea my father – Ben – had remarried. I didn't know who you were.'

'Well, you wouldn't, would you?' my mother snorted again. 'You weren't here, were you? You were gone, weren't you? We didn't know where you were or whether you were ever coming back, did we?' The blunt, rhetorical manner of her speaking was a peculiarity of our region, particularly when expressing scorn and irritation: my mother was doing both. 'What were you, too hard up you couldn't afford a three-ha'penny stamp to send us a letter? You clear off for nineteen years without so much as a thought or a care for anyone, let alone your father, then come creeping back here expecting it to be all the same! Huh! It's a wonder you knew where to come, I should think! It's a wonder you found your way. Who am I indeed?' She left the rest unspoken, but the tone of her voice was explicit: do not question her right to be there.

Once roused, my mother's anger was slow to abate: her questions were abrupt and acerbic: she was determined to have her say, to let Richard know exactly how she felt: it did not matter to her that she had never seen him before, that he was her husband's son and that he had just arrived: she sailed on without giving him a chance to answer: he could do that when she had finished.

'You could have written to him, to Ben, your father, couldn't you? That weren't asking too much, was it? The poor man worried himself half into his grave over you and you couldn't even write a letter to tell him where you were! Where have you been all this time? That's what I should like to know. What have you been doing? What was so important you couldn't write and let us know where you were? You could have been dead for all we knew! Killed in the war. We didn't know, did we? Were you in the war? We don't know what you were doing, do we? We weren't there, were we?'

'I didn't see much of the war,' was Richard's almost apologetic reply: nothing other than that, though he was not really given a chance.

'Huh.' Contempt in my mother's voice. 'We saw plenty of it round here, too much. Doodlebugs and bombings and the planes crashing everywhere. All those planes going over on fire. All those airmen killed. We had our share of the war round here, I can tell you! I wouldn't want to go through that again.'

It was not a boast: it was a truth spoken angrily by someone who would have preferred not to have been bombed and doodlebugged, who would have preferred to have been left in peace. Both Maydun, the hilltop town at the head of the estuary, and Wivencaster, the garrison town thirteen miles away, had been bombed for various reasons, innumerable aircraft had crashed around the Langwater on their way back from bombing raids over Germany, during a dogfight with a Hurricane some Hun had machine-gunned along the northern shore and half-a-dozen doodlebugs had landed either near the estuary mouth or in the fields either side, all within a few miles of us.

It was an idiosyncrasy of my mother, which I never did understand, that she did not just blame the Germans for this, she blamed

Winston Churchill as well: she decried him almost as much as she decried Adolf Hitler. 'Bloody Churchill! Bloody warmonger!' she would exclaim, indignantly, whenever the war was mentioned in her kitchen. 'He wanted a war! He was a bloody warmonger from the start! He couldn't leave things alone, could he? Always going on about war and Hitler and things that were nothing to do with us. Neville Chamberlain was right – people didn't want a war. We didn't want a war. No-one did, except Churchill and Hitler.' I think it had something to do with a miners' strike in Wales years before I was born: two miners were killed and she blamed Churchill for sending in the troops.

By this time, Richard was well inside the kitchen and out of my view, having deemed it safe to sit himself at the table: all I could see of him through the half-open door were the toes of his shoes pointing toward the grate and his overcoat draped over his kitbag: but I could imagine his face reddening under the onslaught of my mother's scorn as she bustled about the kitchen. It was a ploy she often used when wanting to gather her thoughts or distract her mind from something, flying about the kitchen as if she were looking for something and giving each cupboard door or sideboard drawer an angry bang at not finding whatever it was she sought. Now she was at it again.

Over the clatter of cutlery being placed on the table, I heard her ask Richard: 'Whyever didn't you write and let us know you were coming? People don't just come, do they? Look at this place! Fire not properly lit, no kettle boiled, tea not made, no-one up except me! I ask you, what kind of a reception is that for anyone to come back to?' Obviously she had thought up a new line of reprimand and was reluctant to let the matter drop, though I knew, of course, that at the same time she would be getting out the best cutlery, the silver-plated knife and spoon with 'LNER' of the London and North Eastern Railway stamped into their handles, if only to show we had them!

Here Richard made a dreadful mistake. 'It doesn't matter,' he began.

'It matters to me,' my mother cried above his words, because such things did matter to her. 'I like the floor to be swept and the place to be tidy when people come. I like a place to look right, even if they don't tell us they're coming.'

If Richard said anything in reply, a mumbled 'Sorry' perhaps, or a 'Yes, I should have written,' I did not hear it.

Fortunately, my mother, having completed her scolding of someone who till a few minutes before had been a total stranger to her, just a face on a photograph, and not the least fussed or apologetic for having done it, now adopted a more conciliatory tone. When had Richard come, she asked, and how had he come?

'From Wivencaster. I got in late last night,' he replied. 'I walked. I came via Copthall and Cumvirley on the back road to Salter.'

'All that way! Didn't anyone give you a lift? Surely someone could have given you a lift?' My mother's incredulity and anger, that anyone driving one of the few cars then actually on the road, could pass someone walking on a lonely backroad late at night and not offer them a lift, were honestly felt.

'I didn't see many cars. People don't have the petrol in England these days, I suppose,' Richard replied.

My mother grudgingly accepted this explanation, for she made no further comment upon it: there was a brief pause taken up by the sounds of more movement about the kitchen.

Instead, with a slight hesitancy in her voice, unusual for her, she asked: 'Are you back for good then?'

'It all depends,' was Richard's vague reply.

'Depends on what?' my mother wanted to know, her tone sharpening again.

'On many things,' Richard answered. 'On my father mostly, on Ben, I suppose. That and other things.'

She did not ask what 'other things,' enabling Richard to put a question of his own. Almost with embarrassment, he asked: 'How is he, by the way – Ben, my father?'

'Same as always,' replied my mother, grudgingly, with that evident disdain some people adopt when reassuring others of a person's well-being. 'He don't change much. Managing this farm, his oyster beds, shooting in his punt, it's his life. He don't know of no other, does he?' Then, unable to resist the final dig, she added: 'Huh! He's upstairs in his bed asleep right at this minute and he don't even know his own son is back and sitting in his own kitchen!'

If Richard made a reply, again I did not hear it, for any further conversation was drowned by the rattling of the poker in the bars of the grate and a furious puffing, followed by one of my mother's muttered oaths as she attempted to provoke the stubborn fire into life.

'Coke's damp. I'll have to get some more,' I heard her announce and seconds later she came bustling out into the passageway with the scuttle in her hand, making for the back door. I knew she would automatically look up the stairs to see if I were there: anticipating it, I shuffled back into the dark of the landing, holding my breath so as not to give away my presence. I knew, too, that outside she would bypass the coke pile and make straight for the coal bunker and shovel up what she could from our almost exhausted supply: to her way of thinking, any visitor to her house 'deserved a good fire,' even if it meant using up the last of our coal ration at a time when there was no prospect of obtaining more: it was her way. Only when I heard the lumps of coal rattling into the scuttle did I cautiously descend the stairs in an attempt to sneak into the kitchen.

My mother must have sensed this somehow, for she came rushing back into the passageway lugging the heavy scuttle just as I reached the kitchen door: there was a look of fury on her face: she was clearly intent on cutting me off before Richard saw me. Too late, she had to hold back: Richard, sitting with his back to me, half turned in his chair. 'Hullo,' he said, 'who are you?'

FOUR

RICHARD was seated at the table on our one good chair, the one with the back to it: Ben's chair. I say this not to impress upon you the state of our poverty, but simply because it was a fact of our life then. Before him, as expected, were set our one china willow-pattern dinner plate, our best cup and saucer, the London and North Eastern Railways' knife and spoon and one of the only two forks we possessed with any proper shine on it, all of which contrasted somewhat with the handleless cups, chipped plates and assortment of stained, bent and battered cutlery which had been laid in the other places.

In the passageway I had not been able to see him properly, but, as he slowly turned to me, smiling, I saw him first in profile and noticed immediately how unlike Ben he was: Richard clearly took after his mother, whose photograph had once hung in the parlour till my mother had taken it down and shoved it under the tablecloths in the sideboard drawer. Whereas Ben was stocky, muscular, square-faced and nearly bald, Richard was tall and slim, some five-feet-eleven-inches in height, almost gypsyish in appearance, with a sallow skin, high cheekbones, brown eyes and waves of dark hair sweeping back from his straight forehead. His wrists, I noticed particularly, were surprisingly thin and bony for a man of his age, sinewy, without obvious muscle, like someone who had not done any manual work to thicken them or who skimped on his eating. The fingers, too, were long and tapering, like one would expect of a bank clerk or some other office employee who never needed to exert any physical strength in his so-called labour.

It was only when he had turned completely in his chair to greet me that I understood the silence which had followed my mother's first sight of him and realised the shock she must have undergone. The whole of the left side of Richard's face was hideously scarred: it was a mass of crinkled tissue like you see when someone has been burned or perhaps had acid squirted in their face and their skin heals in lumpy patches. One deep scar ran from under the eye to the corner of his mouth: a second ran from the same eye across to his earlobe: a third extended again from the corner of his mouth upward and halfway across to the ear: a fourth curved from the bridge of his nose to meet the third at his cheekbone, forming a cross with it, so to speak: while a fifth ran across the top of his lips and under his nose: following each were the dotted marks of what I would say was improvised stitching!

I had seen wounded soldiers in Gledlang during the war, but nothing like this. Once I had stopped to talk to three soldiers with Commando patches sewn on their uniforms as they sat on the stone steps of Fred Thorn's bakery at the top of Shoe Street eating doughnuts. I had been agog with pride and wonder when they had shown me black-handled daggers marked with the Nazi swastika, which they said they had taken from dead Germans: but, though two had bandaged limbs and the third a bandage-wrapped head, none of them had visible wounds as horrific as I saw on Richard.

My reaction as he half-rose and extended a hand was one of shock, quickly overtaken by revulsion, followed by an acute embarrassment which I was unable to conceal: when one sees people with grotesque faces, such as Richard presented to my eyes that morning, one wants to look at them to find out how they have received those injuries, yet at the same time one feels nauseous and embarrassed by the awfulness of them: you want to look, but know you should not.

Richard's smile, too, I noticed, was on one side of his mouth only, as if the muscles on the other side did not operate at all.

'This is Joey. From my first marriage,' my mother informed him, a marked note of disapproval in her voice. Then, having introduced us and without further ado, she showed her displeasure at my just being there by pushing roughly past to station herself in front of the range so that Richard, still half-turned towards me, could not see the hostility ablaze in her eyes and the clear warning in her look: 'Don't show me up! Don't show you have noticed his face! Don't let him see you staring!'

'Hullo, Joe. I'm pleased to meet you,' Richard smiled his half smile, one hand still extended.

How could I not notice: how could I not stare? I truly hope that in that moment Richard understood the reason for my gawping mouth and my scarlet cheeks as I shuffled sideways past him, staring at his face as if mesmerised by it, too disconcerted even to take the hand he proffered and to shake it. Other than a puzzled frown which quickly vanished and a slight movement of the head, Richard did not appear the least put out by my show of ill manners, but continued to smile his strange smile across the table at me as I sat down on a backless chair opposite. Grotesque and shocking as his looks and twisted smile were to me at that first meeting, there was something about Richard's manner which I also found unsettling and which made me shy of him. Perhaps it was the affability of the smile on so disfigured a face, perhaps it was the brightness of his eyes, or his polite way of speaking which seemed to me as out of place in our kitchen as would be the accent of an educated man in the vault of the Chessman public house in Gledlang on a Saturday night amid all the raucous, vulgar, coughing, grumbling, inarticulate farm labourers who gathered there to drink and to talk and to play their darts and dominoes. Perhaps it was the cleanliness and smartness of his clothes, the blue suit without so much as a splash of mud upon it, foreign-looking to my eyes, lightweight, and so much better cut than the heavy, ill-fitting, chalk-striped, demobilisation suits which other men his age wore about the village for their Sunday best: perhaps it was the starched white shirt with no hint of a fraying collar or fraying cuffs, and the blue-striped tie tucked neatly into the waistband of his trousers, belted, unlike the men I knew who mostly wore braces. Only the polished black shoes, lightly spattered with brown mud, displayed any sign of his having crossed the causeway, all of which contrasted with my crumpled, slept-in shirt, pullover and trousers and mud-caked workboots.

All these things, his looks, his manner and his smartness, combined to make that first meeting between us more traumatic for me than it should have been, notwithstanding my own innate shyness at coming face to face with a grotesque-faced stranger better dressed, better spoken and better mannered than myself. That he should be Ben's son, the mysterious Richard, and my step-brother, only made matters a thousand times worse.

Unhappily, there were unthinking things I did in those days of youthful ignorance at which I now shudder when I recall them: in the turmoil of my embarrassment, I lifted high first one muddy boot, then the other, almost up to the table edge to double-tie my laces: I could hardly have committed a worse sin.

'Do you have to?' wailed my mother from beside the range: and out of Richard's line of sight, one silently mouthed oath, one withering, narrow-eyed stare, one contemptuous twist of the lips and the armistice of the night was ended: a new day of trial and tribulation was about to begin between us, just as it did each and every morning and ceased only with the oblivion of sleep at night. That was the way it always was between my mother and me: as though sometimes nothing I ever did was right. I neither washed properly nor often enough (once a week being enough for me): I did not wash my hands before sitting at the table and when I did sit down, my manners, or lack of them, drove her into a seething frenzy of sarcasm and loathing. I ate too noisily, I drank too noisily and sometimes I forgot myself and, well, licked my plate: it should have been taken as a compliment to her cooking, but it was not.

That awful first meeting between Richard and I was soured even further a few moments later by a brief and spiteful exchange between my mother and myself. Richard had asked, quite politely, how old I was and, having got that answer, enquired where on the island I was working that day: such a question was too good an opportunity for my mother to miss, busy as she was stirring the porridge on the range.

'Work!' she scoffed, pausing and turning to face us. 'He don't know the meaning of the word! Hard work'd kill him – and that creature from round the Maydun road he goes about with. The pair of them couldn't do a proper day's work if their lives depended on it!'

The so-called 'creature from round the Maydun road' was my friend, Billy Garner, with whom I sometimes worked when Ben 'lent me out,' generally for a smaller wage or in exchange for like services, to John Bolt, the grumpy, miserable, mean-spirited, bad-tempered, bullying, slave-driver of a fruit farmer who then owned Boundary farm just across the causeway from us on the mainland itself. This Ben seemed to do at the drop of a hat whenever John Bolt asked, declaring that either there was not enough work on Norsea's two-hundred-and-fifty acres for the both of us at that time, which I never believed, or that what needed to be done could be done by himself alone. In return, I received a pittance of a wage and Ben received help from the Boundary men when he required it most: at harvest time, for the threshing and sometimes for the ploughing and drilling. At the time, I thought Ben did it simply because he wished to get rid of me so that he could perform the needed tasks about the farm on his own: now, in hindsight, I think he did it so that I would at least get away from the confines of Norsea every now and again and work in the company of other men, particularly with my friend Billy. He and I had gone to Gledlang school together, then on to the secondary school at Maydun for three years till we both left at fourteen: it was Billy's company I always sought on those few occasions a month when I could cross easily to the mainland and sit with the other Gledlang boys on the broken ciderstone in the Square to while away the evening hours in banter and idle talk.

I at least received a sympathetic, if unsettling, smile from Richard. Unfortunately, at this point my mother lifted the saucepan of porridge from the fire and advanced to the table, where she proceeded to ladle a substantial portion on to Richard's willow-pattern plate and a much lesser portion on to mine. She also used it as an opportunity to bump me hard with her hip as she came round the table, almost sending me toppling from my chair, while at the same time craftily pushing the milk jug and the sugar bowl across to Richard and out of my reach. Then, he having finished with them, she pointedly whipped them off the table on to the sideboard with a smug smirk, the coldness of her look daring me to protest, yet knowing I would not. I envied him both, the sugar because, being rationed then, seldom if ever was I allowed to sprinkle it on my porridge, and the milk because that morning it was proper milk and not the usual diluted sweetened skimmed tin milk or the awful powdered stuff imported from America during the war and still filling the shelves of Gledlang's post office-cum-grocery store in the Square.

So while I ate my milkless and sugarless, mouth-burning porridge and Richard, unaware of my displeasure, ate his, sweetened and cooled, he asked me various questions about the region and the people he would have known.

FIVE

RICHARD'S first question, perhaps naturally enough, was about Old Hoary, or Horatio Crockshay Volwycke-Hoar as he was ludicrously named, the ageing, eccentric, reclusive, half-barmy scion of a wealthy Norfolk landowning family, who lived alone in the big house down by Norsea's southern shore a couple of hundred yards from our farmhouse. He considered himself to be our employer and would refer to Norsea as 'my island,' even though, in reality, the island was owned lock, stock and barrel by Hoary's older brother, a bigwig somewhere in the Foreign Office in London, who had purchased it from some philanthropic, altruistic mustard manufacturer just after the First War as a safe place for Hoary to live well away from the rest of the world. It was to the bigwig brother's accountants in Wivencaster that Ben sent his income and expenditure figures and it was to the bigwig brother he sent his planting schedules: and had done for twenty-seven years: not that they would have been altered if the bigwig brother had wanted it: Ben did things his way and no one else's.

Hoary, of course, thinking he owned the place and that Ben 'managed' the farm for him, was not one to stint giving orders of his own, though Ben paid him only lip service when he did, agreeing to do something only if he himself considered it should be done and deciding himself when it should be carried out: he was no forelock tugger where Hoary was concerned, but had to accept, grudgingly, that Hoary was the true owner's brother. For that very reason, Hoary seemed to expect me to be beholden to him and at his beck and call for the score or so of different, menial and unnecessary tasks he found for me to do about his house. One Sunday, I might be sweeping his path, the next mending a door on one of his outhouses, or weeding his garden, or planting his spring bulbs, or painting the lower windows of the house itself, or fetching water for him from the pump or his coke or coal ration from the mainland. On a weekday evening, he might ask me to wash a mountain of pots and pans which had accumulated in his sink, or to sharpen the multitude of chisels with which he sculptured great blocks of wood he brought back at times in Sligger Offin's rattletrap village taxi.

Richard, of course, had known Hoary before he went away: the old fool had come to the island in Nineteen-Twenty, straight after the First War, when he was in his mid-thirties, almost the same age as Ben when he was hired as farm bailiff: Richard then would have been aged ten.

Was Old Hoary still as daft as ever? Richard asked, though not exactly in those words. 'The same as ever,' was how he put it. Did he still dress the same way? Still laugh like a hyena? Play the piano half the night? How did I get on with him? Did he still begrudge payment to everyone? I answered all of his questions as best I could in that, yes, Old Hoary was still as cranky as ever: yes, he still walked about half the time dressed like a scarecrow: yes, he still had that awful laugh: yes, he still played the piano at all hours: and, yes, too, where money was concerned, he still seemed to think he was living in his father's big house up in Norfolk and any money he gave me for the extra tasks I performed was no more than a master giving largesse to one of his serfs. Of all things, that rankled the most: a shilling was not much for spending two hours of a Sunday afternoon, my supposed 'day of rest,' hacking at knee-high grass and weeds surrounding his house with a blunt scythe or nailing doors back on their hinges in his house or hosing down his mattresses to wash them and leaving them hung over a washing line to dry.

'Is old Sago Coxwaite still alive?' Richard asked next.

'Just about, though it's a wonder how.' It was my mother interjecting, contemptuously, it has to be said, from her position beside the range. 'A man his age living alone oughtn't to have to go out to work to keep himself fed like he does. The Government don't give old people half enough. They should give him and all the others a proper pension, not the measly amount they dole out.'

'Some of them have more to spend than I do,' I pointedly reminded her.

My mother, equally pointedly, ignored me. 'Huh!' she sniffed. 'The way the Government do it, you'd think they were giving away their own money, not what people have paid in taxes over the years. We had enough of that before the war, people starving on the dole. Don't they know you need money to keep body and soul together? How else are you going to do it? Promises won't do it, will they? If we hadn't had the Threepenny Teapot Club round here, half the old people in the village would have gone before their time because they didn't have enough money to buy proper food. It doesn't matter what Government is in, Churchill and his lot, or Attlee and his lot, they're all the same in my book. Useless! It was the Teapot Club which kept the old people going round here before the war, not the damned Government. Thre'pence a week, we paid. We looked after ourselves. People have just fought a war for better.'

As she was convinced she was right on most things, there was little point in arguing with her: indeed one of her favourite sayings was, 'I know I'm right!' which she used quite frequently in arguments with me. I had to smile at the surprise showing on Richard's face: when he asked the question, he had expected a simple answer: to be told the old man was either dead already or at least on his way, not to receive a diatribe against the Government.

But Old Sago, then in his seventy-fifth year, racked with arthritis, bronchitis and rheumatism, was still very much alive and 'still working': indeed, I had spent many an hour in his company. Richard, of course, had also known Sago before he left Norsea: Hoary had inherited the old man as a general labourer from the mustard manufacturer and Ben had kept him on till Richard left the village school and took his place. He had returned after Richard had left and had remained more or less ever since, though now he came across to work for us only in the pea-picking and bean-picking season or for the high summer harvest period when he stacked sheaves on the wagon while we pitchforked them up to him: or he helped us to thresh the stacks we built in the yard. He did what he could, in view of his age, and Ben was pleased to have him: Sago, though, I suspect, did it as much for something to do, to feel useful still, as for the pittance Old Hoary paid him to go with what little pension he received, or what little he got from the Teapot Club.

Richard went on to ask me about various other village figures: if Jack Spivey still ran the Chessman, if Rex Book still farmed Tithe Farm beside the church, if 'Ma Pop,' Mrs Popple, still taught at the two-roomed, red-brick school, if stuttering Fred Thorn was still the baker and did Ma Rowthey still run people's characters down in the post office-cum-grocery store in the Square? Richard smiled at my replies as I told him and then startled me further when he enquired if John Bolt was still the same miserable, miserly and moaning sod he had always been? To be truthful again, he did not use any of those words, just asked if he still farmed Boundary: but I happily supplied them in my answer!

'He's only got a nephew living with him now – Dennis, the poor sod,' I told Richard. 'You might remember him. He came to live here with his mother, a relative of John Bolt, when he was a baby. She used to keep house. She died when Dennis was about ten, just about the time I was born – bullied to death, most like. Dennis, the poor bugger, is more of a slave than a nephew. Made to work all hours, he is. He'd have been better off in an orphanage, I reckon. A darn sight happier, too.'

My use of the vernacular 'poor bugger' in Richard's presence drew a fierce look from my mother, but other than that she did nothing. Richard just nodded and smiled his twisted smile. 'I vaguely remember a woman being there,' he said. 'Beattie, I think her name was. And I vaguely remember a little kid with dark hair who was always getting shouted at by John Bolt.'

'That's him!' I cried, smiling, pleased that he had at least remembered.

Dennis Bolt was about twenty-six years of age then and would have been only six or seven when Richard left, so he did not pursue the matter. Instead, he asked me about my supposed social life: whether on Saturday nights I went into Maydun and what I did there.

It was the chance for which my mother had been patiently waiting: she was in with her retort before I could even begin to answer: 'He don't do nothing but drink when he goes there,' she snorted. 'All him and that creature from round the Maydun road ever do is go in the pubs. It's all they're fit for – wasting their money on drink! It's all they think about.'

My pained reply, that we always went to the cinema first and only came out at nine after the big picture had finished and only then did we go into a pub, was met with a similar sneer out of Richard's line of sight. Why, I do not know! One-and-a-half-hour's drinking once a week was not going to harm anyone. Billy and I drank only when we went into the small market town because both of us, and the other village boys with whom we went, were all under age and in Gledlang neither Jack Spivey at the Chessman nor Cliff Hinch at the Bowler's Rest up Tithe Street would serve us beer.

And when Richard asked with a grin bordering on the macabre if I went chasing the girls in Maydun – which I did, but never ever with anything like the success my friend Billy had – my mother was in quick to sneer again: 'Who'd have him? I ask you! Who'd have him? What girl in her right mind would want a dreamy lump like him?' Followed by another mocking 'Huh!'

We lapsed into silence for a while after that: we had both finished our porridge so my mother collected the plates and took them into the scullery to wash. While she was clattering about in there, I made another attempt to study Richard's face: the trouble was that I was torn between wanting to look closely to determine how the scarring and lumping had occurred and not wanting to look at all because of that very disfigurement, in case I betrayed what I was thinking. All during my eating, I had tried not to look up too much, but every now and again I felt I had to do so, especially when answering his questions: one cannot mumble down at the tabletop forever.

Richard must have sensed my embarrassment, for, unexpectedly, he leaned towards me and, very quietly and without any malice whatsoever, whispered so my mother could not hear: 'It's all right, Joe. I know my face is a mess. I don't mind you staring at it. I would hardly expect you to do anything else. Take a good look. I would probably do the same if I were in your shoes. It's a souvenir of the war, Joe, a souvenir of the war. Not a very pretty one, I have to admit, but beggars can't be choosers, can they? It's like it is because we didn't have proper medical treatment where I was when I got it. There's not much I can do about it. I'm stuck with it. Some day I'll tell you how it happened – if you're interested?'

Interested! Of course, I was interested! Where was he in the war? That is what I wanted to know. What was he doing? Was he in the Commandos? Had he been in the army? The navy? The air force? Which? Had he been there on D-Day, storming up the beaches, blasting the Jerries to kingdom come? Or at Arnhem, desperately clinging to the bridge, waiting for the tanks to arrive? Had he been in a bomber over Berlin? Or battling it out round the top of Norway on a destroyer bound for Murmansk or Archangel? Which? They were all questions I wanted to ask, and others, and I was determined to ask them the first chance I got: but for now there was the embarrassing matter of my looking at his face.

'I think you'll find, Joe,' he went on, looking straight at me, 'that the best thing to do is to have a good stare and get it over with, get it out of your system. I'm still the same bloke underneath that I always was – it's my face that's messed up, not my brain. You'll get used to it.'

'Oh, I'm not bothered by it,' I lied. 'It's just that – well, you can't help noticing it, can you? I mean it's there, isn't it?'

'I understand, Joe. I've had to live with it for the past two years. I didn't always look like this. But it's there and I can't do anything about it. I wish I could. I realise you don't see many like this round here.'

'We saw plenty of wounded soldiers in Gledlang,' my mother, coming back into the kitchen, interrupted sharply. 'They used to come here from the hospital at Wivencaster to go swimming.' Wise woman that she was, having overheard the last part of the conversation, she had guessed the subject and now proceeded to give me a look of cold fury: that, in her kitchen, a person should ever have to excuse the way they looked and to me of all people!

As if to make amends for my ill manners, she went over to the food cupboard and took out the dripping and two of our precious eggs to fry, rather than taking out the American egg powder with which she usually made our breakfast scrambled egg: then to my astonishment, she also pulled out half of our bacon ration and put that in the frying pan first. There was an awfully smug look on her face as she did so, the kind mothers give their sons when they say, 'I'll show you!'

While we waited, Richard asked me some more questions about Gledlang and Maydun and Wivencaster: I managed to answer most of them without incurring my mother's scorn: at least it did not show. While we ate our egg and bacon, she fried us both some bread, using the horrible grey bread we were getting at that time, which was about all it was fit for. For the most part, while we ate, I still kept my head lowered: despite Richard's understanding and affability, I still found it hard to meet his eyes. I was also anxious, of course, not to catch my mother's eye, for an obvious reason: try as I might, I could not alter the manner of my eating, head bent to within four inches of the plate, elbows out, food scooped up in a tight, windmilling action. Nor could I disguise the noisy slurp I made drinking hot tea, followed by an equally noisy gulp. Being conscious of all these things, I was observant enough to notice how upright Richard sat, compared with me, and how small were the pieces of egg and bacon he cut, again compared to mine. He made no sound as he chewed: he kept his mouth closed and, if I had not seen his Adam's apple moving up and down, I would not have believed he was drinking the tea at all. He also cut his fried bread in half, something I had seen someone do once in a cafe in Maydun, just as I had seen a silly woman in the self-same cafe eating a slice of cake with a fork when she could so easily have picked it up with her fingers!

It is true, for the times, the breakfast Richard and I ate was a hearty one, far better than most people, except the wealthy, ate in towns: but on Norsea we kept our own chickens and a pig, Percy, and always kept back some eggs from the government collector. Being a local man, though, we could always do a deal with him on the side: a half-bag of peas or beans in the early summer or a half-bag of potatoes in the autumn persuaded him to confirm our 'breakages.' Besides, you needed to eat properly if you were to spend a day out in the miserable cold and damp and mud of the fields.

SIX

I HAD just finished my second piece of fried bread when, from above, there was the sound of a pair of boots clumping on to the floor: instantly, a look of alarm spread over my mother's face.

'Good Lord! He's up already and no fresh tea made,' she cried and began to scurry about the kitchen, first to fill the soot-blackened kettle and the equally black saucepan from the pail, then to snatch up the packet of oats and pour them into the saucepan to make a new batch of porridge, before rushing to the table and sawing furiously at the loaf from which she had earlier cut our doorstep slices.

But it was Richard's reaction which held my attention: all of a sudden the colour seemed to drain from his cheeks: a faint shine of perspiration broke out on his brow and he tensed visibly, his eyes staring up at the ceiling as if following the tread of the boots above. As the footsteps clumped down the stairs, he half-rose in his chair, intent, it seemed, on putting what space he could between himself and the door. It was only my mother's calm reassurance which stayed him.

'Don't worry, it'll be all right,' she said, motioning for him to sit down again.

The door opened slowly and Ben shuffled in. A look of utter disbelief passed over Richard's face: nineteen years can bring unimagined changes to a person's appearance, more so when they are approaching old age and you see them again after so long a time. When Ben and Richard had last seen each other, Richard was just seventeen and Ben was just past his forty-fifth birthday, straight standing, well muscled and still with a full head of hair, still much the same as on the photograph taken on the day of his marriage to my mother fifteen years previously. The Ben whom Richard saw again that morning was now bald except for a few wisps of grey hair which straggled across his tanned and shining pate, the face was grizzled and browned even deeper than the dome, almost as if rubbed by a rag soaked in walnut stain. One eye was sunken in its socket and permanently watering and the striding, straight-backed man of before was now stooped and shuffling on bowed legs, a gait made all the more pronounced by the corduroy breeches tucked into leather leggings which he always wore. He seemed almost to have shrunk from the figure he once had been.

That morning, only for a brief instant, no more than the flickering of an eyelid, the involuntary quivering of the muscles around the mouth, the barely discernible trembling of one hand – only for a brief instant did Ben betray that obdurate, emotionless being he presented daily to the world. On seeing Richard, he halted in the doorway, eyes widening in surprise, then in shock, mouth hanging open, framed round the sentence he was about to speak to my mother. In the next instant, the face had been reset, the jaw tightened, the lips compressed over the tobacco-stained teeth, the nostrils flaring with a sudden stubbornness of pride.

Staring straight at Richard, he demanded with a brutal frankness: 'What the bloody hell are you doing back here?' And then almost scoffing: 'And what the bloody hell happened to your face? You look like you lost an argument with a bloody bandsaw, boy! Good God! We thought you were dead. We thought you were long gone. Dead in the war or before it. You might just as well have been for all we knew of ye and for all I care right now. I'll tell you this for nothing, Dick, you ain't welcome in this house n'more. Not now. Not ever. Not after what you did. So you can bloody git. You can bugger off back to where you come from and take that face o' yourn with you! We've managed to live our lives here without you for the last nineteen years and we can go on doing the same. So git! I don't want you in this house! I don't know what happened to your face, but I don't intend to spend the rest of my life looking at it. That I don't.'

To this day, I believe he said it because he considered men should say such things when confronted thus: pride overruled commonsense and compassion: and all else. If the unexpectedness and harshness of his attitude stunned me, it devastated my poor mother: standing as she was beside the range, stirring the saucepan of porridge, ready for Ben's entrance, she had given the faintest smile of greeting when he pulled open the door, anticipating the gladness of the reunion between father and son. Now she stood motionless, stunned, disbelieving her own ears, frozen by the unexpected viciousness of it all: one instant her face seemed drained of colour, the next it was crimson with embarrassment. Then, as women will on such occasions, she gave a stifled sob and tears of disappointment welled up in her eyes: Ben whirled on her at the first sound

'Don't you start that, woman,' he snapped, angrily pushing past her into the kitchen proper and to my side of the table, where he could face Richard, leaving him the only alternative of retreat through the kitchen door still ajar behind him.

Richard completed the rise to his feet and let out a barely discernible sigh, whether of disappointment or resignation, I am not sure. True, there was an air of weariness about his movements, but he kept his head high as he met Ben's hostile gaze and the hands that pushed back the chair were steady and untrembling. Even in that crushing moment, he was determined to remain dignified, as though he had half-anticipated Ben's hostility and had prepared himself for it.

At this point, my mother acted: she came bundling round the table and, using the time as an excuse, roughly evicted me from the chair. 'Come on, creature,' she cried, wet-eyed, 'you haven't got time to sit there gawping.' Unresisting, I was pushed round the table, past the grim-faced Richard, in the process of collecting up his kitbag and his overcoat, and out into the passageway: another violent shove propelled me through the back door into the yard, so I heard nothing more of Richard's and Ben's conversation, if indeed there were any, or what transpired after that.

My greatcoat and cap were unceremoniously thrown after me and any protest on my part or hope of a return were dissuaded by the set of my mother's jaw and the manner in which she blocked the doorway: since I expected little else from her, it made no impression on me, apart from remembering it here.

Yet I was not without feeling, callow youth that I then was: I was not indifferent to her pain: all I know is that I would have liked to have said something comforting to her in that moment, something to heal the rancour and distrust which existed between us and which was bared at almost every exchange.

But it was not to be: when I stopped to put on my greatcoat and she realised I had seen the tears again trickling down her cheeks, she became even angrier: the old hostility blazed once more in her eyes, telling me quite plainly that I had no right to have witnessed her disappointment and shame and still less to have felt any compassion for her. In her anger, she rushed a few steps down the path towards me, one fist clenched and raised and I had to dance quickly across the yard in order to put distance between us.

The last look my mother gave me as she slammed shut the back door was one of contempt and loathing and one which unmistakably excluded me from whatever private grief or sadness she felt at that moment. That was the way it always was between us: that was the way it had always been: all I could do was shrug at it all and go to work.

SEVEN

THAT FIRST day of Richard's return I laboured alone at the far end of the island, hoeing, a detestable task, hated by everyone whoever did it, for me the worst of all farm work since I did so much of it. Anyone who has never hoed a field on a bitterly cold April day with an east wind blowing ceaselessly across the flat, exposed fields along the Langwater estuary can count themselves fortunate that they had better, drier, warmer work in a factory or an office or a shop somewhere. Now most farm work is done by men sitting on machines in warm cabins, but in my youth, just after the war, it was mostly manual still, hard, back-aching labour, often lonely, soul-destroying, monotonous and seemingly never-ending.

Imagine yourself alone in one of Norsea's fields, a mile or more out from either mainland shore amid the vastness of the estuary so no sound reaches you to disturb your thoughts, not even from the squabbling white gulls soaring and diving over the meandering creeks and labyrinthed salting banks far out from the shore. All the time you are shuffling forward over the cloying, saturated earth with spine bent and back aching, arms wielding the hoe in the wearied manner of a slavish automaton as you chop at the earth down between the rows of, say, peas, beet or cabbage or broad beans: left, left, right, right, left, left...forever shuffling forward, forever forward. Ahead of you stretches the row on which you are working: perhaps the first, perhaps the tenth, perhaps the fiftieth you have hoed since you began, two hundred or more yards of it, say: and when finally you finish that row, there is another and another after that: fifty to the acre, two hundred or more to the field and all have to be hoed: and that is only the first field!

Overhead scudding grey clouds sweep in off the sea threatening rain, at best a short shower or fine drizzle, at worst a lashing downpour, icy and chilling, numbing the hands and stinging the face, and soaking through your mud-stained clothes. Too many such soakings, too many hours treading the sodden earth while the chill rises up through your boots into your bones, too many racking, untreated coughs and, inevitably, you know it will lead to all the ills and aches that so plagued Ben and his kind when I was growing up, bronchitis, pneumonia, pleurisy, rheumatism, arthritis and others.

Every half-minute or so you cast an eye up at the sky and pray it will not rain, or that the rain will stop, for there is nowhere to shelter in the middle of a field on an island in the middle of an estuary, except in the hedge and, anyway, sheltering was not allowed, not on Ben's time. You must work on through wind and rain and sleet and snow, work on even if a gale blows up: you just bend your head lower and press on through it all so long as you can stand. You begin in the early morning, say seven o'clock, and labour through all the long, lonely hours of the day when time seems to stand still and any distraction, a bird swooping overhead, an aeroplane high in the sky, a shaft of pale sunlight breaking through the clouds far off, is as welcome as would be a cheery word from a companion alongside you, anything to alleviate the brain-dulling sameness of it all. A half-hour for lunch, seated on a gate perhaps, but more often sitting on the cold earth in the lee of a hedgerow, then you return to your task. Not till the first glow of lamplight from the farmhouse in the purple dusk signals the end of your weary day can you gather up your things and trudge homeward: and as you put away your hoe in the barn or the shed, you know that you will be doing the same thing again tomorrow, and the day after that, and the day after that, perhaps for a whole week or more: and, if you are truly unlucky, as I often was, for a fortnight and beyond.

That is why I hated hoeing. I did it in the November fogs when the whole estuary was blanketed in a grey, saturating shroud and one felt as alone in one of Norsea's flat fields as one would if the whole world had vanished. I did it on freezing February days when blizzards of sleet blocked out the great elms which then lined many of the island's hedgerows and I did it on March, April and May days when the rains were endless and there was no-one to whom I could talk, and only a desperate, angry desire to finish the hated job and put it behind me drove me on from one row to the next, from one field to the next. Whether I did it for Ben because I had to or whether I did it for John Bolt on those occasions when I was 'lent out' to him to work on the arable part of Boundary's extensive acres, such work was the bane of my life.

That first day of Richard's return my mind was invested with a curious excitement, an anxiety which I had not known before: right from the start I wanted to have done with the day so that I might return to the farmhouse and learn more about him and what had happened after I had been ejected so unceremoniously from the kitchen, hoping against hope that he would still be there and had not returned to the mainland, and anxious, too, to put myself in a better light with him than had been possible at the breakfast table.

I found myself forever looking up to scan the far distance, just in the hope of seeing him come strolling along the track beside the field in which I was working or ambling along the headland in the next, renewing his links with the island that once had been his home by visiting and remembering the half-forgotten places. But sight of him there was none: only my mother appeared shortly before noon with some cold sardine sandwiches wrapped in newspaper and a lemonade bottle of warm tea.

'You can eat out here,' she said, pointedly dropping the sandwiches and tea over the gate, then turning on her heel and marching back to the dry and warmth of the farmhouse: and that was how I ate my lunch that first day, the same way I often ate my lunch, perched on a gate leading into a muddy field, huddled inside my greatcoat, and my cap pulled well down against the spits of rain that were just beginning to fall.

As the day dragged to its close, the unease within me grew, so that when at last I went clumping into the kitchen a quarter-of-an-hour before six, I knew immediately from the bad temper my mother was in that Richard and Ben had not made up their differences.

'He's gone to one of the cottages to sleep, if you really want to know,' my mother eventually declared in answer to my question, the curl of her lip signifying how much she resented my interest. 'I've been to see that creature – ' She meant Hoary, whom she detested so thoroughly that she could not bring herself to mention him by name. ' – and he says he can use one of the cottages for now. I've given him some blankets and a pillow off your bed. He can use Old Sago's mattress till I get something better. I said you would take some things round after tea when I had looked them out. You can take him some dinner, too, before your step-father gets in.'

Ben had spent that day working with our old mare, Molly, at the opposite end of the island to where I had passed my miserable and lonely day and, not unexpectedly, he did not come into the kitchen while I was there eating my evening meal. I suspected that he had eaten his cooked dinner at lunchtime and had taken sandwiches to the field for his tea so that he could work on till it got dark, something he often did, because for much of the time there was not much else to do on Norsea except work, eat, listen to the wireless and sleep.

'You had better have yours and keep out of his way,' my mother commanded, pushing a plate of stew and potatoes across the table to me almost before I had sat down. 'He won't want to eat with you or anyone else tonight, or for the next few nights, I shouldn't reckon. Just keep out of his way, will you. You've got plenty to do outside, so you don't need to go bothering him. I don't want him upset any more than he is already. I've had enough upsets for one day and I don't want any more caused by you and your stupid ways.'

My mother, never being one to mince her words, added a further warning: 'And I don't want you saying anything stupid about his face either – ' Meaning Richard's face. ' – It's bad enough as it is without you making it worse.' She gave an involuntary shudder. 'Ugh! To have that happen to you! And him still reasonably young, too. When you see him on the photographs – him and his mother – it's terrible, terrible. I can't get over that! I can't get over that!'

Another shudder followed as she raked at the lower ashes of the fire to get the blaze going again, all the time muttering to herself with scarcely concealed anger. 'Bloody Germans! Bloody, bloody Germans! Bloody, bloody, bloody Germans!'

Not unnaturally, to my mother's way of thinking, the Germans were solely to blame for Richard's disfigurement, no matter who had done it, them or the Italians or the Japanese: she meant, of course, that it probably would never have happened if there had not been a war: and the Germans had started that. Once, when I pointed out that we had declared war on them, not them on us, she had become even angrier. 'You know nothing,' she had snapped, furious that I should even challenge her on such a matter. 'You were too young. It was the bloody Germans who started the war. They wanted a war. If it hadn't have been for us, they would have done a lot more than they did. All those men killed, all those men killed!'

Perhaps there was some logic in what she said? Who knows?

EIGHT

THE COTTAGE to which Richard had retreated was one of a group of eleven single-storey, shiplap bungalows, some one-bedroom, some two-bedroom, which made up a small hamlet in the centre of Norsea, all empty then, built on two sides of an area of green with a flagpole and pump in the centre and forming what were grandly called East and North Streets. They had been erected cheaply before the First War by the philanthropic mustard manufacturer, purely to give the drunks and derelicts among London's dispossessed and downtrodden a holiday amid the fresh air and bracing breezes of the Langwater. At any one time, twenty or thirty of these shambling, dull-eyed, palsied creatures, all men, would have been seen wandering about the island under the watchful eye of their nurses and minders, bathing and paddling off the southern beach, performing calisthenics on the square of green, even helping with what farmwork was done then, all in the vague hope that it would induce a cure: and there they remained summer-long, with no way of getting off the island unless they slipped past the guards at the causeway or swam for it. Such an altruistic endeavour was inevitably doomed: it lasted no more than three years, ending just before the First War began, undermined by cynical locals, who rowed out to Norsea under cover of darkness with cases of ale and bottles of whisky and gin in their punts and sold them to the desperate alcoholics at a good profit. So no one was cured and the whole effort was a waste of time and money, but then the philanthropic mustard manufacturer had plenty of both, unlike us.

In Nineteen-Fifteen, the Government put two coastguards and their families in the cottages because it was feared that, for some unaccountable reason, the German Grand Fleet might steam up to the mouth of the Langwater and shell Maydun from long range like it had shelled Hartlepool, Whitby and Great Yarmouth a few months before. It never did, of course: it had no reason to do so: there was nothing in Maydun worth shelling, except a boatyard, a couple of corn mills, the salt works and a timber yard where trench duckboards were later made for the Western Front. But after the Kaiser's navy had been trounced at Jutland – so they told us at school, anyway – and with the war at an end, both families had moved back to the mainland in the November of Eighteen, wearied by the isolation and the tidal strictures of island living and unwilling to face another winter on Norsea. All this, of course, was before Ben's time.

For the next twenty years, after Hoary's brother bought the island, the cottages were left empty and became somewhat dilapidated: the bats and the mice moved in and, when the Ministry of Something-or-Other commandeered them soon after the start of the Second War, Ben and Old Sago, his sole help again by then, had a devil of a time driving them out so that they could all be painted up and their leaking roofs repaired. For a brief and somewhat exciting few months during the invasion scare of Nineteen-Forty, a motor torpedo boat had tied up on Norsea's southern shore and men had come from Maydun to repair our wooden pier and build a petrol bunker as well as dig two concrete-sided machine-gun pits at either end of the island. At the time the shallow estuary was considered a possible crossing point for Hitler's hordes coming up from the South Coast and we were warned we might have to pack up and quit at very short notice, which did not please my mother over much, especially as she was just harvesting her best ever crop of tomatoes, gooseberries and radishes from her garden at the side of the farmhouse. There was even a seaplane moored in the main creek for a while and two pilots, six torpedo boat sailors, plus their officer, and four Wrens, plus their officer, living in the cottages, fourteen people in all, quite a crowd on a small island. The Wrens operated a wireless station of some kind in a nissen hut erected on one corner of the green and were all city girls, as far as I could make out, for they were not at all like the village women: they wore bright lipsticks and pencilled their eyebrows and blacked their eyelashes every day and at times could be very rude in their gestures and language towards the ordinary sailors and the workmen. They also seemed to spend a lot of the time laughing and joking with the sailors and, in a sense, they were my first introduction to the 'pleasures' of what life had to offer other than school till I was fourteen and the prospect of never-ending work after that. On sunny days I used to watch them bathing in the river in their vests and bloomers because none had a swimming costume. Often the weight of the water would make their bloomers sag and slip down over their bottoms or their hips as they waded ashore, but they never seemed to care: they did not seem to care either if their soaked vests became so transparent that they showed off everything they had, which was all very disturbing to me. They might give a squeal and run up the shingle beach if a man were nearby, but they did it laughing, knowing what he was looking at and why. Once, when their own officer and the young naval lieutenant in charge of the sailors were away on the mainland, I saw one of the Wrens disappear with one of the torpedo boat sailors to the far end of the island, where the grass was longer, but I never got near enough to see what they did.

The Wrens were all very nice to me, though, because I was only nine years of age at the time: they all gave me a smile when they saw me about the island or when I watched each evening as they lowered the flag from their flagpole while one of the sailors blew on a bugle. I even had a ride with the sailors to the mainland on the torpedo boat once, just to go to school, while the Wrens were always happy to invite me into one or other of the cottages for tea and to share their strawberry jam sandwiches and Swiss rolls. One even gave me a kiss and a hug when I fell out of a tree and bruised my leg just as she was walking nearby: I could not tell her that I had climbed the tree in the hope of seeing what her colleague and the sailor were doing a hundred yards away in the long grass.

But, sad to say, they all left after six or seven months: the seaplane pilots took off one day and never came back: a week later the Wrens marched across to the mainland with their arms swinging, climbed on to a lorry and drove off: some sailors came in a big motorised barge to remove the machine guns, the nissen hut, the wireless mast and the petrol bunker and in time the weeds grew back around the concrete pits, while the torpedo boat, which was really a rescue craft for shotdown airmen, was moved five miles downriver to Strood Island right at the estuary mouth because Norsea was too susceptible to low tides and it was no good having a rescue boat that could not be launched.

Ben just went on farming, helped by Old Sago, coming up to seventy then: he tried to get a Land Army girl as a replacement, but never did: they were needed for bigger places, so Old Sago kept coming. 'Working for the war effort and digging for victory,' he said. Now seven years later he was still riding over each spring once the weather grew warmer, the only man in the village prepared to put up with the isolation and discomfort of bedding down in one of Norsea's derelict cottages for three or four days at a time when the tide was against him and there was no prospect of a drink at the Chessman. Apart from a few missing tiles, blown off in some winter storm, and a cracked or broken window pane here and there, the cottages were still quite habitable really and indeed needed only a good coke fire lit in their grates to dispel the damp from their rooms, a brisk sweep with a broom to clear the dust and cobwebs and a good rattle and bang with a stout stick against the rafters and the floorboards to drive out the bats and starlings from under the roof and the field mice and voles from under the foundations. Small as they were, the cottages would have been quite pretty places if someone had taken the trouble to paint the flaking doors and window-frames, weatherproof their outsides and hack down the jungle of brambles, nettles, thistles and docks which choked their sagging-fenced gardens.

Old Hoary had talked rather grandly of letting them out as 'holiday cottages' to some unsuspecting city dwellers who he presumed would want to spend their summers on 'idyllic Norsea,' but then he was always full of absurd ideas. He had even placed an advertisement in one of the London newspapers, which, he said, had cost him a phenomenal amount, but thus far had not received a single reply. Ben was not at all keen on having strangers 'parading about the place,' as he put it, and he and Old Hoary had had a sharp exchange on the matter, but Old Hoary went ahead anyway. He owned the island, he airily declared, or at least his family did, and 'you, Benjamin, are only the farm bailiff,' so he, Hoary, could and would do whatever he pleased! Ben just called him a 'daft, old sod' and told him that no-one in their right mind would want to spend a holiday on Norsea when they could go to Brighton or Bournemouth or Eastbourne or Margate. 'There ain't no sandy beaches round here,' he snorted, 'just mud!' It was true, too.

My mother, with her usual contrariness, simply named them 'the far cottage' or 'the near cottage' or 'the one this side of the pump' or 'the one the other side of the pump' and so on, trusting everyone else's intelligence was equal to her own and they would know immediately which one she meant. Mind you, she did the same with our relatives in Gledlang: there was 'her by the school,' and 'them along Tottle road,' as well as 'the one in the end house,' and 'old Auntie by the Square,' harmless identifications for those with whom she got along. For those with whom she did not get along, especially my dead father's two brothers, Uncle Arthur and Uncle Albert, it was 'him who's always in the pub' and 'that shiftless creature in Tithe Street.' Even then, these were mild compared with some of the others she used about villagers unrelated to us – 'that lot who were barefoot when they come here and now put on their airs and graces like they're better than us,' or 'that bloody traitor who said he didn't care who won the war so long as he didn't have to go and fight and then had the gall to join the rest of us in the Square on VE Night,' not to mention 'her who was always in Maydun on Saturday nights when the soldiers were there.'

NINE

RICHARD had taken up residence in 'the third cottage the other side,' according to my mother: my mistake was to look suitably blank as to where I was to take the cardboard box containing, among other things, a basin of warm stew, a half-loaf of bread, some cheese, butter and jam, a tin of sweetened condensed milk, various cubes of soup, along with a cup, two plates, two well-scrubbed pans, and knife, fork and spoon, all polished till they shone and all supposedly surplus to requirements from our poor stock.

'Good God! Haven't you got any brains?' my mother exploded as I began to ask which cottage she actually meant: the threat of a wet rolled tea-towel across my face saw me quickly on my way.

It was dark by then, but knowing every inch of the island, having lived on it since I was a year old, I had no trouble picking my way round the potholes, puddles and mud patches along the rutted track in the rain and the dark: fortunately, Richard had lit a lamp so I had no trouble finding which was his cottage after all.

After a minute or so of banging on the door, Richard swung it open, yawning and rubbing at his unshaven chin, his tousled hair and dishevilled appearance informing me that he must have just risen from his 'bed.' I had anticipated he would show some grumpiness or displeasure because I was intruding and I was prepared to thrust the heavy box at him and retreat: but he appeared to be genuinely pleased to see me, which heartened me no end, and greeted me with a broad smile on the good side of his face.

'Hullo, young Joe. Come in, come in,' he said, opening the door wider and motioning me past him into the front room, where a smoky coke fire was glowing in the grate.

'I've brought you some things from my mother,' I said, but unfortunately, the words came out sounding far grumpier than I intended. I was horribly aware even then of the crudeness of my speech beside his clearer and more precise pronunciation, for I spoke with the gruff dialect of the region, never having known any different. In fact, so bad was my rural manner of speaking that, when I had gone to the secondary school at Maydun, the English teacher had threatened to give me elocution lessons because, she said, she could hardly understand a word I said! My faux pas on meeting Richard again only made me even more reticent in his company, embarrassed as I was already by the knowledge that he and I were actually 'linked,' if not by blood, by family at least.

Richard did his best to put me at my ease. 'Put them on the table, will you, please, Joe,' he said, nodding towards a rickety collapsible card table under the window, at the same time buttoning his shirtfront and tucking the tail of it into his trousers, 'and be sure to thank your mother for me.' I obeyed the first of Richard's instruction and made a mental not to bother with the second.

'Old Sago sometimes sleeps here,' I said, setting down the box and turning back to face him: really, it was said just for the want of something to say, an apology for the dowdiness of the place.

'I guessed as much,' Richard said with a grin, a gesture of the hand conceding the bareness of the place: the rickety table and a battered, horsehair sofa comprised the only furniture in the room, while on the table itself were Old Sago's only utensils, a chipped cup and a plate gathering mould and an empty ale bottle gathering cobwebs in which was stuck a stub of unlit candle. Apart from the fire, the only source of light was a lopsided paraffin lamp with blackened glass which stood in the hearth alongside a soot-blackened kettle and handleless saucepan.

'We ain't seen much of him since potato-lifting finished last year,' I informed Richard. 'I don't know whether we shall see much of him this year after the winter we've just had. He gets bronchitis bad sometimes and we've just had a real ding-dong of a winter.'

Richard looked puzzled, so I explained: having only recently arrived in England from wherever he had come, he would not have known that the winter just past had been the worst in living memory, so the older people had said: the worst for a century, according to some. Towards the end of January, through all of February and into March, the whole of our region had been blanketed under deep snow: we had had fall after fall and blizzard after blizzard till on Norsea the snow had lain two-feet deep in the fields and four-feet to five-feet deep in places where it had drifted: against our barn, wherever the rutted track was banked and against the hedgerows. The temperature had plummeted below freezing on most days and, worst of all, for weeks on end we never saw the sun: just snow and ice and grey gloom and bitter, knifing winds which blew off the North Sea day after day. Ben and I had been unable to do any work at all in the fields because they were either too deep in snow or the ground was frozen iron-hard. On one Sunday I had seen ice floes drifting upriver on the incoming tide and when it went out again they lay along Norsea's southern shore like large, irregular panes of shattered green glass, five or six feet across in some cases. I had spent much of my time doing jobs in either the barn or the wagon shed till the thaw had come in mid-March, bringing with it the inevitable floods so that our lowest-lying fields resembled lakes rather than arable land. Indeed, I had spent a whole fortnight digging drainage channels to run the water off the fields: in my book, splashing through thick mud and icy water day after day in turned-down wellingtons with a spade in your hand rates second only to standing in the middle of a field with a hoe as the worst of farm jobs.

Consequently, all our crops were late: the spring weather had finally come and there was much for us to catch up on: that was why Ben found it necessary most days to work late into the evenings to get things done which should have been completed weeks before, and why he expected me to do the same. It was also why I was left alone so much, why I hoed alone, dug drainage channels alone, deepened ditches alone, laid hedges alone and riddled potatoes alone from our clamp: he had plenty to do elsewhere.

'Not much of a place, is it?' I said, picking up the mould-covered cup and pretending to inspect it, again for the want of something to do to conceal my nervousness.

Richard gave a shrug as he looked about him. 'I've been in worse,' he said, 'much worse than this.' He offered no explanation. 'I shall just have to lump it, that's all,' he went on. 'It's home of a kind. It'll do for now, anyway.'

That was the first intimation Richard had given that he intended to stay: that he did not intend on the morrow to pick up his kitbag and leave. I found myself strangely pleased, but gave no hint of it: we never did in our family. I just stood there dumbly, trying not to catch Richard's eyes or to look at his face and unsure of what I ought to do next. Having completed my mother's errand and, unable to think of anything else to say, I began to shuffle sideways to the door.

Just as I went out, Richard touched my arm. 'Don't worry about this morning, Joe,' he said. 'I half expected it. I don't blame my father – Ben. It's more my fault than his. Ben and I never did see eye to eye, even when I was here before.' With a sigh he added: 'Things happen in life, Young Joe, that you can't always control. You just have to live with them. I can't say I'm happy about it, but there isn't much I can do about it, except live with it, the same as I have to live with this.' He meant his face.

As I moved off down the path, Richard called out with a laugh: 'I'll probably see you around tomorrow then, Joe – step-brother Joe,' he added after a short pause.

Step-brother! I went home very happy that night.

TEN

FOR THE FIRST week after Richard's return my mother seemed to do everything in her power to ensure that I had no opportunity to aggravate an already fraught situation: somehow she contrived that neither Ben nor I should sit at the same meal table together, calling me a good half-hour before him in the morning and letting him sleep late deliberately so that I breakfasted alone.

When I left for the field to resume my three weeks of hated hoeing, she thrust a packet of either stale cheese or cold sausage sandwiches into my hands, along with a bottle of barely lukewarm tea, the glare in her eyes rather than any spoken word giving the clear warning that on no account should I return to the farmhouse before teatime. And when I did return in the evening and stood warming myself by the range fire, my meal was already cooked in readiness and served ahead of time, separately from her own and Ben's, so that my plate and cup had already been washed and put away in the dark wood sideboard when he eventually came stamping in, having delayed his own return for the very same reason that he did not wish to share his meal table with me either.

'I just don't want you upsetting him. I just want you out of the way till he's got over it,' my mother declared fiercely one such evening. Then with that sneering smirk of hers, she added: 'And it ain't no use you going round there to see him – ' Meaning Richard ' – because he ain't there. He's gone off somewhere. I saw Sligger Offin's taxi come for that other creature this morning and I saw him in it, too. So don't expect him back for a while. You've got enough to do in the evenings anyway.'

It was no surprise that Richard should seek to renew his acquaintance with Hoary, having, as I say, known him in his youth and having worked for him just as I did then, especially as he also needed Hoary's permission to stay in one of the cottages, anyway. My mother, never one to miss a trick, had seen them talking together by the cottages the day after Richard's arrival. 'Lord, I hope he's not going to take up with that creature!' she had wailed, genuinely, I believe. 'Whatever does he think he's doing? That thing of all people!' Her ravings against Old Hoary and the icy indifference she showed towards him whenever he called at our house to talk to Ben never seemed to faze the old man: he always smiled and addressed her politely as 'Mrs Wigboe' and was always the gentleman: she, sad to say, was never the lady and no sooner had she banged shut the door after him than she would launch into one of her usual tirades against him.

Her remark that I had plenty to occupy myself in the evenings was an understatement if ever there were one! No sooner had I finished my tea than I would be chivvied outside to do some of the neverending chores which always needed to be done on a farm and which Ben, having told me once which ones to do and when, expected me to do them without being told again: like feeding the chickens if my mother had not already done so, mashing up our potato peelings and boiling them and other waste for Percy's pig food, shovelling any urine-soaked straw and droppings from Molly's stable or the pigsty on to the manure heap in the corner of the yard, creosoting the outside of the chicken huts, or the stable, or the barn or the tumbledown wagon shed. And if I were not doing any of those delightful tasks, I could be found cleaning, de-rusting and greasing any equipment which we intended to use in the next week or so, the next month or so, or the next year or so, like our plough, our seed drill, our cultivator, harrow, roller, binder, cart and wagon, all of which competed for space in the barn or wagon shed. Or I might be mending a fence or a gate, or humping twenty or so two-and-a-half hundredweight sacks of grain about the barn ready for Ben to do the winnowing, or sharpening implements like hoes, sickles, scythes, haycutters, beet hooks, stack knives, hedge-laying axes or ditch diggers: any of a hundred tasks: even splashing out a couple of hundred yards into the estuary to check on Ben's oyster beds. You do not spend idle hours on a farm: there is always something which needs doing today and something which should have been done yesterday.

And if I was not doing farm chores for Ben or my mother, there were a couple of score others which Hoary was always pressing me to do: the only difference was that from him I was able to extract a modest extra payment for the extra work, not a lot, just a couple of shillings or so, but at least it was something. Happily, though, now the winter was over, I was hoping to pass Hoary's tasks on to a new friend I had made in the past year, Stanley Lobel, a boy from Tottle, the next village to Gledlang, who, for reasons I will explain later, was looking to earn any and all money he could, particularly as he had left school and had no steady job: in fact, he had told me he did not want a steady job, just regular casual paying work. I was hoping he would soon be coming across to help relieve my burden, especially the most detestable task I did for Hoary: emptying his outhouse bucket and burying its contents: Stanley was more than welcome to take that over and all the others: but till he came, I still had to do Hoary's chores as well as the ones Ben demanded about the farm.

Seeing nothing of Richard for several days, I continued with my hoeing during the day and my two hours of chores in the evening. During the day, Ben did not even bother to come to the field to check on my work, which most times he usually did daily, just to ensure I was doing it right, I hoped, rather than whether I was doing it at all: I think we just avoided each other. Even when Ben was in the house and I came in from the yard, any conversation he was having with my mother mysteriously ended the moment I banged shut the door and he was off into his tiny, cubbyhole office at the end of the stone-flagged passageway across from the parlour to do his paperwork at the roll-top desk and smoke his straw-thin cigarettes for the rest of the night. A curt 'Don't you go in there!' from my mother was enough to keep me out.

So for the next five days and evenings we hardly saw each other, even though we lived in the same farmhouse. On two of those evenings, in the hope of escaping my tedious chores, I went round to call on Richard early in the evening to see if he had returned from wherever it was he had gone, but I got no answer when I knocked and, grudgingly, had to return to the farmyard. The first evening I spent my time from seven o'clock till nine in the barn patching ripped grain sacks with fish glue: the next night, still with no sighting of Richard, I creosoted the inside of the chicken shed and splattered my cheeks so badly that the skin on them peeled like the skin of an onion. My mother put some butter on them, naturally all the while cursing me for my stupidity, but at least she did allow me to sit with her in the parlour, uncomfortably so, I must say, listening to the wireless.

We listened to the wireless then as a matter of course on most nights and as a way of passing the time from the end of chores till bed. Some nights, if I were lucky enough not to have any to do, which was seldom, I might catch the six forty-five *Dick Barton* serial with Jock and Snowey or hear the cowboys singing on *Big Bill Campbell's Rocky Mountain Rhythm* or I might get to listen to a comedy programme, say, with Arthur Askey in *Forever Arthur,* or Richard Murdoch, Sam Costa and Kenneth Horne in *Much Binding In The Marsh* or Tommy Handley in *I.T.M.A.* (*It's That Man Again*!): but on other nights, I would have to suffer my mother's favourites, some orchestra playing dance music from a London restaurant, or Anne Zeigler and Webster Booth warbling away on Sunday evenings, followed by *Grand Hotel* and its Palm Court Orchestra.

If I so much as winced at any of it, she would be up out of her chair with her arm raised and her fist clenched. 'Well, I like it,' she would cry. 'They play the old songs. I like the old songs even if you don't!' Or 'I like hymns! I'll listen to what I want!'

The wireless was a large, pre-war cabinet type with a fancy fretwork front which stood on top of the sideboard, with my mother and Ben's wedding photograph alongside: we had no electricity on Norsea so the wireless was battery-operated, which is why my mother rigidly controlled its use: so that the batteries did not run down too quickly.

Only on the fifth evening of that first week of Richard's return, the Friday, did I manage to escape from Norsea on my bicycle and escape, too, the dreaded organ music and prancing dance music which my mother so liked. The trouble with living on an island was that there were only two periods each day, about six hours each, when one could cross the causeway: for the rest of the time, the narrow ribbon of rock and shale was under water, covered either by the outgoing flood or the incoming tide creeping back: so you were stuck on the island unless, of course, you rowed to the mainland or were foolish enough to try and swim the mile or more against the current.

In the village, as usual, I sat talking with Billy Garner and Nick Coxwaite, Sago's grandson, and the other village boys on the broken ciderstone beside the pump in the Square. The five-foot-diameter granite ciderstone had been brought up from Somerset by one of the local farmers on a wagon sixty years before so that he could make cider from his apples: just as it reached Gledlang Square, a wheel broke, the wagon tipped and the ciderstone slid on to the road and broke: the farmer just manoeuvred the two halves to the side beside the pump and left them. Ever after, the broken ciderstone became the place where the youths of the village sat, and still sit, to while away the tedious hours of evening. Sometimes, if we tired of sitting there and someone had a ball, we would play football against the blank wall of the Chessman's beer store, but so many wet tennis balls had thudded against the yellow distemper and covered it with brown blotches that Jack Spivey was forever coming out to chase us off. 'Bugger off, you young sods!' he would shout. 'Go and play in your own backyard,' which meant anywhere but his.

That night we were joined for a change by the stoop-backed, long-striding, mole-faced Lennie Ring, with whom I was not so friendly, enemies really: still, I put up with him and his gruff and grumpy ways because Billy and Nick regarded him as their friend and I was eager to tell them of Richard's return. But when they questioned me about him – where he had been and what he had been doing while he was away all that time – I realised I had very little to tell them, other than that he was back and had a badly scarred face, which I described as best I could. How he had got it – war wound, trapped in a blazing bomber, hit by shrapnel, blown up by a mine? – I still did not know at that time.

'You don't know much then, do you?' was Billy's sarcastic retort when my repetitive 'Don't know. I haven't asked him yet.' failed for the fifth or sixth time to answer any of their questions.

Lennie Ring did sneeringly ask how Ben had reacted on seeing him again. 'All right,' I lied, 'a bit surprised he came back without telling anyone, but all right other than that. Glad to see him.' I certainly was not going to tell him what had really happened, or Billy and Nick for that matter.

'Where's he now, then?' Nick asked.

'I don't know. I haven't seen him since he came back on Monday. Gone off with Hoary somewhere, I think,' I replied feebly. 'I haven't seen either of them this week,' which was true, for despite my mother's crowing, I had still looked for Richard daily. That Old Hoary was missing for the whole of that week, too, was nothing unusual: sometimes we never saw him for days on end: sometimes a fortnight passed without a sign of him, all of which pleased us greatly as it meant we could get on with the business of farming without his interference. If the old man had lain dead somewhere, I doubt that Ben or I would have gone looking for him for at least a month or more: I shudder to think what we might have found if it had ever happened, especially in the heat of summer: we had enough bluebottles on Norsea as it was, especially around the dung heap.

My repeated failure to answer the questions Billy and the others put to me meant that they soon lost interest and went on to talk about more interesting things, interesting to them, anyway, such as the workings of a new Fordson N tractor, which the farmer for whom Lennie Ring and Nick both worked had just bought, or whether Kerry the Milkman would ever get enough clothing coupons from the village women to enable him to buy ten red shirts for the football team he was trying to form. Billy and Nick wanted it called Gledlang Gunners after Arsenal, while Lennie Ring hoped it would be Gledlang Hotspurs. (It eventually played under the name of Gledlang Wanderers, not because Wolverhampton Wanderers were the top team then, but because no farmer would give them a field on which to play anywhere within the village so they played on a field full of cowpats a mile out along the Salter road and strung ropes between surplus army tent poles for the goals, just like back in the Eighteen-Eighties.)

The only time that evening that I again bothered to take part in any debate, which was to prove a great mistake, was when we were joined by Lennie Ring's older brother, Fred, home on leave from Germany, where he was doing his National Service with the British Army of the Rhine. Fred Ring was a boaster, a line-shooter, a braggart and a bully, I always reckoned, and he and I had never been over keen on each other, even before he was called up: to put it bluntly, we detested each other. We had clashed too many times to be friendly towards each other and, where I was concerned, both Lennie Ring and Fred Ring seemed to be adopting an aggressive stance towards me. Fred Ring was in uniform that night and, as he was transferring from one camp in Germany to another, he had brought his rifle home with him and was showing us how soldiers performed their drill, to let us know how difficult it all would be when we 'went in' to do our compulsory two-years of National Service, as in time we were all bound to do.

Too often in the past I had found myself disputing things Fred Ring had said, once or twice to such an extent that he had threatened to give me 'a smack in the mouth.' He never had, but that did not mean he would not have tried, given half a chance. That night I gave him his chance.

As I recall it, he had finished showing us his rifle drill – 'slope arms, porter arms, present, stand at ease!' – and was describing in the most lurid detail the sights and goings on he and his army mates had seen down a certain street in Hamburg, the Reeperbahn, which was notorious for its prostitutes: one in every doorway, he said, and some who sat brazenly in brightly lit windows in their underwear so that you could see everything, while behind them in full view of everyone passing was the actual bed on which you were expected to shag them behind a curtain. Sometimes, he said, in some of the worst of the bombed buildings, there was only a blanket draped over a clothesline between where you were grinding away at the daughter of the house and the rest of the family were sitting around the stove trying to warm themselves. When I challenged him over some of the more far-fetched things he said he had witnessed in the brothels, which he claimed to have visited regularly, he sneeringly produced a sequence of four postcard-size photographs which he had bought in one of them. They showed a naked woman lying on a bed facing the camera with her legs apart and doing something with a cucumber which I found so incredible I refused to believe what the others said she was doing. Surely the photograph had been faked! By the brighter light in the village telephone kiosk, I carefully studied all four photographs, ghastly as each was, convinced that for each of them she must simply have sliced off the top of the cucumber so that it got shorter and shorter. Billy, who had squeezed into the kiosk with me, went into hysterics when I protested that was what she must have done: I just could not believe what he claimed she was doing. No woman would ever do that to herself! At that, Fred Ring, who was waiting outside, called me 'a naive little twerp,' which immediately brought my temper boiling up: I flew out of the telephone kiosk and had swung at him – and missed – before I realised what I was doing. The red mist had descended: I was not in control, especially when the jeering came from the likes of Fred Ring and his brother Lennie.

'Try that again and I'll bloody kill you!' roared soldier Fred, raising his own fists, incredulous that I should even think of challenging him, me a clod of a village boy with no experience of the world, and him a trained soldier, taught to shoot and kill the King's enemies, polish his own boots and make his own bed! At least, I have no doubt that was what he was thinking as we stood glowering at each other with our fists raised: I might have been three years younger than him, but I was four inches taller and I must have had such an expression of rage on my face that he was actually reluctant to engage in a brawl, if only to protect his neatly creased uniform.

In reality, Fred Ring was no super-fit infantryman footslogging thirty miles a day with full pack, but was in the Royal Army Medical Corps, serving as an orderly in the camp hospital, the infectious diseases clinic, so I had heard, which out there meant taking urine samples and penis scrapings from infected soldiers who during their weekend leaves had gone with prostitutes like those in the doorways and windows of Hamburg and then spent the next fortnight worrying whether they had contracted syphilis or gonorrhoea, among other things, from 'some dirty tart.'

Sadly, I made two mistakes that evening: the first was in not stepping back far enough to put myself out of range of Fred Ring's own raised fists and the second was to call him a 'syphilitic arsehole!' Where I got the correct adjective from, I still do not know to this day: it just came out, so I must have heard it somewhere before. It was too much for brave soldier Fred: he rushed at me with arms flailing and managed to land a blow on my chest which sent me staggering back another yard or so, thus allowing him to advance and swing a polished army boot at my knee cap while I was off balance. I had to skip hastily back on my one good leg to avoid a second kick on the other kneecap, which momentarily surrendered to him the advantage of momentum in attack.

'Go on, piss off back to your bloody island, Coe, you little turd!' he yelled, nostrils flaring and jaw jutting out as he squared up to his full height, all five-foot seven-inches of him. I was no hero, but I was no coward either: there was no way I was going to allow myself to be bullied by a bloody bedpan emptier, so I gave him the traditional two-word reply, adding, perhaps a little too sarcastically, that if he was an example of what the British Rhine Army could produce, God help the rest of us because the bloody Russians would walk all over us in the next war! I knew immediately I had overstepped the mark when his face went apoplectic purple.

He gave a great roar of rage. 'Come here, you cheeky effing bastard!' he cried and a chubby, supposedly muscular, arm reached out to grab me by the throat: but I had seen that done in a fight in Maydun and I was too quick for him: years of dodging my mother's swinging arm to avoid the lash of her wet tea-towel had made me too nimble to be caught by someone as clumsy and stupid as Fred Ring. Before he even got near, I was dancing away out of range and jeering back at him.

Private Fred made a half-hearted effort to catch me, but ran only a few paces before stopping because I ran faster and within seconds I had grabbed my bicycle from where I had propped it against the wall and was pedalling off down Shoe Street towards Norsea and home.

'I'll knock your bloody block off next time I see you, you ignorant little twat,' Fred Ring bellowed after me: as a parting gesture, I half-turned in my seat and gave him the traditional two-fingered Agincourt salute. The last I heard from him that night was a shouted warning: 'Don't you come back here while I'm still here, Joe Coe, or there'll be trouble. Stay on your bloody island with that daft old bugger you work for!'

None of that really bothered me: I had been humiliated before: it was water off a duck's back to me: besides, I knew Fred Ring was home on leave for only another two weeks, then he would be going back to Germany and his round of bedpan emptying and consoling syphilis sufferers. He had another ten months to serve, so, with luck, I had almost a year's grace at least before he came home again and by then he might have mellowed or, better still, might have forgotten all about it. No, what upset me was that neither Billy nor Nick had made any effort to come to my defence: I did not expect them to fight my fights, but I did expect them to take my side against the likes of Fred and Lennie Ring and they had not. There had not been a single word of support from either: not a whisper: Nick had slunk away behind the telephone kiosk as soon as the fighting started and Billy, who was supposed to be my best friend, had simply contented himself with yelling, 'Fight! Fight!' like it was all a joke.

Billy had already annoyed me earlier: when Fred Ring and I had stood glowering at each other in the few seconds of calm before the action started properly, Billy had gleefully sniggered: 'Don't you know anything about girls? Some of them stick a rubber dick up it and do it themselves. They buy them from the chemist's. They don't need you to do it. You know your trouble, Joe, you're too shut away on that bloody island of yours for you own good. You want to get yourself a girlfriend, mate, and you might learn a thing or two. What you need is for some bird to take your dick in her hand and give it a good rub because it stands to reason one ain't done it so far!'

He was right about the last thing and may well have been right about the rest: I was sixteen years of age at the time and I had never had a girlfriend, either in Gledlang or Maydun, whereas Billy had had several. My experience of girls was abysmal: mainly the fading memory of the Wrens on Norsea bathing in the river on summer Sundays when I was a nine-year-old and an unexpected breath-catching erotic moment when I had come across a woman visitor to the estuary sunbathing on the seawall near the causeway without her blouse and brassiere, though she had hastily covered herself at my approach. I lived in hope that I would be lucky enough one day to come across a group of village girls dressing in the long grass of the seawall after a swim in the river and that at least one of their towels would slip before they had pulled up their knickers and give me a glimpse of something I was not supposed to see. Other than those, the most potent stirrer was seeing the silhouetted legs of older girls showing through thin cotton summer dresses when they were not wearing a slip or petticoat and inadvertently crossed from shadow into sunshine: when older women did it, I turned away.

Girls just did not seem to find me attractive: in my sixteen years, the only offer of sex I had ever had had come from a man: he was called Hawksley and was the son of some rich family over Inworth way: he had either dodged going to the war somehow or been turned down by the forces because he was supposed to have a weak heart. He used to ride around the villages in a big black open tourer with a folding hood, looking like some California film star in his dark sunglasses, open neck shirt and cravat. Every boy he met he would ask if they wanted to go for a ride in his car: he asked me once: pulled up alongside and just asked. I told him: 'No, thanks.' We had all been warned about Hawksley.

One evening Billy and the rest of us came across his car parked by the ciderstone: Hawksley had gone into the Chessman for a drink, but there was a boy of about twelve sitting on the back seat: he was a good looking boy with dark fringed hair: we asked him who he was and he said he was Hawksley's 'nephew.' Everyone laughed at that and the boy went very red and would not talk to us further. Six months later Hawksley was hauled up in court on buggery charges: the county weekly carried the story of the court case. There was a boy mentioned in it, aged twelve, who had been buggered so much by Hawksley that the ring muscle on his anus no longer functioned: the poor sod was totally incontinent and would be for the rest of his life. There you have it, my only offer of sex – from a raving, shirt-lifting queer!

As I weaved my way back to Norsea the night of the argument, I consoled myself that Billy had taken Fred Ring's side only because he was slightly in awe of him, over impressed by his arms drill: but once Fred Ring had gone back to Germany, we would resume our usual discussions on the ciderstone and talk over such things as the merits of a Fordson tractor, compared with a Massey-Ferguson or an Allis Chalmer, and who was doing what jobs on their respective farms: interesting things like that.

ELEVEN

IT WAS while I was on my way to Richard's on the Sunday morning, again to see if he had returned, that I was finally confronted by Ben: I had sneaked out of the house while my mother was upstairs and made my way round behind the wagon shed to get on to the main track through a gap in the hedge where some brambles had been burned the previous autumn. As I stepped out on to the path, I was confronted by Ben, walking Molly back from where he had been ridging potatoes: it happened so unexpectedly I had no way of avoiding him.

'I've been meaning to talk to you all week, Joe,' he said with evident embarrassment, bringing Molly to a halt. 'I mean away from her, away from your mother.'

'I'm just off to see if Hoary's geese are all right,' I lied, desperate for an excuse to explain why I was creeping about: the cackling geese gave it. At one end of the island, Hoary kept twenty or so of the birds which I sometimes fed as one of my chores: that morning they had been cackling loudly over something, probably no more than a dispute between a gander and a goose hustling him away from her nest: whatever it was, it was loud enough to be heard all over the island. The only problem was that the geese lay in the opposite direction to the one in which I was going.

That morning, I remember, was one of those bright, mid-spring days when the whole estuary shimmered under a clear blue sky: far off the sound of Gledlang's church bells could be heard tolling across the empty salt-sheened wastes, calling to prayer what few faithful there were in the village.

Ben just nodded at my lame excuse: he was not the least interested in my reason for being there: he had other things on his mind. He steadied Molly with a pat, took out his tobacco tin and began to roll himself a cigarette.

'I suppose you think I were wrong in what I did?' he said, questioningly, not looking directly at me, but concentrating on licking the cigarette paper and rolling it into shape.

My dilemma was obvious: if I said 'Yes,' then, in his eyes, I would be siding with Richard: if I said 'No,' then I would be condoning an action which completely mystified me.

'You must have had a reason for it,' I shrugged, hoping to give the impression that I was not bothered either way.

Ben clicked his lighter and put the flame to the end of his cigarette, peering at me from under the peak of his cap. 'You been going round to see him, have you?' he asked.

I could hardly lie: he would know if I did, anyway. 'I went round there last night,' I told him somewhat guiltily, 'but he wasn't in. He's been away all week.'

Ben sniffed and blew out some smoke. 'I can't stop you seeing him,' he said, a gruff displeasure in his tone. 'You're your own man now. You're coming up for seventeen in November, so you'll be in the army soon enough. And he is your step-brother, so to speak, even though you ain't of the same blood. I'm only your step-father, I know that. So I can't really stop you, can I? I just want you to know that I ain't especially proud of what I did, but a man has to have some pride – he has to retain something or he ain't nothing. All I say is that when Dick went like he did after his mother died, he had no reason to go that I could see, but he went just the same. He left me without a word of explanation at a bad time. No word where or anything. I always thought he'd come back sooner or later if only for a visit, like, to explain why he had gone, but he didn't. Nothing – not for month after month, year after year. He's stayed away all this time, never writing, never letting me know how he was or why he'd left. I know the war come in between, it's just that I felt he had turned his back on me, like I weren't good enough. Just an uneducated farmer. Not even that – just a farm bailiff. You see, Joe, I didn't know the reason why he did it, why he left, why he never wrote. It was like he didn't want to come back, ever. That's a hard thing for a man to accept, being rejected by his own son, his own flesh and blood, and never knowing why. It gnaws at your guts. It did mine – and I still don't know why. Then he comes swanning back out of the blue after nineteen years without so much as a word. Well, I just blew my top when I saw him. Exploded. It were all too much, too unexpected, him sitting at the table in the kitchen as large as life as though nothing had happened. All those years gone by and expecting everything to be just as it was. Well, I just wanted to give him back something of what he give me. That's all. Maybe it weren't the Christian thing to do, but, you know me, I ain't no psalm-singing churchgoer. Never was and with good reason –

' No explanation of the last remark. ' – You can't always turn the other cheek. I can't anyway. Sometimes you've got to give as good as you get. Your own pride tells you to, as you'll find out soon enough.'

Ben's voice trembled at this point: I think he was actually on the verge of tears, but he swallowed hard, puffed on his rapidly diminishing cigarette and managed to go on. 'Remember, I was a much younger man then, Joe. The day afore he left I had just buried my first wife, Mary, Dick's mother. Then he disappeared the day after the funeral. Just vanished. I was left here on my own and life weren't no bed of roses then. Farming weren't the best of jobs, not on this island anyway. No one wanted farmers or farm workers. There were farms up for sale all over the place and prices for everything were at rock bottom. It was a struggle. Things are different now, but they weren't then. We managed to keep this one going somehow, Old Sago and me when he come back, working all hours God sent. I didn't mind, it were my livelihood, but it were a lonely life for me all the same, especially on the nights when Old Sago rode back to the mainland. I ain't complaining – it's one I chose, but you know yourself how isolated it can be here, especially in the middle of winter when it gets dark early and the nights are long. Most of the time I had no one to talk to and not much to look forward to but an empty house and my own cooking. But I stuck it out. I think I kept hoping Dick would come back and it would be him and me together again. Father and son. You couldn't talk to Hoary, not like you can to another man – he ain't one of us. He ain't all there, is he? He's got more than a screw loose. You and I know that. We deal with him every day – ' A pause and a half-smile here before his face became set again. ' – After I buried Dick's mother, I was a lonely man till I met your mother when she come over here pea-picking with you in a pram. She were newly widowed after your father had died. Well, we got to liking each other and we got hitched up together. She's been a saviour for me. I know she and you don't always see eye to eye and that she can be a hard woman at times – ' That was an understatement if ever there was one! ' – but she don't mean much by it. Just looking out for your interests, that's all. She's been a rock to me or I'd have left this place long ago. Your mother is the only woman I know who would have stayed here. She ain't never once in the past fifteen years complained about it or wanted to leave it, unlike Dick's mother. She never wanted to come here in the first place and all she ever did was ask to leave it. She never stopped going on about it.'

Ben gave a cough and brown spittle mixed with the mud of the track: then came a flourish of brown and blue as he blew his nose on an oily handkerchief.

'Perhaps I should have left,' he said, wiping one watery eye, 'but it's too late to bother about that now. What's done is done. I can't undo what's already done, no one can. So you see why I blew up at Dick. Nineteen years of hurt was just too much, I suppose. I was sorry to see about his face. That were a real shock, but I can't do anything about it, no one can. He's stuck with it and, well, bad as it is, he'll just have to put up with it, won't he? There ain't nothing you or I can do for him there.'

We could make him welcome in the house, talk to him and end the silly feud, I thought, but I did not say so.

Ben filled in the silence. 'I understand he's considering staying on Norsea for a while,' he added with a sigh. 'I'd rather he didn't, for all our sakes. I'd rather he went off back to the mainland and left us in peace. I can't see any good'll come of it, which brings me to you. To be blunt, if he does stay, I'd rather you didn't go round to see him too often. I know you have that right and I can't stop you, but I'd just rather you didn't, that's all.'

I kept quiet: I could not make such a promise: Richard's return remained a cause of great excitement to me, even though I had seen him only twice since he had arrived – in our kitchen and then in the cottage that first night I took him the food. I dearly hoped to see him again, just to have someone else on the island to whom I could talk, other than Ben, who seldom discussed anything anyway, my mother, who never let me get a word in edgeways, and Old Hoary, who at times treated me like some imbecile country bumpkin who knew nothing about anything. Richard, on the other hand, was, as Ben said, a sort of a step-brother, so we had that affinity: and Richard had himself mentioned the word the night I had visited him. I would like to have explained all this to Ben, but I knew he would not understand. As much as I accepted, grudgingly, Norsea's isolation, with Richard's arrival I now felt less alone upon it: and as Richard clearly was more intelligent and more worldly wise than my normal companions, Billy, Nick and the other village youths who whiled away their boredom on the ciderstone, I felt that here at last was someone to whom I would be able to talk about the subjects in which I was interested, the ones at which I had been good at school: history, for one, geography, for a second, drawing, for a third, even painting, that is, if he knew anything about such things. I would still go across to the mainland, of course, when the tide permitted, to sit with the others once Fred Ring was back in Germany, but, for those other evenings when I could not cross, I now had a step-brother to visit: and that was paradise for me. Best of all, I had an excuse to avoid some of the more onerous chores with which I had been saddled and which took up at least three of my evenings each week and some Saturday afternoons and Sunday mornings, too.

All the time Ben had been speaking, Molly had been waiting patiently, as shire horses will, giving only an occasional swish at the flies with her tail, a toss of the head or a sudden trembling of the flanks to show she was anxious to be off. I somehow sensed Ben had a lot more to say, but, unexpectedly, with a great sigh of weariness, he gave Molly a pat and a gruff, 'Walk on' and she plodded off down the track, with Ben walking beside her holding the bridle.

'Well, think on what I've said, Joe boy,' were his final words as he trudged off, 'think on what I've said.'

As I watched them go, I felt strangely moved: for the first time in all the years I had known him, possibly for the first time ever in his life, Ben Wigboe, my step-father, dour, phlegmatic, plodding Ben, had unburdened his soul. Even then, I think he had cut short our talk because he suddenly realised he was revealing too much of himself to the world, even if that world were represented solely by me. The unemotional, almost unfeeling, image which he presented daily to the world and which he wore almost as a badge of Arcadian stoicism was revealed that day for what it was: a mask, a sham.

It was not that I blamed Ben for what he had done: more that I failed to understand his reasons. I neither thought of nor considered the dejection and unhappiness he must have felt while Richard was away all that time, with never a word from him or a word about him to ease the gnawing cancer of doubt in his heart. So when Ben was at last confronted by the ultimate test – forgiveness of one who had injured him, particularly his pride – he had given in to the angry side of his nature: he had rejected in turn as he had been rejected. Even now I do not think there was any lasting malice in him: rather that he acted from a man's obstinacy, the male's need to conceal from one who has caused him pain the true extent of that hurt.

I suppose that, most of all, I felt let down by the discovery that Ben, to whom I had previously looked for guidance in most things when I could not get it from my mother, had given in to the foolishness of pride for pride's sake. For the first time in my solitary existence, it brought home to me a realisation of the great gulfs that can divide families, the futility of blood squabbling with blood over matters of no real importance, son against father, son against mother, and in my case, mother against son, for I considered myself more sinned against than sinning.

Between Ben and myself, his rejection of Richard was to cast the first real shadow of that year over our relationship, the bond which had existed without any apparent challenge till then between a father and son, or rather a step-father and step-son: for the first time that I could recall, it had become strained.

Ben had married my mother within a year of my birth, after my real father had drowned while duck shooting in his punt on the Othona Flats, a vast expanse of marsh and salting banks which lies in the open sea just beyond the estuary's mouth and thus is more dangerous than the calmer reaches of the Langwater and places like Gledlang Shoe or the Thistley and Lingsea Creeks, which face each other on opposite shores and so broaden the estuary even more. Everyone surmised he must have stood up in the punt for some reason, perhaps to shoot his gun at some wildfowl rising up through the mist-shrouded waters, and had pitched overboard: then, too weighed down by his seaboots, he had gasped out the last of life's breath on the dark seabed, unable to rise to the surface again. His body they found weeks afterwards, washed into one of the lonely creeks, where the crabs had done their gruesome work. I never knew him, of course, so rarely ever thought of him, except when my mother would rant at me about him.

'You're just like him,' she would shout on occasions when I had been found wanting, 'bone idle the pair of you! He didn't want to work either! All he ever wanted to do was shoot that daft gun of his. And look where it got him! Six feet under in Gledlang bloody churchyard, that's where. Bloody fool of a man! Bloody fool of a man!'

Perhaps it was because of the stupidity of his death that the memory of it angered her so: or because he was still young, only thirty-three, a year younger than her, when he died: or that she had not prevented it, for she had said once or twice to me that, 'I told him not to go out in the stupid punt of his, but he would go, wouldn't he? He would go!'

To be fair, there was a sniffle of a tear in her voice when she said it, so, I suppose, in her own way, she still cared for him and remembered him with some affection: but for my benefit, when I was being chastised, he was always described as 'a lazy, ignorant bugger who could never keep a job and didn't want to work, a bloody know-all who thought he knew better than everyone else' or he would not have gone out shooting alone in his punt in such dangerous waters on a freezing, November night so far from the shore. What troubles me now is that, all the time I was growing up on Norsea, I never once went to look for his grave in Gledlang churchyard: he was my father, but, because I had never known him, I felt no sorrow for him, which is the only reason I can think of why people visit graves: sadness for those who lie in them.

Rather, for me, it was Ben who had always been there, ever since I could remember, carrying me about the farm on his shoulders when I was scarcely out of the toddling stage, sitting me squarely on Molly's back when I was no more than four and sometimes even allowing me to stand at the front of the cart and hold the reins so that I thought I was guiding her when all she was doing was plodding along a well-remembered headland path from field to field and gateway to gateway. Ben was there, too, when I went to the little two-roomed school in Tithe Street, alongside the tithe barn and the church, often rowing me across in his grey punt for the start in the morning when the tide was against us, and, till I was seven and old enough to come home on my own, sometimes fetching me back in the late afternoon on his high-handlebar bicycle when the tide was out. The two of us would grimace and laugh together as we bumped and bounced back to the island over the potholed causeway, both well aware of the danger in the black ooze either side, but relishing every moment of it.

It was Ben who taught me to swim in the shallows by the old wooden pier where the motor torpedo boat used to tie up at the start of the war: it was Ben who showed me how to snare a rabbit, where to lay the hoop of wire so it would slip easily round the rabbit's throat and how to put it out of its misery quickly with a blow from a club: it was Ben who taught me how to trap an adder with a double-pronged stick in the rough, gorse-covered, flint-strewn ground of the decoy on John Bolt's Boundary farm: and it was Ben who taught me how to slit a jackdaw's tongue so that it could talk. It was Ben, too, who calmed my mother when she was railing against me as a child, while I cowered under the kitchen table, awaiting my chance to dash for the door and the relative safety of the yard.

All these things and a thousand others formed the bond between us. True, when we worked together, he could be as firm and as impatient as any governor, ever ready to chivvy me along or to criticise me for a task not done well or not done to his satisfaction, which, with me, could be frequently. But then, as Old Hoary's bailiff, that was his job: it was expected of him. We could still laugh together at work, away from my mother, and laugh when listening to the wireless together in the house while my mother was elsewhere, though she generally put a stop to that by a withering look or an acid comment when she came back. Why she was that way, I never knew for sure: all I can say is that I looked up her first marriage certificate once, when I was ten, to find out my father's real names, Robert Joseph Coe, and I discovered she had married him in the June of the year I was born, only five months before my birth in the November, so I suppose there was reason enough there. He was dead and she was saddled with me, a squawking babe.

Do not be misled by all of this about Ben: he could get angry, too, very angry, when his patience wore thin. He could storm and shout as well as anyone if he thought he needed to and, when prompted by my mother, was sometimes over quick to raise his hand to cuff my ear or to swing his boot at my rear: for some reason, he seldom made contact with either and I think he did it solely to satisfy her, deliberately telegraphing his intention and knowing that I would duck and dodge quickly away and be gone before he had a second chance. Once I looked back at him just after he had swung his boot and had missed by a mile and saw on his face a wonderfully sly grin, which my mother behind him could not see: then he gave me a wink as if to say, 'I didn't want to kick you, Joe. I was just pretending for her sake.'

That was the Ben I knew.

TWELVE

SOME NIGHTS on Norsea, if you stood on the track leading to the big house, you would hear the sound of a piano being played so loudly and so passionately that the very notes seemed to reverberate through the surrounding dark, to be picked up by the breeze and carried to the farthest corners of the island. It was Old Hoary playing his classical music on the big upright piano which stood in the parlour of the big house, or the drawing room, as he called it. Sometimes, if I were passing nearby, I would steal up to the house and stand outside the window just to watch and to listen, but mostly, I am sorry to say, to smirk at Hoary's wild eccentricity. There, by the flickering light of a paraffin lamp, with every window thrown wide open so as to allow the music to escape into the encircling blackness – there, in spring, summer, autumn and winter, too, he would sit at his piano for hours on end, often playing long into the night, till dawn sometimes, oblivious to the wind howling through the open windows or the great white curtains billowing about him like demented ghouls. Through the window you would see him one moment bent so low over the piano that his chin almost touched the keys, his eyes screwed so tightly shut it was as if he were momentarily frozen in a trance: the next moment his head would jerk up and his fingers would fly left and right over the keys like running centipedes, moving so quickly and so delicately that they appeared not to touch them at all. Sometimes his whole body would rear up in the chair, his back would arch and he would throw back his head, a great ecstatic smile on his face, as if he were intoxicated by his own brilliance. The hands would rise up and hover like gryphon's claws over the notes for a second or so before crashing down in a dramatic gesture as he pounded out Beethoven or Bach or Wagner or Tchaikovsky or whoever it was he was playing: not that I knew or recognised any of them. To me then, in my ignorance, it was just so much noise, though I have to admit, the old man did play well, I could appreciate that, and I did like some of the tinklier bits and some of the quieter tunes.

In a magazine I used to read regularly in later life, they used to print articles about 'the most amazing character I have ever known.' Horatio Crockshay Volwycke-Hoar was mine: there was no one I knew more amazing than him, or more strange.

He banged away at his piano at all hours, out of loneliness, I suppose. Poor Hoary! Not being one of us, he did not mix too well with the villagers, for they generally disliked him and distrusted him. He was, I think, the loneliest man I have ever known, living his life almost as a recluse upon an island in the middle of a tidal estuary, without true companionship or obvious purpose or any real friends that I knew of, just existing, yet seemingly unperturbed by it. In truth, he was an exile – exiled by his own family, by his own people, his own kind, exiled and mostly forgotten. It is with a sense of some guilt that I recall that while he, through a genuine altruism which he showed towards all people, felt a compassion for us because of what he perceived to be the poverty of our lives, culturally and financially, we for our part regarded him as a deluded crank.

His people lived in another part of the region, up Hunstanton way, true gentry by breeding, it was said, with extensive land and property holdings in that county and in the neighbouring Fen counties. He had gone to Harrow School as a boy and on to Oxford as a young man to study history and languages: from photographs he had shown me in one of his several albums, he had been quite a sportsman in his youth, for there were pictures of him playing tennis, rowing, golfing, taking part in fox hunting, point-to-point and horse-jumping at shows. When the First War broke out, he had become a lieutenant in the cavalry, serving in France with his county's yeomanry, and spending his time, along with the rest of the cavalry, riding from one place to another behind the lines waiting for the great breakthrough which never came while the appalling slaughter at the front went on and the generals tried and failed and tried again ever more desperately to achieve it.

There is a piece of newsreel film of the First War, which I saw later in life, of a cavalry troop riding out on to a road: a German shell lands near them and one rider and his horse disappear in an explosion of dirt and smoke. That rider, I know, was Old Hoary, or young Hoary as he was then. 'There was a man filming us with a camera,' he guffawed, searching through one of his many photographic albums and thrusting into my hand a still photograph taken from the film of that very incident. 'The Germans sent over some shells. And bang! You can just see me and my horse disappearing in the explosion.' All the time he was speaking, he cackled in that mad way of his as if it were all a great joke. The poor horse was killed and Old Hoary received horrific shrapnel wounds which he willingly showed to any of the village boys if they asked: deep clefts gouged in his side and back as if someone had chopped at him with an axe the way one chops at a tree trunk: the next six months he spent in a hospital. In another photograph taken a few days before he was blown up, which he kept in the same album, he is pictured on his horse shepherding in twenty or so German prisoners with nothing but a cavalry sabre across his shoulder. 'Some other soldiers captured them. I just brought them in,' he said with a laugh. They gave him a medal for that: he got nothing for being blown up.

After the war, Hoary had worked briefly as a teacher at a small public school, but the war had changed him too much: his mind had altered. He had become ultra religious, ultra humane, ultra liberal, a complete pacifist, against all wars, all killing, all intolerance, all wealth and all grace and favour, except his own, of course: he thought most of life meaningless. Among his own kind, he had become an outcast, one who, to them, had strange and unpredictable ways: not a communist as such, more of an overtly religious, socialistic, God-fearing, Christian crank. I suppose in reality he had become the black sheep with whom the family did not know how to deal, an embarrassment who shamed them by the weirdness of his thinking, the manner of his dress, the idiosyncrasies of his ways, the things he did, the causes he championed, someone to be hidden away in the depths of the country and forgotten, as unwelcome in their company as would be a leper in the company of the clean.

I only ever saw his bigwig older brother, the actual owner of Norsea, once when he came with Hoary's mother early in the war: because of the scarcity of petrol, they crossed to Norsea in a little pony and trap rented at Wivencaster, she a frail, white-haired old lady dressed all in black, he a bulky, dark-suited, bowler-hatted type who grimaced when he saw me and my shabby clothes: I was eleven then. Hoary and his mother walked round the island arm in arm in the afternoon sunshine, I remember, with the pompous brother tagging along behind: then they disappeared into the big house for tea. The last I saw of them was Old Hoary standing at the island end of the causeway waving to them and smiling as they disappeared back towards the mainland before the tide cut them off, happy to be gone and the one and only time I know of when they acknowledged his existence. His mother must have died soon after, for she never came again: neither did his brother, but that was no surprise.

As well as the strangest character I have ever known, Old Hoary was also the most intelligent, with the mind of an academic rather than a martinet military man. He spoke five languages – Greek, Latin, French, German and Russian – and was passionate about history, ancient history, Roman history, Anglo-Saxon history, medieval history, modern history, everything. As an accomplished pianist, he was not above marching into the Chessman on a Friday night when the air in the vault was as blue with swearing as with tobacco smoke. He would order a half-pint of lemonade, for he never drank beer or spirits, and then go into the big room where the piano was and bang out an hour or more of Bach, Beethoven, Chopin and Rachmaninov for the edification of the farmworkers who crowded in there. They never complained: in fact, they would cheer loudly whenever he paused and shout for more, never knowing or caring whether the music had finished and he was just pausing between one sonata and the next. They would laugh behind their hands when he acknowledged their applause: some would shout, to the tittering of their friends, 'Give us Tipperary,' or 'We want Lily of Laguna' or 'Roll Out the Barrel, Hoary!' or 'Play Springtime in the Rockies' or 'What about something by Al Bowlly?' or Vera Lynn or Leslie Hutchinson, 'Hutch.' If Old Hoary knew they were laughing at him, he never seemed to care: he was happy to play for them, though he always ignored their requests and returned to his Bach or Beethoven. It filled an hour or two of his life, I suppose.

Hoary knew men in Government departments in London with whom he had been at school at Harrow, with whom he had studied at Oxford or with whom he had served in the cavalry in France and it was not uncommon to see him sprawled on the floor of the village's telephone box, talking in a voice loud enough to be heard fifty feet away to some high-up civil servant in the Home Office, or the Foreign Office or the Treasury whom he knew by Christian name. It always amused us to wonder what they in London would have thought, standing amid the gilded splendour of their Whitehall offices in their well-cut jackets, pin-striped trousers and stiff-collared shirts, if they had known that the man who expounded so eloquently on the trials and tribulations of the world was actually lying half in and half out of a red-painted, concrete telephone kiosk in a marshland village square, wearing a holed tennis shoe on one foot, a frayed carpet slipper on the other, invariably sockless, most times unshaven, in warmer weather dressed only in navy-blue running shorts and a collarless striped shirt, with a public school tennis or cricket sweater tied round his middle.

This was Hoary's usual mode of dress whenever one saw him about the village or the island, but that is not to say he could not be smart. The next day, if he was off to London on one of his 'necessary' jaunts, he would appear in a smart brown tweed suit and mustard waistcoat, stiff-collared shirt, brushed homburg hat, suede boots and yellow cravat, very often carrying a silver-topped cane. Just for a laugh we would ask him to doff his hat to us, which he always did with an embarrassed guffaw and a bow, pleased to be the centre of attention, but it rather spoiled the image when he revealed his bald pate, the wild disorder of his ring of overlong, frizzy grey hair and two rows of gapped teeth liberally sprinkled with gold fillings.

The big house in which Hoary passed his lonely existence stood about fifty yards inland from the southern shore, more in its own space than in actual grounds, for no hedge, wall or fence surrounded it on that frontage. It was open to the sea and the winds and the rain and was really more of a mansion than a mere house, built in Edwardian times as a summer retreat by the millionaire mustard manufacturer for himself, his family and his guests and servants. It had three floors, with Mock Tudor beams in the upper storey, high Elizabethan chimneys, large windows and, at each end of the south-facing front, were Gothic towers with slated conical roofs. The centre of the ground floor was taken up by a magnificent multi-windowed bay, fully thirty feet across, which gave panoramic views from the spacious parlour out over the estuary. The main bedroom, in which Hoary still slept when he was not playing his piano till dawn, was immediately above this. All told, there were ten or twelve bedrooms on the two upper floors, those for the servants being dormers high in the roof. On the ground floor there were at least a half-dozen other rooms: in addition to the main drawing room, there was a long dining room, a games room with an unused snooker table (piled high with papers and junk) and a library so dusty you sneezed every time you went in. At the rear of the house were a kitchen the size of our parlour and a pantry the size of our kitchen, plus various outbuildings, all dilapidated. Until the big house was built, our decrepit, old, period farmhouse, with its cracking beams, sloping floors, sagging leaky roof and draughty windows, had been the main building on the island.

But, whereas our house was sparsely furnished through circumstance, Hoary's house was filled with every kind of junk: mountains of books, piles of magazines, all manner of pots and pans, plates, bowls, dishes, saucers, countless cups, mugs, jugs and vases, marble clocks, wooden clocks and glass-cased clocks, statuettes of men, women and animals, all kinds of mementoes, acquisitions and trophies: fox heads, bear heads, antelope heads, silver cups, various animal hides, umbrellas, tennis racquets, golf clubs, spears, sabres, hide shields, all were piled on pieces of broken and useless furniture and on pieces of good and useable furniture, too. In fact, all the bric-a-brac one would expect to find in a backstreet pawnbroker's shop cluttered room after room, piled on tables, chairs and couches, pushed under beds, stuffed into cupboards and cabinets and sideboards and chests of drawers, or strewn about the floor to be walked on by anyone who visited. Among them, to my own disbelief, were centuries-old, leather-bound books with pages of beautifully illuminated vellum in Latin, Greek, French and Old German, painstakingly hand-written in some little cell somewhere long ago by some bowed, half-starved, squinting monk or scribe. Now they littered the floor of Hoary's mansion of a house, to be trodden on by careless visitors like me or peed on by any and all of the half-dozen half-wild cats which strutted or lazed about the place: these Hoary fed simply by throwing down whole fish for them to eat or leaving quarter-pound pats of butter on plates outside the back door for them to lick.

When treading about his house it was not unusual to find scattered among the books and papers an occasional pan of cooked food, which he had set down a month before and forgotten about and which in the meantime had gone mouldy. Or it might be one of the saucers of watered-down tinned milk he had put down for the cats and which over the weeks it had lain there had congealed to the consistency of rancid putty. The number of cats did diminish: Ben and his four-ten accidentally saw to that on several occasions.

Hoary was totally unconcerned about mundane matters like washing dishes and pans, sweeping out the house, cooking food properly, changing his bedding every now and again, the everyday things of life about which others concerned themselves. Only the greater issues exercised his mind: like the fate of the world, the absolute truth of the Bible, the madness of the atomic bomb, the damnation of all dictators like Hitler and Stalin, and how all mankind should be able to live together in peace and harmony.

It never seemed to enter Hoary's mind that he lived in total squalor: most of the clutter had belonged to his late mother and an old spinster aunt, he said: three vanloads of books, furniture and other effects, which his London-based brother either did not want or wrongly thought could be stored safely at Hoary's house for the duration, had arrived on Norsea midway through the war. I remember watching the vans creeping across the causeway one summer afternoon, their drivers absolutely petrified of going over the edge. Because of the tide and not wanting to be trapped on the island, so they said, the van drivers had simply dumped everything on the grass inside two hours and driven off: Ben and I had to carry it all into the house and, not knowing exactly what he had, Old Hoary had seemingly ignored it, though he would occasionally pick up one or other of the illuminated books and make a comment about it: that it was a religious tract which probably had once belonged to some European duke or duchess or lord or lady, or it was the work of some august German poet or scholar of whom I had never heard and to this day have never heard spoken of either.

Given Hoary's forgetfulness, it was perhaps fortunate that his interest in the actual running of the farm was minimal: as I have said, he sometimes intervened to ask why we were not growing a certain crop in a certain field, like roses or sunflowers or Dutch tulips, oblivious to the practice of crop rotation, like the Norfolk four course, where you planted wheat in a field in the first year, turnips, say, in the second year and barley in the third, with an under-sowing of clover which you cut and sold for feed in the fourth. Thankfully, Hoary mostly left the crop-growing to Ben: he just provided the money, via a very generous allowance from his well-to-do brother, of course. He was never short of money, that was for sure, even though he was always protesting that he was: he had money to burn, literally: I lifted some books in his parlour one day and found a half-dozen big white five-pound notes folded flat underneath them. If you are wondering, I left them there.

Whatever expenditure was required, such as Ben's wage, my paltry wages, money for seed, fertiliser, lime, repair or replacement of machinery, buying Molly's feed, or just paying the roving threshing crew once a year, Hoary drew from a bank account in Maydun, which his bigwig brother regularly replenished: Ben kept the books, of course, because Hoary was not to be trusted to do them and did not know what was going on anyway. The farm's accounts were posted at the end of each tax year to the accountants in Wivencaster, who audited them before sending them to the bigwig brother in London. Apart from the crops, that was the only thing about which Ben ever seemed to worry: he need not have bothered: profit or loss, the bigwig brother never complained: I think he wrote off the island as an affordable loss so long as younger brother Horatio stayed on it.

Hoary was even benignly tolerant of Ben's outspokenness towards him, which sometimes could be caustic: not many men then could call their superior and nominal employer a 'bloody old fool' or a 'daft bugger' to his face and get away with it, or harangue him for twenty minutes on his lack of knowledge about the business that provided his income, and have him saying, 'Well, you do as you wish Benjamin, you do as you wish. You are the bailiff, so if you think it should be done that way – I was just thinking it might be better if ...' Whenever he heard any of Ben's epithets, Old Hoary would throw back his head and guffaw with laughter, interpreting Ben's castigation of him with the same fondness perhaps with which a timid teacher might regard unruly pupils when he is the target of their innumerable pranks, believing they did it out of liking for him when, in truth, it was done out of total disrespect.

The one thing which took Hoary away from the island more than anything else was his preoccupation with 'archaeological diggings,' as he called them: he was always exploring along the coastline of that region and even up into the next county, for Roman, Saxon or Viking occupation. We had all three around the estuary: both the Romans and the Vikings at Wivencaster, though several hundred years apart, and the Anglo-Saxons at Maydun from Aelthred's time onwards. Hoary was never happier than when he was climbing into Sligger Offin's smoky taxi, a prewar Morris Ten, to go to the station at Hamwyte or Wivencaster as he set off to wherever it was he was proposing to start his next archaeological dig and annoy everyone there. It was an obsession with him, so much so that he often disappeared for days on end, weeks sometimes, without a word to anyone – not that there was anyone to tell, save myself or Ben, and neither he nor I were the least bit interested. We would not see him for days and then the next thing we would know was he was back in Sligger Offin's Morris, unloading some massive, canvas-covered piece of blackened, rotting, waterlogged timber which he would proudly proclaim was part of a newly discovered Roman pier, or Roman well, or Saxon granary or Viking longship, or some such. Whether they were, of course, we had no way of knowing, nor did we care.

Now that the warmth had begun to return, Old Hoary had already taken to charging about the countryside again in Sligger's taxi, visiting the archaeological digs he had begun the previous summer and left unfinished in October. He was just making sure they were still there as he had left them, I suppose, and had not been tampered with by 'treasure seekers': or for that matter, destroyed by philistine American soldiers driving tanks across them as they had done during the war at the site of one of his greatest archaeological finds, 'an Angle burial ship, better than the Saxon one at Sutton Hoo,' which he claimed to have discovered in Thirty-Nine up in the next county, but had been unable to excavate because the war had intervened.

When he was not doing that, or yapping to civil servants in Whitehall from the village telephone box, or banging away on his piano or off up to London for one of his 'necessary visits,' Old Hoary could usually be found in a small outhouse ankle deep in wood shavings. The old man – he was in his early sixties – considered himself something of a wood carver, a sculptor no less, and had forty or fifty chisels of various kinds, thick, thin, broad, medium, curved and straight, some as thin as wire, some as thick as two fingers, which from time to time I sharpened on a whetstone using olive oil, a task I was hoping to pass on to Stanley Lobel, the boy from Tottle. Mostly I just wore away the points, or blades or cutting edges, which made them quite useless, but he paid me a shilling to do it so I was not one to complain.

The figures which he carved were grotesque: human kind gone wrong: hideous, deformed creatures, like squat tribal idols or pygmy-sized versions of the Easter Island statues. Their heads were misshapen, their arms and legs were out of proportion, often of different length, and mostly they had faces which were screwed up and lopsided, looking for all the world like Charles Laughton's impersonation of poor Quasimodo, the hunchback of Notre Dame. It was clear to me that the man did not have an artistic bone in his body: Ben, not normally one to pass judgment, agreed: my mother just scoffed at the mention of them and raised her eyes to the ceiling, asking Heaven why they allowed it.

It was on the Monday evening of the second week that I went round to Hoary's house in answer to a summons he had given to Ben to sharpen his chisels because Stanley Lobel was not yet able to come over. The sun was just dipping behind Maydun hill to the west and the last of its rays were slanting over the wastes of the mudflats, throwing the reed-topped salting banks into sharp relief. When I reached the rear of the house I came across an unexpected sight: Old Hoary was down on his knees, still in his navy blue gym shorts and collarless shirt, smoothing an area of wet cement on the path near the kitchen door which had cracked and crumbled under the successive onslaughts of winter rain and frost. In one hand he held a trowel with which he was laying and smoothing the cement, in the other he held a pointed stick with which he was meticulously inscribing into the wet cement verses from a Bible which lay open on the ground beside him. Behind him, watching him work, wearing a dark green sweater, blue shirt and worn corduroy trousers and leaning on a shovel with which he had been mixing the cement, stood Richard: and the two of them were having an argument.

THIRTEEN

CLEARLY, Richard had said something which had fired Hoary's religious passions, judging by the gestures he was making with his hands and the volubility of his remarks: for even as I approached I heard the Bible mentioned several times, along with God and Jesus, the Holy Spirit, Moses, Saint Peter, the Angel Gabriel et al, all of which always went over my head because I never gave much credence to any of it.

I had not been to Saint Peter's in Gledlang since I had been ejected from the Sunday school for spitting when I was nine years of age. It happened during a slide show by two travelling Church of England nuns: for some reason Billy, Nick and I, sitting at the back, unobserved as we thought, decided to engage in a competition to see who could spit the farthest over the next pew. Unhappily, the verger saw us, quietly came up behind us, gave each of us a clout around the ear and chased us out for 'defiling God's house.' After that, I did not bother with church: I was too ashamed: besides I had only gone in the first place to collect the coloured stamps they gave for attendance. To my mind, God and Jesus and the rest of them, all the saints, the prophets and the angels, were all right when you were hymn-singing along with a massed congregation in a warm, cosy, flower-bedecked church with the sunlight streaming through the stained-glass windows, revealing the glory of it all: that was a comfort: but there was not much comfort in it when you were standing in the middle of a field in a freezing November fog, topping beets all by yourself for days on end.

Then, when the whole world seems to have vanished, when no sound penetrates the grey murk which surrounds you and every cry fades and dies in the silence of the world's emptiness, when all life is muffled and stilled by an icy, saturating shroud, when you are so frozen and so miserable and so desperate in your loneliness you wonder even whether it would be worth deliberately slicing off the tip of an unneeded finger just as an excuse to get away from it all, when you would willingly make a pact with the Devil himself, if he existed – when you are that low, you do not turn to God and Jesus and the Angel Gabriel, you think of yourself. You do not want to be one of the meek who will inherit the earth: let them that want the earth have it and they can bloody well plough it and hoe it, too! On such days all I ever wanted to be was somewhere warm and dry and cheerful, like our farmhouse kitchen by the light of the oil lamp, with the old range fire glowing red hot and one of my mother's stews bubbling away in a saucepan fierce enough to make the lid rattle.

No, I never really had any time for religion: and neither, it seemed, did Richard. As I approached, I heard him say in answer to some remark by Hoary: 'Oh, I know all about the Bible, Mr Hoar. I know my Bible. If anyone knows their Bible, I do. I had it drummed into me enough – '

He broke off when he saw me coming and greeted me with a hugely cheerful lopsided grin on his scarred face as if to say, 'I've got the old fool going here!' What I did detect immediately was that he appeared to be arguing more for argument's sake than because he actually hoped to convert Hoary to his way of thinking or seriously to question the old man's faith.

Hoary, on the other hand, greeted me with only the faintest of smiles, which was disconcerting bearing in mind I was there because of his summons: Richard and he were obviously discussing the inscriptions: it seemed to have irritated Hoary that I should have chosen to arrive at the very moment he was engaged in a deep and meaningful theological argument. Perhaps he thought he was winning and I had interrupted a vital point: though from the grin on Richard's face as he stood behind the old man's back, it was obvious he did not think Hoary was winning.

As I joined them, Hoary was ranting on about this Book and that Book in that weird, baying voice of his and waving the pointed stick agitatedly in the air before returning to the Biblical passage he was incising in the wet cement. A half-minute of listening to their stuff was enough for me: not understanding or caring overmuch about any of it, anyway, and as a precaution against being considered an ally of Richard, as well as being wary of lightning bolts being flung down from the sky, I left them and went over to the outhouse in which Hoary kept his chisels in a wooden box. Normally I sharpened them inside, but that night I carried the box outside and set it down on the path a good twenty yards from them, far enough away for me to listen, but not close enough to be dragged into their argument. I placed the whetstone block on the ground between my legs, poured on a liberal measure of olive oil from the bottle and set about sharpening, or rather wearing away, Hoary's multitude of chisels. What I marvelled at most was Richard's intelligence in holding his own with Hoary on such an intellectual subject as God and the Universe, the Creation and the meaning of life and all that. At least his arguments sounded reasonable and intelligent to me.

It has to be said that Hoary was generally a good-natured old soul: eccentric yes, dotty yes, half mad yes, but a kindly old soul nevertheless. Though generally disagreeing absolutely with each of Richard's remarks, he did pay him the compliment of answering him calmly and respectfully, countering his arguments with his own careful replies without being the least condescending.

I cannot recall over much detail of their discussion: what I remember of it were just the general remarks which Richard made and which so astonished – and alarmed me – at the time that they have stayed in my memory. According to Richard, for instance, Jesus was just the leader of some weird sect walking around Palestine or Israel a couple of thousand years ago supposedly doing good deeds and championed by his followers with a belief that he could heal the sick and the blind: just a man and certainly not born of any holy virgin by some form of immaculate conception: whatever that was!

The Bible was only a book, the Old Testament just a collection of Jewish legends and the Gospels of Matthew, Mark, Luke and John were probably written from hearsay long after the events described in them by followers of Saint Paul or by monks of some kind in the next century or so.

And Jesus, Richard said at another point in answer to another of Hoary's exclamations, probably did not even die on the Cross: he was probably taken down while still alive after Joseph of Arimathea bribed the Roman guards so that he and someone called Nicodemuas could hide him in the tomb and tend his wounds with myrrh and aloes: and the supposed rolling away of the stone by angels was probably done by them taking Jesus elsewhere to escape the searching Pharisees after drugging the guards

In all my days I had never heard such a discussion: Richard was arguing like someone who had been university educated with someone who had been university educated! At Oxford no less! To my ears, his remarks were all deliberately scurrilous, intended to annoy: and they did. Clearly, Hoary had never had to argue such things before, for every now and again he would let out a long sigh, as if he were saying to Richard, 'How can you be so foolish?' and return to his task of inscribing into the wet cement. But Hoary's pride was such that he could not, would not, let matters rest: and it was not long before he was trying another tack.

According to Hoary, when Jesus appeared among the Disciples after the Crucifixion and let Doubting Thomas put his fingers in his wounds that was proof positive that 'He had risen again from the dead.' To Richard, it simply proved only that Jesus was alive and walking about: and, according to him, when Jesus 'ascended into Heaven,' as the Bible says, he probably either died or fled as far away from Jerusalem and the Pharisees and the Romans as he could get, bearing in mind they had just tried to crucify him and were still looking for him. 'If the truth be known, Jesus probably fled to Persia or India somewhere,' declared the contrary Richard. 'He certainly did not ascend into Heaven with tongues of fire coming down unless they were meteorites. It's all poppycock! If you want to do a real archaeological dig, Mr Hoar, go and look for Jesus's grave – '

The last remark finally seemed to exhaust Hoary's patience, not to mention his goodwill. Like some Hindu holy man kneeling in a street, he threw up his arms as if in supplication to the Heaven in which he believed and climbed to his feet. 'Nonsense, Dick! Nonsense. You do speak such gibberish at times,' he cried. 'What you say is blasphemy, and one should not blaspheme against God. If you persist in mocking the Christian religion, I will not listen to you. You seem to be one of those people who take from the Bible only those parts of it which suit them and ignore the rest if they do not conform to their ideas. That is too easy. Life would be very easy if we could all do that. If you accept the Bible is the word of God, then you must accept all of it, not just those parts which suit you.'

At that he stalked off, declaring: 'I am going in. I have had enough. I shall pray for the forgiveness of your sins tonight, Dick – ' and catching sight of me ' – and yours, Joseph.' Then, with an airy, irritated wave of the hand, he said: 'I may see you tomorrow or I may not. I do not know whether I shall be up to it.'

'What have I done?' I protested. 'I haven't said anything. I've just been sitting here sharpening your bloody chisels and minding my own business!'

But Hoary was not listening: he had gone into the house and slammed the door behind him. Later that night, we were to hear him banging away at his piano, to soothe his wounded soul, I suppose.

Richard was smiling his queer lopsided smile when he came over to me. 'He hasn't changed much, has he?' he said, with a grin. 'He's still as fanatical as ever. It doesn't take much to get him going.'

'He's a bloody lunatic. He needs locking up,' was my unbiased verdict, which made Richard smile all the more. I hasten to add it was not said with any venom on my part, more in sympathy and understanding that the poor man could not help being the way he was: everyone who knew Hoary, us on the island and the villagers in Gledlang, understood the weirdness of his ways, even if we did not agree with them, and so we were never surprised by them.

Only the previous year he had turned up at the opening of the village fete wearing his baggy navy shorts, ready for a running race three hours later. To raise funds for his hoped-for football team, Kerry the Milkman had organised the race around the Gledlang Mile, a triangle of roads which formed the village's shape and, perversely, was a mile-and-a-third around: a pound and a cup were put up as the winner's prize, with ten bob for second and five shillings for third. Amazingly runners who fancied themselves had come from all over the area: Salter, Cobwycke, Cumvirley, the two Tottles, Greater and Lesser, plus Tidwolton, Maydun and Hamwyte: they did it more to test which was the best in the area rather than for the prize itself. In the event, thirty paid the two-shillings entry fee and lined up in three ranks by the grass triangle at the junction of Tithe Street and the Salter road, among them Hoary, pitting himself against boys a quarter of his age and men a third of it. Even Billy and Nick had entered, though Billy smoked too many rolled Darkie Shag cigarettes to have much of a chance: despite that, he still managed to wheeze round in seven-and-a-half minutes, a creditable twentieth, seven places behind Nick. Hoary finished last, of course, collapsing over the line in seventeen minutes-plus, fully eleven minutes after the winner had breasted the tape, or rather a length of binder string stretched across the road: you could have walked round in less time.

The poor old fool had to stop several times to catch his breath and, in fact, Kerry became so concerned about him when he did not appear as expected that he sent two of the younger lads on their bicycles back round the course in case the old fool had had a heart attack. When he finally came into view, grinning away as usual, exalted by his achievement, he received a special derisory cheer from the guffawing spectators. They even restrung the binder string across the road as Hoary staggered on spindly legs over the last fifty yards, crying mockingly to him, 'Come on, Hoary, you can still win! You can still win!' By this time most of the other competitors were sitting on the grass on the triangle having a smoke and watching in bewilderment. Several of them, like Billy, for instance, looked to be near death's door, but they all recovered eventually. Things like that we expected of Hoary: that is why we were never really surprised by them.

After Hoary had stamped back into the big house following his disagreement with Richard, I put away the chisels, making a mental note to get my shilling pay from him the next day, and then walked with Richard back to his cottage. It was as we walked back that Richard gave me the news. 'I've decided to stay on Norsea indefinitely,' he said. 'I can't help what Ben thinks. If he is bothered by me being here, well, that's his problem, not mine.'

It was a callous statement, but a realistic one: it was not up to him to apologise to Ben. 'He'll come round, eventually,' I said.

'Maybe,' said Richard, though not sounding at all sure. 'Maybe he will, maybe he won't. Whatever he does, I'm staying. Hoary says I can have the cottage rent free. He says I can stay as long as I like. I need a summer in the fresh air, maybe the autumn, too, doing odd jobs for him and helping him out with the digging. Handyman and digger-in-chief, that's me from now on. Your friend Stanley and I have already been to a couple of his sites. We'll be going to another next week.'

'It's all right with me,' I said, secretly pleased that he was staying and I would have a companion on the island. It would also relieve me of all the jobs I was expected to do for Hoary: Richard could do those now: it might put Stanley's nose out of joint a bit, though, since he was expecting to come over, but he could still go on the digs with Richard and he could still come over to help us with the pea-picking and bean-picking.

There was a brief pause before Richard spoke again: then, in a quiet, serious voice, he said: 'I have my own reason for staying on Norsea. For a while, anyway. I made a promise to someone and I intend to keep it, Ben or no Ben. It's important to me. I have to be here just in case. And I need some peace and quiet, somewhere I can get away from people for a while.'

Hiding away, more like, I thought: hiding away because of your face: but then who would not? The scars on Richard's face again drew my gaze: they changed colour to a sickly purple-grey in the light: Richard caught me looking.

'I am not doing it because of these,' he said, giving me a stern look in return. 'I can't see them unless I look in the mirror so I don't have to worry about them and neither should you. Half the time I forget about them. If people see them and don't like the look of them, that is their lookout, not mine. The only trouble is I might find it difficult to get a job. I realise that. I can't see anyone wanting to employ me looking like this. I might scare the customers. That's why I have taken up Hoary's offer to stay on Norsea and work for him. I don't have to mix with people so much.'

He was unconvincing. I was just thinking the conversation would end there when Richard made a startling statement. 'There is only one person in the world who I would worry about seeing me as I am, Joe,' he said, 'and she is not here. I would be worried how she would react when she saw them, not anyone else. Not badly, I hope. As for the rest of the world, I don't give a damn!'

'One person in the world! She!' Who was 'she'? That night I was to learn so much more about Richard: where he had been, what he had done and what had happened to him all those years he was away. It amounted to not only the story of his life but his philosophy on life almost.

FOURTEEN

'I SUPPOSE you are wondering how I got them.' Richard pointed a black-nailed finger at his scarred face: there was no irritation in his voice, just an acceptance of my curiosity. 'I got them in the Far East, the same way I got two rib wounds and a punctured lung – from a Jap officer with a sword and a couple of guards with bayonets. I wasn't in the war like others, Joe. I spent my war in a Jap internment camp.'

We were sitting in Richard's parlour after walking back from Hoary's house and I had finally plucked up the courage to ask him where he been all the years he was away: I never expected the answer I got or realised the misfortune that can befall a person by chance in wartime.

Richard had stoked up the smouldering fire as soon as we entered and had placed a kettle of water on the glowing coke to make tea. Now as he spoke, he stood with his back to me, one hand resting on the dusty mantelpiece, staring into the flickering flames, remembering. When he spoke, there was an unmistakable bitterness in his voice as the memories of what had happened came flooding back. Anger was nothing to be surprised at then: being so soon after the war, one was used to people who had fought against the Germans and the Japanese, who had been bombed by them, shot at by them or captured by them, damning them to high heaven, particularly the Japanese because we were just beginning to hear the stories of their brutality and the atrocities they had perpetrated.

Stories about the Death Railway in Thailand and the tortures inflicted on our own British and Australian soldiers captured at Singapore had appeared in several Sunday papers so we had good reason to hate them: it was a cold, hard, vicious and unforgiving hatred, fuelled by numerous gung-ho American war films showing at the Embassy in Maydun as much as by the newspaper accounts. To Billy, Nick, myself and others, the Japanese were 'yellow bastards' and you almost spat out the words when you mentioned their race. Every time some prat of a clergyman spoke about forgiveness of the enemy, people used to wince and say, 'Maybe, the Germans, but never the bloody Japs!'

The hostility towards the Germans was already beginning to wane, even though it was barely two years since the first pictures of Belsen had been shown on the newsreels at Maydun. True, that anger flared every now and again as a new story of their barbarism in the East came out, but Germany was too close to Britain for it to go on forever. Moreover, the Germans were said to be as near to starving as people could be without actually dying and, as the Russians grew ever more bloody-minded, people were beginning to feel sorry for their former enemy, especially as every newsreel seemed to depict them living among the gutted buildings of bombed-out towns and cities. Why, Othona, the village at the head of the estuary, even had a German prisoner-of-war, Red Rudi, playing in their football team! When they came to Gledlang for a friendly against Kerry the Milkman's Wanderers, the burly, red-haired ex-paratrooper had been the best player on the field.

Richard gave the coke lumps several vigorous thrusts with the poker before turning to face me. 'I was unlucky enough to be in the Philippines when the Japs landed in Forty-One just after Pearl Harbor,' he said. 'I just happened to be in Manila, the capital, when they marched in in the January of Forty-Two. I didn't intend to be there. I was just in the wrong place at the wrong time and I couldn't get away.'

Richard pre-empted my question before it had even formed on my lips: how and why was he in Manila when the Japs invaded? 'I was on a passenger ship in the South China Sea at the time, off the Philippines, on my way from Shanghai to India. You have to remember the war was in Europe then and that was a long way off. We read about it, but it didn't affect us. So – ' He shrugged as if there were no answer. ' – So I suppose we just didn't worry about it till the Japs attacked Pearl Harbor.'

'What were you doing in Shanghai?' I asked, astonished. 'Where is it anyway?' I genuinely did not know.

'It's in China. It's a big city and port on the Whangpoo river, a tributary of the Yangtze. I was working there as a shipping clerk. That's how I came to be on the ship heading for India. The firm I worked for had an office in Calcutta. I was heading there. When the Japs bombed Pearl Harbor, our ship, like every other ship in the South China Sea, was ordered to make straight for Manila, where the Americans were. Jap submarines were about and everyone was afraid they would torpedo us. There were a lot of women and children on board, a couple of hundred or more, evacuees from Shanghai, packed off to Singapore and India in case the Japs marched in, which they did the same day they bombed Pearl Harbor. They had already bombed Shanghai while I was there back in Thirty-Seven, killing hundreds, thousands. And they had been camping outside the city for years waiting, so it was only a matter of time. They controlled the countryside all around anyway and weren't averse to killing anyone they came across, European or Chinese. You knew they were there, but you learned to live with it in the International Settlement.' A grimness entered his voice here. 'We all thought we would be safe once we reached Manila, but no sooner had we tied up than the Japs started bombing the harbour. Several ships were hit and several people were killed. One boat burned like a bonfire for days. We were sitting ducks where we were so the captain ordered all passengers ashore. All sailings were supposed to be cancelled, but, while we were ashore dodging the bombs for the next five days, living from hand to mouth in a seedy little hotel, the bloody ship sailed off without us, taking all our luggage, my trunk, other people's baggage, everything. All I had was a small suitcase with a few changes of underwear, my shaving gear and the clothes I stood up in. Fortunately, I had managed to change my money for Filipino pesos, not a lot, but enough to tide me over for a month or two. That's when I helped Jean.'

'Jean? Who's she?'

Richard smiled to himself. 'She's a lady I met on the boat when we sat at dinner together. Jean McLaughlin's her name, a married Scot's lady, one of the Shanghai evacuees. She had a little boy with her, William. The three of us got stranded in the same hotel together. When the bastard of a ship's captain sailed off, he took all her things as well as mine and everybody else's. She had even less money than I did, just a few of her own things and the kiddie's clothes she had been able to take ashore. There wasn't time to grab anything else, not with Jap bombs raining down. It was just sheer bloody panic at the time. I helped Jean and her kiddie because they were in a worse plight than I was. She was grateful for my help.'

He must have caught the look in my eye, for he wagged an admonishing finger. 'Not in that way,' he said, with a reproachful shake of the head.

I reddened: it seemed a natural conclusion to make: how else would a woman 'be grateful'? Richard ignored my mumbled apology and went on: 'The Japs came over bombing five or six times a day –

they even came on Christmas Day. They didn't meet much opposition as far as I could see. Most of the Yank planes were destroyed on the ground at the airfield, Clarke Field, lined up during refuelling as if they were on bloody parade. It was chaos. Half the city was burning, there were dead everywhere, the streets were choked with rubble and smoke from a big oil refinery the Yanks had blown up hung over the place for days. When the Japs came ashore two days before Christmas, we thought the Yanks and the Filipinos would drive them back or at least hold them up till reinforcements arrived. They didn't, they retreated and left the city wide open. The Japs marched in with hardly a fight. I watched the cocky little blighters drive in in their tanks and, believe me, Joe, it was bloody mayhem for a while – and I mean bloody. Some terrible things were going on, so we stayed in our hotel. You couldn't go out in the streets, it was too dangerous. The Jap soldiers were drunk and so were half their officers. Finally, they sobered up and some officer came and told us we all had to go to a sports stadium to register. Then they rounded up all the aliens they could find – three-and-a-half-thousand of us, men, women and children – and stuck us in a compound at the university surrounded by a high barbed-wire fence. Jean and I and her kiddie, William, went in together. I was there for two-and-a-half years. I spent the first year sleeping on a grass mat in a room along with fifty others.'

The iron kettle began to whistle and Richard paused while he lifted it off the flames and poured the boiling water into the teapot my mother had given him a week before.

'The Japs are bastards,' I empathised. 'They need shooting, the lot of them!' Richard made no immediate reply to my comment, but busied himself stirring the tea.

'How bad was it in the camp?' I asked. 'We've heard stories about the Japs and what they did.'

'Bad enough,' was Richard's blunt, gruff answer as he poured the tea and handed me a mug. 'I was in two camps. The first camp at the university was survivable – just – while I was there. It got bad later, but at the start it wasn't too grim. We had a couple of hundred guards to contend with, but it was the overcrowding you noticed most. Ours was a civilian camp, mostly families, all ages, old men, young men, old women, wives, daughters, and odds and sods like me, no soldiers. The majority were Americans, but there were a fair number of British who, like me, had been caught there. Dutch, too, plus a few Poles and Russians and Filipinos who had worked for the Yanks, all kinds of people really, government officials, university teachers, businessmen, doctors, newspaper people, shopkeepers, bankers, and their wives and children, not forgetting the European and American dregs from the local gaol, who were shoved in, too.'

A querying eyebrow raised here. Richard answered it with the same grin: 'We didn't all live together. We were segregated – the women and children were in the main university building and we were in the education block. We had our problems, but we managed. The first commandant was an old Jap called Yagamuchi – ' He ignored my snigger at the weirdness of the name. ' – He wasn't too bad. He let the Filipino traders set up stalls outside the barbed-wire perimeter and we were able to get passes to go out and buy things from them. There was no point in escaping. There was nowhere to go, anyway. The Philippines were swarming with Japs, so you stayed where you were – in the camp. People who had been lucky enough to be able to bring in their possessions were best off. They had something to barter. They were the ones who set up little stalls in the corridors to sell things, clothes, electric razors, shoes, gramophones, gramophone records, pots, pans, cups, coffee percolators, though the Americans wanted those. The unlucky ones were those who had nothing much to trade.'

'And you helped the woman Jean?'

'Yes,' said Richard, suspiciously. 'I had money, she had a kiddie and kiddies need food. And besides, we liked each other by then. We had got to like each other a lot.'

Richard must have noticed how my interest again perked up, for he gave a little shrug the way people do when they accept the inevitable. 'If you are asking,' he said with a shy smile on the half of his face which still operated, 'the answer is, yes, I did like her, I liked her a lot, and, as to the other question – "Would I have?" – the answer again is, yes, I would willingly have married her if she had not already been married. But she was, to some government bod in Shanghai, so there was only ever going to be one outcome there. We looked after each other, we helped each other, we enjoyed each other's company. She wasn't the least stuck up, not like some of the snooty bitches in there. Jean was down-to-earth. She was good company.' Then fingering his scarred face, he said: 'And remember, I didn't have this then.'

'How old was she?'

'Twenty-six when I met her.'

'What about her husband?'

'He got rounded up with the rest of them in Shanghai, probably.' Again the dismissive shrug. 'After a while, Jean and I wanted somewhere we could be together more often so this American guy, John, who also had a girlfriend, he and I built a shanty of sorts out of bamboo and thatch in the grounds of the university, away from the main buildings. It was much cooler and more private there. Nothing sordid. It was somewhere we could be together during the day and somewhere for William to play – and we could make a little garden and grow vegetables. Besides, the dormitories were overcrowded by then. More and more people were coming in and at night the air in them was stifling. There wasn't a lot of room either. The next bloke's mattress would be no more than six inches from yours. The big problem was the Japs frowned on any cohabiting, so to speak, even between husbands and wives, and came down hard on anyone they found together in the shanties at night. They used to mount night patrols and burst in upon you shining torches to see if there were any women with you. We were wise to that. Jean and John's girl only came in the daytime. But others did get caught and got a beating for it, plus a few days in the camp cooler. You just had to make sure you didn't give the game away by getting her pregnant, as some poor sods did. The Japs were fond of beating people. It was their answer to everything.'

Unwittingly, Richard had answered a question I had not even asked, just wondered about. Again there was a pause of a few seconds while he stared into the flickering fire, cradling his cup with both hands and frowning as he remembered: then his face brightened and he went on with his tale: 'Sometimes the four of us played cards together, whist or poker – Jean taught me to play bridge there – or we just read, played music on an old wind-up gramophone or just sat and talked. Other times we did other things – sometimes. But, at least I didn't have to pay for it as some poor blighters did – ' Confirmation! And unsolicited! ' – Oh yes, there was sex for sale in the camp if you had the money. Not that I would have bothered, but there were girls available. The Japs had rounded up half the American, Russian and Filipina bar tarts in Manila and they carried on business as usual wherever they could. There were plenty of places to fornicate undisturbed – ' Fornicate! I did not have a clue what that word meant. ' – There was always a dark corner somewhere at night or a curtained-off room, or the women's showers. People found a way despite the Japs.'

Richard's grin broadened and he gave a little nod in my direction. 'You would have had been very popular in there, Joe. There weren't many young chaps of your age in there, a few, but not many. But there were plenty of young girls of fourteen, fifteen and sixteen, who were all worried they were going to miss out on life and were willing to be taught by any good-looking boy like yourself.' A flush of pride there. 'You would have had no trouble getting a willing girlfriend there. They'd have been fighting over you. American girls are far more forward than English girls. As likely as not, they would have asked you to take a stroll with them round the grounds before lights out. That is, if you could have got them away from their mothers or their grandmothers. There were plenty of bushes where you could have a quick kiss and a cuddle and they were eager to learn.'

Suddenly his face took on a grimmer look. 'Trouble is some of them learned the hard way, poor kids. The Japs weren't above having a go themselves. They used to raid the dormitories at night looking for good looking females. Several poor kids found themselves dragged out by some Jap guard with a rifle and bayonet and forced to do it on the ground outside. Their introduction to sex – rape. It was fairly common. People protested and the Jap officers said the guards would be punished, but no one ever knew if they were.'

An awkward silence ensued. Though his comments brought home one of the horrors of the camp, sadly I have to say that my mind was dwelling more on the American girls and the fascinating thought of easy sex with someone who actually wanted you to have a feel of them and who would actually unbutton your flies and put their hand inside without being asked and without protesting if you asked them to do it! And who would let you put your hand up their skirt or inside their blouse! I almost envied Richard being in there: to a naive, frustrated, adolescent country youth like me, it seemed almost worthwhile to be stuck in a Japanese internment camp with a crowd of Yank girls desperate to let you feel them and finger them and learn what life was all about. The girls of Gledlang and Maydun all seemed to be chastity-belt virgins and determined to remain so till they married. Try anything with them and you never got past their stocking tops: they would get angry and push your hand away and were quite likely to give you a slap, if you kept on trying. Or so I had found.

FIFTEEN

THE NOW blazing fire threw our shadows on to the wall: the lamp flickered on the rickety table behind us and black smoke snaked up from the glass towards the ceiling. Richard had set down his half-drunk tea in the hearth and had pulled a packet of cigarettes from his pocket and was concentrating on lighting one: I half-hoped he would offer me one, but he did not and I felt very self-conscious at having to take out my tobacco tin of pre-rolled wisps and to sit there smoking one of them, knowing it would burn away in no time.

'How did you get to be in Shanghai?' I asked.

'I got sent there,' Richard answered, flatly. 'When I first went to London, I was lucky enough to get a job humping boxes and crates about in a warehouse down by the docks, a shipping company. I was a stacker mostly. I stacked boxes and crates twenty, thirty-feet high, loaded them on to lorries heading for the docks and unloaded them from lorries coming from the docks. Hard work. I was lucky, I got in just before the Big Slump and, when that was at its worst in the mid-Thirties, I was elsewhere. The firm imported things from all over the world, anything from chests of tea from China, elephant tusks from South Africa to bales of cotton and jute from India. They had offices in Cape Town, Rio de Janeiro, Calcutta and Sydney, Australia, as well as Shanghai. I was fortunate, I was a neat writer so I got to do much of the paperwork in the goods inward department, keeping the stock cards up to date, arranging pick-ups at the docks, dispatching the lorries, checking them on their return to make sure no one had pinched anything en route, things like that. I was good at my job, I worked hard and the bosses appreciated it. A couple of years after I started the deputy foreman of the shipping department fell off a stack of crates and broke his leg. While he was in hospital recovering, they made me deputy foreman in his place. For a while, I practically ran the goods inward department, with two other blokes under me. I was just twenty-one – ' A smug smile here. ' – I worked hard, I kept my head down, I did the job. After a while, they took me into the main offices when an older chap retired, or was pushed – ' A shrug.

'You worked in an office!' Honest admiration from me: I had never personally known anyone who had worked in an office.

'It wasn't that great, Joe. Office work can be as boring as anything else – '

Yes, but you would be in the dry and warm, I was thinking, not in the middle of a field being rained on, snowed on and frozen half to death. Working in a warehouse was better than an open field, but an office, that was better still. That was where educated people worked: that was where girls worked, too: girls who wore skirts and tight sweaters!

Richard just went on talking: 'Then I got really lucky. The company directors wanted someone they could trust to go out to Shanghai to replace one of the clerks who wanted to come home because his wife was ill with malaria. They asked me because I was single, unattached and could go straight away and I could do the job. I sailed for Shanghai in the October of Thirty-Four and I was still there seven years later. It just so happened that in December of Forty-One, I was due some leave so I booked passage on a ship to India. I had always wanted to go there. Trouble is, we never made it. The Japs bombed Pearl Harbor, we put in at Manila and the rest you know.'

What could I say, but, 'Rotten luck getting caught like that.'

'Yeah,' Richard agreed, again half lost in thoughts of his own. 'Being behind barbed wire had its bad side. Food was the main problem or rather the lack of it. We never did get enough. Mostly it was oatmeal porridge – we called it mush. You had it more or less every day – mush for breakfast, mush for dinner, mush with cabbage, mush with bananas, mush cakes, mush pudding. You queued for it twice a day behind two thousand others in a long line with your little tin dish in your hand and a cup for your coffee. Other times it was a slop of watery rice, lugao, or whistleweed soup. Most people supplemented their food with whatever they could buy outside from the Filipinos – mungo beans, cabbage if you were lucky, courgettes or sweet potatoes if you were luckier. You could always barter things for food if you had something to swap, or buy them if you had actual money and valuables, a good watch, a ring, or a bracelet, gold cufflinks, Filipino pesos. Everything was available in there – at a price. Cigarettes, razor blades, soap, tobacco. You could even get bootleg whisky. Alcohol was supposed to be banned and the Japs threatened reprisals if anyone was caught with it, but there were always some enterprising blokes fermenting it in secret. They used the mush and added raisins and prunes. Then there were the Filipinos who used to smuggle whisky into the camp inside hollowed-out eggs.' Silence for a few seconds. 'Life wasn't all bad.'

'The worst thing was not knowing how long we were going to have to spend in there, particularly when the Japs seemed to be on top. That was a bad time for us, the British and the Yanks. The Japs would strut around the camp crowing about how they were driving us out of the Far East forever. All we seemed to hear was news of defeat after defeat and the Japs were never slow at telling us they were winning in the Far East and the Germans were winning in Europe. First, we heard Singapore had fallen, then the Americans had given up on Corregidor and then we were in full retreat in Burma and the Japs were about to invade India. The news from Europe was even worse. It was all retreats and defeats, Greece, Crete, North Africa, Russia. That's when some people did doubt we would win, the moaners and groaners and the workshy johnnies. Oh yes, we did some work in the camp. Everyone had a job of some kind – we all pulled together, well, most of us. Jean was in the hospital because we had a lot of sick. When I first went in I was put on the garbage detail, burying the rubbish. Three-and-a-half-thousand people make a lot of rubbish and in that climate you either burn it or bury it or suffer the consequences. We had millions of flies and mosquitoes around the camp – we had nets, but you still got bitten, particularly as there was a marshy area in the grounds and the mosquitoes bred in there by the billion. The Philippines is very hot and very wet at times, ideal for mosquitoes, blackflies and blowflies. It's very humid, too. You sweat all the time. The monsoon season starts in June and it just pours for days and weeks. We also had cockroaches and beetles by the thousand everywhere and we all suffered from head lice and bed bugs. It wasn't all fun – ' Obvious sarcasm. ' – I had various things wrong with me at different times while I was in the first camp, boils, swollen feet, but you put up with those. Really, I was generally fine till I got beri-beri. Ever heard of beri-beri, Joe?'

No, I told him, I had never heard of it. Richard became more serious. 'Just hope you never get it,' he said, blowing smoke into the air. 'There are two kinds of beri-beri, wet beri-beri and dry beri-beri. Fortunately, if you can say that, I had dry beri-beri. Your face bloats up and every joint in your body swells up – ankles, wrists, elbows, knees, even your finger joints. It's very painful and you have difficulty moving about, but it's survivable, given treatment. Others who had wet beri-beri were far worse off. With that, your whole body swells up like a balloon, feet, legs, hands – ' A pause for effect here so I would wince when he said it. ' – and your testicles. A lot of people died of wet beri-beri and things like TB, amoebic dysentery, dengue fever, cholera and septicaemia. Cholera you get from drinking polluted water or stagnant water. Dysentery is like having uncontrollable diarrhoea. We had them all. We were losing ten people a week towards the end. Old people mostly. Heart attacks brought on by anaemia and lack of food and overwork, not to mention despair. They just died. The smaller children and the old and the infirm were always the first to go. After I got out of hospital that first time, I was put on the burial detail by the camp council, making wooden crosses for those who'd died. I was so weak I wasn't really up to that even. When the monsoon came and the graves filled with water, I was the one who had to hold the bodies under with a bamboo pole while the others put earth on top. That was hard, especially when it was a kiddie. It was hard enough burying a child as it was and I helped to bury several. Burying an old man or an old woman is not so bad. They have had their life. But burying a child that way – '

Richard left the sentence unfinished and for a third time sat staring into the fire for fifteen or twenty seconds, remembering again, I suppose, before he went on.

'I went in weighing twelve stone, more or less, and left it weighing just over eight. But I was luckier than most. One of the worst times I had was when I developed the cramps through lack of salt. Salt deprivation, they call it. Every joint in your body aches and you get terrible muscle cramps and I mean terrible. They're agonising. You literally scream with pain. I did. You sweat so much in the heat and the humidity that the salt drains out of your body and you have to replace it because, if you don't, you dehydrate very quickly – lose water to you, Joe. Salt was in short supply all the time. We got a ration, but it was never enough and by that time I had nothing to buy any with from the traders outside the wire. It was Jean who saved me – she bartered her wedding ring to get some salt for me.'

The significance of the last point I did not take in: I was too taken aback by Richard's embarrassing admission that he had screamed with pain: he said it so matter-of-factly that I felt it would be wrong of me even to acknowledge I had heard: so I just lowered my head and made a louder noise sipping my tea.

SIXTEEN

IT SEEMED an obvious question: 'Why didn't you write home? You had plenty of time in there. Other people wrote from PoW camps.'

Richard thought for a few seconds, then he looked across at me: he had finished his tea, the cup was in the hearth and he was leaning forward to put some more coke on the fire.

'We weren't allowed,' he said quite calmly. 'All we got was a postcard to give in to the Red Cross, who were in Manila, "Am prisoner of war. Am well." Or "Am wounded." Cross out what doesn't apply. Except the Japs never handed them over. They were all found later in a cupboard in the Jap admin block – unposted.'

'What happened to the woman Jean?'

'We got separated when the Japs opened a second camp and shipped all the men up to it,' said Richard, letting out a small sigh. 'It was the second camp that was bad. Really bad. The Japs started to get really nasty when it became clear the Allies were winning the war. They brought more and more people into the university compound who had previously been allowed to stay outside and it got vastly overcrowded. By the spring of Forty-Four the place was so jam-packed, people were sleeping everywhere and there was a lot of disease, a lot of disease. People were dying at a much faster rate, too, ten, fifteen, twenty a day, mostly due to the conditions. The Japs decided to open a second camp up in the mountains, at a place where the university had some kind of agricultural buildings on the shores of a big lake. They said we would be better off up there, that it would be much healthier for the children. The air was purer, so they said, and it was much cooler than the heat and humidity of Manila. They told us there were spacious grounds and gardens and running streams in the hills and bungalows to live in. They wanted seven hundred of us to go up to build the nipa and bamboo barracks and dig the wells and latrines. The women and children would follow in the September, after the monsoon – ' A sigh. ' – They asked for volunteers, but not many wanted to go. I didn't. I didn't want to leave Jean. Her little lad, William, was ill and she was two months pregnant – ' He paused here and gave me a severe look as if challenging me to comment: I did not. 'Only a couple of hundred volunteered, so they simply ordered all the fit men on to open trucks at bayonet-point and drove us the ninety miles through the pouring rain to the camp. The Japs had lied, of course. The second camp was no better than the first. We arrived in the rain and we spent the next five months working in the rain, through the monsoon, up to our knees in mud and soaked to the skin. Five months we spent building that bloody camp! Then a bloody hurricane blew in and demolished half of it, so we had to start all over again.'

Another pause while he sought the words. 'We had a bastard for a commandant – a scruffy, sadistic, little bugger called Konochi, Lieutenant Konochi. He ran the place like a concentration camp. The Yanks hanged him after the war. You never saw him without his club. He used to beat people for the most trivial of things. That little bastard had only one intention, as far as we could see, to kill us all one way or another, work us to death or starve us to death. Things got really bad in the February of Forty-Five, after the women and children had come up. They cut the mush ration a second time. They had cut it in half only the week before. People were keeling over just standing in line.' Real bitterness now. 'Then, as if that wasn't bad enough, Konochi also cut the salt ration. He did it as a reprisal as the Yanks were getting nearer and nearer following the landings at Lingayen and the Leyte Gulf. That is when Konochi got me. I had arranged with a Filipino, who traded through the wire, to leave two boiled eggs close enough so I could reach through and lift them in. You needed boiled eggs for your eyes, to stop you going blind. But he wouldn't come any closer than fifty yards so I had to crawl through the wire and through the long grass to get them. The guards got me as I came back. I was lucky, in a way, I was taken to Konochi – if you can call that lucky. Another fellow who tried it a couple of days later was shot out of hand by a guard and another Yank caught outside the wire on a foraging trip was taken off and beheaded. When they took me to him, Konochi went berserk as usual. He knew why I wanted the eggs. He flattened me with a crack across the head with the thick bamboo club he carried, then he set about me with his sword, screaming and yelling and prodding at my face. I think he was trying to take my left eye out because he seemed to be concentrating on that side of my face. Fortunately, dazed as I was, I managed to roll about and protect myself. He must have thought he had done it, there was so much blood, because, after four or five goes, he gave up and went off. He left my face a real mess. After that two of the guards had a go at me as well. They gave me a good kicking and then they both prodded me in the ribs with their bayonets – here and here.' He pointed to two places on his side. 'Luckily there was not a lot of force behind them because I was rolling away at the time and I think they were just prodding me to get up. Two other chaps rushed in and picked me up, but one of the thrusts still went into my left lung, not deep, but deep enough. I was half dead when they carried me to the camp hospital. But again I was lucky. That was all you had really – good luck or bad luck. I had good luck. There was a proper surgeon at the hospital, a Swiss chap, who patched me up as best he could. He plugged my wounds and sewed up the real deep cuts with a darning needle and thread, but I'd been rolling around in muck and mud and some of the wounds became infected. The infection spread from here to here – ' He indicated from his temple to his chin. ' – The whole left side of my face was one great big abscess. They didn't have the medicines to fight that with so they used the only things they had – they put maggots on the wounds. It was standard procedure in the camps. The maggots would eat the pus and clean the wounds. I think some of the buggers they put on mine ate a bit more than they should!' A wicked grin here: then a sigh. 'Still, I was luckier than some. I survived Konochi and his thugs. Other blokes didn't.' Another shrug.

Richard's shrug surprised me. As much as I had heard about these things, he was the first person I had met who had known the victims of them and he seemed to be indifferent to their fate, like there was nothing that could have been done about it so nothing was done about it: it just happened and you forgot about it and got on with life.

'It was touch and go for me for a while,' he went on, 'especially when they thought I had blood poisoning. If you got that, you usually died. Nothing to fight it with. At one stage they must have despaired because I was shoved out on to the veranda along with the others who everyone knew were dying. They needed my mattress. There you got to look at your last sunset. Only a lucky few saw the next dawn after a night out there. I was lucky to be one of them. I managed to pull through. I don't know how, but I did. I'm still not a hundred per cent right from what Konochi and his thugs did, even now. The left lung doesn't operate a hundred per cent, that's why I get so breathless at times. I shouldn't really be smoking, but what the hell! I'm alive and a lot of people aren't.'

A second cigarette was lit. 'The way the Japs were at the time, none of us was sure that we would make it out of there, anyway. We had heard some nasty rumours and I have no doubt they were true. The big rumour on the bamboo telegraph was that Konochi intended to kill us all, men, women and children. No survivors, no witnesses. I think the yellow bastard would have done it, too. Someone said there had been a message from Tokyo to do it. The Japs were losing the war and they knew it. They didn't care anymore. If they were willing to die for their Emperor, they seemed to think we should do the same. That's when people really became worried. Fortunately, that was when the Yanks arrived to rescue us – in the nick of time, believe me.'

Rescue! 'What rescue? How?'

SEVENTEEN

'YANK paratroopers came in and rescued us,' said Richard, with a laugh. 'They dropped into the jungle all round the camp. It was just after the six o'clock roll call. Next thing we knew there were Yank soldiers in the camp, scores of them. Everyone was cheering and shouting and kissing each other. I didn't see much of it, I was still lying on the hospital veranda, but I heard it all. Then this little Yank came up, grinning all over his face, armed to the teeth, he was. It was the happiest day of my life, I can tell you. Suddenly all these amphibious trucks appeared – amtracs, they called them. We were all loaded on them, including me on a stretcher, no messing, and, with soldiers riding shotgun, we were rushed down to the lakeshore and shipped across to the other side where other Yanks were waiting for us, nurses and doctors and cooks. It was a fantastic operation. They got two-thousand or more of us out. As far as I know, we never lost anybody, just three wounded when the Japs fired on us, though some of the paratroopers were killed during the rescue.' A sadness in his voice here, before the excitement of the moment returned.

'There was a lot of shooting going on. The Yanks were firing into the jungle on either side of the road and I know the Japs were firing back because you could hear the bullets whishing overhead and pinging against the sides of the amtrac. The Japs also shelled the beach as we crossed it and, even while we were in the water, there were odd shells landing around us because we were still within artillery range. I was pretty weak at this time. My wounds were festering something awful still. A Yank medic was looking after me and had a tube in my arm putting this stuff into me. All the time the bullets were whistling over the top of the amtrac, he just sat there fully exposed holding this drip up and never flinched, not once. He just sat there chatting away like it was all perfectly normal, asking me about England when he learned I was from there. Marvellous, he was, bloody marvellous!'

An embarrased laugh here and a pause while he thought of what to say next: finally, with a weary sigh, he said: 'After we were rescued, it took me a long time to recover. We couldn't go to Manila, it was in ruins. So they shipped us down to a place called Hollandia in New Guinea, then on to Townsville in north Queensland in Australia. After that to Brisbane. I was in a convalescent hospital there for about four months, till the war ended in August. That's when I first heard about Jean. She hadn't been able to come up to the second camp when the other families came up. Her son, little William, was even worse at the time and she couldn't travel. She was also seven months pregnant.' Another sigh here. 'I learned later her poor little lad died just before they were released. He was only five. A lovely little blond-haired chap. I didn't know all that till later, though. Jean and I got separated when I went up to the second camp and we missed each other after that.

'She had been released well ahead of us and was gone by the time I got to Townsville and I never caught up with her. Being a government bod's wife, she was put on an earlier transport than me. She had the baby in the first camp, a girl, I was told, but I don't know what she called it. The trouble is she probably thinks I'm dead. Everyone else did, even some in the second camp who had seen me carried off. While I was in Australia, I met my friend, John, who had been too sick at the time of the round-up to go up into the mountains. He told me word had got back to those who had stayed at the university that I had died after Konochi gave me a going over. Jean would have heard that, too, so she doesn't even know I am alive. Everyone I met seemed amazed I was still alive. They had good reason to be, I suppose. So many had died and when someone looked like they were dying, you just shrugged and got on with what you were doing. John told me Jean had decided to try and get back to Shanghai to find her husband – to find out if he was still alive. He didn't know whether she had managed it. Everything there was in a state of turmoil after the Japs surrendered. There was a lot of fighting going on around Shanghai, Chinese Communists fighting Chinese Nationalists, so everything was very confused. People were starving, too, and, of course, the Americans had bombed the place to glory.'

The obvious questions which Richard must have thought about: 'Perhaps she's gone back to her husband, permanently? Perhaps she found him and stayed with him?'

Richard shrugged. 'Perhaps she has. It's always a possibility,' he said, slowly blowing out more smoke. 'I won't know till I see her, will I? If I ever see her. Someone in Australia from one of the camps who knows her, someone who was going back to Shanghai themselves, they might tell her I'm still alive and that they had seen me, but I don't know. I just don't know, Joe. In the camp, because of us, because of what happened, when she knew she was going to have the baby, she said she would ask her husband – Robert his name was – for a divorce. That at least is what she told me she would do. But that was when I was with her, before I shipped up to the second camp. I hope that is why she went back to Shanghai, though she owed it to her husband to tell him about the little chap, William, his death. Whether she will get a divorce, I don't know. I don't even know if her husband is alive, whether he survived the camp in Shanghai. Scores of others didn't. And, of course, she may not even know yet I am alive. It's all up in the air, Joe, it's all up in the air.'

For no reason I could think of, I swear, Richard suddenly stared hard at me and stressed: 'Jean was no camp tart, Joe. She was a Sunday school teacher before she married, educated, very religious, unlike me, very correct, a Scottish minister's daughter, church on Sunday and all that. She believed – the exact opposite of me. What happened between us came unexpectedly for both of us. If we hadn't got talking on the boat, about religion strangely enough, I doubt it would have happened at all. We fell in love first. Nothing happened between us for at least five months. It started out as just a friendship, just talking together, looking out for each other. No hopping into bed at the first opportunity, not that you could there. She didn't want to commit adultery, Joe.'

'But she did.'

'Yes, but only after John and I had built the shanty. It was more love than adultery. That's the way I see it. And we weren't at it all the time either. There were too many patrolling Japs for that. Half the time you didn't feel like it, anyway, or you were incapable. When you're half-starved, your main thought is for food, not chasing after women. Plus the humidity there is up over a hundred most days and you do nothing but sweat – '

He left the sentence unfinished, leaving me the option of filling in the mental picture of two threshing, sweat-soaked bodies heaving against each other on a rickety bed: which momentarily I did: all Richard did was pull a face. 'As far as her husband is concerned, I only have what Jean told me in the camp to go on. From what she said, I don't think the marriage was that great anyway. That was one of the reasons she was on the boat, to take a break. She was heading back to England as it was.'

'Perhaps her old man wouldn't give her a divorce?' I suggested.

'Perhaps,' Richard nodded. 'I don't suppose he would be too happy when his wife turned up with a new kid, mine, and told him his own son had died. She would have wanted to square things with him about that. Then she said she wanted to get home to England. She'd made that clear in the camp.'

'Didn't you ever try to find her, to write to her?'

'Oh yes,' Richard replied. 'I asked a couple of people who were also trying to get back to Shanghai to tell her if they met her that I was alive. While I was in Australia, I also wrote to an address in Shanghai she had given me in the camp, but I never got an answer. I wrote to her a couple of times.' He answered the question himself with a shrug. 'Maybe because of her husband.'

'Did you tell her about your face in the letter?'

A much longer pause from Richard here: then a very quiet, almost sorrowful: 'No. No I didn't. I don't know how she would react now, seeing me with this. I didn't have this face when I last saw her. When someone gets badly injured or crippled, it throws some people. They can't take it. They duck out. I'd like to think Jean wouldn't, but then she hasn't seen it, has she? Perhaps someone else told her about it and that's why – ' Again the incomplete thought. 'I hope not. A thing like this can throw people. It threw you when you first saw it, didn't it?'

'It did a bit,' I admitted, reluctantly and hastily changed tack. 'Are you still trying to find her? Now, I mean?'

Another wearied sigh from Richard. 'Yes, that's what I was hoping to do up in London. If she is getting a divorce, I was hoping she would be back in England by now. She lived in London before she went out to Shanghai. I went to the address she gave me, but the block of flats had been badly blitzed. That's where I was one day last week, trying to find her. Some of the flats are still there so I left a letter with some old caretaker chap. I also tried a couple of other addresses, but without any luck. I know her family lived near Aberdeen somewhere, but I don't know exactly where. I don't have an actual address. Jean and I spent two-and-a-half years together, hard years. You don't forget that in a hurry.'

By this time Richard had puffed his second cigarette to a mere stub: he blew out the last of the smoke and watched it curl away in the flickering light of the fire before tossing it into the flames.

'If she was looking for you, surely she would have written by now?' I suggested. Immediately I said it, I felt guilty: there was a painful look on Richard's face: my remark had hit a vulnerable point:

obviously, it was something which had occurred to him, too. 'What will you do if she doesn't come back?'

He answered without any real enthusiasm as if hoping he would never have to do it: 'Find another woman, I suppose. If I can find one who will put up with this.' He pointed at his face again.

'There's plenty of widows about,' I offered, half jokingly. 'Some of them could be a bit desperate. They wouldn't worry about your face. It's all the same in the dark, ain't it? And you could get run over by a bus tomorrow.'

I was not sure that Richard appreciated the remark, but he smiled at it anyway.

My next question, 'Why didn't you stay in Australia? It must be better than here?' seemed a sensible one to me.

'I did think of it for a while. I'd got a clerking job after I came out of hospital, working for the Aussies and the Yanks, helping them process other released prisoners coming through. But I decided Australia wasn't for me. I wanted to get home, back to dear old England, back to Blighty, back to Gledlang even!' A bigger grin now. 'Mainly because of Jean – in case she came. I wanted to make sure I got ahead of her. I only arrived here four weeks ago. I had to wait for a ship. That's why I stayed in Australia so long. There was a shortage of ships and the Yanks were taking their soldiers home first. When I did get a passage, the sea voyage took eight weeks. We came via the Panama Canal, as it was. We landed at Liverpool and I came down to London by train. That's where I learned I'm still not over what the Japs did to me. I've got a damaged kidney from the kicking and my lungs aren't a hundred per cent from being used for bayonet practice. Coming out of Euston station, I tried to run for a bus and just keeled over, breathless. I really ought to see a doctor every now and again for a check-up.'

A pause followed and, in the pause, Richard's mood hardened appreciably. 'One thing I learned in the camps, Joe,' he began, 'is you never know what's going to happen in life. Sometimes you just have to live for the moment. If an opportunity comes, you have to seize it with both hands. Grab it and hang on. Like Jean and me, for instance. If there is one thing I learned about life, it is not to expect anything. Don't rely on others. Do things yourself. I saw enough people die in the camps to know life can be short enough without wasting it. People died so quickly there, the kids and the old people, it was frightening. I think that is why Jean and I got together. At the time, we thought we'd be in there for years. It was a natural thing to do and we did it.'

His philosophy on life rather shocked me at the time, mainly because no one had ever taken the trouble before to discuss such things with me so I had never really contemplated them.

'At least you saw a bit of the world,' I said: it was meant as a compliment: admiration for what he had experienced as much as for what he had suffered: Richard did not see it that way.

He shot me a cold look. 'The bit of the world I saw was the worst part,' he began, not angrily, just correcting my naive impressions of a bold adventurer. 'I've seen things you would never want to see. People don't know how good England is till they have been out East. Shanghai is the arsehole of the universe. I was actually glad when I left it. I saw babies left in the gutter to die, abandoned by their mothers simply because they were girls, useless mouths, left to starve to death and no one seemed to care, except the missionaries and they couldn't save them all. When the Japs cut it off, people were dying in the streets of starvation, mostly refugees. They'd be sitting outside your gates begging in the morning and be dead by the afternoon and no one gave a damn. Oh, the Europeans in the Settlement were all right and those in the French part, but the Chinese themselves – they had nothing. All you ever saw was poverty and disease and death everywhere you looked, outside the city, down the alleyways in the rougher quarters, down by the Whangpoo river. You only had to walk along the waterfront to see the dead floating past on the outgoing tide. I even saw people publicly beheaded in the street in Shanghai, criminals, thieves and that, their heads chopped off right in front of you! Not to mention the poor buggers being publicly strangled. You could sit and watch that for entertainment if you wanted. Watch some poor bugger strangle slowly in an iron cage clamped by their jaws so their feet were just an inch or two off the ground. Manila was no different after the Japs came in. I saw people lying in the streets there who had been beheaded or bayoneted or beaten to death for no other reason than they happened to be standing on the pavement when some Jap soldiers going past decided they wanted some sport. And I heard women screaming as the soldiers dragged them into the big hotels. They knew what was going to happen to them in there. The Japs usually killed the women they raped.'

'At least you've seen other places,' I pouted. 'I ain't seen nothing. I wish I could leave here and get a job up in London, maybe. They say there's plenty of building work up there, clearing the rubble from the bomb sites, rebuilding the buildings, trolley-bus driving, even conductoring. Anywhere would be better than here, especially in the bloody winter. It ain't so bad in the summer, but the winters here can be a bit cold.' That was the usual understatement for 'bloody freezing': we always reckoned the winds in winter blew straight from Siberia, across the steppes of Russia and the plains of Hungary, then the flat parts of Germany and the polder fields of Holland and finally straight across the North Sea to us.

'I did live here,' Richard reminded me with a smile. 'I doubt you would be any happier up there than you would here.'

'Just give me a chance,' I retorted, 'just give me a chance.'

When I returned home that night, my mother was waiting in the kitchen: John Bolt had sent word that I was required on Boundary the next morning – for hoeing! – and Ben had agreed. As well as its vast orchards, Boundary had six arable fields in all, three sown with wheat and three planted with root crops: I was to help them hoe the beet. 'You'll work when you go across there,' my mother declared, rather churlishly. 'You won't be able to do as you like with John Bolt, that you won't!'

I cannot say I was over happy about it: after three weeks of hoeing for Ben, I now was going to have to spend the next week, perhaps even the next two weeks, hoeing for John Bolt. At least, I would have company while I worked: I would be seeing Billy again, so I would be able to make my peace with him: and, as I now had plenty to tell him about Richard, that would not be too difficult.

EIGHTEEN

THAT WAS how, the next morning just after seven o'clock, I found myself bouncing across the causeway on my high-handlebar bicycle with my sandwiches and bottle of tea in a knapsack slung across my shoulders, on my way to Boundary farm.

I was not relishing the prospect: John Bolt was as miserable and heartless a man as I have ever known, full of unreasonable moods and sudden tempers, meanness and unfair practices, who, when I worked for him, forced Billy and I to work much harder than ever we wished to do, demanding always that we should do more than we did, and do that better and more quickly than we had ever done. Neither Billy nor I ever saw any good in him: no task was ever done to his satisfaction, so no word of thanks or praise ever passed his lips.

He was without a doubt the most feared and abusive of all the district's farmers and, in retrospect I wonder how I ever allowed myself to labour so often in his employ, so thoroughly did I detest the man. I suppose, in truth, I did it for Ben, for the 'dropping-off' agreements he had with him, rather than for the pittance which John Bolt paid me: Ben, I think, also did it so that from time to time I would have company other than just him while I worked, so that I would not be so lonely: but he never said so.

A week's labour for John Bolt was like a month's labour on Norsea, so hard was it: and when the time came each Saturday noon for the five older farmworkers, Charlie Mangapp, the foreman, the cringing Tully Jude, Sam Perry, Bob Bird and Ted Oldton, along with Billy, and sometimes myself, to line up in his office to receive our little brown envelopes, his expression as he counted out mine and Billy's money was always such that I knew he begrudged us every copper halfpenny of it. With his squat, spreading bulk squeezed into a polished wooden swivel chair, he would make great play of unlocking the ornate roll-top desk in which he kept his papers, first shifting them about as if looking for money to pay us, then scrabbling in a drawer for the extra ten-shilling or one-pound note and whatever silver and copper coins he could spare, as if to say they were all he had when we knew full well he kept a roll of notes wound up with an elastic band in a locked drawer near his elbow and a small hessian bag of silver coins in the cupboard underneath. Once he had reckoned up the older men's wages, counted them out into the envelopes, sealed the flaps and handed them over to receive a respectful, 'Thank you, Mr Bolt,' he would turn to us. And here my picture of John Bolt never alters: from out of a sullen, florid face, two steely blue pig-like eyes would peer at us over the top of steel-rimmed half-glasses, the ever-burning cigarette would protrude from the thin tight line of his lips and, as he counted out the money, there would be a permanent scowl on his face as if to say we did not deserve so much, that we had not worked well, that he knew we were really idle slackers and it was only a matter of time before he caught us out.

Looking back, I think the only work upon Boundary I ever truly liked was when Billy and I were assigned to loading the bushel boxes of picked and graded fruit on to the lorry taking them to the London markets: that and picking together. When we picked together, we would often work at the tops of our ladders stripped to the waist, our torsos burned a coppery red by the fierceness of the summer sun, calling out to each other as we picked, revelling in the brightness of the day, the blue sky, the puffy white clouds drifting up from the southwest, the panorama of river and countryside all around and the freedom and lack of caring in our lives.

Not unexpectedly, John Bolt was waiting for me when I reached the yard: the crafty sod had hidden himself behind the half-open doorway of the barn, in one hand the brass pocketwatch by which he timed the arrivals and departures of all his workers, in the other a heavy knobbed hazel stick beating out an impatient tattoo against the toe of his boot. I knew he was there even as I approached: Blackie, his flop-eared spaniel, was snuffling among the nettles in search of rodents, rats or mice or voles and where it was, John Bolt was always sure to be.

On top of the nearby hayrick, Charlie Mangapp, the stooping, round-backed, moustacheoed foreman, in his late fifties, was sharpening a curved hayknife preparatory to cutting feed for Peter, the shire: he frantically tried to signal to me, but it was too late: as I skidded to a halt in a spray of mud and stones and let my bicycle fall among the nettles, John Bolt stepped out to confront me, a look of grim satisfaction on his face.

'What time of the bloody morning do you call this, young Joe?' he barked in his usual brusque manner, making a show of consulting his watch, purely for my benefit, of course. 'I pay you to start on time, boy, and to finish on time, not to come when you think you will.'

'I'm sorry, Mr Bolt,' was my apathetic reply, 'I had a flat tyre and had to pump it up.'

John Bolt dismissed my excuse with an angry exclamation and pointed at my bicycle. 'You ain't got no pump!' he snorted: it was a small detail, which in my breathlessness, I had overlooked. 'Don't you lie to me, boy. You're a quarter of an hour late. You either lose a half-hour's money or you make up the time in your lunch hour.'

'I'll make it up in my lunch hour, Mr Bolt,' I reluctantly promised, hoping my show of contrition would appease him.

It did not. 'You bloody will and all!' he informed me curtly, snapping shut the watch and repocketing it. I felt like telling him what he could do with his job, getting on my bicycle and riding back to Norsea, but knew that I dare not: John Bolt's temper and his bullying ways were too well known and, besides, Ben would have sent me back anyway: he needed to stay in John Bolt's good books. 'Now get a bloody hoe out of the barn, Joe, and get to work,' I was told. 'You're with Billy and Dennis hoeing in the top field. Get on with it or I'll dock you an hour and you can explain that to your step-father.'

With that, he gave a sharp command to Blackie and went striding off across the quagmire of a yard towards a line of low, whitewashed storage sheds where the various fruits, picked by the women of the village, were sorted and packed by the men, then loaded on to the lorry for London. The best I could manage to appease my injured pride was a short, two-fingered gesture at John Bolt's disappearing back.

'You'll do that once too often, young Joe,' Charlie Mangapp admonished from his position on the hayrick as I trudged below him on my way to the barn to collect my hoe and a hessian sack to wear as a head covering in case of rain: but I was in no mood for lectures and stamped past him with a show of ill grace and a muttered obscenity.

When I reached the field Billy and Dennis Bolt were a good hundred yards along their rows, hoeing vigorously. In normal circumstances, if I were late joining him, Billy would stop hoeing his row, cross to mine and begin working back towards me, thus allowing me to catch up: that way, the two of us could progress side by side down the field, chatting as we went. This day Billy did not hoe back towards me: instead he kept his head down and his back turned, an obvious surliness about his whole manner: it was Dennis who crossed to my row and hoed the fifty yards back to meet me.

'What's the matter with him?' I asked, nodding towards Billy when eventually we met.

'Got a bollocking off the old man first thing this morning for not doing a job properly yesterday,' Dennis replied, but he said it without a smile, more in despair than actual sympathy, I think. 'The old man really laid into him. Threatened to give him his cards if it happened again. Billy ain't too happy about it, especially as he's lost his new overcoat as well. Wally Ponder's taken it back. Took it off him this morning on his way here. Stopped him in the street and made him give it back.' True enough, Billy was wearing just an ordinary jacket: the army greatcoat like mine he had bought a few months before off one of the village men, Wally Ponder, a demobbed soldier, was nowhere to be seen. Wally Ponder was supposedly on seven years' reserve and had been told to keep his uniform and kit ready for instant recall should the army ever need him again: but, on his demobilisation, he had declared to all and sundry in the Chessman that he had 'done his bit' and there was no way he was going back in the army, not even if they sent the military police after him. No way was he going to fight his socialist brothers, the Russians. The Americans, yes! He would fight them anytime! Bloody swanky Yanks! But the Russians? No way! He had then promptly sold off everything.

Perhaps unwisely, never being one able to save money, Billy had agreed to pay three pounds for his army greatcoat at five shillings a week: payment was not so much late as non-existent: most of it had been spent in the public houses of Maydun on a Saturday night: so Wally Ponder had taken the greatcoat back. It was no wonder Billy was seething: on the land, in spring as well as winter, you needed such coats. In the middle of that field that day, Billy would have been cold, too, and if it rained, as it was threatening, he would get wet, very wet!

I did not mind working with Dennis Bolt, John Bolt's nephew: in fact, I enjoyed it: Dennis could be quite pleasant at times, good company, though a bit naive, with a wry sense of humour. Whenever he and I worked together and I joined him, he positively beamed a greeting: I think he was just glad to have someone other than a sour-faced Billy or the more serious-minded older men with whom he could talk. He and his uncle lived alone in the six-bedroomed Georgian farmhouse: he was ten years older than Billy and I, small in stature, lean framed, with dark straight hair, dark eyes, a bright smile when away from his uncle and a peculiar habit of sniffing and rubbing his nose as he spoke. Of late, he had attempted to grow a small pencil line moustache to counter his boyish looks, but it was not a success, about as successful as his love life, I would say: for he had never had a girlfriend that I knew of – but then neither had I, so that could not be held against him. He was only rarely seen about the village and then was always in his work clothes, muddy gumboots turned down at the tops, grey-brown herringbone overcoat, boiler suit and a cloth cap heavily soiled with grease and oil from repairing farm machinery. Much like myself, I suppose. But unlike us, Billy, Nick, myself, Lennie Ring and other Gledlang youths, he never drank in public houses, in Maydun or anywhere, and never went to the cinema in Maydun on Saturday nights: nor had he ever sat upon the broken ciderstone in Gledlang Square idling away the evening hours, or played football against Jack Spivey's wall, or cricket up the Park where the multi-chimneyed, Eighteenth Century parsonage, stands. Nor had he ever gone swimming on bright July and August Sundays as the other youths did or engaged in noisy, ill-tempered mud fights across the saltings while waiting for the incoming tide. He never seemed to do any of the things a normal person might do: most days he remained by himself on Boundary farm, where John Bolt always found some work to occupy his time. Even as a youth, it was not uncommon to see him performing some day-long task on a Saturday and Sunday afternoon when other landworkers dug their gardens or pedalled slowly home from the Chessman in the early afternoon sunshine for the traditional midday dinner. Quite bluntly, Dennis Bolt worked seven days a week and most evenings, more even than I did (and that was enough) and was never allowed an idle hour to himself. Always hovering in the background was John Bolt, planning some new task for his nephew before he had even completed the one on which he was engaged. It was not uncommon on Boundary for the older landworkers to join Dennis Bolt on some work to find he had completed half of it over a weekend, or the evening before. Everyone in the village felt sorry for him, especially when John Bolt was in one of his mean moods, which was often. In front of the other workers, you reddened yourself sometimes to hear the foul-mouthed, foul-tempered farmer haranguing his poor nephew in a way he never did the other farm-workers, except Billy and myself: and Dennis took it all meekly, quietly, just standing there, offering no defence, no excuse or explanation of any kind for fear perhaps that it would bring even greater wrath down upon his head.

No, you could not help but like Dennis Bolt, ever eager to please, never coarse or offensive in anything he said, always willing to listen to your grumbles, but never grumbling himself, though he had a thousand and more reasons to do so. You liked him and you pitied him.

NINETEEN

WE NEVER did catch up with Billy: while Dennis and I laboured and chatted together in the vastness of that flat field, Billy worked alone a hundred yards ahead of us, determined to remain so. He stopped only once to roll himself a cigarette from his tobacco tin: normally, lighting a cigarette was an excuse to lean on one's hoe for a few minutes and ease aching back muscles. But Billy had taken only a few puffs when he realised we were catching him, so he bent to his task again. Indeed, he seemed to put on a spurt at times to make sure he got away from us and any attempts to talk to him across the rows as he came back down the field past us were met with an initial, 'I ain't talking about it,' followed by a cold silence.

The extent of Billy's anger was evident from what I saw of his work: he did not seem at all bothered that he was hacking up the odd growing plant as well as the weeds around it. When Dennis, whom we regarded as a friend, and as put upon by John Bolt as the both of us, went across to suggest he ought to be more careful, he was met with a curt: 'Piss off! It ain't your bloody farm yet, Dennis! You ain't even the bloody foreman!' Which was quite true: John Bolt would not even make Dennis his head man: but Dennis did it just the same because he was John Bolt's nephew, I think, and also because he knew any blame for what Billy was doing would fall squarely upon him. He came back looking rather sheepish and the two of us hoed together: Billy remained ahead of us and I never did get to tell him what I knew about Richard.

All the while we worked, the tattered outriders of the approaching rain came scudding up from the west and soon a dismal pall of grey encircled us, from horizon in front to horizon behind, over land and estuary alike. It began to rain just after our quarter-hour breakfast break at nine, which Dennis and I took together, and gradually got heavier and heavier. The hessian sack I had brought from the farm I now folded into a cowl to protect my head and shoulders. Dennis, too, fetched a sack from the hedge and folded it into a similar hood, but

Billy, as well as no overcoat, had neither cap nor sack: I can only assume the telling off by John Bolt made him forget to pick one up from the barn. Although he had turned up the collar of his jacket, his hair was soon plastered against his skull and even at that distance I could see the anger and exasperation mounting at each futile attempt to wipe the rain from his eyes. But the rain just teemed down relentlessly.

For a further two hours I continued to slash and dig at the weeds, my own overcoat saturated and my limbs growing steadily more chilled. With the ground becoming ever more muddy, I found that I had to pause every ten minutes or so to scrape the pancake of earth and weeds from my boots merely to be able to shuffle forward without slipping: pausing to roll a cigarette was out of the question: even my conversation with Dennis ceased.

Suddenly, Billy appeared out of the curtain of rain, looking bedraggled and sour-faced, as forlorn a figure as I had ever seen, using his hoe to help himself across the boggy ground like a shepherd uses his crook. As he trudged past towards the shelter of the hedge, barely within speaking distance, he exclaimed: 'I ain't working in this bloody weather! I'm soaked to the bloody skin.' Then directly to Dennis, he said challengingly: 'And if your bloody uncle don't like it, he can shove his job up his arse!'

I tried to dissuade him. 'It ain't even half-eleven yet,' I informed him.

'I don't bloody care! I've had enough.'

'You'll cop it if the old man catches you, especially after this morning,' Dennis tried.

'Bollocks!' It was Billy's standard reply.

I watched him go till he was a faint figure at the far end of the field, blurred by the sweeping rain as he squatted under the overhang of the highest hedgerow: and there he sat for the next forty minutes or so smoking and staring dismally out from under the 'tent' of his jacket, not even bothering to acknowledge either of us when we twice turned at the headland near him. The first time, Dennis again tried to coax him back to work, but was greeted with the same short sharp retort as before.

I idly thought about joining him, but knew I could not leave Dennis to work on alone: it was just as well I did not, for suddenly John Bolt appeared through a gap in the self-same hedgerow with Blackie snuffling at his heels. Billy, huddled as he was under his jacket, did not see him and thus had no chance of leaping to his feet, seizing his hoe and pretending that he was working. He had been caught red-handed, so to speak, and neither Dennis, some twenty yards away, nor I, forty yards away, was able to warn him.

'You idle little blighter!' John Bolt's roar cut through the curtain of rain. 'What the hell do you think you're doing?'

'I'm on my dinner break,' Billy told him, stony-faced.

'I'll tell you when it's your dinner break,' John Bolt shouted back angrily. He had the big brass watch in his hand, checking the time, even as he had emerged from the hedge, almost as if he had expected that he would find someone taking an early dinner out of the rain.

Billy ignored him. 'I'm taking it early,' he said sarcastically.

'I know how to deal with skiving little buggers like you!' snapped John Bolt, repocketing his watch and taking a firmer grip on his hazel stick. The blood drained from Dennis's face and he looked at me in alarm: he knew, just as I did, what was coming next: he knew, too, that he would be blamed for anything that did happen for allowing Billy to leave off hoeing before his time in the first place.

'Oh, bloody hell!' was all Dennis said, pulling the dripping hood further forward to protect his face.

'On your feet, boy,' John Bolt ordered, giving Billy a couple of savage prods in the ribs with his stick.

Angrily, Billy pushed it away. 'It's too wet to hoe properly, so I'm taking my lunch break early,' he yelled up at the farmer towering over him and, in a gesture of defiance, pulled the soaking jacket even more tightly about him as if to declare, 'I'm staying put.'

'Then your dinner break's just about over. When you work for me, you work!' John Bolt snapped and, reaching down with one muscular arm, he hauled Billy to his feet by his hair and, with one vicious push, sent him stumbling across the headland towards where we stood.

Billy regained his balance and swung round to confront the farmer. 'You keep you bloody hands to yourself!' he cried, almost screaming in his fury. As John Bolt moved towards Billy, he raised his hazel stick as if he were going to strike: Billy must have thought he was going to do so, for, without warning, he gripped the hoe firmly at the top of the haft, raised it above his head and brought the metal end down hard on top of John Bolt's skull.

Dennis and I heard the crack of metal striking bone from where we stood. John Bolt's cap went flying and we saw his knees buckle. The next thing I knew was that Dennis was off and running towards them, slipping and slithering across the intervening rows of beet. The only thing I could think to do, however, was to stand and watch, mesmerised by the unexpectedness of it all

'You bloody lunatic!' Dennis shouted at Billy. 'Ain't you got no brains? You could kill someone!'

'Pity I bloody didn't,' sneered Billy, the hoe still raised defensively in front of him like a Civil War pikeman positioning himself to parry an enemy's thrust. 'Try that again and I'll give you another whack,' he told John Bolt defiantly.

The portly farmer, meanwhile, had clamped a hand to his head as if expecting there to be a dent, but there was only a thin trickle of blood mixing with the rain. However, his anger was up and he visibly puffed himself up with the outrage of it all. No one had ever challenged him so blatantly before. With a cry of anger, he charged at Billy, raising his own heavy hazel stick again, this time to strike himself: but Billy saw the blow coming and dodged it easily, which enraged John Bolt all the more. In the same blind fury, he again rushed at Billy, swinging wildly this time, determined to land at least one blow to avenge his wounded pride. Once again Billy contemptuously ducked aside and the blow swished through empty air. Then a second blow from Billy caught the farmer above the ear and his knees buckled again.

It was utter foolishness for a man over sixty: he had run only fifteen or twenty yards, but was out of breath and having to prop himself up on his stick: years of smoking forty cigarettes a day and drinking a couple of glasses of whisky of an evening had taken their toll: he would never catch Billy in a month of Sundays and could only glower at him across the twenty or so feet which Billy had wisely put between them.

By this time Dennis had reached them. 'For God's sake, stop it!' he pleaded.

'Get out of the way, Dennis,' snapped John Bolt, thrusting his nephew aside as he sought to interpose himself between the pair.

'Piss off, Dennis!' was Billy's retort. Then out of a feeling of some friendship and sympathy for the put upon Dennis, he added: 'This ain't your fight. The days when the likes of him think they can push us around are long gone. We've got a Labour Government in now. Him and his kind have had their day.'

For fully five seconds, the three, Dennis and John Bolt on the one side and Billy on the other, stood glaring at each other: all might have ended there, with John Bolt suitably humiliated but intact had not Blackie decided to enter the fray at this point. Rushing forward, the flop-eared spaniel began snapping excitedly at Billy's ankles. Billy looked down disdainfully at the animal tugging at his trouser leg, gave a shout for it to 'Bugger off!' and brought the handle of his hoe down hard across its back, sending the poor dog careering round in a wide circle yelping with pain. When it did finally return, it stood bravely a couple of yards off yapping in an irritating way till one of Billy's hobnailed boots thudded into the poor animal's chest and sent it somersaulting into a large puddle of water and slime which had collected on the track. After that, Blackie maintained a safer distance behind his master's legs, though still snuffling and growling.

John Bolt, however, was not so easily deterred: pride saw to that. In an even greater rage, if that were possible, over Billy's treatment of Blackie, he now made a third lunge, swishing at Billy with his hazel stick: but youth told: Billy skipped away and Dennis deflected the blow with his own hoe.

'For God's sake, give up, the pair of you!'

'He started it,' Billy said with a petulant sniff. John Bolt's stick, meanwhile, had looped harmlessly from his hand on to the muddy earth. The farmer again stood doubled over, grunting aloud like a man having a seizure: the exertion of it all had been too much for him.

'Well, I'm finishing it before the pair of you kill yourselves,' Dennis told them both, though he looked at the sorry figure of his wheezing uncle as he said it. Then turning to Billy he said quietly: 'You had better go, Billy. I don't think you'll be working here any longer.'

Billy did not seem to care. 'I'm bloody going anyway,' he cried, hurling his hoe into the hedge and stamping off along the headland. When he had put a safe distance between himself and the gasping John Bolt, he turned and jeered: 'You're nothing but a bloody slave-driver, Bolt!' Then, just before he disappeared through the curtain of rain: 'I ain't fired – I bloody quit! I wouldn't work for you if you were the last bugger on earth!'

During the pauses in the action, I had myself crossed nearer to them and I now came to stand alongside Dennis, but saying nothing which might exacerbate the situation. Billy was going and there was nothing I could do about that, except wish him well at a later time. Secretly, I was as gleeful as anyone could be that a friend of mine had bested the blustering bully, John Bolt, but I had to control my glee, for now anyway. 'You're fired, boy! You're fired. Tell him he's fired,' the exhausted farmer croaked into the ground as a cock-a-hoop Billy strode off. 'And tell him not to expect any money either. If I catch him on my land again, I'll bloody kill him.'

Dennis was still holding up his sagging uncle. 'Let him go,' he counselled the wheezing farmer when he attempted to react to Billy's parting remarks. 'Let him go or you'll kill yourself.'

Reluctantly, John Bolt gave in. On his own, he might well have gone after Billy a fourth time, such was the unforgiving nature of the man and such was his pride: and he might well have killed himself doing it. But he was too exhausted even to try, more was the pity. For a minute or so, while he gathered himself, he remained bent over and gasping, propping himself with his hands on his knees the way unfit people do when they have overreached themselves. And when he did recover, true to form, he turned on Dennis and then on myself.

'You let him do it, you stupid bugger!' he cried angrily at Dennis, roughly pushing him away and picking up his stick. There was still rage enough in him for me to fear that he might strike Dennis, which he had done in the past, so I had been told. 'You were supposed to be in charge of the hoeing. It's all your bloody fault. You knew what a shirker the little bugger was, but you let him sit under the bloody hedge for half the morning doing nothing. What kind of a useless bugger are you, Dennis? What kind of a useless bugger?'... And so on and so on.

He was apoplectic. I had seen him in rages before, but none such as that day. He must have harangued poor Dennis for fully two minutes, blaming him for just about every trouble that had ever afflicted the farm. Then he turned on me.

'You get back to your work, Joe Coe!' he yelled. 'You're as idle as your mate. You can tell him when you see him that he ain't heard the last of this. I'll have the law on him, the cocky little bugger. You see if I don't. I'm going to phone the Salter constable first chance I get ... ' And so on and so on again.

It was a relief when he went stamping off back towards the farm with the craven Blackie slinking along at his heels. When Dennis and I returned to our hoeing, the nephew looked even more downcast than he had been before. Neither of us spoke for quite a while: Dennis because he did not want to say anything, I because I did not know what to say. Caught in the teeming rain, cold and miserable and working in utter silence, we passed an awkward lunchtime and afternoon. I was glad when five o'clock came and we could put our hoes back in the barn and I could return to Norsea.

The only thing that bothered me was the reaction of my mother if she were to hear of it: Ben would just sniff, unconcerned: but my mother, I knew, would fly into a fury even though I was guilty of being nothing more than an unfortunate bystander: in her eyes, I would be found guilty as an accomplice just by being there and seeing it all.

TWENTY

THE MAYDUN postman brought the news two mornings later: John Bolt was dead. The previous evening he had got up from the table after his meal, walked over to the mantelshelf where he kept his cigarettes and dropped dead on the hearthrug. That at least is what Charlie Mangapp told the postman when he called at the farm to deliver his letters en route to Norsea. According to the postman, Dennis had found his uncle sprawled on the fender in front of the fire when he returned to the house after eventually finishing work at eight: perhaps if he had returned earlier, he might have saved him. Who knows? It was all a matter of conjecture now. Me? I was glad the old sod was dead: it was his own fault for making poor Dennis work so late.

It has to be said that I had not expected John Bolt to die: I was as stunned as Ben and my mother: he had not looked like he was about to die when I had passed him in the yard the morning after the fracas, brass watch in his hand as usual, timing my arrival. I have to admit to a certain disappointment that there was no bandaging protruding from beneath his cap: and after all Billy's efforts! He looked perfectly healthy to me: his usual grumpy self, you could say, so I assumed he was all right.

As I expected he would, John Bolt made some remark about Billy. 'That bloody mate o' yourn is going to get his come-uppance as soon as I get hold of that fool of a constable at Salter,' he growled as I went past, scurried past really, with no more than a nod in his direction, deeming it more prudent to keep going than to answer. All I wanted to do was to join Dennis: even hoeing with him all day was infinitely more preferable than having to listen to a snarling John Bolt, who might take it into his head to think that I was equally as responsible as Billy. Now the blustering bully was dead! Well, well!

'Bit of a t'do about it, though,' the postman, a big jovial man with sideburns and a handlebar moustache, said as he sat in our kitchen drinking tea. 'That drunken fool of a doctor, MacFadden, signed the death certificate saying it was natural causes till it were pointed out to him there weren't nothing natural about a man lying dead on his own hearthrug with three six-inch bruises on the top of his head? It took the old fool an hour to get there as it was after they phoned for him and, when he did turn up, he was smelling of whisky as usual.'

'How did he get the bruises?' my mother asked, innocently, even as my heart sank in my chest.

'The way I heard it from Charlie, Mrs Wigboe,' said the postman, leaning forward conspiratorially, 'is one of the village boys, a boy named Billy Garner, if you know him, cracked him over the head with a hoe a couple of days ago. They had a fight in a field or something and John Bolt got hit over the head. It could be that which killed him, though I hope for the lad's sake it wasn't. But you never know, you never know, do you?'

Instinctively, I felt my mother's eyes swivel upon me, fixing me with that eagle stare of hers: till that moment, she would rather I had not been there so that she and Ben could discuss the unexpected news with the postman on their own. All of a sudden I had become the centre of attention. As soon as I heard the postman telling them about the hoe, I thought: 'Oh God, here it comes! Billy, you stupid bugger, you've done it now!' What puzzled me, though, was that third bruise. Strange that: Billy had hit him only twice, to my knowledge.

The only reason I was there and not already across on Boundary was that this conversation took place at twenty to seven in the morning and I was not due at Boundary till seven. I had been preparing to leave when the postman called: obviously, I would not now be required to go, or so I hoped.

'Oh, yes, we know Billy Garner,' said my mother, her mouth set in a grim line: then in a tone which told me she was sure I knew everything about it, she demanded: 'What do you know about all this? Were you there?'

I wanted to say 'No,' but how could I? I started to say, 'Nothing,' but stopped. 'A bit,' was my reluctant answer, knowing it was never going to be enough for her. They say mothers have an uncanny knack of knowing without being told what their offspring have been up to and what they are likely to get up to: something to do with a basic instinct to ensure the survival of the species, I had heard somewhere, though judging by the number of times my mother had hurled things at me across the kitchen, I sometimes wondered whether she was even bothered about my survival. Anyway, if I had said anything else, she would have just assumed I was lying because, out of self-preservation, most of the excuses I gave her were lies or half-truths of one kind or another.

Ben broke the silence. 'Come on, boy, if you were there, tell us what you know,' he said quietly, looking across the table at me. 'No one's blaming you over it. If you were there when sommat happened, we just want to know, that's all. No one's saying anything that happened is your fault, no more than it could have been anyone else's. If you were there, I want to hear about it.' He eyed my mother into silence as he spoke and there was a calmness and reasonableness about his manner which at least reassured me I would get a fair hearing.

I told them all that I had seen, how Billy had been sitting under the hedge, how John Bolt had found him and poked him with his stick, then grabbed him and pushed him and how Billy had smacked him over the head twice with his hoe. The only fact I left out was the length of time Billy had been sitting in the hedge before John Bolt had come upon him: had I told them that, my mother would have used it as an excuse for some acerbic comment like, 'I suppose you were doing the same. Lazy good-for-nothing pair, the both of you. You shouldn't be allowed to work together. You're both as bad as each other ...' Etcetera, etcetera. So I did not bother. As it was, out of the corner of my eye, I could see her quietly seething over the fact that I should have allowed myself to become a part of it all, unwittingly or not.

When I had finished the postman looked quite grumpy: till then he had been the one with all the news, or so he had thought: now there was I, superceding him. 'Well,' he said after a pause, 'whatever it was that killed him, it don't look too good for the young lad, do it? It don't look good for him at all. Still, they'll know soon enough after the inquest, I expect,'

'Inquest? Will they have to hold an inquest?' My mother sounded alarmed.

'Bound to, Mrs Wigboe, bound to,' the postman replied with a nod. 'A sudden death like that, especially where there's been a blow on the head and someone found dead, they have to have an inquest. It can't be avoided.'

There was an awkward silence: no one wanted to state the obvious about poor Billy, especially with me there. The postman, remembering something amusing, suddenly guffawed loudly: 'I don't want to speak ill of the dead, but the big laugh is, MacFadden called in Charlie Male to measure him up and no sooner had he got the poor blighter all boxed up in his coffin than they had to take him out again. It seems

Charlie was a bit too quick off the mark for the Salter constable's liking. He was there with his tape measure before the poor sod was properly cold. Had him all nailed down and ready to go by ten o'clock, brass handles and all, Charlie Mangapp said. Still, I can't say I blame him. It's bound to be a big funeral, a local farmer and all that, and being local like, he'd want to get there afore anyone else, wouldn't he? Especially afore the Co-op. Trouble is that, when that fool of a doctor, MacFadden, got home and phoned the death through to the Salter constable, as the coroner's officer, he didn't know John Bolt had already tried to get hold of the constable about laying a charge of assault against some young lad who'd hit him over the head with a hoe. The constable's wife had taken the call apparently. So when he heard the man making it had just died, he had no option, did he? He had to send MacFadden back. MacFadden can't have inspected the body properly. Too eager to get back to the bar of the Red Lion at Cobwyke no doubt. Got told in no uncertain terms that he would have to go back, open up the coffin and take a second look and then to cancel the death certificate till they knew for certain. Silly old blighter, MacFadden! Drunk most probably. They took the body to Wivencaster for a post mortem late last night. Sent an ambulance for it. Police come as well. Charlie Mangapp says Dennis is really cut up about the old uncle's death. I don't know where he was this morning, but Charlie was already there – ' A chortle here. ' – I don't suppose there'll be much work done on that farm this week or next week, come to that. Dennis was in tears, Charlie said, when he went round after he found the body. In tears. The shock, I expect. Didn't have a clue what to do himself. Charlie phoned for MacFadden from the phone box in the Square and then got Ma Parrot and Ma Parkinson, the housekeeper, to go in and clean him up, lay him out proper, like, in his Sunday best – ' A special piece of information that for my mother: women are peculiar about knowing such details. 'Pity is poor Dennis don't have any other relations. He's the last, so he gets the farm, don't he? That'll make him a catch for some woman, someone who ain't too fussy about looks.' Another smirk here from the postman and knowing smiles from us.

'They must think there's something in it to call in the coroner,' my mother fished, the way women do: but the postman was reluctant to speculate.

'I wouldn't know anything about that, Mrs Wigboe. Maybe you're right. I couldn't say.' He drained his cup, gave a weary sigh and stood up: it was time to go. It had been a rewarding session for him and, thanks to me, he was leaving with more information than when he came. 'I have to go. Must get on. Got deliveries to make and time's a pressing, time's a pressing.'

Since he had been sitting there for at least a half-hour, had used our lavatory, drunk two mugs of our tea and eaten two slices of our fried bread, his sudden desire to press on struck me as a bit of a joke: what he had was gossip to pass on. Unfortunately, at this point, I gave vent to an accidental snort of derision, which the postman heard: he glowered at me for a few seconds and then, with a sly smirk, informed me: 'Of course, you know what they do at these post mortem examinations, don't you, young Joe, especially when they're looking for a specific cause of death? They saw the top of the head off, boy, that's what they do. Saw it right off and take out the old grey matter. Then they slice it up into strips on a bacon slicer, like, to see what they can find out.' As he spoke, he made first a sawing motion and then that of someone operating a bacon slicer: as all our meagre official bacon ration was cut on just such a machine in Ma Rowthey's post office-cum-grocery store, we all recognised what he was miming.

'Don't! Ugh!' my mother wailed, grimacing at the grisliness of the image. If I went a little green at that moment, no one seemed to notice, for Ben and my mother were following the postman out to the door thanking him for his tale. Once he was on his bicycle and out of earshot, my mother came flying back into the kitchen with a cry of, 'Look what you've got yourself involved in now, you stupid little blighter!' But I had anticipated her and was already departing by the scullery door. The ghastliness of that image, of a man with the top of his head sawn off and his brain exposed to the poking fingers of someone's hand, made me feel distinctly queasy for the rest of the day: the awfulness of the postman's remark has remained with me ever since.

The last I saw of him was his slow-pedalling bulk wobbling back across the causeway: we would not be seeing him again for a week or ten days at the earliest, till the tide allowed him to cross again, and by then events had moved on. Later that day, when I saw Ben, his only admonishment about what I had revealed in the kitchen was, 'Gawd, boy, you should have told us,' delivered with a wearied shake of the head.

'It didn't seem important.' I lied, knowing full well they would never believe me: as anyone knew who lived in a place such as Gledlang, when a farmer got hit over the head with a hoe by a farmworker in our part of the world, that was news: they would be talking about it in the Chessman for months: such a thing had never happened before. All I could really say in my own defence was: 'I didn't know he was going to die, did I?'

And that was it from Ben: apart from one other comment, true to his nature, a gruff: 'You had better give me the hours you worked for John Bolt so I can give them to Dennis. I suppose I'll have to get the money from him now. I shouldn't bother going back just yet unless Dennis sends for you. I shouldn't think he'll be doing much farming this week afore the funeral. I'll find you something to do here for now till things have sorted themselves out.'

There was no sadness at a man's death, no regret, just an acceptance of what God, or nature, or the Fates, had meted out to John Bolt and, in turn, would mete out to each of us: John Bolt's death was just another happening in life, an unavoidable fact and of concern to him only because he was owed money by the dead man, which he was for the time I had worked there.

Philosophically, Ben was very much of the 'We all have to go sometime ...' school. Oh, he would be at the funeral, whenever that was to be, as would my mother and I. Ben would go because it was his duty to attend the funeral of a neighbour and also to talk to the other farmers: he might only be the bailiff on Norsea, but at the funeral he would have equal standing with them and that gave him a sense of importance. My mother would look upon it as a trip to the mainland to gossip with the other village women and perhaps do her shopping afterwards at the post office-cum-grocery store, the baker's at the top of Shoe Street and the butcher's in Hedge Street, opposite the parish hall: and I would go to ensure the old bugger really was dead and buried six feet under with a couple of tons of heavy brown clay holding him down!

TWENTY-ONE

JOHN BOLT'S grave was dug in the churchyard on the next Monday and filled in again on the Thursday, sadly without him in it: though an inquest, at which the deceased was identified, was opened and adjourned on the Tuesday, the Wivencaster coroner would not release the body for burial. Also, it rained for two days and the grave began to fill with water and, as there were no other takers for it among the village's unobliging elderly, the new young vicar, Reverend Thomas Ffawcon, thought it indelicate to have a yawning grave in the churchyard waiting for someone, anyone: so Charlie Male's men shovelled the earth back. Like everyone else not used to the workings of a coroner's court, they, too, had expected the body would be released for burial straight away: instead John Bolt stayed in cold storage at the mortuary in Wivencaster: he was still there when the resumed inquest was held a week later and he was still there a week after it: no one, it seems, wanted to bury the bugger!

I did not go to either inquest simply because no one asked me to go: for some reason, someone decided I was not needed as a witness at either. Dennis told me later that it was probably his fault: when he had spoken to the Salter constable, Dawes by name, he inadvertently told him that I was still fifteen years of age, forgetting a year had passed since my last birthday: it was not something he would have thought about over much and he was more than likely still confused and stunned. Of course, telling him also that Billy and I were the best of friends, 'always going about together,' would not have helped: the Salter constable must have decided that a 'fifteen-year-old' could not be trusted, especially one who was a close friend of the prime suspect, so I was never asked. Not being able to get across to Norsea because of the tide at the particular time he called at Boundary may also have had something to do with it: so on the day of the resumed inquest, I was working.

Charlie Mangapp did go and came across to tell Ben and my mother about it afterwards: unfortunately, I again happened to be in the kitchen at the time – I say 'unfortunately' because, as far as my mother was concerned, it only made matters between us worse, if that were possible.

Dennis and Charlie had driven to Wivencaster in John Bolt's little green van for the resumed inquest. The small coroner's court was quite full when they got there, said Charlie, for there were two inquests that day: apart from the coroner and his officer and the witnesses and counsel for the other inquest, for John Bolt's there were the Salter constable, a police inspector, and eight shopkeepers, who, having closed their premises for the usual half-day, were acting as the jury: even then, they were short and the two young reporters from the town's rival newspapers had to be co-opted on to the panel, so Charlie said, which meant they had to scribble their shorthand notes while supposedly deliberating on the evidence.

The police inspector had risen first and announced that there were 'circumstances surrounding the death of John Bolt' which needed to be clarified: such as, on the very afternoon of the day he died, the deceased had telephoned his constable at Salter asking him to call at Boundary farm the next day as he wished to speak to him on a serious matter, namely that he had been attacked with a hoe.

'The constable was out at the time, but his good wife had taken the message,' said the police inspector. 'She understood the farmer was alleging he had been attacked by one of his workers and wished to lay a charge of assault against that person.'

'Was this person named?' the coroner wanted to know, exasperated that he had not been informed of this before.

'No, sir, not at that time,' replied the police inspector, adding: 'The deceased was very upset and sounded very angry. It appears he had telephoned the previous day as well and the constable had also been out then. He apparently became very enraged and was very abusive to the constable's wife when he found out that her husband was not there a second time. He was swearing a lot, your honour, and slammed down the telephone before she could take all the details.'

'Just like John Bolt,' I thought when Charlie related it. The Salter constable's wife had given the message to her husband when he had got in at tea time and he had intended to call on John Bolt the next day, but, late that same night, he had received a telephone call from Doctor MacFadden, of Cobwycke, informing him, as the local coroner's officer, that a Gledlang farmer, John Bolt, of Boundary farm, had been found dead at his home. It was no more than a courtesy call. In view of what he knew earlier, the Salter constable had suggested the doctor return to the house and arrange for a possible post mortem examination. This had now been done. No mention was made of MacFadden's misdiagnosis: that was quietly hushed up.

'They used a lot of long-winded words, but it all comes down to one thing,' said Charlie. 'They aren't sure how he died. It's not as clear-cut as MacFadden first thought. We don't know whether it was death from natural causes or not.'

They still called Dennis into the witness box to set the scene, so to speak: he told how he had found the body when he went back to the house after finishing that night, how he had gone round to Charlie's house for help and how they had phoned for the doctor from the kiosk in the Square. The coroner, still angry over not being properly briefed beforehand by the police inspector about the deceased's telephone call to the Salter constable, began questioning Dennis at length over for what purpose John Bolt had made it and why he had been so angry: consequently, what had happened in the field came out and was all carefully written down by the coroner with a scratchy pen.

'Dennis couldn't avoid it,' shrugged Charlie, with a shake of the head, 'he had to name young Billy. He had to tell what he saw because it were evidence, like, about the possible cause of death. He named your Joe here, too.'

Even I realised the implications of that: my mother shot me an angry look, but held her temper in check, while Ben just looked rather grim: as a precaution, I edged just a little closer to the door.

'After Doctor MacFadden had gone into the box, another doctor chap come up,' said Charlie, continuing with his tale, 'a pathologist, I think they call them. He gave a lot of medical evidence about John I didn't understand, all about his heart and lungs and arteries and blood vessels in his brain and that. It were all a bit over my head. The coroner took it all down, then announced he was adjourning everything pending further police enquiries and another post mortem. He'd think about releasing the body for Dennis to bury it later and not until.'

'What does all that mean?' my mother asked again, still grim-faced.

'It means this ain't done with yet,' growled Ben, looking across at me. 'You mark my words, boy, they'll be coming over here to see you. I wish I'd damned well not sent you now.'

Him and me both!

I was out of the door like a shot as soon as Charlie stood up to go: for once, my mother did not follow. Outside, I asked him: 'How's Dennis?'

'He's all right. He'll get over it,' Charlie replied flatly. 'A bit down in the mouth, but who wouldn't be after what he found? He'll have to get over it, won't he? He's the boss now. The farm goes to him. I ain't so sure, though, that's he's that lucky a bugger getting it. Farms bring problems. I'd rather go home at night and sleep sound without the worries he's going to have on my shoulders.'

As an afterthought, as he mounted his bicycle, he added: 'By the way, Dennis told me to tell you he'll be over to see you sometime in the next week. Didn't say what for. Something special.'

With that, he rode off on his creaking bicycle towards the causeway, his duty done.

TWENTY-TWO

BEN AND I were working with Molly in the western field, liming the spring wheat when the very thing I feared the most occurred a day later, on the Friday: the Salter constable came straining over to Norsea on his black bicycle.

'Gawd! Bloody hell! What did I tell you, boy,' exclaimed Ben on seeing his black helmet go bobbing along the line of the hedge towards the house. 'This is all down to you, you little bugger.' I hoped he said it just for something to say.

Ben brought Molly to a halt and went forward to unhitch: we left the spreader in the middle of the field and walked Molly to the headland: by the time we had tethered her by the gate, put on her feedbag and walked the hundred yards or so back to the farmhouse, the constable was waiting in our yard, quietly whistling to himself as he leant across his bicycle saddle. It was all nonchalant show, of course, to cover his embarrassment: in front of him stood my mother, glowering at him, arms folded, barring him from entering her house. She had been in the scullery, drying the dinner things, when he had dismounted in the yard and had immediately rushed out to ensure he stayed where he was – in the yard! No way was he going to be allowed to enter her house! She had no time for policemen: as she had so often declared, 'Most of them don't have the brains they were born with!'

Indeed, she had railed against the local constabulary so many times in our kitchen that one could almost imagine the vitriolic tirade which had greeted the unsuspecting Salter constable, even though she knew perfectly well why he had come. Something like: 'What do you want with us? Ain't you got nothing better to do than come over here bothering honest folk? Why don't you go off and catch some real crooks for a change – ' (I never knew quite what she meant by that. However …) ' – There's enough of them over there, all them spivs and wide boys and black marketeers stealing people blind. There's some I could name who don't live too far from here either …' The same old diatribe to which she gave vent on all such occasions.

She probably would have named some of the 'crooks,' too, if asked, for she was not one to be restricted by the laws of slander: when banging on about certain Gledlang-ites, which she did quite frequently, she regularly described two in particular as 'the biggest rogues in the village,' one Denny Caidge and his cohort, Matt Cobb, both thuggish, thirty-year-old farmworkers lately returned from the army, whom I disliked intensely. Neither was averse to stealing a tyre or two off a parked car in Maydun or siphoning petrol from any vehicle foolishly left in a secluded spot in Wivencaster or taking a battery from an unattended vehicle in Hamwyte.

Their other nocturnal activities included, so rumour had it, rustling turkeys in the dead of night just before Christmas, helping themselves to half a lorry-load of bagged peas parked overnight at the roadside near Tottle and selling them on to London barrow boys, plus the usual rabbiting without permission on various farms and regularly shooting without a licence. Nor, if the truth were known, were they averse to buying up 'surplus' petrol from the farmers and selling it on to anyone in the district prepared to pay their price for it.

I mention them here because I was to cross them later, with unfortunate consequences – for me, that is.

The Salter constable took my mother's railing phlegmatically. 'We do our best, Mrs Coe. We do our best,' he was saying as Ben and I pushed through the gate into the yard, the clothing of both of us white with lime.

'The name's Wigboe now,' my mother corrected him sharply, at the same time looking directly past him and giving me one of her withering stares. 'I remarried years ago. I was a Coe when I first married, but he died. Got drowned in the river. I've been remarried fifteen years this year.' Then, in case the constable should have any doubts, she bluntly informed him: 'And I've got the marriage lines to prove it!' So that he should be in no doubt as well where he stood in her estimation, she added for good measure: 'You ought to know who people are, oughtn't you? Especially if you have to deal with them. Lord! If you're an example of the law round here, God help us all, I say!'

It is a fact of life that a woman can sometimes say such things to a policeman and he will only smile resignedly at her scorn, but if a man were to say the same things he most probably would quickly find himself in a tight armlock with a ham-like fist thumping into his face. That day Constable Dawes suffered it all patiently, though I think he was glad when he saw us come through the gate, for he wearily drew himself up to his full height and forced a weak smile of recognition.

Unfortunately, as if his presence on our island were not bad enough, he immediately got off on the wrong foot by saying: 'I've been trying to get across to see you for two days, but I ain't had much luck with the tide. It were against me every time I tried. However do you people live on a place like this? Half the time you can't get on it and the rest of the time you can't get off it.'

It was meant light-heartedly, merely a way of acknowledging our arrival: but it was not received that way. 'We manage,' was Ben's gruff reply. Then, equally as bluntly, he demanded: 'What do you want with us?'

'It's your boy I want,' the constable said: then fixing me with a suspicious stare as if he expected me to deny who I was, he asked: 'Is your name Joe Coe?'

'Yes,' I said, trying to put into a one-word reply as much meekness and puzzlement as one can put as to why he should have crossed to Norsea to see me.

'I've come about John Bolt,' he said, unbuttoning his tunic pocket and taking out a notebook. 'I have to take a statement from you about a recent happening on Boundary farm. I have it on authority that you were there and a witness.'

Behind the policeman I saw my mother's lip curl: Ben just stood to one side with his head lowered, rolling himself a cigarette, listening.

'Now then,' said Constable Dawes, pencil poised, ready to write, one eyebrow raised enquiringly, 'I'd be obliged if you would tell me what you know about the fracas between John Bolt and William Garner, one of his workers at the time. I've already interviewed the nephew, Dennis Bolt, and he tells me there was an argument and blows were exchanged. Is that right? I want to hear your version of events. Everything mind, lad. Don't leave anything out. We don't want any problems there, do we? Just tell the truth, boy, and you'll come to no harm. That's all you can do, boy, tell the truth. Tell me what you saw.'

So I told him the truth: just as I had told Ben, my mother and the Maydun postman. What troubled me were the questions which the Salter constable asked, like he thought I might be trying to hide something: questions like, how far away was I when it all began? What did John Bolt actually say to Billy? What did Billy say to John Bolt? Who struck the first blow? What did Billy hit him with? How many blows did Billy strike? He asked that one twice for some reason. Each answer, I felt, put Billy in a worse light than the one before. The constable took down my answers very slowly, sometimes repeating the words I had spoken phrase by phrase, as if to ensure he had heard them correctly. The whole process took about fifteen unhappy minutes: every sentence I uttered, every fact I confirmed, I sensed my mother's anger building: with the constable's departure, I knew it would explode.

'Well that should do it,' said the constable finally, folding shut his notebook, then adding with a sniff: 'No doubt you'll be hearing from us.'

'Whatever for?' my mother demanded.

'Other people will want to hear this, I reckon, missus,' the constable replied phlegmatically, without elaborating. 'What your boy says is pretty much the same as Dennis Bolt is saying. It ain't up to me to decide, but I reckon there could be some charges come out of this. Your boy may be called, he may not. That won't be up to me. The inspector will decide that. Your boy could be called to give evidence.' The constant reference to 'your boy,' I could tell from my mother's face, was a most unfortunate choice of words: right then, I think my mother would have willingly disowned me!

'Charges! Charges against who?' Ben wanted to know.

'Not your lad,' the constable reassured us. 'Against the lad that hit him. This has become a very serious business indeed, you know.'

'What kind of charges?' Ben asked, refusing to be fobbed off.

'Serious ones,' said the Salter constable grimly, but really not giving anything away, 'very serious, if I'm not mistaken.'

That was enough for my mother. 'You damned little fool!' she screeched: not without reason, I suppose: just by having been there, I was being drawn more and more into the quagmire and, at the same time, I was exposing the family, that is, her and Ben, to a risk of being gossiped about and discussed when she would have preferred being left to live her life free from all that.

'It wasn't my fault, woman,' I shouted back. 'I just happened to be there. I couldn't have done anything to stop it.'

The policeman soothed my injured pride. 'Of course not, lad, of course not. Your mother knows that, I'm sure.' I was not so sure she did, but I did not want an argument on the matter.

'I just have to warn you afore I go,' said the Salter constable, 'that we're dealing with a very serious matter here, very serious indeed. If there is a court hearing, most like you will be subpoenaed to appear. If you are subpoenaed to appear, make sure you're there. I don't want to have to come and get you, do I, sonny?' He gave me a stern look. 'I reckon you'll want to come of your own accord, won't you? You'll want to see justice done, John Bolt being your neighbour, like?'

The Salter constable was smiling smugly to himself as he mounted his oversized bicycle and pedalled slowly back towards the causeway and the mainland: he had repaid the harshness of my mother's earlier greeting by sowing disharmony among us: it pleased him.

No sooner was he out of earshot and out of sight than my mother rushed at me. 'You stupid bugger!' she cried, repeating the time-worn epithet with even greater venom as I fled down the track ten yards ahead of her, just far enough for me to duck and dart sideways the instant I saw her arm come up: the plate she had been drying when the policeman came sailed harmlessly past and splashed into a puddle.

TWENTY-THREE

ONE THOUGHT was uppermost in my mind: how was my friend Billy? The Salter constable would surely have visited him so what would he have asked him? And what had Billy said in reply? I just had to go across and find out.

Unfortunately, two teatime tides and the need to finish our work prevented me from crossing to the mainland over the weekend and then heavy rain, some of it hail, deterred me on the Monday evening. That in itself was to prove a fateful delay: if I had been able to go earlier, things may not have turned out as they did.

I had seen from the look on Billy's face as he walked away that day in the field that he thought I should have done the same: he felt he had been left out on a limb when I chose to continue working with Dennis through the rain. I had to make my peace with him sometime and this was really the first opportunity: and, if he were in an agreeable mood, I might even tell him more about Richard, though I was still debating whether I ought to tell him about what the constable had said about me 'giving evidence in a court case.' I did not want to worry him.

Soon after six on the Tuesday evening, I cycled over the causeway, up through the village and out along the Maydun road to Billy's house. His mother answered the door: she must have seen me coming, for there was a look of black fury on her face. Normally, she would swing open the door and say: 'Hullo, Joe, come on in.' This time she took one look at me and angrily declared: 'You've got a bloody nerve coming here, Joe Coe. Bugger off! Go on, bugger off! You ain't welcome here.' Then she slammed the door shut in my face.

Puzzled, upset and more than a little dispirited by the unexpectedness of her outburst, I was in the act of retrieving my bicycle from the hedge when the door opened again and Billy's father came out: strangely, he was dressed in his best Sunday suit. Herbert Garner, normally, was the most likeable of men, a real old countryman, deferential to his employer and even displaying a Conservative poster in his window at the last election so it would give the Tory farmer for whom he worked no cause to find fault with him: it also explained why he had never joined the Agricultural Workers' Union and never went to any of the Labour meetings in the parish hall when the local firebrand MP, Tom Gridber, an Eton-educated, former Fleet Street newspaper writer, came round, stirring up revolt and revolution among the natives for an evening before getting into his big black Humber and driving back to his big house and three acres of land in Othona-Juxta-Mare the other side of the estuary. Whether Billy's father believed in Tory politics, I do not know: but when you have eight children and a wife to feed and exist on a farm labourer's wage, you do not court controversy with your employer. It was a pity his third son had not learned that lesson.

'Just a minute, Joe,' Billy's father said, coming down the path, one finger raised to indicate he wanted to talk to me.

'Yes, Mr Garner.'

'Have you called to see Billy?'

'Yes, Mr Garner.'

'You ain't heard then?'

'Heard what, Mr Garner? I ain't heard anything.'

'Billy's in gaol. Leastways, he's in the juvenile wing at Melchborough Gaol. Dawes and Tucker come and took him yesterday morning. He's been in there all yesterday and today. The wife and I have only just got back from visiting him. They're saying he might have had something to do with John Bolt's death. Do you know anything about that, Joe?'

The news stunned me. Billy in gaol! Carted off by the Salter constable and the Hamwyte sergeant! Billy's father had spoken the words so quietly he might have been telling me Billy was just along the road at Nick's house, something as totally innocuous as that. For a few seconds I could not think of anything to say.

Billy's father filled in the pause. 'I've spoken with Billy, you know,' he said, eyeing me suspiciously, as if trying to discover what I was thinking. 'The wife and I went to see him this morning and we'll be going again tomorrow if they'll let us. It seems they want to keep him in there. We've had to hire a solicitor and solicitors don't come cheap. I've lost a day's pay already to-ing and fro-ing between here and Melchborough and I'll lose more tomorrow, I dare say. I can't afford to lose hard-earned money. I ain't made of it, as you well know. A man in my position, I've had to apply for this new legal aid thing the Government's brought in, but we don't know whether we'll get it. We'll have to wait and see. I've got a little saved in the Teapot Club, but, if we don't get it, it's going to cost a lot more than I've got in there to get this over and done with.'

Billy's father continued to peer closely at me. 'Billy said you were there the day he and John Bolt had their argument. He said you and Dennis were both there and saw what happened. I hear you had a visit from the Salter constable the other day. There ain't no use denying it – someone saw him pedalling over and coming back.' There was no fooling him.

'Yes, Mr Garner. He came on Friday.'

'Took your time coming over to let us know, didn't you?'

'The tide was against me.'

'The tide was against you! Pah!' He did not think much of that excuse: I decided it would be better if I changed the subject.

'What has Billy been charged with?' I asked, nervously.

'Assault and battery for the moment, but that ain't to say they won't think o' something a lot worse if they puts their minds to it, is it?'

'No, Mr Garner.' Common sense told me to get on my bicycle and ride off at this point: but I could not do so: something kept me there: old friendship, embarrassment, a wish not to hurt his feelings: so I asked the next question: 'So what happens now?'

It was an open invitation. 'Depends on what he's eventually charged with, don't it?' said Billy's father, sagely. 'Solicitor says he most likely will be charged properly tomorrow just so's they can keep him inside. And it'll mean a court case. When that's likely to be, I can't say. September probably, even October, whenever the next Quarter Sessions are. So we'll have this thing hanging over us all summer. I ain't so worried about that. What's troubling me is what the likes of you and Dennis Bolt have already told them will decide what they charge our Billy with – something more serious – something that could mean he'll be locked up a good deal longer than we want him to be. Do you understand what I'm saying?'

'I think so, Mr Garner.'

'Think so! Have you got the vaguest idea of what I mean by "something more serious"?' He was beginning to get angry.

'Well, no. Sorry.' I was flummoxed.

'Manslaughter, boy! Manslaughter! You know what that is?'

'Not exactly, Mr Garner.'

'It's when you kill someone, unintentionally,' he explained. 'You don't mean to kill them, but you do. It might be an accident, but that don't matter to the likes of the police. It still carries a long gaol sentence. Twelve years in some cases, I'm told. The other charge they could lay against Billy don't bear thinking about. I couldn't sleep at night if I were to think about that one. You know what that one is, don't you?'

'Er, no.' Another lie. I was way ahead of him. Surely they could not charge Billy with murder? Herbert Garner was right: it did not bear thinking about.

'The point is, Joe, the Salter constable has been over to see you and he's taken a statement off you and that means you'll probably be giving evidence against Billy, won't you?'

'I can't avoid it really, can I, Mr Garner? If the Salter constable says I have to go and give evidence, then I'll have to go, I suppose.'

'There ain't no suppose about it, Joe,' Billy's father said curtly. 'If you don't, they'll serve you with a summons to make sure you do go, boy. They're bound to. They can't do anything else, can they? It stands to reason, don't it, if you were there at the time, you'll be called as a witness for any court case? It's what you're going to say and how you're going to say it that bothers me.'

Other members of the Garner family were beginning to appear in the doorway, most menacingly Billy's twin ten-year-old brothers, Arthur and Albert, who were prone to throwing stones at anyone they did not like: and right then it was clear by their sullen faces that they did not like me. Fortunately, his two married elder brothers, Jimmy and Ron, were not there or things could have turned really nasty, I felt sure.

'I don't know, Mr Garner, I don't know.' I could see where the conversation was heading and was becoming more apprehensive by the second. 'But if they ask me what happened, I shall have to tell them the truth, won't I?' I pleaded. 'I can't go into court and lie, can I? They'd know if I was lying. I'd have to tell them the same as I've told the Salter constable, if they ask me, won't I?'

'And just what did you tell him, Joe?'

At that moment, Billy's mother pushed through the throng in the doorway and called out: 'Tell him to clear off! Your dinner's on the table going cold. I've told him to clear off once already.'

Herbert Garner was not a man to lose his temper. He simply half turned and quietly ordered her: 'Be quiet, woman! Get inside.' Then, turning back to me, he calmly repeated the question: 'What exactly did you tell the Salter constable, Joe? I've seen Billy. I've had his version of what happened. What's yours?'

Sometimes I think it would have been better if he had been angry: he would at least have got it out of his system: but he was not, he was the same calm man, speaking in the same calm manner as he always did.

There was no other answer I could give. 'Billy gave John Bolt a couple of cracks across the head with his hoe, the blade end,' I told him. 'It was a bloody daft thing to do. He could have killed him there and then.' Immediately I had said it, I wished I had chosen other words.

'I see,' said Billy's father, his face becoming grim. 'And that is what you are going to tell them in court?'

'If they ask me, yes, Mr Garner, I shall have to, won't I?' I replied solemnly. 'What else can I say? I shall have to answer them if they ask, won't I?' The 'won't I?' was the plea of a desperate youth trying to extricate himself from an awkward, if well nigh impossible, situation. As the conversation had progressed and my unease had increased, I had taken the precaution of gripping the handlebars and the saddle of the bicycle, ready to push off quickly if need be.

'Oh, they'll ask you, Joe, they'll ask you. You can bet on that,' declared Herbert Garner. 'The likes of us ain't got no chance against them. What I'm unhappy about is that I always thought you and Billy were friends.'

'We are, Mr Garner. We still are, I hope,'

'Not if you're going to give evidence against him like that,' Billy's father retorted, for the first time showing anger. 'Evidence like that could put him in Borstal, or gaol even, for God knows how many years. Don't you realise, boy, what you say in that court could even put a bloody rope around my son's neck? They could hang him, for Christ's sake! Did you think of that when you were gabbing out the "truth," as you call it, to that bloody bastard of a constable? Did you stop and think of that for one minute even?'

Well, no, I had not: till that moment, I had not given it a thought.

'I – I can't see that happening, Mr Garner,' I blustered, desperate to convince him. 'I don't see that happening. Never!'

'Oh, you don't, don't you? And you would know, would you?' The calm had gone: bitterness was showing now. 'Did you ever think to say you saw nothing, that you had your head down and didn't see anything? Did you not think to say that?'

No, I had not, I had to admit to myself. 'Look, don't blame me,' I wailed. 'It's not my fault. None of it's my doing, none of it – I don't want to give evidence. It was Dennis who told them I was there. Blame him, not me.'

'If things go wrong for Billy – and they could – I'll do more than blame you, boy,' Billy's father said sharply. The tone was icy now. 'You, more than anyone were his friend, or so you say. The two of you grew up together. You've always been friends. We've always made you welcome in our house, you know that. We've treated you like our own son all the time we've known you. You've eaten with us at the tea table. Now you say you're going to give evidence in a court of law that could, if they decide to be bloody-minded about it and charge him with something he didn't do, hang my son!'

Billy's father raised one eyebrow and regarded me through steely unblinking eyes. The logic of his thinking, or the logic of his grievance, was clear: for a few seconds I thought he was going to let me go without further comment. But after a second or so he straightened himself up, gave a great despairing sigh and, in the same calm, measured tone with which he had begun, said: 'You're a bloody Judas, Joe Coe! A bloody Judas! Bugger off afore I set the dog on ye. I don't want to see you round here no more. Just bugger off out of this village, boy, and out of my sight!'

With that, he turned on his heel and, with that peculiar plodding gait of his, walked slowly back up the path where he ushered his hostile brood inside without a backward glance. It was a sickening moment and I rode off in absolute despair. Until then, I had not thought overmuch about what I had related to the Salter constable other than Billy would not like it and would curse me for it and sulk a bit when we met again: now suddenly to find myself being rejected absolutely for telling the truth by someone I had always considered a friend was devastating. I had known Billy's father as long as I had known Billy. To me, he was the epitome of the phlegmatic old countryman who worked the land because he never believed he had the ability to do anything else: he was content with it: he never complained about the low wages paid then to all farm workers: he never joined the union because he knew it would antagonise his governor and he did not willingly court trouble or dismissal: in short, he accepted his lot and got on with life. That is why I was so saddened at his rejection.

It was a very miserable and subdued youth who rode back across the empty estuary that night. In effect, it was the night my friendship with Billy and, in consequence, my friendship with Nick, too, finally ended and was never to be renewed, though I did not know it at the time. On Norsea, there was no cheering light from Richard's window:

his cottage was dark: I could not go home, I felt too shamed, too humiliated, too hurt. So I left my bicycle in the wagon shed and went for a walk along the southern shore, comforting myself that the half-mile width of the island and the mile-wide expanse of the Stumble mudflats lay between me and Gledlang and my troubles.

TWENTY-FOUR

RICHARD had returned to the island by the Saturday: he and Old Hoary and Stanley Lobel, my friend from Tottle, had been digging for two days at a site near Icklesham, up in the next county: Hoary was convinced there had once been an Iron Age village there. They would have been there longer, but, in his enthusiasm to get started, Hoary had neglected to obtain permission from the farmer to dig on his land and Richard was regaling me with a tale of how the poor fool had been chased off, vigorously protesting that the work he was doing was 'vital to the heritage of England.'

'Heritage of England, my arse!' the farmer had roared, propelling a spluttering Hoary through the gate by the scruff of the neck and sending him sprawling on to the road. 'I'll give you bloody heritage of England if you come on my land again! I'll give you a load of buckshot up your arse, that's what I'll give you! Bugger off, you daft old sod! If I see you back here again, I'll plough the bloody lot into the ground!'

There was nothing left for Hoary, Richard and Stanley to do but to pay the bill at the local inn, where they had been staying, and come home: on their way past the farm in a taxi, en route to the railway station, they found the farmer, true to his word, standing by the now padlocked gate with a double-barrelled shotgun under his arm and a pair of horses hitched to a plough, ready and waiting to carry out his threat. So much for the Englishman's reverence for his heritage.

It made me laugh, though, and I was sorely in need of a leavening of some kind: I was glad Richard was back: I have to say it, my spirit actually soared with thankfulness and relief when I saw him unloading the spades and shovels and other implements from Sligger Offin's taxi before that went off in a trail of smoke. After my brush with Billy's father, I had mooched around the island like a lost soul for three evenings after finishing my chores: now Richard and I were again sitting in his parlour drinking tea: he was again lounging on the three-legged sofa and I was seated on my usual seat, the upturned bushel box from Boundary.

It was late afternoon: the rain of the previous days had stopped and early afternoon sunlight was streaming through the windows: Richard's scratchy, wind-up gramophone was playing a record he wanted me to hear, to 'educate' me, he said. It was of some man with an Italian name singing his head off in French about being a Spanish bullfighter, or so Richard told me: about what, I do not know: I did not take much interest: I was too busy telling him about my misfortunes. Richard, I had noticed, played this record regularly on the wind-up gramophone. 'It cheers me up,' he explained. 'It makes me think of Jean. It was one of her favourite records. We played it all the time in the camp.'

I should have thought the memory would have made him sad rather than cheerful: the thought of what I would be missing that evening by staying on Norsea certainly upset me. Normally at that time on a Saturday, I would have been in our kitchen polishing my best boots or pressing creases into the trousers of my suit on the table with one of my mother's hob irons and the help of a damp tea-towel, preparing for my weekly trip to the Embassy at Maydun with the other village boys and the vain hope of meeting a girl: and, if not that, drowning my sorrows with Black and Tans in the White Horse or the Jolly Sailor: underage though most of us may have been, there was always one pub where we could drink unchallenged. However, in view of the hostility of Herbert Garner following Billy's arrest, I deemed it prudent to keep away from the village and from Maydun for a while and to stay on Norsea, where there was more than enough for me to do, if I wanted to do it, that is. The girls of Maydun would have to be patient for another week or two.

When I told Richard about Billy's arrest and his father's hostility, Richard's only comment was: 'Your friend sounds like a bit of a hothead to me. It seems to me he has only got himself to blame.'

He was right there: Billy was a well-known hothead. Though he was only five months older than me and would be seventeen in a month, he had already been to court twice, the first time when he was just twelve for throwing a pared-fuse rook-scarer under the wheels of an aged villager pedalling slowly past on his rickety bicycle: pared-fuse rook-scarers go off within two or three seconds of being lit, which is what Billy intended.

'Maybe he'll go a bit faster if we put a banger up his rear end,' Billy had giggled as he threw it: unfortunately, the bang and the flash sent the old man toppling from his bicycle and he hit his head on the road. We all ran away, but, it being a small village where everyone knew everyone, they knew who the culprit was and it cost Billy's father a five shillings fine at Maydun juvenile court.

The second time Billy went to court, strange as it may seem, was as a witness to a kidnapping – his own! One summer evening, while out with Nick and Lennie Ring, he had crept up on a small blue van parked in the gateway of a field along the Salter road which was rocking vigorously on its rear springs: inside, someone else's husband was shagging someone's else's wife. Billy could not resist the novelty of seeing a man and a woman at it so he had peeped through the rear window: he was spotted almost immediately by the woman, who let out an almighty shriek, whether of shock, anger or fright, I cannot say, but the couple's ardour ended there. Nick and Lennie Ring ran one way and Billy ran another way: the man chased Billy, hauled him back to the van and bundled him inside: then, with the doors locked, he was driven literally kicking and yelling ten miles or so along the back lanes before the couple had had enough of his boots thudding against their rear doors and pitched him out the other side of Inworth.

Nick and Lennie Ring, meanwhile, had rushed back to the village to raise the alarm. 'Billy's been kidnapped by a couple in a blue van! No, he wasn't doing anything. They just grabbed him and threw him in the back and drove off.' Half the village joined in the frantic search, spurred on by all kinds of wild pronouncements by some of the women, ever eager to think the worst: like, 'They could be gypoes. They steal children and sell them, don't they?' And, worse, 'He could be lying in a ditch somewhere with his throat cut!'

Suffice it to say, Billy was alive and well, if not kicking any more, and was eventually found a couple of hours later strolling nonchalantly along a lane back towards the village, unworried by the dark and with a broad grin on his face as two of the desperate searchers rode up on their bicycles. He came home to a hero's welcome perched on Posey Gate's handlebars: the Salter constable came to ask his questions the next morning.

The van was traced a week later and the couple were duly hauled up before the magistrates. In his evidence, Billy said he was innocently walking near the van when he was seized and bundled into the back, but the magistrates were far shrewder than that: they knew there was more to it. When they heard the couple's story, that they had been 'kissing and cuddling' in the back of the van when Billy's smirking face had appeared at the window, that they had not meant to 'kidnap' or 'abduct' him or to deprive his parents permanently of his company, but just took him for a ride to teach him a lesson, the magistrates decided there was a cause for leniency and, rather than send them on to an upper court, fined them five pounds apiece and let them go. The cuckolded husband hustled his unfaithful wife away after the court case: apparently he and the other chap had already come to blows over the incident. The philandering man's grim-faced wife did not look at all happy either as she left with him. Neither did Billy's father: the normally placid Herbert Garner said to his son as they left: 'You need a good leathering, boy, that's what you need.' He never got it, though.

He should have gone to court a third time when he tied the thirteen-year-old Bullace girl, Vera, to a tree in the churchyard, pulled down her drawers and cut off what pubic hairs she had already grown with a pair of scissors after she had laughed at him over something. When the girl told her father, he chased Billy for over a mile before catching him: luckily for Billy, the angry Josh Bullace thought it more prudent to give the violator of his daughter's innocence a good thrashing with the belt rather than take him to court and, that way, have his daughter publicly ridiculed. Billy preferred it that way, too: the so-called thrashing, five swipes with a buckle end across the lower legs, was all over in ten seconds and did not hurt, anyway, or so he said!

And had Billy's father known about the blind piano tuner, who came tap-tapping along the tarred pavement opposite the village school one day, he would have got another belting, too, no doubt: it was Billy who told the poor man that the way ahead was clear and then quietly watched as he went sprawling over Billy's bicycle lying directly in his path: Billy just retrieved the bicycle and rode off laughing: Nick and I had to help the bewildered fellow up.

At one time, Billy would cross to Norsea on a Sunday to help me with Hoary's chores and to earn some extra money: but he would not work properly, treating everything as a lark, and eventually an angry Hoary had banned him and refused to pay him: a short while later I had come across Billy preparing to ride back: Billy had a grin upon his face and a sack slung over his shoulder: in it was one of Hoary's geese, stone dead, its neck rung, all ready for his mother to pluck and cook!

But this was the same Billy who saved me from drowning one summer holiday when I was seven, before Ben taught me to swim: I had crossed to join the other village boys and a half-dozen of us were running about on salting banks as the tide came in: suddenly, I plunged off the end of one of the saltings into a deep channel. I went down once, twice and was just going down for a third time when Billy grabbed my hair and hauled me out: I crossed back to Norsea that evening feeling very sick from the amount of salt water I had swallowed and feeling very sorry for myself. It was the same Billy, too, who, on VE Night, poured white spirit on to the handlebars, forks and metal rims of his bicycle, put a match to it and rode around the Square with the whole thing ablaze: no one else had thought of doing that or would have dared, only Billy!

It was as I related my trials and tribulations to Richard that there was a knock at the door and we opened it to find Dennis Bolt standing there: he had a black diamond patch sewn on to the sleeve of his jacket as a mark of mourning for his uncle, still in cold storage in Wivencaster, and was otherwise dressed in a shirt and tie and grey flannels. If it had been me, I would not have mourned John Bolt with a black patch, I would have worn a red rose! Dennis, naturally, had called first at the farmhouse and my mother had directed him on to us with an acerbic 'It ain't no good you calling here for him, he spends half his time round there!'

Normally, Dennis did not stutter much when we worked together because I paid it no heed and he knew me so well he could talk easily and comfortably in my presence: but the first sight of Richard, a stranger, had him reddening visibly and stammering away in the old manner. 'Your m-m-mother said I'd f-f-find you here,' he managed to blurt out, pointedly remaining in the doorway.

I introduced him to Richard and Richard to him and, to his credit, Richard rose from his lop-sided sofa and acknowledged Dennis with a nod and a polite, 'Hullo, Dennis, pleased to meet you again.'

It may have been the shock of seeing Richard's scarred face close-up for the first time, for Dennis looked quite taken aback and for a few moments was even more flustered than usual: somehow he managed the briefest of nods in return along with one of his nervous 'How are you?' smiles: and, as if in desperation to avoid looking at Richard, fixed his eyes upon me. 'J-Joe,' he stuttered, 'I – I – I've got some rooms to c-c-clear out at the house – the attic, the b-box room, Uncle's b-bedroom and two others and the office – and I w-was hoping you would help me?'

Of course, I would: anything that was different: anything that would make a change from my chores on Norsea.

'There's lots of old p-papers and clutter I have to g-get rid of,' explained Dennis. 'The house is too full. It needs c-clearing out. C-c-could you come over t-tomorrow and give me a hand? I don't want to ask any of the men. U-Uncle wouldn't have l-liked that. He wouldn't have w-wanted just anybody noseying into his things. It's d-different with you. I don't think he w-would have minded about you. H-he liked you.'

I was not sure whether I should have felt flattered or insulted by that last remark: but since it was Dennis and it offered the prospect of passing an otherwise dull and lonely Sunday by doing something interesting, I readily agreed.

'Would you like some help?' Richard asked, unexpectedly. 'I'd be glad to give you a hand. I don't have anything else to do tomorrow. You might need an extra pair of hands.'

Dennis appeared about to refuse, but, to my surprise, he stuttered out his thanks: well, y-yes, he w-would be g-glad of any help. 'Th-th-there's a lot of old V-Victorian stuff that particularly wants throwing out,' he said. 'Some of it is over a hundred years old. I d-doubt anyone would want it. N-No one in the village, anyway. It's f-far too ancient. It needs b-burning. There's a lot of heavy boxes t-to move, too. Piles and p-p-piles of papers as well. It all needs to be b-burned.'

'Happy to oblige,' said Richard, beaming. 'What time do you want us? Ten-thirty? Will that do?' And when Dennis nodded, 'Fine.'

Dennis was about to leave when, looking round Richard's sparsely furnished cottage, he suddenly said: 'Of c-c-course, if there's anything you w-want that I d-don't want, you're w-welcome to it. Help yourself. You t-too, Joe. I'd be p-pleased to let you have it.'

As he closed the door, Richard was positively rubbing his hands in anticipation at the prospect of at last furnishing his home properly: even if it was old and decrepit Victorian cast-outs, it was better than what he had, the lopsided sofa, rickety card table, a couple of upturned boxes for chairs and a mattress on the floor in the bedroom.

You would have thought Hoary would have lent Richard some furniture: after all, he had enough of it: his rooms were cluttered with it and one of the outhouses was bulging with it: but, no the old skinflint would not lend him one stick. Richard had asked soon after his return, in my hearing, but, astonishingly, Hoary had waved him away. 'Oh no, no I could not possibly do that,' he had cried, aghast. 'My things are far too valuable to be given away to just anyone, far too valuable. They were my mother's. They are all family heirlooms. I could not possibly let just any Tom, Dick and Harry have them. You will have to buy some of this utilitarian furniture they make now for your needs? That would be far better for you. All you people want to do today is to throw things away and get in new furniture. You don't know the value of old things, any of you! Ha, ha.'

It had been a surprise: throwing out furniture which had been around since before Victoria's Jubilee sounded logical to me and I told the old fool in no uncertain terms: but he was adamant: he wanted to preserve his clutter – 'for future generations to enjoy,' as he put it. 'They are far better suited to a larger house like mine and for people who would appreciate them. Ha, ha, ha!'

To be honest, Richard did not make a song and dance about it: he just stole – borrowed – the wind-up gramophone and a couple of dozen of Hoary's records. Perhaps if Hoary had lent Richard some of his furniture, a table, say, an armchair, a bed and a sideboard, then Richard and I would not have carted back what we did from Dennis's house because there would have been no need. The cottage would have been furnished already and all that we took out of the attic, the various bedrooms and the drawing room of Boundary's farmhouse would have gone on the bonfire in the yard: then I would never have found what I found and all the things which happened afterwards would never have happened. Perhaps.

TWENTY-FIVE

THE NEXT day, Sunday, at ten-thirty exactly, Richard and I walked over the causeway to Boundary to help Dennis clear out the farmhouse. It was one of those days when you are glad to be alive: the tide was far out beyond the estuary mouth and the vast acres of sucking, salt-sheened mud were sparkling in the brilliant May sunshine, just as a meadow sometimes glistens in the early morning light when a sheen of dew has settled upon it overnight and each droplet is picked out by the rays of the rising sun. Overhead in the cloudless, cerulean air the raucous, squabbling white gulls wheeled and dived over the far off channels of the Thistley Creek, while from the tall, greystone tower of Saint Peter's church, rising amid its clump of greening elms and horsechestnuts by Gledlang Square, came the slow, monotonous tolling of a single bell.

Dennis opened the door, looking tired and unshaven: he had been up for hours, he said, sorting through various drawers and cupboards: now as he led us through the house, it was evident that there was far too much junk in the house: much of it would have to go.

'I've g-got five b-bedrooms full of it,' said Dennis, 'old f-feather mattresses, w-washstands, chests of d-drawers and things. I only n-need one bedroom to sleep in, d-don't I? Same as we've got t-two rooms downstairs with t-two old horsehair sofas in them. We don't n-need them both. There's only me to sit on them. They must be s-seventy or eighty years old if they're a d-day. The stuffing's c-coming out of one of them and the b-back's falling off the other. They need throwing out. You're w-welcome to any of it. I'll be g-glad to get rid of it.'

The wide hallway from the parlour to the backdoor was already filled with pile upon pile of old newspapers, books and magazines: I had a quick perusal and discovered that many dated from long before the First War. Whatever happened, I intended to have a good look through those before we burned them. I was less worried about the other tottering piles: a half-dozen leather-bound editions of the

Wivencaster weekly rag, the Standard, which must have been printed about the time the Corn Laws were repealed, several stacked bundles of Farmers' Weekly, a couple of dozen dog-eared, red-covered account books, plus several well-thumbed ready-reckoners, which had been used to determine piecework rates at fruit-picking times since before the turn of the century. Lying among them in boxes and covered in dust, which wafted up and set us coughing each time we lifted them outside, were forty years or more of the farm's paperwork, box after box of invoices, bills of lading and business letters, every scrap of paper John Bolt had ever read, signed or received: knowing him, I suspect he kept them all the better to argue his case in any disputes about a bill, a payment or a consignment of something or other.

'I've been c-clearing out the c-cupboards and Uncle's office,' Dennis declared. 'They're mostly Uncle's old papers. Most of them are out of date now. Some are from before the First War. I'm keeping some, but the rest can g-go. A bonfire's the best place for them, and a lot of the furniture upstairs as well.'

So we heaved it all outside into the yard to clear a way for the furniture which we had to bring down from the attic and the bedrooms: this we proceeded to do over the next two hours. Between eleven o'clock and one, we manoeuvred down the narrow stairs from the attic and from three of the larger bedrooms a ghastly mahogany Victorian wardrobe full of carvings and crenellations, a lopsided oak armoire, two dressing tables with carvings all over them, a high beechwood bachelor chest of drawers, two iron double bedsteads, both with sagging wire spring frames, plus their mattresses, a red walnut sideboard with an ornate mirrored back which John Bolt's great-grandmother probably peered into, two cupboards, two ordinary chests of drawers of smaller size and some leather-padded chairs with funny bow legs and carved backs which Dennis said were so old Queen Victoria's mother could have sat on them. We practically emptied the attic and the three bedrooms: you could have furnished a four-bedroom farmhouse with the stuff we pitched out: there was not a thing that was not a hundred years old or older: totally useless rubbish that no one would want in a hundred years!

Had we had the gumption, and the time and the inclination, we could have transported the lot into Wivencaster to sell at the auction room: some people might even have bought it: some bombed-out London families were so desperate for furniture of any kind they would even have taken hundred-year-old stuff if they could not get new stuff, which was all utilitarian rubbish, anyway, made out of old orange boxes and packing cases. But we did not have the transport or the inclination, so we did not bother: Dennis wanted it burned so we burned it: anyway, it was a Sunday and none of the auctioneers was open and burning was quicker and more final.

We had just carted out two marble-topped washstands, along with their flower-painted basins and pitchers, when Dennis called out that it was time to put the kettle on for tea: while it was boiling, he cut each of us two thick slices of bread liberally spread with butter and plum jam, which he spooned from a large jar in the kitchen: it was, after all, made from the farm's plums at the Inworth jam factory. To me somehow, it felt very manly for the three of us to be sitting there, with the bright sunlight streaming through the kitchen windows, eating doorstep slices of bread and jam with a mug of hot tea beside us: I was enjoying myself: my recent problems over Billy were forgotten.

I was pleased to see how well Dennis and Richard got on: Dennis had even lost his shyness: his stammering had almost gone and, now that he had got used to looking at Richard's scarred face, he started to act quite normally, or as normal as Dennis could act. Richard, for his part, was very amiable and worked as hard as anyone and, when it came to lifting the bulky furniture, he knew a lot more than I on how to twist and turn the more cumbersome pieces to get them down the narrow stairs and through the various doors: but for him, I do not think we would have managed a quarter of what we achieved, though he did have to pause for breath every now and again: his ribs, I supposed.

During lunch, while they were still eating, I sorted among the old magazines for anything I could take: I retrieved some copies of Punch going back to the Eighteen-Seventies, though much of the cartoon humour defeated me: still, I thought they were interesting. But, best of all, were the two dozen or more copies of the Illustrated London News, some dating back to just before the turn of the century: I loved to flick through such magazines, to look back in pictures to an age long gone. I was especially fascinated by those old photographs and engravings of the Boxer Rebellion and the Boer War, especially the drawings of the Chinese uprising and the siege of Peking. One drawing, in particular, has stuck in my memory: it showed some poor terrified pigtailed Chinaman fleeing for his life along a wooden bridge pursued by a howling mob of bandanaed Boxers armed with swords, spears, knives and axes. Fascinating! I wonder if they caught him? We never saw pictures like that at school.

In some of the magazines, there were these odd, oval-shaped photographs of capped Eton and Harrow schoolboys, who were to play each other at cricket and rugby, all wearing their distinctive hooped caps. It was a peculiarity with me that, whenever I saw a photograph of a young boy of, say, fourteen, fifteen or my own age, sixteen, taken around the turn of the century, I could not but help wonder how they had fared in the carnage of the First War. Did they survive it? Were they alive somewhere even as I looked at their photographs? Or had they been mown down by machine-guns charging across no-man's land with no more than a swagger stick in their hands? I used to find myself staring into their eyes wondering whether they ever had an inkling of what was to come.

It was the same with the photographs of our soldiers in Flanders in one or two of the later editions, smiling for the camera wearing captured German pickelhaubes or coalscuttle helmets: how many of them, I wondered, were dead the next day? Or the day after that?

Richard, meanwhile, had taken a liking to the rosewood bedroom sideboard we had brought down, the one into the mirror of which John Bolt's grandmother's had probably peered. I nearly broke my back manoeuvring it down the stairs, for it was exceedingly cumbersome and heavy: it was also monstrously hideous, in my view, all scrolls and twisted columns and balled feet. As well as an ornate back with a flaking silver mirror, it had a bow-fronted cupboard and a recessed shelf space underneath and at each end were two small drawers: Dennis had cleared one along with the other contents, but the second remained locked: he had no key to it and had decided not to force it. When Richard laughingly told him, 'If I find any money in it, I'll give it to you, I promise,' Dennis laughed, too, and that was good to see: he had not had much to laugh at in his life, poor chap.

'If you want it, take it,' Dennis said: he himself could not see any reason why someone would want so ugly a thing, but promised to lend us the farm's four-wheeled, long-handled cart, on which the men used to pull the filled bushel boxes of fruit between the orchards and the weighing shed, to carry it and anything else we fancied back to Norsea: the cart was eight-feet long, a couple of feet high and four-feet wide with wide-rimmed cast iron wheels and a pulling handle and would just about do so long as we did not add too much to our load.

Richard also asked Dennis if he could take one of the heavy iron-framed single beds we had carted down from the attic, with rod screws to tighten the springs: Richard took the mattress, too, as it was better than the one Old Sago had bequeathed him and cleaner: when he had shaken that out on first taking up residence in the cottage, shredded paper from a mouse's nest had fluttered out.

To add to what I thought was growing into an overload, even for an eight-foot, four-wheeled cart, Richard also chose a battered leather armchair and a small, round, fold-away, dining table with three claw-like feet projecting from a single central pillar: someone had polished and polished it once, for it was a deep nut brown in colour and would have been all right if the worms had not got at it.

By late afternoon, we had cleared the clutter from the attic, both the three main bedrooms and two of the lesser bedrooms, the parlours, the dining room and John Bolt's office: the bonfire in the backyard stood near ten feet high. I am ashamed to say that all three of us gave a whoop of delight when, at the end of our labours, we set fire to it: Dennis sprinkled on some paraffin and, with a whoosh, the hungry flames roared skyward twenty feet or more, all orange, red and crackling like fury: all we needed was a Guy Fawkes on top of it!

Every few minutes or so we would pitch another piece of furniture into the conflagration, a chair, a table, a hatstand, a chest of drawers, even one of the black horsehair sofas. Richard and Dennis did that: my job was to toss on all the unwanted books, papers and magazines, which meant every now and again grabbing an armful, running straight at the bonfire, heaving them into the flames from five or six feet, then retreating hurriedly to avoid being scorched. Dangerous, but fun.

The three of us watched the blaze for an hour or more, standing well back from the searing heat, though every so often Dennis, keen to ensure that everything burned, would creep in close under the heat and give the bonfire a poke with one of the long metal poles the men used to shake down the plums. It hardly needed it: the wood was tinder dry and burned so quickly and so well that half-charred pages of magazines, books and newspapers, some still aflame, were sent fluttering skyward in the vortex of rising heat before the flames had caught them properly.

Eventually, the time came for us to say our goodbyes: it was early evening, the tide was on its way in and we really had to get back across.

TWENTY-SIX

IT WAS Richard's damned sideboard which gave us all the trouble: but for that, we would have been all right. We loaded our salvaged prizes, the sideboard, the fold-up table, the chair and the iron bed frame with its spring and mattress, plus my four-dozen magazines, on to the handcart and, with Richard pulling on the iron handle at the front and me pushing at the back, we trundled it down the rough track.

The only delay was when we reached the 'boards,' the half-dozen, thick oak timbers slotted into concrete posts to fill a ten-foot gap cut into the seawall to allow the passage of small boats and vehicles where the causeway comes ashore, or sets out across the mudflats: they had to be taken out every time anyone went through: and replaced, of course, or the whole of Boundary farm and half of Shoe Street would have been flooded by the incoming tide. The timbers were not just heavy but also cumbersome to lift and you could quite easily lose a finger if you were not careful how you put them back. We lost a good five minutes there and, as we had delayed too long at the house, by the time we were halfway across the tide was already lapping at the foot of the slope where the causeway dips to its lowest. Richard became apprehensive as to whether we would make it, particularly as we had to stop several times to adjust our precarious load. From experience, I knew that the causeway would be under water in a half-hour: it would take us fifteen minutes to complete the crossing at the pace we were going: we could just about do it, I reckoned.

We had tied everything down with ropes, but the sideboard still protruded over the back end and, as we bumped and bounced over the potholes, it twice slipped off. The first time, I managed to stop it before it crashed to the ground and we pushed it back on, readjusted the ropes and set off again: but it really never was secure: when all was said and done, the load was just too big for the size of the cart. Halfway across, Richard and I changed places so that, while I pulled and steered at the front, he did the pushing at the back. It was not my fault that the sideboard fell off a second time: I suppose I should have avoided the patch of loose shale a hundred or so yards out from the island, but I did not: I was so busy worrying about the bouncing cart and that damned sideboard that I forgot it was there.

When it happened, the tide was beginning to seep over the top of the lower part of the causeway: we were still ahead of it – just – but had we been going any slower it would have caught us and we would have had to finish the last fifty yards splashing through water: still, it added a bit of excitement to the journey. We had just begun to hurry to beat it, when the wheel sank, the cart tipped and the sideboard crashed down.

The first I realised that something had happened was when Richard began yelling frantically for me to stop: he had tried to prevent the sideboard from falling, but the weight, the size and the momentum of it had been too much for him and he had fallen backwards with the thing landing on top of him. All I could see of him at first were two hands gripping its sides and his feet protruding from under it, like a man mending a car, though I could hear a lot of swearing. It did not help that I thought it funny enough to start to laugh: Richard's cursing put a stop to that.

He was pinned flat on his back and was struggling to lift the sideboard off himself, but could not manage it because it was too heavy and too cumbersome: eventually, the two of us managed to tilt it on one edge so that he could wriggle free and he lay there for a minute or so, white-faced and gasping, curled up and holding his side: at least the mirror was not broken. 'The bloody thing got me in the ribs,' he said through clenched teeth: apparently, a corner of the sideboard had caught him: no wonder he had yelled in pain.

Fearful that he might have broken something and so mortified by my unwitting part in the accident, I found myself apologising, not something I normally did: 'Sorry, Richard. We hit a patch of shale and it just tipped. I should have looked where I was going.'

'It's all right, Joe, it wasn't your fault,' Richard reassured me through gritted teeth. 'I thought I could hold it. I should have jumped out of the way and let the bloody thing go.' He climbed to his feet and, opening his coat, gingerly tested each rib in turn, then massaged the injured spot. 'There's nothing broken, fortunately. It's just that that's where I got poked by the guards in the camp. It hit me in the exact same spot. I don't want the bloody wound opening up again. That's what I'm afraid of.'

'We'd better get a move on if you are okay,' I said. 'The tide's coming in fast. It'll be over the causeway soon.'

The delay of a couple of minutes or more had allowed the tide to come swirling up the slope, almost to where we stood and we still had a hundred yards to go. There was nothing for it but to run the other stuff up on to the hard and return for the sideboard if we had time: better that than struggling to lift the sideboard back on, readjusting and retying everything and risk losing the lot. Richard managed to push the rest of the way one-handed while still clutching at his ribs, but was so out of breath when we got there, he was all for leaving the sideboard where it was and letting the tide carry it away. However, I had pulled the bloody thing almost the whole way across and I was not going to give up now! Richard, his face still creased with pain, was kneeling on the ground, recovering his breath, so I quickly unloaded the other stuff, my magazines included, wheeled the cart round and went racing back.

Shallow water, ankle deep and rising, covered the causeway: as the low cart now was empty, I was easily able to tip the sideboard on to it, even as the waves rippled around the wheels, and trundle it back. There was no time to take off my boots and socks or to roll up my trousers: I just splashed ashore with the sideboard in tow: another minute and it would have gone floating off toward Maydun. I had the absurd mental picture of a pipe-smoking crewman of one of the Swedish timber boats, which plied their way up the estuary on high tides, staring over the side in astonishment as our sideboard floated past.

When Richard had recovered sufficiently, we reloaded everything and hauled it round to the cottage, where, after unloading, I spent the next couple of hours eating bread and ginger marmalade and drying my socks and boots in front of a glowing coke fire: the red walnut sideboard with its ugly scrolls and twists, flaking mirror and bow-front had been given a place of honour against the back wall: the fold-up table was in position under the window and its precursor, Sago's rickety table, was burning fiercely in the grate: Richard sat in the new leather chair and I was sprawled upon the old lopsided sofa: that left only the bed to be brought in.

After a cup of tea, Richard, who had apparently recovered, though he still winced with pain every now and again, helped me carry Old Sago's mattress out and lug in the new bed and set it up. It was at this point that Richard went 'up the garden,' so to speak, and I wandered back into the parlour and went across to the sideboard where my magazines were piled, intent on flicking through one or two of them.

I did it almost idly and, to this day, I do not know how I managed it: a long-bladed kitchen knife, one my mother had lent Richard, was lying nearby: if it had not been there, I would not have bothered. Just to see what would happen, I pushed the tip of the blade into the keyhole of the unopened drawer and gave it a twist and a bang with my fist: there was a click and the drawer slid out like it was on a spring. It was what was in it that roused my curiosity: inside were a letter and three photographs.

TWENTY-SEVEN

WHEN the drawer clicked open, my first instinct was to call out and tell Richard what I had found, but he was still 'up the garden,' so instead I walked across to the oil-lamp to view the letter and the photographs in a better light: the photographs first.

The largest was a studio portrait of a baby, obviously a girl, no more than a year-old, dressed in a white smock and sitting on a rug, smiling out at the camera: judging by its sepia tone and the clothes and bonnet the child was wearing, it had been taken at least twenty or so years before. What caught my attention was the name of the photographer embossed in gold across the bottom of the stiff card, particularly the words 'Torquay, Devon.' Turning it over, I saw on the back a pencilled inscription, 'Joanne, aged ten months.' The second photograph was an amateur snap, tiny, no more than two inches by one-and-a-half, taken with a box brownie: it showed the same girl, this time as a skinny infant, standing in a field beside a stern-faced woman in a black dress and white apron, with the inscription on the back, 'Joanne, aged six, with Hettie, 1931.'

The third photograph aroused much more interest: it was again an amateur photograph, as tiny as the second and probably taken with the same camera, but this time it showed a girl of about sixteen or seventeen in a long skirt standing by the back door of a stone-built cottage, smiling out at the camera, one hand resting on the doorframe. The pencilled writing on the back I recognised as John Bolt's unmistakable scrawl: 'Niece Joanne, 1939.'

The letter was only a two-page affair on lined, blue paper: it had been sent to John Bolt four years before, in Forty-Three. My first reading of it was a hurried affair as I expected Richard would return at any moment: for some unaccountable reason, when I did hear him coming, I slid the letter inside my shirt: I wanted to read it properly at my leisure and alone, which I did later in the secrecy of my bedroom.

'Dear Cousin John,' the letter began, 'Just a short letter to tell you we are being moved. Our house is being taken over by the authorities.

All the villages round here are being evacuated as they want them for the Americans. I suppose it will be for training for when they invade Europe with our soldiers, if they ever do! They say they want our bit of the coast so the Americans can shoot their guns and practice landing from boats. Since it is mostly cliffs round here, I can't see that it will do them much good! A lot of people have gone already. A few of the farmers, the shopkeepers and the publicans are being allowed to stay, but not us. We have to uproot and go to live somewhere completely different. I have no idea where we will end up, but I will write and let you know when we find out for certain. Rumours are we are going to be moved inland to Wiltshire, Swindon most probably, so long as it is well away from the coast and the guns.'

Here the letter was paragraphed. The writer, having got the main reason for the letter out of the way, now imparted the harder news. 'I am sorry to have to tell you, John, that I had to go to the doctor recently. I have not been feeling well for sometime. He won't tell me what's wrong exactly, but I can give a good guess, just as you probably will in view of our family's history. I am nearly sixty now so we must expect these things, mustn't we? There is not much I can do about it anyway. Therefore, I am taking this opportunity to write and let you know and to send you what spare photographs I have of your niece, Joanne. She has her own, but these are the only ones I have of her. There is no one else now my Harold has gone. No one else would be interested in them. If I do go to join Harold, you and Dennis will be her only living relatives so it is natural that they should go to you two. Joanne is nearly eighteen now and is talking about going into the WAAFs. I'm not against it, a spell in the WAAFs might do her good as she is a bit headstrong at times. She's also one for the boys, especially the soldiers, so a couple of years in the forces might be for the best. I have to say she has been a comfort to me since Harold died. She has a good heart and is pleasant to live with most of the time. Since leaving school, she has been working in a local factory as a machinist, but the factory is closing as well and shifting everything to Swindon along with the workers. What troubles me, more than my health, is having to leave our old home at my time of life. I'm too old at my age to go traipsing about the country, going to live in a new town and having to make new friends. We don't know how long the war is going to last, though I hope it will be over soon. We could be there for years, we just don't know. What worries me is that, if I leave our little cottage now, I might never return to it, in view of what the doctor won't tell me! I know I am going to miss it terribly. Kindest regards to you and Dennis – Your Cousin, Hettie Waters.

'PS – Put some flowers on Beattie's grave for me. She was a dear sister to me and a good mother to Dennis.'

It was such a sad letter, a woman calmly discussing her own death and patiently waiting for it: if the letter were written in Forty-Three, I reasoned, the old girl was probably dead by that time, but her daughter, the girl in the photographs, would still be alive, that is, if she had not been blown to bits by a doodlebug: unlikely, as most of them fell on London or around us rather than in the West Country. It was at this point that realisation dawned: Dennis had a cousin! Not much of a looker, but a cousin, nevertheless. 'He thinks he is the only one of his family left. Won't he be surprised when he learns he's not!' I said to myself, gleefully, for an idea was already forming in my mind.

Why not write to the cousin, Joanne What's-her-name? – Joanne Waters, and tell her about Uncle John Bolt's sad demise and invite her to the funeral and, thus, inform her about Dennis? It was no use writing to the old girl, Hettie: if she had the 'big C' when she wrote that letter in Forty-Three, it was a foregone conclusion she would be six feet under: but that should not stop me writing to her daughter and telling her about Dennis and her uncle's death, should it?

One snag: I did not have an address in Wiltshire to which I could write: if I were to write to anywhere, it would have to be to the address at the top of the first page, the one in Devon: that was the best I could do. 'You never know,' I told myself, 'the daughter might have gone back there after the war and might even be living there now.' I had never heard of the place in Devon where she and her mother had lived and supposed it to be a small village: it was not much to go on, but it was worth a try, just for the sheer hell of it! If Joanne Waters were there, she would get the letter: if she were not, well – it would be no skin off my nose: she would be none the wiser and would go on living wherever she was and Dennis would go on living at Boundary, none the wiser either, till I told him: if I told him.

I did fleetingly consider that I ought to give him the letter when next I saw him, make up some tale about finding it among the magazines and let him decide: but I knew Dennis: if I left it to him, he would not write in a month of Sundays. Where women were concerned, especially those of his own age, he was painfully shy and far too unsure of himself ever to do anything so bold as to write a letter to one, even if she was his own kith and kin, a cousin no less, and probably the last surviving relative he had on this planet. I doubted if he had ever written a letter in his life. No, if I did not write it, Dennis was going to be the only relative at the funeral, whenever that was to be.

I did not spend a lot of time thinking about it: that was my way then: do it, and worry about it afterwards! I swear, I firmly believed that Dennis had a right to know he had a cousin: that he was not the last of the Bolts in this world: and that was my reason for writing the letter: to invite her to the funeral: she would want to be there to see her long lost uncle buried!

I could not find a pen and ink and supposed we did not have any, so I wrote it in pencil, keeping it short so as not to make any mistakes or to say the wrong things and doing it in my neatest handwriting, three versions in all till I thought I had it right: 'Dear Miss Waters, I am sorry to have to tell you that your uncle, John Bolt, has died at Boundary Farm, Gledlang, near Maydun. He lived there with his nephew, your cousin, Dennis. I got your address from a letter written by your mother, Mrs Hettie Waters, four years ago, which we found and I am writing on Dennis's behalf. Your uncle's death was very sudden. Unfortunately, the funeral has been delayed because the coroner won't give us back the body to bury, but we expect to be able to do that next week or the week after, all being well. There should be a good turnout. If you want to come, you will be welcome.'

How to sign it? I thought of ending it 'A Friend' or 'A wellwisher,' but decided against both: it seemed silly. So I just signed it, 'J.C.' No one down in Devon, or Wiltshire, or wherever, would know who 'J.C.' was! Or care.

There, done it! Nothing difficult about that: it reads fine: send the bloody thing! Would Dennis thank me for writing it? With luck, he might never know I had done it: if he did find out, I just had to hope that he would be glad that I had put him in touch with a 'long lost' cousin! He ought to be bloody grateful, was my view, first, because, if Richard had not insisted on having the sideboard, it would have been burned on the bonfire and the photographs and letter with it: and, second, if I had not made a dash back when it had fallen off the handcart, it would have gone bobbing off towards Maydun and eventually sunk through water-logging in a back creek somewhere: and, third, of course, if I had not opened the drawer, no one would have known anything about her anyway.

When my mother and Ben had gone to sleep, I crept downstairs and searched her parlour sideboard drawer for an envelope and a stamp, the same drawer in which she kept her first marriage certificate and a heart-shaped locket with a photograph of my father in it: I knew that because I had rifled through the drawer to take a peek ages before.

Two evenings later, I rode across to the mainland and posted it: there was no one about in the Square so it was no real act of bravado, not at eleven o'clock at night: and that was how, as a favour to Dennis Bolt, I came to write to his cousin, Joanne Waters, then living in a small Devonshire village: sending that letter turned out to be one of the best things I ever did – and one of the worst!

TWENTY-EIGHT

IT CANNOT be an easy thing for a man to pass within fifty yards of his only son and for both of them to turn their heads away: it happened several times on Norsea in the first weeks of Richard's return. Ben, I know, would have preferred Richard to have taken up lodgings elsewhere, in the village, say, or in Maydun: but he had no say in the matter. For all his authority as farm manager or bailiff, Ben could not dictate who lived on the island: Hoary would decide that: it was one of the few things upon which he remained uninfluenced by others. Hoary had given permission for Richard to stay rent-free in the cottage for as long as he needed and had also taken him on as a handyman and that was that: I suspect the old fool was entirely unaware of the friction it caused between father and son.

On an island a little more than a mile long and a half-mile at its widest, Ben and Richard could hardly avoid seeing each other: it was almost impossible not to do so: there were hedgerows around most of the fields then which limited some of the view and tall elms spaced in them and in the corners of some fields: but the island was totally flat and if you stood at one end on the low seawall which ran along the northern shoreline you could always see from one end to the other. When you are working in a field and you see your son walking past the gateway to it, or when you are standing one side of a hedgerow and he is strolling along the track on the other side, it must be hard indeed to avoid lifting your eyes and giving even a flicker of recognition: I would say heart-rendingly so: but then I am guessing.

There was one instance, I recall, when I was riddling and bagging up the last of the previous year's potato crop from our small clamp near where the tracks divide when Richard came up and stopped to talk to me: he had spent the morning at Hoary's place and was on his way back to his cottage: but when he saw me, he turned into the field. To pass the time while we talked, Richard helped me stack some of the filled sacks, a job he laughingly admitted he had not done for almost twenty years. However, when he saw Ben approaching with

Molly and the cart to pick up what I had done, his mood changed abruptly and he set off across the field in the opposite direction.

'And what did he want?' Ben asked suspiciously as he brought Molly up.

'We were just talking,' I replied.

A sniff and a harrumph from Ben. 'The sooner he gets off this island the better it'll bloody be for the both of us, then we won't have to keep on avoiding each other.' He meant it, too. Sad really.

When I mentioned this to Richard later that same evening, he just shrugged and said quite calmly: 'I'm staying, Joe. I like it here. I was brought up here. I've got a rent-free cottage, I've got a job of sorts – one that will do for now, anyway. It is something to do, it keeps me occupied and it is good fun sometimes, especially the digging trips, even if the work is sometimes a bit much for me with my bad lung. Hoary's not a bad old stick. He pays me for what I do, a sort of weekly retainer, and I do whatever jobs he asks. I don't mind. I did worse in the camps. I need somewhere where I don't have to bother over much with people. People can't help themselves when they see a face like mine – they stare. On here, I don't have to worry about them. Summer's coming on and I intend to spend the whole of it out in the fresh air, so why should I leave? And besides I promised Jean I would be here – when she comes.' The latter spoken after a pause.

Thereafter, Richard made no effort to avoid us, Ben and myself, that is: we saw him on the tracks, we saw him over the hedgerows, we saw him on the headlands, we saw him from the fields, we saw him heading for the causeway and coming back across it: and once or twice, when we were with Molly and the cart, we even negotiated the same length of track as him. He also passed the farmhouse front door on occasions: at times it could not be avoided, I suppose, as there was a well-trodden route from the cottages to the big house past the farmhouse and sometimes Richard took it. The only times we did not see him was when he was away on one of his other trips, when he went up to London, hoping to find the woman Jean, or when he went up into the next county with Hoary and Stanley Lobel on an archaeological dig, of which they made three in that first six weeks alone.

The strain of it was all beginning to tell on Ben: he was looking more dour and there was a greater grumpiness in his tone and he was quicker to irritation. Whereas once, if I made a mistake, he would just utter a despairing, 'For Gawd's sake, Joe!' and shake his head wistfully, now he had begun to snap at anything and everything. 'Can't you do any bloody thing right, boy?' he would shout if, for instance, I so much as turned Molly a couple of yards too late at a gateway or halted her in the wrong spot picking up a load of bagged onions, adding: 'Where'd you get your brains from, boy? Gawd, help me! Half the time you ain't worth the money I pay you.' Which was a bit harsh, I thought, as I was only paid two pounds a week and my mother took a pound of that for 'my keep.' And besides, it was Hoary who actually 'paid me': all Ben did was to give me the money.

For six weeks, Ben and Richard had been silently passing each other: I know Richard was content helping Hoary: he had already cut the grass on the old tennis court which I should have cut, clipped the riotous rhododendron bushes (unfortunately, while they were in bud), dug a wide border round the self-same tennis court and planted flowers and some withered-looking rose bushes. He had also finished cementing the path by the scullery backdoor which Hoary had begun (minus the Biblical exhortations), started to paint the woodwork at the front of the house where it weathered the most, rebuilt a low wall four bricks high at the bottom of the slope where the house's flagged terrace drops towards the 'lawn.' His next task, he told me, would be to demolish the dangerously leaning, brick, octagonal summer house, which was being used as Hoary's coke and wood store and which I generally filled quarterly, like everything for Norsea, fetching a load of coke for both our houses from the mainland drop-off point on Boundary on an appointed day each quarter. All in all, this was a fair six weeks' work: Richard was being kept busy all right.

The big surprise was when Richard told me Hoary was even considering buying himself a car! 'I have told him he ought to get one, a Bentley or a Rolls, nothing too pretentious,' said Richard with a laugh. It was a lovely pipedream: no car had appeared as yet and any that did would have to be registered with the local authorities just to get enough coupons to buy the rationed petrol to run it: and it would have to be able to contend with the narrowness of the causeway, which really desperately needed widening and building up. Hoary's hope, I think, was to be able to dispense with Sligger Offin's smoky old taxi and have Richard chauffeur him to the various archaeological sites around the region so he could keep a closer eye on them, for he never ceased to bemoan the 'vandalism' of the Americans during the war: someone in Whitehall got a very irate hour-long telephone call from a man sprawled on the floor of a telephone box in Gledlang Square over that.

Richard had even promised to ask Hoary if I could go on one of the digs with him, just to get away from Norsea for a few days, a week or so. 'You should come some time, Joe. You would enjoy it,' he said. 'The digs are great fun, four or five hours digging in a field, then back to the pub where you're staying for a meal and drinking and Hoary paying for everything. It's marvellous.'

I did not hold out much hope: Ben, I knew, would oppose it: had I dared to ask, I could almost hear his answer: 'What do you want to go looking for extra work for? Ain't there enough on Norsea for you to do without going gallivantin' across half the country looking for it? If there ain't enough to keep you busy, boy, I can soon find you some more. Now get back to the job you get paid to do.'

Once I came across Richard digging holes all over Hoary's 'lawn,' a couple of dozen of them in which he proposed to plant Hoary's wood sculptures which were spread about the grass: I knew Richard had just returned from one of his trips to London and, though he smiled a greeting, I thought he looked a bit glum. 'No luck on your trip then?' I asked, sympathetically, meaning, of course, his search for the woman Jean.

'No,' he said with a shake of the head. 'I went back to the apartments, but the caretaker had heard nothing. Trouble is, a doodlebug hit the Tube station at the end of the street and wiped that out and all the other houses all around, everything within a hundred-yard radius, has gone. All that's left is half her old building at the farthest end. Just my luck, I suppose.'

In an attempt to cheer him up, I made some facetious remark about the carvings, stunted, dwarflike grotesques, with lopsided eyes, deformed arms and hands and oversized feet, not to mention the odd gouging by a slipped chisel. The mental state of the person carving them was beginning to make me wonder. 'Oh Gawd! I hope she don't come here and see them. She'll think we're all barmy,' I exclaimed. 'I tell you, if someone in a lunatic asylum did carvings of things like that, they'd put him in a padded cell and throw away the key.' Well, at least it got Richard smiling again, even if he was not laughing out loud.

It was about this time that we met Old Sago: he came pedalling along the track one Sunday morning on his way to see Ben to ask when he should come over to start work for the summer. When he saw Richard, the old countryman let out a gleeful yell. 'Good Gawd, bless my old eyes, if it ain't Dick Wigboe come back to see us!' he exclaimed, dismounting so that the two of them could shake hands, all feigned as village gossip would have told him long before that Richard was back: but this was their first meeting, so I suppose the acting could be excused: it is what people do.

'Well, how are yer, Dick boy? How are yer?' the old man went on, beaming his toothless grin. 'I'm glad to see you agin all in one piece. I heard you'd come back. I meant to come over to see ye afore this, but the old bones 'on't let me get about like I used to. I must say, I thought you were gorn for good, boy. I didn't expect to see you back here. Where've you bin then? Someone said out East somewhere...'

The two stood talking for a good ten minutes, mostly quietly out of my hearing. One part I did hear was when Sago said, with genuine sadness: 'I'm sorry to hear about you and Ben.' Since I had not told him, I could only suppose it was someone from Boundary, Charlie Mangapp probably, who had got it from Dennis.

Richard nodded almost imperceptibly. 'Yes, well,' he began, giving a shrug of the shoulders, but did not finish the sentence.

'Never mind,' consoled Sago, 'what happens happens, don't it? It's just good to see you're back. Though why you've come back here, I don't know.'

Richard just gave a wry smile. 'It's good to be back, Sago,' he said, 'truly it is. It's like they say, there's no place like home, is there? And after some of the places I've seen, round here's better than a lot of them.'

The old man beamed. 'It's good to hear that the arsehole of England here's as good as any other place,' he chortled. For a global traveller such as Richard to make such a remark was, in a way, comforting for the old man: that all his long years spent in drudgery in that remote and lonely part of the country had not been a waste of his life.

'I have to say, Dick,' said Sago, rubbing a finger along his drooping grey moustache, 'if I hadn't have known it was ye, I wouldn't have recognised you and not just because of your face either. I heard about that from Charlie. It ain't half so bad as they said.' A nice sympathy there. 'It's just that you were a lad when I last saw ye. I remember you a lot differently than y'are now. You seem changed, boy. You're a lot thinner than I remember ye. And you're a lot better spoken than I remember ye. You don't speak like us n'more with our oohs and aahs and that must be a blessing.' A chuckle from the old man.

Richard smiled even more. 'We've all changed, Sago,' he said gravely. 'I think the war did that. It changed everybody one way or another.'

'Yes, maybe you're right, boy,' said Old Sago, remounting his bicycle, 'maybe you're right. Well, I'm off to see Ben, but we'll talk some more, Dick, we'll talk some more.' And with that he wobbled off, calling out again as he departed: 'We'll talk some more, Dick, boy, we'll talk some more.'

Richard's remark to Old Sago about being glad to be back I found strangely disconcerting for some reason: like it was almost a betrayal of my hopes. 'Are you really glad to be back?' I asked as we walked on.

'Yes, Joe, I am,' he answered, nodding and looking at me in some surprise that I should doubt him. 'I'm here for Jean, like I told you, so she can find me. That is what we arranged in the camp. If we got separated and didn't meet up again, I would come here and try and find her at the London address and she would come to London and then come here to look for me. It's as simple as that. We had it all planned. I told her that, if we missed each other, I would make for home when the war was over. I gave her this – ' He sought for the word and then just used the obvious. ' – address. I had not expected I would have to wait in Australia so long. If Jean learns I am still alive, I know she'll make for here. At least, I hope she will.'

'She'll be in for a shock when she gets here.'

Richard's arm swept round in a wide gesture. 'Norsea is normality after what I've seen,' he said sharply. 'Things haven't changed round here for hundreds of years. People still farm the same land, plant the same crops and harvest them the same way. People were farming on Norsea before the Battle of Hastings, before the Normans came. And they'll be farming on it a hundred years from now. If the truth be known, it was probably the Romans who first built the causeway.'

'We might carry on farming here if Hoary doesn't turn the place into a bloody holiday camp first,' I said, only half jokingly. There was already talk in the village that a disused army camp along the coast was being taken over by some enterprising chap specifically as a place where Londoners could take their holidays by the sea: now Hoary was advertising his cottages on Norsea for holidays. Would we be taken over the same way? I did not fancy having whining, nasal-voiced townies traipsing about everywhere, looking at us with contempt: just a bunch of bloody swedes, clodhoppers and country bumpkins!

Had we not been an island twice daily cut off by the tide, remote and privately owned by a high-up civil servant in Whitehall, I daresay we would have had half-a-dozen bombed-out families from London marching across the causeway to us: as it was, even they did not want to come and live on a windswept island in the middle of an estuary with no electricity, no running water, no shops, public houses or streetlights and, worst of all, no buses running past their doorsteps. They would live in empty warehouses, they would live in Nissen huts on deserted army camps, they would live in disused hangers on abandoned airfields, bomb-damaged buildings and even berthed Thames river barges, but they would not live on Norsea, for love or money!

The council had brought two desperate East End families from Hoxton during the winter to show them the cottages, but chose the wrong day in the wrong month in the wrong year to do it: two mothers each with a brood of four or five children came on the very day in January, Friday the twenty-fourth, when the snow of that winter started falling. The women took one look at the bleakness of the place, its isolation, its snow-covered fields, the biting wind whistling up the barren estuary, the bare trees and hedgerows, the puddles and mud, and went back on the next train: better a bombed-out building or abandoned bomb shelter in London than having to live in such a God-forsaken place! They were good judges, for it snowed every day for the next month: after that, no more came: I suspect that was when Hoary telephoned his brother in Whitehall, for it was about that time that he began putting discreet advertisements in the London newspapers advertising the cottages as 'summer residences' and he ignored Ben's protests over that.

To me, the idea of 'holiday cottages' was absurd: cottages were what people in our region lived in all year round and, after six years of war and two of austerity without proper repair, most of them were near uninhabitable. As for myself, it was no use me worrying what Hoary did for the island: I had never had a holiday, not a proper holiday: I just got Christmas Day and Good Friday off and worked the rest the same as Ben and everyone else. Besides, in a year and a few months, I would be in the army, starting my two years' National Service, so there was no point in worrying. My future would be dictated by a buff envelope from the War Department: my call-up.

TWENTY-NINE

THREE DAYS after Richard and Hoary left on another of their trips up into the next county, I met Jan the Polack: not to put too fine a point on it, I rescued him: though he was not really in any great danger of losing his life, just in a state of panic, not knowing what to do next: being a foreigner, that can be excused, I suppose.

It was late evening, about nine o'clock, and, after finishing my chores, I was walking near the Eastern Point, mooching along the shoreline, skimming pebbles across the waves for entertainment, when out in the southern channel I saw a man standing in a rowboat and frantically waving his arms: who he was I had no idea at that time: I had never seen him before. He was a couple of hundred yards out and appeared to be in trouble: as well as waving his arms, he was shouting a lot, though I could not make out what he said. It was obvious what that trouble was: he had lost his single sculling oar and the rowboat was drifting out on the ebb tide towards the estuary mouth: pitiful really: any Gledlang youth worth his salt would have dived overboard and swum to the shore, fully clothed or not. True, the current is much stronger on the south side of Norsea when the tide is running out than when it is coming in and it can be dangerous if you are not used to rowing or sculling through it as Ben and I were. We had punted across it, along it, against it and round in circles on it on duck-hunting trips in every kind of weather ever since I had learned to swim after my near-drowning: so I knew exactly what the so-called 'dangerous current' did, where it flowed strongest and where it had changed its course from the previous year. One mad summer I had even paddled out into it astride a ten-foot plank – my 'canoe' – and spent a couple of happy hours struggling up and down against its flow just to see how strong it was!

The man in the punt had already drifted level with the Eastern Point and was beginning to get frantic: even though he was drifting away, his yells seemed to get louder, especially when I acknowledged his wave and hurried back along the shoreline. I was only going to get

Ben's punt which he kept beached near the wooden pier: it took a matter of seconds for me to untie it, drag it down the beach and launch it into the wind-whipped water. We always kept the oars in the punt so I was able to row after the drifting boat and, with the help of the current itself, pull alongside within a couple of minutes or so. After that, it was a simple matter of tying the mooring rope on to the rowboat prow, telling the frantic man to hang on to it and then pulling both boats out of the stronger flow of the current into slower-moving, less choppy water.

It was then I realised what the man was, if not who: he gabbled something at me which I could not understand, then tried to say the same thing in English, but his teeth were chattering too much for me to make much sense of it. He was soaked to the skin and had obviously fallen overboard while sculling, but had somehow managed to clamber back aboard, though the oar had gone floating off. That week, even though it was almost summer, the weather had been much cooler and the water was cold enough to turn anyone blue: also, evening breezes on the river can be quite chilly and the man had only a jacket over his open-neck shirt and they were soaking wet. He gabbled something again as I towed him towards the shore, but his words were whipped away on the wind: from his accent, loud and guttural, I gathered that he was one of our Polish friends, one of an army of displaced Polacks who, like the still unrepatriated Italian and German PoWs, went around the country helping out with all kinds of work: from spring hoeing, pea and bean picking, fruit picking, grain harvesting, potato and beet lifting on the farms, say, to felling timber in the Scottish forests, hewing coal in the mines of Yorkshire, Lancashire, Nottinghamshire and Durham or working in the clay quarries of the Bedfordshire brick fields for the Government: anything, in fact, which paid a wage.

The poor Polacks could not go back to Poland because the Russians would not let them, which seemed a bit harsh to me, especially as they had fought the Germans as much as we had done: their crime, it seemed, was to have escaped from Poland in the first place, then to compound it by joining the British Army in Palestine and fighting alongside them as infantry in North Africa, Italy and Normandy and as paratroopers at Arnhem. Others had joined the Royal Air Force as pilots and been renowned for their fighting ability. When the war ended, all those wearing British Army khaki or Royal Air Force blue were regarded by that unelected, authoritarian, 'democratic people's' police state – or Soviet satellite, to you and me – as 'tainted' because of their exposure to the West and all the more suspect because they had fought with us. Anyone going back was likely to be stood up against a wall and shot. Bloody fool Communists! Bloody murdering Communists! What a bunch of hypocritical, lunatic arseholes, they were! Nazis in different-coloured uniforms! I am glad the lot of them are gone now.

Some of our Socialists were not much better, the Russian-loving Labourites, the Fabianist university lecturers who lived in their six-bedroomed houses and demanded council houses for everyone else, and the self-proclaimed intellectuals who talked a good fight but never did a damned day's work in their lives: them and the Daily Worker lot and their ilk. They were so enamoured of the new order and its coming that they did not seem to give a tinker's cuss about the poor Poles, or all the other displaced persons traipsing around Europe at that time looking for a country, Jews, Czechoslovaks, Latvians, Lithuanians, Estonians, etcetera. Most of our left-wing intellectuals were too busy sucking up to the Russians to do anything for people who had helped them win the war. Out of a sense of compassion, Clement Attlee's Government did allow most of the poor blighters to stay in England: some did marry English girls and settle to a family life, but many others never did: they went to live in the abandoned army camps in north Wales and remoter parts of the Fen country and twenty-five years later were still there, their lives wasted!

It would be too difficult, and too comical probably, to attempt to reproduce a Polish accent, with all its 'vees' and 'vots' and 'yahs,' so I will report our conversation in plain English as far as is possible.

'Thank you. Thank you. Thank you,' had been the first words the man spoke when I tossed him the rope and began towing him out of the current into the calmer water: of course, he spoke them as 'Zanku, zanku, zanku,' and was still saying the same thing when after the five-minute pull I steered in among the salting banks on the more protected northern side of Norsea and beached the punt at the foot of the low seawall. The final 'thank you' came as he stepped ashore with a great sigh of relief and planted his feet on solid if muddy ground.

The stranger was only about twenty-six years of age, tall and slim, with sharp, handsome features, an untidy mop of near-white-blond hair parted in the centre and combed to each side, and eyebrows so fair that, unless you looked closely, you would have thought he had none at all: his eyes, screwed up because of the cold as they were, had that cold blue look about them that you associate more with Nordic types, Norwegians and Finns and Swedes. In fact, had I not guessed that he was one of the displaced Polacks, I would have taken him for a Swede or, worse, a German PoW working on one of the farms south of the river, fed up with waiting for his repatriation and trying to row back to Germany. One ungrateful bugger had already tried it halfway through the war and had half the Royal Navy – well, the Cobwycke MTB branch of it – hunting him down: luckily, they found him before he froze to death because it was late November and the North Sea can get a bit rough and a bit chilly then, especially if you are in a twelve-foot, narrow marshman's punt with no covering on it other than a loose tarpaulin and fifteen-foot waves of freezing cold water are crashing over you: you would probably freeze to death before you drowned.

The shivering man I had rescued introduced himself as Jan Lakadat. 'I borrow boat,' he explained in his thick, grating Polish accent, which gives no idea at all of the difficulty I had in understanding it. 'Borrowing a boat' in anyone's parlance, was a euphemism for stealing one, or at least taking it without the owner's permission.

'I try to get across river to village Gledlang on other side,' he went on. 'I slip and fall in water and lose oar. I get back, but no oar now. I float away. Tide go – ' A gesture here towards the estuary mouth. ' – I not swim very well. Thank you very much for rescue me. Thank you very much.'

I said it again without thinking. 'It was a pleasure, Jan. My name's Joe, by the way. Joe Coe. Happy to help.'

The rowboat was now bobbing gently in the shallows, with its painter secured around a rock: it had no name on its prow or stern, so I could not tell from where Jan had taken it. Part of the answer he gave next. 'I come from Abbey Farm over there,' he said, pointing across to the Langwater's southern shore and the flat fields where the largest farm estate along the estuary lay, with its massive former abbey farmhouse. Not unusually, in the weirdness of the times, the estate belonged to some Russian-loving Labourite lord, who peculiarly supported the party of the very working classes who had vowed the year before to get rid of him and his kind for all time. Still, it is always easy to be a left-winger and have a socialist conscience when you are rich and own thousands of acres of land and are called Lord Somebody-or-Other: people should try it when they are cold and hungry, standing in the pouring rain in the middle of a field with holes in the soles of their boots. You do not feel like being a working class hero then or a ragged-trousered philanthropist: you feel like being a middle-class clerk and working in a nice dry office where they bring the hot tea and sandwiches round on a trolley, or even an upper class peer lording it over other poor cold and hungry buggers stuck in the middle of a field with the rain teeming down and holes in the soles of their boots wishing they were you!

'Is that where you work?' I asked: I knew of the German and Italian prisoners working on various farms south of the river, but I had not heard there were any Poles there.

'No, I with Catchment Board, building up seawall,' said Jan. 'We have camp there, at Abbey Farm, at Lingsea. I borrow boat from there.'

The two of us were below the level of the seawall at that point and well protected from the wind, but Jan was still shivering and his teeth were chattering like castanets: he needed to be got inside, somewhere where it was warm and where I could light a fire and he could dry himself and his clothes or his next stop would be a sickbed with the diagnosis 'pneumonia.' There really was only one place: Richard's cottage: as I say, he was away, but I knew he would not have locked his door: on Norsea there was no need: no one was likely to go creeping into someone's else's house to burgle it: the only person I could think of who might want to take a peek into someone else's house was my mother being nosey.

We managed to get to the cottage without being seen simply by going along the headlands and always ensuring there was a hedgerow between us and the farmhouse: if my mother or Ben had looked out they would have seen nothing. Once inside Richard's cottage, I went to get the blanket off Richard's bed and when I returned I was somewhat shocked to find Jan had stripped to his underpants and draped his wet clothes across the drying line in front of the fireless grate: having served in the forces with other men, and now living in a camp with a hundred or so of them, he most probably was used to such a thing, but it surprised me. I quickly lit the fire with kindling and newspapers and some logs and paraffin and, fortunately, it blazed up quickly: taking some water from Richard's pail, which I hoped had not been standing too long, I put the kettle on to boil for tea. While the grateful Jan warmed himself by the fire, I searched in Richard's small scullery-kitchen and found a tin of vegetable soup on one of the shelves: five minutes later and Jan was greedily eating the hot soup from the saucepan in which I had heated it, dunking into it the slice of dry bread which I had sawn off Richard's loaf: unhappily, he pulled a face at the tea I made with sweetened tinned milk: so much so I thought he was going to spit it out! As he sipped, grimacing with every swallow, he told me just why he happened to be floating down the river towards the open sea in a leaky rowboat and without an oar.

'I try to get to Gledlang to see girl,' he said. 'You know village called Gledlang?'

'Yes, it's just across the causeway. I went to school there,' I told him. 'You can walk across to it when the tide is out.'

Jan looked at me, disbelievingly. 'Walk across to village?'

'Yes, when the tide's out. There's a causeway.'

'Causeway? What is causeway?'

'A road over the mud, from here to the mainland. It's been there for hundreds of years, ever since the Romans. They probably built it.' I remembered what Richard had said.

Jan frowned: realisation dawned very slowly. 'You say I can walk from here to village?'

'Yes, when the tide is out.'

'How long before tide go out?'

'Three or four hours completely.' Seeing he did not understand, I just held up three fingers. 'Three hours.'

Jan thought for a while, then asked: 'If I go across, can I come back?'

I explained the tidal pattern as best I could, hoping he would understand: from the questions he asked me subsequently, it became apparent he wanted to cross to Gledlang that night, but had to be back at the Catchment Board site early the next morning, 'or I get push,' as he colloquially put it. If he crossed the causeway on foot that night, he would have to wait until after eleven o'clock, almost midnight, when the tide would be properly out: but, of course, when he re-crossed to Norsea in the small hours, there would be no tide for him to row back to Lingsea and I would not have advised anyone to attempt to walk across the mudflats: you can very easily sink and be held fast there until the next tide comes washing back over you. What concerned me, though, was that he was really not in good enough shape to go across to Gledlang, hang around there, then come back three or four hours later and try to get across to Lingsea for the 'morning roll call.' Fortunately, Jan must have realised this himself, huddled as he was in front of the fire, shivering still, because he looked gloomily into the flames and said: 'I not go now. I too cold. It too late. Tomorrow perhaps.' Which was a relief to me because if he were to get himself cut off by the incoming morning tide, there was no way I was going to pick him up from Gledlang Shoe and row him from one side of the estuary to the other, not at five or six o'clock in the morning: I would still be asleep in my bed at that time.

'What's the name of the girl you want to see in Gledlang?' I actually knew the answer to the question before I asked it.

'Girl called Violet, now called Reddy. You know her? You know girl called Violet Reddy, yes?' Jan was peering at me intently. 'She mother, young, beautiful. Has little boy. Little boy my son. She name him Thomas, I think.'

When I nodded to all this, Jan smiled and sighed as if a great weight had been lifted from his shoulders. 'I too cold, too wet, to go now,' he said, disconsolately: then, giving me a pleading look, he asked: 'Can you take letter for me?'

'Sure, I can. No bother.'

'Have you paper? We do letter now, please.'

I found some paper and a pencil and together we drafted the letter: it took three attempts and two re-sharpenings of the pencil before Jan was satisfied with what he wanted to say. While we composed, he asked questions about Violet and little Thomas. You know the kind: 'She pretty girl, no?' and 'Boy Thomas have hair like me, blond, eh?' and 'What her husband like? Big man? Handsome like me?' I think there was a trace of sarcasm in his voice when he asked that.

I gave him chapter and verse. Yes, I thought Violet was very pretty: yes, little Thomas looked just like him, which he did: if you had put the two together, a blind man would have seen how alike they were! Thomas had the same white-blond hair, the same fair eyebrows and the same blue eyes and the same-shaped face, chin and nose. And the husband, Walter Reddy? Well, an out-and-out blockhead really: and ten years older than Violet, if he were a day!

My description of little Thomas pleased Jan no end. 'Like me,' he kept repeating, proud as a peacock, 'like me.'

Jan seemed to think that never having seen his own son required some explanation: when he offered it, I did not discourage him: it was information, it confirmed what I already knew and it passed the time while we smoked and Jan got warm. By merging what I knew already and what Jan told me, I pieced together the following story: a few weeks after D-Day, Jan had been badly wounded in the battles around Falaise in Normandy, trying to close the infamous gap and bottle up a whole German army. A shell had blown him thirty feet across a road and wrapped him around a telephone pole: after convalescing for a couple of months at a Wivencaster military hospital, he and about thirty other wounded fellow Poles, who were also considered not fit enough to return to duty but fit enough to do some work, were marched out of their tents one day, bundled on to lorries and driven to nearby Cobwycke: the tents were wanted for badly wounded Arnhem returnees. The authorities had another job for the recovering Polacks: at Cobwycke, the County Catchment Board, in anticipation of a final victory and eventual peace, had that autumn begun rebuilding the seawalls which run for two hundred miles or more all down our coast-line, twisting and turning round bays and creeks and inlets right to the mouth of the big river itself. All of them had been sadly neglected during the war because people had had other things on their minds and the recovered Polack soldiers, waiting in tents at Wivencaster, were a godsend: they were still at it rebuilding them when the war ended. Like the canal-digging Irish navvies of the Nineteenth Century, the Polacks had dug hundreds of miles of deep delph ditches running parallel to the seawalls, partly to drain the land and also to use the earth to build up the seawalls to a greater height. The Catchment Board gangs lived as they had always lived, in ex-army tents in farmers' fields, with a communal eating tent and an exposed latrine: the camps were always sited well away from the villages, in case the local populace were offended by the smells from them, so they said: though, it was more likely they did not want the Polacks to mix with the locals too much, especially the girls.

Jan and his conscripted gang had worked on building up the seawall at Cobwycke all during the winter of Forty-Four to Forty-Five and it was there that somehow he had met and courted for a few short weeks and eventually impregnated one Violet Goody, maid of that parish: but then a flooding emergency up in Lincolnshire in the May of Forty-Five, just as the war ended, saw Jan's gang shipped up to the flat Fen Country around the Wash to deepen the long, arrow-straight dykes, or cuts, which drain the land up there into the Great Ouse and the Nene. It was an emergency simply because the Fen area was and remains this country's major potato-growing area and there was, too, a danger that the whole newly planted crop would be lost at a time of an acute national shortage. Violet had written to Jan at the start, of course, but the gang was being shunted all round the Fens, even into Huntingdonshire and Cambridgeshire: they were never in the same place for long: every two weeks or so they would uproot and move to another camp twenty or thirty miles away: consequently, the letters never caught up with him. The sadness is that both thought the other was being neglectful, Jan because no letters were forwarded to him and Violet because all those she wrote were returned to her and she received none in return.

Jan's gang had returned to our estuary only a fortnight previously to start rebuilding the sea defences along the south shore: at the specific request – some might call it influence or favouritism – they had begun at the large Abbey Farm estate, directly opposite Norsea and Gledlang: they were to rebuild all the way to the mouth of the Langwater and then turn south past the old Roman fort at Othona. I knew from a single visit I had made years before with Ben that once they left Othona behind and turned south past the Ray Sands, there was nothing but emptiness for mile after mile after mile: you could walk thirty miles along the seawall there and never see a living soul. Once you go into that marshy, treeless country, you virtually disappear off the face of the earth: this is what had bothered Jan and why he had taken the risk and tried to row across to Gledlang to see Violet.

Jan swore – and I believed him – that he had known nothing of her pregnancy when he had left her behind in Cobwycke: it was only through a chance reunion a week previously with another of his Polish comrades, who had married another Cobwycke girl under a special Government licence and was visiting their camp to renew old acquaintances, that he even learned Violet had become pregnant and given birth to a baby boy eight months after he had left: little Thomas was all of seventeen months before Jan knew he existed: it was then, too, that he learned Violet had married and was living across the river from him in Gledlang.

He would not have left her, he assured me forcefully, if he had known about the baby: he would have married her and taken her and the baby with him! I had no reason to disbelieve him. The sad thing was that seven months after Jan left, Violet had gone down the aisle with the recently demobbed Walter Reddy, who had taken a fancy to her and pity on her: she was, of course, also eight months' gone and half of the female population of Cobwycke was waiting outside the church to see if she would marry in white: that I knew from overhearing the Gledlang gossips. Wisely, she decided not to waste her clothing coupons and had borrowed an ordinary dress from a friend, a large one that fitted her changed figure, I suppose. Now almost two years later, here was Jan, the self-same long-vanished lover, back to claim her: it was going to be an interesting time, I thought. I would have known none of this if Jan had done the sensible thing: gone round the estuary by land, but he was too eager to get to see her, I suppose.

As he was writing the note, I tried to explain how the time of each tide was advanced by forty minutes so that no two tides were ever at the same time on the same day: it was second nature to me to work it out.

'When best for me to come?' Jan asked, pencil poised to write. 'Tomorrow?'

'No, no, hold on. I have to get the note to her,' I told him. 'That could take a couple of days. I know you're anxious, but you would be better waiting till Saturday. I can get the note to her by then and it's a three o'clock high tide. You would be better waiting till then, believe me.'

Jan eyed me closely. 'Okay, if you say. I say for her to meet me here on Saturday,' he informed me. 'Please take letter quick. I be here Saturday afternoon you say, when tide let me to come to island.'

It was almost eleven o'clock when we relaunched the dinghy, but there was still enough water for him to get back across the main southern channel, then take to one of the smaller creeks branching off it to get back to the Abbey Farm landing stage: first, I doused the fire in Richard's grate, then sneaked into the barn for one of Ben's older oars to replace the one Jan had lost: as a precaution, I watched him all the way round the prow of Norsea and as far across the channel to Abbey Farm as the darkness would allow.

I went to bed that night with Jan's note safely tucked into the inside pocket of my greatcoat and with a smile upon my face: for I knew the messenger would be well received by Violet Reddy, very well received.

THIRTY

DID I KNOW Violet Reddy? Jan could not have asked a sillier question! Oh, yes, I knew Violet Reddy. She was, I say without any shame or embarrassment, the great lust of my life! If there were one woman among the female population of Gledlang who filled my night-time fantasies, it was Violet Reddy: I had mooned over her and lusted after her ever since she, husband Walter and baby Thomas had come to live in a two-bedroom, clapboard cottage at the bottom of Shoe Street at the beginning of Forty-Six. Shame brought her to us, the shame of falling pregnant with no man to marry her – until Walter Reddy had offered, that is: that and the shame of the wagging tongues in her home village.

Being from Cobwyke, young and new to Gledlang, she did not have any friends among the village women: in fact, they shunned her, regarded her as a 'loose woman' because of her past, the kind who 'hung about outside soldiers' camps,' as they put it, and were forever gossiping about her: and, in what was the most deliberate snub of all, no one ever asked her to join their picking gangs.

During the spring and summer months most of the women left the village daily to work on the various farms around Gledlang: each farmer had his regular picking gang of garrulous mothers: from early June, through July, the heat of August and into the Indian summers of September, sometimes even into the duller days of October, you would see them tramping the various lanes and headland tracks in the early morning, trundling prams in which their babies still slept and on to which they had loaded spare clothing, clanking pails and shopping bags. The pails they used for picking, the shopping bags contained their lunches for themselves and their broods: but both could be, and were, used to smuggle back vegetables or fruit from the farmer's fields or orchards. And always running alongside, hanging on to their skirts or on to the sides of the prams were their whining, fractious, bleating pre-school offspring, begging their mothers to slow down or to pick them up and sometimes just defiantly flopping down on to the track and bawling as much with rage as tiredness, which, of course, only induced a matching rage from their mothers.

In the first months, they mostly lifted or picked early onions, cabbage and sprouts: in mid-June they stripped the pea and bean fields, in July you would see them crouched over rows of strawberries or bending their backs hour after hour down lines of black-currant, red-currant, raspberry and gooseberry bushes. By the time the heat of August came the tribe of mothers would be squatting on their haunches in the plum orchards scrabbling on the grass to fill the bushel boxes with Victorias and Pershaws shaken down by the farmhands. On bright September days you would see them balanced precariously at the tops of high step-ladders, half-hidden among the leaves and branches in the apple orchards, chattering away as they always did and carefully filling their metal pails. The picking season finally ended with the potato-lifting in late September and early October: this was the worst of all the jobs, frequently interrupted when the rains set in and too often completed in mud. The one constant about all this work was that your back was always bent: lesser mortals, I know, who tried to join these women came away at the end of the first day so stiff that they thought their vertebrae had fused together!

It was right at the start of the picking season the previous summer, as we started on our peas, that I first met Violet Reddy: Ben had got my mother to put a notice in Thorn's bakery window at the top of Shoe Street and in the post office-cum-grocery store in the Square asking for pea pickers to help Old Sago, herself and me with our seven acres. No one had come on the first day we picked: then Violet Reddy had turned up on the second day, the only woman from the village willing to cross to Norsea and join us. Perhaps she expected others to be there and she would at last be able to join them in their gossiping, become one of them, so to speak. If she did, she was sadly disappointed: getting pickers to come to Norsea was almost impossible: they just would not come. Most of the women, knowing that they could cross to the island only at certain times and on some days might have to leave before their picking day was halfway done and so lose money, just could not be bothered with the inconvenience of it all: others with tiny children feared being trapped by the tide halfway across and all of them drowned. So my mother, Old Sago and myself did the picking between us – till Violet Reddy came.

She came, I think, for several reasons: for something to do: because she lived at the bottom of Shoe Street and our field, on an island though it was, was the nearest and could be reached in twenty minutes of quick walking, even pushing a pram. She came, too, as I say, because none of the other women asked her to join their gangs when they went off to other farms: and she came also because she and husband Walter needed the money: a farmworker's four pounds ten was not much of a weekly wage with which to feed and clothe yourself and your wife and a toddler and pay the rent man.

She arrived one dismal, rainy, grey-skied mid-morning in June, pushing little Thomas in a pram: the tide was out and was not due back in till seven that evening so she would easily be able to return to the mainland at the end of the day and quite comfortably repeat the crossing over the next three or four days, which would enable her to put in a series of good money-earning sessions: it was enough for Ben: as she was the only one to come from Gledlang, he took her on, pleased to have her.

I was pleased, too: when she wheeled her pram to the end of the next row to mine and greeted me with that glorious, sunny smile of hers, it was one of most memorable moments of my life, insignificant as it may sound to others: it lifted my spirits to the sky and set my pulses racing in a way no female had done before: well, I was only fifteen at the time.

Violet then was only nineteen or twenty, with a pretty, oval face, milk-white skin, bright blue-violet eyes, smiling red lips and a mass of wavy blonde hair: best of all, like many of the younger women, she often wore tight parachute silk blouses, which showed off the shape of her breasts, and cinched skirts, which emphasised the curve of her hips and buttocks: that summer she had also worn thin cotton dresses which became see-through in the bright sunshine and stirred feelings in me which none of the Gledlang girls had been able to do at that time.

The first day she came, my mother and Old Sago were already well down their respective rows, stooping and straightening with the practised rhythm of longtime pickers as they ripped up the pea rice, plucked off the pods in a blur of flying fingers and pitched them into the pails at their feet and moved on. They worked too quickly for me: I was happily dawdling, day-dreaming mostly, already bored with the monotony of the work. I had started at six that morning, but by nine o'clock I was only twenty yards down my row whereas they were fifty yards along: I had picked just two forty-pound bags while they had picked six apiece.

The trouble was I disliked picking of every kind, whether I was picking peas, beans or potatoes: to me, they were all the same and I approached it the same as I approached hoeing: reluctant to start because I knew that, once I had started, there would be row after row to complete before I had finished, so depression set in early. Picking of any kind in the rain is as abysmal as hoeing in the rain: you get just as wet and your fingers get just as cold and bloodless ripping up the pea or bean rice and tearing off the pods as they do scrabbling for potatoes in the sodden earth or gripping the handle of a hoe for hour after hour: you get the same agonising backache and even trying to keep off the rain with a sack hood is just as futile: you get soaked exactly the same.

Happily, even as Violet Reddy came through the gate, the sun burst over the fields, the clouds rolled away and it was suddenly very hot: my sack hood, greatcoat and jacket I pitched on to the pea rice behind me: even my mother discarded her coat and picked in her flowered pinafore, though Old Sago gave the sun a wary glance, took off his outer coat and laid it atop a picked bag, but kept on his jacket. As he rejoined us, I turned to glance at Violet Reddy and saw with great joy that she, too, was taking off her coat and was preparing to pick wearing just her normal dress underneath.

It was not uncommon in the open peafields for mothers to let even the smallest of their children wander among the rows of discarded rice, but still keeping one eye on them while they worked: once out of his pram, off went little Thomas, dressed in his short blue trousers, check shirt and white sunhat, crawling through the lines of discarded pea rice, happy as a sandboy at the expanse of his freedom to roam. Eventually, curiosity brought him to my row to watch me and talk his baby talk: it pleased Violet no end when I responded to him, even though his attempt at speech was just a meaningless babble to me, punctuated by gurgles. I, of course, did most of the talking while he listened and stared up at me with big open eyes, wondering who I was, I suppose: still, it pleased Violet, especially when I took his hand and 'walked' him slowly back to her: I knew from the smile she gave me that those ten minutes with little Thomas had put me in her good books: make friends with the child and you make friends with the mother.

As soon as she had resettled little Thomas in his pram, Violet bent quickly to the task and proved to be as adept and nimble-fingered a picker as my mother, an ability which all the women of that region seemed to share by comparison with me: they picked and chattered and filled their pails with a coordination of hand and eye no man I knew possessed, not even Old Sago, who had been doing it for fifty years or more. Within an hour or so, Violet had already filled two of the half-dozen sacks Ben had given her and had started a third, while I was still just shaking down my own third, which was not much of a return for five hours' labour. As Violet worked her way forward on the row next to mine, it just so happened that I noticed the top two buttons of her dress were undone and that, every time she bent down to pull up the pea rice, her breasts hung inside in full view, soft and round, for, like many countrywomen, she wore no brassiere. It was at that moment that my obsessive lust first manifested itself with an embarrassing stirring in my loins. Whether Violet was aware of why, as she neared me, I was constantly turning back to talk to her, I do not know: all I know is she did not make any attempt to button herself up and it drastically slowed the pace of my own pea-picking. For a short time we worked side by side: the sight of her breasts hanging inside her dress each time she bent forward to tear up the pea rice both fascinated and excited me: mesmerised would be a better word. It was a sight that was unfamiliar to me. I had a wonderful urge just to reach out, slip my hand inside and cup one of those warm, soft orbs – there is nothing else one can call them – just to see what they felt like. It was a distraction and I was happy to have any distraction, especially as I was on a bad row, with pods half the size of everyone else's! And she was happy to have someone with whom she could talk.

Suffice it to say, I got a telling off from Ben when he came at midday to tie the first sacks because, from starting at six o'clock and working till lunchtime, I managed to pick only four sacks of peas, and one of those was underweight, when I ought to have had six or more.

I did work harder after lunch, but not because Ben had torn me off a strip: I worked harder because by then Violet Reddy was just ahead of me on the next row and the afternoon sun was so strong it shone straight through the thin material of her dress, outlining the silhouette of her legs so that you could see the slimness of her thighs, the roundness of her buttocks and the inviting arch of her quim. At the time, my mother and Old Sago were working down the other end of the field so there was no one else to notice. Working flat out, I managed to stay a few yards behind her all the way down the field: the erotic, masturbatory image of Violet Reddy's figure seen through the thin material of her dress that day, bending and straightening as she tore at the pea rice, is one of the abiding memories of my pea-picking days on Norsea.

One afternoon on the second or third day, when little Thomas had again been put to sleep on a bed of pea rice in a circle of full sacks, with an empty sack draped over to provide shade from the sun, Violet and I fell to chatting, and at some point in the conversation she asked me if I had a girlfriend. My answer, of course, was an embarrassed 'No': I did not get much opportunity to mix with girls, living on an island in the middle of a tidal estuary.

'What, a good looking boy like you!' she exclaimed, laughing at the grumpy solemnity of my reply. 'You ought to be able to get a girlfriend easily. There's lots of girls who'd like a nice looking boy like you. I don't reckon you try hard enough, do you?'

She was teasing me, I knew, and my blushing only made her laugh all the more: but I was, despite my shyness, vain enough to believe her flattery: I honestly did not think I was too bad-looking, nothing that a good haircut and a good wash would not fix. I had blue eyes, a haystack thatch of short, fine blond hair, white even teeth, and a face tanned a nice red from exposure to the sun, winds and rain and with just enough prominence to the cheekbones, I thought, to make it interesting, in a lean and hungry way. Standing five-feet-eleven inches, I regarded myself as slim when, in fact, looking at old photographs, I now realise that I was just plain skinny, gangling: I had a bit of muscle on my arms and shoulders from landwork, but I was bone thin everywhere else. When I stood up in the tin bath at home in the kitchen to dry myself, my stomach was almost concave so that my hip bones seemed to press out of the skin either side like my shoulder blades: I also had two sets of ribs you could count from twenty yards. It was on this day my lust to possess Violet Reddy began: in imagination, she was a nightly companion.

It is quite true that Violet had married Walter Reddy, lately of the Pioneer Corps (or battlefield clearer-uppers, as we called them), just to give baby Thomas a name: the women already knew that Walter was not the child's real father and, when she pushed her pram up to the baker's at the top of Shoe Street, or called in at the post office-cum-grocery store, or joined the queue outside the butcher's shed opposite the parish hall in Hedge Street, she would be greeted with those sickly smiles women give to each other when they pretend friendship, but never mean it. No sooner had she gone than some of the more acid-tongued would make some tarty remark, like: 'That's what comes of going with foreigners. Stick to your own, I say. At least they'll marry yer afterwards.' Or 'She's brazen about it, I'll say that for her, pushing that Polish brat about for all to see.' Or about Walter: 'He's just a bloody meal ticket and don't know it. Can't be any love there, not with a man ten years older than herself and with a face like he's got.' Or 'You mark my words, she'll be off with the first good-looking thing in trousers that comes along and asks.'

The knowledge that the child was not his was the prime reason why the older, uglier and more stupid Walter Reddy had left Cobwycke to live in Gledlang in the first place: as I say, he wanted to spare Violet her own village's sneers and no doubt to spare himself the behind-the-hands sniggers and grins of the Cobwycke menfolk whenever he walked into the Rose and Crown or the Red Lion there, snide remarks such as 'bringing up some Polack's sprog' or 'lying on a second-hand nest' or 'used goods is soiled goods.' By coming to live in Gledlang, I think, he more than she hoped that no one there would learn of it, but he reckoned without the gossips who meet on buses and Gledlang folk with relatives in Cobwycke. I do not think Violet was bothered by what the women said: if they did not wish to be friends with her, so be it. But Walter was a proud man and it hurt him: he wanted to protect Violet: he just could not believe that he had got a wife as young and as pretty as her: it made him proud, very proud, too proud really: she was more than he could ever have hoped to marry with a face as pug ugly as was his. Violet had the looks and figure, even after Thomas's birth, that made men turn their heads in the street: dopey Walter could walk out with her on his arm and know that other men were looking and envying him lying between her legs at night, while all they had to look forward to were their own swollen-bellied, lumpy bags where you were likely to spend half your time fingering the wrong crease.

The women were right about Walter's looks: one glance told you he had been a boxer, and a bad one: as a youth, he had fancied himself as the next Tommy Farr, Jack London, Ted 'Kid' Lewis or Jackie Lynch or some such, but among the professionals he was way down the league when it came to skill: his mess of a face showed the beatings he had taken at the hands of some very experienced bruisers. So he had turned to booth fighting and had spent the last two years before the war with a travelling fair, taking on all-comers: some said he had had too many mismatched cash-on-the-barrel fights in Sunday morning 'blood tubs' up North around Manchester and in the colliery clubs of the mining valleys of Wales, even taking on gypsy toughs in no-holds-barred contests staged in remote encampments in Wales and Northumberland: but, as the latter were supposed to be illegal, no one asked him about them.

Billy, my former friend, always described him as 'sixpence short of a shilling': most just considered he was 'punch drunk': I always reckoned that his brain must have been turned to mush inside his skull it had been bounced around so many times. He had the expected cauliflower ear, heavily scarred eyebrows and a horribly flattened nose and he also slurred his speech and was dimwitted almost to the point of imbecility. Sometimes when I spoke to him, there seemed to be a vacuum where his brain should have been, for he struggled to comprehend the simplest points of a conversation. If you told him something, he would look at you blankly for a few seconds before whatever was left of the pulverised porridge in his head sparked into comprehension. Even then, he would only give out a gormless 'Oh yeah, Joe, I know' as confirmation that he understood when you knew full well he did not understand at all: other times it would be just a moronic grunt and his eyes would go blank as if the very effort of thinking were too much for him.

Not surprisingly, with a wife as pretty and as shapely and as young as Violet, he was also a very jealous man: I knew from the way he peered at me sometimes when I called at their cottage, like he was trying to read my mind. Was I lusting after his wife? Could I be trusted while he was at work? Or was I sneaking back during the day to shag her when only he was supposed to? Well, the answer to those three questions was: Yes, I was: no, I could not: and, given even the slightest encouragement, yes, I would have. All youths dream and I was no different to the rest.

THIRTY-ONE

WHY ANYONE ever came to a place as remote and as dull as Gledlang never ceased to amaze me: Gledlang was a true backwater village, down a lane off a B road off an A road. It was not a big village, or a lively one for that matter, or an attractive one: not much ever really happened there, in the eyes of the locals: a few fights, a few squabbles, one day pretty much the same as the rest.

We were no more than three-hundred-and-fifty souls, most of whom lived in the older cottages grouped around the Square and down Shoe Street, plus a few scattered houses up Tithe Street as far the blacksmith's, with a few more squeezed into the first hundred yards of Hedge Street: only the luckier ones, lived in one of the two rows of 'new,' pre-war council houses extending along the west side of the Maydun road and a short way up Renter's Lane. Vast plum and apple orchards surrounded the village to the south, east and north, while to the west there were flat, open fields all the way to Maydun hill and the Greater Tottle ridge, both five or more miles away. There were four shops, the post-office-cum-grocery store in the Square, the baker's in Shoe Street and the butcher's along Hedge Street and a confectionery-cum-tobacconist along the Maydun road: Sligger Offin's garage stood opposite the church: there was a two-roomed, red-brick village school owned by the church which stood alongside Rex Book's tithe barn, and two public houses, the Chessman in the Square and the Bowler's Rest halfway up Tithe Street. Seven of every ten men worked on the various farms around the village, as did most of the boys who had left school and were too young for the army, like myself, about fifteen of us all told, and who were waiting to be called up for National Service.

Most of the older places in the village had no electricity, but were lit by paraffin lamps: very few had taps and most villagers collected their water from the old iron-wheeled pump in the Square. No running water meant no bathrooms and an outhouse at the top of the garden: for these houses, the 'golden cart' from Maydun came round fortnightly late on a Saturday night to empty the buckets of what was euphemistically termed 'night soil' by the rural district council: they usually came just after eleven o'clock, just as the last Bourne Brothers' bus from Maydun reached the village. Invariably, you would find your way 'blocked' by the tanker into which the men were cheerily tipping the contents of the buckets: the only way to escape the overpowering stench was to sprint past holding your breath or take to the fields and risk injury stumbling over ploughed furrows in the utter blackness.

But come people did: unexpectedly, two well-to-do women artists had finally answered one of Hoary's advertisements in the London newspaper: they wanted to come down and spend the whole of the summer and the autumn, too, on Norsea, painting in the quiet idyll of the countryside: from July till October, they said. The reason was quite simple: the Government was banning people from going abroad on holiday and so they were going to have to slum it in the countryside with us: they could not have known anything about Gleldlang when they answered the advertisement, except perhaps where it was on a map, or they would never have come. They certainly could not have known anything about Norsea: they were, I have to admit, the last people I would have expected to find in a place such as Gledlang: even worse to come across to Norsea to live, even if only for a while: but then I was prejudiced: I had been born in Gledlang, I had lived all my life on Norsea and all I ever did was dream of getting away from the place.

Not unexpectedly, the cottages on Norsea were dusty and grimy and full of cobwebs after years of non-use and would obviously need a good clean: Hoary immediately declared he must 'find someone to do it': he meant my mother, of course, but I knew there was no way she would do it. Hoary came round to the farmhouse that evening to ask her if she would be 'a good woman' and sweep out two of the cottages: my mother, recognising his way of knocking and forewarned by me that he was coming, flew to the door before Ben or I had even moved from our chairs.

'I'm not doing your bloody cleaning, I've already told you that!' was her furious reply to his request, just as I expected it would be. 'I've got more than enough of my own to do. Find someone else!'

Silly Hoary should have known she would fly at him: she had done it enough times. He tried to reassure her that it was only a small task and would not take up much of her time: both cottages could be done in a day, he said: and she was, after all, the only woman on the island,

'Benjamin's wife' and he was 'Benjamin's employer and landlord' and so he would have expected her to agree: and, also, there was no one else.

'I don't care how much time it takes, the answer is still no,' I heard my mother retort. 'If I were the last woman on earth, I still wouldn't do it. I'm no one's skivvy, least of all yours. I never have been and never will be. If you want the job done so bad, do it yourself! You've got a pair of hands like the rest of us, haven't you? I'll give you the bucket and mop, you have a go! Do some real work for a change.' And with that, she slammed the door in his face, leaving the poor man standing on the step, looking dismayed and perplexed: he was in a decidedly irritable mood as he marched off.

There the matter might have rested had I not met Jan and learned of his great desire to see his long-lost love and the progeny of a quarter-hour of horizontal passion on a coat behind a roadside hedge on the frozen dirt of some Cobwycke headland: baby Thomas.

At first, when I went round to the big house and knocked on his kitchen door, the old buffoon was not pleased to see me: it was two evenings after Jan's retreat to Lingsea and a week after my mother's blunt refusal: and Hoary was still smarting from the rebuff. 'It was very rude of your mother the way she spoke to me,' he sniffed when I broached the subject. 'I have asked Benjamin to have a word with her. I cannot allow myself to be spoken to in that way by the wife of someone whom I employ.'

There was not much point in me sympathising with him or telling him that Ben was unlikely to do any such thing: after all, we spoke to him like that all the time: so I just put forward my suggestion: 'I know a woman in the village who would be only too happy to clean your cottages, Mr Hoar. She's called Violet Reddy. She's new to Gledlang, but she was over here pea-picking and bean-picking and potato-picking last year so she knows the place. I am sure she would do it if I was to ask her. She'd come this Saturday for certain, I'm sure. I know she's looking for extra money and she'd do a good job. She's a good worker and she's young and capable. She might even agree to cleaning your house once a fortnight like you wanted. It could do with a bloody good clean and clearout, I reckon.'

Hoary's face brightened immediately. 'I'll pay her, of course, I'll pay her,' he cried, enthusiastically, his gap-toothed, gold grin returning.

'Write her a letter so she'll know the offer is genuine,' I instructed, 'and I'll take it across. She only lives at the bottom of Shoe Street so she'll be ideal. I'll ask her to come across about ten o'clock on Saturday. The tide will still be out then. High tide'll be about three so she'll be able to get back to the mainland by early evening teatime.'

It was not merely the tide of which I was thinking when I suggested these times: they were all a part of my plan: for, on the Saturday morning, I knew, my mother and Ben would be making their bi-monthly trip to Melchborough market fifteen miles away, ten miles the other side of Maydun. It was their day out, 'away from this place and him,' meaning Hoary, as my mother so thankfully described it: I think it kept them both sane, especially my mother, cooped up as she was on Norsea for days on end, with only the twice-weekly or thrice-weekly bicycle rides to Gledlang's shops to relieve the monotony.

Richard, too, had said he would be 'going across to the mainland' early that day, but did not say where: back up to London probably, continuing his silly and futile search for the woman Jean.

It meant, of course, that, apart from Hoary, who was unlikely to stray from his house, I would be the only other person on the island, till Violet and Jan came: and what could be better than that? It was the perfect set-up for their meeting.

THIRTY-TWO

I DELIVERED both Jan's message to Violet Reddy and Hoary's letter to her the very next day: I simply told Ben that I had to go across to the Reddys' cottage to take Hoary's letter and he accepted it because going across to their house was something I did at times for various reasons. Whenever the Maydun postman could not deliver our mail because of the tide, which was quite frequently, he simply left any parcels or letters for us or for Hoary at the Reddys' cottage. The arrangement went back to the previous summer when Violet had come pea-picking on Norsea that first time: my mother, taking a liking to her, had asked her if she would mind taking in the mail for us and so save either her or myself the extra half-mile trip up Shoe Street to the post office in the Square. Violet had said, 'Yes, of course.'

In the months since, the Reddys' cottage had become a regular picking-up and dropping-off point for us. As well as the postman, Kerry the Milkman now left our milk there three times a week in a half-gallon can: he would put the urn in a pail of cold water in Walter's shed at the back on a Monday, Wednesday and Friday and my mother would collect this along with any mail on her way back from her trips to the village's shops: and if she did not go, I went.

It was the same with the 'egg man': every two weeks my mother would take any eggs our chickens had laid and leave them at the Reddys' to be collected by the 'egg man' from Maydun: generally there would be about two or three-dozen: they were our quota to comply with the Government's edict. The 'egg man' cycled from village to village, towing his home-made cart and calling fortnightly at every farm and private house where chickens or pullets or geese were kept to pick up their egg production: for years he was a common sight around our area, pedalling along the highways and byways on his creaking bicycle, with the pram-wheeled cart swinging from side to side behind him: it needed only one careless Bourne Brothers' bus driver or lorry driver to come round a corner too fast and the whole of the Gledlang and district's fortnightly egg production would have ended up scrambled on the road.

Of course, we never gave him all our eggs: no one in their right mind ever filled their quota exactly: we always kept some back because there were always times when the chickens were, well, 'not laying' or the rooster was 'off colour' or eggs, being such fragile things, got 'broken': and we always gave Violet a couple or three (for little Thomas) for taking in our mail and milk. Even Hoary ignored the threat of Ministry fines for not fulfilling his quota and kept back duck and geese eggs: he always argued that his birds were 'wild' anyway and 'don't always lay where they should.' Fresh eggs were infinitely better than the waxed packets of dried egg powder we had received in food parcels from America during the war. Fortunately, for the poorer families of the village, those with six or seven kids and no father to bring in a wage, these had been superseded by tins of malt from Canada and chocolate powder from somewhere else, but best of all in Forty-Six and Forty-Seven, along with the peaches and other tinned fruit, were the food parcels containing large tins of boiled sweets – from Tanganyika, of all places!

Sometimes, as I say, my mother rode across specifically, sometimes she called on her way back from the butcher's or the baker's whether Violet was in or not: and sometimes she would ask me to go. Other times, if she did not ask, I would volunteer: really, it was no bother, I always told her: after all, it was no more than a five-minute ride there, was it? Of course, when I rode over, I always hoped that Violet would be in and, when work and the tide allowed, I always tried to call on Violet in the middle of the afternoon when she was alone and little Thomas would, I hoped, be asleep upstairs, so there would be just the two of us sipping tea in her kitchen.

She was, I think, glad to see me and to chat, particularly as husband Walter was out at work all day, from seven o'clock in the morning till almost six at night, and she had no one else in the village to whom she could talk: even after sixteen months in Gledlang she had not made any real friends and was very lonely.

In our kitchen conversations, Violet and I would talk about anything and everything: what I did on the farm, what I did (or once did) when I went to Maydun with Billy and Nick and the others: what I intended to do when the army called me up in a couple of years: the places I might visit, Germany, Palestine, Egypt, Hong Kong, Malaya, Libya: things like that. She was so pleasant and talkative, by comparison with my mother, the only other woman with whom I ever conducted a conversation, that I was only too happy to dawdle there. But I have to be honest: I looked forward to my visits to Shoe Street not really for the conversations but solely in the earnest hope that I might just see down her half-buttoned blouse again when she bent forward across the table to pour the tea or to hand me my cup or when she stooped to pick up one of little Thomas's wooden toys left lying on the floor. Being with her, watching her, talking and laughing, answering her questions, sometimes with great embarrassment, while porridge-brained husband Walter was out working on a farm along the Salter road and Thomas was asleep upstairs, was the high spot of my existence. I always washed my hands and face before I went and plastered down my hair with tapeline (water, to you): and I always pedalled across the causeway much faster than I ever did coming back and always with the same sublime hope in my breast that, by some womanly intuition or need of her own, or sheer devilment, she would fulfil my fantasies. Hope springs eternal, they say: mine never left me: it was always there.

Whether the Violet who smiled at me, laughed with me and chatted to me, who was friendly, welcoming and kind and above all who was pretty and had the right-size soft breasts and wore dresses and skirts that clung to her figure with the steaming damp of the kitchen – whether she ever knew how much I lusted after her, I do not know, but sometimes there would be laughter in her eyes as though she knew why I crossed my legs so awkwardly, avoided her eyes when we sat opposite each other at the table and why, when the time came for me to go, I invariably stood up and shuffled out with my jacket draped in front of my stomach. We all have an ideal woman in our minds whom we hope to meet: Violet Reddy was mine. I am not sure whether I should be ashamed now of the feelings I had for her then: after all, they were only the natural lusts of a sexually frustrated adolescent and did no harm. All I know is that when I sat in Violet Reddy's kitchen, always in my mind was the thought that I wanted to lie between her legs, to have her wrap them around me, to bury my face in her breasts and, as all young men want to do with a desirable woman, to enter into her and pump away at her and then explode within her, to die the little death and collapse exhausted upon her. Each time I crossed that causeway in the early afternoon, each time I pushed open the gate and wheeled my bicycle round the back and each time I caught her with the steam of the copper soaking the thin material of her blouse or dress, I was consumed by that hope, always dreaming as immature sixteen-year-olds do for the unlikeliest of things: that one day, sitting opposite me, she would reach out without being asked and touch me where I wanted her to touch me, saying something like: 'Ooh, have you got a hard on, Joe Coe? Ooh, yes you have! Nice. If you like, we can go upstairs on the bed and I can play with it for you? Don't worry, Walter's out at work. He'll never know. Come on, come upstairs with me. If you're really nice, I might even let you put it in. You'd like that, I bet.' And she would take me by the hand and lead me up to the bedroom ...!

Nothing ever happened, of course, and each time I rode away carrying the packet of letters or the parcel or the can of milk with the same despondency: but I dreamed on, week after week, month after month.

And yet I delivered Jan's love letter to her: why, I do not know even to this day: honour, maybe: because I had promised Jan and I could not break a promise? And because of what it would mean to Violet?

'Oh, my God, Joe! When? When did you see Jan? Where? Where?' was her reaction when I handed over the letter and told her who it was from. She read it twice, the first time with eyes wide, the second time half closed as though she did not believe what she had read the first time and could not bear to read it in case it was different from what she had first read, as if Fate were playing a trick upon her: there were tears of happiness in her eyes as she read the words and she was smiling and smiling and crying and crying and her manner was that of an excited schoolgirl.

'Oh, Joe, Joe,' she said with such a breathless sighing voice that my heart seemed to shrink physically in my chest with the realisation of how much it actually meant to her. 'Oh, Joe, you don't know how much I have longed for this letter to come and now it has and you have brought it to me. Oh, Joe, Joe.'

I knew as I watched her that I had lost her: I saw the brightness in her eyes and in that moment realised that any hope of fulfilling my great fantasy was ended: it would never come to pass now. She literally was crying with happiness the way women do: she had not expected to hear from Jan ever again: after all, he had been gone for more than two years: she had spent months resisting the shouted threats of her father and the tearful entreaties of her mother to find some backstreet harridan in Wivencaster or London and 'get rid of the bloody thing' – 'the bloody thing' which now turned out to be blond-haired little Thomas asleep upstairs. Now here was the man who had brought shame upon her family, who had supposedly deserted her, the cause of all her misfortunes (and I include marrying Walter Reddy as one of her misfortunes and coming to Gledlang as another), here he was writing a letter to her, asking for her forgiveness, telling her he had not known about the baby, that he thought she had forgotten him, that he still loved her and wanted her to meet him and, especially, to show him his little son.

I know because I wrote out the actual letter she was reading: Jan's attempts at the King's English were so lamentable as to be well nigh incomprehensible: even Violet realised I had written the words: he had just signed it. The irony of the situation did not escape me: that I, who lusted after Violet so greatly, should have written a letter of undying love to her, from someone else! I just wanted it to be right for Violet, that's all.

'How can I meet him, Joe? Oh, how can I meet him?' she sighed again, almost in despair now. 'Where? Where? He can't come here. If Walter ever found out, he would kill me. Oh, Joe, where can I meet him, where can we be together, Jan, Thomas and me?'

That was when I gave her the second letter: the answer was on Norsea, of course: isolated Norsea that very Saturday. Violet would show Hoary's letter to Walter and he would accept it for what it was, an offer of cleaning work, albeit from a dotty old man on an island: he would never suspect in a thousand years that Violet would be across there meeting her long lost love. The two London artists could not have decided to come at a more auspicious time.

Her eyes were brimming with tears when I left: that was the only time she ever kissed me: on the cheek, I have to say: still, I did feel the softness of her body briefly pressed against me and the coolness of her skin as her arms went around my neck: there will always be the memory of that.

THIRTY-THREE

VIOLET REDDY came over to Norsea just before ten on the Saturday, pushing young Thomas atop an overloaded pram: the little chap was perched on the apron, squealing half in delight, half in fear each time the rickety machine juddered against an exposed rock or lurched sideways in the mud. Several times it seemed he would be pitched on to the causeway shale, but this only brought even louder cries of terror and delight from him. They were halfway across when I first saw them, so, for the sake of little Thomas, I went out to meet them and to help Violet steer the lopsided pram over the last three-hundred yards.

The reason Thomas sat atop the apron was because into the well of the pram itself Violet had piled all the things she considered she would need to clean Hoary's two cottages: two pails, a mop, a broom, a dustpan and brush, a bundle of Walter's old shirts for use as washing and polishing rags, plus a cardboard box containing such things as Dettol, Brasso, Vim, soap powder, black leading for the grates and even polish for the non-existent furniture, as well as a black kettle and saucepan for boiling water, all of it packed into a tin bath resting on the pram's mattress: it was on top of all this that little Thomas, now all of nineteen months and dressed in his Sunday best, was perched.

Violet, I noticed, had taken great care with her own appearance, too: for Jan's benefit, of course. She had lipsticked her mouth a bright cherry red, her cheeks were powdered a warm pink and her eyes were shadowed in pale blue and carefully outlined and she had washed and waved her blonde hair especially so that its natural gold shone in the morning sun. She was not dressed in anything special: just a pale yellow dress which accentuated the slimness of her figure and the narrowness of her waist and which every now and again flared up in the breeze to reveal a glimpse of a white lace-edged petticoat. Pushing the pram in her flat shoes, white ankle socks and cardigan, she resembled not so much a married woman as an unfortunate schoolgirl caught out by some youth's lust and abandoned to her fate: but to me that day she appeared prettier and more desirable than ever.

'He hasn't come yet, has he?' she asked eagerly as I joined them, forgetting the whole plan I had devised: she was just desperate to see the man, I suppose.

'No, not yet,' I told her, a little irritated by her impatience. 'He won't be here till this afternoon, like I said, not till the tide is up enough for him to cross the channel from Abbey Farm and that won't be till then.' Her face lost its happy smile of greeting and she pouted with displeasure, like lovestruck schoolgirls are apt to do when the fickle male object of their desire fails to respond in the way they wish him to do. Poor Violet: despite her unwillingness to wait, I felt sorry for her.

'Don't worry,' I consoled, giving little Thomas a wink which made him smile. 'He'll be here, I'm sure of it.'

'Oh, I do hope he comes, I do so hope he comes,' she sighed: then as if to cheer herself and counter Thomas's concern at her frowning face, she suddenly leaned forward the way mothers do and rubbed her nose against his to make him laugh, all the time cooing at him: 'You're going to see your daddy today, Thomas, your real daddy. Yes, you are, yes you are, your real daddy. Won't that be nice? Won't that be lovely, Thomas? Your real daddy.' The child just looked at her with a puzzled frown of his own, pleased that he was being shown such attention, but wondering what his mother meant by it.

Violet continued to fuss over the little chap all the way up on to the hard, one minute teasing him, the next acting all wistful and girlish: 'I can't wait to see him, Joe. It's been so long. I just want to see him again and hug him. I'll die if I don't, I'll die!'

'He'll come,' I reassured her and then, as we wheeled the pram along the track, added in a silly show of bravado: 'If he doesn't, I'll bloody well go over in our punt and fetch him!'

It was not such an idle boast as it may seem: for the thought had crossed my mind more than once that, because of fate or circumstance, Jan might not be able to keep his assignation as he intended. For instance, despite what I had told Violet, there was a chance he might not be able to 'borrow' the rowboat again, or he might have had to work and been unable to get away, both possibilities. With this in mind, I had taken the precaution earlier that morning of dragging Ben's punt down on to the shingle beach, ready to launch it and cross to Lingsea if needs be.

As much as I lusted after Violet, I could not bear to have seen her disappointed: I knew, too, in my heart, that, if Jan did not come, she would not turn to me for solace: she would have returned tearful and depressed and bewildered to Walter and I would have been left in the same position as before. Jan, the fair-haired Polack, the father of her child, was the man she loved, the love of her life, and Walter was her husband by law and by marriage lines: if she could not go to one, she would return to the other. Me, she regarded as a friend, nothing more: all I would ever have of her was her image in my mind's eye receiving me in during my night-time fantasies.

'Any problems with Walter?' I asked tentatively: I needed to know just for reassurance.

'No,' sniffed Violet, slightly put out that I had even mentioned him in what were to be her hours of joy. 'I showed him Mr Hoar's letter and he never said a word other than "Be careful crossing." I left him some cold dinner, corned beef, beetroot and potatoes. He'll be on his allotment all this afternoon.'

I thought of poor Walter dourly digging on his allotment while his young wife was joyously and willingly being shagged by another man: well, it was more than likely that is what she would be doing: even I expected that! It was just as well Ben and my mother were not there: they had been gone over an hour already on their bi-monthly trip to Melchborough market before Violet came over. In my eagerness to get them on their way, I had even volunteered to feed Molly, the chickens and the pig, Percy. As my mother mounted her bicycle, she had eyed me suspiciously, as if to say, 'I know you're up to something, but I don't know what – yet.' Had she known of the assignation I had arranged between Violet and Jan, she would have had a few choice words to say on the matter, I am sure, much as she liked Violet, whereas Ben would almost certainly have chased Jan off the island altogether if he had caught him skulking about: a four-ten shotgun can be a powerful persuader when pointed at your crotch.

They had set off for the mainland soon after eight: Ben led as usual, pedalling slowly on his creaking Raleigh because of his arthritic knee, my mother wobbling along behind on her high-handlebar machine like she always did, deliberately going more slowly so as not to overtake him: the man must lead, the woman must follow. Everything about their bi-monthly day out was predictable: they would leave their bicycles at the rear of the Chessman as usual, catch the morning Bourne Brothers' bus into Maydun as usual, take the National double-decker to Melchborough as usual, spend the morning going round the market as usual and the afternoon going round the shops as usual, before catching the five o'clock National back to Maydun and the seven o'clock Bourne Brothers' return bus to Gledlang as usual. They would be back about eight o'clock as usual: it never varied. In the meantime, the tide would have come in and gone out.

Despite the fact that the morning was half gone, Old Hoary was still abed when I banged on the kitchen door at the rear of the big house for the keys to the two cottages which Violet was to clean: it took three or four minutes of sustained hammering before he pulled open the door a matter of inches and peered out into the bright morning light, bleary-eyed and unsmiling.

'What is it? What is it?' he demanded impatiently in the manner of a man who considers he should be disturbed only if his house is on fire and for no reason other than that. From the puzzled expression on his face and the irritation in his voice, it was clear he did not know who Violet was or why she was standing outside his back door with a tot atop a loaded pram: I quickly reminded him.

'It's Mrs Reddy, you daft old fool!' I shouted through the gap. 'She's come to do the cottages. You asked her to, for God's sake!' So he would see better, I gave the door a push and it swung open to reveal Hoary in the full glory of his bedroom attire: blue-striped nightshirt, multi-coloured patterned pullover, odd woollen socks and brown balaclava. Out of the corner of my eye I saw Violet gasp in astonishment: I can only assume that she had never seen such an apparition before. As for little Thomas, they say children have a sixth-sense where peculiar adults are concerned: the little chap took one look at the gap-toothed Hoary standing in the doorway in all his weird wonderment, unshaven, hair disordered, and burst into tears.

Realisation dawned and Hoary shuffled off muttering to himself, then came back a minute later with the keys: I gave him a terse and ungrateful 'Thank you. About bloody time!'

'Do you always talk to him like that?' Violet asked, surprised, as we walked away, me pushing the ungainly pram, she cradling the tearful Thomas in her arms.

'Oh, yes,' I lied. 'It's the only way you can get through to him. He's a bloody lunatic anyway. Completely dotty. He hasn't got a clue how to run a farm. Ben and I run it for him, or, more like, for his brother in London because he's the one who owns it. Even I know a hundred times more about farming than Hoary does. He wasn't brought up to it, was he? Not like me.'

It was all bombast pure and simple to impress Violet: I know that I felt immeasurably more grown-up having said it and, for some peculiar reason, I also considered I might, too, just have grown a little more in her esteem.

When we reached the first of the cottages, we unloaded the pram and I ushered Violet and little Thomas inside: I had been in the cottages before so their condition was less of a shock to me than it was to Violet. The place was dusty and damp and there was a smell of mildew everywhere: the grate had not been raked since the Wrens had left seven years before because my mother had always refused Hoary's pleas and blandishments to do it. A draught from somewhere had blown a covering of fine ash half across the floor: cobwebs of various ages in which desiccated flies and other insects were entangled hung across the windows: dead wasps from the previous autumn lay on the sill: there were mouse droppings underfoot and, as I entered, a black beetle scurried away into a dark corner.

'Oh, my God!' exclaimed Violet in some alarm. 'I didn't think it would be this bad. And I've got my best dress on, too. I wish I hadn't put it on now.'

It was too good an opportunity to miss. 'You can always take it off,' I grinned: it was a cheeky comment, but a deliberately bold one: I wanted to show her that I was not shy of women when, in fact, I was.

'Joe Coe!' Violet cried, looking astonished. 'I'm surprised at you, saying things like that. And if I do,' she added with a coquettish tilt of her head, 'you won't be there to see me.'

Unsure whether her shock was feigned or real, I decided I had to get back in her good books, tentatively asking: 'Is there anything I can do to help?'

'You can fetch me some water,' Violet informed me, sternly. 'I need water and lots of it. You can fill the tin bath for me from that pump outside. A half-dozen bucketsful should be enough for now. While you do that, I'm going to get a fire started somehow. I'll have to boil the water. This place needs scrubbing and disinfecting from top to bottom.'

It did and so did the second cottage: I carried bucket after bucket from the pump to the cottage and tipped it into the tin bath: Violet, meanwhile, had gathered up some pieces of wood from outside to make a fire: to ingratiate myself even more in her good books, I went to Richard's unlocked cottage and filled a bucket with some of his coke and wood. He would not need it: it was early summer and there was plenty of time till the first mists of autumn came and Ben ordered our coke for the winter, which the coal merchant from Maydun dumped at Boundary farm on an appointed date in September and we went across with Molly and the wagon to bring it back.

Violet stood in the centre of the parlour in the first cottage, hands on hips, surveying the task ahead of her.

'Is there anything else I can do?' I asked, in hope.

'Yes, you can look after Thomas for me,' she replied. 'Take him for a walk or something. Show him your horse. He knows you, he'll be all right with you. This is going to take longer than I thought.'

'How long do you want me to take him for?' I hoped she would not notice the dejection in my tone.

'Two hours at least,' she said and my heart sank. 'It'll take me at least two hours to do these properly – maybe longer if the other one is like this one – ' It was. ' – Can you do that for me?'

I could and would, albeit reluctantly. 'Oh yes,' I said cheerfully as I took little Thomas's tiny hand: I would much rather have stayed to watch her work, solely in the hope that I might just accidentally catch a glimpse of something, some part of her that I had not seen and was not supposed to see. It is the way things are with youths: it made life exciting for me then to see parts of a female's anatomy, especially that of a young female, which I was not supposed to see.

It was at this point that Violet extracted a solemn promise from me: it was not 'Look after Thomas, whatever you do,' but a more selfish: 'Joe, when Jan comes, whatever you do, don't let him come here till I say so. Come and tell me first. Please. Please. I don't want him to see me till I'm ready. Promise me.' Vanity.

I promised and spent the next two hours walking and carrying little Thomas round the island: we went on to the beach where we searched for shells and different coloured pebbles: then into the stable where I showed him Molly, and finally on to see the pig and the chickens and Hoary's ducks and geese. He toured the whole of the island, perfectly at ease in my company and happy as a sand boy at being free to roam as he wished, to pick up sticks, peer into ditches, splash through puddles and scale our gates. The two of us had a grand time till he began to smell and I had to carry him back to the cottages: he was asleep in my arms by the time I got there.

As I passed the window of the second of the two cottages I had shown to Violet, I just happened to glance in: she was still down on her hands and knees scrubbing the bare floorboards and I saw why she had been so keen to get rid of me. To do the cleaning, she had stripped off her dress and petticoat to just her underwear and put on a loose pinafore which she had not bothered to tie properly at the back so that it hung loose: it gave me a side view of her unbrassiered breasts hanging down and her red-knickered rear in the way I had always dreamed I would see her: it was a fascinating, erotic sight and I stood transfixed. My dilemma was whether I could summon the courage to barge in upon her, accidentally on purpose, and maybe catch a gloriously fuller view of her, or whether I ought to knock and call out: in the end I gave in to decorum – or was it cowardice? – and called out.

'Wait a minute! Wait a minute!' came Violet's alarmed cry and I heard the scurrying of feet before she appeared at the door, red-faced and perspiring, the pinafore now disappointingly tied and closed to the neck. She made a pretence of scolding me for returning 'too soon' and seeing her like that, then took little Thomas from me and carried him inside, where she laid him gently on the pram mattress so as not to wake him: I noticed that, as she laid the little chap down, she ensured I did not see anything I should not.

'What time is it?' she asked apprehensively: I pulled out my old pocket watch with its battered brass case and told her it was just before half-past-twelve. Violet relaxed at that. 'I've nearly finished in here,' she explained, 'but I've still got things to finish in the other cottage. They'll take me an hour or more. Then I want to get ready. I want to look my best for when Jan comes.'

I fetched some more water for her, as requested, and then was ushered out. 'Go and get some dinner,' Violet ordered. 'I need you to keep a lookout for Jan. I want to know the minute you see him coming. I don't want him sneaking up on me and seeing me looking like this.'

She looked all right to me: she was still attractive and desirable, I thought, even with grey ash on her face and arms and perspiration shining on her cheeks and forehead, and dressed in a flowered pinafore: but that, I suppose, was the last thing on her mind.

So I went off to a dinner of my own corned beef sandwiches spread with mustard, listening to the wireless till some brass band from some colliery town in Yorkshire started playing: then I switched it off and went down to the beach just after two o'clock to keep a lookout for Jan.

THIRTY-FOUR

IT WAS just as well I did go down to the beach to watch for Jan: he was no more than fifty yards from the shore, sculling in with more expertise than I would have imagined: I could only surmise that he had been practising. We hailed each other and Jan beached the boat and leapt nimbly ashore.

'She's here,' I told him before he had even asked the question, 'but she says you're to wait here and I am to go and fetch her.' A white lie, but it sounded reasonable.

'She bring baby Thomas?' Jan wanted to know as we tugged the boat up on to the shingle and secured the painter around a rock. Hardly a baby, Jan! He's very nearly two years of age!

'Yes, he's here. They're both here,' I reassured him. 'Violet wants you to wait here because she wants to put on her make-up first. She wants to look nice for you. I'll go and fetch her.'

In case he did not understand all the words, I gave a short mime of a woman powdering her face and putting on lipstick: I think Jan thought I had gone a little stupid. 'Okay, I wait,' he said, shrugging.

I left him sitting on the low bank at the top of the beach, rather reluctantly and somewhat impatiently, I have to admit, while I went loping off to the cottage to tell Violet. I could not help but grin as I approached: she was standing in the doorway looking pensive and frowning: she had cleaned her face, put on her clothes, redone her make-up and was looking just as good as when she had first crossed that morning. You would not have known she had just spent more than three hours scrubbing floors, cleaning out grates, washing down woodwork, doors and windows, and even washing the fading wallpaper on both parlour walls. She had done a thorough job and I was glad of that: it meant my recommendation of her, slyly and selfishly done as it was, had been vindicated: it also meant Old Hoary would have no reason to dispute payment, which he was quite apt to do at times for the most innocuous of reasons.

'He's come,' I called out while still some thirty yards from her, 'he's come. He's down on the beach.'

My grinning face had given the game away long before I shouted: Violet gave a little squeal of pure joy: one hand flew to her face and she vanished inside the cottage: when she reappeared she was carrying the now awake Thomas in her arms. 'Thank you, Joe,' she cried, tears brimming in her eyes as she rushed past. 'Thank you, thank you.'

Then she was gone, hurrying along the track towards the beach, cradling Thomas: I followed for fifty yards or so, curious to see what happened at their meeting. Violet must have been calling out Jan's name, for he suddenly appeared on the track and stretched out his arms. Perhaps because of the child they did not kiss straight away, as I had expected they would, but just hugged each other: you could see that Violet was weeping, with happiness, I presume, while Jan just enveloped her and the child in a bear hug and buried his face in her hair: it was all very emotional. Poor little Thomas was the one who did not seem happy: as Jan put his arms around his mother, he pulled away in fright and terror and must have burst into tears again, for the two of them, both smiling and laughing at the little chap, spent some time trying to console him: and when Jan took the little fellow in his arms, he struggled and had to be given back to his mother.

The three of them disappeared down on to the beach and I went back to the cottages and spent some time piling Violet's things back into the pram, then I sat and smoked and mooched around for another half-hour or so. Eventually, Jan and Violet came strolling along the track: she had her arm hooked through his in that possessive way young women do when they claim a man, while Jan was carrying Thomas high on his shoulders, gripping the toddler's feet in front so he did not fall: the little chap appeared to have got over his earlier fears, for he was smiling happily at the world, delighted at being so dangerously high up.

I knew what Violet was going to ask even as they approached: the very happiness shining in her eyes and the doleful expression demanding my sympathy and understanding told me that. 'Joe, would you look after little Thomas for me again?' she asked, blinking her eyes at me. 'Just for half an hour or so. Jan and I want to talk.' Talk! It would have been more honest if she had given a knowing wink, but she just smiled shyly and lowered her gaze. Jan at least had the good grace to look embarrassed, even if he did follow it with a huge grin:

only little Thomas seemed perturbed when Jan handed him down to me, turning to his mother and emitting pitiful little cries.

Violet managed to reassure him that she was not leaving him and that it would be all right if I took him off around the island again: it has to be said my mind was not exactly on the task: even as I was leading Violet and Jan's son along the headlands, sitting him on gates and generally trying to keep him interested in something so that he would not get tearful and frightened, I could not dismiss from my thoughts that at that very moment Jan and Violet were engaged in a passionate squeezing, stroking, kissing, groaning, bucking shagging for which they had waited more than two years! I could imagine it, but I could not actually see it and I do not know which vexed me most, the thought of what she was willingly doing with him or the knowledge that she would never ask me to do it now that she had Jan back. Somehow dopey Walter came into my thoughts: the fact that his wife was at that very moment willingly, happily, lovingly committing adultery and I was conniving in it brought a sudden chill sweat of fear to my brow: a few dandelions lost their heads to my agitatedly swishing stick that afternoon. Little Thomas thought it was great fun and, though he could not understand why I swished so hard, he nevertheless followed me along the hedgerow laughing and hacking at everything with a short, thin broken branch-end.

I gave them threequarters-of-an-hour to satiate their lust — that should be enough for anybody — then picked up Thomas and piggybacked him back to the cottages: Violet and Jan must have finished sometime before, for they were sitting outside on the grass: Jan was smoking and Violet was leaning against him, her head resting on his shoulder, the two of them just sitting there, side by side, not talking, content to be together and to bask in the warm late afternoon sunshine. They made such a contented couple that something in me made me say it.

'Wouldn't it be great,' I said, 'if Jan could work on Norsea?' And as Violet's face brightened at the suggestion: 'He could help us with pea-picking when we start. He could even live in one of the cottages while he did it! I'm sure Hoary would let him. He lets Old Sago and Richard. You'd be able to meet whenever you wanted then.'

Violet and Jan looked at each other and Violet's eyes brimmed with tears again. 'Oh, Joe, if only he could?' she sighed. 'Do you think you could ask your step-father?'

'Sure,' I promised. 'As soon as we're ready to start the picking. We'd be glad of the help.'

After Jan had departed on the ebbing tide, with much weeping and sadness from Violet and bemusement from Thomas, I hitched up Molly to the wagon and the two of us loaded it with furniture which Hoary, in an unusual moment of sanity, realising the cottages needed furnishing, had had me pull out of the outhouse where the discards were stored: as the tide ebbed, we trundled it round to the cottages with Thomas standing at the front holding the reins, held by his mother, of course. If I promised Violet once that I would keep her secret, I must have promised her fifty times!

Violet helped me lift in the furniture, taken from the many former servants' bedrooms: she gave it all a final polish, then it was time for her and Thomas to leave, for it was almost six o'clock and by that time the causeway was uncovered enough for them to cross safely: and Walter would be wanting his tea. To be safe, I walked them back across.

Ben and my mother returned just before eight: I expected Ben to ask what I had been doing, but it was my mother who asked instead: when I told her – not everything – she made her views known, as was to be expected. What I remember particularly about that conversation was what she said when I queried why Ben had gone into the front parlour and was slumped in his chair.

'He's worn out,' she said. 'All this business with him is wearing him out. Can't you do something about it?'

By 'this business with him,' she meant, of course, the feud with Richard: I shrugged and muttered something in reply about what could I do that would change the situation? My doings made no impact upon the world whatsoever!

THIRTY-FIVE

THE ONLY actual war damage we ever had on Norsea was our bomb hole: the dilapidated lean-to wagon shed had been shaken by the blast from a doodlebug which fell in the river a mile away near Cobwycke in the autumn of Forty-Four, but had remained standing, just: thus, the bomb hole in the middle of a field at Eastern Point remained our prime example of the wanton destructiveness of the Hun. It had been made in Forty-One by a Heinkel 111, which came sneaking up the river, machine-gunning the cows and everything else and sending the women picking fruit in John Bolt's plum orchards scattering in terror: I know, I was there, aged eleven and on the six-week school holiday at the time.

The first inkling we had of the sneaky bastard was when one of the women came running down the lines of plum trees screaming her head off for everyone to take cover: children were grabbed without ceremony and hurled into the nearest ditch with an adult on top of them. Even I managed to snatch up Mary Chaplin's four-year-old, Joseph, and sprint for the ditch with him in my arms: the only problem was he did not want to go and kicked me violently on the forehead: I had the bruise for a fortnight afterwards.

As the Heinkel wheeled over the river, a Hurricane came roaring up from nowhere and the air was filled with the rat-a-tat-tat of machine-guns. Everyone assumed the lone German was after the motor torpedo boats at Cobwycke or the searchlight battery manned by the small army contingent on Gledlang Park. He missed both and, as the Hurricane dived on his tail, he unloaded his bombs over the river: all the better to get away, I suppose. He dropped a stick of six: five created black geysers in a line across the Stumble mud: the sixth made a fifteen-foot-deep crater in our field. The last I saw of the Heinkel was it disappearing out to sea trailing smoke: I neither know nor care whether the crew made it home: I hope they crashed: after all, the buggers were shooting at me! Well, as far as I was concerned, they were shooting at me.

We wired off the bomb hole, of course, and, when the time came, ploughed around it. We would have gone on doing that if Hoary had not decided it must be filled in so that the foolish townies who were going to come did not fall into it. Of course, I was designated to do it and I railed against it. 'It's a bloody waste of time. I know it's there, you know it's there, even Molly knows it's there! What do I have to waste my time filling it in for?'

'Because I say so, boy,' was Ben's phlegmatic answer.

I was supposed to use some bricks from a demolished partition wall in the wagon shed, lying in our yard, but, for some reason, laziness, perhaps, or sheer bloody-mindedness, I still had not got around to doing it when Ben and Hoary had their argument on the front doorstep: it was early evening the following Saturday and I was in the parlour trying to tune the wireless to one of the European stations, Hilversum, I think, in the hope they would have on better music than the bilge the Light Programme was playing.

'I shall need Joseph tomorrow. I must have him. There is no one else,' were the first words I heard Hoary cry.

'Well, you can't bloody have him.' Ben's voice, angry and adamant. 'He's needed here and, come Monday, he's supposed to be filling in that bloody bomb hole you want done. I've been waiting all week. That'll be his first job on Monday.'

I crept into the passageway to listen: Ben's back was blocking the doorway, but I could see Hoary's bare legs and sandalled feet through the gap. 'But I need him, too, Benjamin. I must have him. There just isn't anyone else.' So nice to be so wanted.

Ben, suspicious now: 'What do you want him for? Not for your bloody daft diggings, is it?'

Hoary's pitiful whine again. 'I am going up into the next county tomorrow. I have only Stanley Lobel from Tottle to help me. I need someone else – Joseph – to help us dig.'

Ben, indignant: 'You've got the other one.' Meaning Richard. 'Why do you want to take him for?' Meaning me.

A bleat from Hoary: he knew he was on dangerous ground here. 'Your son, Richard, is unwell. He is not at all well. He says he is unable go with me this time. He is too ill.'

Ben, disbelieving: 'What's the matter with him?

'He has a bad chest. His lungs, I think. He is much too ill to travel. He is in bed with a fever and his breathing is affected. I cannot possibly ask him to come with us.'

Just a low growl from Ben. 'And what do you want me to do about it?'

'I need Joseph to replace Richard. You cannot expect young Stanley to dig all by himself. Come, come, Benjamin. I am sure you can spare Joseph for a few days.'

A curse from Ben: 'A few days! How long is a few days?'

Hoary, airily: 'Oh, three days, four days. Tomorrow, Monday and Tuesday, Wednesday, possibly. I don't think it will take any longer than that.' A funny nervous laugh here. 'Surely, you can spare Joseph for just three days, Benjamin?'

Ben, exploding: 'Three days! Three bloody days! And what am I supposed to do while he's gallivanting around half the country with you and that bloody Tottle-ite? You tell me. I can't run a bloody farm on my own. I need help sometimes.'

'It's only for three or four days, Benjamin. There is not a lot that needs doing at the present? I am sure things can wait till we return.'

Ben, sarcastic: 'Oh, and you would know that, would you? There's enough that needs doing to keep the both of us busy for the next three bloody months or more. Things don't grow themselves, you know. They need a bit of help from the likes of us. You can't wait around on a farm scratching your arse all day and sucking on a piece of straw. You might be able to, but I can't.'

It was a deliberate insult, but it did not dissuade Hoary: he stuck to his demand: 'I need Joseph, Benjamin. I need him to dig for me. I have no one else.'

'Why can't you do the digging instead of him,' a fuming Ben tried one last time, emphasising the 'you,' 'You're quite capable of picking up a spade and digging a hole, aren't you? You've got two hands and half a brain, why can't you do it?' Shades of my mother there.

Hoary horrified. 'You cannot expect me to do the digging. I have never done manual work. That is why I pay others to do it. Oh no, Benjamin. Oh, no. Ha, ha.'

'Then maybe it's about bloody time you started!'

Ben's unsympathetic retort was met with another manic, gold-glinting 'Ha, ha' from Hoary.

Outright sarcasm now from Ben: 'What are you after this time, King John's treasure lost in The Wash?' Followed by a displeased, even hopeful: 'With luck, you might get lost yourself and do us all a favour.'

An even louder and near screeching 'Ha, ha' from Hoary. 'No, no, Benjamin, I am hoping to uncover a Roman pier in an estuary very like the Langwater. I want to prove that the Romans traded there, too. They did not just sail up to Wivencaster with their merchandise, you know. I believe they had other ports and traded all along this coast. So you see, Benjamin, we shall be uncovering a little bit of England's history.'

'And what good'll that do?' demanded Ben, contemptuous now. 'Even if you find a Roman pier, you won't be able to tie a boat up to it, will you? It'll have rotted away like everything else. It ain't going to be of any use to anybody, is it?'

Hoary, condescendingly: 'I would not expect you to understand, Benjamin. You are not educated enough to understand such things. You are, after all, just a farm worker.'

'I'm your brother's bloody bailiff!'

Hoary, petulantly now: 'There is no need to swear, Benjamin. You have an agreement with my brother that, as part of your duties managing this farm, you are to assist me from time to time should I ever require it. I expect you to adhere to that. I require Joseph and he must come and help me before all else. That is the agreement. That is all I will say on the matter.' Hoary was getting annoyed now.

I had come up behind them in the passageway by this time. Ben heard me and turned. 'Do you want to go on this daft digging lark, boy?' he demanded. I think he knew the answer even as he asked the question.

'I wouldn't mind,' I said, but not too enthusiastically. 'It'd make a change. Be like a holiday. Away from Norsea for a few days.'

I knew instantly I had said the wrong thing. 'A holiday! A bloody holiday! I'd like a bloody holiday myself sometime,' Ben raged. 'But I can't afford it, can I? I've got this farm to run, haven't I? I've got my livelihood to look after. Bloody holiday indeed!'

His anger grew greater. 'Bloody go, if you must! I don't care. If you want to go, go. I'll fill the bloody bomb hole in myself – when I get time – if I get time. It ain't no use asking you to do anything on this farm, boy, because half the time you don't bloody do it!' Then as if to make me feel even more guilty, he railed: 'I suppose I'll have to ride over to Gledlang and ask Old Sago to come across early. I'll have to ask a man of seventy-five to come across and do your work – do more than he should, more than he's capable of doing just because you want to go gallivanting about up in the next county digging bloody holes with him!'

Wheeling back to face Hoary, he cried, 'You can bloody take him for all I care!' and slammed the door in the old man's face: through it,

I heard Hoary calling out: 'Nine-thirty tomorrow morning, Joseph. Nine-thirty tomorrow morning. Mr Offin will be taking us all the way.'

'Yes, Mr Hoar,' I shouted back. 'Nine-thirty.'

Ben had not finished with me yet. 'The next time I tell you to do a job, bloody do it!' he rapped. 'Two weeks ago I told you to shift those bloody bricks in the yard after you'd finished work and tip them into that hole, them and the ones from that old fool's outhouse which your friend – ' He meant Richard again. ' – demolished and left lying about.' I was supposed to have done it using Molly and the four-wheeled wagon: in view of the mood Ben was in, I thought it prudent not to mention Jan the Polack just then.

Later that evening I went round to see what Richard's illness was and found him propped up in bed, looking very weak. 'It's just a cough,' he said. 'It's got on my chest and I seem to be bringing up a lot of stuff.' He coughed even as he said it, his face creased with pain, one arm clutching at his ribs as the violence of the spasm bent him forward: at one point he swayed as though he were going to faint and almost fell sideways out of bed: he would have done had I not steadied him.

'Having the wound the Japs gave me doesn't help,' he gasped as the coughing fit subsided. 'I'd be all right but for that. It makes coughing more painful.'

I made him a cup of tea and a piece of buttered toast and told him we had a bottle of old linctus which MacFadden had prescribed for Ben a couple of years before: I would try and sneak that to him before I left in the morning.

'So you're going after all,' Richard managed to smile. 'I never thought Ben would agree. I told Hoary to ask you. It'll do you good. You'll enjoy it. I'm sorry I'm not going with you. We could have had a laugh together.'

It was a perspiring, grey-faced Richard whom I left in bed. On the quiet, I managed to have a word with my mother. 'I'll go round with some medicine and a hot water bottle when your step-father's not about,' she said. 'I don't want to start no wars, do I?' At least I was thankful for that.

THIRTY-SIX

THE DIGGING trip took us four days: I have to admit to a certain pleasure at the thought of the adventure which lay ahead when, promptly at nine-thirty, I climbed into Sligger Offin's loaded-down taxi and we set off: I did have a slight pang of guilt when I saw Ben, a Sunday though it was, standing in a field with Molly as we set off: but, as I was in the back, screened by the shovels and buckets as the old car wheezed by, I was able to duck down and hide. Then we were out on the causeway, going no more than three or four miles an hour because of the eight or ten stout planks and posts tied on to the roof. As Norsea receded slowly behind us, I felt a great weight fall away from me: I was free of the place, even if it was for only three days: and by the time I got back, Ben would have filled in the bomb hole, though I would have taken a bet that he would do it during the working day and not as an evening chore.

Once through Gledlang, we speeded up and took the Tottle road, picking up Stanley Lobel at the crossroads in the centre of that village: the conversation when Stanley and I met again was much the same as it always was:

'Hi, Joe.'
'Hi, Stanley.'
'How are you?'
'Fine. How are you?'
'Fine. Looking forward to this?'
'Yeah. It'll make a change.'

The wheezing, rattling, clunking old car was so overloaded it was a wonder it got up some of the hills and several times Sligger Offin threatened that, if it did not make it, we would all have to get out and push. As a precaution, we went all the way by the quieter country roads: any policeman worth his whistle would have stopped us, made us unload and turned us back, I am sure: and no doubt he would also have made a few enquiries about how, at a time of extreme austerity (and getting worse), we came to be driving so far and wasting so much petrol on such an unimportant mission when private travel of any kind was frowned upon: and where did we get the petrol? It would have been no good Hoary boasting, 'I have a brother in Whitehall who works in the Ministry of Foreign and Commonwealth Affairs,' or some such. 'I am allowed extra petrol for my work.' But, fortunately, we managed to avoid them all.

Eventually, after about three hours, we crossed a main road and passed down a narrower road which ran across a gorse-covered heath alongside a wide marshy estuary: the road eventually came to an end and we found ourselves among trees and houses, just half a dozen or so, hardly enough to be called a village, but it was one: Waderswick was its name. I was surprised to learn that we had driven over sixty miles since we had left that morning.

Stanley and I unloaded the posts, boards, buckets, shovels and ropes and Hoary paid off Sligger Offin, who was anxious to get going so as to be home before dark because one of his headlamps was not working and 'The last bugger I want to meet tonight is the Hamwyte sergeant,' he said as he got in. I never knew how much Sligger charged Hoary for a trip like that, but it was probably more than anyone else would have charged: Sligger was convenient to Hoary's plans and he knew it and capitalised on it: I only know I saw a folded white fiver pass between them. 'See you Wednesday,' a grinning Sligger cried as he chugged off.

An old fishermen's inn stood at the end of this so-called village, almost on the beach itself: Hoary had booked in advance into two rooms: Stanley and I were in one at the back which smelled of tomcat's urine, Hoary was alone at the front: all beds were single, I am happy to say. After we had inspected our rooms and stowed everything away, putting the boards, posts, buckets and implements round the back, we went into the bar. 'You're too late for a drink,' the surly publican told us when we enquired. 'I stop serving at two.' It was a quarter past. Hoary then asked about a meal and was most put out when the publican and his wife refused to cook for us. 'This ain't no restaurant,' the publican retorted, looking aggrieved, even though we told him we had all brought our ration books: the best he could do, or would do, for us was cold luncheon meat and pickle sandwiches, a packet of potato crisps apiece and a cup of tea, all to be paid for in advance. We did not know it at the time, but we had the same thing at our evening meal for the next two days!

The village lay across a narrow estuary from a little seaside town built on some hard clay cliffs: there would be cafes there and, better still, local girls: I would have liked to have taken a look at them: seeing what girls looked like in a different town or region was one of the perks of travelling, I reckoned: you wanted to see if they were any different from your own down in Maydun and Gledlang. Unhappily, there was no way across, no bridge and no ferry because the tide was out anyway: a rowboat ferry did run from Monday to Saturday, but this was a Sunday and the ferryman was observing the Sabbath, so we were told: drinking in one or several of the town's two dozen pubs more like, I thought.

The little inn on the beach was not opening its doors till seven-thirty so Stanley and I went for a walk along the strand, watching the waves crashing against the exposed shoreline: then we explored the heathland around the village: it was almost dusk when we got back. Across the river a lighthouse of all things soared above the rooftops of the houses right in the middle of the small town and Stanley and I watched it flashing out its warning to passing ships heading for the ports north and south of where we were. Neither of us had ever seen one in operation before and we were both fascinated by it.

Though the inn had opened for custom at seven-thirty, there was no one in the main bar when we got back: Stanley was able to deceive the publican into believing he was nineteen and so we were able to sit in one corner till bedtime, drinking our bitter shandies: I half-suspected the landlord knew we were both under age, but was glad that night to have custom of any kind and turned a blind eye: then we went to bed.

Next morning, after a breakfast of stale bread fried in dripping, a single oatmeal sausage, scrambled powdered egg and tea thickened with condensed milk and sweetened with saccharin, two each, we began our dig. First, we carried all boards, posts, buckets, shovels and ropes down to a mud and shingle beach which runs a short way along the estuary, and then, in bare feet, with our trousers rolled up to our thighs, splashed out into the mud carrying our loads, sinking deeper and deeper the farther we went from the shore. By the time we reached the spot where we were to dig, fifty yards out where a solitary, spear-pointed black stake protruded a few inches skyward, we were knee-deep in the black ooze and it was a struggle to move forward under the weight of the boards, posts and implements we shouldered.

When all was assembled, a square was marked out, two posts were banged in with spades at each corner and the first of the planks slotted between them: not to keep the tide out, but to stop the mud we were about to bail out from flowing back in. This was to be our primary digging area: if we widened it, or lengthened it, as was more likely, we would just have to fetch more posts and more heavy boards. They would all cost money, of course, and have to come from a local timber yard: yet such was Hoary's enthusiasm that he blithely wasted a hundred pounds or more a year on his silly digging trips. 'The man must have money to burn,' my mother said.

The salt-sheened surface mud was quickly cleared from this redoubt, no more than eight feet by eight feet, then we were down into the black ooze: Hoary did not dig, but still clambered into the redoubt 'to supervise': all he did was get in our way! In so confined a space, with both Stanley and I shovelling mud into a bucket apiece before slopping it over the side, we could not help splattering each other: in no time at all our faces, hair, arms, legs, shirts and trousers were caked in it. From start to finish, it was a constant struggle to preserve what we had done: for as fast as we pitched the mud out, most of it seemed to ooze back.

That was how we spent the first day, throwing evil-smelling mud out of a redoubt in the middle of a tidal estuary, bumping and barging into each other, getting blacker and blacker by the hour and generally having a good laugh at the stupidity of it all.

All good things must come to an end: and when the tide reached the estuary mouth, we gathered up our buckets and spades and plodded back to the shore, leaving the redoubt to submerge beneath the waves after marking it with a pole in case any sailboats bumped into it at low water. A half-hour later and the three of us – Hoary in a rolled-down one-piece – were splashing about in our costumes in the shallows off the main beach till we were thoroughly cleansed: then it was back to the inn and the moody innkeeper, luncheon meat sandwiches again and a piece of jam Swiss roll apiece, followed by a quiet night of talking and drinking: shandies again for Stanley and myself: pink gins for Hoary: then to bed.

The second day of digging was spent very much the same as the first: except that we had wait for the morning tide to go out and then clear out all the mud which had washed back into the excavation before we could dig down even further. Hoary was right about one thing: there had been a pier there in Roman times, though it was more than two feet down when we reached it: we managed to uncover enough of its length for him to set up his tripod camera and take a series of plates, which, for some reason, he said he would be sending to the British Museum: though why they would be interested in two rows of blackened, spear-pointed stakes, eighteen-inches high sticking up out of the mud of a river bed like the blackened bottom teeth of a sunken crocodile, I failed to see. Hoary, however, was ecstatic and photographed them from every conceivable angle, even taking close-ups!

When the three of us squeezed back into Sligger Offin's smoky Morris just before midday on the Wednesday to drive home, I was rather sorry to leave: it had been a happy, if a slogging, 'holiday,' but at least it had been a break from the routine of Norsea: I had seen a different part of the world and I had seen all the countryside between Waderswick and Gledlang which normally I would never have seen: my only disappointment was that I had not seen any girls. Still, to me it was worthwhile: to Stanley it was worthwhile because it earned him money: to Hoary it was worthwhile because it proved he had been right about whatever it was he was trying to prove he was right about: and to Sligger Offin it was worthwhile because he had charged through the nose for the trip, as he did all trips: no wonder Hoary was starting to talk more and more about getting his own car and having Richard drive it.

To Ben, however, it was 'a complete bloody waste of time and petrol' and he said so as soon as we got back. One thing I did notice, the bricks from the octagonal outhouse behind Hoary's big house which Richard had demolished were still in an untidy pile beside the lawn and the bricks from our demolished wall were still stacked in our yard: Ben had not touched either: the bomb hole had still not been filled in!

'I ain't had time. I've had other things to do,' was his terse comment as we passed them: and when I offered to carry out the task as my first duty back the following day, he snapped: 'You leave the bloody things where they are! I'll shift them myself when I get time and not before! Then I'll know the job'll get done and get done properly.'

So be it: and when a fortnight later he did move them, he chose completely the wrong day on which to do it.

THIRTY-SEVEN

THE DAY Ben moved the bricks was the day of the storm: the heat had been building since the start of the month, even while we were up in Waderswick: on three successive days the temperature had soared into the mid-eighties and on one it had topped ninety in London, according to the wireless. Peculiar weather indeed when one considers that in three months we had passed from the harshest winter in memory to searing summer heat and violent, crashing thunderstorms. Great flat-topped anvil clouds would rear up over Maydun hill and you would know by the lurid light that you were in for a deluge: we had had five already: the day of the sixth storm was the day it happened.

I was working alone in the middle of a field a quarter-mile from the farmhouse, cutting the last of the cabbages and tossing them into piles at intervals down the field ready to be sacked-up and loaded on to the four-wheeled wagon when Ben brought it at the end of the day after finishing the job I should have done: moving the bricks.

Thunder was rumbling away south of the river and so muggy had it become that I had stripped off my jacket and pullover and was working in my shirtsleeves, dry-mouthed and perspiring, at the same time keeping one eye on Maydun hill: when that vanished in a curtain of rain, it would be time for me to dash for the shelter of the barn or the wagon shed, though never the house.

Perhaps if Ben had been shifting just our small load of bricks and had not decided to include the heap of rubble from Hoary's demolished outhouse, it would have been over and done with long before the lightning came. One intense flash seemed to fill half the sky and there was an almost instantaneous crash of thunder directly overhead: it was as if the sky had split open or a high-explosive shell had burst thirty feet above my head. It made me duck, anyway, and wonder about the knife I was holding in my hand: would a bolt of lightning strike that? I was not sure and spent a nervous half-hour watching and waiting.

I had just looked up again to check on the threatening rain when I saw a breathless Old Sago, who now joined us daily, come staggering up to the gate, clutching at his chest as though he were having a heart attack: in fact, I thought he was having an attack when I ran over to him. For several seconds, the poor old man was bent double, unable to speak, gulping in air: one arm was clutched across his chest and he was wheezing like an old concertina: not unsurprising in view of the fact that he had hobbled nearly two hundred yards as fast as his old legs would carry him in the muggy heat.

At last he found breath to speak. 'Quick, boy, get on your bike and goo for a doctor,' he gasped, half slumping against the gate. 'It's Ben. He's had an accident. He's lying in the field back there. We think the cart wheels have gone over him. He looks in a bad way. You'll have to goo for MacFadden.'

Briefly, I had a sickening vision of Ben slipping under the rolling wheels of the wagon and being crushed into the muddy earth while old Molly plodded on oblivious to the agonies of her master lying on the ground behind her: then I was off and running. 'There's no need to goo and look, boy,' Old Sago found breath to shout after me, 'your mother's already with him. Get your bike, boy, get your bike and goo for the doctor!'

But panic and fear, and maybe even curiosity, overrode common sense: determined to see for myself, I reached the scene to find my mother on her knees beside a prone Ben, cradling his head in her lap. The thunder was rumbling closer again and in her pathetic attempt at succour she had taken off her apron and placed it across his chest as a covering against the likelihood of rain.

When she saw me approaching, she just let out a scream of rage. 'I don't need you here!' she cried. 'Get the doctor, you little fool. Get the doctor! He needs a doctor, not you!' It was one of the few times in her life when I recognised her rage and desperation were real and not merely being acted out for my benefit. Ben was lying on his back, eyes closed, face creased with pain, letting out small cries of agony every time he so much as shifted a half-inch: that he was badly injured was obvious. My mother was in tears and too distraught and too hysterical to do anything other than comfort him: Old Sago was still making his way back: it needed a cool head, someone who could think and make a decision – me: and that is not boasting.

The deluge was nearly upon us and Ben could not be left where he was: he would be soaked in seconds and could die of pneumonia with his poor lungs. 'We have to get him under cover,' I shouted to my mother. 'He can't stay out here. There's going to be a thunderstorm in a minute.' Even as I spoke, there was another violent sky-splitting flash of lightning over the estuary to the west, followed three or four seconds later by a long, deep rumble: the storm would be upon us in minutes.

'We can't move him,' my mother screamed, incredulous at my suggestion. 'His back could be broken.'

I looked at the marks where the two wheels had gone over Ben, one across his pelvis, the other across his thighs just below the groin: it was unlikely his back was broken: I was not an expert, but I was prepared to take that chance.

'We're bloody well going to have to,' I shouted back. 'We can't leave him lying out here. We've got to get him on the wagon somehow, put some sacks under him for a cushion and get him back to the wagon shed or the barn. The storm's coming and there isn't any shelter out here.' There was common sense, as well as desperation, in that: perhaps it was the fierceness in my voice, for my mother just cursed silently and started crying again.

'I'm going for that old door in the yard and some sacks,' I said, wheeling away. 'The three of us can lift him on to the wagon on the door. You'll have to unload the bricks and make a space for him.'

My mother was none too pleased at being told what to do, but it was a matter of urgency and not a time for arguing: heavy drops of rain were already beginning to spatter the earth and several hard spits had already struck my hair: as I ran back to the farm, I saw her climbing up on to the wagon and heaving bricks over the side. I know they say you should never move an injured man unless you are an experienced first-aider, but the people who made that rule did not make it for an injured man with legs and pelvis crushed by a couple of wagon wheels lying in the middle of a muddy field on an isolated island in the middle of an estuary miles from anywhere with a storm about to break overhead and a long wait for a doctor. It was made for townies who expect an ambulance to arrive at the scene of their accident within twenty minutes if they so much as sprain an ankle on a raised paving stone or tumble from a ladder trying to fix the leak in their guttering. In the country then, it was different: you waited, and waited, and maybe kept on waiting, hours if need be, till the doctor arrived. Sometimes half a day or a whole night might pass before he would come: then, and only then, would he send for an ambulance if he considered your injury warranted it: till he arrived, you gritted your teeth and lumped it.

My idea to use the door as a stretcher and lift Ben up so he could be taken out of the rain came from a piece of ingenuity shown by three Land Army girls working on a farm near the coast during the war. The crew of one of the returning American bombers, on fire and struggling home on two engines, had pushed out a seriously wounded airman, knowing that he would be found and taken to a hospital and receive treatment far more quickly than if he had remained in the aircraft for a further threequarter-hour's flight, then on landing faced a thirty-minute ride in the back of an ambulance to the nearest hospital: and, of course, there had always been the possibility that they themselves would not make it in their crippled aircraft. The Land Army girls saw the parachute come down, rushed to it and carted the badly wounded airman more than a mile on a five-bar gate to the nearest road, where they flagged down the first vehicle that came along, a cattle lorry. The airman was on the operating table in Wivencaster hospital, it was said, before the aeroplane had even touched down at Framlingham.

It was admiration for them that fed my ego that day: just backing the wagon over Ben as a protection and unhitching Molly so she did not run over him a second time never occurred to me.

How long Ben had lain there before Old Sago had looked into the field and seen him did not bear thinking about: meanwhile, the culprit of all this, Molly, was standing nearby, occasionally shifting her position and jingling her harness, waiting patiently for the next command from her master: except that none would come: I think that was the only day I ever truly cursed her and cursed, too, the fact that we lived on an island.

The door was an old one taken off the chicken shed and discarded a couple of years before: we were fortunate that it had not been chopped up for firewood: it was light and narrow and just long enough to take Ben's length. I heaved it out of the bed of nettles and, grabbing a pile of folded sacks and a spade from just inside the barn, was back beside my mother and Ben even as Old Sago tottered up: the poor old chap could scarcely manage a wobbly thirty yards before he had to pause and rest.

He did not look too sure when I explained what we needed to do and my mother was at her hand-wringing best: but I ignored them and went ahead anyway. Very carefully, I scooped a shallow trench with the spade the length of Ben's body and as far under it as I could: when I had done enough, I tipped one edge of the door into the trench at a shallow angle and inserted it under Ben's prone form: then, with my mother and Old Sago positioned at his shoulders, I wiggled the makeshift stretcher very carefully, very slowly and very gently, inch by inch under Ben's legs, hips, and upper torso. It was fortunate that the ground was muddy, for the door slipped under Ben without too much trouble. In fact, the only bad moment came when Ben's eyes rolled upwards and his mouth flopped open as though he was having difficulty in breathing: he had turned a weird purple colour, too, and was shaking rather than shivering: I will say this for him, though, he never uttered a sound all the time I was wriggling the door under him: probably because of the shock.

Of course, it did not help matters that, all the while I was pushing the makeshift stretcher under him, my mother was exhorting 'Be careful!' 'Steady! You're hurting him!' and 'He's in pain! Look at him! Do you know what you are doing?' None of which was very encouraging, but it had to be done: we had to get him under cover and out of the rain. Once we had got him on the stretcher, it was an easy matter for the three of us to lift him and carefully lower him on to the treble cushion of sacks my mother had already spread on the wagon floor so that any jolting on the way to the wagon shed would be kept to a minimum: Ben never uttered one cry of pain: he just lay there with his eyes closed!

That done, I started off at a loping run for the farm, only to be called back angrily by Old Sago as he trundled the cart round, holding on to Molly's halter: my mother was up beside Ben, her face creased with anxiety.

In emergencies, one cannot be expected to think of everything. 'Have you got money for the phone, boy?' Old Sago demanded.

'No,' I answered, embarrassed.

'God! You clown,' said Sago, reaching into his pocket and pulling out fourpence. 'Use that.' I took it and ran.

Behind me, I heard my mother's wail by way of adding to the urgency of my mission. 'He's unconscious. He's in a coma. Tell MacFadden it's bad. Run, you useless thing, run!'

At the farm, I dragged my bicycle out of the wagon shed and raced down the track and out over the causeway, bumping and bouncing over the self-same potholes and splashing through the self-same puddles which at any other time would have been a lark, but which that day became a hindrance to be cursed. The deluge hit me as I was halfway across and in no time I was saturated: a flash of lightning greeted me as I flung my bicycle up the slope of the seawall at the Boundary boards and down the other side and pedalled on through the long lines of the orchards. I must have halved my usual time from the farm to Gledlang Square and it was with a sense of undeniable exhilaration that I skidded to a halt and hurled my machine down beside the red telephone box: the adrenalin must have been pumping strongly that day.

Fortunately, the phone box was empty and I was able to get straight through to the operator and ask for MacFadden's house: four pence in the slot and press button A (I would press button B at the end of the call, like I always did, in an attempt to get my money back, just in case.)

'Yes?' a woman's voice answered with a certain irritation in the tone: MacFadden's wife.

'Can I speak to Doctor MacFadden, please?' I shouted my question down the telephone.

'No, I'm sorry, you can't,' MacFadden's wife said stiffly. 'He's out. And there is no need to shout. I can hear you perfectly well. I am not deaf.'

'Sorry.' I apologised, not wanting to upset the old biddy and have her slam the telephone down on me. 'When will he be back?'

It was about half-past-two when I reached the phone box so MacFadden should have been just about wending his way home after his lunchtime session in the bar of the Red Lion at Cobwycke: that was my guess where he was anyway, according to stories I had heard.

Outside there was another flash of lighting over the church and the thunder crashed again like it was trying to split the tall elms along the churchyard path: rain was bouncing off the road and drumming furiously against the panes of glass.

The doctor's wife broke the silence. 'The doctor is out on his rounds,' she said. 'He has had to go over to Greater Tottle to see a patient, then he has to go on to Hamwyte. I do not expect him back before tea. What do you want the doctor for anyway? Can't it wait? Is it that urgent?'

'Yes, sorry, it is urgent,' I shouted back above the crash of the thunder. 'I'm sorry to bother you, but it's my step-father. He's been injured. We found him lying in a field. We think he's been run over by the wheels of the wagon.' Think! It was bloody obvious he had. 'His name's Ben Wigboe, from Norsea Island farm.'

Silence for a few seconds, then a peevish 'I see,' followed by another silence. 'Well, if the doctor rings in, I'll tell him to come straight to you. That's the best I can do.'

'How long do you think that will be?' I asked, hoping the time would shorten.

'I have no idea,' said the voice on the other end of the telephone: she obviously did not like being asked the same question twice. 'I will send him over to you as soon as he comes in. That is the best I can do.'

Not good enough: not nearly good enough: outside the rain was coming down harder: there was a flash of lightning towards Norsea and then almost immediately a great peeling roll of thunder lasting several seconds. I thought of Ben being trundled across the uneven ground and hoped that my mother and Old Sago had got him under cover somehow before the deluge had begun.

'Mum says we really need an ambulance to get him to hospital.' I had to shout again over the noise of the thunder.

'Please, I have asked you once. Do not shout down the phone,' commanded the doctor's wife. 'I can hear you perfectly well without you shouting.'

'Sorry, I'm not used to phoning.' It was a lie: I often telephoned Ben's seed orders through to the corn merchant at Tidwolton, the potato seed merchant at Hamwyte, the threshing machine boss at Tudwick and the coke merchant at Maydun: but it would do for her.

'Obviously,' was the scoffing reply: there was a second or two pause before she asked: 'Is that all?' And without waiting for my answer, she added: 'I suggest you keep the patient as still as possible and do not move him. Keep him covered and dry if you can. I will tell the doctor as soon as I can. I'm sorry, I have said all I can.' And with that, she banged down the phone.

Do not move him! Keep him dry! What in the middle of a field in a raging thunderstorm! The stupid woman! It was then that anger got the better of me and I made a decision: it might be two, three, even four hours before MacFadden got over to Norsea, particularly if he were sleeping off a hangover, as I suspected he most probably was. I could not leave Ben lying in the back of a wagon for four or five hours with the rain teeming down, thunder rolling overhead and lightning flashing all around, could I? If he was unconscious when I left, he could be dead by the time MacFadden arrived: if he arrived at all.

I still believe I was right in what I did: it would have been too terrible if we had had to wait all that time for MacFadden: and then there was the risk he might not be sober when he got there, and of him bungling everything the way he had with one poor girl in the village who broke her leg falling down the stairs. MacFadden was under the influence when he arrived at the house, the mother said, and he had set the broken thighbone crooked so that ever afterwards the girl, a pretty young thing named Alice, walked with one foot bent outwards. For months afterwards, the mother had begged MacFadden to take the girl to hospital so the bone could be re-broken and reset straight, gruesome as that might be: but, unwilling perhaps to admit his earlier incompetence, MacFadden had refused. Then there was the second possibility, that he would not come before the tide came in that evening and so would be unable to cross when he did arrive: knowing him, he would not wait, but would turn round and go home and come back in the morning: and I could not allow that.

For once in my life I used my initiative: I dialled the emergency number and asked for the ambulance station at Maydun.

THIRTY-EIGHT

'CAN YOU afford to pay if you have to, sonny?' the man at the other end of the telephone asked as I gave him the details of the accident. 'You might have to, you know, being farmers.'

'Yes, we can,' I lied and briefly contemplated telling him we were bailiffs and ordinary workers like everyone else, but decided against it in case it deterred him from sending the ambulance: at least, he accepted that the accident sounded serious enough to warrant one being sent. Whether we could or could not pay, whether we would or would not be asked to pay, I did not care: I just wanted to get an ambulance there and get Ben to hospital out of the rain: the matter of paying for it could be sorted out later. At that time, the Government was still trying to bring in some kind of a National Health Service, but it was still a year away because half the country's doctors were refusing to join.

Having satisfied the ambulance dispatcher, he said a vehicle would be sent immediately, though he seemed puzzled when I told him: 'Our farm's after Boundary, at the bottom of Shoe Street.'

'Don't worry, sonny, we'll find it,' he said. 'You're lucky calling like you have. We've just got our new ambulance. I'll send that. It'll get there quicker. This'll be its first run out.'

He was as good as his word and within half-an-hour a shiny, brand new, cream-white ambulance, bearing the county's curved red seaxes on its doors and large black Maltese cross on its side, arrived in the Square: even its black and white numberplate was clean and shiny: it was then that I ran into my second problem that day.

I had decided to wait rather than risk them trying to find me: I signalled the two men aboard to follow me and led them down Shoe Street and along the rough track through Boundary's orchards. The heavy rain had stopped for the minute, but the thunder was still rumbling all around and there were occasional lightning flashes away to the west. It was as the ambulance jolted over the potholes and I looked back to ensure they were still following that I saw the first signs of concern on the faces of the two ambulancemen, especially a portly little man named Percy, who was driving: every bump and bounce was accompanied by a silently mouthed oath: the problem came to a head when we reached the boards.

'What the hell do you call this?' portly Percy, being the senior, demanded, climbing out of the cab and beginning to inspect the side of his now mud-spattered vehicle. The rain started again at that moment, stair-rod stuff, drumming on the bonnet and roof of the ambulance, and Percy quickly climbed back inside.

'It's just a farm track, like any other,' I shouted above the noise, not understanding his hostility.

'Some bloody track this is!' exclaimed his companion, who was named Ted, poking his head out of his window and taking off his peak cap to scratch his forehead: he soon put it on again when the stair-rods bounced off his bald pate.

'And where do you want us to go next, sonny? Where is this bloody farm of yours?' Percy demanded.

'Over the causeway,' I said, 'through the boards and across to the island.'

'The boards?'

'Yes, the boards.' I pointed towards the heavy oak timbers slotted into their concrete posts and explained that we needed to remove them to allow the ambulance through and down on to the causeway itself.

'You're not expecting us to shift those, are you?' exclaimed Percy.

Well, yes, I was: at the very least, I expected them to help me lift them out, even if they did not put them back.

'That ain't part of our job,' Percy grumbled, with a shake of the head, 'not in this bloody rain! You should have removed them before we come.'

How could I have done? I had been waiting for them in the Square. Besides, I was the one who was standing astride my bicycle in the teeming rain: and I was the one who was already soaked to the skin while they sat in the dry cab. 'I'll do it now – by my bloody self, if you won't help me!' I retorted angrily.

'Hold your horses first, sonny,' said Percy when he realised how adamant I was. 'I suppose we had better take a look at this causeway of yours first.'

The swearing began as they got out of the cab to pull on their county issue waterproofs and the full force of the pelting rain hit them: it increased when they clambered up to the top of the seawall and looked out over the rainswept estuary, lit by lightning flashes: both let out similar exclamations and expletives as they disappeared down the other side. By the time I had wheeled my bicycle to the top, they were out on the causeway, ostensibly inspecting it, but I think their minds were made up as soon as they saw it: the driving rain did not help. They were soon back: their inspection amounted to little more than a cursory glance, a kick at a rock, a series of shrugs, exaggerated shakes of the head for my benefit and then one long moan as they came scrambling back up the seawall, eager to get back into their cab.

'It's too dangerous,' said Percy, with a shake of the head, sucking at his teeth. 'It's far too narrow for this ambulance.'

'What!' I was dumbfounded.

'How wide is it?' asked his companion, Ted.

'Nine feet,' I lied: it was seven feet at its widest.

'And what about in the middle? It's a long way across.'

'The same,' I lied again: the causeway actually dipped two feet in mid-channel and narrowed to about six feet, just wide enough for Molly pulling our wagon, or Peter pulling Boundary's wagon, and just wide enough, too, for Sligger Offin's taxi, the late, unlamented John Bolt's little green van and the furniture vans which delivered Hoary's mother's stuff midway through the war: so long as one went slowly, of course. My hope was that once they got started, they would have to keep going as there was nowhere they could turn round and any attempt at reversing back to the mainland in that rain would have sent them sliding into the mud for sure.

'You might get a car across, sonny, if it was small enough,' sniffed Percy, again sucking at his teeth and continuing to shake his head, 'but you wouldn't get an ambulance across. Not one this wide. Not in this rain. No room to manoeuvre. This is a brand new ambulance and I ain't risking a brand new ambulance on its first trip out.'

The ambulance did not look that wide to me: I estimated that, at the narrowest part of the causeway, the wheels would have four or five inches of clearance either side before the slope began: all they had to do was to drive carefully and slowly: I just wished my mother had been there to hear them: she would have given them a piece of her mind they would not have forgotten in a hurry! But she was not: and, though I protested in her place, I dared not say too much in case they turned round and went back to Maydun.

'One of you could walk in front to check,' I suggested, hopefully, and quite seriously.

'Like bloody hell we will!' snorted Percy. 'This ain't no bloody village taxi, sonny, it's a brand new ambulance and I'm not risking it out there. Can't you bring the patient to us? Ain't you got a farm cart or something you could put him on? Where would I be if I lost an ambulance in the middle of a river? Up the bloody creek with no job, that's where!'

Their refusal staggered me: stupid bloody-minded townies, I thought: surely, it was their job to go out and fetch the sick and the injured in their ambulance and take them off to hospital? But there they were, refusing because they were too frightened to cross a causeway in the rain.

When he saw my face drop, Ted, trying to be helpful, I suppose, suggested a compromise: 'Look, lad, ride across and tell them that, if they can bring him across to us on a cart, we'd be only too willing to take him to hospital. I'll come across with you and explain to your mother. I'll take a look at the injured chap and, if he needs splinting-up or bandaging, I can do that. Percy and I can't both go. One of us needs to stay with the ambulance. I'll go, Percy will stay. How's that?'

Better than nothing: I had to agree because there was no other option. So while the chubby Percy sat smoking in the cab of his brand new ambulance, Ted followed me across to Norsea on foot in his waterproofs through the teeming rain, all the way chuntering on about how surprised he was that we should live on such an isolated place. 'What do you want to live in such a God-forsaken place like this for, anyway?' he asked. 'Especially when it's so awkward to get to. You'd be better off living on the mainland than being cut off on Norsea half the day.'

He got a silent two-word answer for that one before I told him: 'It's only awkward if you make it bloody awkward!' After that, I left him to walk the rest of the way in the rain on his own: by the time I reached the hard, I had put a good two-hundred yards between us: and, lightning or no lightning, I waited gleefully under the overhang of a tree as he completed the last hundred in another drenching downpour.

When we reached the wagon shed, Ben, still in a coma, was lying under a tarpaulin which my mother had made into a tent: she was cradling his upper body and casting anxious eyes up at the thunder still crashing around overhead: Old Sago was sitting on the end of the wagon, dangling his legs and puffing away at his pipe from under a sack hood.

'We can't get the vehicle across to you, missus,' Ted told my mother bluntly as soon as he climbed up beside Ben. 'That track's too narrow for it and we could damage the springs or break an axle and then where would we be? We'll have to take him on the cart. I've come across to make him comfortable so he doesn't get jarred about too much.'

It has never ceased to amaze me how some people respect a uniform, irrespective of its wearer: just because some chap in a uniform tells them something cannot be done, or has to be done a different way, people will accept it without question: my mother did that day, blithely agreeing to Ted's suggestion without a murmur of protest. So did Old Sago: I can only assume they were just grateful that the ambulanceman was there to take the responsibility of seeing to Ben out of their inexperienced hands.

The ambulanceman gingerly felt Ben's legs where a line of dried mud now showed where the first wagon wheel had rolled across the top of both and the second had jolted over his stomach and pelvis: he gave a shake of the head, exhaled deeply and announced grimly: 'Both his thighs are broken, missus. Breaks of the upper femur. He could have other damage, a cracked pelvis, crushed organs or something in the duodenum, but it's his spine that's the real worry. You can see where the wheels went over him. His lower vertebrae could be damaged. He doesn't look too good at all, missus. He needs to be got to a hospital urgent.'

Bloody hell! I could have told him that! That's why I had sent for him! What the hell did he expect when a man has been run over by two six-foot-diameter, iron-rimmed wheels of a wagon loaded with bricks!

To give Ted the ambulanceman his due, he did a proper job on Ben: two brooms were quickly brought, their brushes knocked off, and then tied with bandages from Ted's knapsack all the way up Ben's body to his armpits: cushions from the parlour and a couple of pillows from my bedroom which my mother also fetched were wedged against him to prevent him rolling, then, using his own and Sago's belt, Ted bound him firmly to the chicken hut door. And that was how we took Ben across to the mainland and the waiting ambulance, with my mother and the ambulanceman holding up the tarpaulin like a tent to protect the three of them from the teeming rain and Sago and I leading a subdued Molly, while all around the thunder rumbled on and the lightning flashed as threatening as ever. My mother had already fetched her coat, hat, purse and a dry set of clothes from the house and so was able to go off with Ben in the ambulance.

'How'd it happen?' I asked Sago as the two of us walked back with Molly.

'That big thunderclap, I reckon,' Sago said grimly. 'The one right overhead. Molly must hev took fright and lurched forward, poor old gel. Ben must hev been walking at the front and slipped under the wheels. The first wheel went over his legs, I reckon, the second over his middle. I didn't see it happen, but soon as I saw him lying there I knew straight away he was in a bad way so I went for your mother and she said to get you. I called in at Richard's as I passed his cottage, thinking he might help, like, but he weren't there. Is he away?'

'Been away for the past two days,' I told him. 'Up in the next county again with Hoary and Stanley.'

Sago was quiet for a few seconds, then he said solemnly: 'I don't know where this leaves you and me, boy, but I ain't a young man no more. I don't mind helping out when you need me, like, but I ain't good for much these days. I can do some things, bean-picking, pea-picking, tying the sacks, stabling Molly, clearing her out, helping with the harvest and the like, but I ain't good for much else' That would do for a start, I thought, but kept it to myself.

To end a bad day, MacFadden came bouncing across the causeway three hours later in his new Riley car: the thunder had ceased and the sun was glinting on the brown puddles as it came splashing into the yard. Old Sago had gone and my mother by that time would have been sitting in the hospital waiting room at Melchborough working herself into a frenzy of anxiety, and unlikely to be back before morning: she had already indicated she would probably be staying the night with Old Auntie opposite the parish hall because of the late night tide.

MacFadden was not at all pleased when I told him that an ambulance had taken Ben to hospital three hours earlier because we felt we could not wait for him as we did not know when he would come.

'Who said he should go to hospital?' he began.

'The ambulanceman.'

'And who called the ambulance?'

'I'm afraid I did.' I saw the anger blaze in his eyes and added hurriedly: 'My mother sent me on my bike. I rang you, but you weren't there.'

MacFadden regarded me for a moment, gave a sniff and stalked back to his car. As he wrenched open the door and threw his bag inside, he paused and, looking straight at me, said with polite Irish sarcasm: 'I have just driven fifteen miles through a thunderstorm to get here. It has taken me fifteen minutes to get across your causeway. In future, should you have reason to ring for a doctor, I trust you will have the good manners to allow me to see the patient before you call an ambulance. It is my job to tend to the patient and then and only then will I call for an ambulance if I think one is needed. A broken leg does not necessarily need hospital treatment. I could have set it here.'

'My mother thought both his legs were broken – up here – and he might have injuries inside,' I interrupted, a little too triumphantly perhaps, at the same time indicating the upper thigh and stomach. 'And to his back and spine,' I added for good measure. Of course, I should have said 'the ambulanceman said,' but did not and immediately regretted the mistake.

'Your mother? I see,' said MacFadden, with the same sarcasm. 'And she is qualified to diagnose such things, is she?'

'Well, no.'

'Then have the goodness to tell your mother that the next time she sends for me at least to wait until I arrive before sending the patient to hospital. I am not at all happy that I have driven all this way for nothing in the middle of a thunderstorm – ' Which was over by then! ' – It is both a waste of my petrol and my time. Next time you may not find me so amenable. I have other patients to call upon, you know. Tell your mother that.'

Then he was gone. I do not know why he was so sore at me: it was not my fault he had been 'out' when I had telephoned.

My mother returned the next day soon after breakfast, weary, bitter and short-tempered after a bad night's sleep at Auntie's: her usual self: I forgot to mention MacFadden and, instead asked about Ben.

'How the bloody hell do you think he is?' exploded my mother. 'How the bloody hell do you think a man is when he's lying in a hospital bed with two broken legs, half his organs crushed, his spine all bruised and his legs not working and no feeling at all below his waist! Months he's going to be in there! Months! If you had shifted those bricks when he asked, he wouldn't be lying half-dead in Melchborough hospital ...' And so on and so on.

She railed on, too, all the dinner hour about fate, luck, God, Old Hoary and me, so, come the end of the day, rather than go back to the house and suffer the same during tea, I deemed it a safer idea to go over and see Dennis and tell him about it all.

THIRTY-NINE

IF YOU had been standing in Gledlang Square at about six o'clock that evening, a half-hour after I had cycled across to Boundary, you would have seen a slim, fair-haired girl get off the Bourne Brothers' bus from Maydun, carrying a battered brown leather suitcase. If you had been a man riding past on your way home from work, it is unlikely you would have given her much more than a cursory glance: you might even have smiled at the girl's waif-like thinness, her wide mouth and funny nose, the tip of which was not so much turned up as curved up. To be honest, she did not have much that would attract a man: she was not pretty, she was not really attractive, though she did have a smiling face and laughing blue-grey eyes.

If you had been a woman on your way home, say, from the baker's in Shoe Street clutching a loaf still warm from the oven, or returning from the butcher's in Hedge Street with a wrapped parcel of bread and herb sausages, or coming from the post office-cum-grocery store in the Square with a little blue bag of rationed sugar in your shopping bag, you would have smiled at the girl's dowdy, old-fashioned appearance, her darned red cardigan, home-made floral-patterned blue dress, flat down-at-heel black shoes and white ankle socks, topped by a brown beret: all of which marked her down as an obvious country girl or would have to any sophisticated reader of the newspaper women's sections in which the dreamy, frothy marvels of the New Look were being daily enthused over.

It was her thinness which was deceptive to the casual passer-by, plus her height, which was no more than five-feet-two or thereabouts: from a distance, she appeared to be only in her middle 'teens, but on a closer inspection you would have realised that she was actually in her early twenties, twenty-two or twenty-three.

Ma Rowthey, in the post office-cum-grocery store on the north side of the Square, saw her arrive and knew, of course, that she was a stranger, first, because she had never seen her before and, second, because she set down her suitcase and immediately looked about her as if she were unsure where to go next and was content to wait for someone to come along whom she could ask.

Being closed for post, but still open for grocery business, helpful, nosey and with no one to serve, Ma Rowthey obliged and went out to assist the newcomer, and also, of course, to find out who she was and why she was standing amid the puddles in Gledlang Square with a suitcase at her feet and a brown overcoat draped over it.

The girl, or rather the woman, was looking for Boundary farm, she said: she did not know the village and did not know which way to go.

'John Bolt's farm?' said the postmistress by way of a question and, by habit, using the old description.

'Yes,' said the girl.

The postmistress gave her directions which amounted to little more than pointing across the Square to where Shoe Street sloped away and telling her to keep going down the hill, through the white gates at the bottom and along a track that led through some big orchards: follow it round to the right and there was the farm, about a one-and-a-half-mile walk.

'Do I know you?' asked the postmistress, struggling over the girl's broad 'burring' accent: it was not a local accent, or a county one, or a regional one, and definitely not a London one either: West Country, the post mistress decided.

The girl gave a little laugh. 'No,' she said, picking up her coat and suitcase, 'I've never been here in my life before.' And without saying anything further, she set off across the Square, swinging the suitcase as she went.

Dennis and I were in the farmhouse kitchen discussing Ben's accident and bemoaning our bad luck when the knock came on the front door and Blackie set off down the hallway barking furiously: few people ever knocked at John Bolt's front door: the farm men always went round the back, as did his cleaning lady, Old Ma Parkinson. Dennis was standing by the stove, frying some oatmeal sausages and bread and heating some baked beans and could not answer the door: so I went to open it.

I knew straight away who she was: it did not take a genius to guess: besides, I had seen her photograph and, though she was older by three or four years and her hair style was different, she had the same look about her. Most families have characteristics of face, figure, speech, walk, stance and the like which are found in other members of the wider family, in uncles, aunts, nephews, nieces, cousins, etcetera: Joanne Waters was no exception: she had the family look about her and indeed appeared to me to be almost as malnourished as Dennis: the difference was her wide stare-straight-at-you eyes and the boldness in her manner. 'Are you Dennis Bolt?' she asked with a giggle.

'No, he's in the kitchen. Do you want him?' A stupid question, especially as she had just asked for him.

'Yes, please. Can you tell him his cousin, Joanne, is here to see him, Joanne Waters, from Devon.' She made no attempt to enter, but was content to wait on the doorstep, still smiling away and patting Blackie as he sniffed around her ankles, furiously wagging his tail. As I turned away, she asked me in her deep, burring accent, looking me up and down: 'Are you Dennis's brother?' Did I detect a note of hope in her voice?

I laughed at that one: I did not mean to be rude, but for me to have been Dennis's brother would have meant I would also have had to have been related to John Bolt and that would never have done: I would sooner have been the son of the Devil than a nephew of that man, dead or otherwise.

'No,' I replied, with a shake of the head, 'my name's Joe Coe. I'm just a friend of Dennis.'

'Oh,' said Joanne Waters, her smile widening, 'you're J.C., the one who sent me the letter.'

'Er, yes,' I replied, now a little nervous lest Dennis hear, 'but don't tell anyone, please.' In truth, once I had posted the letter, I had forgotten about it, especially when, after a week or so, nobody had come: to have the matter raised now would be an embarrassment: better that Dennis should not know I had sent anything. 'Dennis doesn't know I wrote to you. To be honest, I didn't really expect you would get it. I only had the one address.'

'Oh, I got it,' she said, which was obvious, since she was there, 'so I thought I would come over and see everybody. I'm pleased you sent it if no one else is.' Not many people thanked me for what I did: it was a bit of a novelty and I blushed: but I was still worried about what Dennis's reaction might be.

'You're too late for the funeral. It's already been held,' I told her, begging: 'Can you just say you come anyway? Just say you heard about him somewhere – or read it somewhere. Please.'

'Like in the Farmer's Weekly?' suggested Joanne Waters, laughing herself at the subterfuge.

'Yes,' I said, eagerly seizing on the lie: well, half-lie: Dennis had put a death notice in the paper, giving his uncle's Boundary address, so there would be a certain plausibility about Joanne Waters's story. 'No one'll know but me and you.'

'Okay, if you say so,' said Joanne Waters, still smiling, 'but if he finds out different, I'll have to tell the truth.'

That was all right with me. 'Fine,' I said, 'fine.' Then to hide my embarrassment and to get things over with quickly: 'Do you want to come in?'

'Yes, thank you,' she said, stepping into the house's wide parqueted hallway and letting out a little 'Oooh' of admiration: despite our big clearout, the oil paintings in their gold frames remained as did two bow-legged side tables and five ornate, similarly bow-legged chairs upholstered in fading green silk stripes. She seemed particularly impressed by the sweep and width of the staircase and its sturdy balustrade: after all the farmhouse was Georgian and, more through a lack of will than a lack of money on the part of the Bolts, it had remained untouched over the intervening two-hundred years, the only additions being indoor plumbing and electricity: the rest was unchanged.

My first reaction to Joanne Waters was that she was not at all my type: too thin, with no real bust and 'matchstick' legs. 'She'd be all right on a dark night with a sack over her head,' is how Billy would have described her, but not really worth a good stare. Only Blackie, trotting ahead of her down the hall and turning back to look up at her, seemed to consider she was worth a second glance and a wag of the tail.

'There's someone here to see you, Dennis,' I called out as I led her towards the kitchen

Dennis appeared at the kitchen door wearing his usual soiled blue dungarees, a mug of tea in one hand and a tablespoon with which he had been stirring the baked beans in the other: he had not even taken off his greasy cap, though he had discarded his wellingtons and was in his holed socks.

'Hullo, I'm your cousin Joanne, from Devon. Your mother, Beattie, and my mother, Hettie, were sisters,' Joanne Waters said, holding out her hand and giving Dennis an even broader smile than she had given me: her eyes were twinkling, her personality was literally radiating and it destroyed him: poor Dennis, it destroyed him: straight away, immediately, instantly.

In all my years of seeing girls meet boys on Maydun Promenade and women chase after men, I have seldom seen a man blush so deeply as Dennis did that day: you could see his cheeks redden even under the tan and grime of farmwork: the poor chap went to pieces. His supposed 'Hullo' was an incomprehensible mumble, accompanied by a silly embarrassed smile: if it had not been for her reaching out to take his hand, I doubt the two of them would ever have touched, his arm was wavering so much. The effect on Dennis of that touch was even more electrifying than the meeting of their eyes: before you knew what was happening, he was backing away into the kitchen and round the big, square table, colliding with a chair and almost falling over.

He was not the brightest of fellows, as I have said, but all of a sudden he became the clumsiest: like he could not do anything without knocking something or dropping something or tipping it over. As if not wanting to meet her eyes, he returned to the stove and tried to busy himself stirring his baked beans and turning his sausages and bread in the frying pan: but, in attempting to transfer the sausages from the pan on to his plate, when he lifted the plate with his bare hands, he discovered it had become too hot from being perched on the hob and he dropped the lot on the floor with a cry, which only made Joanne Waters smile all the more: even I had a chuckle. And when a flustered Dennis ducked down to pick them up, he knocked the handle of the saucepan and upset the beans and then banged into the table itself.

Remembering my manners from some distant confrontation with my mother, I offered her a chair and a cup of tea: fortunately, during Dennis's little calamity, I was holding the cup and saucer into which I was about to pour the tea so we were spared that catastrophe.

'My mother died in Nineteen Forty-Four when we lived in Swindon,' Joanne went on by way of explanation as she settled herself gracefully on the chair. 'We got moved there in Forty-Three. I read a notice about Uncle's death in the Farmer's Weekly – ' She said it without so much as a blink as she looked at me, the impish smile still there: from me an almost audible sigh of relief. ' – so I thought I'd come over and see everyone.'

Dennis looked a little puzzled by her 'everyone.'

'There's only me,' he said, bluntly. 'There ain't no one else.'

'Oh,' was all Joanne said as I placed the tea in front of her: there seemed to be a definite arousal of interest there: looking about her, she asked: 'Is this all yours then?'

'T'is now, I suppose,' Dennis answered with a shrug, 'or it will be once Uncle's will has been probated, I expect.'

Joanne was impressed: her smiling eyes followed him as he went to run his painful fingers under the cold tap: she was not afraid to be caught looking straight at a man, that girl, and, when she was, she just smiled all the more broadly.

'Do you mind if I smoke?' she asked, clicking open her handbag and withdrawing a packet of cigarettes and a small silver lighter.

A hasty 'No, no' from me and a similar mumbled negative and shake of the head from Dennis, now nervously seated opposite her and sawing at the crisped edges of his fried bread. As Joanne Waters carefully lit her cigarette, I noticed for the first time the length of her fingernails and that they were painted a bright red, like her lipstick. To my way of thinking, there was a certain calm elegance and assuredness about the way she sat there sipping her tea, one leg crossed over the other, foot gently swinging, her body upright against the back of the chair, one elbow resting on the table: and each time, she blew out smoke there was an exaggerated movement of the wrist and hand so that the 'V' of the fingers holding the cigarette finished on a level with her ear while pointing straight up at the ceiling well away from her face. It was something I had seen a lot of girls do in Maydun, an attempt at sophistication, I suppose. Most blokes would have kept the cigarette in front of their mouths or clamped it between their lips if they were out in the field: I always did when I hoed or topped sugar beet because you needed both hands with which to work. Joanne Waters, I thought, is out to make an impression: on Dennis, not on me!

Another thing I noticed was that, though Dennis did not look directly at Joanne Waters when she was smiling at him, he did take a half-second peep at her every now and again from under his cap, each time blushing a deeper crimson. The poor man did not know whether to speak or not to speak, to stand up or not to stand up, to smile or not to smile, what to say, when to say it or whether to say it at all. If I had not been there, I think the two of them would have sat together in that kitchen without saying a single word to each other, simply because poor Dennis was too tongue-tied to speak and she was the kind who would just sit and smile and stare at a man, smoking in her affected manner and casually swinging one leg.

'Have you just come today?' I asked: I know it was as daft a question as I could ask since the girl had just dropped a large suitcase in the hallway, but at least it relieved the pressure on Dennis, chomping away to clear his plate.

'Yes, I came up from Devon this morning,' said Joanne Waters, looking straight at Dennis. 'I just came to meet everybody. I always knew I had relatives in East Anglia, but Mum never said where exactly. I would never have guessed here.'

Dennis looked up from slicing one of his sausages and blushed as their eyes met again: I thought he was going to say something, like 'I'm glad you've come,' but he just lowered his head again and chomped on: what he would have done if he had not had his food upon which to concentrate, I really cannot think.

It was left to Joanne Waters to keep the conversation going. 'What was Uncle John like?' she asked, innocently.

Dennis just looked more embarrassed than ever, probably because he was confounded by the question and was unable to think of anything to say, so I said it for him: 'He was an old sod, a right bastard, even if Dennis doesn't think so. You've not missed anything, missing him. Dennis here has been taking it easy since he went, haven't you, Dennis?' He grinned at my chiding as much as my description of his uncle, but he did not dispute it. 'It's just a pity there's all that fuss about him going,' I added.

'There's a b-b-bit of controversy over his death,' Dennis explained quickly, at last finding his voice again. 'He g-got h-hit on the head with a h-hoe by one of the farmhands and he's being ch-ch-charged with m-manslaughter, we think, or c-causing his death somehow. Joe and I expect we'll have to g-go and give evidence when the case comes up at W-Wivencaster Assizes, but we don't think that will be till October at the e-earliest. They t-take their time with these things.'

'Oh dear,' was all Joanne Waters said, giving a reasonable impression of lip-biting concern: and Dennis, having found his voice and realised she would not bite him if he looked at her and spoke directly to her, was able to go on and tell her all the sordid details of Billy's stupidity, thankfully omitting that he was my best friend.

'Oer,' Joanne Waters repeated at intervals, before adding when he had finished: 'So you live here all on your own then?'

Did Dennis detect a meaning in the question that I missed? 'Yes,' he said, and the crimson flush under his brown face changed to carmine.

Since it was past seven o'clock by then, I gave a cough at that question and pointedly asked: 'Where are you staying tonight then?'

'I was hoping to stay here,' said Joanne Waters, fixing Dennis with those bright eyes of hers, 'if Cousin Dennis doesn't mind?' Cousin Dennis should have said something like, 'You can't possibly do that,' as decorum required: you cannot have an unmarried girl sleeping in the same house alone with an unmarried man: well, you could not in those days and Dennis was to get into trouble over it later. When he spotted my raised eyebrow, the silly grin reappeared: her use of his name had been as electrifying as had been the eye contact and touch of her hand. But he did not utter a single word and the request was acquiesced in silence with just a weak smile from him and a brighter smile of 'Thank you' from her: he was afraid to refuse, I thought: or he did not want to refuse!

It did not seem to faze Joanne Waters one bit. 'Would you mind if I cooked myself something to eat,' she asked blithely, getting up from the chair. 'I haven't had anything to eat since I left Devon this morning.'

Well, again Dennis could hardly say 'No,' could he? So Joanne Waters cooked herself a scrambled egg thing with bits of cheese in it, and made a fresh pot of tea: and sly Dennis watched her all the time she did it out of the corner of his eye: he could not keep his eyes off her. The only comment she made about spending the night there was in asking him a second time in that wheedling voice women adopt when they want a man to agree to something: 'You don't mind if I stay here, do you, Dennis?' This time Dennis did actually say, 'No, no, I don't mind. We've got plenty of room. For tonight anyway.'

'I hope your beds are nice and comfortable,' said Joanne Waters, turning round to give him a smile from where she stood at the stove. 'I like a nice comfortable bed to sleep in, don't you? I like to be tucked up at night.' That was too much for me, a mention of women and beds and sleeping: since I needed to get back to Norsea before eight o'clock, I made my excuses and left, as the reporters always said in the *News of the World* when they had exposed some Maltese-run prostitution ring up in London. Dennis followed me out and still had that bemused, silly look on his face when he closed the door. Joanne Waters also gave me a nice smile as I went: I think she was pleased to have met a friend of Dennis who was so nice: that is what I thought, anyway. Dennis was a strangely happier and a perkier man when I left him just after seven-thirty and rode back to Norsea.

FORTY

ALL THE WAY across to Norsea, I kept thinking of Joanne Waters and Dennis in the house together: if her arrival had been a surprise, her manner when she sat in the kitchen had been startling, to say the least: bold and a bit brassy, I would have said. In my mind's eye, I had an image of the two of them sleeping in their separate bedrooms in the darkened house that night, each listening to the movements of the other. Which one would bolt their door? Dennis, I reckoned. Somehow, I did not think Joanne Waters would even think of it. One thing: she would be better company for him than his uncle had been: thankfully for me, he was finally six-feet under in Gledlang churchyard.

John Bolt's funeral had been held the week after my return from Waderswick when the coroner had finally released the body, or at least what remained of it after they had finished cutting it up: half the village was there – well, to be charitable, threequarters of it – and more than a few of them, like me, smiled inwardly if not openly when they lowered the coffin into the grave: goodbye John Bolt!

It being before Ben's accident, he was able to go and, rightfully, to sit among the other farmers: my mother went to be with him and I went to support Dennis and to see him through it: and Hoary went because he had talked the Reverend Ffawcon, much to the chagrin of the regular organist, into allowing him to play a doleful piece of funeral music for the waiting mourners.

All the other district's farmers and their wives were there: the Stanson sisters from opposite the school, grumpy Dick Witney from Hollymount, Bernie and Joan Hampe from Curlew's Hall, Rex Book and his wife and son, all the Pontings, all the Godwin clan led by Old Josh and his four sons, as well as the Pudneys and the Mussetts and the Hammonds and the Ponders from as far afield as Salter, the Peakmans from halfway to Maydun and the Olivers from Little Luton farm, plus a few even I did not know.

Richard did not go: when I had asked him, he just said: 'No, I don't think I'll bother. Nobody will miss me. I saw enough funerals in the camps.' Just that: I think he stayed away because Ben was going.

The funeral was at eleven-fifteen, nicely timed so that Jack Spivey at the Chessman next door could open up at twelve and guarantee at least forty or fifty would pack into the big room at Dennis's invitation to drink and to eat a standing lunch of spam, corned beef, spring onions, radishes, and leeks, egg and cheese and ham sandwiches, pork pies, oatmeal sausages, jam swiss roll, jam sponge cake and currant rock cakes and lemon curd tarts which Jack's wife, Vera, had laid on, at a price, of course. Jack Spivey did well that afternoon, as most of the farmers and their wives drank till well after two o'clock with the doors closed against the law. To me, it was noticeable that none of the other farm workers joined them: only Old Sago and myself: even the men from Boundary sloped off after the ceremony to get changed and were back at work by two o'clock: such were the times then.

All in all, Joanne Waters missed a good blowout: when I got back to Norsea the evening of her arrival, my mother's mood was no better: apart from the fact that I had not shown for tea, which she had left on the table to go cold so it was near inedible, with gravy the consistency of drying glue, to her way of thinking I had been over at Boundary 'hanging round that loon Dennis Bolt, who ain't half there' when I should have been doing work about the farm.

At some point during the argument, she stated something which had been worrying me. 'It's going to take more than you and Old Sago to run this place,' she declared. 'Where are you going to get extra help from because you'll need it? Is he –' Meaning Richard ' – going to give us any help? We've got bean-picking and pea-picking about to start and harvesting to come. You can't do that on your own! You're going to need help from someone and I can't see Dennis Bolt lending us anyone. He's one short himself now that creature from round the road has gone and he won't be doing much himself, will he?'

When, through youthful pride, I rather foolishly protested, 'Old Sago and me'll be all right,' meaning for what we were doing at that time, she nearly hurled the tea caddy at me.

'You bloody daft thing!' she exploded. 'You can't run this place like your step-father does. You're too stupid – and Sago's too old. He ain't got the strength to do half the jobs he used to do. He's over seventy, for Gawd's sake! Working this place with just you and him would see him off inside a month. And, as for you, you don't know the first thing about running a farm properly. You ain't never learned.

You ain't never been willing to learn. All you have ever thought about is ...' Etcetera, etcetera for a full minute or so before she suddenly suggested: 'You'll have to go round to that creature – ' Meaning Hoary. '– and tell him he'll have to give us someone else.' The 'someone else' she meant was, of course, Richard: who else? He was available and in Hoary's employ, the same as us: had, of course, worked on the farm before, as a boy, and was, despite his current more educated persona, a one-time farmboy just like me: he would have been a natural had I asked him.

But I had someone else in mind – Jan. I deliberately waited till she had finished her ranting: then, sneeringly, I played my trump card. 'There's a young Polish chap who's looking for work.' I declared scornfully. 'He came over in a boat from Abbey Farm a week or two back when you and Ben were in Melchborough. He's working for the Catchment Board at the moment.' Then the two lies: 'He asked me about farm work. I told him we always needed pickers for piece work.'

Mother turned to face me, eyes looking hard at me as if she were trying to determine why I should have suddenly blurted it out. 'What Polish chap? What's his name?' she asked bluntly.

'Jan – Janislav Something-or-other.'

'How old is he?'

'Mid-twenties. He's over at the Abbey Farm now, building up the seawall, but he'd like to stay around as they're due to pack up and leave soon. They're going further along the coast to Othona and beyond and he's got a girlfriend in Gledlang.' Foolish me! That was a giveaway.

My mother had a favourite saying, which she trotted out regularly when she had outwitted or outguessed me in my attempts at deceit or artfulness. 'There's only one to get over when you get over me and that's the Devil himself!' she would declare: this time she did not need to say it: it was in her eyes.

'Violet Reddy!' she declared, flapping the tea-towel in triumph. 'Who else could it be? It could only be her! Is that why she's started coming over here to clean that creature's house? To meet him? What other reason could there be? No one in their right mind would take it on willingly. This Polish chap, he's the one who left her with the baby, isn't he?'

The answer to my mother's question must have been written on my face. 'I knew it!' she exulted. 'I knew it. The little fool! The bloody little fool! She's married, for God's sake!'

Mind you, when you consider that the whole village knew Violet's baby was fathered by a missing Polack, it did not take much to put two and two together and get four when one turned up on the doorstep, did it?

My mother just ranted on, mostly to herself, not really addressing me: 'Ain't one man enough for her? What does she want to run after another one for? She should be thankful for the one she's got. Huh, I hope she knows what she'll get if he finds out. Bloody fool of a girl! I don't want her on my conscience if he finds out. I like the girl, but what she's doing only ever leads to trouble. It can't lead to anything else.' She seemed genuinely concerned for poor Violet's well-being.

I tried to explain about Jan being taken up into the Fens, the letters that had been returned and the letters that had not been received, and how he had come back to the area only in the past month and had only wanted to see the child: but all I got from my mother was another sniff of disbelief. 'Huh. He's a bit late coming back for the child now, isn't he?' she said, a contemptuous twist to her mouth. 'He's got a father now, he don't want another one.' Then the warning: 'Don't you get involved in any of it! Don't you dare!'

'Oh, I won't,' I assured her, playing the innocent. 'Not me. It's nothing to do with me. If he wants to come and work here, fine. If he wants to chase after Violet Reddy, that's his lookout.'

A glower from my mother and a quick slam of a sideboard cupboard door. 'You just make sure you get that creature to hire him – not us. I don't want us to have anything to do with it. He can work here – we need all the help we can get – but we're not hiring him. If things go wrong, I am not taking the blame and neither are you.'

'He is the father of her kid, little Thomas, and he'd have married her most like if he'd have stayed around,' I tried in Violet's defence.

'That's as may be,' replied my mother, bristling, 'but she upped and married someone else, didn't she, dopey as he is? He's her husband now. There was enough of what she's doing going on in the war. We don't want any more of it. If you're asked, we don't know anything about it. Understand? Nothing. We didn't hire him. That creature did.'

After another cupboard-banging pause, she enquired: 'When's she coming again?'

'She'll be here on Saturday, cleaning for Hoary. So will he, most like.'

'Ask him then. If we weren't in such a pickle, I wouldn't bother. I'd say "no," but we need the help. Silly bloody girl! I've a good mind to give her a talking to she won't forget in a hurry.' She did not, though.

Our conversation finished and I went walking round the island, aimlessly beheading stalks of cow parsley and marsh marigolds with a stick: later on I spent a half hour or so 'bombing' a piece of driftwood floating past the southern beach. Strangely, even though I was alone, I did not feel the least bit lonely: I felt strangely invigorated at what lay ahead. Richard and Hoary would be back on the morrow or the day after and now there was the prospect of Jan the Polack joining me full-time in the fields. As much as I liked Old Sago, what my mother said was true: he really was getting too old, especially for the heavier work.

FORTY-ONE

THE funny-looking foreign car with the two women in it plunged off the causeway about two hundred yards out from Norsea's shore, just where a short straight stretch ends and the track curves to the right before beginning its run across the fringing salting banks and up on to the island. It just seemed to miss the turn: then it slewed through the mud for fifteen yards and came to an abrupt halt with its rear end up and its radiator and front wheels embedded axle deep in the black ooze.

Only minutes earlier I had let it through the boards at the end of the Boundary track after a wait of more than one-and-a-half hours in a cool, easterly morning breeze, sheltering in the lee of the seawall, huddled inside my army greatcoat. Hoary had volunteered me for the task the previous evening. 'I need Joseph to do it, I need Joseph to do it!' he had pleaded to my mother from the relative safety of our front gate: and so I had risen at six-thirty that morning, a full two hours before I normally did on a Sunday, and crossed to the mainland just after seven. I had been told the car would be there at seven-thirty at the latest, in good time to cross before the tide reached us at nine-forty: all I had to do was remove the boards and then replace them once the car had passed through: it was late by a good hour when it came bouncing along the Boundary track.

A blonde-haired woman opened the passenger-side door and got out, visibly flinching in the chill airflow. 'Is this the road to Norsea village, please?' she asked, frowning. She was in her late twenties, slim, with shoulder-length hair nicely waved: she looked quite city smart in a dark blue skirt and a white lace-edged silk blouse under a short dark blue jacket which, being unbuttoned, immediately drew my eyes to the obvious display of her sex: after that, they moved down to where the blowing wind pressed the front of the skirt tightly up against her body to show the lower contours and depressions: I think she had blue eyes. Without a doubt, she was the most attractive woman I had seen: the kind I had seen only on Pathe Newsreels at Maydun pictures parading women's fashions with long cigarette holders in their hands.

Norsea village? Oh well, I suppose you could call the cottages a 'village.'

'Yes, miss. Keep going straight on, through the boards and over the causeway, miss.'

'Over the causeway?' She sounded as unsure as the cantankerous ambulancemen had been.

'Yes, miss, through the boards and across the causeway.'

The woman's weak smile was more one of bewilderment than thanks as, still frowning, she got back into the car and said something to her companion. Now her companion, the driver, she was altogether different: nearer forty than thirty, I reckoned, with black hair cut very short about her ears and fringed at the front: man-faced, I considered, dark and foreign-looking, Italian perhaps, or Greek, I thought, and none too tall from the low way she sat in the driving seat.

She looked distinctly sour-faced when her companion pointed to the gap in the boards and indicated that was the way she was to go: it was several seconds before she released the handbrake and the car jerked forward in a cloud of exhaust fumes. I waved them through with as cheery a smile as one can muster when kept waiting in a chill breeze for one-and-a-half hours. Both women eyed me with some surprise as they went by, like they were looking at the village idiot: admittedly, I had tied my frayed and mud-caked army greatcoat round with binder string and my headgear was a grey scarf turned inside out, Commando-style, and pulled well down over my forehead and ears.

No one could have anticipated what happened next: for some reason, perhaps in the belief that the causeway was just another road or through sheer foolhardiness, the car suddenly accelerated as it went out on to the causeway proper. It was madness! Those silly women must have been doing twenty or twenty-five miles an hour on the straight bit! I ran a short way down the hard after them, shouting for them to slow down and waving my arms: but, either they did not see me or hear me, or paid no attention if they did.

Whatever I did, I had first to put back the boards or the whole of Boundary farm and half the houses at the bottom of Shoe Street would have been under three or four feet of water when the tide came in: this took me all of four or five minutes as the boards are cumbersome for one person to lift if doing it alone and, if you are careless, you risk trapping your fingers in the slot or having one of the timbers drop on your foot. I kept my eye on the car as much as I could: that was when I saw it disappear over the edge.

The last board safely in place, I jumped on my bicycle and pedalled furiously after the women: when I reached the spot where the car had gone off the causeway and let my bicycle drop, they were just climbing out, looking very shaken. The soft surface mud there is about two-feet deep and makes a horrible sucking sound each time you drag one foot out of one black hole and plunge it into another: each step is an effort: every time a calf-deep leg is pulled free as you lean forward, it happens so suddenly that, if you are not careful, you can easily pitch headlong: and if you have two feet stuck in it at the same time, it is almost impossible to move forward at all. The blonde-haired one was just struggling towards the causeway, squelching her way through the foul-smelling black ooze, and, more by luck than judgment, just avoided that fate.

'Oh, my God! What awful stuff!' she cried and it seemed to me she was near to tears through disgust alone when she reached the bottom of the causeway slope.

'Give me your hand,' I said, slithering down and reaching out, at the same time trying not to grin at the sight of them both. I managed to pull the blonde one up the slope and received a cursory 'Thank you,' though once upon the hard she seemed more intent on examining how badly her clothes were splattered. 'Look at me,' she wailed to no one in particular, 'I'm covered in it, absolutely covered in it!'

She was, too: the black ooze was almost up to her knees, and, in her exertions, she had managed to splatter her jacket and blouse as well and she had lost both shoes.

Her shorter, dark-haired companion was at this time standing on one leg by the car's open door, holding on and reaching inside to tug at something, all the time loudly cursing to herself: her right leg was peculiarly raised to keep it out of the mud and she looked to be in some considerable pain: she, too, was barefoot, but her shoes were tied round her neck and she had already rolled up the legs of her black slacks, though without much luck as there was mud on them, too.

'Damn this bloody car, damn this bloody road and damn this bloody holiday!' She almost snarled the words: it only needed for her to kick the car to complete the comedy of the moment. Then, on hearing the wailing of her friend safe upon the hard, she angrily rapped out: 'Oh, do shut up, Laura! It's not the end of the bloody world, is it? It's my car. I didn't crash the effing thing on purpose.' Her easy use of the swearword was a shock to me: men used it – some times, yes –

like Ben and the Boundary workers, but I had never heard a woman using it: my mother would not have dreamed of doing so: somehow, it sounded very crude when the dark-haired, man-faced one spoke it.

That she had injured herself quite badly became obvious when she attempted to cross from the car to the hard: she had pulled a large umbrella almost as big as herself from the back of the car and, using it as a crutch, she half-hopped, half-sloshed, half-dragged herself on one leg through the deep mud in small twists and wriggles. Several times I thought she was going to pitch forward on to her face as the point of the umbrella sank a good eighteen inches or more into the black ooze: but she reached the slope through sheer exertion and willpower alone, accompanied by angry exclamations and curses spoken through gritted teeth.

I was quite prepared to splosh out and help her, but something about her manner told me to hold back: I was right: she was going to do this by herself and did not need assistance from anyone, especially a mere boy. When she got close, I did offer my hand, but she angrily waved it away. 'I can manage, boy, I can manage,' she cried: so I let her 'manage' and was rewarded when, with the very last effort of pulling herself free from the sucking ooze, she fell flat on her face, sadly on the slope of the hard rather than the churned black mud: the language only got worse after that.

She appeared to have twisted or wrenched the ligaments of her right knee and ankle, for she was unwilling to put even the slightest weight upon the leg and kept it off the ground all the while she sat on the slope recovering her breath. From what I gleaned between the epithets, when the car went off the track, her foot had become jammed under the brake pedal and had received the full impact as the vehicle rammed into the mud and upended itself: it would have been like hitting a brick wall.

Eventually, she turned to me. 'What the hell kind of road do you call this, boy?' she demanded: she said it, I think, without expecting an answer, for she immediately plunged on: 'The bloody thing's hardly wide enough to ride an effing bicycle on, let alone drive a car on. Couldn't you have widened the bloody thing? It's not a road, it's a – a – an effing farm track!'

'It's a causeway,' I informed her, the same as I had informed the complaining ambulancemen.

'Whatever it is, it's a bloody disgrace, boy,' the sour-faced one snorted. 'If I have broken my ankle, there will be hell to pay over this, hell to pay! And God help you if I lose my car. I'll sue you for every penny you've got! That's a special car. It cost a lot of money pre-war, more than you've got.'

No argument there: you would not get much out of us, was my first thought, because we have not got any money anyway. Instead, I settled for a petulant putdown: 'It's not my island, miss. I only live on it.' I did not see why I should get the blame. 'We mend the causeway as best we can, but the tide washes it away again, bit by bit. The currents do it. Anyway, you were going too fast. You have to go slow to get across.'

'Fast! Twenty miles an hour fast?' More like thirty, I thought.

'That's far too fast for going across the way the track is,' I told her, smugly. 'No one round here goes much over five miles an hour.'

'Five miles an hour! I could walk quicker than that.' The short one looked flabbergasted. 'You didn't say anything when you saw us.'

I felt like saying, 'Common sense should have told you,' but said instead: 'I thought you knew. Didn't Mr Hoar tell you about the causeway?'

'Who's Mr Hoar?'

'He owns Norsea. Well, sort of! He put the ad in the papers.'

'Who are you then, his son?'

'No, I bloody well am not!' I replied: my turn to swear now. 'Joe Coe's my name. We're the island's bailiffs.' I was now that Ben was in hospital.

'Well, Joe, as you call yourself,' the dark-haired one said in a sneering voice, 'no one said anything about a bloody island or an effing causeway. If I had known it was going to be on a bloody island like this, I wouldn't have bloody come.'

Her blonde companion, Laura, chose this moment to ask plaintively: 'What about our things? And the car?'

The sour-faced one glared at me for a moment as if I were responsible for their misfortune. 'Well?' she said. 'What do we do now?'

A shrug from me: the car was well embedded, tilted up on its nose fifteen yards out and the mud was already oozing back into the five-foot-wide furrow it had gouged: the tide was well on its way in: one glance down towards the estuary mouth told me that. It had already crept past Thistley Creek just a mile or so away as the crow flies and the channel branching towards the Shoe was beginning to fill and widen with the inflow: soon the water would be swirling across the Stumble mudflats towards us: in three-quarters-of-an-hour, give or take ten minutes, it would be lapping over the top of the causeway at that precise point.

'I don't want to alarm you,' I said, bluntly, 'but I don't know whether you've got time to pull it out. The tide's on its way in. It'll be up soon.' If ever a statement was calculated to cause alarm, that was and I was quite pleased at their consternation: I just wanted to get back at the dark one for her snottiness.

'Oh my God! Greta!' Panic from the blonde Laura: she looked at me in total disbelief, as if she expected me to hold back the tide till someone came along and pulled the car out: a latterday King Canute I was not!

'Eff,' exploded the foul-mouthed one, Greta. 'Eff this island and eff this effing road!'

'Causeway,' I corrected her and instantly wished I had not.

'Don't you try and be smart with me, boy,' she snapped, pushing herself upright with the aid of the large umbrella so that she could survey the upended car: I was pleased to see the simple act of getting up caused her great pain. 'How long before this tide of yours comes in?' she demanded.

It was not my tide: the Moon governed it. 'Thirty minutes before it reaches here,' I said: fifty was nearer the mark, but she was being snide and I wanted to panic them a bit more. 'An hour and it'll be covered, I reckon.'

That immediately set off more cries of alarm from the blonde Laura: the short, dark-haired Greta just swore again and demanded: 'Haven't you got a tractor or something to pull it out with? You could put a rope on it and pull it out in no time.'

We could if we had a tractor, madam, I thought to myself, but we do not have one: I tried to keep the glee out of my voice as I told her: then, as their faces fell, I added with a casual shrug: 'We've got a horse, a mare called Molly.'

'I don't care what the bloody horse's name is,' the man-faced one snapped, 'it will have to do.' From the peevish look on her face I think she would have preferred a tractor: she appeared angry that I had let her down by having only a horse and a mare at that. For the sake of the good-looking blonde, Laura, I felt that I needed to be helpful. 'Is there much in the car, miss? I could get it out for you, if you like?'

'Oh, no, not much,' the fuming Greta replied, her tone heavy with sarcasm. 'Just all our clothes, all our art gear, all our paints, our oils, our water-colours, our canvases, our brushes, pastels, bed linen, pots, pans! Just about everything we own, that's all. Not much really.'

I was only asking. 'I'll get them for you,' I said, sitting down and beginning to unlace my boots.

'Can't we pull the car out first somehow?' Laura, the blonde, bleated.

'It would be better to empty it just in case, miss,' I suggested, sensibly, I thought. 'I can get your stuff out now, up on to the hard and on to the island, and then go and get the mare and try to pull it out – ' A pause for effect here. ' – if we've got time.'

The dark-haired Greta thought for a few seconds, then said ungraciously: 'Oh, all right. Get the bloody stuff out. Better safe than sorry, I suppose. At least we'll have that if we don't have anything else. And get a bloody move on!'

Yes, madam. Certainly, madam. At your service, madam …

FORTY-TWO

THE CAR really was embedded axle deep: the mud was almost up to the doors, but, fortunately, it was not sinking: well, not yet anyway. The radiator and the engine would obviously be fouled, one headlamp was pointing skywards, the right-side front mudguard was bent inwards and the tyre there had been pierced: they would not like that: new tyres were almost impossible to get then: the best anyone could get were retreads.

The luggage attached to the back I managed to carry across to the causeway and pitch up on to the top, though even this did not please them, but drew cries of 'Be careful with that, boy!' and 'Mind that, for God's sake!' from the bossy Greta and pleas from the blonde Laura of 'Oh, can you look for my handbag, please? It was down by the passenger seat. I've left it there.' And 'Can you please bring the brown suitcase next? All my clothes are in that.'

Her friend swore at her for that and ordered me instead to bring some cardboard boxes containing a couple of dozen small canvases, plus two folding easels and two flat wooden cases which I supposed contained their oil paints and brushes: but since the blonde was more polite, more appreciative and less bossy, I made out I had not heard and got all of what I thought were her things first. It took me ten minutes to clear the car of six boxes, three suitcases, their art materials and several 'odds and ends' from the glove compartment. I balanced the two heavier suitcases on the handlebars of my bicycle and wheeled them the two hundred yards to the safety of the island: then went back for the rest, which I brought ashore in two further trips over the next twenty minutes: all done without any thanks.

The two women seemed to leave everything to me: the blonde Laura, being barefoot, grimaced all the way to the land as the causeway stones dug into the soles of her feet: her foul-mouthed companion, one hand on her friend's shoulder, let out half-stifled grunts of pain, and muttered inaudible swearwords and other curses through gritted teeth as she hopped beside her on the umbrella crutch, like

Wallace Beery's portrayal of Long John Silver I had seen once at Maydun cinema.

Fifteen minutes later, in what I knew was going to be a futile attempt, I trotted Molly down on to the causeway with a forty-foot length of rope looped round the collar: even on my bicycle, it had taken me ten minutes to fetch her from the small paddock where she had been grazing, harness her and find the rope. When I reached the point at which the car had plunged off, the tide was no more than thirty yards from the causeway and swirling fast across the mud: I estimated that I had ten minutes at the most: not nearly enough time. I wished either Ben or Richard had been there to help me, but Ben was in hospital and Richard was away somewhere that weekend, in London, I think he had said, and unlikely to be back before Tuesday.

I managed to attach one end of the rope round the back axle and to pull the car down on to an even keel and I even managed to drag it a foot or so nearer the causeway, well, Molly did, but really it was only for show: there was no way that car was going to come out, not with just Molly pulling, even if she did stand sixteen hands high: she just did not have the weight and the mud just held it. The water was already swirling past my feet when I finally gave up, unhitched the rope and turned Molly for home and safety: as we went back, the old mare turned her head towards me and looked at me as if to say, 'Whatever are you doing out here, Joe Coe? Whatever am I doing out here plodding through water? Get us off this causeway on to dry land do!'

I did, however, find the blonde Laura's shoes in the mud. 'Thank you,' she said when I handed them to her, albeit full of smelly ooze, which was very nice of her. 'Thank you.'

Man-face was in a different frame of mind, though, mouth open in disbelief and absolutely fuming. 'I would have thought your bloody horse could have pulled the car out!' she snarled as, from a safe distance, she watched the water swirling round it, already up to the axles. 'Did you really give it a good go? I mean a proper try, boy, not some half-hearted, pussy-footing attempt?'

'Yes, miss. It was just too far out and embedded too deep. Your car's too heavy. It'd need two horses pulling together to haul that out,' I informed her, managing to keep my cool despite her inference: then to try and calm her, I suggested: 'We can always have another go later.'

'Later!' she exploded. 'Later! The bloody car'll be twenty feet under water by then. Washed out to sea most likely.'

That was silly: a strong current might shift it a foot or two, but not much more: the tidal flow was not strong enough and the car was far too heavy: but, if that was her attitude, I was not going to tell her different: let them think that, let them suffer, her in particular!

I tied two of the suitcases on to Molly's halter and carried the third myself as I led them round to the cottages: the blonde Laura, still barefoot, wheeled my bicycle with her mud-filled shoes hanging from the handlebars and two painting easels strapped to the crossbar and across the saddle: the rest I left to be picked up on a second and third journey. Grumpy Greta carried nothing, but just hopped along slowly and painfully on her 'crutch,' with one shoe on, moaning and cursing and complaining the whole way.

As we walked along the track, it was: 'How much farther is this place?' And when I halted Molly by the two cottages: 'Is this it? God almighty!' And then when I pushed open the door and they saw inside: 'Oh my God, it's positively bloody primitive!'

Then the questions came: 'Where's the electric light?'

'We don't have electric light on Norsea. We use paraffin lamps.' Concern on their faces as I pointed to the lopsided lamp on the sideboard which I had brought from Hoary's along with the other furniture.

We passed into the kitchen: more bewilderment as they looked about. 'Where are the taps?'

'There are no taps, miss. We get the water from the pump outside in a bucket.' Utter disbelief on their faces.

'And the toilet? Where's that?'

'The what?'

'The toilet, the bathroom, the lavatory?'

'Oh, there ain't no bathroom. The lav's up the garden.'

'Up the garden! An outhouse?' Stupefaction now.

'Where do you wash then?' The blonde this time. 'I mean how do you have a bath?'

A sniggering smile from me. 'You have to heat your own water, miss. Light a fire, get a couple of buckets from the pump, fill a kettle and pour it in the old tin bath there.' I had put one from Hoary's outhouse in the kitchen, leaning it against the tapless sink. 'Half-a-dozen kettles'll fill it. Well, enough to have a wash in, anyway. Then there's always the river? You can always go for a swim. It's quite good round here. We've got a beach.'

'What, swim in the river! Do you actually swim in it?'

'Oh, yes, miss. It's salt water, but it's clean. There ain't nothing floating around in it like in other places.' I did not elaborate.

Their protests were not yet over: the blonde Laura was first into the bedroom off the parlour: no sooner had she entered than she let out a howl of dismay. 'They've put in single beds!' she cried.

The dark, man-faced one quickly followed her in, then turned on me accusingly. 'These are no good,' she declared sharply. 'We asked for a double bed in here.'

Puzzled, I was about to ask 'Why?' when something about the way in which she glared at me dissuaded me: instead I just shrugged. 'I don't know anything about that, missus.' She flinched at my use of the word. 'I only put in what Mr Hoar told me to. You'll have to ask him, if you want it changed.'

Why make a fuss over a couple of single beds? They were perfectly good beds to sleep on: they may have been the old black, iron-framed, lumpy-mattress ones from the old servants' quarters, but they were comfortable enough: Old Hoary slept on one in his starlight room and what was good enough for him was good enough for them. Anyway, I should have thought they would both have slept better in single beds rather than trying to cram together into one, waking each other each time they tossed and turned and pulling the blankets off each other. Still, how these two silly women chose to sleep was their business, not mine.

At that stage, I still did not know their full names, just their first names, what they had called each other: only later did I learn that the pleasant blonde was called Laura Wilchard, and the dark-haired, sour-faced one was named Greta Pocklington. Though both were painters from London, the dark-haired one was supposed to be well-known: all the while she was on Norsea, she demanded to be called 'Pocklington' by anyone who addressed her and repeatedly reminded Old Hoary that she was 'an ARA,' though what that meant I did not then know. What I did know is that I did not like her: she had already shown how haughty and bossy and demanding she could be, as well as foul mouthed. The blonde Laura, I did like: she was altogether more pleasant, more feminine and a damned sight more attractive: and more polite: though, from the way the other one spoke to her, she seemed to be very much the 'whipping girl' of the pair. Inside the cottage, as I walked Molly off to get the rest of their things, there seemed to be a lot of shouting going on: I was not sure, but one of them may have been crying: the blonde one most likely. The way they acted towards each other, you would have thought they were married!

FORTY-THREE

WE TOWED the car out two days later after it had been covered three more times by the tide: its position had not shifted at all, though it had sunk another six inches into the mud: given a week and it would have been a good eighteen inches down: two weeks and it would have been buried to its door handles.

This time we doubled our horsepower: as a gesture in Ben's absence, Charlie Mangapp brought Peter over from Boundary so the two horses could pull together: they had been unable to come on the Monday because of work commitments, which meant the car had had another two drownings: and that had not gone down at all well with the grumpy Pocklington. 'Does nobody round here do anything when they should?' she had wailed at poor old Hoary, who was crimson with embarrassment over the whole business.

Everybody was there to watch the recovery: Hoary had to be and was fussing about all over the place: Old Sago, who was about to start on the bean picking that very day, walked over with Charlie and was having a quiet laugh as he leaned on his bicycle, sucking at his empty pipe: even my mother was there, watching from a distance atop the low seawall, with arms folded and a sour look on her face, though I suspect she was more concerned about my handling of Molly than whether we got the car out. She kept herself well away from grumpy Greta, who stood on the north side of the causeway, while my mother watched from the south side.

The big surprise was not that Richard was also there but that he should come strolling up with Laura Wilchard just as we were about to start, chatting away as though he had known her all his life.

'Well in there, ain't he, boy?' growled Old Sago, a clear note of disapproval in his tone.

Richard had returned only the previous evening from wherever he had been on another of his solo trips, so how he had got to know Laura Wilchard in so short a time mystified me: but however he had done it, he certainly was 'well in,' as Old Sago put it.

I have to admit I was more than envious of Richard, watching the two of them talking so easily together as they walked out to where Sago, Molly and I and Charlie and Peter were waiting, though Laura Wilchard appeared to be doing most of the talking: she seemed to be very interested in Richard, overly interested, I thought. Strangely, she did not seem the least bit bothered by his scarred face, as I had expected she would have been: as I expected most people would have been: it made me wonder whether she had seen it or things like it before: she just looked up at him as she spoke and kept on talking.

She was wearing a straw sunhat and a bright blue, flower-patterned dress, which was a mistake in the breezy river conditions, because several times while they were walking along and while they were standing watching, the dress billowed up and I got quite a good view of everything underneath from the bottom of the causeway slope simply because she was also carrying a drawing pad under one arm and was using the other hand to keep the sunhat from blowing away and paying no attention whatsoever to her billowing dress.

The trousered grumpy Greta, still on her 'crutch,' the foot bandaged now, had given me a scowl as I led Molly past: if anyone had asked, I would have said she was peeved because she had to remain at a distance and the thought did cross my mind that she resented the fact that Richard was accompanying her friend: afraid she might be talking about her, perhaps?

My first task was to wade out with a shovel and clear what black slime I could from the rear wheels: this I did at Hoary's suggestion, but anyone who knows the river would have known that the mud would just ooze back in again: still I did it, and it did.

We attached a length of rope from the collar of each horse to the rear axles of the car, a task which necessitated me stripping off my shirt and vest so as not to get them any dirtier than they were: of course, all that happened was my chest, arms and face became caked instead. When I looked up to tell Charlie and Sago to get the horses ready to pull, I saw Laura Wilchard grimace with disgust: Richard looked at me, grinned and just raised his eyebrows: he seemed to think the whole thing funny.

At Charlie's suggestion, I had also taken out two planks and some old sacks and these I now wedged under the rear wheels, with the sacks laid on top, so we could haul the big car backwards without, it was to be hoped, too much resistance: then I went to check the handbrake was off. That was when I saw how much mud the swirling tides had deposited inside the car: the seats, the dashboard, the floor were covered in it: it was everywhere and it stank. 'Serve the silly women right for leaving the windows open and one of the doors ajar,' I thought: it would not have made much difference if they had closed the windows, of course: the mud would have got in just the same.

It took a strong pull to get the front wheels unstuck, but once the car started to move Molly and Peter just ambled forwards together: with two horses pulling, the car came out easily: all I had to do was to shift the planks and sacks a couple of times under the rear wheels and it was up on to the hard of the causeway in less than five minutes: ten minutes later and we had towed it up on to Norsea.

It all looked so easy that the po-faced Pocklington gave me a particularly hard stare as she hobbled forwards to meet us, muttering something to herself about 'We could have done all this before.' She and friend Laura had a real shock when they put their heads through the open window to peer inside, for the mud was an inch or more deep on the floor. 'Oh, God! The smell – it's vile! The seats are ruined! Ugh! It's awful! We will never be able to clean that out!' from a horrified Laura. And 'Bugger, bugger, bugger! Well, that's it then!' from grumpy Greta. Silly bloody women! Who cares about bloody carpets and upholstery or the smell?

Charlie Mangapp lifted the bonnet and told them what really mattered. 'Your engine's clogged to buggery, missus,' he informed the fuming Pocklington, fussing around the car. 'I don't reckon she'll start without a good clean. She'll need a few new bits, too, I reckon. Salt water won't have done her any good. A new battery for a start, most like. New electrics. A new carburettor, too, I reckon. Pump, brake linings, spark plugs, an oil change, new rubbers, new tyre. And everything'll have to be sluiced out, petrol tank, everything. To get rid of the salt.' As if to underscore his words, he gave the starting handle a few turns – but nothing.

'How long will all that take?' demanded Pocklington, almost choking with anger.

Charlie laid it on nicely: he gave the engine a long look, poked at it, stroked his chin a few times, gave a couple of sniffs and a 'Hmm' and said in his gravest voice: 'Two or three weeks, missus, maybe a month, round here anyway. It's difficult to say. It ain't like it's an English car, is it? French, is it?'

'It's Italian, a Bugatti,' snapped Pocklington angrily.

'Ah,' said Charlie, nodding sagely, 'if it needs new parts, I doubt you'll be able to get them round here, not straight away, anyway, not for a Musso car. We've only got the one garage in Gledlang and I know he won't have 'em. Not for an Itie car. And there ain't much chance anyone in Maydun'll have any either. You may have to go to Wivencaster or Melchborough and even then you 'on't know till you get there, will you?'

It was just as well the bonnet flap was up because it masked Old Sago and myself and meant we could smirk unseen: even Richard was trying to look concerned and not to grin. Pocklington spent her time muttering to herself and glowering at everybody as though it were all a conspiracy against her, while Laura Wilchard made suitable noises in sympathy.

Hoary spoiled it all. 'Don't worry, ladies,' he cried, 'all is not lost. We shall try to buy a car to take you on your trips. Richard and I have been talking about purchasing a car in which to drive around. I normally use Mr Offin's taxi service from the village, but Richard has convinced me that it would be more economic to buy a car for myself and for us to drive around in that. I have seen one for sale at quite a reasonable price. If I purchase that, I am quite sure I shall be able to register it with the authorities for petrol coupons. I shall ask for extra, of course. We shall need more than the basic ration. My brother is in Government in Whitehall so there should be no difficulty there. I shall ask him to help me. You ladies would be welcome to use the car at any time.'

'Except I've got this and can't bloody drive it,' an ungrateful Pocklington interrupted, pointing to her bandaged foot, before pointing at her companion and adding: 'And she can't drive. So who'll drive the bloody thing? You?'

'Oh, no, not me, not me,' chortled Hoary. 'That would never do. I couldn't do that. I would not be safe on the road and I do not have the time.' Then, like he had plucked the answer out of the air, he declared triumphantly: 'Richard will drive it, won't you, Richard? I am sure Richard would be delighted to take you anywhere you wish. I should be delighted to lend the car to you while yours is being repaired. In the meantime, I will get Charles and Joseph to tow your car across to the mainland to Mr Offin's garage to have it repaired. How is that?'

The women perked up at that: well, Laura Wilchard did: I distinctly saw her look across at Richard and smile: Pocklington just scowled even more, while Richard gave me a surprised grin at the announcement: whether at the prospect of getting a car or driving the women about in it, I do not know. 'I'd be happy to drive them,' he confirmed. 'Delighted.' Then with overstated politeness: 'Anywhere you wish to go, ladies, anywhere you wish to go. I shall be at your service.'

I had to say it: in an aside to Richard just before I left, I whispered: 'I didn't know you could drive?'

'Oh yes,' Richard confirmed, nodding. 'I drove an American jeep while I was working in Australia and I drove the lorry several times when I was working at the warehouse in London.'

'Well, you'll have no trouble then, will you, so long as you've passed your test?'

'Test? What test?' Richard sounded perplexed.

'You need to take a driving test now,' I informed him.

'Brought it in before the war in Thirty-Four,' Charlie elaborated to a frowning Richard. 'You have to take a test to drive in England now to show you're competent. You can't get a licence without one, leastways not a full licence.'

'To hell with all that,' scoffed Richard. 'I can drive, what more do they want?'

Charlie and Old Sago both laughed. 'You'll cop it, boy, if the law catches up with you,' Old Sago chortled.

I watched as Richard and Hoary went off with the women: to their cottage, I presumed: Sago, too, went off to begin his bean-picking with my mother, leaving Charlie and I to tow the car back across the causeway to Sligger Offin's garage opposite the church. Charlie hitched up the horses again and, with him guiding, I sat in the muddy driving seat steering it.

The crossing to the village took us half an hour: we had to go extra slow because of the punctured tyre: it was a most uncomfortable half-hour for me, sitting on a seat caked in black slime: I tried various ways of doing it, crouching on the seat, even just standing, but, whatever I did, I generally ended up with the seat of my trousers soaking wet and coated in mud:.

One peculiar thing: as Laura Wilchard had walked away, Charlie had caught me looking after her and had growled: 'It ain't no use you looking at her, boy. She and the other one ain't exactly your sort.'

I knew that and I told him so: he did not have to tell me that, in her eyes, I was a country yokel, while she was a sophisticated, well-to-do Londoner, trained in the arts, travelling in an expensive Italian car, even if it were defunct and half-full of mud at that precise moment: she obviously had plenty of money to be able to paint for a living and to be able to afford a holiday in the first place, even if it was on Norsea: but a boy can look at a sophisticated, well-bred woman and wonder and use his imagination, can he not?

'That ain't exactly what I meant,' said Charlie, with a sniff.

FORTY-FOUR

CHARLIE told me the tale of Joanne Waters as we walked the horses back down Shoe Street after delivering the women's car to an unenthusiastic Sligger Offin: cousin or no cousin, Joanne Waters's arrival and determination to stay in Boundary farmhouse had caused something of a stir in the village: I was just surprised that she was still there, a week or more after turning up on Dennis's doorstep: knowing the particular characters of the people involved, Charlie's tale made me laugh.

It had all started the morning following her arrival when Old Ma Parkinson, who had cleaned and dusted for John Bolt for a half-dozen or more years, arrived at the back door just as Charlie also called to find out what new orders Dennis had for the men that day. Joanne Waters was standing in the kitchen in just her slip, washing her underwear: the prudish Ma Parkinson was outraged and demanded to know who she was and what did she think she was doing? According to Charlie, she was told by Joanne Waters in no uncertain terms to 'Mind your own bloody business!' That got the old girl's back up.

'You haven't been here all night, have you?' the dried-up old lady demanded.

'Of course, I have!' Joanne Waters answered. 'I only got here yesterday evening. Where else would I go? I don't know anyone else here, do I?'

'Good God, girl! You don't sleep in the same house as a man unless you're married to him,' a horrified Ma Parkinson declared.

'Don't be so bloody daft!' Joanne Waters retorted.

'Daft! Daft! You brazen hussy,' Ma Parkinson scolded back. 'People don't do such things, not decent people anyway. And you just a slip of a girl! How do I know you weren't in his bed last night?'

'You don't. And, even if I had been, it wouldn't be any of your business,' replied an infuriated Joanne. 'What I do is my business. This is the Nineteen-Forties not the Nineteenth Century!'

'Anything could have happened with you and him here on your own!' Ma Parkinson tried again, meaning only one thing. 'Anything!'

'Well, it didn't. And if you mean what I think you mean, that happened long before I ever come here,' was the bold reply from Joanne Waters, 'and I hope it'll happen again, as often as possible if I have my way.' The reply left poor Ma Parkinson speechless.

Charlie admitted he had taken a good look at Joanne Waters while she stood there and, like me, had not been overly impressed. 'Too skinny for my liking,' he said shaking his head and laughing. 'I like a woman that's got something to grab hold of and a bit o' flesh you can sink into when you're poking the fire.' As his wife was a sixteen-stoner, you knew what he meant.

Charlie continued his tale: the idea that Dennis could have been getting up to anything struck him and me as very funny, but Ma Parkinson was of a more suspicious and disbelieving nature and had gone upstairs to make sure both beds had been slept in: and by a single person. No sooner had she finished her work than she was straining at the pedals of her creaking, unoiled bicycle, wobbling up Shoe Street and through the Square and up Tithe Street to the new parsonage: an hour later, just as the men on Boundary were about to start their dinner in one of the packing sheds, the new vicar, Reverend Ffawcon, came bowling along the track on his bicycle, heading for the farmhouse.

'Ho, ho, Dennis is in for it now,' exclaimed a grinning Ted Oldton: the men had all been told about Joanne Waters's arrival and her overnight stay: so they knew what was about to happen. Before that day, Reverend Ffawcon had never been seen on the farm, not even at harvest festival time: John Bolt, late and unlamented, would have chased him off if he had. So it did not take a genius to know why he had suddenly decided to make a call on the very first day after Joanne Waters's arrival: Dennis and she were both in for some moral correction.

To me, it seemed a bit churlish of him to deny Dennis some fun: especially as the Reverend Ffawcon himself was in need of a little 'moral correction,' at least according to the village choirgirls: they told a story that our new vicar had taken one of their number into the belfry to administer his brand of 'moral correction' after catching her misbehaving at evening practice: he had told her to bend over to give her a smack on the behind and then lifted her dress to do it, so the girls said. All the more churlish, too, as he had a buxom, blonde wife at home, the bespectacled Anne Ffawcon, with shapely legs and large breasts that wobbled when she walked, a joy, I would have thought, for any man to lie beside in bed at night and reach out and touch.

But I suppose that when a villager, particularly one who helps to clean the church after services on a Sunday, complains that a young couple of the parish, who are neither married nor engaged, are sharing a house together, then the Reverend Ffawcon must have felt it his bounden duty to point out to them the potential for sin and to tell them that, in communities such as Gledlang, such actions were frowned upon. What he could not say, for decorum's sake, was that all those who were old and spinstered because of the First War (there were fifteen soldiers' names on our war memorial) or who were widowed and dried up by the passage of time, like old Ma Parkinson herself, were just soured and jealous. It was his moral duty, therefore, to suggest a compromise: that, till such time as Joanne Waters returned to Devon, Ma Parkinson herself should take up residence in the self-same house and be the housekeeper-cum-chaperone to preserve moral decency and quieten wagging tongues. Not unnaturally, Ma Parkinson was more than willing to do this as it meant she would be on hand to undertake her usual dusting and washing duties in the morning and also able to cook meals for the both of them in the evening: it also meant she would get free meals and lodging for herself and live in a big house which was light, spacious and airy and a good deal more grand than the dingy, damp, decaying cottage up past the Bowler's Rest in which she lived out her lonely days. She would also, of course, still be paid.

The Reverend Ffawcon must have presumed it would not be long before Joanne Waters went home, just a couple of weeks or so: but Charlie and the men were not so sure: they saw the evidence for that on that first full day after Joanne Waters's arrival, before the Reverend Ffawcon had even ridden through the white gates on his moral crusade. When Dennis had joined them first thing after breakfast to supervise their work, spraying the trees against blight, he was washed and shaved, which he normally was not, he had changed his tattered, greasy cap for a cleaner one and his blue overalls appeared to have been washed overnight, while his turned-down wellingtons, which no landworker ever washes, had been given something of a hosing down to make them shine. He even appeared to be embarrassed to be in their company: like he was wondering what they were thinking after hearing from Charlie Mangapp that a girl had been staying overnight in a farmhouse bed with just him there. The question which formed in their minds was the obvious one: Did old Dennis give it a try during the night? Small wonder then that the poor man was agitated and nervous for the short time he was with them.

It did not take an intelligent man to realise where Dennis wanted to be: they saw the reason in the distance later that afternoon, Dennis showing Joanne Waters around the farm. The men did not actually meet her till they all trooped into the yard at teatime to put away the sprayers and tanks and retrieve their bicycles and came upon the two of them just leaving the barn: a sheepish Dennis blushed a deep crimson and grinned in that inane, embarrassed fashion of his all the way through the introductions, while, according to Charlie, Joanne Waters smiled boldly back at the men as if she had known them all her life. Like Charlie and I, none of the men, Ted Oldton, Bob Bird, Sam Perry and Tully Jude, thought overmuch of Joanne now that they had met her and seen her close up.

'I've seen more fat on a butcher's pencil,' said a normally unopinionated Bob Bird, once Dennis and Joanne Waters had gone into the house to eat the tea which Ma Parkinson was cooking for them at that very moment, having made her peace with her employer and his guest: it was really a case of having to, especially as she now would be staying under the same roof with them.

'Thighs like matchsticks, tits like poached eggs, and a fanny like a keyhole no doubt,' expounded Sam Perry sniffily, partway underscoring my own judgment.

It was Tully Jude who surprised them all. 'The nearer the bone, the sweeter the meat, they say,' the scrawny, stoop-backed, squint-eyed bachelor cackled, giving his toothless grin. His unexpected comment brought tears of laughter welling up in the other men's eyes: they knew that Tully Jude had never once dipped his wick in all of his sixty-plus years, so what would he know about it? The men were laughing all the way up Shoe Street: and Tully, not realising they were laughing at him rather than with him, laughed as well, thinking he had cracked a joke.

'They say there's a woman for every man, somewhere, and this could be the one for Dennis,' an unexpectedly prescient Charlie Mangapp said as he prepared to take his leave of Molly and I at the junction of the Boundary track. 'It's about bloody time Dennis got himself a woman and found out what it's all about. A man don't live by bread alone. He needs something more'n that. I'll say this for Dennis, he and that cousin o' his suit each other. Neither of them's what you'd call an oil painting and neither of them's that bright. They'd go well together. I reckon she could be staying for a lot longer yet, a lot longer, if I ain't a bad judge. Time will tell, though, time will tell.'

FORTY-FIVE

HOARY bought the promised car a week later: I went round one evening to see Richard in his cottage, but he was not there: it was a disappointment: that day I was low in spirits and needed someone to whom I could talk. That day, the hospital authorities had told us, Ben would be undergoing an operation on his stomach, just 'a minor operation,' they called it, to 'correct' something inside his gut. Any operation was a worry for us: people died during them: but for my mother, knowing that he was being sliced open on an operating table even as she stood in the beanfield alongside Old Sago, it must have been unnerving: I imagined all kinds of things myself, all of them gruesome.

My mother had left the beanfield early as soon as we had finished in the afternoon and then had spent over an hour waiting by the telephone kiosk in Gledlang Square to call the hospital for news: she was not in a good mood when she returned and, when I asked her how Ben was, she just gave me a curt, 'It's over. They've got to wait now,' which was as much as her temper would allow her to say. She was, I think, quite fearful, tearful even when by herself in the kitchen, though she would not show it, especially to me. A couple of times, glancing into the scullery while I ate my tea, I caught her wiping her eyes as she stood over the washing-up basin, but all I got was an angry look for seeing her. Had it not been for the fact that we needed to get in the bean crop, I think she would have gone over to Melchborough just to be at the hospital when Ben came out of the operating theatre and most probably would have stayed at his bedside all night if they had let her: she was sentimental like that. But when she flared up at my presence around her, I scuttled away and went to find Richard to tell him what I knew.

As it was, I had spent a miserable day, just as I had spent a miserable week, bean-picking: my mother and Old Sago had naturally picked side by side, and Jan the Polack, starting work on Norsea that very week, and a happy Violet Reddy had also picked side by side, which meant, that with the non-appearance of Stanley Lobel, I had passed most of the time working on my own on a row way behind the rest. Only when Sago fetched Molly from the small paddock just before four o'clock to hitch her up to the wagon and I joined him to load the sacks and carry them across to the Boundary pick-up point for the five o'clock market lorry did I have someone to whom I could talk.

Once I had given my mother the driver's consignment note, as she was now doing Ben's books, I went in search of Richard and eventually found him round at Hoary's house – where else? – and that is where I got the surprise which made me forget about Ben and my mother's troubles: parked on the 'lawn' alongside his now embedded statues was the car which Hoary had promised the women he would buy so that Richard could chauffeur them about till their own car was repaired, whenever that would be.

Richard was nearby. 'What do you think of it?' he asked, coming over when he saw me inspecting it.

Disappointing. 'It's not exactly new, is it?' I said.

The car was a very second-hand Austin Seven, third-hand or fourth-hand, I would have said, a tin can on wheels, a spindly boneshaker, with painted-over bits of rust here and there and one or two dents in the black mudguards: the boot was very small and would never take their fold-up easels, stools and painting boxes: they, like the big umbrellas they had brought, would have to go on the back seat. True, the car was polished up well enough: it was just that I had expected something bigger, something brand new which would make the villagers' eyes boggle: but that was being naive. You could buy new cars then, if you had the money: all you had to do was to promise not to sell it inside a couple of years (done to beat the wideboys), though there was not a lot of choice. Because of the war there were no really new designs at that time and the best went abroad anyway: postwar Britain, so the miserable Chancellor of the Exchequer, Hugh Dalton, kept telling us, was on the verge of bankruptcy and any decent cars we made had to go for export: seventy-five per cent, they said. The best that most buyers could hope for was a prewar, second-hand Morris, Vauxhall, Austin or Ford, bought off a bombsite lot and, because for most that is all there was, they were charged an exorbitant price (in some case, several times the car's prewar purchase price). No one in Gledlang, other than Sligger Offin, had a motor, except the farmers, of course, like Dennis with his little green van who got a supplementary petrol ration. Still, I thought Hoary's might have been at least a Humber or a sleek new Riley saloon (like MacFadden).

'How much did he pay for that?' I asked Richard.

'Just over three hundred,' was Richard's astonishing answer: when you have never had more than a pound note in your pocket ever, the knowledge that someone could cheerily produce three hundred to buy a twelve-year-old car, even if that was the going price, was quite startling.

'It's a bit small, especially if there are going to be three of you in it.'

'It'll do. It's a bit of a squeeze, but it'll do,' said Richard. He gave his usual macabre, lop-sided smile, but there was something in the way he said it and the way he looked at me, which suggested he was relishing the prospect of driving the two women about, particularly one of them.

To my mind, the car was hardly big enough for two people to sit in comfortably, so what it would be like when there were three in it, plus all their easels and canvases and such, I could not imagine: they would be bumping into each other every time they got in and out as there were only two doors and so squashed up against each other they would hardly be able to move. On second thoughts, that might be a pleasant experience, having Laura Wilchard's rear end brushing past your face as she struggled into the back.

'We'll manage,' said Richard. 'The first trip is tomorrow. I'm taking them up to Beckenden Woods for the day. They can paint there.'

'What will you do while they're doing that?' I asked.

'Park the car and wait for them till they have finished, I expect,' he said, casually.

'It beats bean-picking, I suppose,' I said, grudgingly.

As much as I envied Richard driving around the countryside in a car with Laura Wilchard in it, I did not envy him driving the sour-faced Pocklington: no one would volunteer to chauffeur her, especially if she were sitting in the front seat, which I expected she would insist upon doing in view of her injured leg. Sligger Offin's taxi had called the day after we had dragged their car out to take her across to MacFadden's surgery in Lil Brown's front room at the top of Shoe Street: there, through Hoary and Old Sago, I had learned, a sober MacFadden had diagnosed badly torn knee and ankle ligaments and a couple of bone fractures, which made it quite remarkable that she should have been able to limp ashore as she had. Now she was hobbling about on a stick, with her plastered leg stiff as a board and was likely to be that way for at least a month.

'How long is all that going to last?' I asked.

'Until their car is mended. Two or three weeks. Not too long, I hope,' replied Richard. 'Hoary wants to resume his digging trips as soon as he can. He wants to go up to some place the other side of Saxmundham, where he thinks he will find some Roman brick-making kilns like the red earth ones he found near Cobwycke last year. We can't do that while I'm driving them around. The sooner Sligger Offin repairs their car the better.'

I did not like to tell him that it could be sometime before Sligger Offin even started work on it: he had not taken too kindly to the news, inadvertently given by me, when I had mentioned in passing: 'Old Hoary's looking for a car. He wants Richard to drive him about.'

'The bugger he does!' exclaimed a flabbergasted Sligger: the old man's regular taxi trips to Hamwyte station and to Wivencaster station as Hoary set off on his digging trips up into the next county constituted a lucrative source of his income: enough for him to buy his wife a new mangle, which was a disappointment to her as she thought she was going to get one of the new-fangled twin-tub washing machines. The crafty Sligger had been able to run his car all throughout the war when others had had to put theirs up on bricks or run them off gasbags: he managed to get more than the basic monthly five gallons at the start because he offered his car for 'war work,' delivering evacuees to homes in rural locations, or so he said: though most got fed up with waiting at stations and walked to their destinations. Later on, when the ration was cut altogether, Sligger still wangled his share by saying he was picking up servicemen at railways stations who were going home on leave or dropping off those going back to their units: a likely story! He ran a few here and there, but mostly his petrol was used to run a more profitable taxi business on the sly for Yanks and their girls and to take his wife and children shopping and on picnics to the beach at Yalton fifteen or so miles up the coast.

When Charlie and I had left Pocklington's car with him, Sligger Offin had taken one look at it and declared that he was not going to start trying to repair a car in the condition it was in: I managed to clear some of the mud out before I left: even then he was not satisfied, grumbling that he was quite sure he would not be able to get the new parts for a month or more: he might just as well have added 'if I'm lucky' or 'as if I bloody care!' He also pushed it to the back of his yard: out of sight, out of mind, I suppose: he was paying Old Hoary back, obviously.

'Fancy a trip out?' Richard asked, jerking his head in the direction of the mainland.

'I wouldn't mind,' I replied, enthusiastically: a run-out would be interesting at the least, just to see if the old car went. 'But won't it waste petrol?'

Richard dismissed my concern with a wave of the hand. 'Who cares?' he said. 'Hoary's wangled himself extra. He's got coupons for ten gallons a month.' Then with a laugh: 'It pays to have a brother high up in Whitehall.'

Richard went up the 'Repent ye ...' path to the open kitchen window where Hoary, in his usual assortment of clothing, was crunching to and fro over the refuse on the kitchen floor, brewing some of his treacly, black Turkish coffee, which he somehow managed to acquire: you would not have thought Violet Reddy had cleaned the place twice already! Even cash-short Violet had bridled at sweeping out all of Hoary's twenty or so rooms for the money he offered and had struck a bargain with him: she would clean and dust and polish his two parlours, the large one overlooking the estuary where he played his piano on his lonely nights and a smaller one at the western end where he piled his illuminated vellum books and from which he watched his sunsets: she would also clean his kitchen, pantry, scullery and hallway: and, of the dozen bedrooms, she would sweep, dust, polish and tidy just the two main ones, the one in which he slept on cold or cloudy nights and the second one with a skylight where on summer nights he would lie abed with the skylight open staring up at the stars and pondering no doubt upon the vastness of the universe and the meaning of all things, most of which there was no point in worrying about as neither he nor we could change them. The other rooms, of course, were too full of things for her to do anything with them.

'I'm just going to the Pool garage in Maydun to put some petrol in the tank ready for tomorrow,' Richard informed him, poking his head through the window. 'Have you got the coupons and some money?'

After a minute or so, Hoary's hand appeared through the window to pass Richard the booklet of coupons and a white five-pound note. Then the car was cranked and we were off, bumping across the causeway at five miles an hour, removing and reslotting the boards, then tootling up Shoe Street. The hunched group on the ciderstone in the Square stared in disbelief as we rattled by, particularly Nick, who, when he saw I was looking at him, averted his gaze, like he felt guilty about something.

Eventually, as if he had been waiting for the right moment, Richard enquired about Ben: siding with no one, my mother had made it a point of keeping him informed of the forthcoming operation.

'Mum says he's okay. He's ruptured something in his guts, but they say they've been able to put that right, that and one or two other things they found. He's doing better, they say.'

'I'd like to go and see him,' said Richard, 'but, you know – ' He released one hand and waved it in a gesture of frustration.

'I suppose I shall have to go myself soon,' I told him in a tone more grudging than I intended, 'just to let him know I'm still alive and tell him how the farm's doing.'

My reluctance was born of guilt, I think, as much as experience: Molly may have been pulling the wagon, but what happened would not have happened if I had shifted the bricks when I had been told to do so. I was reluctant also because I knew Ben's temperament: he was bad enough when he had to stay in bed for just a few days with a bronchial inflammation, which he often got in the winter through smoking his cigarettes: he could be cantankerous, angry, harsh, demanding, unhelpful and downright unappreciative of everything anyone tried to do for him: so what he would be like facing the prospect of several months in hospital, I dreaded to think.

When I remarked on this to Richard, he said quite surprisingly: 'He's always been like that. He was the same when I was at home. My mother always said – ' He stopped suddenly: it was the first time I had heard Richard mention his mother: Ben and my mother always referred to his first wife as 'she' or 'her' or 'the first one,' like she had no name, just as they used to refer to Richard as 'him' and 'he' before he came back: and they always seemed to choose their words as though they did not want to dredge up old memories, painful memories.

'What did your mother say?' I began, hoping to pick up the conversation following Richard's pause.

Richard suddenly looked flustered and shot me an angry glance, though it was just a flash of mood passing across his face. 'Never mind, Joe,' he said curtly. 'I'll tell you some other time. Not now.'

We motored on in silence for a while after that: it was not till we reached Boundary and repeated the unxious business of removing and replacing the boards a second time, before bumping back over to the island just an hour ahead of the incoming tide, that Richard regained his cheerfulness. Even so, the drive had been great fun: something different: at least it made me forget the troubles with my mother and with the others: I was glad, though, to see that the Square was empty and the ciderstone deserted when we came back through.

That was to be my one and only ride in the car for some time: after that, I was too busy working and Richard's time was taken up during the day, and sometimes well into the evening, driving the women about.

FORTY-SIX

WHAT a wonderful life it must be, I thought one mid-morning a week or so later, standing in our second beanfield rubbing an aching back and watching for the umpteenth time the little car and its occupants bump and bounce past the field, heading for the causeway and who knew where beyond – what a wonderful life it must be to sit all day on a roadside verge covered with cow parsley and dandelions, or to sit at the edge of a field of waving corn, or in the middle of a meadow of daisies with the sun high and bright in the sky overhead, butterflies dancing along the hedgerows and the birds singing all around you, painting whatever took your fancy, with no one to trouble you, no one to curse you, no one to make you work faster, doing everything at your own pace, painting pictures while the rest of the world was working for a living!

When they had set off on their first painting trip to Beckenden woods the morning after Richard and I had made our trip out, you would have thought it was some great event: Hoary turned out to wave them all off like he was seeing off the contestants at the start of a Paris-to-Peking car race: he stood on the seawall waving a great big scarf, a woman's, as they chugged out on to the causeway: it was all a bit ridiculous, I thought. So did my mother, Old Sago, Violet Reddy and a very bemused Jan the Polack, who must have wondered what it was all about and thought he had joined a lunatic asylum: the only one who got excited about it was little Thomas, who ran to the gate of the field in which we were working, pursued by Violet. As the little car chugged past before setting out across the causeway, Richard turned and gave a grin and a wave of his hand.

When they returned in the evenings, Richard took to parking the car outside his cottage overnight: each morning the two women would climb into the little Austin after breakfast or mid-morning, whenever was appropriate, and, with the limping, stiff-legged, man-faced, grumpy Greta in the front passenger seat, chug across the causeway and then the three of them would vanish down the maze of narrow, high-hedged backlanes which lie between Gledlang and the Roman road twelve miles off and which wind along ridges and dive into valleys and sometimes twist back upon themselves so that the unknowing driver can, if not careful, end up at the same spot three or four times over. In the course of a month, Richard took them to lonely, twisting creeks at Copthall, Cobwyke and Cumvirley where the gulls screech and the wind always blows: he took them to elm-shaded churchyards so overgrown they could hardly make out the gravestones of the forgotten dead: he took them down narrow, twisting dead-end lanes to cornfields where they sat on exposed headlands under the shade of their big umbrellas and painted views of distant sleepy villages and church towers rising from clumps of trees: and he took them to places where the roadside verges were thick with cow parsley, campions, thistle and dock, where they set up their easels and painted humble, clapboard cottages with sagging moss-covered roofs and crazily leaning chimneys.

Sad to say, theirs is probably the last record of many of those old cottages: for most were gone within a few years: none of the country folk wanted to live in such tumbledown places: they preferred the new Utopia of smart, spartan council houses on nice tidy estates with electricity, running water and a flushable lavatory in a bathroom, not an outhouse with a bucket thirty yards up the garden. Consequently, many fell derelict and eventually the well-to-do Londoners came out and bought them and flattened them to make way for their sprawling, soulless bungalows, then started complaining about the smell of manure piles in the nearby fields, cockerels crowing in nearby farmyards, cows which blocked their paths in narrow lanes and left pats all along the roads, sheep which ran about the fields bleating pitiably when shorn, not to mention the curtains of dust which blow across the land at harvest time and cover any washing which has been foolishly left out by some unsuspecting newcomer.

Our intrepid painters sat in sunlit meadows, where milk cows grazed and head-bowed sheep munched in a never-ending crawl across the grass, to paint pink and creamwalled farmhouses and black creosoted barns huddled under their stands of tall, nest-topped elms: they twice visited Maydun quay to paint the old sail barges there, with the backdrop of the old houses climbing up the hill past the whitewood steeple of St Mary's church: and, on one scorching day, they even sat among the debris of the timber wharf at the foot of Maydun hill to paint the bow-fronted Georgian houses straggling down to the river.

Most of the trips were short, just around the immediate area, eight or nine miles out and eight or nine miles back: to Salter, say, Foliot Magna, the two Tottles, Hamwyte, Cobwycke, south of the river once or twice, west to the hill at Nadbury. But, with Hoary's monthly ten gallons supplemented by Pocklington's five gallons from her basic ration because she had no car in which to put it herself, Richard was able to take the women almost anywhere they wanted to go: even over the county boundary once, Richard told me, up to where the Gap is: and, on their way back, he said, they called at a place where a famous painter had worked in his father's flour mill. Even so, both Hoary's ten gallons and Pocklington's five were all used up by the end of the third week and the car had to stay on Norsea for a few days till both could use the next month's coupons.

Sometimes on his trips, Richard took the two women to the same spot for three days in succession, especially when they were painting in oils, which I thought was a complete waste of petrol: and frustrating, too, for someone who did not paint himself, just sitting in the car reading a book or a newspaper and watching two women camped on stools on the grass verge slowly daubing away. I could not have stood three weeks of that! If it had been me chauffeuring them, I would have said 'Sod the petrol!' and driven off into Hamwyte or Wivencaster or Levendon or Shallford, especially the latter, which is a picturesque market town, full of old shops and half-timbered pubs, astride the Roman road between Wivencaster and Melchborough. At least he could have looked at the shop girls or sat in a pub over lunchtime eyeing the barmaids (if there were any), then dawdled back to pick up his passengers at a prearranged time: all he had to do was keep one eye on the weather and, as it was such a scorching month, his job was very easy.

In fact, our two painters could hardly have picked a better month in which to paint than that July: over those first three weeks, it got drier and hotter as the month progressed and temperatures of ninety-plus were broadcast on the wireless news: consequently, the women painters seemed to be out every fine day that came.

Even Richard was persuaded to try his hand at painting a couple of water-colours: but not with any success: that I can confirm by the examples he showed me: very poor. I was not there, of course, but some instinct told me it was Laura Wilchard who made the suggestion: several times I saw Richard helping her out of the car, taking her by the hand as she wriggled between the folded-down passenger seat: and she always said 'Thank you, Richard' in that smiling way of hers.

Pocklington, of course, got out on her own as she always sat in the front seat because of her stiff leg: had she not had to do that, she might well have had competition from Laura Wilchard to see which would sit beside Richard: and for Laura Wilchard it would not just have been to see who would get to look through the windscreen, either, I reckoned!

At times Laura Wilchard addressed Richard directly to his face, as though she were paying no attention whatever to his disfigurement: she had even drawn a portrait of him, showing the scarred side: I know it was her drawing because she had signed and dated it, like the famous artists did and given it to him. More than once it crossed my mind that a friendship of some kind was brewing between the two of them: it interested me to know what kind. If you look, you will see the signs: how people laugh easily together, talk easily together, smile at each other a lot: you will see a woman touch a man's arm, move closer to him, put herself in his line of sight: one could not help but notice how Laura Wilchard sought out his company now, especially in the evenings. Every time I went anywhere near his cottage in the evening, I seemed to find Laura Wilchard sitting in his parlour, drinking tea, smoking or talking while the gramophone would be playing that dreary music I sometimes heard on the Third Programme whenever I attempted to tune our wireless past it to one of the foreign channels.

The umpteenth time I had been round to Richard's cottage and heard her laughter inside and returned home, my mother had sneered, sarcastically: 'Prefers them to you, does he? Well what do you expect, you daft little fool! Though a lot of good it'll do him. Women like that! Ugh!' Whatever that meant?

FORTY-SEVEN

I NEVER stood in one particular peafield to the west of the farmhouse then without thinking back to a bright sunlit afternoon four years before when I stood on the self-same spot watching high in the sky the burning bombers coming back from Germany. They were American B17s: several had already crossed the lakes of blue between the clouds: then three of them came in a line astern together and the middle one was on fire, trailing black smoke, with one of its four engines stopped and another feathering. It seemed to be jerking along, like it was struggling to stay in the air: the plane just ahead of it looked like it was guiding the stricken one home, while the one flying close behind, so close they appeared to be touching, seemed to be nudging the faltering one forward, shepherding it. Everyone in the field was looking up, my mother, Ben, Old Sago, me: all of us, I think, were uttering a silent prayer for those desperate men up there in that burning plane: I have thought of them many times since: even now I wonder if they made it home.

After two grinding weeks, we had finished the last of the beans a few days earlier and now, after a wait of another week, we were starting on the peas: Ben and I had been late in planting them because of the frozen ground in March and then the waterlogged fields which followed, not completing the work till late April, so both our fields of peas were late that year. The fine weather of the past two weeks, in particular, had brought on the first-sown field, though in some places, on some tree-shaded rows near the headlands, the pods were still flat on the vine, while filled out in others. Sago and I decided to start the first field, anyway, as we could not leave them any longer or they would start to shrivel in the next spell of heat and, besides, we were in danger of missing the market if we delayed further. Others on other farms had started picking a week before while we were still finishing the beans and the price had already started to drop, so Old Sago had reported on one of his return trips with a load to the pick-up point on

Boundary. By the time we had finished the first field, we hoped the second would be ready and better filled out.

Fortunately, that morning Stanley Lobel had finally deigned to come across from Tottle to join us and help us pick, a great grin on his tanned face as he rode up and skidded to a halt alongside me as I trudged to the field: we had our usual conversation on meeting.

'Hullo, Joe.'

'Hullo, Stanley. Nice to see you again.'

'How're things, Joe?'

'Fine. How're things with you?'

'Fine.'

'Did you ever get your money from Hoary for that trip?'

'Yeah, I've just called at the old skinflint's house for it. He said you would be here. How's your step-father, by the way? I heard he had a bad accident?'

'Still in hospital, but getting better. He's had an operation, but he's healing. It'll take time, though.'

'Who's in charge now then? You?'

'Why not? Someone has to be.' Then the reality. 'No, Sago's in charge really. At least he knows what he is doing.'

'Tell me, is it true there are some women artists staying on the island?'

'Yeah. They're staying in one of the cottages. A couple from London. I don't know much about them, though. I don't even know whether they're any good. They're supposed to be professional artists. They've just gone out. You must have passed the car on the track.'

'Was that them? A pity. I would have liked to have met them. Ah well, another time perhaps.'

'When do you go up to London?' Emphasis on 'London.'

'Middle of September, I hope...'

That was about the only time it varied. As Stanley had missed the two fields of bean-picking, I was even more glad to see him: both bean-picking and pea-picking, you will have guessed, I rated the same as topping beet in fields shrouded by November fogs, hedging and ditching in freezing December rains and sleeting Januaries or hoeing down between the never-ending rows of vegetables through the blustery winds and sudden icy showers of March and April: it was the same dreary, drudging work.

That day, most peculiarly, we had another thunderstorm and got wet: soaked, in fact. Stanley and I were picking together and, when the thunder and lightning crashed and flashed together directly above us, we took one look at each other, thought 'Blow this for a laugh!' and sprinted through the spitting rain for the shelter of the hedge to put distance between ourselves and our galvanised metal pails: the pea-picking could wait.

It was not long before the deluge came and my mother and Old Sago and Jan the Polack and Violet, with little Thomas, joined us, all sheltering under the overhang of the hedgerow, with sacks over our heads as cowls, watching the rain teeming down. Violet was comforting little Thomas, whom she had put in his pram and who did not like the 'clouds banging together.'

Having Stanley alongside me, someone to whom I could talk, had at least distracted me from continually looking at Violet, whose dress was very damp and clinging in the muggy heat, more so when it got soaking wet, so that I could not help staring: whatever I did, I did not want my mother to know I was looking and, for that matter, I did not want Jan to know I was looking, either.

Apart from one time, my mother had made no further comment about Violet and Jan: she would have put it in that order as she always reckoned it was the woman who made the running in such instances. 'Men are what they are,' she had said contemptuously in the kitchen after the first day of seeing them together: I had no idea what she meant by it. Mostly, in her presence and in Old Sago's presence, Violet and Jan limited themselves to hand-holding, a furtive touch now and again, working together, taking their dinner in the field together and generally happy just to be in each other's company. My mother, I know, kept her silence because she knew that she needed Violet's help in the fields: if we had had a glut of pickers, things might have been said: but she could not afford to do so.

We all knew that if Walter had come along the track on his bicycle at any time during those days, as Old Sago, my mother and I all feared he might, murder would have been done. To me, it was the most daring thing I had ever seen, a man openly consorting with another man's wife as if it were perfectly all right: it gave me a slightly sickening feeling in my stomach that a woman could do such a thing, betray her husband so easily and willingly, doing it with smiles and shining eyes, even if her husband was the dopey Walter Reddy.

'He's playing with fire there all right, your Polack friend,' Old Sago said of Jan one time. 'If Walter Reddy catches him, he 'on't be capable of going with a woman for six months or more, if ever agin. We'll just have to hope that he don't find out, boy.'

'It ain't none of our business,' I said, reiterating my earlier argument.

'I doubt that Walter'd see it that way,' said Old Sago with a shake of the head. 'I doubt his two brothers from Cobwycke would see it that way either, if he asked them.'

That was when I really did start to get worried for Jan: Walter's two brothers in Cobwycke were only a year or so younger than him and, like him, both had been boxers: till the war intervened, they had also briefly followed their brother around the fairground booths of England, though it was more his blood trail than his footsteps from what I had heard: the one time I ever saw them together on the Bourne Brothers' bus, they were as battered about the face as was he.

Not that Jan and Violet ever did anything in anyone's presence at which any of us could take offence: a couple of times in that first week, they did slip away at lunch time to 'take little Thomas for a walk,' but they were back within the hour to lay the sleeping lad on to a bed of pea-rice and resume picking. It was nice to see the tenderness between the two when at four o'clock Violet packed up her things and departed after Sago and I had tied her bags: Jan would give her a peck on the lips and Thomas would then kiss him and they would walk together, pushing the pram to the start of the causeway. I used to think it only needed some busybody with binoculars or a telescope to be standing on the seawall directly opposite and all would be up with them. Fortunately, no one ever did see them and Old Sago never told.

During the week when the weather turned peculiar, Laura Wilchard and Pocklington did not go out in the car as much: instead, on three of the thundery days, they actually remained on Norsea and painted around the island. I will say one thing for them, they were dedicated painters: not only did they go on what they rather strangely called 'plien air' painting trips three or four days a week with Richard, but, when they painted and sketched around Norsea, they seemed completely undeterred by the thunderstorms which the summer heat brought on. Two or three times I saw them sitting with their easels at various places while on the horizon the clouds bubbled in great pillars of white and grey, presaging another violent afternoon of lightning flashes.

In my opinion, having drawn many of the island's trees and views myself at one time or another, there were enough worthwhile subjects to keep them occupied for a fortnight or more, even if they worked every day, so their time was not wasted.

On one of the sunnier, drier days towards the end of that first pea-picking week, Laura Wilchard even came into the field where we were all working and set up her easel and canvas among the furrows about twenty yards from us: she then sat there all afternoon painting us in oils. My mother did not take kindly to someone idling away painting pictures while she was working and said so aloud, specifically so that Laura Wilchard would hear. 'Some people want to do some proper work for a change, not sit there painting silly pictures all the time,' she declared. 'Pictures won't put bread on the table or pay the rent, will they? They won't feed the people up in London either. You need the food honest people work to grow for that!' Then, when she saw us grinning, she raised a clenched fist and contemptuously cried: 'Up the workers!' It was all very comical: I had never thought of my mother as a revolutionary before!

Laura Wilchard pretended she had not heard and just carried on painting, but I saw the red blush come to her cheeks: and alongside me, I saw Stanley's cheeks redden, too, for a good reason, as I shall explain later. He gave a sheepish grin when he saw me smirking and, later, when he was leaving the field to go home, as if to make up for her overhearing my mother's remarks, he stopped beside Laura Wilchard and the two of them talked together for a good quarter-hour or more. I was more than fifty yards away, but I knew exactly what he was telling her from the look of astonishment that appeared on her face. Her whole demeanour towards him changed: from a casual politeness, she suddenly became very interested in what he had to say: she smiled a lot and pointed several times at various things on her picture as if asking Stanley's opinion of them.

It was a different story when I decided to take a look at her painting myself a half-hour after Stanley had gone: when I stopped some ten yards away, she shifted her position trying to block my view. I still saw the picture, though, and I have to admit, I thought it very good: you could tell it was my mother and Old Sago doing the pea-picking: they were right at the front of the picture, he bending to pick up the pea-rice, she standing there in her flowered pinafore and wellingtons stripping off the pods from the vines in her hand and dropping them in a steady stream into the pail at her feet, while behind stood three or four sacks already picked. The rest of us were placed in the background: we were no more than squiggles of paint: I know I was there because I was wearing a blue shirt that day and there was a squiggle of blue near the picture's edge: so someone somewhere may have a picture of me on their wall.

My mother, of course, had to have the last word: walking right up to Laura Wilchard as she left the field, she declared boldly: 'I wouldn't pay hard-earned money for that. You can't even tell who the people are!' With that, she strode off towards the farmhouse. Laura Wilchard just stared after her in stunned silence.

FORTY-EIGHT

I MADE only two visits to see Ben in all the time he was in hospital at Melchborough and they were both strained affairs: I had never been inside a hospital and was not keen to go: as far as I was concerned, hospitals were places to which most people went to die: of all the old people I had known who had been taken into hospital, none had ever come back, to my knowledge.

Ben had been in hospital for well over a month by the time I got there and, in the intervening period, I was quite happy to hear the reports of his progress from my mother, who early each Saturday morning rode over to the village on her high-handlebar bicycle to take the bus to Maydun, and then on to Melchborough, a two-and-a-half-hour trip, and was quite happy to keep me away: it gave her an excuse to vent her anger when she arrived home after a long day out.

For example, after Ben had been in hospital a week, in answer to my query of when, rather than whether, I ought to go and see him, she had exclaimed: 'Don't you go near him! You're the last person he wants to see. It's your fault he's in there. If you had done your bloody job when he asked you to do it, he wouldn't be lying in there with two legs broken and paralysed from the waist down and God knows what else wrong with him! He doesn't want to see you or anybody. I'm the only one he wants to see.'

After the second visit, in answer to my query of how he was progressing: 'The poor man's lucky to be alive, the doctor says, lucky to be alive! No thanks to you, you lazy blighter! So just stay away! Just stay away!'

And after another visit during the third week following his operation: 'Don't ask! Don't bloody ask! He's lucky they decided to operate when they did. If they had waited any longer, he could have died. The doctor said so. Nobody knows yet how things will turn out. He can't move at the moment. He could be paralysed for life. He could die of pneumonia like that. His lungs aren't good at the best of times. They're having to drain his chest as it is. Just stay away till I tell you!'

Other outbursts followed at various times, even without my prompting, outbursts such as: 'He may never walk again because of you' and 'He could be crippled for life because of you' and 'He'll get better a lot quicker without you bothering him.'

I think it was more touch-and-go with Ben than my mother ever let on: after the operation, Ben's progress back towards health of some kind, if not good health, was grudgingly admitted to by her on her return from the hospital with a terse, 'He's doing better than he ought to considering the problems he's had, no thanks to you ...' From that remark, spoken a week before I eventually went to see him, I deduced that he was at last on the mend, which was a great relief.

By the time I went – on a Sunday so that I did not skive off on a Saturday – Ben's doping had been reduced, his pain had eased and he had become more aware of his surroundings: the best news was that the doctors were of the opinion his paralysis would ease eventually and feeling would return below the waist: he would walk again! The bad news was that he would have to remain in hospital for several more months, lying flat on his back on a board for most of that time, being washed and ministered to by nurses and poked and prodded by every passing doctor: he had just been told that when my mother, finally and reluctantly, decided I had better go and see him, as a penance, I think: but with her: she was finally going to tell him about Jan working for us: she had not dared or been able to do so before: now she wanted me to be there to take the flak.

My first sighting of Ben came as a shock: he was lying stretched out on a bed, encased in a chicken wire cage from his chest to his toes, with both legs plastered right up to his groin: there was a greyness about his face which I had never seen before and he seemed to have aged five to ten years from when I had last seen him and looked nearer Old Sago's age than his own. He may have come off the worst of the painkillers they had been giving him, but he was nowhere near a hundred per cent, not even the seventy per cent I had expected him to be: more like fifty per cent, I would have said. All the time we spoke, his breath came in short gasps and he seemed to be thoroughly angry and irritated about everything. Not surprising when poor Ben's movement was restricted entirely by the contraption in which they had encased him: there are not many ways you can occupy your time when you are half-drugged and lying on your back in a hospital bed staring at the ceiling. He was no reader of books so the cheap-paper Sexton Blake novel my mother had bought at the bus station kiosk did not suit and he said so as soon as she pulled it out of her shopping bag: at least he still had the breath to get angry.

'What do you want to buy something daft like that for, woman?' he snapped: well, it was more of a hoarse whisper really, a croak, rather than an actual outburst, like someone speaking with a very sore throat. 'How the hell am I going to read a book in my state?'

'Well, I didn't know what to bring you,' my mother bristled up. 'You've got two hands haven't you? You can hold a book up in front of you even if you can't do anything else.' Then tossing it on to the bed, she sniffed: 'Either read it or don't read it. I don't care. I'll know what to bring next time, won't I? Nothing.' Followed by, as if to justify her sharpness: 'It's not my fault you're lying there with nothing to do. I've come all this way to see you and what do I get?'

They went on like that for a minute or so, snapping, though not actually snarling, at each other: I had seen it and heard it all before: it was just the usual sniping the way they did it at home when having one of their domestic disagreements. It was fuelled, of course, by Ben's frustration at being trapped in a hospital bed and her frustration at having to expend time and money, not to mention effort, in travelling to see him, and this time with me as company.

Finally, Ben acknowledged that I was there. 'I see you've finally found time to come,' he croaked, glowering toward the end of bed where I stood. 'About bloody time since it's your bloody fault I'm lying here.' After a fraught journey with my mother, I was already beginning to wish I had not bothered: there was nothing much I could say: I just had to look suitably penitent. Fortunately for me, my mother must have thought enough had been said already by her about my complicity and she changed the subject. 'That creature on Norsea has hired someone to help Joey,' she said flatly, 'just for the summer, while you're in here, he says.'

Ben exploded with anger: well, exploded in a coughing fit, really, spitting phlegm into a bowl which he took from the top of a small bedside cupboard. 'He's what!' he spluttered. 'I do any hiring and firing on that farm, not bloody Hoary, not you, not him – ' looking at me ' – I do it. Me! No one else.'

'Well you aren't there, are you?' my mother shot back, which angered him even more.

'Who the hell has he hired anyway?' Ben demanded.

My mother could not pronounce the surname properly. 'A young chap off one of the Catchment Board gangs, Yan Something.'

'Who the hell is he when he's at home?' Ben snorted: he was staring straight at me again. 'Where the hell did he come from?'

'He's a Polack bloke,' I said: then gleefully corrected my mother. 'His name's Jan Lakadat. He's come over from the Catchment Board gang building up the wall round Lawling Creek at Lingsea looking for farm work because he don't get on with the head ganger over there.' This Jan had told me: the English Catchment Board ganger seemed to regard all Poles the same as Germans, or the next worst thing, because, to him, they all had the same accents. 'He's a hard worker,' I informed Ben. 'He knows what he's doing, knows the job and he gets on with it. He's all right. He's been helping us with the picking and he's done all right.'

I did not tell him the real reason Jan had come to Norsea and neither did my mother: with luck, Jan would be gone before Ben was discharged and he would be none the wiser.

Jan had worked on the land back in his native Poland and knew about things, particularly horses: he was very good with horses, I told Ben: even Old Sago had commented on how good he was working with Molly. 'He looks after her better than I could,' I stated and was pleased for once to see my mother nodding agreement.

'He is good with horses,' my mother confirmed. 'He's been doing the stabling. Better than this lazy thing.' She meant me, of course.

The reason Jan knew about horses was because, at the start of the war, he had been a seventeen-year-old trooper in the Polish cavalry and had been lucky not to get his head shot off when some fool officer ordered them to charge German tanks with their lances. When Poland was overrun, he had made his way through Romania into Bulgaria, Greece and Egypt, finally making his way to England just about the same time as our lot were scuttling back from Dunkirk in the little ships.

The knowledge that Jan 'knew about horses' and that even Old Sago approved of him seemed to placate Ben's temper: if there was one thing which worried him while he was absent from the island, it was how Molly was faring at my hands when Old Sago could not get across. According to my mother, the first thing he had said when he came round soon after arriving at the hospital, just after the doctors had reset both his legs and plastered them up, was, 'Don't let Joe near Molly. If anything needs doing, get Sago to do it or do it yourself.' My mother had promised she would, but, like so many of her promises, she had promptly 'forgotten' about it once she got home: I only learned about it that day on the bus to Melchborough when she was telling me what I should say and what I should not say to Ben. 'Don't get him worried any more than he needs to be,' she had said. Perhaps she had more faith in me than I had imagined? She still told Old Sago to keep an eye on me while he was there: she was no fool. Now Jan's arrival had eased all her worries on that score: if Old Sago could not get across to us, there was always Jan to look after Molly properly. I slept easier at nights knowing he was there to tend her.

'Is he staying on the island?' Ben wanted to know.

My mother paused for a few seconds before she answered. 'He's in one of the cottages, the one just down from – down from his,' she said matter-of-factly, with a little disdainful sniff at the end. Even she could not bring herself to say Richard's name in Ben's presence: it was still all 'his' and 'him.'

Ben's face remained a mask of studied sullenness.

'We're going to need help, all we can get, especially with the harvest,' I reminded Ben. 'The chap, Jan, only wants to stay the summer, till he's got himself sorted out. He just wants a few weeks' work, a couple of months, that's all.' Another warning look from my mother made me pause: Ben accepted the explanation with a grunt.

My mother interrupted before I could think of what to say next. 'Joey needs someone to help him,' she said quickly. 'Old Sago isn't up to much now. He can do some things, but you can't expect him to go lifting two-and-a-half hundredweight sacks of grain at his age, can you? And Joey can't do it all. We need someone to help out, if only for the summer. Hoary's hired him and so far he's worked well, just as Joey says.'

'I'd still like to have seen him first,' grunted Ben, a little sulkily, perhaps feeling somewhat redundant. 'I run that farm, not Hoary. That's what I'm paid for.' Then, I think, to cheer himself up, he added the warning: 'If I find this Polish chap ain't no good when I get back, he'll be gone sharpish with a flea in his ear.'

That was perfectly fine with me: I had seen Jan working and knew that even Ben would have approved. Obviously he was repaying me the favour I had done for him: and he had an ulterior motive in mind: one Violet Reddy and little Thomas: he needed to stay close to them: and Ben, from what my mother had told me, was unlikely to be home for months, maybe three! Or four! Or five!

FORTY-NINE

THE ANTICIPATED grilling about the farm came after that: question after croaking question, punctuated by bouts of coughing, sips of water, spitting, grunts and groans and innumerable sighs: Was there any sign of blight on the pea crop? Had I checked? Had I kept my eyes open for that new Colorado beetle everyone was talking about on the potatoes? Had I checked the corn and the barley for smut, leaf stripe or wireworm? Aphis on the potatoes? Better check again. And had I checked on the drainage in the end field after the thunderstorms? Maybe I needed to dig out the ditch again? Etcetera, etcetera. My answers reassured him, to a degree, but he was still grumping and gave me no thanks. 'If you hadn't have called that bloody ambulance, I wouldn't be here now, boy, would I?' he said, gruffly and unkindly. 'I'd still be at home and on the spot and able to see to things for myself.'

It was not for me to say, 'And bloody well dead, too!' I thought it, but I did not say it.

My mother said it instead. 'He had to call an ambulance. Be sensible, man, do! You're better off in here than at home.' Unfortunately, she spoiled her earlier sympathy, by saying with another of her disdainful sniffs: 'Besides, we didn't have to pay anything for it, thanks to me, so what are you complaining about?'

When she had arrived in the ambulance with Ben, against the ambulancemen's wishes, she had had to sit through a very uncomfortable half-hour answering questions from the hospital's relieving officer and the matron in order to get Ben into a ward. By her stony-faced answers, she had managed to convince them that, though our address was The Old Farmhouse, Norsea Island, Gledlang, near Maydun, Ben was, in fact, no more than the bailiff, a fancy name for the chief labourer, and not the owner of the farm or the island and paid only a pound or so more per week than the four-pounds-ten other farm workers received: though we paid no rent, out of that all bills had to be paid, the same as everyone else. The indignity of it still rankled with my mother: she was reminded of it every time she went to the hospital: at best, it meant we would not be asked to make a contribution towards the costs: at worst, it was 'charity,' and, as she was quick to say, 'I don't want other people's charity. Half the time, it ain't even charity, it's just busy-bodying into your affairs!'

In Forty-Seven, the now universal National Health Scheme, in which all treatment and prescriptions were to be free for everyone, was still a year away: like us, most people paid into a state insurance scheme which entitled them to the services of a doctor and hoped that, if they went to hospital, it would be a local authority one in which treatment would be free of charge. Unfortunately, the hospital in Melchborough to which Ben had been taken was not: it was the town's most prestigious, voluntary one for the well-to-do, supported by flag days and fetes. Ben had been taken there simply because they had an up-to-date X-ray room and it had been feared that the wagon wheels had broken not only both his thighs and his pelvis but also his lower spinal vertebrae: everything is possible when a heavy wagon rolls over you loaded with bricks.

'They tell me I'm going to be in here for bloody months till my legs are mended,' Ben growled in his hoarse whisper, true to form, when I had answered all I could answer. 'I can't do a damned thing for myself. Nothing. If I even want a pee, I have to call one of the bloody nurses. Nothing but bloody fussing nurses in here. And there's too many of the buggers they bring in here who are dying for my liking. Fellah two beds away kicked the bucket the other night. Heart attack. Gawd, I itch! I itch more'n I hurt now! The trouble with these bloody plaster casts is you can't scratch anywhere.'

If he was itching, I thought, he must be getting better: I could understand a man complaining about itching which he could not scratch, but I could not understand what his complaint was about the nurses: standing by the window now, because I had no chair on which to sit, I watched them hurrying up and down the ward: they all looked very nice to me, very young, many of them, and quite pretty, some.

There was one sandy-haired nurse, who came bustling through the swing doors, fastening her apron front and checking her watch, who gave me such a cheerful smile as she went by that I blushed visibly: I know I did because I saw her laugh, nicely though: and when she came back a few minutes later she made sure she caught my eye and gave me another smile and I had to turn away because I could not look at her. She was very pretty, with lovely white skin, and everything about her was wonderfully slim and delicate, neck, arms, hands, waist, hips, legs. My mother would have described her as 'no more than a slip of a girl,' but I thought how wonderful it would be to have a girl such as her for a wife: cheerful, pretty and beautifully slim, not like some of the other podgy ones there.

The sandy-haired girl could not have been more than four or five years older than me, but she looked and sounded very efficient from the way I saw her directing the other nurses and writing on the patients' cards at the far end of the ward, talking to them and calling out a greeting or a comment to each in turn as she moved from bed to bed. She seemed to know all the patients' names and, when she came to our bed, she gave me that same disconcerting smile and called out gaily: 'Good afternoon, Mr Wigboe. I see you have got all your family with you today.' An obvious reference to my appearance at last. 'I hope you are feeling better today?' Surprisingly, after his earlier grump, Ben gave what in the dark might have passed for a smile and replied: 'Much better, thank you, nurse.' Even my mother gave him a huffy, old-fashioned look for that one.

What made it more painful for me, especially where the prettier nurses were concerned, was that I knew they were most likely all grammar school or high school girls, educated well beyond my level, the 'B' class at Maydun secondary (when the tide allowed me to attend). They would be clever at exams, unlike me, better read and better bred, unlike me, and unlikely to think of me as anything but a gawky youth even though, at my mother's insistence, I had put on my navy blue suit and a tie and had my hair cut by Fred Oldton, Ted's brother, who would cut boys' hair for threepence and men's for sixpence: trouble was, he was no expert and it showed. He used his wife's dress scissors and his method was to give everyone a basin cut without the basin, short back and sides all round, then comb the top forwards into a fringe and snip off as high as possible so that you left his cottage with a haircut that looked like the thatch covering the cottages which bordered the green at Tottle. I had combed a parting in mine with water from the public conveniences at the bus station, but by the time we had walked to the hospital the water had dried and my hair had fluffed out again: perhaps that was what the sandy-haired nurse was smiling at: young men are conscious of such things when attractive girls are walking up and down.

As I watched the nurses, I could not help but wonder what they thought when they saw a man undressed, stark naked, and had to wash him all over. One of the older village youths, Teddy Pamplin, who was then in the army, had told us of the time when, at the age of sixteen, he had to go into hospital to have his appendix removed and the nurse had lifted up his willie with two fingers like it was a worm as she started to shave his pubic hairs: when his willie started to harden because she was touching it, she took a pencil out of her top pocket and rapped it sharply on the end to make it go down. The girl was no more than twenty, he said: in other circumstances, she might have been kind enough to have finished what she had started, if he had asked her.

FIFTY

THERE WAS definitely something up with Dennis Bolt: he was smiling a lot and looking very sheepish: I had met him three times on my daily trips across to the Boundary dropping-off point with our loads of peas and it was not the Dennis of old. Even Old Sago, who accompanied me before riding off for home, commented upon it. 'Something's stirred him up, boy,' he said. 'Something's definitely stirred him up!' That 'something' could be only be someone: one person – his cousin, Joanne Waters.

Confirmation for me came one evening when Sago and I made our usual crossing with Molly and the wagon to the usual dropping-off point, the open weighing shed near the junction of the tracks, where Boundary's boxes and punnets were stored. It was about eight o'clock: we had unloaded, Sago had ridden off after helping me to replace the boards and I had just set out on the return journey back over the causeway, dangling my legs at the front of the wagon, when I saw way off, halfway towards the flour mills at Tidwoldton Basin, two figures walking along the top of the seawall. They must have been almost a mile from me, but because the seawall twists and turns round creeks and bays, often turning back upon itself, they were at that moment lit full face, so to speak, by the evening sun sinking behind Maydun hill. Even at that distance, I was able to recognise Dennis Bolt: and since there was a girl with him and she was wearing a bright blue skirt which was blowing in the breeze, it could only be Joanne Waters: and from the way they were walking, slowly, it was obvious he had his arm round her shoulders and she was leaning against him.

Suddenly, to my surprise, they disappeared from view down the side of the seawall: now every villager in Gledlang knew that when a courting couple disappeared into the long grass down the seawall, it was for one reason only: to do some kissing and cuddling and fumbling inside each other's clothes. It was with a certain sense of annoyance and frustration and jealousy that I bumped and bounced on the wagon back over to Norsea, knowing that at that precise moment Dennis Bolt of all people, shy, timid, skinny, yellow-toothed Dennis, probably had his hand inside Joanne Waters's blouse fondling her poached egg breasts or was sliding it up her dress inside the elastic of her knickers, fingering her there. And knowing her, first from what I had seen that first time she came into the kitchen, and from what Charlie Mangapp had told me, she probably had his old man out and was rubbing it with a wicked smile on her face, because she was the type who would look straight into a man's face and smile bright-eyed encouragement as she did it, coaxing him till he exploded in the time-honoured way and collapsed limp and groaning across her: and she then would smile happily for him when he had done it. Dennis Bolt had discovered sex and Joanne Waters was teaching him!

Of course, I was jealous! What youth would not be if he fantasised nightly about it, had only a wet stomach to satisfy himself, was desperate for it and knew that a friend was getting it and not him? All I had to keep me from going berserk sometimes, chucking in the whole rotten life and going off somewhere where I would meet women, proper girls who knew what to do and would do it without any fuss or bother, perhaps even saying a nice 'Thank you' if they liked it – all I had was the thought that my time would come, down the line my time would come!

The next evening after Jan and I had stabled Molly and he had gone off to his cottage to cook his awful food, and I had fed the chickens and the pig, I went round to Hoary and asked if I could borrow his battered brass telescope, telling the old fool, much to his delight and astonishment, that I wanted to look at the shell duck and waders out on the mudflats. It cost me a five-minute lecture on what other species of bird to look for before I managed to get away, impatient to start, I told him: but it was worth it. Richard, I should add, on that day was still away somewhere with the two women.

Standing atop the low seawall on the north side of Norsea and peering out across the Stumble, through the telescope, I was able to make out the distant figures of Dennis and Joanne Waters again strolling arm in arm along the top of the meandering seawall on the eastern side of the Shoe: in the ten days I had the telescope before Hoary asked for it back, I must have seen them four or five times in the late evening as dusk came creeping down, sometimes almost halfway to Salter, other times halfway to Tidwoldton. There are some long and lonely stretches of seawall around the Langwater where you can disappear into the long grass on the landward side or go down on to the shingle beach in the lee of the seawall or in one of the secluded bays and no one would know you were there unless they came across you unexpectedly. And that is unlikely if you are in some of the remoter spots where only the cows graze: they are truly lonely places: if you sat for a week in some of them, you most probably would not be passed by a single human soul. Whether they thought they were going to keep it a secret, I do not know: they may have done all their 'courting' away from the house in an attempt to fool Old Ma Parkinson, but there was no way they were going to keep it a secret forever: eventually, I think, they just decided to let gossip take its course. That, I suspect, is why they came across to Boundary one evening a week or so later: I was just coming out of the barn when they came chugging into the yard in Dennis's little green van. Dennis said he wanted to visit Ben now that he was getting better and had come to say he would also take me, for what would be my second trip.

I think Dennis did not expect to meet anyone other than me in the yard, for he looked very sheepish when he found my mother standing with me: she was not much taken with Joanne Waters and gave a rather sniffy and abrupt 'How do you do?' and not much else when she was introduced, before retreating inside with her tea-towel.

As it was early evening still, I decided to give Joanne Waters a tour of Norsea, just to show her what it was like. All the time the three of us were walking around the island, she had her arm linked though his, clinging to him like she thought some femme fatale was going to sidle out of the hedge and lure him off somewhere. What Dennis! He would not know if he was being lured off somewhere if he were given directions! All throughout the tour, he was blushing and grinning away like a Cheshire cat and had that unmistakable 'Hey, look at me, I've got a girlfriend!' manner about him. From the way he acted, you would have thought he wanted to know what I thought of him now that he had a girl on his arm and what I thought of her as well. Not much in either case, Dennis, not much in either case.

Before we parted, we agreed the time and place of the pick-up for the visit on the coming Sunday, one o'clock by the punnet shed, allowing ourselves an hour to get to the Melchborough hospital before visiting began at two. I know that I should have gone to see Ben more often than the two visits I actually made, but I was deterred from doing so by the fact that I always had work to do on Norsea and it took most of the day to go there and back.

That Sunday I went with Dennis I had another surprise: when the van came bumping along the track from the farmhouse to pick me up, Joanne Waters was occupying the passenger seat. She had never met Ben and knew nothing about him, other than that he was my stepfather, a friend of Dennis, and a neighbouring farmer who had been injured by the wheels of a wagon going over him: that and whatever else Dennis had told her about him. Yet there she was, sitting in the passenger seat, as large as life, dressed in her Sunday best, while I, in my one and only navy blue suit, damp and shining from the midday ironing, was relegated to a pile of sacks in the back and where all I could do was watch the road speed away behind us.

All through the journey, cousin Joanne seemed to spend most of her time twisted in her seat facing Dennis, watching him drive, as if she were admiring him, and clutching at his arm like she was fascinated by him: at one point she even laid her head briefly on his shoulder and a couple of times when we came to a halt sign, she nuzzled her face up against his and whispered something which made both of them laugh. The sight and sound of Dennis Bolt giggling was something I had never witnessed before: it was all very embarrassing.

I was in the back of the van, as I say, and so I did not have a good view, but I am certain that, as we were trundling up the high hill at Nadbury, I saw her hand settle on Dennis's thigh and then rub the inside of it and he did not even bat an eyelid, just concentrated on driving, enjoying it from the half-smiling grimace on his face. Clearly, from the bold way she did it, Joanne Waters had done it before to others: she was no innocent maid, as the secret seawall walks had shown: she knew what men liked and was prepared to do it to them. All the time her hand was massaging Dennis's thigh, she was looking into his face and smiling: a couple of times she even turned round to look at me, laughing, as if to see whether I had noticed what she was doing – and not caring if I had!

I was just glad when we got there: not much was said between Dennis and myself on the thirty-minute journey because of his preoccupation with Joanne, or rather her preoccupation with him, though Dennis did speak for a few minutes when we first set off, till we got to Maydun and she began distracting him. Most of what he said was 'Joanne and me ...' or 'The two of us ...' or 'We went ...' or 'We're thinking of going ...' Apparently, they had been to the Maydun pictures on the Thursday night to see a film and were thinking of going again the following week: that Dennis was even talking about going to the pictures was startling enough in itself: in all his twenty-six years, I do not think he had ever been near a cinema till he went with Joanne Waters.

At the hospital Ben was pretty much the same as he had been on my last visit, grumpy, bored and still itching inside his plaster casts, they were still giving him medication so he was part doped-up: he still managed to mumble out a host of questions about how I was coping on the farm: Was I doing this? Was I doing that? Was 'the new chap,' Jan, still there? All of them I answered in my own inimitable way, with a shrug, a pulled face, and an 'All right, I suppose …' or a 'Yeah, he's still there.' To be fair, he asked Dennis the same work questions, too, about how he was coping and, in his own way, seemed quite amused to see Joanne Waters clinging on to Dennis's arm as the two of them sat there beside his bed. It raised an eyebrow from him anyway and I believe we marginally cheered him up in the hour we were there, till right at the end I remembered to tell him that Old Hoary had said he was thinking of visiting him sometime in the next week or two. 'He's always asking about you,' I said. That brought a look of alarm to Ben's face and the cry: 'I don't want to see that daft bugger in here! Gawd, can't a man have some peace? Keep him away!' He was still swearing to himself when we went out: if he could have sunk lower into the bed, I think he would have done so.

Dennis and Joanne were much the same on the return journey as they had been going, so wrapped up in each other that my attempts at conversation were mostly ignored: questions were met with sparse answers, comments greeted with a grunt and not much else: so I lapsed into silence out of sheer frustration and stared out of the back window again.

FIFTY-ONE

ONE NIGHT on the track near the cottages I heard voices: Richard, Laura Wilchard and Hoary were all standing in the dark staring up at the stars: Pocklington was not there: she was missing a wonderful view. Deep in the country, away from the light of the towns, the dark was total, velvet black, especially on Norsea where there were no lights whatsoever to pollute the sky: those were the nights to view the stars and this was one of them: the heavens were brilliant with them, millions upon millions studding the blackness or stretched in an opalescent pathway from horizon to horizon. That night on Norsea it was so pitch black that, for safety's sake, you needed to know every twist and turn of the track, where every cart rut, pothole and puddle lay along it: as the night was so dark, I was able to stand in the gateway unobserved: just watching, curious.

Richard and Laura Wilchard seemed to be standing together, passing Hoary's battered brass telescope between them, pointing it up at the stars: she seemed to be smiling a lot and commenting in wonderment: though I could not see her, it was her voice and the way she spoke to Richard that attracted my attention.

Hoary, being a keen astronomer and prone to spending half the night lying on his mattress staring up through the opened skylight of his 'astral' bedroom, was explaining to a marvelling Laura Wilchard which stars were which: those two were Castor and Pollux, the large one low in the southern hemisphere was Sirius, directly overhead were the Great Bear or Plough, the Lesser Bear and Cassiopeia, with the North Star winking pale and cold beyond them, the three in a line were Orion's belt with the sword hanging down, the tight triangular cluster were the Seven Sisters and the bright, bright star was really the planet Jupiter.

It was at that precise moment that the door of the women's cottage was pulled open and a shaft of light illuminated the three figures: Pocklington's voice was heard, loud, irritated and demanding: 'Laura! It's past eleven o'clock. Are you coming to bed now?'

She could have said 'No,' but she did not: she meekly acquiesced with a pitiful 'Coming, Greta,' thanked Richard and Hoary and was gone: for several seconds after the door closed I heard Pocklington's voice: it was still loud and the tone was scolding.

I had witnessed examples of Pocklington's temper just going about the island in the normal course of a week: on such a small place, you cannot avoid people as Richard and Ben had discovered. There was no way I could avoid the women: sometimes you saw them at a distance, sometimes you passed them on the track or on a headland: at any time, night or day, you were likely to come across them. I always gave them a 'Good morning' or a 'Good afternoon,' 'Good evening' or 'Good night,' but I did not always get a reply.

The real trouble began with the incident of Pocklington's spoiled paintings during the thundery period. Pedalling along the track one day in my usual fashion, fast and oblivious to any thought of others, I almost crashed into the silly woman: for some stupid reason she was sitting on a small fold-up stool right in the centre of the path, painting. That I managed to avoid her at all was a miracle, down to pure luck rather than my own skill at swerving. I came round the bend so fast that the best I could do was to wrench at the handlebars the instant I saw her horrified face: I missed her by inches. Unfortunately, I did not miss the jam jar of water she had placed by her foot: my pedal clipped it and flipped it sideways. It was not my fault that her portfolio was lying open and two other pictures she had painted that day were on top, weighted by a stone: the water sluiced right across them and, sad to say, they lost some of their detail.

'My pictures! My paintings!' she screamed. 'You stupid bloody oaf! You bloody arsehole, boy! You – you – ' Well, I do not need to go on: she called me most of the things she could call me, before finishing with a long wailing: 'Do you have to go roaring around like a maniac? Don't you ever think of riding more slowly? My God, boy, why can't you watch where you're going?'

I had grown up on Norsea and had never come across an obstacle on that track in the ten years I had been riding along it, except for the odd flint, that is, and I knew where they were: certainly, I had never come across a foolish female sitting in the middle of the track on a blind corner painting a watercolour of a row of elms as seen across one of our cornfields through a weed-clogged gateway. That made no difference to La Pocklington: I was to blame: I was the 'clumsy oaf ... the reckless idiot ... the imbecile boy ... the effing lunatic.' I meekly offered my apologies, but she was in no mood to accept. 'Just go away, boy,' she cried as she tipped the water off her two pictures: so I did: I remounted my bicycle and rode off with as straight a face as I could muster, though it did deteriorate into a smirk before I had gone twenty yards: the last I saw of Pocklington that day was her screwing up the two soaked paintings and hurling them to the ground in a fury.

Then there was the swimming incident. The weather being continually hot and sticky, Laura Wilchard had quickly overcome her earlier aversion to bathing in the river: I supposed she, like me, found it easier to go for a swim to wash off the sweat, dust and dirt of the day than to lug a half-dozen buckets of water from the pump to the cottage each time she wanted a bath and then have to heat it kettleful by kettleful. Because of her injured leg, Pocklington did not go: she always remained at the cottage: but Laura Wilchard went down to the southern beach to swim at least once a week, sometimes twice: generally, she went when the two of them returned in the late afternoon and there was a six or seven o'clock tide, though sometimes, like at weekends when they did not go over to the mainland to paint, she would go during the day, noon or late afternoon. After all, the beach was there (it was mostly shingle, but with some sand), it was secluded and when the tide was in you would never have guessed there were about fifty square miles of black, sucking mud all around you. When the water was lapping at the sloping shingle, it could have been a seaside beach anywhere.

I also swam whenever I could, sometimes even during the dinner break, sometimes before tea in the evening, sometimes after tea before I did my chores, and more or less every Saturday or Sunday afternoon if the weather were warm and the tide were right and I had a half-hour to spare, which was not often. At high tide, it was the most natural thing in the world to grab an old torn towel and my costume from the washing line and rush down to the beach for a ten-minute or fifteen-minute dip: at mid-day, it refreshed you and helped you carry on working through the afternoon: in the evening, it gave a brief respite from the onerous, never-ending chores I was expected to complete. It also meant that in the summer you took four or five seawater 'baths' instead of the normal one freshwater bath a week, or one a fortnight that you took in winter. So you see, it was not all work, work, work on Norsea: just ninety per cent of the time, that was all.

Early one evening I went for a swim and found Laura Wilchard was already on the beach: she was by herself, lying on a towel in her blue swimming costume, reading, wearing sunglasses: she had obviously already been in, for, as I walked past along the top of the bank, I could see the shape of her nipples sticking up through the damp material of her costume: even so, when I went in, I kept well away, a good hundred yards at least. It was while I was trawling up and down about fifty yards out from the shore that, to my surprise, Richard came along the low seawall: he saw me and gave his customary acknowledgement, but continued on to where Laura Wilchard was lying. He had taken the precaution of putting on his swimming costume under his trousers so that when he joined her it was an easy and less embarrassing matter to get undressed: no sooner had he stripped off and they had spoken a few words to each other than she had put down her book and the two of them were picking their way down the beach together towards the water. As they went in, I came out, towelled myself and then retreated to a clump of bushes to dress: I could hear them calling out to each other and laughing as they swam up and down, but I could not make out what they said.

I was sitting smoking when they came out and began to towel down: to my astonishment, instead of retiring to somewhere where they could do it privately, they began to take off their costumes right in front of each other, though with their backs turned and cloaked by just their towels. A fatal mistake! They were midway through their dressing, he with no trousers yet on and his legs exposed, she just stepping into her knickers, when who should come hobbling along the seawall at precisely the wrong moment but Pocklington on her stick: I have never seen such fury on a woman's face when she saw Laura Wilchard struggling to pull up her knickers under her dress and no more than ten feet away Richard pulling up his trousers and tucking in his shirt. She hurried a red-faced and protesting Laura Wilchard away from Richard's presence like a parent ushering away their child from the company of another who might 'contaminate' them. They had to come past where I was sitting and, from the fuss Pocklington was making once they were out of Richard's earshot, you would have thought they had been doing something else. All very strange.

Then there was Pocklington's drinking. If on a Friday or a Saturday evening the tide were out and likely to remain out, Richard would run the two women over to the Chessman public house in Gledlang Square: he even drank with them a couple of times, according to Old Sago. But on one particular evening, soon after the swimming kerfuffle, he had returned instead to Norsea to tinker with the car's engine because it had been giving trouble: he was still tinkering with it when

I left him. Injured leg or no, Pocklington would have to hobble home: but in what condition? I soon found out.

When you go into the Chessman, the entrance to the bar is through a doorway on the left, halfway along a passageway where the stairs run overhead: there were always a few of the locals who liked to stand at the tiny snug bar at the end of a second wider flagged passageway, formed by a partition wall which divides off the vault: but most of the farmworkers preferred to sit in the vault, particularly in winter when they could crowd on to the benches to warm themselves before the open hearth where a fire was kept blazing every evening. The doorway to the vault is to the left: straight ahead is the doorway to the Big Room, a cold and draughty place, where Hoary banged out his Bach and Beethoven on the piano: mostly it was kept closed and only strangers and farmers ever went in there. Naturally, that is where Laura Wilchard and Pocklington drank – and Richard when he joined them –well away from the blue air, part smoke, part profanity, coming out of the vault.

The particular Saturday evening that Richard spent tinkering with the car was the evening I met Laura Wilchard, late on, walking back from the Chessman: hurrying back, in fact. She did not look at all happy: indeed, she looked quite tearful and several times she glanced behind her as though she were anxious to keep someone at a distance. I gave her a 'Good evening,' but either she did not hear me or she just ignored me, for she hurried on into the darkness without a word.

I guessed what was up and retreated into the shadows to await what, by then, late July, I knew I was about to see: a minute later I was rewarded when Pocklington came lurching along the track on her stick: she had a clear-glass bottle in her free hand, which I presumed was gin, and was obviously well under the influence. I was hoping to see her fall flat on her face, but, by some miracle and some deft use of her stick, she managed to stay upright: then she saw me.

'What are you staring at, you shitty boy?' she snarled, pausing momentarily as if to focus her eyes.

I should have said, 'You, you daft cow!' but I did not: instead I just watched her hobble away, weaving along the track as she went, still hoping she would fall and give me a good laugh.

The shouting started in their cottage a few minutes later: and, just as Hoary's piano-playing resounded around the stillness of the island, so Pocklington's voice reverberated, too, among the trees and hedgerows: she was in a real temper. Suddenly I realised that the shouting was much louder: she must have come out into the open: it was loud enough to draw me creeping back through the shadows in the hope of witnessing another spectacle: anything to liven up what had been an otherwise dull evening.

All I know is that I saw Richard's door open and, by the light of his lamp, briefly saw the silhouette of Laura Wilchard hurrying inside: she had one hand up to her face and appeared to be crying. Pocklington followed her and stood outside shouting for a couple of minutes, then lurched back inside her own cottage. I waited a while, but neither Laura Wilchard nor Pocklington re-appeared, so I finally made my way home. Whether Laura Wilchard stayed in Richard's cottage overnight, sleeping in the 'new' leather armchair or whether she eventually went back to her own cottage, I do not know.

Most of what I observed between Richard and these women, I observed from afar, for I was never directly a part of any of it, so most of my beliefs were based on supposition, assumptions, deductions, and observations. What I did observe was that, between Richard and Laura Wilchard, there had been a definite friendship right from the day of their first meeting when Charlie Mangapp and I had towed the car out of the mud. From the start she was calling him by his Christian name: it was 'Richard, would you be so kind …?' or 'Richard, do you think …?' or 'Are you ready to go, Richard…?': and when they returned from their painting trips, there would always be a polite 'Thank you, Richard, it has been a lovely day' or 'I hope tomorrow is just as nice as today has been, Richard.' Pocklington, on the other hand, with a look on her face sour enough to curdle milk, would hobble off into the cottage without a word of thanks and no comment at all about the next day.

Yes, there was definitely something brewing between Laura Wilchard and Richard, in my opinion. How far things had got, I had not the faintest idea: though several times, when the evening sun was slanting low across the fields, down the length of the estuary, I followed the track past the cottages and saw Richard and Laura Wilchard sitting on chairs on the little patch of green outside their respective dwellings, talking and smiling and sometimes laughing together, but always across an intervening twenty yards or so: they never drew their chairs together that I could see. He might perhaps be smoking: she might be reading a book with her sunglasses on: or they might just be basking in the warm evening sunlight. I never saw Pocklington join them: she always seemed to be hovering in the background, appearing in the doorway with something in her hand, a saucepan, a plate, a mixing bowl, a towel, as if she were keeping an eye on them: then she would disappear inside. Funny that. She was like a mother spying on a daughter because she did not trust her in the presence of a man: but which one did she not trust, the woman or the man?

FIFTY-TWO

ON THOSE evenings when Richard was absent from the island, either still not returned from chauffeuring the women or driving Hoary somewhere, I would, after completing a few chores, go round and sit with Jan while he ate his awful oversalted cooking: potatoes, onions, carrots, cabbages, swede and other vegetables all tipped into a saucepan I had snaffled from Hoary's kitchen and boiled: and generally burnt! Conversations were somewhat stilted and sometimes I nodded an understanding to things about which I did not have an inkling: I just hoped the next nod or smile or shake of the head was not a contradiction of the previous one. Still, we managed and I had someone to whom I could talk and it helped to pass the lonely evenings.

Jan was pleased to see me, too, I think, because it passed the lonely evenings for him as well: his cottage was well away from the women and Richard, at the end of the line in East Street, and I do not think Pocklington and Laura Wilchard took to him at all: so most of his evenings he spent alone, though Richard did stop and chat with him a couple of times, I was pleased to see. When he had first arrived, Jan had brought his own food, some utensils, a cup and a plate and two blankets from the camp: the only furniture in his place was a single iron bed and mattress, an oak gateleg table and a broken wicker chair, all of which I had taken from among the stuff in Hoary's crammed outhouse. He would never miss them: I did not care if he did: Jan was one of his workers now and he had a right to be properly housed, and rent free!

It was during those conversations that I sensed something was troubling him. Violet was still coming across daily during the week to help us to pick the last of our late peas and every other Saturday morning, from nine o'clock onwards, tide allowing, to go to Hoary's house: so they were together a lot. At least it was not a lack of her company which was troubling him: and Jan's mattress was being well used, I thought one day when Violet went past on her way home, pushing little Thomas and giving me an embarrassed and guilty smile.

It just so happened that early one Saturday evening, while Richard was away chauffeuring the women, I again went round to Jan's cottage: and it was on that evening that I accepted an invitation to accompany him across to the village of Lingsea, which lies up a long twisting creek on the southern shore and is smaller and more desolate even than Gledlang. Jan said he wanted to see 'a man who help me with my problem': he did not say what that problem was, but I suspected it had something to do with Violet and Thomas, just as I suspect he asked me so that we would take the punt rather than risk being seen in his 'borrowed' rowboat, then beached high and dry on our southern shore. It took me no more than ten minutes to put on a cleaner pair of trousers and a less frayed shirt and jumper and to meet him down by the rickety pier.

We sculled across the mile of water to the estuary's south bank early on an incoming tide so there would be no worry about being stranded and having to splash back through the mud. The Catchment Board camp was located in a marshy field in the lee of the seawall, a dreary, muddy hole of a place about a mile from the village, so it was to be expected that no one would want to stay there on a Saturday night. Consequently, we found most of Jan's friends in the village pub and they greeted him like a long lost brother, even though he had been away from them for only a short time. Jan was all smiles, too: I think he was just happy to be among his own kind and to be able to converse in his own language again.

They were all relatively young men and cheery company, mostly in their late twenties and early thirties, bachelors all still because of the war, though one or two of the local girls were quite friendly towards them and no doubt hopeful. Some had caught the train from the nearby overgrown village of Eastminster, which called itself a town, and had gone up to London: well, men must if men must: but there were still about fifteen of us, so it was not too bad. The man Jan was hoping to meet was there and the two of them spent the whole time in furtive conversation together, so much so that I was left pretty much to my own devices.

Midway through the evening, one of the Poles began to play the public house's yellow-keyed piano and a second got out an accordion to accompany him: suddenly one man began to sing, another joined in, then a couple more, and another couple, till the whole group was singing together. What they sang, I do not know, but it sounded very sad and very nostalgic: if you had asked me, I would have said it was men longing for their homeland: sad at leaving it: a Polish version of

'Danny Boy,' say! Even the locals came out of their room to stand in the doorway and to listen in silence: no sarcastic remarks, no talking over the singing, no requests for silly British songs, just quiet admiration. Two of the men had particularly harmonious voices: one of them was like a deep rumble, the other sang high like a girl almost. Wonderful stuff when they combined. I looked at their faces as they sang, particularly their eyes, and those of their friends: I would swear that one or two of them seemed to be crying quietly: not outward tears, but inwardly, as men do. Even Jan and his friend had stopped talking to listen and to join in.

The Polacks bought all my drinks, insisting that, as a friend of Jan, I did not pay for anything: I had at least four pints of Black and Tan, which is mild and bitter mixed, and left the pub drunk for the first time in my life. Jan had to half-carry me back to the punt and row back to Norsea on his own: it was quite a feat that he managed it, though he could hardly miss the island, even at night: just get in the boat and point it straight north at the line of tall trees, readjusting every now and again for the outward flow of the current.

I was not so drunk that I do not remember the trip: I remember lying in the bottom of the punt for what seemed an eternity and I remember falling flat on my face on the beach when I got out: I remember Jan helping me to our farmhouse gate and I remember pushing open the door and stumbling up the stairs. My mother was already abed so I was able to creep into my room without any worries: it was the effects of the drinks as I lay there which worried me: I remember the ceiling going over and over as my whole body seemed to somersault as if I were tied to a wheel: my head replaced my feet, then my feet replaced my head, again and again. Fortunately, the last thing I did before I got into bed was to put a copy of one of my old *Daily Expresses* on the floor so that when I was sick, as sick I knew I was going to be, it went all over Desmond Hackett and William Hickey rather than my mother's rag-clipping rug.

After the visit, Jan seemed even more troubled, like he was wrestling with his conscience: you could sense it, by the way he spoke, by the way he sometimes did not speak, by the set of his face when he was thinking. It finally came out as the two of us were walking back with Molly and the wagon on the Tuesday evening after dropping off the latest load of bagged peas.

'Joe,' he said, laying a hand on my arm, 'Joe, I tell you something very important. You tell no one, please. You promise?'

'I promise.' Even as I said it I had that sinking feeling that whatever he was about to tell me was for his benefit and not for mine.

Jan looked about him as if to ensure there was no one near enough who might overhear: as we had been the only two in the field, it was unlikely anyone else was going to hear what he had to say: Old Sago was in the adjoining field, a full hundred yards from us, still raking up the bean rice to burn so he was unlikely to earwig: Violet and Stanley were long gone, Richard and the two women were still on the mainland, my mother was in the house, Ben was still in hospital and Hoary was God knows where!

'You good friend, Joe,' Jan said, looking earnestly at me. 'You help me see Violet and boy Thomas. You help us be together again.' It was nice to hear that someone thought I was not all bad. 'I tell you so you know. Violet and me, one day soon, we go away. Take Thomas. I sorry, I not want to let you down, but I not stay here longer. I go soon.'

I was stunned. 'Go! Why? What for?' I said it more as something to say than anything else: he was going to tell me anyway.

'I tell you as you my friend. I tell no one else,' Jan replied. Again he paused and looked about him: dark grey columns of smoke were rising from the next field where Sago was heaping his bonfires. 'I have friend in county of Bedshire.'

'Bedfordshire!'

Jan ignored my correction. 'I see man in Lingsea. He give him message. My friend sergeant in army, Parachute Regiment, Polish like me. Now he make bricks. Make plenty of money, too. He write and say plenty of work for brickmakers in brickfields?' Jan raised an eyebrow in query at the word 'brickfield': I nodded to confirm that it was correct. 'Everyone need bricks, lots of bricks. To build houses. Replace houses bombed by bastard Germans. New houses. Brickfields better than coalmines working with Bevin Boys. I not want to dig coal in coalmine. I prefer work in brickfield, in open air, in sunshine. Brick-making pay good. I get job through friend. He say come, work for month, two months, three months, get flat or caravan, come back, get Violet, get Thomas, leave. Go away. Violet leave husband she not love, come with me. Husband not find us, ever.' Suddenly he became fiercely proud. 'Thomas my son, not his. I father. I look after child. Thomas our baby, Violet and me.'

Why did I have a sense of foreboding as he talked? Because I knew Walter Reddy, that is why! So far, he could not have known anything of Jan's almost daily assignations with Violet or there would have been blood on the causeway: he probably did not even know a 'foreigner,' Jan, was working on Norsea and had been for a month by then or he might have put two and two together. But secrets cannot be kept forever and sooner or later someone was going to tell: Sago would not say anything, we knew that: but it needed only for someone to let slip a guffawing comment in the Chessman and the cuckolded Walter would be on the rampage with a vengeance, him and his two brothers from Cobwycke. I did not fancy Jan's chances if he were caught by that trio.

'When are you going? You know we'll be starting the harvest in a couple of weeks? We'll need you for that.' The petulance in my voice was part contrived to get my thoughts away from the last image.

Jan looked suitably penitent. 'I sorry, Joe,' he said quietly, again placing his hand on my arm. 'I go tomorrow. I take train to London, then to friend in Bedfordshire. Start work next week. All arranged.'

The thought occurred to me so I asked anyway. 'Does Violet know you're leaving?'

Jan suddenly looked very guilty. 'No, I not tell her yet. I go secret so she not know till I gone.' He reached into his pocket and pulled out a piece of paper folded over. 'I have letter for her. You give her letter when she come to island, please? Everything in letter. Better this way. She cry if I tell her and I not go. So I go now. You give her letter, please, Joe, and tell her, I come back. I come back for her and Thomas. Not to worry. I come back as soon as I have money and proper place for them.'

'Yes, but when?'

Jan was looking downcast again. 'I not know,' he said with a sigh and a shrug. 'One month, two months, three months, six months. I not know. But I come back. You tell her? Tell her I write to you. You give her this letter, others I send to you. Okay?' A shrug from me: okay.

And that was how Jan left us the very next evening, saying nothing at all to Violet even though they worked alongside each other all day: that evening he asked Hoary for what money he was owed and slipped away without even coming to say a final goodbye. I knew he had gone when he was not waiting on the track the following morning. Instead I was waiting by the turn when Violet came up pushing Thomas in the rickety pram: I tried to return her cheery greeting, but failed miserably: the instant she saw my expression, the hereditary mournful Coe look, her own smile vanished: alarm, disbelief, fear replaced it: tears were already forming in her eyes.

'He says he will be back,' I said as I handed her the letter. 'A couple of months. Maybe three. But he'll be back. He said to tell you that. And that he'll write via me, so he said, so that Walter won't ever find out. I'll give them to you when he does.'

I think she nodded: it was difficult to say: she just took the letter, opened it, read it and turned away with tears streaming down her cheeks: she did not even ask a question: just walked off pushing Thomas: it was the saddest thing I had ever seen. The romantics would say that, in that moment, her heart was broken: the realists would say it was no such thing: all I will say is that the quiet sobbing of Violet Reddy as she left me was the nearest thing to actual heartbreak I have ever seen or ever want to see.

My mother was incandescent with rage when I told her – as was to be expected, of course. 'And you let him go, you bloody little, fool! Why the hell didn't you try to stop him?' To be honest, I was sorry Jan had gone, but, since he was an older man, the thought of stopping him never occurred to me: I just accepted it as his decision, inconvenient as it was.

'You expect that kind of thing from foreigners,' my mother said waspishly when she had calmed down: then, referring directly to Violet, she added: 'Well, she'll have to go back to her husband now, won't she?' She meant bedwise, I think.

Her words struck a curious chord in me: I just could not understand how Jan could leave the woman he said he loved, the woman with whom he intended to spend the rest of his life, knowing that, while he was away, she would be climbing into bed each night with another man for the next three or four months, even if that man was her husband. All the worse, I would have thought, when you know that, during those months, every other night or so he would be pawing at her, parting her legs with his hands, forcibly if needs be, inserting his finger, demanding she take him, then grinding away on top of her two or three times a week and emptying himself into her while you lay alone in your own bed trying not to think about it. I could not have done that, definitely not: I could not have left Violet, or any woman for that matter, to someone else's groping hands or their lust: to me, it would have tarnished any love that might have existed between us: but such a thing did not seem to enter into Jan's thinking.

FIFTY-THREE

THEN, right near the end of pea-picking, it happened! Two thousand or so miles away from Gledlang and Norsea, members of a Jewish gang, the Irgun, kidnapped two British Army sergeants from Natanya beach in Palestine and hanged them in a citrus grove: their booby-trapped bodies were found that same week. When the news broke in the papers in England, any and every known Jew was a target for a punch in the face: and Stanley Lobel was a Jew.

Stanley was riding down Tithe Street just before seven o'clock on the Friday on his way to join us for the very last day of pea-picking when he was hit by a stone the size of a bantam's egg: just the one, just before he reached the Square. Two stones came sailing out of the early morning shadows as he passed along by the church wall where the Crucified Christ hangs on the First War memorial on the patch of hallowed greensward in front of the flint and Roman brick tower of St Peter's church. Stanley saw the first bounce on the road beside him, but, before he could take evasive action, the second hit him on the top of the head, right on the crown, and sent him crashing on to the road. It was several seconds before he was able to get to his feet: as he lay in the road, he heard a man's voice cry out: 'How do you like a bit of your own medicine, you effing Jew?' The only people likely to be in that area at that time were the men going into Rex Book's farm beside the church: and two of them were named Denny Caidge and Matt Cobb.

Stanley was too dazed from the blow on the head, too winded by his fall and hurting too much from grazed arms and knees to bother overmuch about the stone throwers: so much blood was pouring from the head wound that you would have thought he had cracked his skull open: but it was just one of those things that happen when you cut your scalp on the crown: you bleed profusely. I had done it myself when Ben was hammering in some fence posts and my head banged against the post as I held it upright: it was only a pinprick scalp wound, but it bled till my hair was as red as tomato sauce.

Not unnaturally, Stanley was more interested in getting away than starting an argument or a stone-throwing fight: he managed to remount his bicycle and pedal away, weaving as much from dizziness and pain as planned evasiveness, just as two more stones came bouncing along the road after him.

His hair was matted with blood and it was running in rivulets down his face when he rode through the gate into our field: we did not realise anything was wrong till he fell off his bicycle. 'You clown, Stanley,' I thought and started to laugh, thinking he had just skidded on a patch of mud: but my mother and Old Sago, who were nearest the gate, saw straight away that he was in some distress: how he had got across the causeway in his condition without steering over the edge was a minor miracle.

My mother was across to him immediately. 'Get him cleaned up, for Christ's sake!' she ordered as I joined her and helped Old Sago lift him to his feet: it was almost as if she knew what had happened and why, for, in a voice of sheer exasperation, she exclaimed to God and the world in general: 'Why do people do these things? Why can't they just let people be, let them get on with their lives in peace? They ain't hurting nobody.'

With Violet, a much sadder, wearier, unsmiling Violet now, looking on in some consternation, especially as Thomas had wandered over to see why Stanley had fallen off his bicycle, I led him down the track to the squeaky-handled pump on the square of green in front of the cottages and worked the handle while he sluiced off the blood: the water was freezing cold, coming from a well sixty feet down into the clay of the region so it stemmed the bleeding eventually: that and a handkerchief held to the wound.

We both knew why it had happened, just as I guessed who were the likeliest culprits among Rex Book's men: but as Stanley had not actually seen who had thrown the stone which hit him, or the stones which had missed him, there was not a lot he could do about it: and telling the Salter constable would have been totally futile: it was unlikely to evoke much sympathy from him at that time: nor was he likely to institute any kind of proper investigation. Chances were he was more likely to ride up to Stanley and tell him, 'You got what you bloody deserve, Jew boy,' than he was to ride up to Matt Cobb and Denny Caidge and give them a good telling off or charge them with throwing a stone at 'some Jew kid' a couple of days after they had found the two sergeants.

I felt guilty because Stanley was on his way to us when it happened: it was not the first incident to occur involving Stanley: but the others involved youths of the village, not grown men.

As far as I knew, Stanley was the only Jewish boy in the district, an orphan of the war, who lived with a reasonably well-to-do couple in a house with a walled garden on a back road between Tottle and Budwick: he was a year older than I, had gone to the same school as me at Maydun, but not with a great deal of academic success, I think.

He had come over as a nine-year-old on one of the last refugee boats into Harwich before the outbreak of war: they said it docked on the very day the Germans invaded Poland and closed their borders to all trains: it was that close for Stanley. Two days later, on the Sunday, Neville Chamberlain, the Prime Minister, spoke to the nation from the Cabinet room of 10 Downing Street and told us all that the British Ambassador in Berlin had delivered a Note to Herr Hitler stating that, unless we heard that Germany was prepared to withdraw its forces from Poland, 'a state of war would exist between us.' They did not, it did, and we won, so they told us. (We did not actually hear Chamberlain's broadcast on Norsea: the batteries in our wireless had gone and we still had not obtained any replacements when the war started on the Sunday: so for us, the war started on the Tuesday when Old Sago came across and told us.)

By the time I got to know him properly, Stanley had lost his foreign accent and spoke English like a native. I had known vaguely of him at Maydun secondary and I had seen him waiting outside the school gates to go home on the bus that went by the back roads to Tottle, a different bus to the one on which I travelled: and our paths had crossed briefly a couple of times, but I had never actually spoken to him at any length till the year before of which I write. It was my love of drawing which led to our meeting: one Sunday I escaped my chores on Norsea and rode over to Tottle by the back roads to draw the Swan Inn and some of the old thatched clapboard cottages surrounding the bramble-bushed green there. Stanley, who had left school by then, had come riding by on his shiny bicycle and, seeing me sitting on the verge sketching, had stopped to look and to talk, which was all very flattering to me, and with good reason.

The two of us sat and talked for an hour or more: I think he was genuinely pleased to have someone with whom he could talk, for, by all accounts, he led a pretty lonely life, a lot like me: he had not bothered to get a job since leaving school and was just 'hanging about,' as he put it, riding round and round the district: but that could have had something to do with the news coming out of Europe. We talked about all kinds of things and I liked him straight away because he smiled so much. Stanley always smiled: it was the great thing about him, his pleasantness and his willingness to be friends: after all, he had no one else in England except the couple who fostered him: and after what had happened in the East on the Continent no one else in the world, probably. He never said anything about it, but it could not have been easy for him to stand there chatting to me and knowing all the time that his mother and father, elder brother and sister, uncles, aunts, cousins and grandparents, his whole family, were gone forever and he would never see them again.

It was while we were talking that I told him about Norsea, about Hoary and his diggings and the fact that he was always looking for boys to help: to my astonishment, a week or so later in that early summer of Forty-Six, Stanley had come riding over to Norsea to see Hoary and ask if he needed any help with his diggings: yes, he did and Stanley was 'hired' for the next expedition. We had just started our pea-picking and, seeing me in the field as he rode back, Stanley had come through the gate to speak to me and to thank me for putting him 'on to such a good one': his description, not mine!

Ben, realising he was keen to earn money any way, quickly roped him in for pea-picking at three shillings a bag: Stanley leaned his bicycle against the hedge and started there and then. Ben, I know, was glad to have him, Stanley was glad of the work and I was glad of his company, especially as he picked at the same slower rate as I did, by comparison with my mother and Old Sago, and we could work side by side. The rest of the summer, Stanley had spent much of his time with Hoary, helping him on his excavations around the estuary and up in the next county: this he had continued in the second year, Forty-Seven.

The reason that Stanley came pea-picking on Norsea and went digging in the mud for Hoary was simply because he was desperate to earn as much money as possible for when he went 'up to London.' Among the boys of the area, he was acknowledged as a brilliant artist: in fact, he was so accomplished that, on seeing some of his work once, I had despaired of my own and, rather than trying to emulate him, I had consigned several of my poorer drawings to the range fire in our kitchen. Pushed by the art master at our school, a one-time Commando, Stanley had joined the local art society at Maydun and in that winter of Forty-Six had become the youngest ever of its members to have a one-man exhibition of his work in the Moot Hall at the top of Maydun hill, to which I went. It was well known that Stanley was earmarked for the Royal Academy School: he had been up to London for an interview and to show the big-wigs some of his work and was waiting to be called: he was that good. I have to say that I was more than a little jealous, not in a vicious way, but in an envious way. His art was vastly superior to mine: it was real art by comparison, done in proper water colours, oils or pastels, whereas my art was simple pencil drawings scrawled on pages torn from old exercise books I had stolen in my last term at school or on the backs of pieces of wallpaper with which my mother lined our drawers: often the shading was poor, the pencil work erratic and the perspective not always correct. So you will understand how flattered and pleased I was when he stopped to talk to me that first time and complimented me on how I had drawn the cottages at Tottle: I had done them very well, he said.

The day of the stone-throwing, we had been sitting by the pump for half-an-hour while Stanley recovered himself before my mother came to chivvy me back to the peafield: Stanley, much better now, though his head was still sore, followed, though he should have stayed where he was a bit longer: but it was in his nature not to let anyone down. When we returned to the field, I went back down his row to meet him so that the two of us could again pick alongside each other for the rest of the day. After all, my mother and Old Sago picked at the same approximate rate and stayed together, Violet Reddy was picking just behind them so all three could talk together and keep an eye on little Thomas, so why should Stanley and I not pick together?

We also took our lunch together, sitting among the pea rice, although we did not share our sandwiches because I had Spam and chutney and Stanley would not eat that, though he ate almost anything else: he was not a strict, Orthodox, rabbi-fearing Jew, just Jewish, because that is what he had been born to, just as a Catholic is a Catholic because they are born to it and Protestants are Protestants. That is why, I think, I never became overly religious: I never knew whether being a Jew was being part of a race or just part of a religion, or both: likewise, I never saw the need for any difference between the Catholics and the Protestants and why they went to separate churches and one would not set foot inside the other's. Or, for that matter, why some people were chapel, or Methodist or Baptist or Congregationalist or Spiritualist: it all seemed the same to me: and, of course, the two questions which kept coming to my agnostic mind were: What did

God, if he really were there – what did He think of it all? And: Did they carry on fighting and arguing up in Heaven, if there were one?

Because of the incoming tide, Violet and little Thomas had to leave at three: at four-thirty, my mother went off to cut some jam sandwiches and make a bottle of tea, which she brought to the field and which I shared with Stanley. Sago came and sat with us while we ate and we talked about various things, though no mention was made of Palestine: we steered well clear of that: it was not Stanley's fault what had happened: after tea, we resumed our work: it was as dreary as that.

We picked on late into the evening, mainly because it was the last day and we wanted to get it all finished: I excelled myself and picked eight bags, the most ever in a day: Old Sago was most impressed when he tied them up and Stanley and I pitched them on to the wagon. Stanley picked only five all day because he had to go slower and sometimes even to rest: the continual bending and straightening as he pulled up the pea-rice made him feel dizzy.

When Stanley left that night, splashing through the puddles left by the tide, he had Old Sago and me for company: he rode back across the causeway hanging on to the back of the wagon as we trundled the last sacks of peas across to the Boundary shed ready for the nine o'clock morning pick-up by the Hamwyte lorry which would put them on the train to London for sale the next day at the big market there. No one would throw stones while Old Sago was with him: not because they feared the old man (who would fear a man of seventy-five?), but because he was one of the most liked and respected men in the village, revered almost, because he was the best darts chalker in the Chessman. Hardly had a thrower's dart hit the board than Old Sago would have subtracted it from the total and be telling him three different ways to get out: 'Treble seventeen, double top ... bull, one, double top ... or treble eighteen, seven, double fifteen ...' Stanley was safe with him.

Sadly, it was to be some time before I saw him again and, when I did, it was not the same old Stanley.

FIFTY-FOUR

IN A WAY, I could understand how people felt about the murder of two British soldiers by a ruthless bunch like the Irgun, half of whom, if not all, had served in the British Army fighting against the Germans: the Jewish Brigade had fought well in Italy during the war and had a record of which to be proud.

To be honest, the first ever time I had seen Stanley I had not even realised he was Jewish, or what being 'Jewish' was: it was the autumn of Forty-Three, I was eleven and had just started a week before at Maydun secondary: that evening I had crossed to the village to be with the other village boys and a whole gang of us were walking past the little redbrick school in Tithe Street on our way to sit on the ciderstone after conkering up on the Park where the army searchlight and ack-ack battery were stationed. A tanned and handsome thirteen-year-old Stanley had cycled leisurely past with his hands stuck in his pockets and relying solely on his skill to keep his balance: to me then he was still a stranger who might have come from any of the surrounding villages, Salter, Tottle, Beckenden or Foliot Magna.

On seeing the village boys, Stanley had nervously raised one hand in greeting and had smiled and I had raised my hand in return and smiled right back: I was the only one.

Fred Ring, then fifteen and at that time the loud-mouthed leader of our group, gave me an angry look. 'Bloody Jew boy!' he muttered once Stanley had passed out of earshot: it was the first of many times I was to hear that epithet.

'What do you want to say a thing like that for?' I had demanded rather naively, puzzled by the unnecessary vehemence of the remark.

'Because I hate bloody Jews,' Fred Ring had snapped back, angry that I should even query his opinions.

'Why for God's sake?'

'Because we bloody do!' was the snarling reply from Lennie Ring walking alongside his brother: all I could do was shrug to let them know that I did not think such a thing was worthwhile: Germans, yes:

Japs, yes: but why Jews? It just made no sense to me: horrific rumours about massacres of Jews in the East by the Germans had been appearing at times in the newspapers, but that did not deter Fred Ring. Yes, Stanley looked different from us: yes, we knew he was a foreigner: but it was not till the day that Fred Ring called him a 'Jew boy' that I first wondered why his being Jewish could make him any different from me.

Admittedly, his looks did mark him down in our parts as 'not being one of us': he was sallow-skinned, with dark wavy hair and dark brown eyes, and was what I now know to be as Jewish looking, in my opinion, as I was Anglo-Saxon looking. What was worse, in summer he had a tendency to go nut brown in the sun and, with his dark hair and dark eyes, was an obvious 'foreigner': till I spoke to Stanley, I had never met a Jew whom I knew to be a Jew and would not have known had I done so.

Stanley was not the cause of the troubles between myself and the boys who nightly sat upon the ciderstone: they had been brewing for sometime: my defence of him was just an outcome of it. It really all began when Lennie Ring and his five older brothers had first come to Gledlang after being evacuated from their own village down south following Dunkirk because the army wanted it. At our very first meeting on the ciderstone, Lennie Ring and I had taken an intense dislike to each other and, after a bout of sullenness, sneering, baiting and bravado challenges, had briefly fought each other on a triangle of land up near Gledlang House, where Tithe Street joins the Salter road. It was a very brief affair: I had punched Lennie Ring in the chest and he had fallen backwards: the fight ended there: he claimed he fell over the wire support of a telegraph pole: I claimed I had knocked him down. He never forgot it and never forgave me for it either: every time I joined the others on the ciderstone in Gledlang Square, the mere sight of me riding up seemed to be enough to bring the sullenness to his face. I could see the 'Oh, bloody hell, here comes Joe Coe!' look in his eyes before I had even leaned my bicycle against the allotment wall. And no sooner had I joined in whatever discussion they were having and offered an opinion than he would be making scathing comments, like, 'Here we go again!' or 'All you ever bloody do when you sit with us is bloody argue!' or 'You only come over here to upset us because you're bored over there.'

'What the hell are you doing sitting here night after night if you aren't bored yourself?' I had retorted to that on one occasion, adding for good measure: 'It's not exactly the greatest thing in the world sitting here listening to you lot yapping about tractor engines and car engines and motorbike engines, is it?'

'What do you want us to talk about?' Lennie Ring had asked, sarcastically, in the manner of one who would have dismissed out of hand any suggestion I made.

'Christ! Anything!' I exploded, not meaning Jesus, of course. 'You could talk about anything other than car engines and tractor engines! There's more things in the world than them.'

'We talk about what we want to talk about, not what you want,' an indignant Lennie Ring had snapped back. 'Why should we have to talk about what you want to talk about? You don't have to join us if you don't like it. Bugger off back to Norsea if you don't like what we talk about.'

Billy had surprised me that evening by adding his support. 'No one forces you to come over,' he grumbled.

'I come because I like to come,' I had retorted, unwilling to be put down. 'I don't have to ask you or anyone else.' The usual reply when pride is at stake.

'No one's stopping you coming, but we don't have to sit here and listen to you when you get here,' Lennie Ring had snorted and, with a jerk of the head to Billy and some of the others, he had led them off to their second favoured position, the long church wall the other side of the Square, opposite Sligger Offin's garage, where they sat smugly sniggering as I recovered my bicycle and prepared to depart.

That particular argument occurred long before my fracas with Fred Ring. That, as things turned out, was to be the last time I ever sat with them on the ciderstone: and even that was not unexpected. For some time, I had discerned that Billy's greetings to me had become more casual, indifferent almost, and his hostility when argument flared more obvious and quicker to rise. More and more he seemed to have begun to accept that what Lennie Ring decreed he and the others should do. None of the Ring family, Lennie included, was known for their brains and yet Billy and the others seemed to agree with his opinions no matter how daft they were, even reinforcing them with similar arguments of their own. The other boys, Dick Hobson, Chris Huffle, Ted Chaffy, Jimmy Johnson and George Meaney, all seemed to be criticising me as well: bit by bit, I realised I was being excluded from the brotherhood of the ciderstone: not that I cared overmuch: I was a misfit and I knew it.

Only Nick seemed to maintain an outward neutrality during our many differences of opinion. 'You are an argumentative bugger when you get going, Joe,' he declared the evening they all tramped off and left me sitting alone on the ciderstone. 'You ought not to argue so much. Other people have opinions, too, you know.' Then he trudged after them, shaking his head sadly as if to say it could all have been avoided if I had not been so stubborn.

Somewhat chastened by Nick's admonishment, I had ridden home that night pondering on what he had said. I could not help that I argued with them, it was in my nature to debate: I was a natural-born debater: 'an argumentative bugger.' To Billy, Nick and Lennie Ring, or anyone else with whom I disagreed, it was an argument: to me, it was a discussion, an exchange of views, the simple airing of diverse opinions: nothing to get angry about, nothing to raise your fists over, nothing to threaten to punch someone in the teeth over. I liked arguing, or discussing things. Trouble was I knew that I 'argued' for argument's sake and enjoyed it: perhaps I did it because I worked alone so much that just to hear other people expressing views, nonsensical as I thought most of them were, was a challenge to me.

I was not a vicious arguer: I just liked to talk about things: I did not want to talk solely about tractors and ploughing and drilling and hoeing and the like: I did enough of the latter not to want to talk about it after I had finished it. We never took newspapers on Norsea because there was no guarantee they would be delivered daily: also because neither my mother nor Ben would give them house room, except to use to light the kitchen fire: and the ones they used for that, I provided. Whenever I could afford it, on my trips across to Gledlang, I always tried to buy a *Daily Express* from the post office: I would even wait till the next day sometimes before sitting down to read it in the parlour while listening to the wireless: it was another way of passing the long and lonely hours between completing my chores and going to bed. There was nothing else to do: we had no books to read on Norsea:, not a single one in the house: Hoary had hundreds, but he would never lend me any of them.

I suppose I was just more curious about things than the other village boys: they always wanted to talk about inlet manifolds, pistons and crankshafts and firing systems: I was interested in politics, for one, history and reading for another, and drawing. But it was my interest in politics which annoyed the other youths the most: for some unaccountable reason, politics, especially Joe Stalin and Russia, the Jews and Arabs in Palestine, the Americans and the atom bomb were as interesting to me as they were anathema to them. My daily boundaries were the shorelines of Norsea, one mile long and half a mile wide, peopled by just the four of us, myself, Ben, my mother and Old Hoary, till Richard and the women artists came. I was willing to discuss almost any subject within reason: discussion was the only way open to me to learn: there were things about the world outside Norsea and Gledlang about which I knew nothing: I wanted to learn about them: but the others just did not seem to care one way or the other.

'It's buggers like you who start wars,' were Lennie Ring's final words just before he had stamped off that final evening I sat with them, followed by Billy, the others and finally Nick.

And what kind of things did I want to talk about? The affairs of the world, no less: particularly as I was soon to be a part of it. In just over a year, the army would be sending me a buff envelope with my call-up papers in it, along with a travel warrant to go somewhere or other for a medical: I knew that I would pass the medical and that, within a month, I would be on a train to Aldershot or Tidmarsh, marched up and down for six weeks by some raving lunatic of a drill sergeant, taught how to polish my boots, Blanco my webbing, fold my socks into little squares, fold my blankets into neat piles, paint coal black, shovel white snow on top of dirtied snow and clip grass with a pair of scissors. Eventually I might be taught to point a rifle for King and Country and kill some poor sod in the Middle East, the Far East or along the banks of the Rhine whom I had never met and with whom I had no quarrel.

Politics did not play a big part in the discussions in the Chessman or the Bowler's Rest either: mostly they talked of the problems of crop growing, the imminent arrival of a tractor on a farm to replace a loved but plodding shire or other farming matters. If the men grumbled at all about politics, it was that coal was rationed, bread was rationed, bacon was rationed, clothing was rationed, petrol was rationed, even potatoes were rationed: and, worse for their children, sweets were rationed and chocolate of any kind was virtually unobtainable from the post office's grocery counter or anywhere else: and that two years after the war had ended! Some jokers were even saying the Germans were getting more than we were, except in Berlin, where Uncle Joe's Russians were full of bloody-mindedness. Who would have thought we had won the war!

Grain ships from America were being diverted to India, where the people were supposed to be starving: the Hindus and the Muslims, it seemed, were too busy fighting each other to grow food: they had asked for their independence and we had granted it, but instead of building a country all they were doing was massacring each other, burning each other's homes and raping each other's young women. The Pathe newsreels at the Embassy in Maydun were very disappointing: they never showed any of the girls who had been raped, like the Chinese girl in Nanking being dragged away by Japanese soldiers: you knew what was going to happen to her! All we got of the riots were distant shots of dead bodies scattered in a street somewhere, some buildings burning and khaki-clad policemen in baggy shorts and turbans thwacking people with sticks while some horse-faced, topeed British officer directed them from the rear.

The troubles in Palestine had been brewing since the end of the war: Jewish survivors from the Nazi concentration camps had been arriving in the Promised Land by the boatload: almost every week the screen was filled by pathetic, silently staring faces of children and young people standing forlornly on the decks of steamers trying to get into Palestine, or sitting in displaced persons' camps. The poor bloody British soldiers were trying to keep the peace and ensure that Jewish immigration was controlled enough so that the Arabs would not start an all-out war: but it was futile as both sides were already arming. Still, I felt sorry for those people after what they had endured: they needed a home somewhere. Getting ashore in Palestine, as thousands did, was no guarantee that their suffering was at an end: those not murdered by Arabs were rounded up by our soldiers and shipped back to Cyprus, those who did not blow up themselves and their ship, that is. On Cyprus, they were herded into new barbed-wire holding camps – 'concentration camps,' the Americans viciously called them, though there were no gas chambers, crematoria, gallows or starvation blocks and medical attention was given by the Red Cross as well as British Army doctors. We saw plenty of pictures of British soldiers guarding people in barbed-wire cages: it was not an easy time to be proud and British and the knowledge that I might be doing the same in a year or so made me doubly apprehensive.

The atrocity by the Irgun had only made things worse.

FIFTY-FIVE

ONLY A MAN with a near childish faith in the Almighty would have climbed the crumbling stone steps to the belfry of St Peter's church tower, squeezed through a small leaded window forty feet up and walked without fear along the ridge coping to inspect the roof for holes: but Hoary did it in his plimsolled feet. Why, I do not know: on a whim, I suppose, like all the other daft things he did. What he found there led to an emergency meeting of the churchwardens being called the very next evening: I know who it was at that meeting who suggested we hold a fete and flower show on Gledlang House Park to raise funds for church repairs: but I am not sure who it was who conceived the idea of holding an art exhibition in conjunction with that fete.

My suspicion is that it was Hoary himself who suggested it: unusually for him, he was at the churchwardens' meeting, having invited himself and then, once there, ignored polite suggestions that he should leave. He came back to Norsea chirping all about it, positively rubbing his hands with glee: that is why I think it was him. I think he saw it as an opportunity to exhibit his grotesque sculptures because otherwise no one else would see them if they remained scattered about his 'lawn': and also, of course, to display the 'proper painting' of his two guests, Laura Wilchard and Pocklington, for the edification of the culturally deprived of Gledlang. Whoever it was who made the suggestion, an art exhibition is what we got, to be run in conjunction with the fete and flower show on the second Saturday of August, all proceeds to go towards the church's fabric fund.

An art exhibition in Gledlang! That must have caused some mirth in Salter, where they actually had an artists' society for amateur weekend daubers and there was even one man living there who professed to be an actual professional artist who made his living from painting people's portraits: he lived in a big house with half-a-dozen children so he must have had some success at it. Unlike in Gledlang: until Laura Wilchard and Pocklington came to stay on Norsea, we had no one in the village who aspired to being a proper artist: there was no call for one: who in their right mind was going to pay five pounds for an artistic picture of a view they could see twenty times a day for nothing? Living in Gledlang, they saw nothing about the estuary remotely worth painting: just bleak saltings and even bleaker mudflats under the vast grey dome of the sky. 'Ain't nothing there but mud and seaweed and bloody seagulls,' was the consensus. 'And the land around ain't no better. It's as flat as a bloody pancake everywhere you look! People want to see mountains, hills and trees, don't they? And lakes and things. Something to look at, not flat bloody mudbanks, flat fields and flat everything else.'

So they must have had a good laugh in Salter when the posters went up on the telegraph poles: there had always had been a certain jealousy between the inhabitants of Gledlang and the much larger Salter: it had taken a turn for the worse the previous year when Salter had achieved a claim to fame which we envied even more. One sunny June weekend, a certain royal personage, who liked playing cricket and was courting a certain princess, had come down from London unannounced with a team of some Honorable Company or Other and had played against the village team, scoring half a dozen runs and taking a couple of wickets with his slow spinners. No one had spotted who he was till the teams took tea in the Blue Lion and the poor landlord nearly dropped the plate of sandwiches he was handing round when he saw who was sitting at his table in the snug: it was on the front pages of all the Sunday papers the next day. We hoped the royal personage would come to Gledlang, just to even things out, but he never did.

All we got was some *Manchester Guardian* writer, who came a couple of months later in that same summer of Forty-Six and took a photograph of the village cricket team playing on the Park for a book he was writing about idyllic England. News of his coming was put up in the village post office by Sir Garstang Judkin, who owned the Park surrounding his twelve-roomed, seven-chimneyed, mullion-windowed, Eighteenth Century former parsonage and graciously allowed us to play on it: he knew the writer chap apparently. About fifty people turned up just to get on the photograph: the picture is taken from behind and shows the villagers of rural England lounging on the grass in the shade of tall, spreading-branched elms, watching a game of cricket, all on a sunny summer's day, with the unmown outfield covered in flowers. 'Buttercups and daisies cricket' the writer chap captioned it: all very nice. He was not there the next weekend when hailstones as big as marbles flattened the corn in the field across the road, cracked the panes in greenhouses and dented the roof of John Bolt's van just as if someone had been pounding on it with a hammer: nor was he there a month or so later when the farmers came with their twelve-bore shotguns and blasted up through the branches of those self-same elms till the ground beneath was strewn with the black, gunshot-frayed corpses and loose feathers of the rooks which nested in the tops of those very trees.

Billy, Nick and I are on the photograph somewhere half-visible in the shadow: out in the sunlight, padded up and waiting to go in, are Sir Garstang and the then new vicar, Reverend Ffawcon: that was the only day I knew that they played and they only did that because they had whites and proper school-hooped cricket caps and it would look better on the photograph. Most of the village men usually played in white shirts, if they had one, grey flannels and whitened plimsolls: except our best bowler, Tony Bow, who always turned up in his hob-nailed workboots and a blue working shirt with the sleeves rolled up: he played that day, but he is not on the picture.

Still, the coming of the writer meant there is actually a picture of Gledlang as it used to be in a book somewhere, which is something of which to be proud, just as we should have been pleased that, in a preamble, he described Gledlang itself as 'the last unspoiled village' along the Langwater estuary. The locals laughed at that. 'If we're unspoiled, it's because no bugger wants to live here!' declared one wag in the Chessman.

The so-called Park on which the fete and art exhibition were to be held was really no more than three large rough-grassed meadows, about twenty acres all told, divided by barbed wire fencing on which the Stanson sisters grazed their dairy cattle. Sir Garstang's gardener mowed the wicket especially for that one game and even put a chain mower over the outfield a fortnight before to get the daisies and buttercups growing properly: that was the only time he did it: the rest of the time the players had to do it themselves.

The gardener and his family lived in, so to speak: his wife cooked and cleaned for her Ladyship, while their plump, bespectacled daughter acted as a secretarial dogsbody and flower changer for the old harridan. Her Ladyship was a horse-faced woman whose idea of entering into the life of the village was to smile benignly at the locals when she passed them trotting around in her pony and trap, take the front pew for herself in the church, have her groceries delivered from the post office-cum-grocery store and to preside as more-or-less permanent honorary president of the fledgling Women's Institute, to which, being university educated like her husband, she gave talks on all manner of subjects about which she knew very little and judged the handicraft and cooking competitions, as well as drawing the raffle: still, she got her name each time in the WI Notes in the local paper. She also served as the unelected chairwoman of the churchwardens and saw herself as the governor-in-chief, unappointed, of the village's church school. Just your normal sort of village squire's wife really.

Needless to say, Sir Garstang and Lady Judkin were staunch supporters of the Labour Party – what else! – just so long as they did not have to live like us, work like us, get the same pay as us and have to mix too much with us. Sir Garstang held a senior post on the administrative side at the Labour Party's headquarters at Transport House in London: each weekday morning at nine-fifteen, the portly, grey-haired, grey-moustacheoed Sir Garstang, looking every inch a city gent in black jacket, pinstripe trousers and bowler hat and carrying his brief case and rolled umbrella, would climb into a special black handsome cab driven over from Hamwyte, to be taken to the station there to catch the ten o'clock express up to London. No rattletrap taxi from Sligger Offin's garage for him: and no worries about austerity, petrol rationing or unnecessary motor trips which his own Government was even then threatening to clamp down upon: just like Hoary.

Of course, being a supporter of the Labour Party, not to mention a benign, munificent, squire-like figure to the labouring classes, did not mean Sir Garstang would allow the ruffian youths of the village to erect their goalposts on his Park and turn his precious meadowland into a quagmire each winter kicking a ball about: any other field would do for Kerry the Milkman's Wanderers: and they could always take a shovel with them if they needed to clear the cowpats and flatten the molehills before erecting their tent posts and rope crossbars for each game.

Oh yes, I knew Sir Garstang and Lady Judkin well: twice a year, I delivered a quarter-sack of Ben's oysters to the backdoor of the big house and pocketed the twelve-and-six the cook gave me: I gave it to Ben, of course: it was his way of making a little extra money on the side.

It was in her capacity as occupant of the front pew, senior churchwarden and president of the Women's Institute and wife of our self-appointed squire that Lady Judkin allowed the fete, flower show and exhibition to be held partly on the Park and partly on the lawns of Gledlang House. The two main marquees, one for the flower exhibits and handicrafts and one for the fruit and vegetables, would be on the rougher grass of the Park and cowpats would have to be tolerated: a third, smaller marquee for the paintings, being cultural, would be on the back lawn: a section of the hurdle fencing which surrounded the house would be removed and anyone who wished to visit the art exhibition would be charged an extra threepence to go through the gap to that marquee: there they would see Laura Wilchard's and Pocklington's paintings, along with Hoary's rubbish sculptures.

Stanley Lobel, my 'Jew boy' friend and digging and pea-picking companion, was not even asked to exhibit: news that 'someone' had thrown a stone at Stanley and knocked him off his bicycle following the Palestine incident had seeped round the village by then and the fete and flower show committee decided not to tempt providence. From what I gleaned later, the proposal 'not to ask him because of what's happened out there in Palestine' was accepted without comment, even by the vicar! They did not even take a vote on it: it was a great disappointment to me.

Most people in the village who knew Stanley, whether they liked him or not, blamed him or not, knew he was a very good painter: even the Philistines who could not tell a landscape from a vase of flowers accepted that you had to be good to have an exhibition of your own pictures in Maydun Moot Hall when aged just fifteen and be invited up to London at seventeen to see if you were good enough to study proper art at the Royal Academy School. What a feather in our cap it would have been to have included him in our art show! We could easily have called him a 'Gledlang boy' since he regularly rode through the village and on several occasions had painted various bits of it: and, of course, he did work for Hoary and on Norsea, too!

Just ten or fifteen of Stanley's paintings would, in my humble opinion, have turned Gledlang's first ever proper art exhibition into a great little show, better than anything Salter could have put on. As it was, the exhibition was open to everyone else, just not to Stanley. A half-dozen others did enter: the vicar's plump little wife, Anne Ffawcon, for instance, put in some water colours of vases of various flowers, variety unknown: and the new young infants' mistress at the school, a twenty-two-year-old beanpole of a girl, whom the children called 'Miss Lewis,' dashed off a couple of local water-colour scenes and entered those, as did one of the flower arrangers at the church, who encased hers in cheap photographic frames after consigning Great Uncle Harry's bewhiskered visage and Aunt Matilda's haughty stare to a sideboard drawer. Even her ladyship herself put in a couple of excruciating daubs done especially for the occasion – portraits of the King and Queen and the Princesses Elizabeth and Margaret copied from newspaper photographs – where every colour, it seemed, was mixed with white and everything came out pasty and tonally flat: beige faces and beige hair!

I entered four of my own drawings, unframed, but, sadly, they were not on display with the real artists, that is, the grown-ups, but were hung separately in a children's exhibition. As a concession to the villagers and also to get them to attend, a small open exhibition for 'children' was established at one end of the art exhibition marquee. Prizes of two-shillings and sixpence were to be given for the best picture by someone sixteen-and-under, twelve-and-under and seven-and-under. I entered four of what I considered to be my very best, which had been gathering dust on top of the bedroom wardrobe: they were our barn on Norsea, an angled view of the ivy-clad village church across the gravestones, the higgledy-piggledy houses straggling down Shoe Street as seen across the top of Rex Book's orchard, and a view of the old Swan Inn and thatched cottages on the green at Tottle, drawn when I first met Stanley. They were worth a shilling apiece, in my book, so I wrote a two-and-six price on each and crossed my fingers.

The sad thing about that art exhibition is that it was to be the final undoing between Billy and Nick and myself: but for that we might have made up our differences over the other divisions and disagreements between us, like my argumentative nature, my exasperation at the banality of their conversation when we sat together on the ciderstone, even my having to give evidence against Billy in the court case. I just hoped that Billy would understand that, when I was called to tell what I had seen, I would do it because there was nothing else I could do but tell the truth and that I did it wishing him no ill. But the art show and what happened there changed all that, irrevocably: after that, I had neither the inclination nor a wish to seek out Billy or any of them to make up our differences. When eventually I was to face Billy in court and give my evidence there was an unbridgeable bitterness between us: and, in such a small place as Gledlang, they are the things around which lives revolved.

FIFTY-SIX

SUMMER strangers came regularly to the Langwater: Laura Wilchard and Pocklington were not the first city types to dwell there for a few weeks and then depart: but most came only for a day, a few hours. What they saw, or thought they saw, was a tranquil paradise of unalterable calm, a timeless haven where the sun beat down from an azure sky and laughing bathers splashed in the shallows of the twice-daily tide, where distant upon a sparkling swell red-sailed timber barges glided before the cooling rush of the breeze and in the fields all around the speeding arrows of swift and swallow skimmed rippling acres of red-golden grain, finch and martin weaved along the courses of deep delph ditches and drowsy butterflies danced in heat hazes before distant hedgerows hung thick with the profusion of summer.

That was the false idyll of their memory: for they departed before the tide had completed its ebb and knew nothing of the hideousness of the place when it lay empty and brooding between the floods of the sea. They did not look out over the brown-sheened wastes stretching to the misted line of the opposite shore, or walk by lonely inlets where the ribbed, skeletal hulks of long-sunken nameless boats rotted beneath their decades of glistening green slime. Nor did they suspect or care that far out from the land, where the webbed arrow prints of gulls and geese track across the brown salt sheen, a man can, in the space of a single step, sink to his thighs in the treacherous black ooze and, if sunk too deep, or too weighted down by seaboots or too panic-stricken to drag himself free, be held fast there till the tide creeps back over the wastes and silences forever his anguished cries. A man called Coker, who collected winkles and tended oyster beds and knew the Langwater better than any man on it, had died that way only twenty years before: three years later the father I had never known had drowned out on the Othona Flats while hunting alone in his punt: and the estuary was still taking lives. The year before that of which I write, a young farmer, Lester Peakman, second of Old Man Peakman's sons, had set off on a sea fishing trip with two village men: he had got himself a little dinghy and wanted to try out his new outboard engine. Somewhere off Cobwycke they hit a metal pylon sunk into the mud to moor the naval boats prior to D-Day and never removed: the pylon ripped the bottom out of the little boat and pitched all three overboard. The two village men had on only ordinary boots and so were able to swim ashore: the young farmer had a new pair of thigh-high seaboots and could not free himself: they filled with water and he drowned, struggling on the bottom just like my father all those years before. So you see the estuary was idyllic to some, a place of brooding ugliness to others, and, for the unlucky few, a death trap.

It was one of these summer strangers whom Sir Garstang persuaded to open the fete, the beknighted film-actor father of a famous 'thespian family,' who occasionally came during the hotter days of July and August to spend a week or fortnight at Gledlang House. Sometimes we would see him and his red-haired wife, and their snooty brood, a lanky girl called 'Vee,' a plump younger sister called 'Ellen' and a sour-faced boy, 'Kay,' all red-haired like their mother, strolling leisurely down Shoe Street to the river to bathe, gawping in utter disbelief at the local youth.

On one occasion, just as they came down Shoe Street carrying their towels, I rode up towards the Square from Boundary, begrimed and in my work clothes: I had to smile because I had just crossed from Norsea: the tide was out or how else would I have done it? There would be no swimming for them that day. I received the usual sympathetic stare from the children – sympathetic in the way of 'how could anyone go about looking so dirty and dressed in such old clothes?' Everything between the husband and the wife was prefaced by a strident 'I say, Darling ...' and, from the children, all answers and comments seemed to include an equally vocal 'Oh, look Daddy...' or 'Oh, look, Mummy...' followed by a 'Yes, Darling...' or a 'No, Darling...' One of the girls later became a left-wing revolutionary fighting to free the working class from people just like themselves and the boy became a union hothead, but I always reckoned that what they knew about us you could have written on the inside flap of a packet of ten Park Drive cigarettes! It is easy to champion the working class when you earn a lot of money, live, say, in a big ten-roomed house in Hampstead or Highgate among the other genteel London folk, and have rich friends round for candlelit dinners with wine and champagne to drink while you discuss the privations being inflicted upon the long-suffering masses and which you, by dint of status then, a fair bit of wealth and always knowing someone on the black market who could get you what you wanted, were always able to circumvent.

You try being working class slaving away on Norsea all winter through cold and sleet and rain and snow and fog and winds and hail: and drinking cold tea from a Tizer bottle sitting under a hedge and unwrapping cold oatmeal sausage sandwiches from a piece of newspaper before you plod back through pools of mud and water to stand in a drainage ditch for the next five hours. Sod being working class! I would have given my right arm to be middle class or upper class and never have to do another bloody day's work as long as I lived!

Richard transported Hoary's wooden Easter Island statues to Gledlang House in the car on the Friday evening: I was entrusted with loading them and, as there were so many of them, at least twenty, ranging in size from eighteen inches high to four feet, I piled them on to the back seat: they were a bit higgledy-piggledy and there was not much room so I had to ram the last ones in. As was to be expected, Hoary found fault with the way I did that and went almost hair-tearingly spare at some damage or other he said he could see: it was nothing much: one of the idols lost its nose and another was chipped over one of its eyes, that's all: no one in Gledlang would have known the difference!

They caused quite a bit of mirth among those villagers who were helping to prepare the site when we rolled up and began unloading. 'Good Gawd! What the bloody hell are they?' seemed to be the general reaction. 'They look like things you'd find outside a bloody witchdoctor's hut in Africa or on top of an Indian totem pole.' Some were laughing so much they had tears in their eyes and had to put their hands over their mouths to stifle it.

Hoary had jammed himself in the front of the car with Richard, leaving me to cycle over after them, and so, unfortunately, was on hand to discuss the positioning of each with Lady Judkin, who was supervising the arty side of the fete.

I handed in my four drawings for the children's exhibition at the marquee and went back out: by this time Richard had driven off, heading back to Norsea to pick up Laura Wilchard and Greta Pocklington and their paintings. Lady Judkin and Hoary, meanwhile, were attempting to arrange the sculptures in a roped-off section of the lawn some thirty feet by thirty feet and I was seconded to help. Hoary had pinned a price on each – 'forty pounds' some of them! – and it took them a half-hour or more to agree on the 'final positioning,' after which it took them another half-hour to agree on the 'final, final positioning.' The trouble was whenever one suggested a position in relation to another sculpture, the other might agree, but then proceeded to adjust everything around: so all the time I was moving 'this one left and 'that one right' and 'that one back' and 'that one forward' and 'that one over there' and 'that one over here,' from one side of the lawn to the other and back again.

By the time they had settled everything, to the complete satisfaction of neither, Richard had returned from Norsea with Pocklington and Laura Wilchard and was helping them to carry their pictures into the marquee on the lawn: the flap was pulled across and no one, except Hoary and Lady Judkin, was allowed to follow them in. So, having finished what I had to do, I cycled back down Tithe Street into the Square and got a shock.

Billy, of all people, was sitting there on the ciderstone with Nick, Lennie Ring and a half-dozen other younger village boys: I had not known he had been let out of gaol: I was pleased to see he was out, but made sure I did not show it: I rode past and went down Shoe Street without acknowledging them and they all turned their backs on me, except Nick, who turned and gave a feeble grin like before. That was something at least. I hoped Richard would come up behind me with the car before I reached Norsea, but he did not: he was still with the two women and Hoary, I supposed. All I got from my mother when I walked into the kitchen was a contemptuous look: she did not approve of me wasting my time drawing pictures and showed it: she would never understand what entering my pictures and going to the fete and seeing them on display, maybe with a farmer later offering to buy one, meant to me.

FIFTY-SEVEN

THE TIMING of the fete and flower show-cum-art exhibition could not have been better for me: we were in a lull after finishing the pea-picking and the exhibition gave me an excuse not to work on a Saturday afternoon and to flee the island, if only for a few hours: there would not be many more opportunities for some time. Once we started on the grain harvest, weather allowing, I would be working long, gruelling hours, non-stop almost, till the harvest was safely gathered in and the stacks sheeted down awaiting the arrival of the threshing gang from Budwick sometime in September. This would be my last free Saturday for three or four weeks: so for me, the art exhibition was a more than welcome distraction.

The day of the fete dawned, I spent an impatient morning waiting for the clock to tick round and then crossed to Gledlang alone just before two o'clock: Richard had driven Hoary, Laura Wilchard and Pocklington across a half-hour earlier because they wanted to meet the 'invited celebrity.' My mother, too, had gone on ahead for once: she wanted to see the flowers, the cakes, the bread and the knitted handicrafts. The fete did not open till two o'clock so, with luck, I might arrive, if not after the opening speeches at least towards the end of them. I was out of luck: they were just starting when I rode up to the gate and paid my entrance fee and I had to wait with the rest of the crowd before the famous thespian and film actor declared the fete 'open.' At least, his presence drew a crowd: there must have been a hundred or more people at the opening, all eager to trample the lawns of Gledlang House, and effectively blocking my route to the exhibition marquee to see if I had won a prize.

The famous film actor gave the usual blather which people speak at such events: you know, 'how good it is to be here' when they wished they were elsewhere, 'all the lovely exhibits' when they thought most of them were laughable rural rubbish produced by clodhopping nobodies whose wives made wine from parsnips and beetroot and damsons, rugs from old rags and pullovers from the remnants of old socks. Then there were 'the children's lovely wild flowers' when they had just viewed a line of two-dozen scruffy jam jars half-filled with tapwater into which clumsy young fingers had crammed a few dandelions, daisies and dog roses, some a few campions, and others the odd sprig of cow parsley or other weed, ragwort or thistle. A tour of the vegetables and fruit and handicraft and flower marquees followed, the official party comprising the actor and his wife, of course, Sir Garstang and Lady Judkin, Pocklington and Laura Wilchard, and the Reverend Ffawcon and his wife: oh, and Hoary, who bayed away all the way round in his usual manner, trod in a cowpat which someone had neglected to clear away and tripped over a guide rope: just his usual inanity. Trailing behind were the film actor's children, looking haughty and sullen and thoroughly bored.

The poor film actor must have wished he had not allowed himself to be talked into it after he had inspected his fifteenth plate of gooseberries the size of golf balls, twenty more of strawberries the size of plums, ten more of raspberries the size of strawberries, not to mention plate after plate of damsons, purple plums, golden plums, greengages, pears with one sliced in half for taste, bunches of black currants and red currants, perfectly straight cucumbers, scrubbed potatoes so big you would need only one for a meal for three, not to mention in the next marquee trestle table after trestle table of newly knitted cardigans, jumpers, socks, rag rugs and tea-cosies followed by vase after vase of flowers of every hue and description, big flowers, little flowers, blue flowers, red flowers, yellow flowers ... Consequently, no one was allowed to enter any of the marquees till the official party had passed round them: once they were clear, there was the usual push and shove of hopeful prize-winners, all eager to see who had been awarded a yellow card first, a red second or a blue third.

What I had seen of the children's art section in handing in my own four pictures was so bad that an honest judge would have hesitated to nominate anyone's as being more outstanding than the rest, except for mine, of course: so I had high hopes of taking at least one, maybe even two, perhaps even all three of the prizes, a first, second and a third. After all, I had walked off with the main drawing prize in the sixteen-and-under section on the previous two occasions the fete and flower show had been held, mostly because I was the only one who had entered that section: no one else had bothered. It may have been only a half-crown, but then it was only a village fete and flower show, so one could not expect anything more.

Suffice it to say, I did not win the sixteen-and-under prize this time: I did not win anything: I did not win simply because there were none of my pictures on display. Anne Ffawcon saw me looking along the line of screens on which they had been pinned and came over to tell me: she was very sympathetic and very sorry: I could hardly believe what she told me.

During the night someone had slipped in under the canvas of the art marquee, taken down my four drawings, torn them up and scattered the pieces between there and the gate like someone laying a trail in a paper chase. There had not been any security simply because no one had thought they would need it: not in a village like Gledlang: such things just did not happen! She really was very, very sorry: she then gave me a brown paper bag: inside were my drawings, torn to pieces and stained with mud.

I knew exactly who had done it: just before I had turned into the gate where the entrance table had been set up, I had seen Billy and Lennie Ring standing astride their bicycles about thirty yards off, on the triangle of green where Tithe Street divides towards Salter and Tottle. When they saw me, they began laughing, looking at each other and laughing. The anger just welled up inside me: in moments I was out of that tent, retrieving my bicycle and pedalling furiously out of the gate: I intended to wipe the smile off their faces: pay them back for the hurt they had inflicted on me.

Immediately they saw me, Billy and Lennie Ring wheeled their bicycles round and attempted to ride off: they were laughing again as they did so: the prospect of a chase along the Salter road appealed to them. It takes a few yards to get a bicycle going at any speed and Billy was a bit slow: I had the momentum in my favour. As he dragged his bicycle round and started to pedal away, I deliberately crashed into his back wheel, sending bicycle and rider tumbling to the ground in a heap. I let my bicycle fall and stood over Billy as he got painfully to his feet: then I hit him, in the mouth with my right fist and then on the cheek with my left: I was aiming for his nose, but he turned his head away. He staggered a bit and I hit him a third time, this time on the nose, and he fell backwards on to the bank, clutching at his face. I know, that as I did it, I was swearing at him: what I said exactly is lost in the mists of rage, but it had enough vehemence and hate in it for shock to register in Billy's eyes. Lennie Ring had stopped some fifty yards off and was circling in the road, unsure whether to come back, but I was not going to chase him: I had got the better of Billy and I was not going to risk my luck a second time. As I walked back to my own bicycle lying in the road nearby, in a final act of viciousness, I stamped my boot on the spokes of Billy's back wheel, bending several of them: then I seized his pump and sent it flying over the hedge into Rex Book's red currant field.

I did not go back to the fete: I did not have the heart: I rode back to Norsea and beheaded every flower and weed in sight.

FIFTY-EIGHT

WITH JAN gone and Stanley failing to appear, and Richard still driving the women about or helping Old Hoary, there was just Old Sago and I to get in the harvest. My mother would help, of course: women had always helped with the harvesting in our region: but a man of seventy-five, a sixteen-year-old and a woman nearing fifty, even if she was my mother and used to field work, would struggle to get in five fields of wheat and barley, especially if the weather broke: and that was what I feared the most. We had had an unbroken run of sunny days since the thunderstorms left us in the middle of July: temperatures in the eighties and nineties some days: cloudless skies. The cynic would say, by the law of averages, the weather had to break some time: and, if the Fates really were as perverse as people said, they would do their worst in the middle of harvest time.

I owed it to Ben to get in the harvest: he had spent the whole of the past year worrying about our growing grain crop: he had worried at the breakfast table, he had worried at the dinner table: I had stood with him in all of our five fields at one time or another and watched him ruminating on the state of the growth. Ours was winter wheat, dressed and well limed because wheat land should always be well limed and we always gave it a top dressing in the spring and rolled it to push the stones back down: and sometimes we lightly harrowed in clover to keep the other weeds out. Winter wheat gave a better yield generally than spring wheat and we grew more of it simply because it was a good cash crop: a good yield would be about one-and-a-half tonnes of grain to the acre, with a tonne of straw per acre to sell across to the mainland for those who needed it for littering their livestock as wheat straw was no good for feed: there were always takers. The profit from a year's hard and frustrating endeavour may have gone to Hoary, or to Hoary's bigwig brother in London, but it was a matter of pride to Ben that the farm on Norsea did show a profit from the crops it produced: then a man could hold up his head in the company of others: I was not about to let him down.

From the time we had ploughed in the previous September and drilled in the first two weeks of October, right through Christmas and the dreadful months of January and February, when the fields lay buried under two to three feet of snow, Ben just worried: he had gone on worrying when the big thaw came in mid-March and he and I had spent a whole week hastily digging drainage channels across the fields at the eastern end to run off the surface water from the melting snow down to our sluice at the Eastern Point. He had worried again when the first nodes were detected on the stem of the wheat, for there was always the fear of mildew or eyespot: the second nodes had begun to appear towards the end of June, just at the time Ben had his accident, so I knew that, even lying in his hospital bed, he would have gone on worrying about red rust and yellow rust despite the dressings he had applied to the seedbed, all the time hoping Sago and I were not delayed too long in getting in the wheat because there was a danger that soot mould would spread through it and we would have to burn it and plough it back into the ground.

If he were not worrying about the three fields of wheat, Ben was worrying about the barley: we had drilled two fields of winter barley between September and November, again making sure the land was well limed as barley will fail without it: barley needs a seed bed finer than for wheat and you drill about two inches deep: with barley, you worried about leaf diseases, net blotch, smut, leaf stripe or wireworm: you harrowed against weeds and harvested after the ears had 'necked,' that is, turned downwards.

Wheat must be 'dead ripe' to harvest, Ben had always told me: the grain must be hard and dry: if you waited too long before you cut, it would 'shallow': that is, some of the grain would be lost on the ground. If the weather were wet, as sometimes it can be, sheeting rain and thunderstorms flattening everything, you harvested it and hoped you would be able to save some of it: enough to break even on the expenditures even if you did not make a profit. Thankfully, Old Sago inspected the five fields with me on the Friday before the disastrous flower show and fete: and it was he who adjudged the wheat was ready for cutting and that the barley would be by the time we had finished getting in the first wheat. He plucked a couple of ears from a different spot in each field, each time rubbing first one and then the other in the palm of his hand, testing some of the grains between his thumb and forefinger before smelling them and tasting them. 'Time to get this lot in, young Joe,' he announced. 'We'll start Monday.' It was then, with just the two of us standing in the field, that the thought first struck me: how the hell were a man of his age and a youth my age, plus a woman of indeterminate usefulness, going to do all that?

But it was ready and get it in I would, by hook or by crook: I had it all planned: for the cutting, Sago would be on the binder, with Molly pulling: my mother and I would be walking round the field behind the binder, picking up the tied sheaves as they were ejected and stacking a half-dozen into stooks, where they would be left to dry for anything from a few days to a week, again depending on the weather. Then they would have to be collected on the wagon, with 'ladders' added at each end to take the load. Generally, two pitch up to a third who builds the load to twelve or fifteen feet high, standing in the centre of each layer and forking the sheaves around him so that they bind and the load does not topple when it is trundled back to the yard. A sure stacker like Old Sago would ride his own load, even at age seventy-five, safe in the knowledge that it would not topple. In the yard, you built your wheat stack or barley stack to await the arrival of the threshing gang. If you were a well-to-do farmer, you might have an elevator to take the sheaves up to the higher levels of the stack: if you were like us, you pitched them, not by brute force but by timing and motion so there was no waste of energy. Once you had done that, you trundled back to the field for the next load: and the next after that and you did that every day fine weather was sent, including Saturdays and Sundays, working late into the evening, till ten o'clock and dark if needs be. The harvest came first: all else came second.

The, once all was safely gathered in and the stacks had been sheeted down with tarpaulins (ours were bought up cheap after covering roofs of blitzed London houses), after two or three weeks, the threshing gang would arrive. We always threshed our stacks in the same week as Boundary threshed the wheat or barley from their two grain fields so that the threshing machine from Budwick, which toured all the farms in the area, had only to make the journey down Shoe Street once. Even when John Bolt had ruled Boundary like some baronial squire, he and Ben had had a reciprocal arrangement which always amazed me: Ben, it seemed, was the only one who ever got on with the cantankerous old bugger: he was the only one who ever called him 'John' and was accorded a 'Ben, mate' in return, in between puffs of cigarette smoke. At threshing time, Ben and I would go across to help the Boundary men and a couple of them, usually the foreman, Charlie Mangapp and the pleasant Ted Oldton, would come across to help us: it was the done thing. As the threshing machine governor refused to risk driving his steam tractor across to us and we had no electricity,

Charlie would bring Peter to help Molly with the horse-gear drive, the two of them working in tandem to rotate the conveyor belts which powered the thresher and the combined elevator for the loose straw stack. Some farmers winnowed as they threshed, pushing the grain through two winnowing blowers to get rid of the chaff and dust and small stones before it emerged into the sacks: a 'double blaster,' we called them. We were never happy till we had carted the last load of sacked grain across the causeway to the pick-up shed to be loaded with Boundary's on to the lorry and hence to the flour mills at Tidwoldton Basin, just where the Melchborough canal exits into the estuary through lock gates.

So you will understand some of the tasks which lay ahead for me and Old Sago, and, of course, my mother, and why I was so downcast when Charlie Mangapp knocked on our front door at six o'clock on the very Monday morning we were due to begin: he had bad news and had ridden over expressly to give it to us.

'Albert,' which was Old Sago's real name, 'won't be with you this morning,' he told my mother, who answered his knock. 'His son come round mine last night and said the old chap had a bad chest. Bronchial trouble, he says. He's under the doctor and they say he's going to be in bed for at least a fortnight, maybe longer. He don't know when he'll be able to make it across.'

Charlie must have read my mother's thoughts. 'I'm sorry, Clara. I realise this has come at a bad time for you,' he said, apologetically, 'but we can't spare anyone from Boundary this year to help you, not just at the moment, anyway. Our picking's still in full swing and we're down one since that hothead Billy Garner left. He ent been replaced and Dennis is too busy now organising and doing his uncle's old job, so he ent doing a lot alongside us n'more. So by rights, that makes us two down. We're so short, he even had that cousin o' his scrabbling up the plums off the orchard floor with the other women, though she ent much good at it from what I saw. Picked a whole box o' green'uns the other day. Factory work's more in her line, I should think. She ent much use in the country.'

I was standing behind my mother in the passageway while Charlie was telling us the bad news. 'Sorry, Joe,' he said. 'It puts everything on to your shoulders. You'll just have to do the best you can, boy. You can't do nothing else, can you?'

When Charlie had gone, I said, rather too boldly for my mother's liking: 'I'll just have to do it all by my bloody self, won't I?'

'Don't be so bloody daft,' she scoffed, whirling round. 'You can't do that work on your own. You'd kill yourself!' Nice of her to be so concerned, I thought.

FIFTY-NINE

THERE WAS an answer to our dilemma, of course: it was to ask Richard: after all, he had worked on the farm as a youth: and, no matter how long since he had sat astride a binder, piled sheaves into a stable, tented stook, or pitched them up on to a wagon or from it up on to a rising straw stack, he would at least know how to do those things. It was just that I fought shy of asking, out of deference to Ben, I suppose: I kept wondering what he would think: would he think I was taking sides against him because I know he would not have asked Richard? It was my mother who put me right on that one. 'Go and ask him, you bloody little fool,' she angrily declared. 'You need the help so ask him. He – ' Meaning Ben ' – don't need to know. Tell Richard we need his help more than a couple of silly women.'

So I did: what else could I do! That evening, after a frustrating day, after I had stabled and fed Molly, I went round to see Richard: the car was parked outside his cottage as usual: he had just returned from a long day trip when I knocked and was lolling in the armchair, drinking tea and listening to his music. He was pleased to see me and greeted me cheerily, but, when I put my problem to him, he was hesitant, reluctant almost, which disappointed me. Maybe it was the unexpectedness of the request: maybe he thought he had enough on his hands doing Hoary's odd jobs and chauffeuring the two women around. He took so long to answer that at first I thought he was going to refuse: finally, he gave a weary sigh, the sign of submission, I always thought. 'All right, I'll help you if you need it, if Hoary agrees. One thing, though, I don't want him, Ben, your step-father, to know. I don't want him to hear of it, ever. I'll do it for you and your mother, and Old Hoary, of course, but no one else. Do you understand?' I said I did understand, but really I did not: I just thought, 'Curious usage that, saying 'Ben, your step-father' rather than just 'my father.'

'It'll be like old times for you, won't it?' I suggested, rather too cheerily, as I went out: Richard just looked at me, stony-faced.

From Richard's, I went straight round to Hoary's to tell him about Old Sago: I found him in his front parlour sitting at his piano, lost in a world of his own as usual, and looking his normal sartorially elegant self in his gym shorts, odd carpet slippers, bare skinny arms and bare spindly legs, with just the holed tennis sweater over his bony, scar-gouged, frame. Straight to the point, I told him we needed Richard to help us gather in the harvest and that he was willing to do it and, if I did not get his help, 'there won't be a bloody harvest to gather in because I can't do it on my own.'

I could do certain things: I could work the reaper, or 'binder,' as we called it, but I would need others to help me with the other tasks which follow on from the cutting. For the uninitiated, I will explain: we had a Grantham-made Hornsby self-binding, open-back reaper, with revolving, paddle-style 'sails,' or 'rakes,' which forced the standing corn down on to a serrated cutting bar and then took the cut swathes along a canvas conveyor to the binding mechanism at the side: from there, the tied sheaves were ejected on to the ground so the field walker coming along behind could gather them up and stack them into stooks. The binder was a rickety, old affair, with an Eighteen-Ninety maker's date stamped on its frame, so it was over fifty years old when I used it that day.

I had helped Old Sago drag it out of the wagon shed the week before and, in the last few days he was with us before his illness, the old farmworker had done a good job of cleaning and greasing the cutting bar and repairing one of the sails as well as sewing a slit in the canvas conveyor and oiling the wheels and cogs and chains. Hoary had bought it third-hand somewhere about the year I was born, so Ben said: the best thing about it was, it was just about light enough for Molly to pull on her own without too much effort and, if oiled and greased in the morning, would run all day and evening without further attention.

'My mother can pick up the sheaves, but she and I can't do everything,' I told Hoary. 'We need help, especially with the loading and the stack-building. We need three, we need Richard.'

Hoary, of course did his usual moaning: he could not possibly spare Richard, he protested: he needed him for this and he needed him for that and a few other things he had not yet thought up. 'It is most inconvenient,' he said, 'most inconvenient. I have promised the ladies that Richard will always be available to take them on their painting trips till their own car is repaired and I cannot go back on my word.' It was as though the old fool thought I ought to be able to do all the work on my own: that is, go round with the binder cutting the five fields, then go round on foot picking up the sheaves in each and standing them in their stooks to dry. Then, perhaps, when I had stacked all the stooks in the final field, I could lead in Molly and the wagon, pitch up the sheaves, climb on to the wagon, spread them, jump down, move the wagon along and repeat the whole process up and down the field fifty or sixty times till the wagon was top-loaded twelve to fifteen feet high, just about enough for Molly to pull with me pushing. After that, all I had to do was trundle the lot to the yard and build the stack, or stacks. Repeat daily till all five fields were harvested! I did not ask him, but I am certain, too, after the harvesting, he would have expected me to lift the two fields of potatoes on my own as well, plough all the fields which needed ploughing after that, then harrow them, lime them, drill them and roll them. And in the second week…!

'I'll leave the bloody lot in the fields to rot unless I get the help I need, you daft old bugger!' I told him, the anger and sheer frustration of trying to convince the man of the obvious the cause of my rudeness.

'You have your mother to help you. Cannot the two of you do it between yourselves?' Hoary demanded, petulantly. 'Your mother ought to be able to do that kind of work, she is a countrywoman.'

'We'll need a bit more help than she can give,' I stormed back. 'You can't bloody expect a woman of her age to pitch up sheaves all day long on her own, build stacks and be the only one from Norsea helping me when the threshing time comes. It's a man's job at the best of times.'

Suffice it to say, I eventually managed to persuade the old fool to see my point of view: that the farm, and most particularly the harvest, must come first. There was, however, one snag: while Richard was helping us, who was going to drive the women about? Hoary, for once used his brains, and said they could hire Sligger Offin's taxi if necessary: as it turned out, Laura Wilchard and Pocklington did not seem at all bothered at losing Richard's services: well, Pocklington did not! They had a few days of 'work,' as they called it, that they could do in the 'studio' cottage, so they said. So be it: what Laura Wilchard said, I do not know.

When I told my mother during a suppertime conversation how Hoary had finally acquiesced with his usual grumpy grace, she bridled at my defence of her capabilities. 'I'm not that old that I can't pitch up sheaves,' she snorted, 'and I'm not afraid of hard work. I was helping with the harvest the first five summers I was on Norsea. The three of us –' Meaning Ben, her and Old Sago ' – did it between us when you were still in your pram. So don't you go thinking I'm not capable.'

Fortunately, the weather was with us from the very start: in fact, it was to prove the best harvesting weather for decades, a blessed relief: there had been no rain for almost five weeks and it was a gloriously bright, sunlit day, the tenth in succession, as I led Molly towing our binder into the field just after nine, with my mother following with her shopping bag of sandwiches and drink. Richard was waiting with a small parcel of his own sandwiches and drink, which he left with ours in the shade under the hedgerow: it would save having to walk back to the farm or to his cottage at lunchtime and wasting time.

As I took my place on the binder and set Molly in motion that first time, I felt a great sense of exhilaration: like at last this was a useful purpose in life: I still made a hash of it, though. It may have been the presence of my mother and her overly critical gaze, or it may have been Richard's presence, but I steered a decidedly wavy line for the first fifty yards: after that I was able to keep Molly reasonably straight and soon clouds of fine dust were wafting about as the old binder clacked round and round the field, each time cutting a five-to-six-foot swathe through our ripened grain. As I came round a second time, Richard gave me a nod and a grin, as if to inform me that I was doing it all right, though I am not so sure my mother was over happy: if Richard had not been there, I sensed she would have found fault with something.

Richard, I was pleased to see, pitched in from the start and seemed quite cheery as he worked with my mother, gathering up the sheaves and building the stooks: it is not a strenuous job, but you do get scratched about the arms and face, often the air is dust-laden and you do a lot of walking over uneven ground under a burning sun, so it is not exactly a picnic: but Richard seemed happy enough. Indeed, I think he was actually enjoying himself, for he seemed quite chatty and he and my mother talked all the time they were working. They waited till I had been round the field twice before they began and when I came round a third time, a neat row of spaced-out stooks lined the outside of the field: Norsea's harvesting was well and truly under way.

Looking at Richard as he worked, you would not have known he had been away from a farm for nineteen years: he was eager and quick, his stooks were tidy and none fell down that I saw, unlike mine sometimes did, so he obviously had not forgotten the technique from all those years ago. With his sleeves rolled up, a cap on to protect his head and a cigarette in his mouth, he looked very much the average farm worker. In a way, you sensed that he was glad to be out working in the sunshine, hot as it was, glad to be doing the work, perhaps remembering images from his own boyhood when he had worked alongside Ben and Old Sago doing much the same task: it must have brought back memories to him: happy ones, I hoped.

It was well into the afternoon as the clock ticked round to three-thirty and we stopped for a quarter-hour's teabreak that I first noticed Richard start to flag: once, when I had come round the field on an umpteenth circuit, I found him squatting on his haunches, cap in his hand, mopping his face and breathing hard: he was clutching at his chest and seemed to be short of breath. Later, when we took our short afternoon break, it was a good three or four minutes after my mother and I had resumed work before Richard climbed to his feet. I just assumed it was because of the heat which had been building all day so that by three o'clock, the hottest part of the afternoon, the sun really was scorching down. The fact that our summer heat was far less than the extreme temperatures of the Philippines, where he had spent the war years, never occurred to me: eighty-five degrees was scorching hot to me. In fact, it had become so hot that by then I had discarded my shirt and vest and was sitting on the seat of the clacking machine stripped to the waist in the hope of obtaining that golden brown tan which all village boys coveted then: all I ever managed, though, was a tan as red as the skin of a North American Indian, raw and painful, which blistered and peeled within days.

We worked on into the evening after another break for tea and sandwiches at five: it was during this period that Richard had to stop several times as if sucking in breath: my mother, who had gone off to feed the pig and the chickens, noticed it as she came back into the field and found Richard crouched by one of the stooks, holding his ribs. She said nothing to him, of course, pretending she had not seen him, for he stood up as soon as he saw her: but when we finished for the day at nine o'clock and she and I led Molly towards the farmhouse and a hoped for bowl of soup and bread (no cooked meal because it was 'too late to peel potatoes'), she caught my eye and bluntly asked: 'Is he all right, do you think?'

Since I did not want to lose Richard on some whim of my mother on his very first day, I had to make light of it: 'Oh yes, he's just not used to it, that's all. He'll be all right after a couple of days.' As if to confirm this, when Richard saw us turning to observe him, thinking we were actually bidding him a final 'Good evening,' albeit from fifty yards away, he smiled and gave us a brief wave of the hand and continued on his way: but there was a definite heaviness to his step as he walked off.

I was thankful just to see him come into the field the next morning, though, after another long session in the gruelling heat of the sun, I never saw a man sink so wearily into the shadow of the hedgerow to take his rest and eat his sandwiches as he did at half-twelve. When my mother and I rose again at one, Richard was still lolling under the hedge: really, I think we should have told him to stay there and take the full hour's rest, as if to say to him, 'It's all right, you are not used to what we are doing.' But he got up as soon as he saw us looking and the concern my mother expressed was again waved away: we finished at ten that night and he left us with the same heavy, wearied tread as before.

However, he was back on the third day, smiling his morning greeting and eager to get on: as if, keen to show us he was fit and capable, he even made a half-hearted attempt to chase after a rabbit, which broke cover from the shrinking oblong of standing corn and dashed for the safety of the hedgerow. Normally such diversions as rabbit-chasing were joined in by all: the previous year, helping the Boundary men with their grain harvest, I had joined Billy, Dennis Bolt, Tully Jude and Ted Oldton all chasing a single rabbit, the whole gang of us 'whooping and hollering' after the petrified animal and trying to strike it with our sticks in the hope of breaking its back. None of us did, though: it dodged us all: a pity as stewed rabbit was a meal that cost you nothing. This time I could only watch from my seat on the binder: Richard's attempt faltered after thirty or so yards, by which time the rabbit had already disappeared into the hedgerow, and he was bent over again, gasping for breath just like before. My concern was purely selfish: if we lost Richard because he could not do the work and he went back to chauffeuring, there would be just my mother and me to do all the work: and I did not relish working alone with her for the next three weeks.

SIXTY

FORTUNATELY, our worries about Richard returning to chauffeuring evaporated after a visit to the mainland by Hoary and no doubt an exchange of money between him and Sligger Offin: for the funny-looking foreign car came chugging along the track on the fourth morning just as we were starting on the second field. It was blowing blue-grey smoke everywhere, but at least it was going and it solved the problem of who was going to take the women on their painting trips. Sligger said he had managed to fix it with parts he had eventually obtained after 'great effort': no doubt he repaired it with parts found at the back of his garage and charged Hoary treble for 'new parts and labour'!

Pocklington, now able to discard her stick and with her injured leg much better, declared herself fit to drive her own car and the two women set off for the mainland that very day by themselves. Hoary went across to see Dennis and he had Bob Bird remove and replace the boards each time they went through, which he continued to do every morning as soon as he arrived for work (so long as the tide was not up or due up, of course) and repeated each evening, as and when necessary. Hoary paid for the service, though: Bob charged him five shillings a week: handy money then.

Then, on the fifth day, Old Sago turned up out of the blue: we had been told he would be in bed for at least two weeks, so it was a great relief to see him wheeling his bicycle through the gate just after eight o'clock on the Friday morning, with three shopping bags hanging from his handlebars containing all the food and things he would need to stay on Norsea for the next couple of weeks. In view of his age and the nature of his illness, I have to admit I had been sceptical whether we would see him again inside a month, if ever again: but there he was, leaning wearily against the machine and wheezing almost as much as Richard had done.

'I'm sorry Joe, boy, I'm sorry, Clara,' he said in between pauses for breath. 'This damned chest of mine let me down again. I wouldn't hev picked this time to fall ill for all the tea in China – not during harvesting – that I wouldn't. I'll put in extra to make up for the time I've missed. I've brought some things to keep me going and I can sleep in one of the other cottages till we're done.'

He finished his statement with a deep, retching cough: I suppose I should have sent the old fool home there and then, but there was such a pathetic look on his face, apologetic and pleading at one and the same time, that you would have thought he was begging forgiveness for having committed a cardinal sin by taking to his bed with inflamed lungs and narrowed bronchial tubes and goodness knows what else! And besides, to my way of thinking, two half-cripples, Sago and Richard, made a whole and that was better than nothing: if they wanted to work, let them: we needed them both and who was I to stop them?

Old Sago was as good as his word as far as putting in extra time was concerned: he set himself up in the empty cottage Jan had vacated and worked like a coolie for the rest of the time we were cutting: he was up ahead of me each morning to feed and water Molly and had the binder greased and ready each day and Molly harnessed into the shafts before I even got to the field. The only change to the field routine was that Old Sago went up on the binder seat, where he could cough and spit with impunity, and I joined Richard stooking the sheaves over the next four or five days as we went into the barley: at least with Old Sago on the binder, the cutting was straighter. His arrival at least released my mother for half the day to go off and do the other tasks about the house and the farm which she had complained she had been forced to neglect.

When we began loading and stacking the dried sheaves in the third week, for some reason, Old Sago did not want to be on top of the wagon as he normally was: he said he was having bouts of giddiness and asked me if I would take his place. Normally, I would have been on the ground, pitching up and leading Molly: being trusted with the stacking of the load, layering and binding the sheaves as Ben had taught me, was an honour and I jumped at the chance. When you stacked on top of the load, you did it with a sense of pride: you also did it with a great deal of care as the last thing you wanted was for the whole lot to topple sideways on the journey back to the farmyard and bring the curses of those who had just helped you to load it down on your head: not to mention the fact that a fall of twenty feet or more from a tipping load can be extremely painful, dangerous even: I did not want a broken arm or a broken leg, or a broken neck for that matter!

I also built the stacks in the yard for the first time ever, another great honour, I felt, though at the end of each day Old Sago helped me ensure they were properly sheeted for the night.

The three weeks I worked with Richard, and the fortnight with Sago, were, I think, the best of my life: the work wearied us, the sun blistered us, the dust choked us, the sharp cut ends of the corn and the barley scratched us, particularly me as I often worked stripped to the waist. We worked long hours parched and hungry: we worked Saturdays, we worked Sundays: we ate our lunches of sandwiches and warm tea which my mother brought to the field either sitting under a hedgerow away from the swirling dust devils that danced across the emptying fields or at other times sprawled on the freshly cut stubble in the shade of the wagon to avoid the fierce heat of the sun. Often we were still working long after the sun had sunk like a large red Jupiter into the haze of dust curtaining the lower sky to the west: sometimes we worked on even as the harvest moon, huge and swollen, climbed from the east above the tops of the trees like a red Mars.

In those three weeks, the world passed us by: all the time we worked, India had become independent and divided in a welter of blood and flame: the Russians were laying down mile after hundred mile of barbed-wire frontier to divide East from West: London was preparing for the Royal wedding: there was fighting in Indonesia, China, Indo-China, Burma and Palestine. Yet for me, it was the satisfaction of looking back at an empty field, cleared of all its stooks, as I left it and moved on to the next that I remember most: they were the best weeks of my life.

Then Old Sago's death blighted it all.

SIXTY-ONE

OLD SAGO died on the very last day of harvesting during a shimmering heat-hazed lunchtime, leaning back against a pile of sheaves in the middle of a field, resting after a long morning's work in the sun. He settled back, closed his eyes and appeared to be trying to doze: his feet were spread out into the stubble, his head was tilted back and his cap was pulled down to shade his eyes against the glare. After a few moments, his mouth fell open with a sigh like he was going to snore, except no sound came: he just slipped away in the bright sunshine.

For me, that awful day was the day the summer idyll ended: after three wearying weeks of pitchforking sheaves in the blistering heat of August, of arms scratched and raw from stacking them, of dry-mouthed thirsts, tiredness, aching limbs and a back burnt and peeling from too much exposure to the sun, after three weeks of choking dust that seemed to hang everywhere and to cover everything, and the all-too-slow passing of time, this was to be the end to it all for another year. Our five fields of wheat and barley were bare expanses of sun-bleached stubble, the stacks were already in place alongside the barn, the two wheat ones completed, thatched and covered by a tarpaulin, the barley one awaiting the final load.

Everywhere about us there were the unmistakable signs of summer fading into autumn: it was the first day of September and the early morning air had taken on a sharper chill: dew-pearled cobwebs were already beginning to appear on the hedgerows and when I led Molly along the headland to begin the day, a faint mist was still hanging over the fields. Overhead, the birds were already gathering, preparing to fly south, hundreds upon hundreds of them, great swooping and swishing clusters, filling the early evening sky as they darted left and right and round and back in long trailing arrows. Once they had gone, September would slip into October: the ploughing would begin: on some farms the new tractors would bump and bounce ahead of their multiple-bladed ploughs, on others stooped, leaning figures would still stumble and struggle with the old ploughs behind plodding horses. Soon the days of unending rain would come: the icy mists of November would return to blanket the fields and the cold blows of December would sweep up the estuary, to be cursed as only those who work out in them can curse them, but all to be borne with a reluctant fortitude: for, as I and the others knew, in that region Januaries and Februaries could, and most probably would, be ten times worse.

Old Sago would miss all that: he had gathered in his last harvest: in that last week he had worked from eight in the morning till nine and ten at night without the slightest complaint: just an old countryman doing his job because it needed to be done and making no fuss about it: happy to do it, pleased to be needed: that is not sentimental twaddle, just plain fact.

Just before Old Sago lay back and died, I saw him prop the half-drunk bottle of tea against his hip and snap shut the biscuit tin in which he kept his sandwiches: the last words I heard him speak were to Richard, a prophetic: 'Dick, boy, I shall be glad when we're done and I can have a good long rest.' A minute or so later his heart gave out: he had got his long rest.

At the time, I was perched high on the ladder at the front of the wagon, smoking a rolled cigarette and idly watching Molly flick her tail at the flies settling on her hindquarters: Richard was lolling in the shade of the cart, with his back against one of the wheels, not talking, just smoking and staring out at the lines of stubble stretching away before him, lost in private thoughts, it seemed. Around us, the midday heat bounced off the parched earth: small dust devils sprang up, whirled for a few seconds across the emptiness of the field and then vanished: fork-tailed swallows weaved and skimmed low as they hunted flies on the wing and buff-brown corncrakes fluttered up from the headland grasses. On such days men are glad to be alive: but on such days, too, men die.

Did I have a premonition? I do not know: but I do remember looking across at Old Sago as he lay sprawled on the stubble, berry brown, grizzled, white-haired and toothless, and thinking he was sleeping the sleep of a tired old man. Even as I looked, I felt a sadness within me: this surely would be his last harvest, I thought: he would be seventy-six later that year and could not really carry on for much longer: his working life had to end sometime and the Fates had been kind enough to give him such a long, hot, dry summer. He had spent his lifetime on the land, more than sixty years in all, working in the fields around

Gledlang: five seconds after that thought, his life ended in one of them.

Richard was the first to notice: he had seen men die: he knew the signs: the smell, the lolling head, the change in pallor: suddenly he was jumping to his feet and bending over Sago's prone form, shaking him by the shoulder and calling his name: 'Sago! Sago! Wake up, old fellah! Wake up!'

My mother, who had been helping us that morning, came up just as Old Sago died: she had gone off to the farmhouse during our break and was just returning. She was still twenty yards from us when his body slipped sideways: his cap fell off and his face banged into the dirt, still with the mouth open, spittle drooling from the lips: the eyes, however, remained shut. I just happened to be looking at her and I saw the instant sadness pass across her face.

'Oh God, he ain't died, has he?' I heard her ask in quiet, sympathetic disbelief.

Just to hear those dreadful words and see Richard bending over his prone, lifeless form was too much for me: I had never seen a dead body before, let alone witnessed the actual moment of death: I had never seen how lifeless, how empty is the shell left behind when the spirit departs from it: and how silent and final it all is. True, I had seen dead chickens, I had seen dead rabbits which I had helped to snare and dead birds I had killed with a catapult: but never a man, never a man with whom I had talked and laughed that morning when life still existed within him: indeed had heard the last words he had spoken before the breath of life left him like a fleeing whisper. I could not help myself: the shock of it overwhelmed me and, to my great embarrassment, tears welled up from somewhere deep inside: childish tears, mortifying and unexpected.

For fully two minutes I cried silently and unnoticed, slumped on the floor of the cart so as to be out of their view, my head hung in sorrow. By the time I had recovered my composure, Richard and my mother had stretched Sago out on the stubble and were stooping to lift his lifeless form up on to the cart upon which I was sprawled. 'He was asleep, Joe,' Richard said quietly, when at last I clambered to my feet to help them, vigorously rubbing at my eyes and highly embarrassed by my show of unmanliness. 'He didn't know anything about it. He went in his sleep. It was his time. You can't do anything about that.' There was a grim set to his mouth as he said it.

My mother just looked sad and wearied: there was no harshness in her manner now: the only words she spoke were a soft and sympathetic plea, 'Be careful with him,' directed at me, as we laid him carefully on the straw-strewn floor and covered him with a jacket: then we trundled him to the house.

There, Richard asked me to ride across to Sago's son, Jack Coxwaite, Nick's father, to tell him the sad news, while he and my mother followed with the wagon. This I did, but neither Nick nor his father were there, of course: they were at work: Nick's mother was there, however.

It is strange how some people accept death: when Nick's mother opened the back door of the council house to my knocking and I gave her the news and told her Richard and my mother were bringing him home on the wagon, not so much as a single tear moistened her eye. 'Oh Gawd! The silly bugger!' she exclaimed. 'He would go. We didn't want him to go with his chest the way it was, but he seemed to think you were counting on him. Now look where it's got him! Bloody dead!' She heaved a great sigh of exasperation, before adding: 'Give me a knock when he gets here.' Then she retreated inside and closed the door.

When my mother and Richard arrived with Old Sago's body on the wagon, Nick's mother came out again: she gave his corpse no more than a cursory glance, like she did not want to see it, and with a gesture of the hand towards the house directed us to carry the poor man inside. We laid him out in the back bedroom, Nick's bedroom: at least, I thought, he will be in company of a kind that night, not lying alone in a dark cottage, even if Nick did sleep downstairs. Then Nick's mother ushered us out. 'I suppose I'll have to wash him myself?' she grumbled, half to herself as we went down the path, refusing even my mother's offer of help with the same ill-graced 'No, I can manage, Clara, I can manage.' To my way of thinking, there was not a flicker of sorrow from her anywhere: at the back of my mind, for some reason, was the nagging thought that she might be thinking that, by employing him so soon after his illness, we had killed him! That we had worked the old man to his death! Was that what we had done? Worked the old man to his death? Oh, no. That would have been too much.

What I had not known when he came wheeling his bicycle into the yard was that the stupid old bugger had got out of his sickbed to join us! Country pride, you see, country pride: he had to be there at the harvesting, he had to be there: he had not missed a harvest in over sixty years and he was not going to miss one now: and it killed him.

SIXTY-TWO

OLD SAGO'S funeral was held three days later and most of the village turned out: I went with Richard and my mother, though even in her formidable presence I felt that I was taking a risk. Did I imagine it or were there a few hostile looks directed our way as the three of us pushed into the church just as the service began? True, no one actually accused me or spat at me or shook their fist in my face, but, I sensed one or two would have liked to have done: though perhaps I was just imagining things. Fortunately, the church was so crowded we found ourselves right at the back, almost forced through the door into the bell chamber so that parts of the service were drowned out by the single bell which was tolled mournfully throughout: and Reverend Ffawcon was not the loudest of speakers.

A good two-hundred or more were there, the old man was that popular: I was pleased to see that: and they all sang properly, too: no faltering, embarrassed, lowered-head croaking and feigned hoarseness. The more tuneful women sent their voices soaring up among the beams and carved faces in the vaulted roof, way above the groan of the organ, and all done with a passion that suggested they really did want their words heard in Heaven: Old Sago's family must have been grateful to them. Nick was at the front, with Billy and Lennie Ring: when the congregation knelt to pray, I could see the backs of their heads over all the other heads in between: mostly they kept their backs to me, though midway through the service Nick did give a quick glance over his shoulder: he saw me and we looked at each other for a few seconds, but his expression did not change, though even from the back of the church I could see there was moisture glistening on his cheeks.

After they carried the coffin out and everyone filed after it, Richard and I remained in the porch for a smoke: my mother, defiant as ever, went down to the graveside to stand with the other women: she knew that no one would get sniffy with her because of me and anyone who tried, they knew, would have got short thrift from Clara Coe-

Wigboe, funeral or no funeral. I think both Richard and I felt we had already said our goodbyes mentally to Sago when we had trundled him lifeless out of the field and back to the village on the wagon. I, for one, did not want to watch him being put into a hole in the ground: I liked to think that, since he had died on Norsea, his spirit, if there is one in the human body, remained there and it was just his empty shell which we had been taken back to the mainland and which they were burying.

As the graveside ceremony neared its end and the Reverend Ffawcon began intoning the committal prayer, Richard and I finished our cigarettes and were about to depart ahead of the crowd when Violet Reddy came hurrying up the path from the graveside, wheeling little Thomas in his pram. 'Joe, wait. I'm glad you're here, I need to ask you something,' she said, joining us in the porch: then with that pleading voice women adopt to cajole men, she asked: 'Have you heard anything from Jan, a letter or something, anything? I haven't heard a thing from him since he left and I am beginning to get worried. I was expecting to get something before now via you, Joe. He said in the letter he wrote when he went he'd write to you, because he can't write straight to me, can he? He said he'd let you know when he was coming back. I need to know, Joe, I need to know when he is coming back. I don't know how much longer I can go on like I am, not knowing, living with him – ' Meaning Walter ' – I'm living on my nerves as it is. I wish now I had gone with him. It would all have been over by now. I wouldn't have all this worry.' The tears started at this point, rolling down her cheeks and hanging like small glistening beads on her chin while she searched for a handkerchief with which to wipe them away and dab at her eyes.

I shook my head. 'Sorry, Violet. I haven't heard anything from him –' I had never expected I would, to be honest: but I had to give her hope. ' – If he does write, I'll certainly pass anything on to you, on the sly, of course, so Walter won't know, but so far we haven't heard anything. Sorry.' Then, when her tears started again, a more reassuring, 'There's still plenty of time, though, Violet, isn't there?'

Violet seemed to be reassured, for she sniffed back the tears and reached into her coat pocket. 'I've written a short letter back, just in case,' she declared, holding out a single sheet of blue letter paper. 'I did it while we were in church to save time, in case you can't get Jan's letter to me for some reason. If he does write, you can just send this back to him at the address he gives without waiting for me. It's just a note from me telling him how much I miss him, but it contains some information which I won't be able to keep secret for much longer and which he needs to know about.' The weeping and handkerchief dabbing started again here. 'I honestly don't know how much longer I can go on living with Walter. I want my Jan to come back and soon. I need him.' It was all very embarrassing for us, listening to a married woman declaring herself in that way, her eyes brimming with tears as she said it.

Just as she thrust the note towards me, one of the village women appeared out of the darkness of the church interior: she was one of the church cleaners and she, like us, had not joined the graveside throng, but had remained behind to gather up the hymn books and take down the hymn numbers and do whatever else there was to be done. Now, as the graveside service was ending, she was hurrying to the parish hall where she had been delegated to switch on the urn to make the tea for the big after-funeral gathering. She could hardly miss seeing the letter in Violet's hand, suspended halfway between her and me, even though Richard, with more presence of mind than myself, quickly reached out and snatched it from her and slipped it inside the small pocket of his dark overcoat. Had she seen or heard anything? We did not know: though, as she pushed between us, she lowered her head and averted her gaze as if pretending she had not, but could not prevent herself from casting a quick sideways glance at Violet, one that spoke of disdain.

I was never to read the letter: the only words on it that I had seen, as Violet was passing it over, were 'Dearest Love...' The reason, quite simply, was that when we returned to Norsea and parted, Richard still had the letter in the inside pocket of his overcoat and I forgot to ask him for it so I could pass it on to Jan when he returned: it was still in his overcoat pocket when he walked off.

SIXTY-THREE

LAURA WILCHARD and Pocklington were still lucky with the weather: the perfect summer was just shimmering on into a full and glorious autumn.

One thing I did observe was that, in the evenings, Laura Wilchard still seemed to be forever going to or coming from Richard's cottage even though he was no longer driving them about: whether Pocklington approved, I did not know: though I suspected she did not and that she was always on the watch.

On at least three occasions, on my way to spend the later hours with Richard, I was forced to turn back because Laura Wilchard was standing outside his doorway and the two of them were talking and laughing together: and there was no way I was going to join them, not in my work clothes, not with my face and hands unwashed from the day's work: I had my pride.

Such a thing was, I suppose, to be expected of people living as neighbours in an out-of-the-way place like Norsea and not much to do in the evening except to talk or to listen to the wireless, if you had one, which Pocklington and Laura Wilchard did: I had put one of Hoary's old battery sets in their cottage specifically at their request right at the start.

My trouble was that I was jealous and I knew it: jealous that Richard had female friendship in the desirable shape of Laura Wilchard, even if it were just platonic, and I had none: and as I no longer went to Maydun, I had no prospects of finding any either (not that I ever had when I went there!), but that was what I wished for most. Perhaps I was just too young: or perhaps girls did not want to get involved with a boy who would soon – well, in a year, anyhow – be going off to the army: a boy in the army was no good to a girl dreaming of wedding dresses and bridesmaids and bridal bouquets, as they all seemed to do. I had heard of boys who had courted girls for less than a year and had suddenly found themselves talked into 'getting engaged' and buying a ring they could ill afford: usually they were nagged into it, poor blighters, or gave into her tearful cajolings, like 'You've had your fun, now you can ...' A month or two later and they were coming out of the church porch, with some grasping female clinging to their arm like grim death, being showered with rice, a bemused look on their faces and all wondering how they had let it happen: married, independence gone and only the shackling ball and chain of wife, children, weekly rent and neverending debt to which to look forward.

    I did not want that to happen to me: I wanted a girlfriend then just to have someone whom I could kiss and feel and have them put their hand down my trousers and do what Billy said they had done to him. I wanted nothing serious, nothing long: when I went into the army, I did not want to be tied down by some sour-faced English country girl, especially if I got a posting to BOAR in Germany or Austria, say, where, I had heard you only had to give a girl a bar of chocolate and she would let you do it: according to the talk on the ciderstone, anyway. If I were really lucky, my thinking went then, I might even end up in Hong Kong with one of those Chinese 'taxi' dancers, who, it was said, were not averse to taking you upstairs from the dance hall to earn a bit of extra money on the side: and then down in the harbour, so a couple of younger men who had been out East with the navy described, there were thirteen-year-old and fourteen-year-old girls who plied their trade from the family sampan with little red lights on them and you could pay them a couple of shillings for it while their family sat the other side of a curtain eating their rice and sour pork. I did not want to miss out on any of that just because some simpering English girl back home had nagged me into putting a ring on her finger. When I came across some fraulein in Hamburg or Vienna or some Hong Kong dance hall girl with a red silk skirt split up to the thigh, the last thing I wanted to be was inhibited by guilt about some girl back home, did I?

    Then, one evening during the second week, going past Richard's cottage on my way back from rehanging a gate at the far end of the island, I heard a strange sound coming from inside: it was the kind of whimpering noise a woman might make if, say, she were being ill treated, like if someone were cruelly twisting her arm or she was being violently shaken: a cry which was part pain, part anguish and part pleading. The only thing I could think was that it was the women's battery radio which Richard had borrowed while they were out: for a quarter-hour earlier I had seen Pocklington's funny foreign car go bouncing along the track, heading for the mainland and the Chessman snug, I assumed.

Normally, I would have lifted the latch, pushed open Richard's front door and strode right in: but such was the peculiarity of the noise, one that I had not heard before, anyway, that it sent me creeping round to the back window to peer in: I was thankful that I did. Oh, what a sight I saw! What an unexpected sight! There in the lamplight, lying on Richard's bed, with her skirt up round her waist, knickerless, her naked buttocks resting on a pillow and her legs splayed to the ceiling, was Laura Wilchard! And pumping vigorously at her, trouserless and shirtless, one hand squeezing hard at a bared breast, was Richard, scar-faced, half-face Richard! All the while she was uttering the cries which I had heard outside, cries of what I supposed were her ecstasy and driving back up at Richard as though she wanted more than he could give her. I was so flabbergasted that I forgot to duck, remaining transfixed at the window, silhouetted against the twilight, just staring in and feasting my eyes on the glorious eroticism of the scene. Had either of them glanced sideways on noticing a change in the light caused by my silhouette filling the window, then I should have been discovered. Suddenly Richard seemed to have finished his exertions, for he collapsed upon her, the agony of his effort showing upon his face as he lay there: she, meanwhile, had folded her legs around him, reluctant to let him withdraw, and was quietly kissing his scars and smiling in contentment.

Evenings on Norsea can be so still sometimes that sounds carry for hundreds of yards: so quiet can it be that, when you hold your breath, you can hear a single goose hiss at the other end of the island or catch the piping of a curlew out on a headland. It was another noise which at that moment brought me to my senses and sent me stepping back into the deeper shadows: the sound of car tyres rolling slowly over dirt before coming to a stop: the next thing I heard were running footsteps on Richard's path, coming towards his front door.

The voyeur in me was determined not to miss what was about to happen and I stepped forward to the window again just as Pocklington appeared in the doorway to the bedroom, a furious anger ablaze in her eyes. A half-sobbing, half-terrified howl of anguish came from Laura Wilchard as she slipped off the bed clutching at her unbuttoned skirt, desperately trying to pull it across in front of her and fasten it, as if by so doing she could deny what had just occurred.

Pocklington knew exactly what she had been doing. 'You effing cow! You effing deceitful cow!' she screamed as she rushed into the room, seized the half-naked Laura by the arm and began dragging her out through the door with such violence that the poor woman cannoned into the frame: not that that made any difference to the raging Pocklington: poor Laura Wilchard was simply wrenched through the second doorway and sent sprawling on to the grass outside.

Behind them, Richard rolled off the bed and sat upon it for a few seconds as if he were thinking what to do next, if anything: then, taking up his trousers, he pulled them on, tucked in his shirt and almost wearily followed the two women out of the door.

I, meanwhile, not wishing to be thought of as a Peeping Tom, even if I had been one, darted round by way of the hedge and came out farther along the row to ensure I could see what was going on at the front of the cottage. A distraught Laura Wilchard was lying on the ground, still half dressed, with Pocklington standing over her, ranting and raving away like a madwoman: Laura Wilchard, for her part, was in tears, pleading with her friend.

The more Laura Wilchard pleaded, the nastier friend Greta got. 'You cow! You effing bitch!' she shouted. 'You (something), you (something else). I told you what would happen if you ever did anything like that again! I warned you the last time, I bloody warned you! I told you, you bitch, you effing bitch! I told you! You're like a bitch on heat when you see a man. Anything in trousers for you, anything in trousers. Well, I'm finished with you. You can go to hell for all I care! I've had enough of you and your silly ways. I've put up with them long enough. You've been at it from the first day we came. I'm sick of it. I'm sick of him smarming around you and you smarming around him. Don't think I haven't noticed, I have. I bloody well have, since the first day we came. You're a rotten bloody bitch, Laura Wilchard, a rotten bloody bitch! If that's the way you want it, you can have it! I'm off back to London. I've had enough of this bloody place and you! I've spent three months in this godforsaken hole and I don't intend to spend another bloody day on this bloody island. Stay if you want to, I'm leaving.' Except she did not so much as say these things as scream them down at the prostrated Laura: then, for good measure, she gave her three hard slaps across the top of her head, like a mother cuffing a wailing child to stop it from wailing.

'No, no, Greta, please, no,' pleaded Laura Wilchard. 'Please don't go, Greta. I'm sorry, truly sorry. It was nothing. It won't happen again. I promise, I promise. Please, Greta, please. Believe me. Please, Greta!' She had hold of Greta's leg as if trying to pull her back: but the sour-faced one was having none of it and was trying to get away

All the while, Richard was just standing in his doorway, watching: what surprised me was that he made no attempt to save poor Laura from the slaps or to mediate between the two, if only to calm Pocklington down. The expression on his face was just a blank: well, I could not read it, anyway: it was almost as if he had decided that an argument between the two of them was none of his business, even if Pockington's screeching fury was so loud that my mother heard it several hundred yards away and came out into our yard, straining her ears to hear more. Astonishingly, Richard suddenly closed his door: this seemed to infuriate Pocklington even more, as if she were angered now at being denied an audience: for she raised her arm again and cuffed Laura Wilchard several more times, harder, more vicious blows than before, which sent her friend sprawling full length on to the track: then she wrenched herself free of the clutching hand and stormed back inside their cottage, banging the door shut. The sound of the slamming door must have had some sort of a finality about it as far as the distraught Laura Wilchard was concerned: her whole body sagged visibly and her whole frame shook with sobbing. Like one resigned to her fate, she remained down upon the track for several minutes, weeping uncontrollably, brushing at her tears with dirt-soiled fingers.

With Pocklington gone, I thought that Richard might come out again to talk to Laura, perhaps even to lift her up: but he did not. Eventually, after a few minutes, her sobbing subsided to lip-biting and snivelling: she climbed slowly to her feet, brushed the dirt from her clothes and her limbs, then, disconsolately, walked slowly towards her own cottage door, lifted the latch and went inside. That was when the shouting and the wailing started up again: there was a lot of anger being thrown about inside, judging by the bangs and crashes and shouts and cries coming from within.

It was no surprise when Pocklington came round a half-hour later in her car to demand, rather than to ask politely, that I remove the boards at the Boundary end of the causeway so she could leave and miss the late night tide: for once, I was happy to do so. When I wheeled my bicycle past her car, it was loaded with her equipment and was noticeably lacking in Laura Wilchard's things.

Grumpy Greta had at least learned her lesson, for she crawled across the causeway at five miles an hour, whereas I was able to race across on my bicycle: I had the boards removed before she even drove up on to the hard. It was too much to expect her to acknowledge it with a 'Thank you,' even one mouthed silently through the glass of the windscreen, or even a gesture of the hand: instead, sulky faced, she revved the engine and charged through the gap. The last I saw of her was the car disappearing down the track into the darkness between Boundary's orchards at a speed fast enough to break the springs and leaving a trail of blue-grey exhaust spiralling in its wake. Behind on Norsea, I assumed, Laura Wilchard was sitting alone in her cottage.

SIXTY-FOUR

THE THRESHING gang was due the next morning to thresh our three stacks in the yard: after breakfast, I harnessed Molly and took her to the start of the causeway, ready to go across to meet them when they appeared at Boundary's boards. While I was there, Richard came up: I could not reveal that I had been there the previous evening or what I had seen: I could not even mention Pocklington's sudden departure since, apart from removing and replacing the boards, I was not supposed to know that she had gone for good: and certainly I could not discuss why.

No such inhibitions from my mother when she joined us, ostensibly to see if there was 'any sign of the threshers' on the far side: it was, of course, a perfect opportunity for her to ask about Pocklington. The question was put as soon as she came up: why had 'the miserable one, the one who dresses like a man,' had to go so suddenly that she needed to come knocking at the farmhouse door so late at night to say she was leaving and demanding that 'Joey here' remove the boards?

'No please or thank you either,' snorted my mother in disgust. 'Just "I'm leaving! I want the boards taken down!" Some people don't have the manners they were born with!'

If my mother expected a full and frank discussion on the subject, she was disappointed: all she got from Richard was a gruff: 'It's not surprising she's gone. She never liked living on Norsea in the first place.'

'You knew about it then?'

'Yes, I knew she was going,' noncommittally from Richard.

Not to be put off, my mother put the next question equally directly. 'What was all that commotion about we heard outside their cottage last night, the two of them shouting at each other like that? Did that have something to do with it? You were there, you must have heard it? You could hear them a mile off. What was that all about?'

I was watching Richard's face, but it revealed nothing. 'Something and nothing, I daresay,' he answered with his usual casualness. 'As far as I know, it was simply because one wanted to leave and the other didn't.'

'What's the other one going to do now then?' my mother demanded to know, eying him suspiciously: her instinct told her something different.

Another shrug from Richard, as if to say he was unsure and it did not matter to him anyway. 'She says she's going to stay. She says she has rented the cottage till the end of October and she's going to stay till then. She has that right.'

Oh, yes, and I wonder why, I thought.

'Funny goings on,' said my mother, shaking her head, 'funny goings on.'

After that, my time was taken up by the arrival of the threshing gang across the causeway: actually, they were the three Brown brothers, Artie, Hubert and John, from Budwick, a small village halfway to Wivencaster, who after harvest went round all the farms in turn with their threshing machinery, thus saving each farmer having to pay out several hundred pounds for a thresher and an elevator of his own which he used only for a few days each twelve-month, not to mention the maintenance of them over the year. For obvious reasons, they combined their visit to us with the threshing on Boundary, who only ever had two or three fields of grain to harvest and at most two stacks to thresh because they were eighty-per-cent fruit-growing. The contractor always started with us to get us out of the way because we were the farthest distance from Budwick and the most awkward to get to.

A slow, clanking, tall-chimneyed, black steam tractor towed the thresher and elevator and an accompanying caravan in train down the back lanes to Gledlang and always brought the children running to the school gates to watch it puff by: it never came across to Norsea simply because the causeway was too narrow. The men parked the steam tractor and their caravan near Boundary's boards and we took Molly across to meet them: the causeway was just wide enough for the thresher and the elevator to be towed across, but no way would you risk a lumbering steam tractor weighing twenty or more tons.

In the past, Ben and Old Sago had always taken Molly across: generally, they also fetched Peter from Boundary at the same time to pull one or other of the machines over, as well as to help Molly turn the gears which drove the belts. Fortunately, Charlie Mangapp had not forgotten our need and was already walking Peter down to the boards where the gang were waiting: at least Dennis had agreed to that: Charlie made him, I reckon.

Charlie, it seems, had warned the three about Richard's disfigurement ahead of the crossing, so that when they trundled the threshing machine and the elevator into the yard, where he and my mother were waiting, they were able to greet him normally, or as normally as people can in such circumstances. Like anyone else who sees a badly scarred or disfigured person, they could not help but cast occasional glances at him and several times, out of Richard's line of sight, I saw them exchange little grimaces of disgust or horror with each other, just as I had seen other people do. No doubt, too, that was the reason why they put Richard on top of the now unsheeted stack to cut the string binding the sheaves and feed them into the thresher's hopper: so that they would not have to look too often at his scarred face!

Richard, if he realised why they did it, did not appear to mind, but willingly climbed the ladder to the top of the stack and pitched the sheaves into the hopper with gusto. In the old-fashioned thresher such as they had, the sheaves were whirled round a drum which removed most of the grain from the husks: the grain then fell through a series of riddles to clean it further of stones, grit, dirt and other detritus: a winnowing fan separated out the chaff and the cleaned grain was carried off to a chute and poured into sacks hooked on at the side of the machine.

Being the elder and, therefore, senior hands, John and Hubert did the sacking up: you had to be nippy and know what you were doing, for you could not afford to let a sack overflow. When it was filled, you had to shut off the flow, unhook it, hook up another, release the flow again, whisk the filled sack away, weigh it on the scales to two-and-a-half hundredweight, tie it, then carry it into the barn. John and Hubert were also responsible for keeping the thresher running, greasing the flywheels and ensuring all the bands were operating properly. Meanwhile, straw expelled from the rear of the threshing machine was carried up the elevator to where Artie pitchforked it about all around himself as he built a straw stack.

I was the general dogsbody, helping everybody: one minute, I would be bagging up the chaff which blew out the back in a storm of dust and dirt, the worst of the jobs: the next minute, I would be helping John and Hubert hump the sacks to the storage area in the barn. Then, in the absence of Charlie, who had returned to his work on Boundary, I would be leading either Molly and Peter by the bridles to ensure they maintained their plodding momentum circling round and round the mechanized gears which provided the power to drive the flywheels keeping the various belts operating: and after that I might have to climb the ladder to help Artie, pitching straw across to him so he could lay the stack better, before climbing down again and starting all over again: at the end of the day, I would return Peter to Boundary and fetch him again on the second morning.

All the time we worked, I kept thinking how nice it would have been if Old Sago had been there for one last time to see his stacks being threshed and the grain pouring into sacks: but he was dead, poor bugger.

Richard had the last laugh over the thresher men, though: if they pitied him because of his disfigurement, they envied him when, on the second day, just as we were finishing, late in the evening, Laura Wilchard of all people came past our farmyard. She was slightly puffy-eyed, but otherwise appeared to be normal: she must have come seeking Richard, for she came from the direction of the cottages.

You should have seen the look on the faces of the three Brown brothers when they saw her: for she was wearing tight green slacks and a white silk blouse which left nothing to my imagination anyway, not after what I had seen! You could see the envy in the older men's eyes when Richard climbed down from the last stack and went over to speak to her and she gave him one of her weak smiles: there was outright envy showing among the three brothers as they watched the two of them stroll off a little way, away from all the noise of the rattling thresher, to talk. It was perhaps just as well my mother had gone back into the house by then or she might have had something to say and the words would not have been kind or sympathetic. One can only guess what they talked about: as they parted, I saw Richard reach out and touch her hand as she turned away, as if to console her: it made me wonder how else he was consoling her. In the usual way, I assumed, since I had seen her standing in his cottage at least twice since the evening of the fight: or was that just my jealous mind?

SIXTY-FIVE

IT WAS as we prepared to begin our potato-picking the following week that Richard came round to the farmhouse and, with a certain guilty look, it has to be said, announced that he and Hoary were off on another of Hoary's useless trips. The bombshell was the length of time they expected to be away: three weeks! Maybe four! Doing what? Photographing old houses and pubs and churches and old barns and fields and woods up in the next three counties, that is what! What a useless occupation, I thought, and I told Richard so when he came to tell me the bad news: he just shrugged and said they had to do it then because Hoary wanted the clearer autumn light by which to take his photographs: and he had to go because someone had to drive him up there and lug his bulky tripod and camera and heavy case of glass plates about.

My mother banged about in the kitchen in a temper for a good half-hour after he had gone. 'Is he working on this farm or is he just a bloody servant for that creature?' she exploded. 'I thought he was helping us. We need his help. Doesn't he realise that?' Then the usual: 'Fancy spending your time taking photographs! Useless bloody photographs!'

Despite our protests, Richard and Hoary left early the following morning: too early for my mother to go round and attempt to dissuade Richard, as she had threatened. I do not suppose Laura Wilchard was too pleased either at being left to her own devices for a fortnight or more, alone in a cottage on an isolated island. If anything were to impress upon her the isolation of the place that would: especially having to live there with no one to whom she could talk, for she would not talk to us, and each day the same as the next, with all the inconvenience of the tides with which to contend. She still painted daily, though, I will say that for her: that was something to be admired: her dedication. Perhaps it took her mind off things or maybe it was obstinacy: several times I saw her crossing the causeway on foot, a forlorn figure amid the vastness of the estuary, carrying her board and water colours, a sketchpad or a canvas: she was always back by teatime and the lamp was already lit each evening when I passed by the cottage.

For us, Richard's departure was of greater concern: it meant that there would be only three potato-pickers to get the crop in before the weather turned, myself, my mother and Violet Reddy, who, to my great relief, had agreed to come over in the vain hope, I have no doubt, that by some miracle of mind communication Jan would know she was there and return to Norsea or at least write a letter to me: he did neither. Each morning when Violet came into the field, even when she was still yards away, I saw the desperate pleading in her eyes: 'Has he written yet?'

'No, Violet, not yet. Sorry.' The truth, that he was unlikely to write, I kept to myself.

The previous year we had had Stanley and Old Sago to help us, with Ben doing the turning-up: but Ben was in hospital, Old Sago was dead and we had not seen Stanley since the stone-throwing. As it was late-September by then and he had been accepted by the Royal Academy School, I imagined that at that very moment he was probably sitting in an art classroom up in London somewhere, drawing some real live nude female model and taking a good look at everything.

We had only the two fields of potatoes to lift, but, with just the three of us, it would take us a minimum of two weeks to do the two, working all hours we could. Before you picked potatoes, they had to be turned up out of the ridged soil so that the pickers could scrabble them off the top into their pails and then, when the pails were full, empty them into their sacks. Each day I spent the first half of the morning turning them up with Molly while my mother and Violet began working slowly along the rows: once I had done enough for that day, I turned Molly into her little paddock and joined them: that was when I discovered that there was some consolation to be had from potato-picking.

A couple of times, by chance, and by luck, I happened to be working ten or fifteen yards ahead of Violet as she came up the row behind me: women sometimes do not realise that they are showing everything that they should not be showing and the crouching figure of Violet was no exception: she was squatting on her haunches with her chin down level with her knees and was so engrossed in scrabbling the loose potatoes into her bucket as she worked her way forward that she did not realise or care what she was revealing to the world: or, most particularly, to me. You cannot blame a frustrated boy for looking up a young woman's skirt at 'the Promised Land,' as we called it.

Violet that day was wearing light blue knickers: it was something to remember that night.

As she caught up with me, picking at a faster rate, she stood up to ease her back and aching legs and to call Thomas over to her to wipe his nose: while we rested, we talked: all she wanted to talk about, though, was Jan.

'I know he has not left me,' she said, 'whatever your mother thinks. I know he'll be back sometime. I know he'll come back for me and little Thomas.'

'You won't be able to keep it from Walter forever,' I said. 'He's bound to find out sooner or later.' To me, it was a wonder the woman at the church had not told him already.

Violet looked round to see how close my mother was and whispered: 'I don't care. Not any more. I only married Walter for Thomas's sake. It gave him a name. Don't get me wrong, I was prepared to make a go of it till Jan came back, but not now. Not now. If I had known Jan was coming back, I would never have said yes to Walter, no matter what they said. I'd have waited for him. Oh, Walter's all right. He's good to Thomas, dotes on him, but he's not Jan, is he?' A little giggle there. 'I want to be with Jan, not Walter, and I will be when he comes back. I love Jan. Walter may be my husband, but I don't love him. I love Jan. I think of him all the time. When he comes back, the three of us are going with him.'

'The three of you?'

In reply, Violet gave a mischievous smile and patted her stomach. 'The three of us,' she repeated and seemed immensely pleased about it: I do not think my mother would have been if she had known. That must have been what she meant when she had given Richard the letter, which, as far as I knew he still had in his overcoat.

After that Violet moved away and I spent the next hour talking to little Thomas, who tried to help me by putting the odd potato in my sack, but put in more clods than potatoes before wandering back towards his mother.

The three of us picked all week: day after day of it, in cloud, drizzle and sunshine: and on at least four evenings that week my mother and I went back after tea and picked on by ourselves till eight o'clock and darkness, nine on one day, so that we had taken up all the first lift by the Thursday: on the Friday, we went back with the lifting plough over the rows we had already done to turn up any potatoes that we had missed the first time. We did the same the second week: I was never so glad as when that second Friday came and we had loaded the last of the sacks on to the wagon and I was trundling them into the barn. Eventually, I would re-load them on to the wagon and take them over to the collection point on Boundary and telephone the market lorry from the Square: eventually: when I was less tired. Even my mother complained of an aching back and exclaimed as we left the field: 'Thank God that job's over for another year!'

SIXTY-SIX

LAURA WILCHARD left Norsea while Richard was still away and without telling anyone the day after I gave her the letter from Pocklington: I know it was from the man-faced one because who else would have written to her from London and written the number of the cottage, six, on the envelope? In between rain squalls, my mother had broken off from picking to ride across to the village post office to get a new battery for our fading wireless: she gave me the letter as I came out of the potato field because there was no way she was going to take it round to Laura Wilchard.

The lamp was already lit when I called: Laura Wilchard looked tired and distracted when she opened the door: as far as I know, she had not spoken to anyone for two weeks: she seemed almost relieved to have the opportunity to say something, anything, even if it was just 'Thank you for bringing it.' Her shoulders seemed to slump as she scanned the envelope and recognised the handwriting: the letter was the first which she had been sent that I knew of all the time she had been on Norsea: sadness, unhappiness and loneliness were all showing in her eyes as she closed the door.

That evening the curtains were not drawn: as I walked away past her window, I instinctively looked in, curious to see what I might see: by the lamplight, I saw Laura Wilchard tear open the letter and sink slowly on to a chair: at the end of the second page, she placed the letter on the table beside her and bowed her head: I walked off and left her.

Of course, her sudden departure could have been brought about by the sudden change in the weather and not the letter at all. Arriving in the heat at the start of a long, hot summer, Laura Wilchard had, I think, developed a romantic view of the countryside, the townie's view, the artist's view. She saw it as an idyllic place to visit and in which to sojourn while the summer sun shone and the trees and hedgerows were thick with greenery: then, it was a place of colour and of light, of peace and harmony, a place where birds sang, butterflies fluttered and fields of rippling red-golden grain stretched away to the flat horizon under a cornflower blue sky: where God was in his Heaven and all was right with the world.

Now, all that had changed: prolonged heavy rain had fallen during the previous two days: during the night I had been awakened at least twice by the rain lashing against my bedroom window: when I looked out, the tops of the trees were whipping backwards and forwards in an obvious gale. It had subsided when I went out into the yard soon after seven to feed and harness Molly, the morning calm: but within an hour the wind had risen again and was gleefully ripping the rest of the leaves from the trees and hedgerows and scattering them in great floating streams the length and breadth of the island. Grey gloom was everywhere: the clouds hung above us in dark tatters: the light was as dim and as eerie as any twilight: it was one of those days when you could readily believe the sun was skulking somewhere else, refusing to come out.

Norsea was no longer an idyll: it was cold and bleak and remote, isolated by the broadness of the estuary, far from the bustling Highgate area she knew, with its fine four-storey houses, its comforting, closed-in streets, bright lamplight and warm window glows, rumbling traffic and hurrying figures. On Norsea there were just empty fields, a dark blanket of cloud above, trees and hedgerows brown and bare in the rain, their branches capillaried against the sky, and no movement of any kind outside a fragile window pane other than a curtain of rain sweeping across the flatness.

The next day my mother and I were just sitting down to our midday meal when we heard a tentative knocking at the door: Laura Wilchard was standing on the step, looking rather pale, like she had not slept well or had not slept at all: she apologised for bothering us.

'I was wondering' she said, 'if you would you be so kind as to go over to the village and ask the taxi man if he would come across this afternoon if he is able?'

'Now? Today?' Not reluctance, just surprise at the shortness of the notice.

'If you would be so kind. I do not have a bicycle and it is a long way to walk in the rain.'

'No, no, I'll go, I'll go,' I promised. Never mind me getting wet, I thought, as I closed the door.

I got an old fashioned look from my mother when I went back into the kitchen. 'Fool,' was all she said.

I took Laura Wilchard's message over straight after lunch to give her a chance to beat the evening tide if she were driving somewhere and returning that day. 'Tell her I'll be over straight after dinner,' was Sligger's happy response: business was looking up again, or so he thought.

I did not think anything of it at the time, not till I was walking Molly back to the field I had begun cultivating that day and my way went past Laura Wilchard's door: she was out the back and the front-door was wide open so I peeped in: it was the only time I ever actually was able to see inside properly. I was surprised at the clutter: there seemed to be an awful lot of things lying about the parlour, not what you would have expected from a woman. The table was stacked with canvases, boxes even her suitcase, as well as sheets of drawing paper rolled into 'pipes': other things lay on the floor, pots, pans, plates, tins, brushes, even bedsheets. I just thought it was the way she lived: had I known then that she was about to leave, I would have realised that what she was actually doing was packing.

Later, I saw Sligger's taxi standing outside with its boot and back doors open and he was putting her painting things inside: it was only the next day that I realised she had gone.

SIXTY-SEVEN

I HAD other things on my mind than Laura Wilchard's departure: for instance, how the ploughing was to be done with no one but me to do it.

It must have been my sulky demeanour and slumped posture at breakfast the next day, that past caring look, which alerted my mother to what was going through my mind.

'Don't be so bloody daft!' she snorted. 'Ploughing's a man's work. You can't do everything yourself. You aren't strong enough. You'll have to go across to Boundary and ask Dennis to lend you someone, Charlie Mangapp or Ted Oldton or one of the other creatures. Anyone, so long as they know what they're doing because you don't. And I can't help you. I've never done ploughing. Your step-father always did it with Sago. Lord help me! Have sense do!'

She was right about the ploughing: it was a complicated business if it were to be done right and I wanted to do it right for Ben's sake: I did need help.

For instance, there were three different ways the old ploughmen would horse-plough. One method, 'round-and-round' ploughing, which was sometimes used on Norsea, was best suited to where the fields are fairly level and of a good shape: you started at a short ridge in the centre of the field and ploughed round and round to the outside of the field: or you started at the outside of the field and ploughed round and round till you reached the ridge in the centre.

Then there was 'one-way ploughing,' where you started at one side of the field and continued going up and down ploughing furrow after furrow till you had done the whole field across to the other side: but you needed a reversible plough for that, one with two sets of mouldboards, one turning furrows to the left, one turning furrows to the right, which could be switched over at the end of each furrow so that when you went back down the field all the ridges fell in the same direction. We did not have one of those: our plough was a remodelled 'Improved Ransome,' which only turned the furrows one way, to the right, and was so old it could only have been new when Hodge was a boy. It had an elegant frame and handle made of curved iron, a land wheel which was much smaller than the furrow wheel, and an iron share bolted on to the breastplate: but it was sturdy enough to do the job and was just about enough for me to handle and for Molly to pull on her own.

A third way was systematic ploughing, which was how Ben and Old Sago had mostly done it, but which they had neglected to teach me: I know it now, of course. First, you marked out a headland with sticks about eight or nine yards from the hedge all round the field, then ploughed a marker furrow from stick to stick to circle the field to give horse and plough turning room at the end of each furrow. After that, using the same sticks, you marked out four full 'lands,' or strips, each about twenty-two yards wide running from headland to headland: at either side, dictated by the field shape, were two threequarter lands. From headland to headland, in line with the sticks, you then ploughed an arable ridge to divide each land: after that, starting with the threequarter land, you reduced it to a quarter land by ploughing between the first ridge and the headland mark, turning to the left each time you came into or went out of work, 'casting,' as it is known. When that was done, you ploughed around the ridge, turning to the right each time, 'gathering,' as that was known: that way, you completed the threequarter land first and reduced the full land to a threequarter land width. This you repeated right across the field till the last two lands had been reduced to a quarter each and you could finish on open furrows. The final task was always to plough the headland in the opposite direction to which it had been ploughed the previous year to avoid forming a ridge. So you see, ploughing was more of a science than you thought. I know of these methods now: the trouble was at the time, with Ben and Old Sago always there, I had never been allowed to practice any of them.

'Get on your bike and go!' my mother screamed again when, a few minutes after her first outburst, she came back from the yard and found me still sitting at the breakfast table. A few minutes after that, I was pedalling rather disconsolately across to Boundary: what I really needed was someone to spend two or three days teaching me how proper ploughing should be done: what to do, how to set things up: then I could do it by myself and save my pride!

I found Dennis in the kitchen: he and Joanne Waters were sitting at the table eating breakfast like an old married couple: she even had her hair in paper curlers, which I always thought made women look hideous, but Dennis did not seem to mind. They were sitting very close to each other, both on the same side of the table: I would not have been surprised if things were not being done under that tablecloth: some more of Joanne Waters's thigh massaging perhaps, especially as Ma Parkinson, the supposed chaperone, was banging about in the front parlour, dusting. It was either that or Dennis was creeping along the landing at night and wondering if anyone had noticed anything different about him.

'Richard's still away. I don't know when he'll be back. I'm desperate for some help on Norsea with the ploughing,' I wearily informed Dennis, half-ashamed at having to be there at all. 'I've never ploughed by myself before. Ben and Old Sago always used to do it. Ben wouldn't trust me. I don't even know how to set up properly. I can do the cultivating and the harrowing, but ploughing's different. I need Charlie or Ted to come over and help me for a few days, just to get me started, to show me the ropes, that's all. Just for a couple of days, if you can spare them.'

Dennis was sympathetic, but that day he disappointed me, especially in view of our friendship over the years. 'I can't spare anyone, Joe,' he said, though apologetically, 'not even for a couple of days. We're still grading and packing. We've only just started grading the Coxes and the Russets and next week I'll need the others to start picking the late Salter Spice. Sorry, Joe, but we've just got too much to do. I couldn't even lend you Tully. I would if I could, but I can't, I just can't.'

There was something about the way Dennis said it which unsettled me: I did not like having to beg for help when previously it would have been given without hesitation. I was conscious of the fact that this was a 'new' Dennis I was seeing: no longer was he the put-upon, harangued, bullied and hectored Dennis of old: he was the guv'nor now, more confident, more authoritative, more assured of his place, the decision-maker. He had changed out of all recognition since Joanne Waters's arrival: he smiled more, he dressed better and, if not quite the gentleman farmer, he no longer wore mud-spattered and grease-stained coveralls, but went about in a tweed jacket and new corduroy trousers: he had even bought himself new wellingtons. He also shaved every day, combed his hair, cleaned his teeth and had a new cap: and he no longer smoked rolled Old Holborn, but bought brand packet cigarettes, Goldflake, Senior Service or Player's, and had got himself a silver lighter, all on display on the table. Both the change in him and his refusal were enough to anger me.

It was the first time I had been back in the kitchen since the day of Joanne Waters's arrival: I had just been too busy till then: Joanne Waters, I could not help noticing, had certainly made herself at home: her stockings and underwear were drying on a wooden clothes horse in front of the range and one of her brassieres was dangling in full view from a line suspended across the kitchen above our heads along with other garments: she seemed not to mind one bit that other people, namely me, would see them.

As I turned to go, somewhat disheartened, I realised for the first time that, all through the short conversation, Joanne Waters had been sitting there smiling guiltily: now Dennis was grinning, too. For a moment, I hoped that Dennis's refusal had been part of a joke, but it was not and he was not about to change his mind.

'What are you grinning about?' I demanded.

'We're getting engaged – married,' Dennis blurted out, a look on his face which can only be described as one of sheepish happiness.

'We've asked the vicar to read the banns,' said Joanne Waters. 'When he does, we're going to be there. Do you want to come?'

No, I bloody well did not! I was still upset by Dennis's refusal and told him so. 'I'll have too much to do on Norsea, won't I?' I said, sarcastically, but it was lost on Dennis. Joanne Waters's face, however, did drop a little at my reply. 'Besides,' I added, referring to my spitting shame, 'churches and me don't get on.'

'We hope to get married at the end of this month, once Dennis has finished all the grading and packing. You're invited,' Joanne Waters declared, reaching out and putting her arm round Dennis's neck, which only produced a broader grin and a redder face from Dennis.

For a horrible minute I thought Dennis was going to ask me to be his best man: in the sour mood I was in, inwardly seething, I would have given him a very curt answer: but, blessed relief, that honour had already gone to Charlie Mangapp: after all, he had worked alongside the prospective bridegroom longer than anyone else.

I was both depressed and angry when I rode back to Norsea: and when I stamped into the kitchen and told my mother the bad news, she let out an angry yell: 'And after all we've done for him!' As for the wedding, 'You won't see me there,' she asserted. 'I shan't go. Why should I? If he can't help us here – '

That evening, I went on my customary cursing, stick-swishing, beheading walk around the island, decapitating any and every plant that showed its head above the grass.

SIXTY-EIGHT

THE MAGNITUDE of the task facing me almost overwhelmed me: eight fields had to be cultivated, manured or limed as was necessary, ploughed, harrowed, rolled and drilled in the next five or so weeks before the winter set in: and there was only me to do it. Three were to be drilled with wheat, two with barley, two with winter beans and the other with other crops, onions and cabbage, say: and there still was only me to do it!

Norsea's other fields would remain fallow over the winter and be ploughed and drilled in March with peas and whatever else Ben wanted to put in: and if he were not back with us, there would still be only me to do it!

On my own, I knew that I was unlikely to do even half of it before the weather broke for good, as it almost certainly would sooner or later: I even spent one whole morning, wasted it, really, walking round and round the island, visiting each field in turn wondering just how I was going to set about it all: in the end, I just had to make a start.

Up in Yorkshire that summer, I heard on the wireless, the coalminers, who already earned four times more than I did, had gone on strike for more money, bigger bonuses, shorter working hours, baths at the pithead to wash and two weeks' holidays with pay: they got the lot: but then they had a union behind them. On Norsea, there was just me: often I found myself working ten, twelve or fourteen hours a day, Saturdays and Sundays as well, just to get the job done, and I never even thought of asking Hoary for more money: I would not have got any if I had, not from that old skinflint!

By myself, I managed to complete the cultivating of five of the fields I intended to plough first. Cultivating is tilling the top soil to break the hard ground and grub up the weeds and cover them so they would rot down: it was not so bad doing that with our old rigid-tined 'Dauntless' cultivator, a turn-of-the-century model Ben had bought cheaply at a farm clearance auction ten years earlier. He had wanted to buy a better one, a later, stronger model, plus a Cotswold clod-crusher with a roller which had iron discs free to turn on an axle and was far better for breaking up the lumpy earth: but Hoary had been with him and the old skinflint had refused to stump up the money for either: Ben had had to settle for what we got.

After cultivating, I did the liming and the manuring as was required from the two piles we had in the yard: the worst of liming is that you get covered in the fine white chalk whether the wind is blowing or not and, though a scarf tied round your mouth will keep out most of it, it can still get into your eyes and cause irritation. The worst of manuring is you know exactly what it is splattering your face and caking your clothes as you heave it about: and exactly from where it has come! To load it, I had to stand atop the eight-feet-high mound and carve the compacted dung with a long, two-handed knife into forkable segments, then pitch it on to the cart backed up against the pile. Each load was about fifteen hundredweight and Molly and I took about seven or eight loads a day to the fields before spreading it about, a slow and tedious business: I was at it so late one evening, determined to finish the field, that the moon had risen and my mother had to come into the field to stop me: and that was most unusual.

The first day I ploughed I found out why Ben had never let me plough before: he knew I was not really up to it: not at sixteen and bone thin. It was hard, hard work: my arms quickly began to ache from the constant buffeting and jarring, I stumbled several times and twisted my ankle and the chaffing of the wooden handles soon brought up painful blisters on the palms of my hands: all the time old Molly just plodded along at a steady two miles an hour.

Ploughing a field, you walked seven or eight miles to the acre: and that first day, I ploughed about an acre, after a fashion: by anyone's reckoning then, an acre a day, was considered to be a good stint for ploughing with a horse. For each furrow you ploughed, you walked anywhere between two-hundred-and-twenty and two-hundred-and-fifty yards, hence the furrowlong, or furlong, of two-hundred-and-twenty yards. It took Molly about five minutes to plod from one headland to the other: at the end of each furrow, the time taken to turn a horse has to be added and you try to plough with a minimal time as possible with the plough 'travelling out of work.' In a field of fifty turns to the acre, a half-hour might be added to the actual ploughing time: a hundred turns in two acres might add more than an hour, plus resting time.

The trouble was, it was bad ploughing: unnoticed by me, one of the chains slipped off during one of my traverses and I had trouble controlling Molly's direction: due to inexperience, it was some time before I realised what was wrong. Result: some of the furrows, well, a lot of them really, were not straight, not parallel with each other, so that in places there were thin strips of unploughed stubble in between: had Ben seen it he would have gone berserk: in fact, any decent ploughman would have gnashed his teeth in frustration.

When my mother came to see how I was getting on, she simply confined herself to a bitter 'I told you that you couldn't do it!'

My huffy reply of 'It'll bloody well have to do, won't it?' did not improve her temper and she went off back to the farmhouse expounding to the trees and sky about my supposed inadequacies.

If I learned anything from that first day it was that you needed strong forearms, strong shoulders and a strong back to hang on to the twisting and jarring of a plough hour after hour: the arms are tensed most of the time so you will understand the aches and pains it causes as you go up and down the field for furrow after furrow. By the time I sat in our kitchen and slowly ate my tea, trying to ignore my mother's scathing remarks, my arms and shoulders and back and legs ached as though every muscle was bruised from a beating.

SIXTY-NINE

THEN SUDDENLY Richard was back! Late one evening, just as I was walking Molly back towards the stable after a second disastrous day's ploughing, feeling dejected, angry and humiliated, Sligger Offin's taxi came along the track, belching smoke, and turned off towards Hoary's house. Five minutes later, when it came back towards the causeway, I was waiting at the junction with Molly: Sligger pulled up when he saw me and wound down the window.

'I've just dropped off your step-brother and Hoary,' he declared, a smug smile on his face. 'Picked 'em up from the station in Wivencaster. Your step-brother's gorn and put their bloody car in a ditch and injured hisself. Skidded on a mud patch the other side o' Icklesford a couple o' days back. Wrote the bloody car off good and proper, I hear. Both on'em's been in hospital up at Medundbury. They 'on't be goin' on no more trips for a while. Hoary'll have to use me agin now. I 'on't half charge him!' He was almost gloating.

'Are they both all right?' I asked, though I was more concerned about Richard than Hoary.

Sligger revved up his engine and smothered me in acrid blue smoke. 'Your Dick's a bit shaken up. Hurt his chest, but he'll live,' he said with a sniff, almost as if he wanted to be able to tell me his injuries were worse. 'The other daft bugger's just banged his knee. Pity he didn't bang his head. It might have knocked some sense into him!'

He left the island with the same broad grin on his face as he had when he arrived and the gleeful thought to accompany it that 'Everything comes to he who waits.'

I felt some concern that Richard had hurt himself in a car crash, but somehow the significance of it did not register: I went straight round to see him, pleased that he was back. Injured or not, fit or not, I had something to ask him something important: there was no one else to whom I could turn.

Dusk was falling when I pushed open the door: Richard was standing by the window with his back to me, staring silently out at the darkening sky like a man depressed: he had lit a fire and the kettle was just beginning to boil. For the first time I could recall there was no smile in return when I called out my greeting: no flippant remark about whether I had completed my chores before calling: no jocular question of whether I was hiding from my mother: instead, his mood was pensive, to say the least.

It was obvious why. 'She left three days ago,' I told him.

'I know. She left me a note,' Richard said, with his old weary sigh: then, after a moment or two, during which nothing at all was said, he suddenly crossed to the small bedroom off the parlour, flicking a screwed-up piece of paper into the fire as he did so: Laura Wilchard's note. Unfortunately, it caught alight immediately so I was unable to pull it out to read it.

'I need to change my shirt. I've had this one on since Sunday,' he announced. 'I'll only be a minute.'

When, after five minutes, Richard had not reappeared, I got up from the armchair and crossed to the bedroom in time to see him just starting to pull on the second shirt: he did it very gingerly: it was then that I saw his ribs were bandaged right across his chest, from his armpit to his waist and over one shoulder: in two places there were bumps, like padding: he winced several times as he pulled on the shirt: discreetly, I returned to my seat beside the fire and concentrated on watching the flames licking at the coke.

A couple of times that evening, too, I noticed Richard wince if he stretched too far or too quickly: he never said anything or gasped aloud: just screwed up his eyes and pretended nothing had happened.

I thought about the question I had gone there to ask: in the end I decided I had to ask it: there was no one else, only Richard. Once during one of our long ago evening conversations, Richard had mentioned how he had often helped Ben with the ploughing when he had lived on Norsea as a boy: it was the one job on the farm, he said, he had always enjoyed and which he had always been able to do well. That sentence had stuck in my memory: now I needed to ask for his help.

'Can you help me with the ploughing and the harrowing and the drilling?' I said, putting as much 'please, please' as I could into the words without actually saying them. 'I really need help. I can't do it by myself. I'm desperate. You helped me with the harvest, will you help me with these?'

A moment's pause from Richard before he said with a sigh of resignation: 'If you're desperate, I'll give you a hand. I've not much else to do. I've no car to drive.' Then, with the old smile flickering across his face: 'I think I can still remember what to do. I hope I can. It's been a few years.'

It had been my mother's scorn at my pathetic attempts to emulate Ben as much as the magnitude of the task which had sent me scurrying round to ask him: when he said 'Yes,' I was so relieved that I did not stop to consider the bravado of his reply: and when the next morning he and I stood in the field ready to start and he seemed none the worse for his injuries, I forgot about them: indeed Richard himself was back to his old cheerier self.

'Your furrows are a bit crooked, Joe,' he said with a rueful smile on inspecting the diverging lines of turned earth I had made the previous two days: and then, looking immediately about him as I harnessed Molly to the plough, he exclaimed almost with a sigh at my incompetence: 'And you've left almost as much unploughed as you've actually ploughed!'

I do not think he was serious: it was just friendly chiding to cheer me, I hoped.

The first thing Richard did before we even began that day was to check I had correctly set the depth of the coulter, the part of the plough shaped like a long knife blade, which goes into the ground and makes the vertical cut so that the ploughshare blade slicing along behind follows the same line to turn over the earth. He also checked the height of the land wheel, harnessed up Molly, checked the chains and couplings, then with a 'Git on there, girl!' in our (and his former) vernacular, he guided Molly a short way, cutting a furrow along the headland as a test run: then, before his return, he made some further adjustments.

I could not help marvelling that he remembered what he did after being so long away from it: truly, he made it all look so easy, it made me wonder why I had found it so difficult. I also found it incongruous that someone with Richard's way of speaking should be tramping behind a plough when the only men I knew who did it all had rural 'aahs' and 'goos' and 'boys.' It made me smile.

'You don't forget it, even after all this time,' he remarked on seeing my surprise. 'You just do it. I will say this for Ben, before I left, he did try and teach me everything. A pity I wasn't really interested. He wanted me to learn what he knew.' A hollow laugh here. 'A father passing on his trade to his son, I suppose. He just assumed I was going to be here forever.'

Richard's remarks at least explained why Ben was sometimes so short-tempered with me: why he was unwilling, or at least reluctant, to teach me overmuch: after Richard, he probably did not want to put too much trust in another person: especially someone who might leave: and, as I was due to go into the army in the next year or so, I suppose it made sense. It was a measure of how badly he felt he had been let down.

Richard's method of ploughing was the systematic kind, marking out a headland with sticks, then pacing out four full lands across the field, each twenty-two yards wide, and marking them with sticks, before we began the actual ploughing. When it came to that, Richard walked down the field beside me as I stumbled along wrestling with the plough: he patiently corrected me, showing me when to begin my turn at the headland and how to sweep round in a curve to get back on line with the sticks marking out the 'lands.' That was the marvel of it to me: Richard had been nineteen years away from Norsea, yet he still remembered what Ben had taught him: like he said, you never forgot!

'Keep it straight, keep it straight,' he called out, walking beside me as we went down the field: and more than once, when his exasperation got the better of him, he added his weight to the bucking plough or took the handles himself. 'You're lifting, Joe, you're lifting.' he would cry as the plough came up: and then looking back at a furrow I had just completed, he would admonish: 'You haven't ploughed half deep enough. You've got to go deeper. Put some weight on the plough, Joe, put some weight on it!'

In a week of walking behind a plough a man can walk nigh on sixty miles: small wonder that at least three times after tea during that first week Richard and I worked together, I was to fall asleep in Ben's chair, exhausted. Somehow I did not mind the tiredness: in a strange way I exulted in it: I was doing a man's work, doing it for Ben lying in hospital, doing it for the sake of the farm, to prove to myself that I could do it, to prove to my mother that I could do it: and also because it needed to be done.

SEVENTY

I DID NOT see Richard fall the first time: he was already on the ground when I saw him: I know now that I should never have asked him to help me, but I did and he came: even to this day, I still shudder whenever I think of the effect all that effort had on him.

It happened on his second morning: he was again waiting for me at the gate as I walked up with Molly: in his corduroys and cap and with a packet of sandwiches and a Tizer bottle of water in his hand, he looked more like a farmworker than I had ever seen him, though I doubt he would have wanted me to have told him so: had Laura Wilchard seen him like that, she might not have been so keen: a hoity-toity city woman and a farmworker?

For the first two hours or so we again shared the ploughing, taking turns of a half-hour apiece, though when Richard took the handles I would walk beside him the length of the field and back several times over, just to talk to him: and when my stint came, he walked beside me the same.

Midway through the morning, as Richard started on the last three-quarter land, I went off to mark out the next field as I had been shown the previous day. Near to noon, I was returning, having been away for about an hour, when, as I came through the gate, I saw Richard sprawled on the ground in the middle of the field, lying half in a furrow and half out of it. For a moment, I thought he had just tripped, but then I realised he was not moving: a few yards ahead of him, Molly was waiting patiently, swishing her tail and occasionally looking back, one ear cocked for the command which never came.

As I ran across the field, Richard began to stir: perhaps it was my shouting which penetrated his consciousness, for when I reached him he was struggling to his feet: how long he had been lying there, I do not know and I do not think he did either: he looked white and shaken.

'Are you all right? What happened?'

'I tripped,' Richard replied, but unconvincingly. 'I've just winded myself, that's all.' I noticed that he was gingerly massaging his ribs as he said it.

You don't have to do any more,' I told him. 'I can do the rest myself, now I know what to do.'

Commonsense should have told me there and then that Richard was not fit to work: if it told Richard, he ignored it.

'No, no, I'm all right,' he insisted, brushing the dirt off his coat and trousers and taking up the reins again: nor would he surrender them at the end of the furrow. As he came up on to the headland and guided Molly round ready to go down the field again, he said: 'I'll be all right, Joe. I'll be all right,' but he said it through clenched teeth. 'I just need to work it off, that's all.' And off he went, gritting his teeth, determined not to be beaten by the pain.

He tried to hide it when he came back, but I know he was still in pain when he returned to where I was waiting: this time I insisted on taking over and he was glad to let me do it, I think. However, he still insisted on doing his half-hour-long stints all through the afternoon.

Two days later he fell a second time: I was sitting at one end of the field, having a smoke when I saw him pitch forwards: he still had hold of the handles and was dragged several yards before Molly halted. When I jumped up and started to go towards him, he waved me away as before and called out that I was not to worry: he had 'just stumbled. That was all.' The third time it happened, a couple of days later on still, I was walking along by the hedgerow, again returning to the field from marking out: this time he was just picking himself up, holding his side. When I asked him if he were all right, he said he had just stepped on a clod which had crumbled beneath his foot: he was laughing as he said it, like a person smiling at their own foolishness.

Perhaps a more worldly aware, or more discerning, youth might have known things were not right, but then I was neither worldly aware nor discerning: the nature of the job dictated that sometimes you just gritted your teeth and kept going because you could do nothing else: if you did not do the work, no other bugger would do it for you! When lesser mortals in offices, factories and shops took to their beds with a cold or a cough, the landworkers I knew slogged on because they could not afford to be docked wages. They remembered the bad days before the war when men were put on half-pay in the winter-time, or laid off altogether, because there was no work to keep them on while the fields were turned into quagmires by incessant rain or frozen hard as iron by savage frosts: wages were so poor for rural workers that, if they were breathing, they would go to work. That is what Richard did: he gritted his teeth and carried on working.

'Stop fussing, Joe, stop fussing,' he would say, waving away my concern when expressed in words and responding with a gritty smile when he saw it showing on my face. 'It's just that I'm not used to walking over clods, that's all. You go off and do what you have to do. Get those fields marked out. I'll be all right. I'll be all right.' What else could I do, but shrug, go off and do my work and let him continue.

I know Richard did it to help me, but I am not such a fool that I do not know that he also did it for his father: not in the hope that Ben and he would be reconciled, but because, despite all that had happened, Ben was still his father and, when your father is lying in hospital, you do not let him down by allowing his livelihood to go to rack and ruin: or, for that matter, leave his incompetent step-son to struggle along on his own.

How many times Richard fell during the weeks we worked together, I do not know: I saw him fall three times, but there could have been other occasions while I was away marking out or doing other things which needed to be done. But Richard would not give up: he just would not give up! He worked and worked: he even worked with me on the harrowing on the three Sundays that Dennis Bolt and Joanne Waters were sitting in church listening to their banns being read and she no doubt was fondling him under his new overcoat.

SEVENTY-ONE

THE MOST curious thing was that all during this time my mother's attitude towards me underwent a dramatic change: she no longer cursed me or harangued me or corrected me or threatened me, or did any of the things which had been normal between us all the years I had been growing up: it was almost as if she respected the effort of my labour. Several times, while I lay slumped in the armchair in the parlour late in the evening after a day's work, she asked me if I was all right. Was I tired? Had I had enough dinner? Did I want another cup of tea? The kind of service Ben used to get. It was as though, being the sole male in the house, I was suddenly elevated to the status of the man in it: no longer a child to be harried about the place and chased from it.

No more was I scolded from my bed just after six in the morning, but was allowed to stay in my cocoon till at least six-thirty: no knotted tea-towel was brandished, no spoons or forks or scissors were thrown at my head, no insults came my way, no scorn, no criticism, no vehemence: all was calm and peace of a kind I had not known before.

When I got up in the morning, I always saw to Molly first and then took my own breakfast: the bread was the same awful stuff people ate then, all they could get, almost grey in colour, fit only for frying in dripping, but it would be there on my plate as soon as I returned and sat down, with a pot of tea under the cosy: two eggs would follow, scrambled, fried, boiled or poached. I ate them almost every breakfast time, while the rest of the world, or at least the rest of the country, had to make do with the return of the dreaded wartime powdered egg. Ghastly stuff! Of course, our fortnightly egg quota was short by quite a few during those weeks: five eggs per chicken a week dropped to three per chicken a week: my mother believed in going to work on a couple of eggs long before some smartarse advertiser did. I suspect, too, I may even have got the whole of what rationed bacon she could obtain from the butcher's in the village: and if we had toast, there was always a pot of ginger marmalade on the table to take away the taste of the bread.

Richard, too, she made welcome, as if in acknowledgement of the effort he was putting in: sometimes, if we could spare the time, we would call at the house for a half-hour's dinner and my mother would heat a tin of soup, oxtail, celery or kidney, for the both of us, and cut and butter a couple of doorsteps for us to dip in the bowl. She also insisted that he eat with us in the evenings after we had stabled Molly and, if he looked overly weary after his stint behind the plough, this always seemed to put new life into him. Invariably, my mother had a stew, with onions, carrots, and dumplings waiting for us: we were never short of meat for a stew at teatime, even if it was unrationed horse meat from Argentina. Pork and breadcrumb sausages were regulars on our menu with mashed potatoes and peas and gravy: being potato-growers ourselves, we simply ignored the Government's potato-rationing edicts.

All this may be tedious to those who know only plenty, but we did not: we lived in a world of frugality, shortage and rationing: the rest of the world was better off than we were, it seemed. No wonder there were queues outside the Dominion embassies in London to go to Australia, Canada and New Zealand: you paid your ten pounds and caught the next boat: six weeks later and you were in Australia: that was the favourite: it had sunshine all the year round, so people said.

It was good to see Richard again sitting in our kitchen eating alongside us: it was where he should always have been, I thought more than once: it was as if my mother were thumbing her nose at Ben for his stupidity: trying to make amends for his coldness towards his own son, his anger and his stubborn pride in not even acknowledging his existence.

In my opinion, Richard had earned his place there by dint of sheer hard work alone: following Molly up and down day after day, he more than did his fair share of a ploughman's weekly sixty miles! Small wonder then that, one evening when I hurried after him with something my mother wished him to have, ten minutes after he had entered his own cottage I found him fast asleep in his armchair, a cup of tea he had brewed going cold in the hearth beside him. I fell asleep in Ben's armchair several times myself: somehow I did not mind the tiredness and, in a strange way, even exulted in it!

My mother even allowed me to tune in to whatever programme I wished: not only *Dick Barton* but the madcap antics of Jimmy Jewel and Ben Warriss in *Up The Pole*, or four weird people all talking lunatic rubbish on *Ignorance Is Bliss* to make us laugh, all of which my mother hated: and *The Adventures of PC 49,* which she thought was just plain silly, but then she never did like policemen.

She still made her Sunday visits to Ben, of course, so he was weekly apprised of the work I was doing, though, pointedly, she made no mention of Richard helping me: as far as Ben was concerned, the men from Boundary had come across to help and were teaching me how things should be done.

When she returned, more cheerful now, she would relate how Ben was faring: how his legs had almost mended, how feeling was returning to them, and how he was walking on sticks in a special department they had at the hospital and how he hoped to be home soon. Really, I suppose, I could have gone with her one more Sunday to see him, but I did not: Richard and I had too many things to do.

For instance, we had to prepare for drilling: and the first thing we had to do was to dress the seed: Richard, remembering from his earlier years, actually showed me how to do it, adding the right amount of chemicals against the various pests, moulds, fungi and blotches which can always devastate your crop: for, be it beet, beans or barley, peas or potatoes, cabbages, mangels, onions, turnips or wheat, there was always something to settle on it or grow on it, in it or from it. It was something Ben had again neglected to teach me: he had, however, remembered to put in his order with the seed merchant at Tidwolton just before his accident so at least it was all delivered to the Boundary drop-off point on the right day for Richard and I to pick up.

Our seed drill was as ancient as the rest of our machinery: it was one invented by some vicar mid-way through the Eighteen-Hundreds, with its own peculiar design of seed box, large carriage wheels almost as high as me and a geared drive from the main axle: you could not have got a piece more ancient than that which we dragged out of the wagon shed. It took us two whole weeks, but by the end of that fortnight we had drilled and rolled all eight fields. Wonderful! Especially when I recalled my earlier anxieties: especially, too, as the weather was worsening daily: the grey fogs were already clamping round the island: the clouds seemed to be darker, to hang lower and the rain to fall longer: everywhere was grey and brown and barren.

I would never have done half of what had been done without Richard's help, I know that: he was still gasping for breath at times, and rubbing his side, but even that was forgotten amid the smiling as we left the last field that final evening. To be truthful, by the time we finished the final rolling, I was more concerned about Molly: she, poor old girl, was looking very sluggish after hauling a plough up and down our fields day after day, then a harrow, then a seed drill: she needed a rest, a proper rest. A horse will tell you with their eyes if they are tired: each toss of the head when you try to harness them in the morning, each snort of effort as they lurch forward to get the machinery moving, each plodding weary turn will tell you: but their eyes tell you most: and Molly's told me she was tired, dead tired. I had to give her a good rest: if anything happened to the old mare, Ben, I knew, would never forgive me: neither would my mother. I was in sole charge of her: it was my responsibility.

So at the end of that final Saturday morning, I took her to the paddock and turned her loose: she gave me a look as if to say, 'Are you really doing this?' Then kicked her heels like a daft colt, swished her tail a half-dozen times at imaginary flies and lumbered off: when I left her, she was happily trotting round and round in circles as if unable to believe she was free: later, when I went to give her some hay, she was contentedly grazing: she must have thought I had come to take her back to work, for she trotted off to the farthest corner of the field and would not come while I was there.

Completing the work had at least soothed my mother's animosity towards Dennis Bolt: what we had done, we had done without his or anyone else's help. 'I might even go to the wedding after all,' she said, sniffily, 'if only to tell him that we didn't need him – if I can get the stain out of my blue dress – if ...'

But first Dennis and I had an appointment in Wivencaster: the Maydun postman had visited again, bringing a letter informing me that Billy Garner's trial would be held at the Quarter Sessions there on the very next Monday and I was summoned to appear: somehow, the prospect cast a shadow over the pleasure I felt in looking back at all we had achieved.

SEVENTY-TWO

ON THAT Saturday morning I released Molly into her paddock, a small incident occurred which at least gave me hope and raised my spirits a little: Nick came over to Norsea on his bicycle: it was just after twelve: so he would have ridden straight from his morning's farm work.

I was idly hurling pebbles out into the mud near the Western Point, watching them plop into the ooze and throw up small black geysers like crater marks on the moon: then across on the mainland shore, through the dazzling sunlight reflecting off the channel and the salt-sheened mudflats, I made out the lone figure of a cyclist starting to pick his way past the potholes and puddles: even at that distance I knew it was Nick, simply by the silhouette and the way he rode. His visit was so unexpected it cheered me just to see him, but it would have been a weakness on my part to let him know it or to go out to meet him: so I waited for him at the very top of the incline where the causeway comes ashore, as if to say he need come no farther than that.

Nick stopped about twenty yards from me and remained straddling the crossbar, as boys do, one foot on a pedal, gripping the handlebars, ready perhaps for a quick getaway if things turned nasty.

'I've just come to tell you Bournes are running a special bus to Wivencaster on Monday,' he said, sheepishly. 'Denny Caidge and Matt Cobb have hired a single-decker. They say they're taking the day off no matter what Rex Book says. Time owing, or something. You know how thick they are with Billy's brother Ron. I don't think you should try and catch it because it'll be full most likely. There's quite a few going, about thirty, I reckon, a show of support, like, for Billy. I just thought you should know.'

I thanked him for that: he would not have known that I had already arranged to go with Dennis and Richard in the van: at least three of us in the van meant there would be no room for Joanne Waters.

'Are you going?'

Nick reddened, looked even more sheepish and averted his gaze. 'No, I can't afford the time off,' was the best I could get out of him, which suggested he had thought about it, pressured into it most likely by Billy and Lennie Ring.

He did add one hopeful point: 'They say Billy's going to plead guilty to something or other so it'll be a quick trial, no more'n a day, they reckon. He's willing to say he hit old Bolty, but that's all. The solicitor chap says it's the best thing he can do. He's got a barrister bloke to help him. His dad seems to think things won't be too bad after all.'

There was an uncomfortable pause while Nick scraped a toe in the shale and thought of what to say next. 'I hope things turn out all right,' he offered eventually. 'Billy says he's going to volunteer for the army if he gets off. He says there ain't much in Gledlang to keep him here. No-one'll take him on now, will they? Too afraid of getting a whack over the head with a hoe, I expect.' A sly grin at his own humour. 'He reckons the army will take him, despite this. He says they'll take anybody who'll volunteer, especially if they sign on for seven or twelve years. There's no way I'm going yet, though. I'll wait till they call me. I'm in no hurry. You the same, I suppose?'

'Yeah. They'll have to come and get me. I'm not volunteering for anything.' Spoken in a defiant tone: the exchange was becoming awkward.

A pause while Nick shifted his bicycle round. 'Well, I'll be seeing you,' he said, casually. 'Don't let anyone know I told you.' Then he was off, heading back to the mainland. I watched him go, thankful that he had come to warn me, but unable through pride to cross that divide between us. I would have liked to have sat and talked with him the way we used to, just the two of us perched on the top of the island's low seawall in the bright sunlight, discussing things the way we once did: but I let him leave.

I felt buoyed by Nick's visit, although there was still the worry about what Billy's two older brothers, Jimmy and Ron, might do to me. They might not take it out on Richard and Dennis, Richard because he was not involved and Dennis because he was, after all, a farmer: but I knew that, if they felt like it and got the chance, they would certainly take it out on me and I did not fancy a bloody nose or a split lip and a few loosened teeth. That, more than their ostracism, is what worried me most: the threat of violence and the pain rather than the humiliation it would inflict upon me: I was consoled by one thought, that they were unlikely to kill me: were they?

At times while I waited, I was not so sure: the eldest of Billy's brothers, Jimmy, had been in Athens during the bloody battle our troops had had with the Greek Communists when they tried to take over that country: no quarter had been given in that affair. I had seen pictures on the cinema news at Maydun of British tanks crashing through houses in Piraeus and firing their shells down alleyways at Communist positions. Jimmy had been shipped in with his regiment at short notice from Italy when the emergency arose and would have been in the thick of it: so punching me in the face was not going to bother someone who had shot point-blank at young Communists, girls among them, rushing at him and his mates in their defensive strongpoints around the Acropolis.

The day of the court case Richard and I crossed to the mainland just after eight: if my mother showed any concern for me, she concealed it: her parting words, as I slammed shut the door on my way to meet Richard, were: 'You stupid fool! I can't get over how stupid you are!'

Dennis was already waiting at the boards with his van: Richard sat in the front passenger seat and I sat in the back on some sacks: we were ready for anything, I think. Even as we bumped down the track towards Shoe Street, Richard kept a lookout and Dennis repeatedly revved the engine, ready to put his foot down hard on the accelerator the instant the first stone came sailing out of the trees or over the top of a hedge: none came and we passed up Shoe Street, through the Square, up past the school and the blacksmith's in Tithe Street and out along the Salter road without seeing a soul.

We eventually rattled up East Hill into Wivencaster High Street about nine-thirty and parked in a backstreet near the old Norman castle just as the rain began: from there, it was only a short walk to the courthouse farther up the High Street. Unfortunately, we arrived before the oak doors had been opened and, to my consternation, there was a crowd of thirty or so people waiting outside, among them at least twenty Gledlang-ites. Billy's family, not unexpectedly, was out in force: Jimmy and his wife, Ron and his wife, and his younger brothers, Arthur and Albert: Billy's father and mother, I assumed, were inside with Billy and their solicitor. At least six other men and about eight women from Gledlang were there standing on the grass each side of the flagged path that led up to the doors: the Bourne Brothers' bus must have got in early, for several of the women were clutching bulging shopping bags: clearly, combining their support for

Billy with a rare opportunity to go round Wivencaster's bigger stores, Woolworth's and Marks and Spencer's.

It was an English-style protest: just a chorus of jeers, hisses and boos to greet our arrival: I saw poor Dennis blanch as he recognised the hostile faces: but Richard did not seem the least bit bothered.

'Keep going. There's nothing to be scared of from this lot,' he said, giving me a push when I slowed at the edge of the pavement, reluctant to run the gauntlet, especially as I was at the front of our trio and most likely to be the first to be punched. The determination in Richard's voice drove me on: there may not have been anything to fear from most of them, but there was from Billy's brothers and men like Denny Caidge and Matt Cobb: they were likely to do anything. Right at the entrance, I spotted Lennie Ring, baying as much as the rest of the bedraggled bunch, but I was glad to see that Nick had kept his word and was not there: at least I had half a friend in Gledlang still.

'Keep going, Joe! Shove the blighters out of the way if you have to,' Richard shouted above the noise and he must have given someone a push, for there were yells and oaths behind me and I saw several people stagger back and one person fall. Someone struck out at Dennis and I saw him strike back: then someone struck out at me: it was more of a woman's slap than anything: nothing really.

I only grew alarmed when we were halfway down the pathway, too far to retreat, and Jimmy and Ron Garner and their wives, stepped out on to the pathway to block our approach. The men had their fists clenched, shaking them at us and mouthing obscenities, while the women were screaming hysterically: I had no doubt about what they intended: a mouthful of abuse and perhaps even a kick as we ran past: courtroom precincts or no, they would let us know what they thought of us.

Fortunately, at that moment a fresh-faced young constable swung open one of the doors to see what all the commotion was about: for some reason, inexperience perhaps, he made no move to assist us in the pushing match which had developed – us pushing forward, them pushing us back – but just gawped at the milling throng with a puzzled frown. Luckily, a quicker-thinking older constable did realise what was happening: by shoving against those blocking the doorway, he created a way through for us and we entered to a barrage of jeers.

It was only on seeing all the barristers in their gowns and wigs that it actually dawned on me how serious this was for Billy: till then, I had only seen such things in films: this was in earnest: I suddenly felt sick. I would have quite happily done a bunk, but for the fact that both Dennis and Richard were sitting beside me in the antechamber where the witnesses all waited: plus, a gowned court official had ticked off our names when he directed us there.

SEVENTY-THREE

THE CASE itself was not called till eleven: after a while, bored with sitting in the antechamber staring at the ceiling and counting the red tiles on the lower half of the wall, the three of us slipped into the back of the courtroom to watch the proceedings. It was the first time I had ever been in a proper courtroom: I have to say I found it all very interesting, if a little alarming, knowing that people's lives were being decided upon right before my eyes.

They were sentencing cases mostly: a soldier home on leave got seven years for supposedly raping an old girlfriend he met at a fair: he said she was quite willing to let him shag her as he walked her home from a fairground after having saved her from the lustful attentions of the dodgem car attendant, but, after they had had it on a piece of waste ground, he had foolishly told her he was engaged to another girl near his camp and preferred her: the old girlfriend cried rape out of spite and they believed her!

Two married men came up next, caught together doing 'indecent' things in the back of a car: they did not enlarge on what those 'indecent' things were so I was none the wiser, but they each got three years and seemed stunned by it, tearful even. The skull-faced old judge just turned away as they were taken down. Third up was a frail, visibly shaking old age pensioner, sent for sentence for stealing a bottle of milk off a doorstep: I thought, 'You poor old sod!' Then they read out his record: over a forty-year criminal career, he had done everything, from pimping off his wife and daughter, running a brothel, armed robbery, bank robbery, grievous bodily harm to running protection rackets! I learned that day never to go on appearances!

Suddenly, Billy came up into the dock from the cells below: our eyes met only briefly as Dennis and I, being witnesses, had to scurry back to the antechamber to wait to be called. I was astonished to see how smart he looked: his dad had got him a single-breasted black, chalk-stripe suit from somewhere, probably one of his brothers' demob suits: and, even though it was a size too big for him and made him look like his grandfather, it was the smartest I had ever seen him. He was clean shaven, too, for a change, and was even wearing a blue striped tie, rather than the one with the hand-painted hula girl on it which he usually wore in Maydun: he looked so different I had to look twice to make sure it was him.

Just as we left, the Gledlang crowd came noisily into the gallery and had to be told to be quiet: most had never been in a court before and so were quite excited at the experience: well, it would be something to tell the neighbours or gossip about in the Chessman, would it not?

Richard, of course, remained in court as the barrister outlined the case that one John Bolt had collapsed and died at his home in the village of Gleldlang two days after receiving blows on the head from a hoe wielded by the defendant. The best thing was that, though Billy was being charged with manslaughter, when his counsel stood up, he said Billy was quite prepared to plead guilty to a lesser charge, say, causing grievous bodily harm, rather than actual manslaughter: that was what the judge and jury had to decide. Billy did not deny what had happened, but claimed it was self-defence against the deceased, who had been trying to hit him with a heavy, brass-bound stick: the court was trying to determine whether he had played any part in John Bolt's death.

Dennis was first into the witness box: he told the story as it had happened, just the same as he had told it at the inquest: it did not prevent the hissed intakes of breath and mutterings among the villagers in the gallery, especially from Billy's family and Denny Caidge and Matt Cobb, which caused the judge to look up sternly. They clearly did not like what Dennis had said any more than they were going to like what I said: but at least Dennis had an excuse: it was his uncle who had died.

When I went into the box, a clerk in a black gown thrust a Bible into my hands and told me to read off a card that I would tell the truth, the whole truth and nothing but the truth, 'so help me God.' I was not too happy about saying the last bit, but I said it anyway: if that is what they wanted me to say, then so be it. What did I care?

I looked across at Billy hoping to catch his eye again and see what he was thinking: but there was just a snarl and the word 'Bastard!' mouthed silently before he turned away to glower straight ahead at the rest of the scene: the judge in his red robe seated on high, the barristers and their juniors in their black gowns and grey-white wigs below him, and facing them all from one side the twelve nervous members of the jury. What I told the judge under the prosecution barrister's questioning, was no different from what I had told the Salter constable: more or less word for word, except for the 'sirs': the Salter constable did not merit a 'sir.'

'Did you see the deceased struck a blow with a hoe?'

'Yes, sir.'

'More than one?'

'Yes, sir. Two.'

'Two blows only?'

'Yes, sir.'

'Were they hard blows?'

'Fairly hard, sir.'

'How hard is fairly hard?'

What else could I say? 'Fairly hard, sir. One of them made his knees buckle, anyway.'

'Hard enough to make the deceased, John Bolt, stagger, you say?'

'Yes, sir. Billy gave him a right couple of whacks?'

'Where exactly?'

'Here, sir,' I replied, indicating, 'right across the top of his head.'

'And how far away were you at the time?'

'About thirty yards, sir.'

'And you saw the heavy part of the hoe, held by the defendant – the metal blade end – strike Mr. Bolt on the head?'

'Yes, sir. Saw it and heard it, sir.'

The lawyer for Billy did not look too pleased and there were intakes of breath from those up in the gallery: I did not need to look up there: I knew what they were thinking: but I was telling the truth, the whole truth and nothing but the truth, though I did not see what help I was going to get from God.

'The two were arguing when the blows were struck, were they not?'

'Yes, Billy had gone under the hedge because it was raining and John Bolt caught him. He told him to get back to work and Billy said he was on his dinner. That was when the fight started.'

'The fight?'

'The argument. Billy and John Bolt were shouting at each other.'

'Did John Bolt strike the defendant, William Garner, before he was himself struck?'

'Not exactly, sir. Bolty – John Bolt – had his walking stick in his hand and he gave Billy a couple of prods to get him back to work, then he grabbed him by the hair and pushed him.'

'Pushed him? How far?'

I did not see the trap. 'Five or six feet, maybe more.'

'Seven or eight feet? Out of range of John Bolt's stick?'

'Yes, I suppose so. John Bolt just had a hazel walking stick he was waving about.'

'How long was the stick? About three feet long?'

'About that.'

'So the defendant did not have to turn round and strike John Bolt, did he? He was out of range, as you say, and, therefore, in no immediate danger himself?'

'Well, no, but – '

'No buts, Mr. Coe. You have said he was out of range and in no danger and thus did not have to strike back. That will be all, thank you.' And he sat down.

I had a feeling I had said something which was not quite the way it should have been said: not so much that I should not have said it, but that what I had said had been taken the wrong way: that he had interpreted my words to satisfy his picture of things, as he wanted it to be and not as it should be or as it was.

Billy's lawyer stood up: there was a look of contempt in his eyes and his nostrils were flared in a sneer.

'You were friends with the accused till quite recently, were you not?' he asked, fixing me with what he assumed was an eagle-eyed stare, but which was rather spoiled by the fact that he had one blue eye and one brown one.

'Yes, sir. Billy and I have been friends since we went to school together.'

'And subsequently, you have fallen out?'

'Yes, sir.'

'More than just fallen out? You avoid each other? You do not go about together? You have ceased to be friends?'

'I suppose so.' Spoken reluctantly. 'We used to go to the pictures together, but we don't any more, not since the day Billy hit John Bolt over the head. We've fallen out, that's all.'

'Fallen out enough not to have spoken to each other for several months and to have attacked him quite recently and not for the first time either, Mr. Coe?'

I felt my face reddening again: I looked across at Billy and saw he was smirking at my discomfort, but, as soon as he saw me looking, he again turned away and stared straight ahead, all grim-jawed and uncaring once more.

Yes, I had attacked him a couple of months back, but I had provocation: four torn-up pictures! And I had had a punch-up with him a couple of years before that, after he had lobbed an oversize flint on to my head during one of our periodic stone fights on the dried-up decoy pond: Billy had broken the rules of stone fighting: that is why I charged at him in my rage. I tried to explain the rules to the barrister, but he just stood there, smirking at me.

'Stone fights, Mr. Coe! Stone fights! Whatever next will you do for your amusement?' Even the prosecution barrister and the court officials were sniggering.

'Having a stone fight's nothing unusual,' I told him. 'We have them all the time.' It was true: having a stone fight was nothing unusual for the boys of Gledlang: we had had several over the years: the old dried-up duck decoy down the seawall was perfect for it: all hillocks of piled, flint-strewn earth and narrow valleys through thick gorse bushes where one could hide, lob a few stones at an opponent and then retreat: the only rules were no big stones and no stones to be thrown nearer than ten yards: we divided into two sides to do it, like football teams.

'You know what a dictionary is, do you, Mr. Coe?' More sarcasm from the barrister.

'Yes, a book of words and their meanings and that.' Defiance and pride from me. 'I have used one for spelling.' I emphasised the 'have' just to show that I was not as ignorant as he obviously thought I was: for some reason, people were smirking again: even the barrister was having a cynical smile.

'Well, the opposite of friend is enemy, is it not, Mr. Coe?' I did not like being called 'Mr. Coe' by him: he said it in such a sneering fashion.

I tried to shrug the question off as though I did not think it much of a point to make, but he repeated it, more sharply, this time, eyes narrowing to a ludicrous squinting stare: 'The opposite of friend is enemy, is it not?'

'I suppose so,' I agreed, half-heartedly.

'Do you know the definition of the word "enemy" in the dictionary?'

'Yes, sir. People who fight against each other.'

The barrister let out a sigh and supplied the proper answer. 'One who is "antagonistic to another, especially one seeking to injure or confound, doing something harmful." Not just people who fight against each other, but also people who say things against each other, people who are harmful towards others, who seek to do them harm. People who turn against their friends, Mr. Coe. Like you?'

'Pardon.' I was genuinely confused at what point he was seeking to make.

'The point I am making, Mr. Coe, is that what you are saying here today could be tainted by your enmity towards the defendant?'

'My what?'

'Never mind.' A dismissive wave of the hand from the barrister as though he did not care what I answered. 'No further questions.'

I left the witness box smarting under fifty pairs of laughing eyes: only Richard, sitting at the back of the court, showed any sympathy: fortunately, the judge called for the lunch break and I was able to flee the courtroom and the hostility of the Gledlang-ites.

We sat in the van to eat our sandwiches at lunchtime, not knowing really what to think about the outcome: good or bad? You just could not tell.

SEVENTY-FOUR

IT WAS the pathologist from some big London hospital who 'saved' Billy, if that is not a contradiction in terms: he had been called in to help the local man and had had good poke through John Bolt's body and a peep inside his skull while he was lying in the Wivencaster mortuary. He gave his evidence at the start of the afternoon: if they had called him first, my evidence would not have been necessary.

According to the pathologist, two of the bruises on John Bolt's head were consistent with blows from a hoe – Billy's hoe – but the third was indeterminate and was caused by something else: he could not say what.

Richard said he saw several of the jury shift in their seats at that: they did the same when the defence barrister drew the surprising answer that John Bolt's excessive drinking and smoking could have caused a weakness in the blood vessels in his skull, making his collapse from a relatively ordinary blow more likely than unlikely.

'Any kind of a blow?'

'Yes, almost any kind of a blow, if it were hard enough. Banging his skull accidentally, say, against a low oak beam, if it were done hard enough. A bump, in effect.' The defending barrister seized on that.

'A bump, you say, such as tripping and falling against the sharp edge of a marble mantelpiece, perhaps?'

'Possibly,' said the pathologist, nodding several times. 'Possibly.'

'Or perhaps knocking his head against a fender following a sudden collapse, from a heart attack or a seizure, say?'

'Possibly, yes,' repeated the pathologist, nodding again.

One or other of them had to be the cause of the third bruise. Billy had hit John Bolt only twice!

Such was the condition of John Bolt's innards, too, the pathologist said, that even he was unable to determine whether a blood vessel had burst in his brain first or an artery had ruptured in his chest first, or whether both had occurred at the exact same time or within a few seconds of each other before he fell or when he fell or because he fell. But a rupture and a burst there had been and either would have caused him to collapse against the mantelpiece or fall on to the metal rim of the fender.

Years of heavy smoking had damaged John Bolt's heart and lungs to such an extent and clogged up his arteries to such a point that he could have died at any time, any moment! The pathologist couched it in medical terms, which I do not recall precisely, but this is a fair summary. It made sense to me: John Bolt was forever coughing and spitting while he smoked and always out of breath.

The defending barrister preened himself after that and, according to Richard, made it the main point of his address to the jury: he also suggested that there were mitigating circumstances and Billy's actions 'could be construed as acting in self-defence' since John Bolt had 'poked him, seized him by the hair and pushed him and may even have been about to strike him.' The John Bolt I saw was just waving his stick about really, albeit at Billy till he whacked him one: only then had he charged at Billy, intent on hitting him in return.

Since Billy had already admitted, through his lawyer, to striking the blows, the summings up were mercifully brief. It was ticking on to a quarter past four when the jury went out and when they sent a note back in to say they would have to deliberate longer, the judge adjourned the case till the following day.

Richard, Dennis and I managed to dodge the other Gledlang-ites as we retrieved Dennis's van: we drove back mostly in silence, though Richard seemed to think that the pathologist's remark that John Bolt's arteries had made him susceptible to a collapse stood Billy in good stead. Dennis did not comment: I do not think he knew what to say.

As it happened, Richard was proved right, but not before I had spent another bad night: I had not slept well the night before the court hearing and did not sleep well after it either, thinking of Billy and what punishment he might get: as a result, I went about like a zombie for the rest of the next day: I could not concentrate on what I was doing and poor Molly suffered some rather harsher slaps than she deserved.

I was in the barn when I heard Richard call my name: he did it several times before I answered: I suppose that I just did not want to hear the news I knew he was bringing.

'I've just met Charlie Mangapp. Dennis and his girlfriend went over to the court in the van to hear the verdict. They gave your friend three years in Borstal for the assault. The judge was lenient because he had admitted what he had done and had shown remorse for it. Apparently, they accepted that he may not have been the actual cause of John Bolt's death. He's a very lucky lad, your friend, Billy.'

Oh, I was so glad to hear that! So relieved, so pleased. The one thing I had feared, indeed the one thing everyone had feared, was that Billy would get something like seven years in Melchborough Gaol. But Borstal! Ha! Billy would thrive in Borstal: what a feather in his cap! Billy a Borstal boy! My old mate, Billy! At that moment I had a mental picture of Billy smiling as he got off a bus with twenty or so other bad lads somewhere in the deeper regions of Kent or Sussex or wherever the Borstal was located. Three years in the country doing landwork as a punishment, all meals found! Ha! That would suit Billy down to the ground. It would be like living round Gledlang: a home from home almost. You lucky sod, Billy, I thought, you lucky sod! I was half-jealous. He had whacked that miserable, slave-driving, bastard John Bolt over the head and got away with it. Borstal, heh! When he came out, Billy would be able to get almost any girl he wanted, especially some of them in Maydun: there were girls there who would love to have a Borstal boy on their arm. And three years in Borstal would be something for Billy to tell his grandchildren about, as the saying goes – if he ever had any.

When I crossed to Boundary the next day and met Dennis in the company of Joanne Waters, he looked a little downcast, like he would have expected Billy to have received a longer sentence, if only as a form of revenge for his uncle's death.

'I thought they'd at least give him five years,' he said somewhat disconsolately.

'It's not the sort of thing you ought to be worried about just now, Dennis,' I told him. 'You're getting married on Saturday, you ought to be worrying about that, mate!'

I did not mean it to come out that way and received a hard-eyed stare from Joanne Waters: she was clinging to Dennis's arm like he might blow away in the wind and was staring at me with a peculiar defiance in her eyes: she did not need to say anything: her look said it all: 'Come Saturday, I'm going to be Mrs. Dennis Bolt. I've got my man and I'm hanging on to him.'

SEVENTY-FIVE

THE DAY of the wedding dawned grey and misty. My mother and I were not due at Boundary till two just to make sure Dennis got to the church before three and also to ensure that he walked up Shoe Street in his new suit, with a buttonhole in place, his shoes polished and his hair properly brylcreamed and that he did not drive up in his little green van wearing his new wellingtons.

She had even gone across to the church the previous evening to help Ma Parkinson with the flowers and to give the pews a good polish because, in view of the court case, she did not expect anyone else would: some proper caterers from Maydun had been brought in to lay on a buffet in the parish hall: and, among the farming families, the post office-cum-grocery store had done a fair trade in quarter-ounce bags of rice, which people threw at weddings then. Also, I should add, the blushing bride, who, thankfully, my mother said, would be marrying in a blue suit, had been hustled out of the farmhouse and had gone to Ma Parkinson's sister's in the old bakehouse cottage at the top of Shoe Street for the night. For decorum's sake, I suppose.

This was the first wedding to which I had ever been asked, so I have to admit I was curious and did not quite know what to expect, other than a short service, some women crying like I had seen in a couple films in Maydun, some rice throwing and a couple of photographs being taken if someone had brought a camera. Then there would be lots of eating and drinking in the parish hall afterwards, where Jack Spivey had set up two barrels, one of mild, one of bitter, and had laid on a half-dozen cases of light brown ale for the men, with gin, whisky, port, sherry and soft drinks for the ladies. My mother had even ironed my 'new' blue chalk-striped suit, bought second-hand for the occasion the week before. It had actually belonged to Old Man Howard in the village, who had died a fortnight before, three hours after his wife had departed this world while dozing in the parlour armchair: when the neighbours told the old man she was dead, he had simply followed them upstairs, lain down beside her on the bed and died himself within a couple of hours – of a broken heart, they said. Sad. Still, it meant I had a suit which fitted my still-growing frame.

Wonder of wonders, my mother had even put proper, knife-edge creases in the trousers, straight down the front from top to bottom, unlike mine which sometimes would finish inside or outside of the ankle. 'I don't want you going there all scruffy and showing me up,' she had snapped in offering an explanation for this unexpected display of motherhood. 'People have their pride, you know.' I had borrowed one of Ben's clean shirts and one of his stiff celluloid button-on collars, while Richard had lent me a clean tie and I had polished my boots: all in all, I was going to look quite smart.

Richard himself was not with us: he just said he was not in the mood for a wedding, so my mother and I crossed to Norsea by ourselves just about one-thirty, early, in fact: my mother hurried well ahead, as I expected she would do, leaving me to trail behind: it was just like old times. We rapped the knocker on Dennis's front door and waited: no one came: we knocked again: still no one came. Finally my mother let out an exasperated wail: 'Wherever is he? Whatever does he think he's doing?'

Done a bunk if he has any sense at all, I thought to myself, but said nothing aloud, except, 'I'll take a look round the back, see if he's in the yard.'

My mother said it more to herself than to me as I walked away: 'I don't understand it. I don't expect Ma Parkinson to be here, but I would have expected him to be here. On his wedding day. Where is the man?'

I knocked on the back door, but still no one answered: I peered in at the kitchen window, but could see no one: I circled the house twice, calling out Dennis's name, but got no reply: no one appeared at his bedroom window, no water came sluicing down the pipe from the bathroom to indicate he was there: I even peered through the letter box and all the other downstairs windows, but of Dennis Bolt there was neither sight nor sound.

'Where is the man?' my mother kept repeating, growing ever more agitated and circling the house herself and doing all the things I had just done. 'He must be in there somewhere.'

'He isn't there,' I retorted, put out by her distrust of my efforts and then, hoping to be helpful, blandly suggested: 'Perhaps he's forgotten he's getting married.'

A withering look from my mother: how could she have given birth to such a dopey son? 'You don't forget your own wedding day!' she cried. 'Gawd! I wonder sometimes where you get your ideas from! Not from me, you don't. Have sense do!' The last words were spoken in her usual despairing wail.

I went over to the barn, all the time calling out Dennis's name, but he was not there: neither was he in the packing shed, nor in the weighing shed, or in the row of lavatories behind the barn which the women pickers used for their needs in the summer. Peter was in his paddock, munching on grass and he was not with him: the farm's half-dozen milk cows were in the meadow a half-mile away and there was no sign of Dennis there: nor was he standing in the arable fields ruminating on something: he had vanished. The house was empty, locked up, the windows all closed: everywhere was silent except for the ticking of the grandfather clock in the hall.

We spent a good quarter-hour searching for him, mostly going round in circles. 'Oh, come on,' my mother cried at last, giving up, too exasperated to continue. 'We'll go up to the church. You can look in the Chessman on the way. He's probably in there.'

All things were possible, particularly with the new Dennis under the influence of Joanne Waters: perhaps he had gone to the Chessman for a drink to calm his nerves, I thought: men have been known to call in at a public house on their way to their wedding, have they not? But somehow I did not think Dennis would have done that: he would have waited for me. I kept one eye open for him as we walked along the track through the orchards, looking down each row of trees in turn to make sure he was not doing something there, still dressed in his wellingtons, boiler suit and cap, unaware of the time. Where had he gone, the bloody idiot? I was beginning to feel apprehensive more than merely mystified when we reached the Square.

Gledlang Square has always been a gathering place: for weddings, for funerals, or just waiting for the two o'clock Bourne Brothers' bus from Cobwycke to Maydun, not just for the boys of the village who gather there to sit on the ciderstone. Just over two years before the whole delirious villagers had gathered in the Square to pile all the rubbish they could collect into the centre and light their VE bonfire the night the war ended in Europe: some over exuberant villagers had even dragged a four-wheeled haywain from outside the blacksmith's up Tithe Street and set that on fire to keep the blaze going: and crazy Tom Link had hung backwards out of an American jeep wearing a pail on his head as a helmet: it was bouncing on the road all the way up Shoe Street before the Yank driver halted outside the Chessman with a squeal of brakes.

Three months later they had repeated the whole process for VJ night when Japan surrendered and old man Goddard had come reeling drunk out of the Chessman and staggered right through the middle of the red hot embers before anyone could stop him: he was not even singed.

Now the villagers were gathering again: some twenty or thirty of them, predominantly women, were huddled in four groups, talking among themselves: concern, disbelief, shock, all of these, showed on their faces. Several turned to look at us as we approached and there was sympathy and sadness in their eyes rather than the scorn I had expected after our little outing to the court at Wivencaster. My mother was called across by name, 'Clara, Clara,' to the nearest group by Aunt Annie Taylor, one of her great aunts, and I saw the shock and disbelief register on her face as she was told what had occurred.

Just over two-and-a-half hours earlier, about eleven-thirty, a smart black Wolseley and an older silver-grey Singer had come down Tithe Street and driven straight down Shoe Street. The black Wolseley had stopped forty yards down outside the old bakehouse: the Maydun police sergeant, a woman police constable and, surprisingly, the vicar's wife, Anne Ffawcon, had got out and knocked on the door: Ma Parkinson's sister had opened it and, after a brief word from the vicar's wife, she had let them inside.

Ted Oldton, who lived in the former millhouse directly opposite and happened to be standing at his window when the police car drew up, called his wife over so that she would not miss what was going on: clearly something was up and together the two of them waited. Others also waited: like Lil Brown, who was in her front garden dead-heading her rose bushes: and Percy Forkes, the proud bemedalled veteran of the Boer War and India, who was washing his front ground-floor windows while his midget companion, Little Lou Ponder, sat on the roadside step smoking his pipe. Coming out of the new bakehouse with their weekly bread ration wrapped in tissue paper were Vera Cokeham and Billy Atgove's wife: all gravitated together to watch and wait.

There was a lull of a minute or so: then suddenly they heard a woman's piercing shriek through the half-opened bedroom window, followed by long moaning cries of protest and disbelief. A short while later the door opened and the limp figure of Joanne Waters was helped down the short path: she looked near to collapse and had to be helped into the back of the car by the police sergeant and the woman constable, who were each gripping one arm. The sergeant got into the driving seat, the woman constable followed Joanne Waters into the back and Anne Ffawcon and Old Ma Parkinson's sister just stood on the step watching, white faced: you did not need to be close to see that both women were crying. The car then did a three-point turn, drove back up into the Square, turned into Hedge Street and set off towards Maydun.

The silver-grey Singer, meanwhile, had continued its way down Shoe Street at a sedate twenty miles an hour: anyone observing it would have noticed that it was well down on its springs and that there were two bulky figures in the two front seats, both in uniform. At precisely eleven thirty-seven, it passed through the white gates at the bottom and bumped slowly at a speed of some ten miles an hour along the potholed track before drawing up at the front door of Boundary's Georgian farmhouse. The doors swung open and from the driver's side emerged the burly, square-jawed figure of the Hamwyte sergeant, Tucker, sixteen stone, white-haired and wearing his peak cap: from the other side the giant six-foot-six, seventeen-stone figure of the Salter constable, Dawes, struggled to get out. As they did so, a smaller, lighter, third figure emerged from the back: the Reverend Ffawcon, grim-faced and apprehensive. The Hamwyte sergeant rapped on the door and after a minute or so it was answered by a puzzled Dennis as Ma Parkinson had taken herself off to her own cottage to allow him to get ready for his wedding in peace and also, of course, to prepare herself for the big day.

A half-hour later, round about noon, the car came back up Shoe Street, still doing a modest twenty miles an hour, went straight up Tithe Street, past the church, the little redbrick school and the blacksmith's and Bowler's Rest and turned right on to the Salter road, from which it would eventually divert to Hamwyte. This time the sergeant was alone in the front and the Salter constable was sitting upright in the back: and if you had been able to look properly into the darkened interior as it went past, you would have seen a stunned, silent figure slumped forwards on the rear seat beside him, holding his head in his hands: it was Dennis Bolt: he had been arrested, too!

What the hell was going on? Ted Oldton asked his wife. Why had the police suddenly arrested a girl whose wedding was that very day and only a couple of hours before the ceremony? He needed to know because he was supposed to be a going, was he not? His wife had a different reason for wanting to know: a woman's curiosity: she was already out the door and halfway down the path even as he let the curtain fall back into place: and she was knocking on Ma Parkinson's sister's door before the Wolseley carrying the distraught Joanne Waters had got halfway along Hedge Street on its way out of the village: satisfaction was that she beat Lil Brown by a good six seconds.

All Ma Parkinson's grim-faced sister would say through the narrow gap in the door was that she had been told by the police sergeant not to say anything to anybody. She was about to close the door when, behind her, Anne Ffawcon called out that an explanation would be given by her husband as soon as he came back up from Boundary farm.

So they had gone down there, too, had they? Something was up.

SEVENTY-SIX

A SOLEMN-FACED Reverend Ffawcon eventually walked up from Boundary thirty minutes later: he went straight into Ma Parkinson's sister's, where he remained for a good hour: then as the clock ticked on towards two, he reappeared and walked slowly up into the Square, past the people already gathered there, and through the church gates. There, he took up a position outside the church porch and waited. He could do little else: he did not know who would be attending the wedding till they turned up.

As it happened, most of the farm-owning, and thus the car-owning, community in a ten-mile radius around Gledlang had been invited: they all knew Dennis and were more than willing to put on their Sunday best, pocket their bags of rice and celebrate the wedding of one of their own, even if he were John Bolt's strange, one-time workaholic nephew. The only actual farmworkers invited were Boundary's own men and their wives, those who had them, like Charlie Mangapp and his missus, and Ted Oldton and his missus and Bob Bird and his missus, Sam Perry and Tully Jude on their own and Old Ma Parkinson and us, of course.

The news, that both Dennis and Joanne had been driven away in police cars, went round the village fast enough: those who had intended to watch the wedding, mostly the women, had already been in the Square or walking to it: now they were being joined by a few of the men who had not intended to watch, but just happened to be drinking in the Chessman next door and looking out of the window at the crowd gathering. All around the Square, they now congregated in small groups to gossip and to speculate: and, of course, they would be on hand to watch the invited guests arrive and smile smugly at their embarrassment in turning up for a wedding that was not to be, possibly never to be.

The Ponting farming family were the first to arrive, followed in quick succession by the Godwins, the Peakmans, the Kemps and others, all the district's land-owning community, in fact: some of the younger wives were even dressed up to the nines in their interpretation of the so-called New Look: others, however, the older ones, were wearing what passed for their pre-war finery. Being farmers and employers, no one among the watching farmworkers or their wives was prepared to push himself or herself forward to stop them and tell them of the morning's events: everyone just stood and watched from a distance as they went up the sandy path to where the Reverend Ffawcon waited: and returned with utter disbelief registering on their faces. Some of the women were crying when they came back, dabbing at their eyes with white lace handkerchiefs, while the men trudged down the path solemn-faced, avoiding the smug faces of the onlookers. They just climbed back into their cars without saying anything and drove off.

Eventually, Charlie Mangapp cycled up, leaned his bicycle against the church wall and went hurrying up the path to speak to the vicar: someone had had the good sense to go round and tell him the bad news: after all, he was to have been Dennis's best man, so he had a right to know where they had taken the would-be bride and bridegroom. When Charlie came back down the path, he looked as stunned and ashen-faced as the others: it was while the Reverend Ffawcon was giving out his statement to Charlie that we came up into the Square.

Spotting us waiting in a small group, Charlie came over: our little group of seven or eight suddenly became twenty-eight, with more joining.

'Dennis has been arrested on a charge of something called incest,' Charlie said grimly. 'He's been taken to Hamwyte by the sergeant. I don't know when he'll be back, if at all. Most probably, after they've finished questioning him. Could be he'll be locked up in Melchborough Gaol for a while, for his own good. Whatever happens, the wedding's off. Off for good. She's been taken to Maydun, I understand, to see a doctor and to be given sedation of some kind.'

When Charlie used the word 'incest,' I saw a look of horror cross the faces of several of the women, while several of the men shifted uneasily and stared at their feet.

'Oh my Gawd!' cried one women in an anguished voice.

'Good Gawd, not that,' cried another. 'Not that!'

'Whatever next, whatever next?' exclaimed a third.

'Who'd have believed it? Who'd have believed something like that?' said a fourth, her eyes brimming with tears. 'Not that, not that of all things, and on her wedding day!'

'Better before than after it,' exclaimed a fifth, soberly.

'Makes you wonder what the world is coming to, don't it?' added a sixth.

My mother said nothing: just stood there looking as stunned as the rest: then the large group broke up into smaller groups all muttering and whispering among themselves, and all looking as confused and embarrassed as each other.

From that day forward, Dennis never set foot on Boundary again: on the Monday, Charlie Mangapp and the other men went to work as usual: they could do little else, for the animals needed to be fed and watered and there were all kinds of things to be seen to if the next year's fruit crop was to be as good as the last: even Ma Parkinson went in to dust and took Blackie into her own home, temporarily, when it became obvious Dennis would not be back.

The Salter constable eventually brought them the news which all feared, but some expected: Dennis was being kept in gaol, in the psychiatric wing, because they reckoned he might try to commit suicide if he were released and returned to live on his own. It was poppycock, in my view: Dennis might hide himself away for a few months, keeping to the farm, not venturing into the village or anything like that, but he would never have taken his own life: we knew him: we knew he would never do that. But the know-all doctors thought he might and kept him in gaol. As it turned out, because of that, I was never to see him again.

SEVENTY-SEVEN

THE FULL FACTS only came out in the court case three months later, in the January, when poor Dennis was brought up before the assizes' judge: the same one who had sentenced Billy to three years in Borstal. Most people read about it in the county weekly when it came out on the Friday, a long, ponderous, near-verbatim report which filled a whole page in the broadsheet, seven columns in all. They headlined it 'Tragic tale of farming family!' and 'Marriage of Gledlang couple called off on wedding day!' You knew it was big news by the fact that they set the headline in their biggest forty-eight-point type and added exclamation marks.

'A 26-year-old Gledlang man appeared at Melchborough Assizes on Tuesday and admitted to having committed incest with his 23-year-old sister,' the introduction ran. 'The Gledlang man, Dennis Ernest Bolt, a farmer ...' Etcetera.

Sister! Joanne Waters his sister! My God, Dennis had been shagging his sister for at least a couple of months: he had been taking her into the long grass along the seawall since the second week she had come to Gledlang. And she was his sister! Oh my God, Dennis! Oh my God, what a laugh! Still, it did explain a few things which people had suddenly begun to recall: that they looked very alike: had similar features, same nose, same smile, same eyes, same build, same way of laughing even. That's why people were pleased when it was announced that they were going to get married: they were made for each other. Yes, it was obvious now: you could see it as plain as day: brother and sister, of course: but not knowing it. Poor buggers! That's why they got on so well together: they were the same: born to the same mother. And different fathers? Well, no, as it turned out: Dennis Bolt and Joanne Waters had been born to the same father as well, so they were not half-brother and half-sister, but truly were brother and sister.

But how? They had different names: she was a Waters, he was a Bolt: she had lived most of her life in Devon and Wiltshire: Dennis had grown up in Gledlang since he was a toddler, since his mother, Beattie, had brought him to Boundary when he was four: so how could they be brother and sister? Simple: Beattie was not Dennis's real mother and Hettie Waters was not Joanne's real mother: there was a third sister, Miriam, much younger than the other two and wayward, very wayward, it seems: she was the mother of both of them!

The county weekly's headline was taken from the defending barrister's opening speech: 'As tragic a tale as you are ever likely to hear, m'Lud,' he told the judge. 'The mother of these two unfortunates was a weak-minded girl, named Miriam Bolt, who came from a good farming family, who were of yeoman stock and lived in a remote area in the county of Hampshire. She was the youngest of three sisters by all of fifteen years and, by all accounts, her late birth to an ageing mother already in her forties, unfortunately, as it sometimes does, rendered her somewhat deficient, backward, m'Lud, and retarded morally, as well as mentally. When she was a girl of about twenty, her mother having died, she quarrelled bitterly with her father and left the family home and went to live in Portsmouth, where she met, and subsequently began co-habiting with, a merchant seaman. They lived off his money when he was at home, but, as he was away at sea for long periods, six months or more at times, she obtained work waitressing to support herself and refused her family's pleas to return home. She and the seaman, one Ernest Edgar Spencer, did not marry, m'Lud and, by all accounts, there was intemperate drinking at times and both were known to the local constabulary. After a year of co-habitation, the girl, Miriam Bolt, gave birth out of wedlock to a son, the first of her children, whom she named Dennis, and who retained her family name as she was still unmarried, though her co-habitué's name does appear on the birth certificate as the father, as indeed he does on the birth certificates of both these unfortunate people. After the birth of the son, Dennis, the father Ernest Spencer returned to sea and, while he was away, the woman's own father, the last of her elderly parents, also died. It was at this time, m'Lud, that the daughter, Miriam, became certifiably mentally ill. She had a severe breakdown, became deranged and, due to her state of mind and to the fact that she was unmarried, in intemperate company, living on her own and unable properly to look after the child, it was decided that she be sectioned and committed and the child, Dennis, taken from her. In due course, the child, went to live with the woman Miriam's two older spinster sisters at the family home in Hampshire, adopted, so to speak, by one of those sisters, Beattie Bolt. In the event, the family's farm had to be sold to meet the debts of the father and the eldest of the two sisters, Beattie, brought the boy to live with a relative – actually a second cousin – one John Bolt, a bachelor, of Boundary Farm, Gledlang, where, I understand, she kept house and the boy has lived ever since. I am told he grew up knowing nothing of his family's history, especially of his true mother and true father. All details of his true mother's incarceration were kept from him. Indeed, I understand that the sister Beattie, having no children of her own, told both the child and his so-called "uncle" that she was the mother, he having been born out of wedlock, and that was generally believed by all who knew her. Certainly, from his earliest years, the defendant Dennis Bolt believed her to be his mother and even on her deathbed no one told him anything different. I should add, m'Lud, he has never seen his own birth certificate. About a year after the defendant Dennis Bolt had been taken to Gledlang, his mother, the woman Miriam, was released from the institution and immediately took up again with the seaman Spencer. She made no attempt to contact her son and neither, it seems, did her common-law husband, the boy's father, if indeed he knew or cared where he was. In due course, as a result of her renewed liaison with Spencer, a second child, a girl, was born, again out of wedlock, whom she named Joanne. I can confirm that, according to records kept by the registrar at the Portsmouth maternity hospital, the name of the father appearing on the record of birth is the same as the name of the father appearing on the record of birth of the first child, Dennis, by that time living in Gledlang. Sad to say that, soon after the birth of the second child, Spencer, the father, returned to sea and was killed in a shipboard accident. The shock to the woman Miriam was such that she was re-incarcerated and subsequently died soon after by her own hand. Suicide by drowning, m'Lud, in a stream running alongside the institution. In a sisterly act of compassion, as the first sister had taken the boy, Dennis, the second sister, Hettie, who had by this time married a bachelor farmer named Waters and gone to live in Devon, agreed to take the second child, Joanne. In doing so, she gave the child her own married name of Waters, though no formal application for adoption or change of name was ever made. The baby girl was simply passed off as Joanne Waters, child of Hettie and Harold Waters. The aunt herself was childless, having married in her forties, so it is understandable, m'Lud, that she should take her sister's infant and rear it entirely as her own. They were simple people, m'Lud, totally unaware of the precepts of the law. Like her brother before her, Joanne Waters, grew up believing the woman with whom she lived was her mother and was never told anything different, either by her supposed mother or her supposed father. When he died, she continued to live with her supposed mother using the name Waters. Like her brother, she did not learn of the deception and the details of her parentage and his parentage till the time of her arrest. That is the full and complicated tale, m'Lud.'

A 'humph' from the judge most likely at this point, not recorded by the county weekly.

The defending barrister continued. 'Thus the two children, who were brother and sister, remained with their supposed parents for the next twenty years and more, not knowing of each other's existence, one at Gledlang, the other in Devonshire, and each believing the person with whom they were living was their true mother. Beattie Bolt, the elder sister, who had taken the child Dennis, died before the war when the boy was eleven and he was reared by his uncle once removed, John Bolt, himself now dead. The second sister, Hettie Waters, who had taken in the girl, died during the war. It was only when the uncle, John Bolt, died earlier this year, rather tragically, that the two defendants learned of each other's existence through a letter, informing her of her uncle's death and her "cousin's" existence, though we now know, m'Lud, that he was not, in fact, her cousin, but her brother.'

The judge: 'So a letter passed between them provoked this whole sorry affair? Who sent that?'

'We do not know, m'Lud. We only know it was someone who thought they were doing good, whereas they succeeded only in doing harm. It were better it had never been sent, m'Lud. I think we all agree on that?'

That bit I read several times: I could not believe what the barrister had said: I sent the letter to help Dennis: there is no dishonour in that!

'Whoever sent the letter, m'Lud,' the barrister continued, 'it arrived at the house in Devon, where the girl, still calling herself Joanne Waters, had formerly lived with her supposed mother, Hettie Waters, and it was passed on to her. Until that time, she knew nothing of her cousin's – or, I should say, her brother's – existence and he nothing of her existence. I do stress, m'Lud, that when the defendant Waters went to Gledlang, it was her intention to seek out family ties which thus far had been denied her. She went to meet a man whom she was told was her cousin, and who believed himself to be that and who, subsequently, we are sad to inform you, acted in a manner in which it is quite legal for cousins to act, but not brother and sister. That is, certain incidents occurred which have brought us here today.'

'You mean they had sexual intercourse together?'

'Yes, m'Lud, repeated sexual intercourse.'

'How many times? Are we talking several times, more than a few times or many times?'

'More than several, m'Lud. At least twenty-five or thirty times, according to the two defendants, in the few months they have known each other.'

A raised eyebrow by the judge, again not recorded, and a shuffling of his papers as he peered at his pre-trial depositions. 'Twenty-five or thirty times in four months! Goodness gracious! And they were not yet married?' But then they were young and the judge was well over sixty and probably had not been able to do it for years.

The defending barrister just spread his hands as if to say, 'What can I say?'

What he actually did say was: 'Yes, m'Lud, repeated sexual intercourse.' Or, as it was described in the sniggering conversations in the Chessman: 'They were going at it like two rabbits in a sack!'

The judge again: 'And they both admit all of this? There is no question that it did not happen?'

'None whatsoever, m'Lud. They both admit that sexual intercourse took place on the number of occasions specified. It was not wild abandon, m'Lud. The two had become engaged to be married and, indeed, the sadness of this tale is that, they were both arrested and informed of the facts of their relationship to each other on the very morning of their wedding.'

'Three hours beforehand, so I understand, Mr. Buthnot?'

'You are indeed correct, m'Lud. Three hours before they were due to be married. I do stress, m'Lud, that at no time, when they indulged in sexual intercourse, when the banns were read, right up to the morning of their wedding, did the woman, Joanne Waters, have any idea whatsoever that her "cousin" Dennis Bolt, was, in truth, her brother. And he had no idea whatsoever that she, in truth, was his sister.'

'How did all this come to light then?' asked the judge, thoroughly relishing the tale, though that, too, was never reported by the county weekly.

'The woman's birth certificate was required as proof of her status as a United Kingdom resident and as a spinster. She did not have one of her own, but knew she had been born in a Portsmouth maternity hospital. The brother, Dennis Bolt, also had no birth certificate to hand either, but also knew he had been born in a Portsmouth maternity hospital. The priest sent for both certificates. There was some delay in obtaining them due to the severe bombing inflicted on that city during the war and the dislocation that ensued. It took several weeks, m'Lud. The calling of the banns of marriage had gone ahead, pending their arrival. Eventually, through birth dates alone, the registrar was able to track down the record of their births in the same maternity hospital and he sent the details to the Reverend Ffawcon as requested. It was only on receipt of both certificates late on the Friday afternoon before the wedding on the Saturday that the picture became clear, that indeed they were brother and sister, born of the same mother and the same father, but separated for over twenty years. The vicar in charge was about his business and did not return till late to read them. Due to the nature of the matter, he immediately contacted the sergeant at Hamwyte police station and on the Saturday morning he telephoned through to Portsmouth to verify the facts as we know them.'

Poor old Dennis! Poor Joanne Waters! Their story was printed in the daily newspapers as well: the whole of England read about them in varying degrees of newsworthiness: a splash headline in the *Daily Mirror* and ten tightly written paragraphs, a second page lead in the *Daily Express*, the *Daily Graphic* and the *Daily Mail* and smaller pieces of four long-winded paragraphs in the greyer papers, the *Daily Telegraph* and the *Manchester Guardian*. *The Times*, as was to be expected, never printed a word of it.

They gave Dennis two years in Melchborough Gaol and reckoned that was lenient: he had admitted to having had sexual relations thirty times over with someone who turned out to be his unknown sister: probably due to the number of times he had done it, the law blamed him first and her second. The blind ass of the law saw him as the instigator of any and all activity between the two when those who, like me, knew Dennis and who had seen Joanne fawning over him, squeezing his arm, rubbing the inside of his thigh right in front of me while he was driving the van and smiling as she did it, and letting him squeeze her breasts while she was standing in front of me – they, like me, knew it was not his fault. Ten to one, she had taken him by the hand the first couple of times and led him down into the long grass: the chances are, too, that she had unbuttoned her blouse for him and unfastened her own brassiere as he would not have known how the first time: she probably unbuttoned his flies and pulled up her own dress. That is my belief, anyway, but they punished Dennis for it: but then nobody ever listened to me.

Joanne? Oh, she was placed on probation for a year: she went back to Devon and was never heard from again.

SEVENTY-EIGHT

IF ONE WEEK after the wedding was called off, with the whole district talking about it, bloody Hoary had not attended Gledlang's Remembrance Day service and parade, perhaps what happened would not have happened: but he did and it did.

Six years of war, bombings, privations, hope without hope till the Americans came in, and pride in the eventual victory, meant that on that Sunday there was a full patriotic turnout of both marchers and onlookers. I will not make fun of them because they were remembering the three from Gledlang who had died in the Second War – Ted Ponder's son, Peter, in North Africa, Arthur Townsend in Burma, and chubby Charlie Kempen lost at sea. The widow and two mothers of the three dead were to lead the parade and those who had served were to follow: like many who fought in uniform, the latter were in civvies, but wearing their medals: behind them, all in uniform, came Bert Brite's Home Guard detachment, who never fired a shot in anger. In fact, the only shots they fired were when the Home Guard were trying out a new kind of improvised mortar: we all watched one Sunday morning as they aimed it at a derelict farm cart set up as a target in a field down by the Shoe: they missed with all three shots. Just as well it was not an approaching Tiger tank!

Two serving soldiers home on leave, Chris Huffy's older brother Charlie and Don Kempen, National Servicemen both and only two years older than me, were in the parade, along with a couple of Land Army girls, a half-dozen bemedalled older men from the First War, and the village's four Women's Royal Voluntary Service members, also in uniform, led by Lady Judkin in slouch hat and gold braid. Sam Gale, the special constable, was on hand to direct the 'traffic,' two cars, the Bourne Brothers' single-decker noonday bus and a dozen village boys riding on bicycles to keep up with the marchers.

And, of course, Hoary was there, too, with his homburg hat, gold-topped cane and a row of impressive medals which shamed a few who questioned whether pacifists like him should be allowed to attend at all: but he had dead friends, too, and as much right to be there as his detractors: more so, as one of his medals was the Military Cross or some such.

Standing before the crucified Christ on the sacred ground in front of the church as the wreaths of poppies and the individual wreaths were laid, the old fool had looked about him and noted how scruffy the churchyard appeared: then he had one of his madcap ideas. For some reason he decided that the dead would be happier if the place were tidied: if the long grass growing between the graves and obliterating some were cut, if the weeds were all hacked down, if the leaves which had been falling from the elms all through October were swept up and if the smaller, wrought-iron grave markers, which had sagged sideways over the decades because no one tended them, were straightened.

'And wouldn't it be nice if we planted some daffodils and tulip bulbs and some snowdrops and bluebells to flower in the spring?' he said to the Reverend Ffawcon after the marchers had dispersed, mostly into the Chessman. The Reverend Ffawcon thought it a 'capital idea': after all, that way he would get work done which needed doing and get it done for nothing.

'I'll get Richard and young Joseph to do it,' Hoary declared. 'And young Stanley. He has written to say he is due back from London next weekend and has asked if he can earn a few shillings. We'll do it next week.' Hoary was as oblivious to the stone-throwing incident involving Stanley as he was to the disaster of Dennis Bolt's and Joanne Waters's wedding a week previously, simply because no one had bothered to tell him about either.

So, along with Richard and I, Stanley was recruited: in truth, I had enough work still to do on Norsea, but, after the exertions of August and September and then October, I decided I needed a break from work, well, from farm work: and what better way to have a break from work than to join one of Hoary's mad excursions. So I agreed to do it: at least it would get me off Norsea and would be something different to do.

The following Sunday, I just told my mother I was going to the mainland with Hoary and Richard and that I would not be back till teatime: I did not tell her why: had she known exactly what I was going to do, she almost certainly would have said something like: 'Why can't those lazy blighters in the village do it?' The answer was quite simple: because the tight-fisted churchwardens were not willing to pay anyone to do it: they wanted it done by volunteers and no one had volunteered. The church council had purchased a scythe, but as yet no one had used it or so much as offered to pull up a weed and there were plenty of them: it was like a jungle in there. The whole churchyard, except for the small square of lawn in front of the Calvary memorial, which the vicar himself had cut, was a tangle of high grass, spreading bushes, low-branched trees, docks, thistles, dandelions, ragwort, stinging nettles and brambles.

With no car, we had to rely on a smug Sligger Offin to pick us up early on the Sunday with the implements lodged on the back seat between Richard and myself: for some reason, Richard was not in a good mood that day: perhaps his ribs still smarted, or perhaps he had just got out of the wrong side of the bed: who knows? From the first, I was apprehensive about him joining us: though he tried to hide it, he still flinched on occasions when he made a sudden movement. He was mostly back 'helping' Hoary by then: the only work I was planning to do on Norsea in the following two weeks or so was to lift the sugar beet and my mother and I could do that on our own. When I asked the inevitable questions, he said, dismissively: 'Don't worry, I'll be all right' and 'Yes, I'm sure.'

Although a week had passed since the Remembrance Day parade, the poppy wreaths and the other flowers were still leaning against the base of the Calvary memorial or spread before it on the grass: flowers lying before a memorial to the dead always bring a lump to my throat and make me blink a little more quickly as I go past.

Stanley Lobel was waiting for us right at the back of the churchyard, with his bicycle nearby as if he were ready for a quick getaway: he was looking about him apprehensively and appeared very relieved when he saw Richard and I unloading the implements, though he never came forward to the front of the church to help us. Still, I was pleased to have him there as I could not imagine Richard doing overmuch of the heavier work in his condition.

We dumped the spades, shovels, forks, planks, shears and hooks near the porch. First we had to clear the grass: so I fetched the church council's unused scythe from the shed and set about scything with it, which is as monotonous a task as any other, while Richard and Stanley, at Hoary's direction, cleared an area near the path of rubbish, small fragments of marble from broken grave surrounds, various rusty bits and pieces, a broken gardening fork and some smashed and useless vases which had once adorned older and now forgotten graves. Hoary had obtained some rose bushes from somewhere and, while I continued scything, Stanley and Richard began digging a circle in which to plant them, in their carelessness and a certain grumpy callousness, judging from Hoary's anguished cries, totally obliterating the grave of some poor old biddy who had been lowered into the earth there in the middle of the Nineteenth Century when Victoria was on the throne, when our Empire was still growing and the cowboys were still fighting the Indians in America. Still, she would not know, would she? She had been dead for over eighty years and no one living remembered her.

When it got near to half-ten, I worked my way nearer to the path just to see who among the village's religious would come through the gate before eleven: about forty did in all, the usual gaggle of village girls, who smiled at me because they were amused by my appearance and the work I was doing there, especially as Hoary was very prominent nearby, barking out directions to Richard and Stanley. They both got some queer looks from some of the adults, Richard because of his face, I presume, and Stanley because he was a known Jew and was working in a Christian graveyard: a few lips curled at that sight of him.

I know my Ten Commandments, if I know little else, and there were a few hypocrites going into the church that morning: one or two did stop to pass comment on what we were doing, generally of the order 'About bloody time someone did summat,' or 'See if you can bury that daft bugger, Hoary, while you're at it!'

The two biggest hypocrites came up the path together just before the service began – Denny Caidge and Matt Cobb, of all people, with their waddling wives, sundry relatives and offspring moping along behind. You did not see those two reprobates near a church very often, unless they were stealing the lead from the roof, or in one unless they were stealing the candlesticks off the altar: actually to see them go into a church for a service in their Sunday-best suits, albeit their demob suits, chalk stripe, navy blue, single-breasted and the wrong fit on both of them, was a revelation!

Daft Hoary just happened to have chosen to begin the work the very morning that Denny Caidge's new baby was to be christened: what started my laughter was the sight of Denny Caidge himself proudly wheeling the pram, cigarette in mouth, hair plastered back, brood all around him: there was something so incongruous about it that I could not help myself. It was more of a broad grin than a laugh, but it did not escape the hawk eyes of Matt Cobb walking alongside him: he, I supposed, was there to offer himself as a godparent, something else which made the brain boggle.

When he saw the three of us, he whispered something out of the corner of his mouth to Denny Caidge and I had to turn quickly away: it may have been about me, it could have been about Richard or even about Hoary: but I sensed it was about Stanley being there, for both Denny Caidge and Matt Cobb glowered in his direction and I saw Denny Caidge's anxious-faced wife tug at his sleeve as they turned into the porch: his face was still turned to look towards Stanley when they disappeared from view.

SEVENTY-NINE

WHEN THE churchgoers started to come out at noon, I made sure that I was scything at the farthest end of the churchyard, tucked away in a corner, well out of view, especially that of Denny Caidge and Matt Cobb. Stanley, Richard and Old Hoary were digging a second circular flower bed and putting in the tulip, daffodil and crocus bulbs: our two friends took another long, hard look at Stanley as they headed off down the path towards the Chessman and a celebration drink with their wives: it was enough to make me go cold. Only when they had gone did I work back into the centre, lay my scythe and hook aside and perch myself on one of the table-top tombs to eat my lunch.

Richard and Stanley joined me, but it was not a happy mealtime: all I wanted to do was to eat my jam sandwiches and my apple, drink my bottle of cold tea, smoke a cigarette and then get on with the job: but, between the two of them, they managed to bore me rigid.

On the one side was Stanley, pontificating about art and boasting about the sights and temptations of London and the art school girls, who, according to him, all seemed to believe in 'free love' and were giving it away to anybody they fancied: it just made me angry and jealous.

Stanley had changed in the few weeks he had been up in London: he was certainly not the old Stanley I had known, the laughing and joking, glad-to-have-a-friend Stanley. No longer was he the rural boy from a backroad the other side of Tottle: he had become the big city student. Artists, he seemed to be saying, were, by the nature of their profession, intellectual and, therefore, he was an intellectual. 'If you are that much of an intellectual, Stanley,' I thought, 'what are you doing digging holes in an overgrown churchyard in a back-of-beyond village like Gledlang?' Perhaps I should have asked him, just to bring him down a peg or two?

Richard was no better, banging on about life, God and religion, the way he did sometimes with Hoary: I suppose it was inevitable that, sitting in a graveyard surrounded by the dead, you would discuss death: it was just that it was one subject I did not wish to discuss, or to be lectured about. I knew he had been back up to London the previous day because I had seen him dressed up and crossing the causeway: he had returned late at night, depressed and embittered, and it did not take a genius to understand why. I doubt that he went to see Laura Wilchard, if he even knew her address: Pocklington would not have let him in, anyway. My guess was that he had been back to the half-demolished block of apartments, hoping, with 'one last try,' to establish contact somehow with the woman Jean and had returned disillusioned and frustrated: there was still no letter and no news. Now he was taking that frustration out on anyone with whom he got into conversation: namely, Stanley and myself.

Seeing the Reverend Ffawcon disappearing down the church path towards the gate, Richard gestured towards all the leaning gravestones and mounds of hummocked grass and asked with a sneer: 'All these dead people him and all the other vicars have buried over the years – do you think for one moment that they're up in Heaven looking down at us the way they tell you?' He answered his own question before I could reply. 'Of course, they're bloody not! People don't go to Heaven. They don't have souls. They lie in the ground and rot. The dead are just bloody skeletons now, what remains of them, still six feet down where they were put when they died – just like my mother.' Being young I gave the prospect of Heaven and death no thought whatsoever: there would be time enough for that when I neared old age.

The vehemence of Richard's outburst startled me, as did what he said next. Pointing to an overgrown corner, he said with an unexpected coldness: 'That's my mother's grave over there. Where those bushes are. I had a look at it when I first came back to see how I felt about her. Nineteen years on and nothing has changed. My own mother and I did not feel a thing. I just thought, "This is my mother's grave and I'm standing here. It's her down there." Nothing else. No sadness, no sorrow. Just "This is where my mother is now." This may be so-called consecrated ground, but I tell you, Joe, it doesn't matter whether you are six feet under in a churchyard like Gledlang's or buried in some swampy mudpatch of a cemetery in the two camps I was in the Philippines, it's all the same. When you are dead, you are dead forever, whatever else other people might say, all the priests and all the vicars like – like Ffawcon – 'A sideways glance at Stanley here. ' – or your rabbis.'

I had heard Richard say similar things a dozen times before in his cottage parlour, so it was not so shocking to me as it must have been to Stanley, religious or not, hearing it for the first time. What he thought of it all, he did not say, but it was enough to make him jump down off the table-top tomb, on the pretext of going for a pee, and to escape round the side of the church.

Stanley's disappearance did not stop Richard and I suffered another couple of minutes of it before I, too, jumped down. Just as I did so, I heard a shout from the front of the churchyard, near the road, followed by other shouts. I knew whose voices they were straight away: those of Denny Caidge and Matt Cobb: and the one that gave the cry of pain was Stanley Lobel's.

EIGHTY

WHAT MAKES people do things they should never attempt would fill a book: why I did what I did, I will never know: it was not out of gallantry or anything foolish like that: I suppose I just wanted to see what exactly was happening because an untrimmed cypress tree was blocking my view and what happened came naturally because of that. When I heard the shouts, I was off and running, straight towards the fracas: what had happened I took in at a glance.

Stanley was sprawled on the ground on top of the wreaths which had been laid before the concrete Christ: and standing over him, kicking at him with their size ten boots, were Denny Caidge and Matt Cobb.

After he left us, Stanley had gone round to the front of the church and, casually, as one would, had begun reading the cards on the wreaths of poppies and flowers laid before the memorial: all told, there must have been twenty there, from the widow, the two mothers, aunts and uncles, brothers and old friends: though, mercifully, none from any fatherless children. As fate would have it, the window of the Chessman big room looks out directly on to the front of the churchyard: Denny Caidge and Matt Cobb, drinking with their wives and relations, had seen Stanley. He must have been too intent on turning over the black-edged cards to read what was written upon them to hear the pair as they came running through the church gate: so they were upon him before he had a chance to flee, which anyone with any sense would have done from those two. As Stanley jumped to his feet, Denny Caidge floored him with a haymaker punch and, as I ran up, he and his cohort, Matt Cobb, had already begun to put the boot in, one positioning himself to kick at Stanley's legs and groin, the other at his ribs and head.

'We don't want bloody Jew boys like you buggering about with our flowers,' Matt Cobb shouted as his boot thudded into Stanley's groin. 'We've had enough of your effing lot in Palestine. We don't want your effing mitts on our effing flowers!'

'It's a pity Hitler didn't get you as well, you bloody bastard Jew boy!' Denny Caidge was snarling, aiming his kick at Stanley's head. He, meanwhile, had tucked up his legs to protect himself as best he could down below, with one arm raised before his face to ward off the blows aimed there.

To this day I do not know what made me do what I did: a sudden rush of blood to the head? Or more likely it was because the softness of the mown grass there allowed me to run up behind Denny Caidge and catch him unawares. He had just aimed a third kick at Stanley's face when, to my own surprise, I found myself swinging my own boot at his backside. I even adopted the Ronnie Rooke stance as I did it, balancing on one leg, left knee slightly bent, arm folding across the chest as your foot flies through, just as you saw the footballers doing on the cigarette cards: it was a kick that would have graced a Wembley Cup Final. The only trouble was I was slightly off target and connected with the bottom of Denny Caidge's spine rather than the fat bulge of his behind: better still, I thought, as I felt my steel-rimmed toecap strike bone.

Denny Caidge gave a yelp of pain like a castrated dog and swung round, a look of black fury on his face: I saw his arm draw back and the clenched fist start its swing, but I was unable to avoid the blow. My shot for 'goal' had taken me well within range and, being slightly off balance, I was unable to get away. There was a sickeningly violent blow against the left side of my face, encompassing nose, cheekbone and eye socket: I remember going upwards briefly and then toppling backwards. All the breath was knocked out of me as I hit the ground and the curtain descended: my head throbbed in waves of pain and dizziness. I suddenly realised I was on my knees, head hanging down, blood pouring from my nose and a gashed eye. The next second what I can only suppose was the toe end of Denny Caidge's boot thudded into my mouth and lower jaw, for I tasted and smelled black boot polish: a second kick struck me hard on the bridge of the nose and across the eyes.

'That one's for your friend Billy,' I heard Denny Caidge shout.

Scarcely able to breathe, with my head swimming and half the stars in the universe whirling in a red haze before my eyes, I could only gasp with the pain and await the third kick, knowing that it would be the one to send me under and desperately trying, yet failing, to get to my feet.

The kick never came: somewhere nearby, vaguely, I heard a shout, like an angry warning, then there was a ringing clang of metal striking what I supposed was hard bone, followed by an angry bellow of pain, another blow, more shouting, yet another blow, more of a dull thud this time, and another different angry cry of pain followed by a fourth dull thud, all to the accompaniment of shouts and curses.

It was Richard: when he had heard the shouting begin and had seen me start to run, he had realised immediately what was happening and had followed: but so intent had I been on getting there and stopping Denny Caidge and Matt Cobb from kicking Stanley – well, deterring them – I had not even realised he was following or that he was carrying a shovel. He told me later that his first blow with the back of the shovel caught Denny Caidge smack in the face just as he was about to land the third kick on me: the force of it sent him crashing to the grass like a pole-axed Nepalese bull, with blood streaming from his mouth and nose and from a four-inch gash above his left eye where the edge of the shovel had sliced open the skin.

Richard gave him a second to keep him down and then turned on Matt Cobb: his third blow caught Matt Cobb across the upper left arm and shoulder before he could dodge away and a fourth hit him on the chest, sending him toppling backwards to crush most of the flowers he was trying to protect from Stanley's 'taint.' The yells I heard were him mouthing obscenities as he clutched at both arm and shoulder, bleating that he thought they were broken: unhappily, they were not.

I saw none of this: I only heard it: there was still shouting going on as I felt Richard's arms lifting me to my feet: I heard him asking me if I were all right and I remember mumbling a reply through painful lips. The left side of my face was already beginning to throb and to swell: my left eye had closed and my right eye was closing: one cheek felt as though it had been split to the bone: my lips felt as though someone had sliced half of them off and my jaw was so numb I was convinced it was not there.

The next couple of hours are something of a blur to me: I was so groggy that all I remember is the feel of Richard's arms around my waist as he helped me towards the gate. I vaguely remember being half-carried, half-walked past the cottages down Shoe Street: I also remember being carried for a time and then stood on the gravel of Boundary's chase and on the shale of the causeway while whoever was carrying me rested, then being lifted and shouldered again. My next memory is of my mother bending over me as I lay on my bed, not so much scolding me as being critical of my state and the stupidity of how I had achieved it: then warm water was being wiped across my mouth, eyes and cheek with a flannel, followed by the sting of iodine being applied.

The last thing I recall before I fell asleep was my mother saying to someone standing the other side of the haze curtain: 'He'll be all right now. Perhaps next time he'll keep his nose out of other people's business! Bloody little fool! However did I have him?'

EIGHTY-ONE

I AWOKE to find my mother's blurred shape yet again standing by the side of the bed, looking down at me.

'I've brought you some bread and butter and soup,' she said, touching my shoulder.

Soup! 'Soup for breakfast?'

'It's not breakfast, it's lunchtime,' snapped my mother, irritated because I had not worked that one out for myself: how was I to know I had been asleep for almost twenty hours and with a fever?

When I struggled up to look in the washstand mirror, my face was a nasty shade of purple and yellow, swollen on one side like a child with mumps. I could just about see out of one eye, the right, as the left was still closed: I looked like some boxer who had taken a twelve-round battering from Joe Louis. I was just pleased to see all my teeth were still there.

'I've been round to see Richard and he says he will see to Molly,' my mother said before departing. 'He says he doesn't mind feeding and watering her and putting her out to grass till you're better.'

I stayed in bed all that day and the next: not a bad way to spend your seventeenth birthday! I was still recovering on the Thursday, when Princess Elizabeth married Prince Philip in London: at least, I got a day off and was able to listen to it on the wireless in the parlour along with my mother, which is more than the rest of the country did. The skinflint Labour Prime Minister, Clement Attlee, refused to declare the day a public holiday to allow the people to celebrate: he gave some feeble excuse that he could not permit 'the luxury of a public holiday while potatoes were still rationed!' What poppycock! I bet the potato rationing did not prevent all those champagne socialists from Eton and Harrow in the Government, who claimed to represent the working classes to whom they never spoke, from enjoying themselves at the taxpayers' expense.

Richard called to see me twice, coming the first time in the evening after I had awoken: he was most concerned about the way I looked, but in the end, as people do, we managed to make a joke of it. 'Your face looks like one of those abstract paintings Stanley was talking about,' he said with a laugh, 'all purple, yellow, pink and red.' My mother, who was standing with Richard, gave him a queer old-fashioned look as if to say, 'Whatever are you talking about?'

'How is Stanley?' I asked.

'Oh, he's all right, I think,' replied Richard. 'He'll live. He's a bit bruised around the legs and ribs, but he'll be okay. I think your intervention stopped them before they had done too much damage. His face looks a bit like yours and he won't be riding his bicycle for a while, but otherwise he'll be fine. He's gone back to London, I understand.'

Lucky Stanley, he was out of it. It would be a good few months before I set foot in Gledlang on my own again while Denny Caidge and Matt Cobb were around, I thought: passing through it quickly on my bicycle was one thing, dawdling in the Square or pedalling slowly up Shoe Street hill was another. From now on, I would stay on Norsea and hope that Denny Caidge, especially Denny Caidge, would forget it was I who had kicked him up the backside, or at least had attempted to do so. Just possibly, I tried to convince myself, he might not even care, especially as he had already taken his revenge. Yes, he might not bother: but, just in case, when I did go back to work two days later, I kept one eye on the track while the tide was down: knowing Ben was not with us, Denny Caidge, might, just might, decide to pay me a visit.

But Denny Caidge did not come and when I went back to work, as I had to, my mother and I spent the whole of the next two weeks or so lifting the first of the two fields of sugar beet, myself topping them more carefully this time. The fog and drizzle came soon after we had started and we spent two miserable, grey, freezing weeks completing it, working from seven in the morning till five at night, with feet pancaked by mud and clothes and hoods soaked by the steady drizzle. Still, between us, in those two weeks we had the beet of the first field all piled in a great heap by the gate, ready to be forked into our cart and trundled across to Boundary in a dozen or more loads for the pick-up lorry from the sugar factory at Inworth: when I felt brave enough to go across and telephone him.

Eventually, I summoned up my courage and went trundling out across the causeway with Molly and the loaded-down cart. Boundary was already looking very forlorn: the farmhouse itself was shut up and dark, with the curtains drawn across all the windows like they do when someone dies: the grass was already growing long on the front lawn and unswept leaves were piled on the red-tiled step against the front door. Only Charlie Mangapp of the men had been kept on by Dennis's solicitors and then only to maintain the farm: Ted Oldton, Bob Bird and Sam Perry had already scouted out other farm jobs and Tully Jude was road-sweeping.

Charlie, since he was about the place, had taken Blackie off Ma Parkinson, kept the old dog in his own home because it fretted so much and now took it to the farm with him so that it could run about the place, sniffing for its old master, not knowing, of course, that Dennis was still locked up in the psychiatric ward at Melchborough Gaol and would not be coming back – ever: he was too ashamed. The farm was up for sale and already 'For sale by auction' notices had begun to appear on the telegraph poles along the Salter, Maydun and Tottle roads.

When I heard footfalls coming round the corner of the shed, I half expected it to be Dennis, but it was Charlie: he had been in the nearby orchard, setting rabbit snares and checking the rabbit guards round the trunks of the trees: fruit tree bark is a food source for rabbits in hard weather and young trees can be killed by them gnawing at the bark, or 'ringing' the tree, as we called it.

'I heard about your little trouble with Denny Caidge and Matt Cobb,' he commiserated, though trying not to guffaw. 'I didn't think it was that bad!'

He was still grinning as he showed me where to tip the first load beside the punnet shed so the sugar factory lorry driver would find it: fortunately for me, Charlie said he would make the call to the sugar factory so I would not need to go up into the Square: then the two of us sat talking. Charlie had been over to Melchborough Gaol on the Sunday, he told me, but poor Dennis was so mortified by the disgrace he had brought upon himself that he would not see his foreman. 'A bloody wasted journey,' said Charlie.

It was then that Charlie spoke words that sent a chill through me. 'Still,' he began, matter-of-factly, 'none of it'll matter soon, anyway.' And sweeping an arm towards the dark-shadowed orchards, he said: 'You'd better take a good look at all this, young Joe, so's you remember it, because it might not be here much longer. All this could be gone soon – all the orchards, all the plum trees, all the cherry trees, the apple trees, everything! Come, this time next year there likely 'on't be nothing between you and the Maydun road but open fields full of potatoes, I reckon.'

What did he mean?

'The Rosses from Tottle are looking to buy Boundary,' Charlie informed me, bluntly: it was stunning, devastating news.

The Rosses were a family of farmers who were known as 'the potato kings.' They were newcomers to our area, from the Lowlands of Scotland, and had already bought up two farms at Tottle. They had quickly gained a bad name among us, for they grew nothing but potatoes, field after field of them. Nothing wrong with that, of course: there was a potato shortage the length and breadth of the land and the Government encouraged it.

But, if the Rosses bought Boundary, I knew their first act would be to chop down all the orchards: all the thousands of trees. There would be no more tunnels of pink and white blossom for me to ride through in the spring, no more Golden Victorias, purple Pershaws, black cherries, Cox's Orange, Worcester Pearmain, Red Pippin or Salter Spice apples or Conference pears to steal off the trees and hide in my coat: there would be nothing but bare brown earth and flatness, and endless lines of potato plants as far as the eyes could see.

Please, God, if you are there, I remember thinking, not my fruit trees, not my beautiful fruit trees: over a hundred-and-fifty years of fruit farming gone forever: row after row of old, rough-trunked trees, under which I and the village women had scrabbled and against which I had rested my back on many a sunlit lunchtime working with Billy and the others – please do not let them be sawn down and piled into heaps to be burned like so much waste: just to grow potatoes! What a horrible prospect: I suddenly felt very nauseous.

Was this to be the outcome of my sending that letter to Joanne Waters all those months before, the destruction of the orchards, my beautiful orchards? I was so upset at the thought of the thousands of trees being hewn down, trees I loved, all lying on the grass, that I had to wipe a bit of dirt from my eye...

EIGHTY-TWO

AS WE SAT there on the wooden benches of the punnet shed, I was at first too stunned to think of anything to say: to hide my mortification, I busied myself fumbling in my tobacco tin so as to roll one of my Darkie Shag wisps: Charlie calmly did the same. In the end, in desperation to break the silence, just to make conversation somehow, I asked him about Richard's mother: had he known her? What was she like? What happened between Richard and her and Ben? Ever since Richard's outburst in the churchyard, I had again taken to wondering about him and his mother and how the few facts I knew fitted what I had overheard between Ben and my mother.

'She were a funny one, Dick's mother. She weren't right up here,' said Charlie, tapping his temple, 'more's the pity, because she were a real good-looker, at least she were when she first come here, so you can't blame Ben for having married her. She were the daughter of a Congregational preacher over Inworth way. Used to take the Sunday school there and, by all accounts, she were a bright woman, a teaching assistant in the infants' school there when Ben met her so she must have had a brain in her head. Ben were a good looking chap hisself when he were younger. Farm bailiff on the Inworth estate. Had prospects. I don't want to cast any – any – ' He fumbled for the word. ' – aspersions on anyone, but if you look at Dick's birth date and then the date of her and Ben's wedding, you'll see they ain't too far apart, if you gets my meaning. Not that she's the first to go down that road and nothing agin her if she did. But I reckon Ben had to marry her, if you gets my meaning, and that ain't a good way to start a marriage, is it? Dick took after his mother in one thing at least – his brains. She saw to that. Always schooling him, she were, making him learn – Bible lessons, English lessons, reading books, counting and that. It were solely down to her that Dick were one of the brightest boys they've ever had at the village school – brightest by a long chalk – couldn't help but be with a mother like her – but he paid a high price for it, a high price. One thing's for sure, he were never cut out to be a farm worker. Not like you and I. Nor was he ever going to turn out like Ben.'

Charlie blew out smoke. 'My missus says it were Dick's birth that turned her funny. It does some women. Something goes wrong inside their heads. Just seeing her on the track, she looked no different to any other woman. But when you'd talked to her a few times, you'd realise she weren't all there. She used to have these weird turns, so Old Sago said. He used to work over there with Ben till Dick left school. He told me that some days Ben would go back to the house at dinnertime and find her sitting bolt upright in an armchair, not moving, not hardly breathing, like her heart had stopped and her brain had frozen. She'd be like it for an hour or more, not talking, hearing or seeing. Then she'd be as right as rain, like nothing had happened. Normal agin. Weird, it was. Catatonic shock, I think they call it.'

Charlie shifted his position, gave a sigh, another shake of the head and blew out more smoke.

'I always reckoned Ben knew there was something up soon after he married her, but he had married her and they had had Dick by then so he had to stick by the both on'em, didn't he? By all accounts, she just got worse – that's why he took the job on Norsea when Dick were a lad, back in the Twenties, to get her out of the way, isolate her so he wouldn't have to commit her. Certainly, there weren't much of a marriage left by the time they come here, but he must have still had some feelings for her because he still put up with it all. Yes, I reckon he brought her here to get her out of the way. No one'd come here by choice, would they? I don't think he were ashamed of her, poor gal. He just thought it would be better, safer, like. What I do know is she worrn't cut out to be the wife of a farm bailiff and she knew it. So did Ben. Not on Norsea of all places!'

More smoke spiralling into the air: the cigarette clamped between his lips, moving to the rhythm of his words.

'Her trouble was she were too religious by half, always harping on about the Bible and God and Jesus and Sin and that. Believed everything the Bible told her. Thought the Bible answered everything. Word of the Lord and all that. Some people do, don't they?'

'A religious maniac,' I offered: it explained a lot of what Richard had spoken about to me: his own sceptical beliefs, or rather absence of all belief.

'Near enough, near enough,' Charlie agreed, nodding. 'She'd have a goo at anybody, us included – me, Tully, Ted, John Bolt, even Beattie Bolt, if she felt like it. She had a goo at all of us at one time or another. It got so's you'd avoid her if you saw her coming. You didn't want your ears filled by all that. She turned Dick off it – that's for sure – and one day, just afore she died, he told her so, so Old Sago said. If you want to know anything about religion, young Joe, you ask Dick. He'll tell you. He had it drummed into him most days.'

Another shift of position as Charlie began to pocket his things.

'Don't run away with the idea she were a bad mother, she weren't, just a strange'un at times. She looked after Dick, doted on him, but she weren't above having a go at him with a broom handle if she thought he needed it. I remember one day she come up our track, asking if we'd seen Dick. "He's at school, missus," we said. "No, he's run away," she said. "No, he'll be at school, missus," we said agin. "He's not, he's run away." He hadn't, of course. He was at school. Ben were in Wivencaster that day – at the market – so we couldn't get him. It were pouring with rain that day, but she sat in this very shed all afternoon, soaked to the skin, dress, coat everything, shivering like she'd got pneumonia. When Dick come, she laid about him, slapping him for leaving her, cursing him, but he – he just took it all, then he took her by the hand and walked her back across to Norsea. I saw it so I know! Weird, she was, weird.'

Charlie was on his feet now, finishing the last of his cigarette. 'The real problem came at the end, though, when she took to banging her head agin the wall not long afore she died. I know Ben found her more'n once bleeding all over the place, so I expect Dick did, too. She should have been committed, but she weren't. I suppose Ben just couldn't bring himself to do it. It takes a lot to put your own wife into an asylum, knowing what those places were like then: and knowing, that once she went in, she wouldn't be coming out. Dick and Ben both tried to look after her as best they could, I suppose, but she just got worse.'

'When did she die?' I asked, wanting to get to the end of the story.

Charlie paused to scuff the toe of his boot in the dirt, at an imaginary beetle perhaps. 'Died in the January o' Twenty-Eight. Some sort of queer brain disease, they reckoned. It shrunk the brain. That's why she went funny. Trouble was, a week afore she died, she and Dick had a real set-to in their yard. A bad one. She went at him with the broom handle for some reason or other, like she used to do when he were a kid. But this time he took it off her and laid into her with it. Shouldn't hev done it, of course, not to his own mother, but I expect he'd just about had it by then. Old Sago was pieceworking over there at the time and he had to run into the yard to stop Dick or he reckons he would have killed her. Said Dick were in a terrible state after that. Wouldn't go back in the house, not even for his meals. Remorse, I reckon, especially as she went down hill fast after that, Took to sleeping in one of the cottages, he did. Same one he's in now. Washed under the pump. Ben had to take his meals to him. It were just bad luck she died a week later. Nothing to do with Dick. It were natural causes brought on by her disease. But he wouldn't go to the funeral. I remember that. Refused point-blank. Ben were real cut up about it. Their only son not wanting to see his mother off! They had a real argument about it on the day she were buried. Shouting and that. Came to blows in the end, so Sago said. Ben won, I suppose, but Dick still didn't go. That was when he and Dick parted company, so to speak. I think Ben were always hoping Dick would stay with him on the farm, you know, work alongside him, keep him company, father and son together, like, but he couldn't after that. The fight ended any hope of that. No sooner had she been buried than Dick up and left. Packed his bags in the middle of the night and cleared off the day after the funeral. No reason given. Just went. Disappeared off the face of the earth. We never saw hide nor hair on'im till he come back this year, nineteen years later. It were no wonder Ben took on the way he did.'

Again a toe scuffed in the dirt, as if he were embarrassed at having to reveal his secrets. 'Remember, Ben were an orphan himself. Dick and her had been his only family and, within a week, she'd died and Dick had done a bunk. You knew Ben were an orphan hisself, didn't you?'

I nodded: yes, my mother had told me: that is why we never had visitors from his side of the family.

'So he had no one to come visiting, no company,' said Charlie. 'He were so cut up in the months after Dick left, I think he would have topped himself if your mother hadn't come along when she did. Small wonder he were bitter when Dick come back.'

I was stunned into silence: at that moment, I felt anything I said would have sounded wrong, imbecilic, unsympathetic: so I left it to Charlie to break the silence again.

'Dick and Ben parted wrong. That's why they ain't talking. When she died, they should have come together, but they went further apart because Dick didn't stay around. Ben never did understand why. It never seemed to occur to him that it were Dick's own mother who educated the farm out of him. She schooled him as much as the old village schoolteacher herself. She wanted him to goo, I reckon. Get him away from Norsea. Take her with him! That's what I think she were at, anyway. Showing him there was more to life than landworking. She wanted him to goo and take her with him. But he stuck around with Ben, didn't he, after he left school? That's what I think the fight between Dick and his mother were about. Tragedy was, when he did goo, she were already dead. I reckon he were ashamed of what had happened, a boy striking his mother. It's sad, ain't it? Because Ben now blames Dick for leaving him on his own when he needed him most. I don't think Dick gave a thought to how bad Ben would take his going. You don't when you're young. He just wanted to get away. Felt guilty, I reckon, 'cause she'd died so soon afterwards. No more'n a week, Sago said. Now Dick's come back, he's stirred up old memories for Ben. Painful memories. You know Ben looks on you as his son now, Joe. I hope you realise that?'

I did: it was a sobering thought: and that and the possible loss of my beloved orchards remained with me all the way back to Norsea: it kept appearing at the front of my mind: at least, it did till I walked into the kitchen and found my mother standing there holding a letter and, of all things, smiling, her scorn revitalised!

'They're sending your step-father home,' she crowed, brandishing a letter at me. 'From now on, you won't be able to do as you like. You'll have to do things properly. He'll see to that.'

We were back to normal.

EIGHTY-THREE

WHEN Ben came home, we lied to him: when he asked who had done all the work on the farm, my mother and I said we had done it, with some help from Stanley Lobel, Violet Reddy, Jan the missing Polack and Old Sago while he was still with us: and Charlie Mangapp and Ted Oldton when we had ploughed and drilled. Most of it was true in one form or another: it was just the last bit which was a blatant lie. The reply from Ben was a rasping, throat-clearing cough-cum-grunt from somewhere deep down round his sternum: whether of approval or disapproval, or just phlegm-clearing, you could not tell.

After so many months in Melchborough hospital, with his innards crushed, his lower spinal cord bruised, both his thighbones broken, hip bone fractured, paralysed from the waist down half the time, doped up for weeks on end, plastered from toe to groin and having to lie flat on his back on planks, I would have thought he would have been pleased to be home. You would have expected him to be cheerful and jokey when, on the Sunday, he came home in Sligger Offin's taxi, the trip all the way from Melchborough being paid for by the authorities: you would have thought he would have been glad to be out of his hospital bed, glad to be out of hospital, glad to be home to my mother's cooking, away from the tripe they served up there: just glad to be home, in fact. If he were, he had a funny way of showing it: he was moody, morose, irritable, bad-tempered, argumentative and, above all, suspicious of everything, like he guessed there was something which we were not telling him, but which he could not yet figure out.

For a start, I hoped he would at least have acknowledged the work I had done on the farm, with a 'Thanks for keeping things going' or even, wonder of wonders, an out-of-character, even embarrassing 'Well done, Joe, boy. You've done a good job.' He did nothing of the kind: the first thing he did when he hobbled into the parlour on his two sticks and sat down in his old armchair was to ask what the bloody hell was I doing leaving the beet-lifting so late. So I told him.

Told him! It was a shouting match. Answer: the reason the lifting was so late was because we had planted them late, anyway, and because there was only my mother and me to do it!

After that came all the other questions: Had I done this? Had I done that? Why had I not done this? Why had I not done that? Because I had not had the bloody time and I was too bloody tired most days, that is why! Those and a hundred other questions.

Eventually, Ben did get round to the one question I was expecting. 'I suppose you've been seeing a lot of him?' he asked with a sour-faced grunt the next day, forking a piece of fried bread into his mouth as we sat together at our first breakfast

'Who the hell else is there to talk to on here?' I retorted. I wanted to tell him how much Richard had helped me – helped him – helped us all – helped the bloody country for that matter! – but, at my mother's insistence, I had sworn a near biblical oath not to tell: under no circumstances was I to mention how Richard had worked ten, twelve hours a day with us during harvesting, how he had helped me with the ploughing and the drilling with his injured side, short of breath and damn near to collapsing – I was to say nothing of that on pain of death or something equally as bad, like my mother's knotted wet tea-towel round my face when I was least expecting it.

Ben bristled and fixed me with one of his stares which said, 'Don't you get uppity with me, boy! I ain't so sure you're telling me the whole truth, but I'll find out what you ain't telling me, I'll find out.'

When our first breakfast ended, Ben got to his feet with difficulty: now he was home, he was eager to get round the farm: there was to be no sitting in the parlour listening to *Housewives' Choice* and *A Pause For Thought* while waiting for his strength and vigour to return: sticks or no sticks, he wanted to be out there looking. He went round with my mother and myself immediately after breakfast, slowly and painfully, gritting his teeth, determined. Though his legs were mended – at least the bones had knitted – he would be on sticks for some time to come, months, in fact: he could not put a great deal of weight on his legs as the muscles were still wasted and there was little strength in them: but at least the feeling had returned and, on his sticks, he could shuffle along reasonably well so long as the ground was not too uneven.

The months of inactivity lying in bed in Melchborough hospital had left him very thin: frail really, like an old man: it took us fully two hours of painfully slow walking, in both meanings of the phrase, to get him round and even then we did not see everything he wanted to see. He had to stop and rest about every hundred yards, then heave himself up again and shuffle along grimacing for another hundred yards: and, of course, he would not take any help from me and only from my mother as a last resort.

'I can do it, I can do it. I don't need any help,' was his constant cry, when clearly he did need help: he was in pain still, but he gritted his teeth and wheezed and wobbled along on the sticks, determined to show us he could do it: he walked more like a ninety-year-old than a sixty-year-old: it took us ten minutes to go a hundred yards. In fact, he would have been better being pushed round in a bathchair: I did think of suggesting I could get the wheelbarrow and wheel him round in that, but thought better of it: in his grumpy mood, he was bound to take that the wrong way as well.

I showed him in which field Richard and I had drilled and with what seed: perhaps our lines did weave a bit as they went down the field, but that was neither here nor there: the seeds were in and growing and come March there would be a field of luscious green sproutings. Five fields, in fact.

That still did not stop Ben criticising: the real reason for the tour was so that he could mull over what had been done and what still needed to be done: so his criticism was to be expected and it did not bother me overmuch: it was just the usual griping one would expect from a man of experience viewing a younger one's work.

My mother, of course, took umbrage: she had, after all, done much of the work with me – and Richard. 'There's no satisfying some people!' she sniffed, and added for good measure: 'You can always do the work yourself next time.'

'I was only saying, woman,' protested Ben.

'Well don't,' my mother snapped after one particular comment. 'Keep your thoughts to yourself. We did our best. You can't expect any more than that.'

I thought: 'Well, that's a good start. He's been home less than twenty-four hours and the two of them are at it already!'

Even then, things might have been all right, bearable if not enjoyable, had we not come across Hoary and Richard outside Hoary's house in Sligger Offin's taxi: the three of them were just about to set off somewhere. It was Hoary, of course, who let the cat out of the bag.

'Benjamin, Benjamin, so delighted to see you,' the old fool cried as Sligger stopped the car at the old man's insistence and he got out.

'Are you better? Are you well? I was so sorry I was unable to get to see you, but – '

I was watching Ben's face while the old fool was speaking: so was my mother: Ben was staring straight through the car's windscreen at Richard in the front passenger seat and he was staring straight back at Ben: both their faces were masks of, well, nothing: inscrutability, I suppose you would call it. To me, their features might just as well have been set in ice: there was not a flicker of emotion from either of them, not the blink of an eyelid or the twitch of a muscle: just absolute coldness, absolute indifference: feigned for pride's sake or not, it was chilling to watch. Ben just stood there staring at Richard and he just sat there staring back nervously drumming his fingers on the old man's camera tripod he held: the two of them might just as well have been looking straight through each other. If it were a confrontation of willpower, Ben lost: distracted by Hoary's questioning, he finally looked away.

'The farm has been in good hands while you have been away, Benjamin,' he cried. 'Richard and Young Joseph have worked wonderfully well together. Between them, they have kept the farm running well all the weeks you have been in hospital.'

I was already on my way down the track before he had finished, leaving my mother to help Ben home and wondering what the hell I was going to say when we faced each other again at the tea table.

When late that evening I returned to the farmhouse and nervously pushed open the kitchen door, I expected a tirade, but it did not come: Ben never said anything. In fact, he did not speak to me at all, but over the next week or so took to locking himself in the bedroom when I was about: he remained in bed till I had gone to work in the morning and was back there before I returned for my tea, having already had his own. Work, rather than being the bane of my life, became a thankful means of escape: at least I was away from the house and away from Ben sulking in his bedroom. My mother and I finished lifting, topping and carting the rest of the beet, she fed the chickens as usual and I stabled Molly as usual each evening before the dark closed in: sometimes I went round to sit with Richard as another means of escaping Ben. Quite simply, he and I just avoided each other almost as if by a sullen agreement: hardly a word passed between us: if any communicating needed to be done, my mother did it. She of all of us was the most pained, felt the sadness of the occasion the most: Ben and I were just two stubborn bulls snorting at each other from a distance. On those evenings I did not go round to Richard's, I sat in the barn till well past supper time, till I knew I could safely go to bed.

Christmas came and Christmas went with the atmosphere in the house as chill as the air outside: even Christmas day passed without a cheery remark between us: we were still not speaking to each other when Big Ben chimed in the New Year on the wireless.

EIGHTY-FOUR

I KNEW who it was hiding in the shadows even before he spoke. 'Hullo, Jan. You're back then?' I said, as casually as I could, as the figure stepped out into the moonlight.

It was a couple of weeks after the New Year: a few days before, there had been a heavy fall of snow: the whiteness of it reflected the light like it was daytime: you could see from one end of the island to the other with no difficulty at all so it was no great feat to know who it was standing under the tree. I had seen Jan's huddled figure from fifty yards off even as I walked along the track towards him, heading back to the farmhouse. He was cold and he was shivering: he had his arms folded across his chest and his teeth were chattering.

Jan greeted me and, somewhat to my embarrassment, shook my hand. 'I come back, Joe, like I say I will. I come back for Violet and Thomas. I walk across your causeway and hide till I see you. But I need somewhere to sleep, Joe. Very cold, very tired, very hungry.'

'You daft bugger,' I scolded, but not angrily, to the clicking of Jan's chattering teeth, 'you'll catch your death of cold standing out here. You need to get inside and quick or you'll freeze to death.'

There was only one place to take him – the deserted women's cottage: there was still furniture in it, a couple of chairs, the two single beds, and a table: it was also still reasonably clean. Once I had got him inside, I went off to fetch some wood from our pile: we managed to light a fire, which put a rosier complexion on things: at least it stopped Jan's shivering.

Fortunately, there was no one else on the island other than Ben and my mother: Richard, I knew, had gone up to London with Hoary on one of the latter's periodical 'essential' visits. I had been with him myself once. When I went, I had to kick my heels for an hour or so at Liverpool Street railway station on my own while Hoary took a taxi ride to Soho for whatever purpose he had in mind there, then he came back, picked me up and drove to a posh Strand hotel. While he went in the front door to dine alone in the restaurant, I went round the back where a white fiver from Hoary crossed the palm of the head waiter and I was given a cold pork and pickle sandwich and found myself loading sacks of six-day-old stale buns and cakes into a waiting taxi. When Hoary came out, we drove back to Liverpool Street and home: the stale buns and cakes were fed to Hoary's geese, though one or two were still just about edible.

So I felt no qualms when I slipped into Richard's cottage and took some water from his pail, plus a tin of soup, a saucepan, some slices of bread, some sugar and a small pat of margarine from his larder: at least it would ease Jan's hunger and give him the chance of a good sleep. He needed it, poor blighter: he told me he had been on the road for two days without eating, sleeping in the railway terminus in London before coming on to us. He had counted on his friends being in their camp somewhere nearby, but they were well away by then: fifteen or twenty miles down the coast, I would have thought.

But pleased as I was to see him, I was also irritated. 'You must want your head tested,' I told him sharply. 'You come back for her in the middle of the bloody winter. How are you going to get her and the boy away?'

'I have plan, Joe,' answered Jan. 'I go to village across causeway, bring Violet and Thomas to island. Walter never know where we are. He not think we cross river. If he look for us, he look north of river, but we on island, waiting for sea to come in. When sea come in, you row us in your long boat to Lingsea on south shore. We take bus to railway station at Eastminster, catch train to London and vanish. Poof! We are gone to Bedfordshire. Simple.'

I did not like being part of his plan, but felt I could not refuse, especially as he had come so far to carry it out: I was not going to be the one to deter him. At least, I thought, it was a reasonable plan of sorts: the question was whether he could carry it out successfully and, more to the point, secretly, without anyone seeing him. 'God help you if Walter catches you,' I told him. 'He'll bloody kill you!' And God help me, too!

'Huh, I take chance,' an affronted Jan retorted. 'I not care damn in hell about husband Walter. He stupid. You say so. I come for Violet and Thomas. I take her and him and we go. I not leave till she come and bring boy. I not care about Walter. We family together, not him.'

I had to admire the man. 'Well, it's your bloody funeral, Jan,' I said and hoped my words were not prophetic.

I got Jan bedded down for the night and went back to the farmhouse, promising to take him something else to eat the following day:

I did not tell my mother he was back and there was no point in telling Ben as he was still on his sticks and unlikely to go outside with the ground all icy and covered in compacted snow.

As it was, Jan kept himself well out of the way for the whole of that day and then slipped across the causeway just after seven o'clock, when it was pitch dark: if all went well, he would be back with Violet in an hour, the tide would be over the causeway by about nine-thirty to cut off the island and, thus, forestall any pursuit and I would be able to row them in the punt across to Lingsea and, it was to be hoped, the three of them would be on the last train to Liverpool Street at eleven o'clock.

Violet would be watching for him: I had seen to that, for, in what I thought was a great feat of daring, I had already slipped across to tell her he was coming! Late that afternoon, as late as I dared, I had made one of my now rare trips across to their cottage on the pretext of picking up any post and the can which Kerry the Milkman would have left. So as not to arouse my mother's suspicions, I had volunteered at breakfast to do it to forestall her going across in the snow and ice, which she never liked doing. I gave Violet the note Jan had written outside the backdoor where it was dark and watched her face positively glow with happiness when I silently mouthed the word 'Jan' as I handed it over. I made sure she destroyed it, of course.

Just as well I did: on my way back down the path with the milk and the post, I met Walter at the gate dismounting from his bicycle, for once returning early from work. As luck would have it, Walter, I knew, was going with a whole busload of others to Wivencaster to watch a boxing promotion: someone had organised a Bourne Brothers' bus from all the villages: the notices had been up in the parish notice board for a fortnight. As casually as I could, I confirmed that he would be going by saying 'I wish I was going, too.' I got the right answers: wild horses would not keep Walter away from a boxing match: both his brothers from Cobwycke were also going. The bus would be picking up the Gledlang crowd from the Square at six-forty-five. Perfect! All Jan had to do was wait till Walter was out the way.

Boxing was very popular then, just after the war: everyone listened to it on the wireless and the names of Britain's boxers and commentators were known by every kid: Rinty Monaghan singing *'When Irish Eyes Are Smiling'* after each victory was always a throat-tightener. The Wivencaster promotions may not have been Bruce Woodcock battering Freddie Mills or Gus Lesnivich battering Freddie Mills or heartless Joe Baski battering Freddie Mills and Bruce Woodcock, or

Joe Louis battering everybody, but it was boxing, of a sorts: it was cheap to put on and it was gory. The men went because they appreciated the finer points of the noble art, the adroit footwork, the bobbing and weaving in defence, the jabs, the blows to the solar plexus, the left and right hooks, the uppercuts: the women went because they wanted to see two sweating, half-naked, muscular men hammering away at each other till one lay crushed and bloodied on the canvas: it gave them a nice feeling between their legs, I suppose.

Even as he set off, I thought Jan was foolish to risk it, but did not tell him: it was not my concern if he went chasing someone else's wife, even if that person were the imbecilic Walter Reddy, so dumb, that when someone told him the atomic bombs they had dropped on the Japs at Hiroshima and Nagasaki were no bigger than tennis balls, he had believed it!

I told him I would wait for him in the cottage, ready to row them across to Lingsea. It was then that I made my big mistake, the worst mistake of my life: it was bitterly cold that night, no night to go punting across a river with a toddler. Jan was wearing just his jacket over his shirt and sweater: he really needed an overcoat, at least till he got back, for the wind was really keen and whipping the snow into small drifts along the track. I did not have an overcoat which would fit him, but Richard did: he had two overcoats, a thinner, dark Australian one and a thicker one he had bought in Wivencaster. He only wore the thick one now: but I was sure he would not mind if Jan borrowed the other, his dark one, the one he had worn at Old Sago's funeral, just for a short while, just to go across to Gledlang and back. So I slipped into his cottage and took it from behind the door: it was a spur of the moment thing, carelessly and arrogantly done, done without a thought really, just to please a friend and hoping it would be all right when he returned.

'Richard's out, he won't mind,' I informed Jan when he queried my generosity. I had seen Richard set off for the causeway at the start of the day and he had not yet returned. It was all done so quickly, I did not even think to empty the pockets!

EIGHTY-FIVE

PLANS NEVER go the way they should: bad luck and lust ruined this plan: Jan's bad luck and Violet's lust: or was it the other way round? How was I to know that, when they met for the first time in five months, they would take the opportunity to celebrate their reunion with a feverish half-hour up in the bedroom and her seven months pregnant as well? The bad luck is that they were still at it when Walter walked in the back door: the boxing promotion had been cancelled because snow had fallen much more thickly up in the next county, which it usually did, and half the touring circus of boxers were snowed in by three-foot drifts somewhere up near Sudborough. Thirty disappointed boxing supporters returned to Gledlang: most went into the Chessman to drown their sorrows, literally, but Walter headed off down Shoe Street for home.

Fortunately, Jan heard the gate clicking shut and was able to jump out of the bedroom window and run as Walter came through the back door: but he had to leave Violet and the kiddie behind: even a man of Walter's limited intelligence could work out what had been going on when his wife was standing half-naked beside a wide-open window, desperately trying to pull her knickers up over her bump and the black figure of a man was vaulting the front garden fence clutching at his trousers!

There were some terrible screams coming from the house that night, so I heard later via Charlie Mangapp: none of the neighbours interfered: what went on between a man and his wife in the privacy of their bedroom was their affair and no one else's, they reasoned, whether she was pregnant or not: and, anyway, who was going to take on Walter Reddy, a one-time boxer?

Obviously Walter would have wanted to know who the man was from Violet's own lips: but for some reason, she did not tell him: either would not or could not: probably because the rain of punches to her mouth, nose and eyes started too soon, before he even asked the question, and then was such that I doubt she would have been able to tell even if he had paused. She was probably too busy screaming for her life after the first two or three: after the next five or six, her lips would have been too swollen and her mouth too full of blood for her to speak at all and she probably had too many broken teeth.

The reason I know that Violet never told him Jan's name was because, according to Charlie, who got it from the neighbours, when Walter had finished beating his wife, he went up and down Shoe Street half the night, right up into the Square, yelling like a madman: 'Come out, you bastard! Come out whoever you are!' So it was obvious he did not know who had cuckolded him, which is a pretty poor description to apply when a man's wife allows some other chap to pump away at her, enjoying every minute of it, and wishing he was inside her every time rather than her lummox of a husband! Betrayal would be a better word.

While Walter was out waking up half the village, well, those in Shoe Street, anyway – and he was not going to be shut up by anyone telling him to stop either – a very battered, bruised and bloodied Violet seized the bewildered Thomas from his bed, wrapped him in a blanket and fled over the fields at the back of the house. After struggling across three snow-filled ditches and through four hedges, she eventually came out at the Maydun road, where, fortunately, a passing motorist stopped and gave her a lift or mother and toddler-in-arms would most probably have frozen to death that night: and the unborn baby with her. Whether she hoped to find Jan, I do not know, but she never did: he was haring back across the causeway to where I was waiting: or supposed to be waiting. Thinking I had an hour or so to spare, I was in the barn with Molly and somehow we missed each other. If Jan went to the cottage, I never saw him or heard him call out: I can only suppose that, in his panic, he went straight down to the beach because next morning our punt was gone from the southern beach where it had been tied up ready for him. I never saw him again. My problem was how to get the punt back from some creek at Lingsea, where I hoped it would be tied up, and before Ben found out, though that was unlikely to be for some time in the state he was in.

Violet ended up staying with a married sister somewhere over Greater Tottle way: someone who saw her two weeks later said the bruises which Walter had inflicted were not even starting to fade so he must have given her a terrible beating: and she had lost half her teeth: a person with fists the size of Walter's would do a lot of damage to a man if he were pummelling them, never mind a seven-stone weaker woman.

The problem for me was that somehow Richard's overcoat got left behind and the next day Walter found it lying by the side of the road only ten yards from the house, along with footprints which led towards Boundary's white gates. It had stopped snowing soon after Jan had fled and there was a perfect line of prints on the road: and, since there was no one living at Boundary farmhouse, there was only one place after that: Norsea. Walter, I suppose, put two and two together and got, that whoever had been up in the bedroom with Violet, he must have fled back to Norsea: the overcoat had to be 'his coat,' whoever he was: and when she left, Violet had taken the secret with her. Walter might find out in time, but he was not prepared to wait: he had the answer in his hands: not many people had an overcoat like that in Gledlang with an Australian label: and Richard, of course, had been seen wearing it at various times, like at Old Sago's funeral. In anyone's parlance, two and two make four: especially when his name was written in black ink on the label.

Then there was the 'Dearest Love ...' note in Violet's handwriting which he found in the small inside 'comb' pocket, telling someone she was having his baby, how happy she was it was his and not Walter's and how she longed for the time they could be together. The note, which had been there since Sago's funeral, was frayed, but still readable: Richard, obviously, had forgotten all about it: and, as Jan had never written to me, so had I: when I gave Jan the coat, I did not even think to look to see if it was still there.

But Walter was not to know that: all he knew was that his wife had been going across to Norsea all that summer, first to clean the cottages, then to help with the bean-picking and the pea-picking and later the potato-picking and also going across fortnightly on a Saturday to clean Hoary's downstairs. He knew there had been a man across there other than Hoary and I because he had seen him driving the car. Now he had found her up in their bedroom pulling up her knickers just as another man jumped out of the window and legged it, dropping his overcoat on the way and heading back towards Norsea: and he had found a barely decipherable note written in her handwriting declaring the child he thought was his was actually someone else's, the person who had dropped the overcoat, obviously. Two and two certainly did make four: even Walter could count that far!

When Jan came back without the overcoat, I did the only thing I could do: I kept silent: I suppose that I hoped Richard might think he had left it somewhere, at Hoary's, for instance: or that he would just forget he had it. If he did not, I would have to tell him, eventually, but not yet, not yet.

EIGHTY-SIX

I HAD LOOKED to my left merely by chance: till that moment my head had been bent to the right away from the blizzard sweeping down the length of the estuary and only a sudden drop in the wind and a lessening of the snow driving into my eyes allowed me to turn my head briefly to the left in order to check my path on the causeway. It was then that I saw the white mound move at the bottom of the slope some two hundred yards out from Norsea: only then did I realise that it was the prone form of a man lying half in the mud and half against the shale bank and so shrouded by a four-inch covering of snow as to be nearly invisible. It was Richard.

In seconds I was kneeling beside him, lifting his head and brushing the snow from his face and shoulders as though that act alone would be sufficient to revive him, like those who drag a man from a collapsed trench first clear the clay from his nose, eyes and mouth to permit him to breathe, to see and, hopefully, to speak.

The snow had formed a thin cap of brittle ice on his hair and his face which over large areas of his forehead and cheeks and around his eyes was adhering to a darker surface beneath: gently, I brushed at the encrusting snow with my sock-mittened hands: only when his face was cleared did the true horror of Richard's plight become clear. The darker surface was blood which had congealed and frozen: Richard had been severely beaten, beaten with a brutality and a fury that could only have been done by someone mad with rage.

'I need help, Joe,' he gasped in a voice so faint as to be almost inaudible in the rush of the wind: his teeth were chattering and I lip-read more than I heard. 'I can't make it on my own. Get me back to the cottage. I'm freezing to death here.'

When I raised him in my arms to drag him up the slope, he let out such a cry of pain that I almost let him slip back down rather than cause such agony again. His jacket, trousers and shirt were soaked where he had tumbled into one of the shallow pools which collect at various places at the bottom: too injured and too weak to crawl up again, he had lain there ever since. How long he had been lying there, I do not know, but from the covering of snow upon him, it must have been two or three hours: one thing I did know, however, was that I had to get him back to his cottage or he would develop pneumonia.

It took an effort to get Richard on to the hard, for he was virtually a dead weight: once there, though, I managed with some difficulty to stand him upright, but again not without causing him pain. I was unused to such a thing and lifted him as I would have lifted a drunk, by encircling my arms under his armpits from behind. He gasped and grimaced at every movement and several times cried out and rolled his eyes as if he were about to pass out. He had no strength in his legs and seemed unable to take even a single step on his own, but remained slumped against me, a dead weight, like a man unconscious. Yet I could think of no other way: in my clumsiness, all I succeeded in doing as I dragged him towards the island, I know, was to make the pain well nigh unbearable.

Only when we had reached the island track did Richard finally make an effort to help himself, though still leaning heavily against me for support: it was as if the movement itself of my dragging him revived the flow of his blood so that at least some strength returned: he managed a step forward, but in reality it was no more than a stagger: a second, a third, a fourth and, gradually, slowly, painfully, we made our way along the track.

Several times we had to stop, as much to create a pause in the pain which afflicted Richard as to regather our strength: in two minutes we had covered thirty yards, in five minutes barely a hundred: only after fifteen minutes of buffeting by the fierce, icy wind, with our heads bent against the whipping lines of sleet, did we eventually reach his cottage. Fortunately, the door was unlocked as usual: had it not been, I would have kicked it in to get him inside.

As best as I was able, I did what I could for him: I laid him carefully on the rush matting before the hearth, went into the bedroom, dragged the mattress off his bed and lugged it back into the parlour: then it was a matter of going back for the blankets and coats. Somehow, without too much groaning from Richard, I rolled him on to the mattress and slipped a pillow under his head. My immediate concern was that he should be warm: I needed to light a fire and quickly. Fortunately, there was kindling wood and coke in the bucket in the hearth and newspaper on a chair nearby. However, my frantic efforts were not immediately successful: the wood was damp and did not catch straight away and I repeatedly had to stuff twists of paper under it and fan it for nigh on ten minutes before it caught: and it was a good ten minutes after that before the coke caught sufficiently to give off heat enough for me even to contemplate boiling a kettle of water and ten more minutes for that to happen.

While the fire struggled up, I removed his wet clothing, socks, trousers, underpants, jacket, shirt, and vest: they were saturated and stuck to his skin and he must have endured agony as I wrestled each of them off. Richard's eyes remained closed throughout my struggle, though his teeth were chattering: whether he slipped into unconsciousness from time to time as he lay there, I am not sure: but, concerned as I was by his silence, I was still thankful that he did not cry out as it might have deterred me from doing what I knew had to be done. Once I had stripped him, I dried him all over with another shirt from the bedroom as I could not find a towel: then, carefully, I rubbed the warmth back into his legs, feet, stomach, chest, arms, being extra careful around the left rib cage, for more bruising was beginning to show there. Whoever had beaten Richard so savagely had kicked him, too, several times, angrily, brutally, violently, full of hate. When I had done that, I wrapped a blanket around him like a cocoon, covered him with the other blankets and coats, laid a cushion either side of him to stop him from rolling and tugged the mattress back in front of the now blazing fire.

Once the kettle had boiled, I poured some water into a bowl and carefully set about bathing his injured face, using another of his shirts for a cloth simply because it was to hand: I did it as much to warm his skin as to wipe away the congealed blood on his face and melting ice on his hair. The extra water I poured on top of a tomato soup cube, one of several lying on the table nearby, which I dropped into a cup, but, though I managed to spoon some of it down Richard's throat, most of it trickled down his chin and on to the blankets.

I desperately wanted to hear him speak: one, to let me know that he was all right, and, two, to tell me what to do: even in his terrible state, I could not take him to the farmhouse because Ben would not have allowed it. So I contented myself with stoking up the fire, piling on as much wood and coke as I could safely get away with, ensuring that he was not too near the blaze when it finally took that it would scorch him or the mattress and not too far away that he would not feel the benefit of it: and I stayed with him all night while the wind moaned round the cottage and flurries of snow spattered against the windows.

It was, I think, the worst night of my life: I spent the greater part of it dozing fitfully in the old armchair, fearful lest the fire should go out: no fire I doubt has ever blazed so fiercely in that room: you could feel its heat from ten feet back against the opposite wall: I had to move Richard back several feet when the heat was at its greatest: but at least he was warm, overly warm.

No one was more glad the next morning than I to see the first lightening of the sky to the east: when I awoke from my doze, Richard was looking across at me: he made a brief attempt to sit up, but winced immediately with the pain of it and gave up.

'Did you bring me home?' he asked, still gasping for breath, as though even to speak was an effort for him.

I told him that I had. 'I found you at the bottom of the causeway covered in snow. You were lucky I was passing.' He was: it was only by chance I had left the island to return a creosote sprayer to Charlie Mangapp on Boundary: it was chance, too, that I was walking because of the blizzard and not riding: had I been on my bicycle, I should have been past him before he moved.

'Thanks, Joe. You're a life-saver,' he complimented. 'I tried to get back on my own, but I must have blacked out or something. I remember falling, but I don't remember much else, getting up or whatever. Who helped you? Anyone?'

There was a flicker of disappointment, or was it resignation, upon Richard's face when I answered: perhaps he was hoping that Ben had helped me: but he had not. 'No one. I was by myself.' I said it more as a simple statement of fact rather than an attempt at boasting. 'I had to drag you here, well most of the way. I'm sorry if it was a bit painful.'

'I can't say I remember any of it. I was in a pretty bad way. Still am, I think.' There was a rueful look upon his face as he spoke which was again replaced immediately by a pained expression when he again tried to move. 'God!' he exclaimed. 'I seem to be bruised all over.'

'You are,' I informed him bluntly. 'You've probably got a few ribs cracked – they may even be broken. I'm no doctor. Who the hell did it to you and what for?'

'Some lunatics – two blokes.'

'But why?' I had to ask to conceal the fears of my own guilt.

'I don't know. I didn't see them. They were waiting for me by the boards. They came out of the darkness behind me. I never saw them. I felt a blow across the back of the head and the next thing I knew I was face down in the dirt seeing stars so they must have hit me with something heavy. I tried to twist up to see their faces, but I could not see anything. They were just two black figures seen through a haze. They never even spoke so I would not recognise their voices even.'

'Could it have been Denny Caidge and Matt Cobb?' I ventured, actually hoping it was because then it would rule out the two most likely: Walter Reddy's two brothers from Cobwycke.

'Your guess is as good as mine, Joe,' said Richard, giving a sharp intake of breath as he tried to move: despite his attempt at nonchalance, the pain on his face was marked and distressing. 'Whoever they were, they gave me a proper going over. What they didn't punch, they kicked. I thought they'd never stop.'

'I know, I've seen the bruises,' I reminded him, reddening a little. 'I had to take your shirt and trousers off because they were soaking wet.'

Richard forced a painful smile. 'I thank you for that and the fire. With luck I might avoid pneumonia. I could do with getting a shirt and vest or something on. I feel a bit chilly. There's a shirt and vest in the drawer in the bedroom, and some socks and underpants. Can you get them and bring them to me? I'll need your help, though. Things are a bit painful round the ribcage.'

I did as he requested and over five painful minutes helped him to sit up with the loose armchair seat at his back, slip on a vest and shirt and some socks: he did the underpants himself, I am glad to say, after I had worked them up over his ankles, but it was clearly painful.

I made him some porridge, buttered toast and a cup of tea, put some more coke on the fire and, with a promise that I would look in at midday if I were able, and certainly that evening, I left him to return to the farmhouse.

EIGHTY-SEVEN

THE GUILT stayed with me all the way back to the farmhouse: each time Richard had moved and winced with pain, it had been a reminder to me of how stupid I had been in lending Jan the overcoat. Richard may not have known who had done what they had done to him, or why, but I had a fairly good idea. To my way of thinking, there were four candidates, or two pairs of candidates, I should say: Walter Reddy's two brothers from Cobwycke, doing the job at his instigation, or Denny Caidge and Matt Cobb, getting their own back after the churchyard fracas.

My money, if I had been a betting man, would have been odds-on the Reddys: for the moment, however, I decided to keep my thoughts to myself: I might tell Richard later perhaps. Perhaps.

There was a third vague possibility, of course: that the man-faced Pocklington had hired a couple of London bruisers to do the job for her, to avenge her honour or some such: but I quickly discounted that one as absurd.

My mother was already up despite the earliness of the hour: it was not a happy homecoming: when I walked into the kitchen, stamping the snow off my boots, she was standing by the range as usual, preparing the porridge as usual.

'Taken to sleeping round there now have you?' she sniffed, meaning Richard's cottage. 'If you like it so much, why don't you go and live there? And take your bloody clothes with you.'

I bit my tongue and kept my answer to a pithy, 'I might just do that, woman. What I do is my own bloody business.'

'Not here,' snapped my mother. 'Not here. What goes on in this house is my business.'

'You're welcome to it,' I retorted, trying to control my anger.

We went on like that all through the usual breakfast of porridge, tea, fried egg and fried bread before the inevitable question came in the same inevitable way: 'And what time are you going to start work this morning then, midday?'

I left the kitchen after that and went out to give Molly her feed, change her water, brush her down, fork out the old straw and spread the new: the same with the chickens: it was work of a kind and kept me busy. As Ben was still abed, there was not much else I could do, not with the ground under four inches of snow: and besides, there was no one to make me do much more anyway. The snow was falling intermittently again, so I did not much fancy finishing the drainage ditch I should have been digging in the far-end field: once I had done what was necessary to salve my conscience, I lounged about in the barn, thinking mostly of what to say to Richard when, or if, I ever told him about the overcoat. It was going to be a difficult thing to explain: thinking up the words I would use was easy: doing it was going to be the difficult part.

I suppose I should have told my mother about Richard and the injuries he had suffered and that he was lying on a mattress in front of the fire in his cottage, covered in blankets and coats and in some considerable pain, probably with a couple or more of his ribs bruised, busted or cracked, the same ribs the Japs had stuck a bayonet into and the same ribs which had been bruised in the car crash. A sensible person would have done so: but then questions would have been asked about who had done it: and after 'Who had done it?' comes 'Why did they do it?'

That first day I managed to look in on him at lunchtime unbeknownst to my mother, who, when I did not return to the kitchen at midday, must have thought I was sulking from her breakfast-time churlishness. Richard was dozing when I entered: I had left the wireless on so that he would at least have something to cheer him while he lay there, though *Housewives' Choice* and *Mrs. Dale's Diary* and *Lift Up Your Hearts* would not have been everyone's cup of tea: still there was the *Morning Story*: he would appreciate that, I was sure, so long as the batteries did not run out.

I made some more soup and buttered some bread, but Richard did not eat much of his during the half-hour I sat with him: the fire was low so I raked out the ash and put on some more coke, bringing it in from outside and placing the bucket near the grate so that he could throw some on himself if it got too low. He must have fallen asleep again or been too weak and in too much pain because it was down again when I went back in the evening.

I did go back to the farmhouse for my tea, but there was not much of a conversation between my mother and myself: she was more fussed with Ben, cooking his stew and dumplings and taking it upstairs to him. Tea over, I slipped out of the house while she was in the parlour and went round to the cottage, where I found Richard awake and listening to the wireless. There I stayed till late, ten or eleven o'clock, before I went home, as usual making up the fire with a pile of coke before leaving so that it would burn for the greater part of the night, if not all night. Richard's only request before I left was that I place a bucket nearby on which he could squat if needs be during the night: next morning I emptied it into the hole dug for this purpose at the bottom of the garden.

Each morning, for the next three days, as soon as I had finished my own hurried breakfast, I slipped into Richard's cottage to rake out the grate, and lay and light a new fire, then I would make him tea and toast or tea and porridge before going off to do whatever Ben thought I should be doing about the farm: seeing to Molly, seeing to the chickens, seeing to Hoary's geese, having a go, albeit unsuccessfully, at laying one of the blackthorn hedges, or just resuming my deepening of the drainage ditches: anything useful while I waited for the snow to clear. In the evening, again after a tea bolted down so hurriedly it drew my mother's ire, I made Richard drinks and soup and buttered him some bread: when the soup ran out I took some more from our pantry and once even boiled some potatoes, carrots and peas and made some very ropey dumplings to put in the soup: all the while, I kept the fire going, day by day, emptied his bucket each morning and each evening and generally did what one has to do when looking after a weak and sickly patient.

The only person I told that Richard was ill was Hoary: I called at the big house on the very first day in case he began wondering where Richard was: fortunately, the old man was in his own annual hibernation mood: he was never one to venture out into the snow overmuch and was a little surprised to see me crunching up the path. He came to the door swathed in five or six pullovers with a long scarf wrapped round his neck and trailing down his back.

'Richard's sorry he hasn't been able to come round, but he's got a bad dose of the flu,' I lied. 'It's real bad. I wouldn't go round there if I were you, if you don't want to catch anything. I'm helping feed him and light the fire and that, so he's all right. He's just staying in bed, that's all.'

In an extraordinary act of daring (for me), I threw caution to the wind and made one of my now rare trips up into Gledlang Square to buy a loaf of bread from Fred Thorn's bakery and a few groceries from Ma Rowthey: butter, jam, cheese, tinned milk, a packet of sugar, some soup cubes and a tin apiece of stew, savoury rice and sausages and processed peas. I went in the mid-afternoon when I knew the village would be quiet, when I knew, too, all the other farmworkers, specifically Denny Caidge, Matt Cobb and Walter Reddy, would be at work. I still drew some strange looks from Ma Rowthey, particularly as my mother had collected her weekly groceries the previous day. 'They're for Old Hoary,' I lied yet again, handing over the money I had taken from Richard's pocket: who they were for was none of her business!

Despite all my efforts, Richard ate very little of what I cooked for him, even turning his nose up at my concoction of mashed potatoes, peas, corned beef and beetroot slices which I found in an old jar. He was beginning to have coughing fits which worried me, particularly when he retched and gasped for breath.

EIGHTY-EIGHT

IT WAS sometime after half-eight on the evening of the fifth day that I pushed open the cottage door and found Richard in the parlour on his hands and knees, coughing and retching horribly, his head hanging down like a sick dog, clutching at his ribs with one hand as if the pressure alone would ease his pain. He was hot and shivering. I managed to get him into bed, where I covered him once more as best I could, then sat with him in the hope he would be all right: but he just grew steadily worse: his breathing changed, becoming shorter and more forced: he tossed and turned, moaned and groaned and once or twice cried out. The name he spoke was quite clearly 'Jean – Jean.' His forehead was alternately hot and cold and sometimes he shivered so much his teeth chattered audibly. In the end, after two or three hours, I realised there was nothing else for it: I went straight round to the farmhouse and told my mother. Not everything, of course. Just 'I've just come from Richard's. He's a bit poorly. He's coughing a lot and his ribs hurt. He goes all hot and cold. He's been like it for a couple of days.'

There was cold contempt in her eyes as she pushed past me to take her coat and scarf from off the hook behind the kitchen door. 'A couple of days! You stupid little fool!' she cried as she hurried out without so much as a backward glance. 'Whyever didn't you tell me earlier? Don't you know anything? He could have pneumonia or something.' The sentences were repeated, with minor variations, as I followed her round to Richard's cottage: as a precaution, I trailed a safe ten yards in her wake.

At the cottage, my mother slammed the door behind her so I could not follow her in: she must have diagnosed his condition immediately, for she came rushing out again before a minute had elapsed and rushed at me with a shriek of anger and a swing of the arm.

'He's got pleurisy,' she screamed. 'He's burning up with fever. He can hardly breathe. How long has he been like that?'

'I found him on his knees when I came round this evening,' I told her, truthfully, forgetting to mention the past five days when he had lain first on the mattress, coughing. 'How do you know it's pleurisy, anyway?'

'I know pleurisy when I see it!' she snapped. 'My own father had it. Don't you try and tell me what I know and what I don't know. He's got pleurisy. I know it from his breathing. You'll have to go for MacFadden.'

'I can't go now,' I told her, 'the tide's on its way in. The causeway won't be clear till one.'

'Then get the punt and row across,' she shouted back.

'I can't. It ain't there.'

'Where is it then?' Anger and an accusing look.

'I don't know.' A shrug to accompany the fib.

My mother was not to be fooled. 'You know,' she accused, angrily. 'You know very well where it is. Don't you tell me such lies.'

'I don't know,' I protested, knowing it was hopeless even as I said it: in truth, I did not know where Jan had left it when he had bolted from Walter Reddy, though I hoped it might be moored up some creek near Lingsea, probably full of water. Just as a way of supporting my innocence, I suggested helpfully: 'Perhaps that Polish chap, Jan, took it to get back to Lingsea when he came back to see Violet Reddy and Walter chased him off. He knew it was there. Who else could have taken it? I didn't notice it had gone till a couple of days ago. Honest.' Even my mother on Norsea had heard of Walter's night-long rampage and the mysterious man fleeing the house.

'And you didn't say anything?'

'I thought at first perhaps Hoary might have shifted it, or Richard. I didn't know, did I?' It was the wail of the guilty: my mother did not believe one word of it: she was not that daft. 'You're a bloody liar, you stupid bugger, you!' she exclaimed in frustration. 'I've never met anyone as useless as you. You'll have to go across as soon as the tide is down at one o'clock. If I had my way, I'd make you bloody swim. Now get out of my sight, you useless thing. Go on, get out of my sight!'

She turned on her heel and slammed the door shut: I returned to the kitchen at the farmhouse and was still sitting there heavy with sleep when she came storming back into the kitchen just after midnight, banging the door shut behind her.

Ben must have been awake waiting, for I heard his limping, shuffling tread as he came along the landing on his sticks to the top of the stairs: then his voice rasped out: 'What's going on down there? It's gone midnight, woman. Where have you been all this time? What's up? Something's up, I know it.'

My mother gave me a fierce look. 'Nothing's up,' she declared, exiting the kitchen into the passageway and starting up the stairs: then she contradicted herself in the very next second: 'Joey came round to tell me. Richard's ill. He's got a fever of some kind. I've just been round to see him, that's all. Go back to bed. I've only come for a hot water bottle to give him.'

'Leave him be, woman, and come to bed. If he's ill, it's his own fault,' came Ben's angry response. 'It ain't nothing to do with you. I don't want you getting involved with him. What's between him and me ain't nobody's business but ours. It ain't your business, none of it.'

When my mother set her mind on doing something, she did it no matter what: she just ignored Ben's plea, pushed past him into the bedroom and seconds later came out clutching two hot water bottles.

'I told you to let him be, woman,' Ben exclaimed angrily, clamping a gnarled hand forcefully on her arm as she attempted to pass him on the landing. My mother's response was to set her lips in that grim way of hers and, just as angrily, wrench her arm free and push the unsteady figure of Ben aside: she was going to take the hot water bottles to Richard and no one was going to stop her!

As she came down the stairs, roughly pushing me aside, so Ben started to follow, calling out again: 'I'm warning you, woman – '

'I'll do what I have to,' was my mother's sole comment, flung over her shoulder as she began unbolting the front door. It was then that I intervened, more to ensure she carried out her mission and was not dissuaded by Ben's ire than to provoke an actual confrontation: but a confrontation was what I got. I was on the third step when Ben, coming slowly down the stairs, reached me. 'For Christ's sake,' I pleaded, blocking his path, 'Richard's ill! He's your bloody son! What do you expect us to do, let him die just to please you?'

The answer came in a low, snarling growl: 'Out of my way, boy. I don't give a damn what happens to him. He can bloody die for all I care.'

Did Ben actually mean it? Did he really not care? To this day, I do not know, but it was the breaking point between us. It was the first time he had spoken more than two sentences to me face to face for over a fortnight, and I to him, ever since our falling out: for me, what he said was such a sad and shocking thing to hear that I could not help myself.

In a moment of madness that at some time or other infects us all, I yelled up at him from no more than an arm's length away, almost spitting the words out: 'It's a pity you didn't bloody well die yourself when you got run over by the wagon, then none of this would have happened! Richard's bloody ill! He needs help from me and Mum and he's going to get it whether you like it or not! So bugger you!'

I do not know what made me do it: I had never done such a thing before, nor, I think, would I have dared had he not been half crippled and on sticks: but at that moment I was prepared to say anything that would hurt him in return.

After a declaration like that, an arm's length was too close: Ben moved quickly, more quickly than I expected: switching all his weight to one side on one stick, he let go the other and cuffed me hard and angrily across the side of the head: it was more a closed-fist punch than a slap and it sent me reeling against the banisters, almost tumbling to the foot of the stairs.

'Don't you get bloody cheeky with me, boy!' Ben shouted again. 'This is my bloody house and I'll say what people do and don't do here.'

'Not me you won't!' I yelled back as I regained my balance. 'I ain't taking orders on the bloody farm now.' And then I did it: I clenched my fist, rushed up the stairs and drove my fist upward and hard into his face, so hard that he fell backwards on to the stairs and sat down with a bump.

Ben clapped one hand to his nose and stared at me in the same shock at which I stared at him, our two faces now level: it was as much a surprise to me as it was to him that I could hit so hard. There was something about the anger in his eyes as he looked at me: a resurgent anger you see in people's eyes before they strike back at you. So, to forestall him, I hit him again: and again. To my great shame, twice more I hammered my fist into his face, short angry hooks aimed at his eye and his already bleeding nose, while he, crippled and immobile on the steps and struggling to work his single stick into position to lever himself up, was unable to defend himself. Then I was off, following my mother through the front door and down the path with Ben's threats echoing behind me.

While I waited for the eleven o'clock tide to go down, I sat in Richard's parlour: my mother sat with him in the bedroom to which she had helped him return: we did not speak much: she had the troubles of Richard on her mind and I had the troubles of Ben on mine: first, the shame at what I had done and, second, the fear of his certain reprisal.

EIGHTY-NINE

JUST BEFORE one-thirty, I wheeled my old bicycle out on to the causeway and set off towards the mainland: even though the rocks and shale were exposed enough for me to begin to cycle across, I had to dismount halfway and splash through a couple of hundred yards of water four or five inches deep at the lowest part. The water was absolutely icy: there was a wind off the sea, but I gritted my teeth and plunged on. Fortunately, I knew every curve and, despite the darkness, I was soon up on to the hard by the Boundary boards and pedalling furiously along the potholed chase with water squelching in my boots at every turn of the crank.

Briefly, in the red phone box in a deserted Square, I did think about ringing straightway for an ambulance, but my last encounter with Percy and Ted and a wish not to incur MacFadden's disapproval again deterred me. MacFadden's telephone rang for almost two minutes before a sleepy Irish voice answered: 'Yes, what do you want? Do you not know what time it is? I was asleep in bed. Is it an emergency?' He was as irritable as a bear with a sore backside, as the saying goes: if I were not mistaken, Doctor MacFadden had been on the whisky again and had been sleeping off a hangover.

'I don't know if it is an emergency,' I told him, truthfully. 'I'm ringing from Gledlang. Mum asks, "Can you come over as soon as possible?" My name's Coe. We live on Norsea Island. We've got someone sick, my step-brother.'

All I got was a loud 'Hmmph.' Then he said, again brusquely: 'Aren't you the boy I saw the last time I came to Norsea?'

'Yes, that was me.'

'You were the one who called me out in the summer, during that thunderstorm, when the patient was taken to hospital by ambulance before I got there, were you not?'

'Yes. I'm sorry about that, Doctor.' I felt I had to apologise if only to placate him, an impossible task since he had already taken a sniffy attitude towards me, all compounded by the fact that I had awoken him at two in the morning.

'Well, you know it is snowing outside, don't you?'

'Yes, doctor.' Flakes of snow were streaming diagonally past the phone box windows.

'So what exactly is the problem?'

'It's my step-brother Richard, Richard Wigboe. He's in bed with a fever. Mum's with him. She thinks he's got pleurisy. She's says she's seen it before. Her father had it.'

No doctor likes to be given a diagnosis before he has seen his patient and MacFadden was no different. 'Pleurisy, you say?' he repeated, dismissively. 'It could be just the 'flu, you know. There's a lot of it about. I have seen four cases this week already, none of them serious. How is his breathing?'

'Very painful. And he's sweating a lot.' I stopped short of telling him about Richard's bruises: he would see them when he came.

'Hmmmm,' was all he said this time, before adding after a pause: 'I think, at worst, it could be an inflammation of the bronchial tubes. Norsea is an awfully damp place, you know.' Now how could a man make a diagnosis like that over the telephone? MacFadden must have a sixth sense on such things, for he next asked: 'Have you taken his temperature?'

'Not properly. We don't have a thermometer. Mum just said he is very hot one minute and freezing cold the next. He shivers sometimes, then he gets a fever.'

Another 'Hmmm' from MacFadden.

'Can you come over?' I needed to know.

'There is no way I can come now,' came the sharp answer. 'The roads are very icy. There has been a lot of snow over the past few days. I should not like to chance it tonight. I will try and visit sometime tomorrow, but I cannot make any promises as to what time. I have a busy schedule, you know. What time is high tide tomorrow?'

I told him. 'Eleven-forty. The causeway'll be clear by two.'

'That would mean I would need to cross a minimum of three hours ahead of high-water to be able to see the patient and get back to the mainland comfortably. That is impossible. Eight-forty is much too early for me to come to Gledlang. I have a surgery here in Cobwycke from eight-thirty, then one at Salter at eleven and one at Tottle at two o'clock. Then I have to visit several other patients. This is a busy time of the year, you know, what with the old people. I cannot see myself being able to get over to Gledlang till four or five o'clock at the earliest, nearer teatime. I cannot risk being trapped on Norsea.' A pause and the inevitable question: 'Is there any way you could bring him across to the mainland, to the surgery in Shoe Street, for midday? I could perhaps manage that.'

'I don't know whether we can get him across. He's definitely not fit to walk all that way, not in this weather and there ain't no other way.' We could take him in the cart, I thought at this point, but why should we?

Another thoughtful if weary silence from MacFadden before he added, slyly: 'It would be much easier if you could get him across to see me at the surgery at midday, you know.'

Yes, I did know: but my mother had said he should not be moved and I told him so. 'Very well,' he relented, 'I will try to get across by teatime tomorrow when the tide is out. I've got too many others to visit in the morning. That is the best I can do. I hope this is not going to be a wasted journey like the last?'

There was nothing I could say: he was the doctor and he made the decisions about whom he saw and when: but I felt it was an awful long time to wait.

'Keep the patient warm and give him plenty of hot drinks,' MacFadden calmly advised. 'Put a hot water bottle in his bed. Tell your mother I'll be there about four and, in future, don't ring me in the middle of the night. Eight o'clock in the morning would have done.'

There was a click as he put down the receiver: I had expected he would come immediately, not in fifteen hours' time: but that was the way things were in the country then. There was nothing I could do about it, so I went back to Norsea.

NINETY

I KNEW there was something wrong as soon I pushed open the cottage door: the fire was blazing in the grate, the cottage was warm and my mother was sitting on the edge of Richard's single bed: there were tears rolling down her cheeks.

'He's died,' she said simply. 'He died ten minutes ago.' And then as if the act of telling me suddenly made her aware of it, she reared up and came rushing at me, tears rolling faster down her cheeks, shrieking in the same old way: 'You fool! You bloody little fool!'

Richard dead! I could not comprehend: true, he had a fever: true, he was coughing: true his breathing hurt him: but how could he die? How could he die just like that? It did not seem possible to me: I was stunned by the news, stunned and bewildered, and in my bewilderment I made the mistake of questioning her judgment. 'Are you sure?' was all I asked.

It was too much for my mother: the next instant she was pushing me angrily towards the door. 'Of course, I'm bloody sure!' she raged. 'He's dead, dead because of you, you stupid little bugger.' And with her expletives and curses ringing in my ears, I found myself once more outside on the rutted, iron-hard track with snow falling and a keen wind whipping in off the estuary over the white fields.

I did no work that day: I sat in the barn, thinking and smoking, but really I was too stunned to grasp at any thought: in truth, I was hiding, too frightened to face the light of day and the wrath it would bring, not from Ben, but from my mother. To be accused as I had been accused was too much for me: I cried, not the way a woman cries, all sobbing and wailing, but the way a man cries, a moistening of the eyes and any trickling tear quickly brushed away.

Whatever her failings, my mother was a practical woman: death was something which happened and had to be dealt with, however sad it was, however hard it was for those who had witnessed it. Sometime after five she came into the barn, knowing I would be there carrying a basin of soup and some buttered bread on a tray covered with a cloth:

I was in such a state of shock that, till I saw her approaching, I did not even notice the day had gone by and that the dark had descended over Norsea.

'I've brought this,' she said stiffly, laying the tray on the sacks of grain on which I was sitting. 'You've got to eat something. You ain't had nothing all day, have you?' There was no need for me to thank her: she did not expect it and I did not bother: while I ate, sullen faced and without any real appetite, just a need to fill the hole in my stomach, she told me what had happened, keeping her comments to matters of fact.

MacFadden had come just after six, later than he said he would: I heard his car go past the barn to the farmhouse, but I was too afraid to go out: I did not wish to see anyone and kept myself hidden, even when a white-faced Hoary went hurrying past. When my mother told MacFadden the full story of how Richard had got his scars (which I had told her long before), MacFadden said he did not think there was any need for an inquest as it would only be an inconvenience for everyone, particularly himself, I suspect, and because he thought that she, poor woman, had suffered enough. He wrote out a death certificate there and then: 'Natural causes. Death from myocardial respiratory failure aggravated by...' I think she and MacFadden agreed it all between themselves: he agreed with her that Richard had had pleurisy and did not think the bruises to Richard's face, arms and legs contributed in any way to his death: more likely, his pleurisy was a result of, or made worse by, his rib wounds, he thought.

How Ben took the news I have no idea: my mother did not volunteer the information and I did not ask: nor did I care. My mother, worried perhaps that I might freeze to death in the barn, returned to collect the tray and said in a voice that was unexpectedly wary: 'It's warmer in the house. You'd be better off in there.' Then just before she went out of the barn, she turned in the doorway and, as if sympathising with me or at least understanding my dilemma, she added very gently: 'You needn't worry about him. He's gone back to bed. He's hurt his face. Slipped on the stairs or something, he says.' Her use of 'he says' told me she did not believe what Ben had told her: perhaps that was why she was wary of me, fearing I might suddenly spring up in a mad rage and attack her, too.

'No I'll stay here for now.'

My mother just sighed and went out and I stayed: I stayed late, till well after ten, just smoking and thinking and staring at things around me as I had been doing all day: the same thoughts, the same questions, kept coming back to haunt me and they all began with 'What if...' or 'If only...' They would not go away and so I stayed till the last of my tobacco ran out: only when the tin was empty did I creep into the house and up the stairs: once in my own room, I locked the door and pushed the washstand against it, just in case: I was taking no chances. Then I slept.

When I awoke the next morning, the sun was streaming through the window: outside the sky was a cold icy blue: there had been another fall of snow and the tall elms were dark skeletal giants standing gaunt against the dark hedgerows and blanketed fields. It was just after seven and from Ben's bedroom came the usual hoarse, wheezing sound of his breathing: my mother was already up, busying herself with boiling some washing in the copper in the scullery, her face and arms all shiny and damp from the steam: she was doing it, I suppose, as much to take her mind off the events of the previous night as a need to do it.

For me, the second worst part, one of the most unbearable, was when Charlie Male's men came over with the coffin, asked for by my mother, sent by MacFadden. Richard was laid in it after my mother had washed him: all I saw of it was the back of the four-wheeled, hand-pulled wooden hearse disappearing down the track towards the causeway, pulled by three men, all silhouetted against the snow.

I knew where Richard would be taken, to Charlie Male's so-called 'mortuary,' no more than a lean-to at the rear of his barn-like carpentry shed off the Square where he kept lengths of seasoned wood on trestles. It was cold in there and the best place to keep a body, so long as there was not a delay with the funeral: a couple of days at the most. No doubt Charlie Male and his men would clear the stored wood off a couple of the trestles and put Richard's coffin on them instead: he did for everyone else: almost everyone went via Charlie Male's timber store.

'The funeral will be in two days time,' my mother said when I went in later: she did not expect many would be there, 'things being what they are.' She was right there.

NINETY-ONE

ONLY MY mother, Hoary, Charlie Mangapp and myself were at the funeral: not enough even to sing a hymn: Reverend Ffawcon seemed somewhat embarrassed by the low turnout: at the start of the service he kept glancing towards the door as though he expected others to walk in: no one did. In the end, he took down the two hymn numbers and, after a short service read from a book and a mention of Richard's name – as if to remind God who was coming – signalled the organist to call in Male's men waiting in the porch outside to take the coffin out: there was no eulogy, no comfort, no real sadness from anyone except my mother, Charlie and me, just a couple of incomprehensible prayers and it was all over: in fifteen minutes or less.

Ben refused to come with us Hoary offered to convey him over in Sligger's taxi and Sligger would have done it, ice or no ice on the causeway, but Ben just refused: he had his own reasons, I suppose. I had not seen him since the night Richard had died: he stayed up in his bedroom and did not come down, to my knowledge: and for once my mother did not argue about it.

Somehow as Richard was lowered into the cold earth, I suddenly formed a mental picture of him in his coffin, white-faced, frozen, immobile, the way some people do before someone disappears forever into the grave: one last memory of them. In that moment a strange sense of relief came over me: relief that it was all over: relief, too, that I was no longer under obligation to anyone: my last obligation, friendship and companionship to Richard, had ceased as the coffin was lowered into the hole at my feet.

We tossed our earth on to the coffin, our symbolic act of burial, and the men from Male's began to shovel the brown clay into the hole so that it drummed on to the coffin lid.

Hoary was the first to go: throughout, as the preacher had recited his last words at the graveside, he had remained by himself at one end of the grave, fidgeting and looking embarrassed: no sooner had Male's men begun their work than he declared loudly: 'I have to go,' letting out that nervous baying laugh of his which showed his gold teeth. Then, without further ado, he hurried away.

The vicar, his duty done, was himself already walking slowly back towards the church porch.

'Will you be all right, Joe boy?' Charlie Mangapp paused on his way past and gripped my arm: when I assured him that I would, he gave it a second squeeze, nodded understandingly and trudged off after the others.

Beside me, my mother's eyes were again moist with tears: I cannot say whether they were proper tears of grief for Richard or just 'women's tears' – tears that women 'cry' on such occasions, like tears at weddings: simply a display of female emotion. I would like to think that they were real tears and that in that moment she and I at least shared something which had eluded us over the years of argument and bitterness.

'Are you coming, Joey?' she asked after a while, the tenderness in her voice and the unexpected use of 'Joey,' which she had used all the time when I was much younger, jolting me out of my own sad reverie.

'No, I'll stay awhile,' I said, feeling that I had to remain till the mound had been patted down and our three wreaths laid upon it: I just could not put Richard's corpse into a hole in the ground and coldly walk away, like some so-called mourners do at funerals, as though anxious to get on with life when in reality most of them are anxious to get back to the widow's house and open the bottles of ale lined up on the kitchen table. To me, it has always been the saddest part of a funeral: walking away at the end of it all and leaving the newly dead alone among the other dead, to 'sleep the sleep from which no one wakes,' as Old Sago had been so fond of euphemistically putting it: but then he was sleeping that 'sleep' himself now just ten feet away.

'Well, I'll go,' my mother said quietly, turning away a little reluctantly and going off down the path.

I remained in the churchyard for an hour or so after all the others had gone, after the vicar had closed the church and crept silently away, after Hoary had hurried off to do whatever he had to do, after Male's men had put away their shovels and plodded off down the path, pausing at the gate to look back at me and to shrug their shoulders. Most of the time I sat perched atop one of the table tombs near the porch, smoking and thinking, thinking and smoking, swinging my boot heels against the stonework, going over the years of my life, particularly the last ten months since Richard had returned.

In the end, the cold drove me home: that and a morbid fear of sitting in a dark churchyard with all those dead people lying all around me, even though one of them was Richard.

In the days which followed, Ben and I avoided each other: we hardly spoke: we had nothing to say to each other, leastways I had nothing to say to him. On the few occasions he did deign to speak to me, it was with a brusqueness that did not sit well with me and he received the same back. Most of the time, he stayed in the house, mostly in the bedroom still while I was there, grumbling and mumbling to my mother, who passed it all on to me. To get away from the atmosphere in the house, I spent as much of my time as the weather allowed out and about the farm doing as little as I could get away with not doing, on the bad days of rain and sleet, skulking in the barn out of sight of everybody, wishing and praying the brown envelope would come from the War Office.

NINETY-TWO

THE GALE came towards the end of February, howling down the length of the estuary from the open sea: overhead, the vast bowl of the sky was filled by dark, rushing clouds: windborne spray was everywhere. At Norsea's eastern prow, waves four-feet, five-feet and six-feet high were crashing against the low seawall: it was quite spectacular, the best storm I had ever seen: yet, I nearly missed it. I only went to look to reassure my mother: she had been apprehensive ever since getting up that morning and hearing the wind and rain battering against the window panes. Every time there was a sudden rush of wind around the house or a door banged upstairs, her eyes darted towards the outside like she expected a tree to come crashing through the wall: you could see the anxiety on her face: but then women are like that, always fearing the worst.

We had never had more than two or three gales a year on average on Norsea all the time I had been growing up there: and most of them I had either walked through or worked through. Apart from broken branches strewn about the place, tiles blown off the farmhouse, the barn or the wagon shed and a couple of downed trees one time, there had never been anything to worry about. Certainly, the sea had never come flooding in, even when at its angriest. Being five miles upriver from the mouth of the Langwater, a wave of any height, say five feet, starting its journey at the mouth during a particularly violent gale, would be reduced to no more than a couple of feet by the time it reached us: so the waves I saw that day were exceptional so far as their height was concerned.

I just wished I had someone with me to see it all, someone with whom I could share the excitement, someone like Billy, but he was in Borstal, or Nick, but I never saw him now, or Richard, but he was in Gledlang churchyard. He at least would have appreciated the splendour of the heaving grey sea, as well as the danger of standing atop the low seawall and watching the waves come rushing in straight at you and claw at the slope only a few feet below you.

As the waves hit the seawall, plumes of spray exploded skyward like geysers, twenty to thirty feet up, and then drifted on the wind in long, drenching cascades thirty or forty yards inland: it was like standing on the prow of a ship ploughing through a heaving sea while the waves crashed all around you. The only curious thing I noticed was that there was not a seagull in the sky: it was like they had all been blown inland: most peculiar, I thought.

There was no real danger that I could see: the island was just taking a spectacular wave-battering, that was all. The interior of Norsea does look as flat as a pancake, but actually it slopes very, very gradually upwards from the eastern end to the western point and was higher again on the unseawalled southern side: which is why the big house and the farmhouse were built there. Only the seaward end of the island actually lies below sea level: the rest is slightly above sea level and the highest point is about a foot above the level of the highest spring tide, I would say: so there was no real danger. The seawall along the northern shore round to the eastern prow was seven-feet high and ten-feet wide at its base, though, of course, it was sloped and only a couple of feet wide at the top. It was still enough to keep out the seas we received: even when chased along by a force six gale.

But my mother refused to be convinced. 'Go and look!' she had commanded in her usual way when I had churlishly told her it was 'only a bloody gale' blowing. 'Go and look!' So I went and looked: I am glad I did. The high tide that day was about one-thirty: it was just before twelve when I ran up the slope of the seawall at the eastern prow and almost toppled straight back down as the force of the wind hit me: I had to hang on to my cap and bow my head and shoulders and lean into the wind just to stand up: it was a real laugh and a real struggle.

I could have watched those waves hitting the eastern point all afternoon: they were a marvellous spectacle: but I had been ordered to check the whole damned island: what for, I do not know: leaks? The only water coming in was actually coming over the top of the seawall in the form of spray: all it had created thus far was a long series of puddles on the lower lying land.

I walked, or more correctly was blown along at a trotting pace, all along the top of the low seawall on the northern side as far as the western point where the causeway rises up a foot or so on a compacted low ramp to cross the top of the seawall before dropping down again: if we had a vulnerable point, I would have said that was it, but, though spray was also spewing over the top of the seawall there, it was not half so spectacular as at the eastern point. The southern shore was the same: the waves were sweeping up against the bank at the top of the shingle beach where there was no actual seawall and cascades of seawater were spraying across the grass: but they were neither as high nor as long as the plumes and cascades at the prow. Again, no danger there, even if the seawall at that point was really no more than just a natural bank eroded by the wind and rain, with a three-foot drop down on to the shingle beach, which itself sloped down to the mud of the riverbed, two or three feet, say, over twenty-five yards. A normal high tide only ever came halfway up the beach: we knew that by the seaweed tidemark: we had had fluke tides lapping at the foot of the bank where you step up off the sand and shingle on to the grass, but I had never known the tide to be high enough to flood across. That day it was slapping up against the bank and spray was blowing across the intervening space on to Hoary's 'lawn' fifty feet away, but that was all.

It was my bad luck that Hoary saw me walking along the bank and came out from the house to join me and spoil my enjoyment: he was swathed in a long flowing scarf and huddled inside an old herring bone overcoat: just his face from his eyes up was showing: he looked most peculiar with what was left of his hair almost standing up in the wind. He seemed quite delighted by the whole experience and prattled on about 'violent Nature' and hurricanes and typhoons and the like. Fortunately, most of what he said was blown away on the wind: the old fool was actually smiling and chuckling to himself as the spray cascaded over us: he was enjoying himself. I will not bore you with all of the inane comments he made: suffice it to say they were mostly along the lines of 'God's wrath' and 'God's wonders to behold' and 'Heaven's fury at the sins of mankind' and 'Only Jesus can command the waves to be still.' That kind of thing: rubbish really.

Hoary seemed most concerned that we could not see the rickety old pier: I told him it was submerged at least five feet under the grey surge, which set him praying that it would not be damaged and moaning that he could not afford the cost of repairing it. As it turned out, he did not have to repair it: it was not so much submerged, I found out later, as washed away: bits of it were probably floating past Tidwoldton Basin halfway to Maydun even as we stood there. It also solved the problem of the punt: I did not have to try and find where Jan had left it: when Ben saw it had gone from its beach mooring, he would assume, I hoped, it too had been carried off: he might rail against me having left it tied up there, but what else could he do?

'It's high tide about now,' I called to my mother as I re-entered the kitchen an hour later. 'I don't think it will get any higher, maybe an inch or two.' Then sarcastically, I added: 'I think we've survived this one.'

'You don't know what's going to happen, you ain't that smart yet,' my mother shot back, irritated by my flippancy.

I had enjoyed the sight of the waves battering Norsea. True, spray had come over the seawall and there were small lakes at the eastern end: and we had lost some tiles off the roof of the house and the barn and there were broken branches lying everywhere: but otherwise Norsea was still dry: Norsea had been spared.

So I felt quite justified in jeering back: 'You worry over nothing, woman.'

NINETY-THREE

THEY SAY a deep depression to the north of Scotland suddenly moved very rapidly eastward that day so that there were two areas of extremely low pressure following each other somewhere out in the middle of the North Sea off the east coast of Scotland. The first one had sent the sea surging southward accompanied by the gale, which lasted until about midday and then gradually subsided inland: but not out at sea: there the gale continued to blow straight down the North Sea. Then a phenomenon occurred which had never been experienced before: the first tide did not go out: the strong winds kept it in the creeks and estuaries and inlets all along the low-lying East Coast: the tide stayed in the whole length of the estuary. Twelve hours later, just after two o'clock in the morning, a second tide came surging over the top of the first: that is how the Langwater flood occurred.

I heard my mother screaming as I lay in bed: then suddenly the bedroom door flew open and she was wrenching the blankets off me. 'Get up, you lazy sod!' she yelled. 'We're flooded out. I can't get down the bottom of the stairs!'

Moonlight was streaming through the window: it was still the middle of the night and bitterly cold. The panic in my mother's voice triggered my reactions: but, even without that, I sensed something was wrong: there were sounds in the house which I had not heard before. I was up in an instant and buttoning my trousers and stumbling along the landing to the top of the stairs: from below, I could hear the slapping sound of water: my mother was right: we were flooded out! I had never seen a sight like it before: muddy brown water was lapping at the fourth or fifth stair: a chair from the kitchen was floating at a crazy angle along the passageway and a saucepan was banging up against the back door: there were papers from Ben's office everywhere: the hallstand by the back door had toppled against one wall and all our coats were half under water: from everywhere in the house there seemed to be sounds of splashing water.

I did not bother to roll up my trousers: it would have been futile anyway: the water was too deep: I just plunged straight into it: it came up to my waist and was freezing cold: enough to take my breath away and shrink everything instantly. Upstairs I could hear my mother trying to rouse Ben, shouting at him the same way she had shouted at me.

My first thought was to wade along the passageway towards the front door, thinking it must have somehow blown open or been forced open during the night: stupid thinking really: it was not, it was still firmly shut. As I waded forwards, I could feel the flow of the water against me: it was pouring in from somewhere: there were also things under my feet which, from the feel of them, were most probably my mother's cushions, washed out of the parlour through the open door by the turbulence which had then sunk in the passageway.

Both the parlour and Ben's cubbyhole office were awash: I could see only a small way into the office because I could not open the door properly: Ben's chair had become jammed up against it under water, which was already at the level of his desk top: it was probably too heavy to float: what papers had been lying on it were now bobbing past me, a swirling parade of bills and invoices and receipts no one would read again. The parlour had fared no better: there, the water was pouring in through a shattered window pane: Ben's armchair had tipped over and had almost disappeared: only one arm of it was showing above the surface. Worst of all, the sideboard-cum-cabinet had crashed forward away from the wall: the glass front was shattered and what few knick-knacks my mother had had on the shelves, heirlooms from her own mother, were now lying under three feet of water. It was then that I realised that, in the short time it had taken me to push open the door and assess the scene, the water had stopped pouring through the shattered window pane because the bottom of the window itself was now under water: the water was still rising fast and now was above my waist.

'It's a bloody mess down here,' I shouted back along the passageway to my mother at the top of the stairs. 'The sideboard's fallen over. The glass is all smashed and everything's gone. The chairs and the small table are all under water, too. His papers are everywhere.'

'Never mind the bloody papers!' came my mother's angry reply. 'Get out there and see if Molly's all right. The bloody papers aren't important. She is.'

I made a quick assessment: there was a current, but it was not a fierce one: if I could keep to the wall and work my way along the front of the house and then down the side, hanging on to whatever was there, fence, drainpipe, gatepost, the two-wheeled cart, bushes, I might be able to make it. The front door opened easily, helped by the in-rush of water, and I was soon working my way chest-deep along the front of the house to the corner, then down the side towards the barn, grabbing at anything I could. All I could think of was that I was glad I had sometimes continued swimming into September: it seemed to have inured me against the cold. Fortunately, too, I was moving with the flow and was across the yard pretty quickly, although I missed the barn's double doors by a good five feet and wound up flattened against the wall nearer to one end. One of the big double doors was open, but I decided it was far too dangerous to go in that way: both the plough and the harrow had been left just inside the entrance and I did not want to have to try and negotiate my way over or around them and struggle against a flood at the same time. There were also, I knew, various implements, pitchforks, hay cutters, turnip cutters, machetes, hoes, hooks, not to mention our six-foot, long-bladed 'Father Time' scythe, just inside the door: any of them could be strewn about the floor, washed away from the wall against which I usually leant them: so I worked my way round to the side door and after a couple of attempts managed to force that open. We had so many planks or sections of plank missing that the water was just streaming through the barn almost uninterrupted, foaming through the holes and splashing up against the wood supports and then gurgling on as it found a way round and out. This was the only dangerous bit: moonlight or no, the interior was too dark for me to see much: the only light I got was that reflected off the rushing water. To reach Molly's corner, I had to feel my way in darkness against the flow, which was strong enough to pull me down if I were not careful, in freezing water, chest high, and always with the thought that there were razor-sharp implements under foot: and I was barefoot.

Molly was not there: she had gone: there was just the broken rope by which we tethered her: she must have jerked the rope free when the water started to flood in: she could only have got out one way, through the wide open barn door: the poor old mare must have panicked, broken the tether and fought her way outside. Damn! I could not go and look for her: that would have been too stupid, suicidal in that cold: my teeth were chattering as it was and I was shivering uncontrollably. Just in crossing the yard, I had stumbled and gone under twice, so I was in no mood to go looking for her: we would have to wait till daylight: she could be anywhere. The water was up to my armpits by then so it had to be more than four feet deep: I could only hope that she had gone into a field somewhere and was standing on a banked-up section by a hedge to put herself a few inches higher. Even if she were not, the water would be only just past her belly, so it would not be too high if she stood still: but would she? And it was bitterly, bitterly cold.

My struggle back to the house, though only sixty or so feet across the yard, took all of five minutes against the current: finally, near to frozen, with the blood drained from my hands and feet, teeth chattering, shivering like a pleurisy victim myself, I splashed back through the front door again: Ben and my mother were waiting at the top of the stairs.

'Is she all right?' Ben yelled as soon as he saw me: no concern for me, just for the horse: but then, since I had managed to return undrowned, that was to be expected, I suppose. By then I was numb from the chest down: the circulation seemed to have stopped round about my waist and my feet seemed to have shrivelled into white bloodless blobs of flesh.

'She's gone. She broke her tether. She's out there somewhere.' The words were shouted at the both of them.

'Oh good God!' said my mother and sank down on the top step.

'Gawd Christ!' Ben swore angrily. 'Didn't you go and look for her?'

'Yes, I looked,' I lied, putting as much indignation as I could into my reply. 'She wasn't anywhere around the barn or the yard. I couldn't see her. I had a good look.' The look of despair on his face made me add the next lie. 'She's made for higher ground, I reckon. She could be up near the western end, in one of the fields, sheltering. Up on a bank or something. She ain't daft, that horse. She knows what's what.'

It hardly placated Ben: I was climbing the stairs as I said it, with the water still washing around my feet, keen to get up and into the dry if not the warm: I needed to strip, dry myself on a bedsheet and put on warm dry clothes: socks, trousers and a double set of vests, shirts and pullovers. As I warily mounted the stairs, I braced myself to receive the full vehemence of Ben's anger, ready to counter it with my own: but it did not come. Looking up through the gloom of the landing, I saw Ben was actually quietly crying: or at least tears were welling up in his eyes and trickling down his cheeks, actually trickling down his cheeks.

'How long did you look, a couple of seconds?' my mother sniffed, rising. Her arm was around Ben as he shuffled back towards the bedroom. 'I wouldn't want the old girl to come to any harm,' he said, 'not if we can prevent it.'

'I looked for her. I couldn't see her anywhere. I don't see what harm she could come to, a great heavy horse like her,' I said.

Fortunately, the darkness of the landing hid my shame.

NINETY-FOUR

WHEN DAWN finally came, the water was already receding: the downstairs was a shambles: when my mother and I went down, there were still three or four inches of water washing over the floors where it could not flow back out over the step and we had to splash through that. Mud covered everything, the floor, the walls, the furniture, the food, the pots, the pans, the chairs, the tables, everything. A brown tidemark ran around the bottom half of the walls in all the rooms, kitchen, scullery, parlour, passageway, Ben's office: in places you could run your finger along it and scrape off the slime: and it stank. It was a smell we all recognised: sewage from our outhouse in the yard mixed with mud from the fields, rank and horrible: a smell that would cling for days, for weeks, and which would not easily wash away.

In several places, the plaster had worked loose from the walls and lay in clumps upon the floor. In the kitchen, where I had not been, all the chairs were overturned though the table was still upright: the food in the lower cupboards was ruined. There were cups and plates, utensils, pots and pans, bowls and basins, tins and packets all covered by the same layer of sludge: it also covered the linoleum, the flagstones in the scullery and along the passageway, the bare black boards in the office and the frayed patterned carpet in the parlour. The kitchen range was now brown with mud rather than black with lead as before: the first thing my mother did was to try to relight the fire, if only to boil some water to start washing things: but as the wood was virtually waterlogged and the coke too wet, in the end, I had to slosh through the mud and water in the yard to the barn and wrench a piece of dry timber from it and use that. Ben would not have been pleased if he had known, but then I was not going to tell him.

Outside, the passage of the gale had left its mark: broken branches were lying everywhere, entangled in the hedgerows, littering the track and piled against the front fence: two of the gates were hanging off their hinges and two others had just vanished, borne off on the tide. I kept my eyes open for Molly, but could not see her anywhere. That was really my first task: to find Molly. I went all round the island, from end to end along the top of the seawall, shouting her name just to let her know I was about, but she was nowhere to be seen. The daft horse had obviously panicked and bolted somewhere: and, if she was not on Norsea, there was really only one place she could have gone: I just had to hope that she had lumbered across the causeway to the mainland after the ebb, revelling in her unexpected freedom.

But what worried me was that there was still a lot of water about: too much: it was almost five hours after the flooding and the tide should have been ebbing more than it was, but it was not. The gale had subsided to half its former strength, but the wind still seemed to be strong enough to delay, if not actually to prevent, the full ebb of the tide. When I looked down the estuary towards the mouth, the tide had not even gone beyond Cobwycke and in seven or eight hours the next tide would be coming in: we could be in for a second flood! That was when I really began to worry, about Molly, myself and everyone else. Though our seawall had not been breached, all the fields at the eastern end and along the northern shoreline right up to the track, about seven in all, were under a foot of salt water: field after field, with only the trees and hedgerows, showing above it: the waves were just rippling across them, trapped within the confines of the island, sloshing around the headlands and spilling out through the gaps on to the track in places. The cottages, too, were awash and two of them had been shifted sideways on their brick supports: it would be several days before the flood waters either drained away or evaporated completely in the wind. By the looks of things, I thought, I would be employed for a month digging channels to take it away: it would have to be done, I knew that: but, even as I stood there surveying the sorry scene, I knew there would not be much point. Our crops were ruined, the seawater would have seen to that: the land would be useless for at least two or three years till it recovered and then only after treatment. All that effort which I had put in, which Richard and I had put in together, was wasted: useless! But there was no time even to think of that yet: I must find Molly. Where the hell had she got to?

There was still a strong wind blowing as I made my way back round by the southern shore: on my way past the big house, I called in on Hoary to make sure that he was all right: the poor man was in tears when he answered the door: it was one of the only times I actually felt really sorry for him. He had been playing the piano the night before, probably as some kind of weird accompaniment to the wind when it had got up again, and, when he had gone to bed, he had left two of the windows of the main parlour wide open. When the second tide surged up the estuary over the top of the first, it had been like a tidal bore rushing through his house: it had poured through the open windows with nothing to divert it or delay it. The brown tidemark around his rooms may have been a foot lower than the one around ours, but the water had done the same amount of damage: the force of it had picked up the heavy old piano and carried it over to the opposite wall: the legs had collapsed and it lay jammed amid other furniture like a huge black barge rudder from some wreck beached amid jetsam: other furniture was piled against it: none of it was upright.

As I walked across the carpet, water squelched around my boots: not that it mattered, they were sodden by that time anyway because the water was still everywhere, inches deep in places. Everywhere, floor, furniture and walls, there was the same foul-smelling slime as covered our floor and our furniture: pictures were hanging askew, all kinds of vases, clocks, cushions and other objects littered the floor. I spotted Hoary's brass-fronted camera and tripod wedged under a rosewood sideboard and almost tripped over his brass telescope, the one I had used to spy on Dennis: it was so covered in mud I did not know what it was till I trod on it. Worst of all were the scores of priceless, ornate, calf-skin-covered, illuminated, vellum-paged books lying about in the mud, his lifetime's collection: the rush of water had just swept them off the places where they had been stacked. There must have been fifty or sixty of them strewn about the parlour floor: more again were lying all over the place in the second parlour and the along the wide hallway: even those stacked on the lower stairs had been swept away: his whole 'library' was gone.

I helped the poor man pick up some of the books and straightened his furniture for him, for he seemed unable to do much himself but wander aimlessly from room to room, wringing his hands and bemoaning his ill luck and the loss of his treasures. I should have told him that, if he had had his windows closed, it might not have been half so bad: it would not have stopped the water coming in, but it might not have come in at such a rush, just seeping under the doors and through the air bricks and doing only half the damage it did: but that would have been churlish in the circumstances. The loss of the books, or at least the damage to them, was by far the worst thing: other things could be repaired or replaced, they could not. On some, you could hardly distinguish the script, others had pages stuck together, all were sodden wet and covered in mud: some were unreadable in places where the ink had run or faded: it was like someone had started to paint a watercolour on the same page as the script.

Really, there was little else I could do: I was looking for Molly: she was more important to us and I told him so: I promised I would return to help him once I had found Molly and we had cleaned up our own house. The last thing I told him was not to drink any water or eat any of the food which had been under water: if he needed more food or something to drink, he should cross to the mainland and fetch it. Our outhouse had vanished from the corner of the yard, I had noticed, and our bucket with it: so most probably had the one Richard had used and the one I had never emptied belonging to the women's cottage after Laura Wilchard had left. As I walked near the farmhouse and the cottages, I knew from the smell that I was treading through sewage in places: most of it would be taken out by the receding water, but it was better to be safe than sorry: so I skirted round it and made for the causeway: maybe Molly was grazing somewhere on Boundary? Maybe she had gone off to find old Peter in the hope of finding comfort with him? She might at that very minute be sheltering under the branches in one of the orchards.

It was Charlie Mangapp who came up to meet me just as I reached the Boundary boards. 'I was just coming across to see how you were,' he said solemnly, 'and to tell you we've got your Molly.'

Somehow, in the wind, I missed the import of what he was trying to say and, instead, half-cursing and half-excited plunged into my own tale, believing that was what he wanted to hear. 'I know. I'm looking for her now,' I informed him above the noise of the wind. 'She did a bolt from the barn when the tide came over the top of the wall. I couldn't find her when I went out looking for her. I reckon she must have made for the higher ground up near the Western Point, then waited till the tide went out and crossed to Boundary. We've been flooded out in the farmhouse. Four-foot deep, it was, downstairs. All the furniture was floating everywhere, Ben's papers. Everything. Made a right mess of the parlour and the kitchen and Ben's office, it did. Hoary got flooded out, too. Had his bloody windows open, didn't he? The silly bugger! Water poured in. Ruined all his books. Soaked to buggery, they are. You can't read half of them. The old fool. It even wrecked his piano. He won't be playing that for a while. And the mud! Bloody mud everywhere! Our house stinks to high heaven. It'll take days to clear up. My mother's going barmy!'

Charlie listened to my babbling without comment, then said quietly: 'You had better come with me, young Joe.' And with that, he turned on his heel and went back up the slope. It was only when I saw the other side that I realised how great was the damage done by the storm: Boundary had suffered the same as us: the whole farm was a vast lake, stretching from the boards to halfway up Shoe Street: small waves of cold grey seawater were washing through every orchard.

'Seawall's been breached up near Tidwoldton mills,' said a grim-faced Charlie as I surveyed the scene. 'There's a seventy-yard gap. It took the old sluice away up near Peakman's farm and flooded everywhere right up to the Maydun road and right back to us. Boundary's flooded out. Everywhere's under water, the farmhouse, the barn, the storage sheds, everything. I'm just glad Dennis ent here to see it. It'd tip him right over the edge, I reckon.'

The second tide had poured through, flooding farmland already green with the first blush of corn, drowning orchards. Midway between Gledlang and Maydun caravans from a small holiday site floated upside down: dead cows washed against barbed wire fences: trees and hedgerows stood out stark against the grey flood. In all, fifteen square miles of arable land and orchard, field and farm around the village, were under four or five feet or more of water: I know that because the waves of this inland sea were almost as high as the 'Trespassers will be prosecuted' sign John Bolt had had the men erect near a barbed wire-topped gate to keep the village boys and occasional courting couples out of his orchards.

Charlie led me westward along the top of the seawall: ahead of us, a line of young village boys, wrapped in scarves and balaclavas, were bowing into the full force of the wind, struggling to reach the breach at Tidwoldton and gaze in awe at the most exciting thing that had happened around Gledlang for years: well, since the near miss by the doodlebug had blown over pea-pickers in a field a half mile away and the Heinkel crash near Charity farm.

Charlie and I did not speak for a mile or more because of the wind: he led and I just followed him: finally we rounded a bend and no more than a hundred yards from where the village boys were already gawping at the seventy-yard breach, through which the tide was still flowing out in an angry white foam, Charlie stopped, turned and, putting his hand on my shoulder, said stony-faced: 'This is what I've got to show you. Like I said, we've got your Molly.'

I knew from the look on his face what he meant: just below me, three of the former Boundary men, Bob Bird, Ted Oldton and Sam Perry, were hauling at something with a rope: it was about twenty-feet out in the mud and they were trying to drag it ashore: it was bulky and it was brown: it was Molly, lying on her side half-covered with mud.

'She got drowned or died of exposure,' said Charlie bluntly, but with a certain sympathy. 'Sam found the poor old gal lying on the mud this morning when he come along to find the breach. She must have bolted for the causeway and tried to swim over to the mainland, thinking that were safer. Got taken by the current, I reckon. Wouldn't have known much about it. Cold would have got her, most like. I'm sorry, Joe boy. There ain't much we can do but bury her. That'll be a job and a half once we git her ashore.'

The other men were very sad-faced when I joined them: they tried not to notice my watering eyes as I crunched down the sand and shingle and stared out at the old horse's lifeless carcass and the indignity of the ropes tied round her legs. 'Sorry about this, young Joe,' said Ted Oldton, partly relaxing the tension on one of the ropes, as though my seeing the three of them tugging at the old horse was an affront to me somehow.

'Real sorry,' echoed Sam Perry, while Bob Bird just looked down at his feet, not wanting to say anything.

'We'll get her ashore first and then bury her somewhere when the water goes down,' said a sympathetic Charlie Mangapp, placing a hand on my shoulder before taking hold of one of the ropes himself: almost in a daze, I did the same, thinking only that I must help the men to haul their burden ashore. That it was Molly's lifeless carcass we were straining to drag over the last few feet of mud up on to the hard of the shingle and sand hardly seemed to register: shock, I suppose.

'There aint no need for you to stay now,' Charlie Mangapp said when we had hauled the brown and glistening mud-stained carcass of the old mare under the lee of the seawall. 'We'll take it from here, boy. We'll bury her once the water's gone down. Best you get off and tell Ben and your mother what's happened to her. They'll be wanting to know. And Hoary. It weren't your fault she got drowned, boy. It was just fate, that's all.'

'Tell that to Ben,' I thought, as I stumbled back across the causeway to Norsea. 'Bloody tell that to Ben.'

But tell him I did. 'Molly's been found drowned,' I said, standing at the bottom of the stairs while they stood at the top. 'Charlie Mangapp and the other men dragged her ashore up near Tidwoldton. She must have gone for the mainland and got caught by the current. She's dead anyway. I've seen her. They say they'll bury her once the flood goes down. They'll dig a pit on the shoreline. They say they'll try and do it before the next tide.'

Neither Ben nor my mother was really listening: they just stood there with tears rolling down their cheeks: I managed to hold back my own tears: my eyes were wet simply because of the wind as I had made my way back across the causeway.

I left them to it: after all, someone had to inform Hoary that he was short of one horse.

NINETY-FIVE

THE BREACH at Tidwoldton took six days to repair: they brought the Catchment Board gang from the south of the river to do it: Jan's Polack friends, since they were the nearest: only thirty miles away from us near the Rea Sands, halfway down the long and lonely stretch. First, they heaved in hundreds upon hundreds of concrete-filled sandbags to bring the hollow where the sluice had been gouged away up to land level, all held in place by upright posts like sawn-down telegraph poles driven into the clay the width of the gap: these were then infilled on top with tonne after tonne of rock, all brought in from Wales somewhere by lorries which turned Peakman's farm track and fields into a quagmire that was worse than the flooding: in fact, it got so bad they had to pause for two days while they laid a corrugated sheet-steel road.

Of course, the men could only work at low tide: till they had filled in the whole of the gap to a height of five feet, the seawater just poured back through with every tide and Peakman's and Boundary were flooded twice daily for four of those days. But, once the base of the breach had been filled by rocks and concrete, the Catchment Board gang was able to build on top with earth and concrete slabs infilled with tar. Even so we were luckier than others: the clay cliffs up in Lincolnshire crumbled in places and two houses fell into the sea: the seawalls around the Wash apparently took a worse battering than did ours and the rivers Nene and Ouse backed up half way across the Fenland, flooding the low-lying polder almost as far inland as Peterborough. Coastal areas farther up our part of the coast were inundated, too: at one holiday camp, they found the bodies of five caravan dwellers, who thought they were leaving the housing troubles of London behind them, but left the troubles of the world behind instead.

Because of the lie of the land on Norsea, below sea level at one end, at sea level in the middle and above sea level at the western end, it was almost two weeks before the water drained off: and for a further week, the fields were too sodden to tread anywhere so I did very little: I just waited for them to dry. Because our water was tainted, I cycled daily across to Gledlang to get buckets of water from the village pump: otherwise I mooched about the farmyard between the barn and the wagon shed, still keeping out of Ben's way as much as I could. His bitterness at the loss of Molly was understandable, I suppose: what I could not understand was his railing against me: how I should have found her that first night when I went out in the dark to look for her and how, if I had done so and brought her back, she would be alive now. I think it was that which ended it for me: his own son was dead, buried in Gledlang churchyard, and he was ranting on about a horse, even if it were Molly! I swore at him over that.

'You never even went to your own son's bloody funeral! Yet you bloody well sit there bellyaching about a bloody horse! What kind of a man are you, for God's sake?' I shouted at him in the kitchen one evening. It was not often I invoked the Deity to my cause, though that troubled me less than hearing myself, in my anger, calling old Molly a 'bloody horse!' She was not just any horse, she had been our horse, our workmate, and, for the past seven or eight months, she had been my horse, mine alone: and now she was dead.

Ben tried to come round the table after me, but I was away before he had levered himself up: away from him and my mother, who came rushing in from the passageway to chase me out. The next day, for no reason I could think of, and with the tide out, I just walked across to the village, forgetting work, not caring who saw me and in a mood to take on all-comers if anyone objected. Again, for no reason I know of, I went into the churchyard to look at Richard's grave: it was the first time I had been back since the funeral. As soon as I saw it, still a low mound of muddy, ungrassed earth, with our flowers shrivelled and pathetic looking upon it, a profound melancholy settled over me, as grey as the day all around. Richard was lying beneath my feet, covered in six feet of earth: he was gone: I would see and speak to him no more. I no longer had any friends, certainly none of my own age, to whom I could turn: Billy was gone, Nick was diffident, Old Sago was gone, Dennis was gone, Jan was gone, Stanley was gone: now even Molly was gone: few if any of the villagers spoke to me, except the dour, phlegmatic Charlie Mangapp and the other one-time Boundary men.

It was late when I returned to the farmhouse: I did not speak to my mother or to Ben. That night, while they slept, I packed what clothes I had in my mother's old suitcase, emptied her purse of six shillings and Ben's bureau drawer of seven pounds for the unpaid wages I considered I was owed and, just before the sun came up and the tide cut off the causeway, I crossed to the mainland on foot, leaving behind my faithful old bicycle. At the top of Shoe Street, I turned left into Hedge Street, then out on to the Maydun road and past Billy's house, its windows still curtained and dark except for the glow of lamplight from the kitchen where his mother would already have risen. An hour later, with the help of a lift from one of the flour mill lorries, I reached Maydun, where I knew I could get an early National bus to Melchborough and from there take the train up to London, single, one way.

I just wanted to get away, away from Norsea, away from Gledlang, away from Ben and my mother, but most of all, away from the memories. I have to admit that, as I walked, before I got my lift, there was an unexpected spring in my step: I was anticipating the adventure upon which I was setting out, even excited by it: it was going to be me against the world, or, as I saw it then, the world against me: and hell would freeze over before I went back: whatever happened I was damned well not going back!

NINETY-SIX

AND I never did go back! Well, not till my mother's funeral twenty-four years later, a sad and disillusioning pilgrimage into the cherished images of the mind. Why? Because three months after I left, as soon as he could walk properly, Ben had waded out into the estuary and drowned himself! Just walked up to his chest, opened his mouth, ducked under and was gone: and my mother blamed me.

'He would never have killed himself if you had been here,' she wrote, all angry and accusing, in the only letter I ever received from her in reply to one of my own. 'He looked on you as his own son and what did you do to him? You left him just like the other one. He couldn't sleep after you left. He'd get up in the night and go walking round and round the island, night after night on his sticks despite the pain it caused him. You should have been here to help him because that other creature was no help, bothering him all the time about the money the farm was losing because he couldn't do the work he should have been doing and he couldn't get anybody to come and help. He was a farm bailiff from the age of twenty, he knew what to do and when to do it. He didn't need a fool like that creature telling him all the time. When your legs are broken and paralysed, they take time to mend and he had other troubles. You knew he would not be able to do much till he was better. He needed you here to help him, yet you went off and left him. He'd lost his son and damn near his livelihood and you go off and leave him just like he did that first time! Do you think he didn't feel it when his own son died, especially after what they had been through? It near broke him. I know, he was my husband! I know how he felt!' She ended it: 'So don't you think you can come creeping back here when you see fit, because you won't...' After that, I could not go back: so I never did.

To this day, I ask the question: Did I really cause Ben to kill himself? Did my leaving unbalance his mind that much? Did he commit suicide because of me? I do not know, I really do not know. I hope not, I truly hope not. If I thought he had killed himself because I had deserted him, just as Richard had deserted him, I do not think I could bear it. I believe it was just my mother venting her own bitterness. A wound in me mourns Ben still, even after all these years: in law, we were step-father and step-son, in life we were father and son: till the quarrelling started.

I had only written to her thinking, or hoping, she might be worried about where I was and what I was doing: obviously she was not. I spent my first months in London working on building sites, clearing rubble so that the penny-pinching Government could erect hideous, prefabricated boxes for homeless Londoners: then I went into the army as a seven-year regular. I saw service in the Korean War, I saw death and disease, pain and poverty, hunger and hatred, all the outside things from which on Norsea I believed myself to have been sheltered. I was in my mid-forties, married, with a family and living in a grimy northern mill town when my mother died: she never met my wife or saw her grandchildren. Over the years I sent her a photograph of my wedding and photographs of our children when they were born, but I never got another letter back in all that time.

My mother lived on in the farmhouse until her death simply because Hoary could not find a new bailiff willing to live in so isolated a place for the money he paid: in time, the new tenant of Boundary took over the running of Norsea and his men used to go over two or three days a week to work it – when the tide allowed. They grew potatoes, fields and fields and fields of them! My mother eked out a living as a cook and cleaner for various farmers in the district, including the new owners of Boundary.

Old Hoary himself lived on in the big house till he was well into his seventies and caused his own death: he trod on a rusty nail in his overgrown garden or in the cluttered house somewhere, got gangrene in two of his toes and tried to slice them off with a breadknife. He collapsed from loss of blood and might have died there and then had the men from Boundary not found him: they took him to hospital and his foot was amputated on the new National Health Service. He returned to Norsea and hopped about the place with a broomhandle crutch for a while, but the shock of it eventually killed him inside a year. They held his funeral up in Norfolk: no one from the village went: it was too far to go.

Dennis, as I say, never came back to Boundary: he disappeared for a while after he came out of gaol: he had no farm to come back to anyway: the Ross 'potato kings' bought it, sawed down the serried ranks of old trees and planted their acres of potatoes in hedgeless fields, which I saw when I went back for my mother's funeral. It was at that I learned that, in later years, Dennis had written unexpectedly to Charlie Mangapp from New Zealand: he had taken the money from the sale of Boundary and bought passage on a ship to Auckland, where he was able to set himself up on an apple farm on the North Island: he got married, too.

Violet Reddy? She eventually went back to Walter, who forgave her, I suppose, as she forgave him his temper: she was standing outside the churchyard on the day I buried my mother. She smiled at me as the hearse trundled past, but it was a weak smile, full of sadness: my return must have brought back painful memories for her: memories of long ago: memories of lost love and, worse, an end to happiness.

Stanley Lobel? He did become a well-known artist, but not for his painting: after leaving the Royal Academy School, he went off to Rome on a scholarship and, while there, took to slicing blank folios from antique books in museums and then drawing on them figures and scenes 'in the style of the Old Masters,' even reproducing their three-hundred-year-old inks somehow and ageing the paper with tea and coffee stains. The drawings are in national galleries all over the world, it is said. Stanley made a lot of money and achieved a certain notoriety among his peers when he revealed his secret: it did not please everybody: someone bludgeoned him to death one night as he crossed a square in Rome in a drunken stupor.

My friend Billy went in the army and Nick went in the navy: neither of them came back to live in Gledlang: I do not know if they are still alive or where they live even: I hope it is better than where I am.

Where I now live, halfway up a hill in a grimy industrial town, I do not see trees and hedgerows when I look out of my window: or fields of waving corn or acres of plum and apple orchards in blossom: instead, I see rows of grey-slate rooftops and red-brick chimneys and the taller smokestacks of the closed-down factories. I have lived in the street for thirty years and I still do not know more than a dozen neighbours on either side, whereas in Gledlang I knew every face, from the newest baby to the oldest pensioner. At the foot of the hill, long lorries thunder past in clouds of exhaust fumes, heading for a concrete-pillared motorway: there is no freshness in the air here, no scent of flowers or blossom, no smell of the earth after a fall of cleansing rain, just the smell of carbon monoxide. I am here in body, but my heart is still in Gledlang, my spirit on Norsea.

Life for me has become a reverie of nostalgic memories: in unexpected moments, my mind drifts back down the years to the sixteen-year-old boy I then was and I see again the vast dome of the sky over the flat fields turning to a sea of orange at sunset: and silhouetted against it all the tall elms of Norsea. Images come to mind of a plodding, snorting Molly trudging from hedgerow to hedgerow pulling our Ransome plough on a crisp autumn day while behind her hordes of screeching gulls swoop over the turned shiny earth: or of a summer afternoon as rabbits dart from cover at the approach of the clacking binder. In my nostalgia, the days are always sunny: there are bees and birds and butterflies everywhere and I forget the rain and the snow and the frost and the fogs...

But there is sadness, too: I hear again the death squeal of a rabbit gripped in the jaws of a stoat or a weasel somewhere out in the encircling dark of Boundary and I listen once more to the frenzied cawing of the rooks wheeling over their nesting places high up in the tall elms of the Park as the farmers gather below with their guns. In my imagination, I can still taste the salt from the river borne upon the breeze, still smell the Langwater's black mud through which Billy, Nick and I and the other village boys once waded, impatient to meet the incoming tide: and I hear, too, the silence of the empty estuary, so absolute at times that it seems to rustle in your ears.

Oh, one other thing: as I plodded along the Maydun road through the sleet the day I left, before I got my lift, a small car coming from the direction of Maydun drew up in front of me and a woman wound down the window and asked if she was on the right road to Gledlang. She was a very good-looking woman, well dressed, maybe thirty years of age, with red hair, white skin and bright blue eyes: her accent was unmistakably Scottish, but it was a cultured one. On the backseat behind her, a small child of maybe three or four years of age, a girl, I think, was asleep on some coats.

Yes, I knew where Gledlang was, I told her. 'Just a mile along the road turn right at the two big elms just after the road curves sharply to the left. You can't miss it. That's Hedge Street and it leads directly into the Square.'

And did I know a farm called Boundary Farm? It had white gates and plum and apple orchards. Oh yes. 'When you reach the village square, turn right down Shoe Street at the old iron-wheeled pump and the big broken ciderstone beside it. Go down the hill past the bakehouse and some cottages for threequarters of a mile and Boundary's gates are at the bottom. Just follow the track through the orchards.'

'Thank you,' said the woman with a smile. 'I've just driven from London. I've been driving all night through the snow. I never knew it was so far out and in such an isolated place.'

The best I could do was just to smile in return as she wound up the window and drove off towards Gledlang. I have often wondered who she was…

Made in the USA
Charleston, SC
17 June 2015